I shook my head in disbelief and cried, "You're infuriating!"

"And you love every second."

My mouth made a "poof" noise at such a display of arrogance and I pushed against his chest. His hand slid up my spine, bringing me closer, pinning my hands between us as I watched his neck bend.

I had a feeling I knew where this was going.

"Max," I warned, my body bracing.

"Quiet," he ordered softly. "Got a point to make, honey."

"Max!" I snapped.

"Let's see how good this could be," he muttered, his eyes on my mouth and I knew, I just knew he was going to kiss me.

"Max, don't you—"

But his fingers had sifted into my hair against my scalp cupping my head, holding me steady and his mouth came down on mine, cutting off my words. And considering my mouth was open, he didn't miss the opportunity to slide his tongue inside. My body froze when his tongue touched mine. Then my hands curled into his shirt and my body melted.

His tongue felt good, it tasted good, it was all just *good*. Not just good. It was better than good. I missed this. Lord, did I miss it. My eyes drifted closed, my head tilted and that was it, I was lost...

LIVINGSTON PUBLIC LIBRARY
10 Robert H. Harp Drive
Livingston, NJ 07039

Acclaim for
KRISTEN ASHLEY AND HER NOVELS

"A unique, not-to-be-missed voice in romance. Kristen Ashley is a star in the making!"

—Carly Phillips, *New York Times* bestselling author

"I adore Kristen Ashley's books. She writes engaging, romantic stories with intriguing, colorful, and larger-than-life characters. Her stories grab you by the throat from page one and don't let go until well after the last page. They continue to dwell in your mind days after you finish the story and you'll find yourself anxiously awaiting the next. Ashley is an addicting read no matter which of her stories you find yourself picking up."

—Maya Banks, *New York Times* bestselling author

"There is something about them [Ashley's books] that I find crackalicious."　　　　　—Kati Brown, DearAuthor.com

"Run, don't walk…to get [the Dream Man] series. I love [Kristen Ashley's] rough, tough, hard-loving men. And I love the cosmo-girl club!"　　　　　—NocturneReads.com

"[*Law Man* is an] excellent addition to a phenomenal series!"
—ReadingBetweentheWinesBookclub.blogspot.com

"[*Law Man*] made me laugh out loud. Kristen Ashley is an amazing writer!"　　　　　—TotallyBookedblog.com

"I felt all of the rushes, the adrenaline surges, the anger spikes…my heart pumping in fury. My eyes tearing up when my heart (I mean…*her* heart) would break."

—Maryse's Book Blog (Maryse.net) on *Motorcycle Man*

The
Gamble

The Gamble

KRISTEN ASHLEY

FOREVER

NEW YORK   BOSTON

This book is a work of fiction. Names, characters, places, and incidents are the product of the author's imagination or are used fictitiously. Any resemblance to actual events, locales, or persons, living or dead, is coincidental.

Copyright © 2012 by Kristen Ashley
Excerpt from *Sweet Dreams* copyright © 2012 by Kristen Ashley

All rights reserved. In accordance with the U.S. Copyright Act of 1976, the scanning, uploading, and electronic sharing of any part of this book without the permission of the publisher is unlawful piracy and theft of the author's intellectual property. If you would like to use material from the book (other than for review purposes), prior written permission must be obtained by contacting the publisher at permissions@hbgusa.com. Thank you for your support of the author's rights.

Forever
Hachette Book Group
237 Park Avenue
New York, NY 10017

www.HachetteBookGroup.com

Printed in the United States of America

Originally published as an ebook

First mass market edition: May 2014
10 9 8 7 6 5 4 3 2 1

OPM

Forever is an imprint of Grand Central Publishing.
The Forever name and logo are trademarks of Hachette Book Group, Inc.

The Hachette Speakers Bureau provides a wide range of authors for speaking events. To find out more, go to www.hachettespeakersbureau.com or call (866) 376-6591.

The publisher is not responsible for websites (or their content) that are not owned by the publisher.

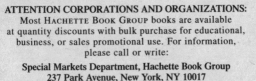

ATTENTION CORPORATIONS AND ORGANIZATIONS:
Most HACHETTE BOOK GROUP books are available
at quantity discounts with bulk purchase for educational,
business, or sales promotional use. For information,
please call or write:

Special Markets Department, Hachette Book Group
237 Park Avenue, New York, NY 10017
Telephone: 1-800-222-6747 Fax: 1-800-477-5925

The
Gamble

CHAPTER ONE

Time-out

I LOOKED AT the clock on the dash of the rental car, then back out at the snow.

I was already twenty minutes late to meet the caretaker. Not only was I worried that I was late, I was also worried that, after I eventually made it there, he had to drive home in this storm. The roads were worsening by the second. The slick had turned to black ice in some places, snow cover in others. I just hoped he lived close to the A-frame.

Then again, he was probably used to this, living in a small mountain town in Colorado. This was probably nothing to him.

It scared the hell out of me.

I resisted the urge to look at the directions I'd memorized on the plane (or, more accurately, before I even got on the plane), which were sitting by my purse in the passenger seat. There was no telling how far away I was and what made matters worse was that I was doing half of what I suspected, but wasn't sure, was the speed limit.

Not to mention the fact that I was exhausted and jet-lagged, having been either on the road, on a plane, or in a grocery store the last seventeen hours.

And not to mention the fact that yesterday (or was it the day before? I couldn't figure out which in changing time zones), I got that weird feeling in my sinuses that either meant a head cold was coming or something worse and that feeling was not going away.

Not to mention the *further* fact that night had fallen and with it a snowstorm that was building as the moments ticked by. Starting with flurries now I could barely see five feet in front of the car. I'd checked the weather reports and it was supposed to be clear skies for the next few days. It was nearing on April, only two days away. How could there be this much snow?

I wondered what Niles was thinking, though he probably wasn't thinking anything since he was likely sleeping. Whereas, if *he* was off on some adventure by himself, or even if he was with friends (which was unlikely, as Niles didn't have many friends), *I* would be awake, worried and wondering if he made it to his destination alive and breathing. Especially if he had that niggling feeling in his sinuses that I told him I had before I left.

I had to admit, he didn't tell me he wanted me to ring when I got to the A-frame safe and sound. He didn't say much at all. Even when I told him before we decided on churches and dates that I needed a two-week time-out. Time to think about our relationship and our future. Time to myself to get my head together. Time to have a bit of adventure, shake up my life a little, clear out the cobwebs in my head and the ones I fancied were attached (and getting thicker by the day) to every facet of my boring, staid, predictable life.

And, I also had to admit, no matter where I went and what I did, Niles didn't seem bothered with whether I arrived safe and sound. He didn't check in, even if I was traveling for work and would be away for a few days. And when I checked in, he didn't seem bothered with the fact that I was checking in. Or, lately (because I tested it a couple of times), when I *didn't* check in and then arrived home safely, sometimes days later, he didn't seem bothered by the fact that I hadn't checked in.

The unpleasant direction of my thoughts shifted when I saw my turn and I was glad of it. It meant I was close, not far away at all now. If it had been a clear night, I figured from what it said in the directions, I'd be there in five minutes. I carefully turned right and concentrated on the ever decreasing visibility of the landscape. Making a left turn, then another right before heading straight up an incline that I feared my car wouldn't make. But I saw it, shining like a beacon all lit up for me to see.

The A-frame, just like it looked on the Internet, except without the pine trees all around it, the mountain backdrop, and the bright shining sun. Of course, they were probably there (except the sun, seeing as it was night); I just couldn't see them.

It was perfect.

"Come on, baby, come on, you can make it," I cooed to the car, relief sweeping through me at the idea of my journey being at an end. I leaned forward as if that would build the car's momentum to get up the incline.

Fortune belatedly shined on me (and the car) and we made it to the postbox with the partially snow-covered letters that said "Maxwell," signifying the beginning of the drive that ran along the front of the house. I turned right again and drove carefully toward the Jeep Cherokee that was parked in front of the house.

"Thank God," I whispered when I'd stopped and pulled up the parking brake, my mind moving immediately to what was next.

Meet caretaker, get keys and instructions.

Empty car of suitcases and copious bags of groceries, two weeks' worth of holiday food—in other words, stuff that was good for me, as per usual, but also stuff that was definitely not, as was *not* per usual.

Put away perishables.

Make bed (if necessary).

Shower.

Take cold medicine I bought at the grocery store.

Call Niles if even just to leave a voice mail message.

Sleep.

It was the sleep I was most looking forward to. I didn't think I'd ever been that exhausted.

In order to make the trips back and forth to the car one less, I grabbed my purse, exited the car, and slung my bag over my shoulder. Then I went to the boot, taking as many grocery bags by the handle as I could carry. I was cautious; the snow had carpeted the front drive and the five steps that led up to the porch that ran the length of the A-frame and I was in high-heeled boots. Even though it was far too late (though I *had* checked the weather forecast and thought I was safe), I was rethinking my choice of wearing high-heeled boots by the time I hit the porch.

I didn't get one step across it before the glass front door opened and a man stood in its frame, his front shadowed by the night, his back silhouetted by the lights from inside.

"Oh, hi, so, so, so sorry I'm late. The storm held me up." I hastily explained my easily explainable rudeness (for anyone could see it was snowing, which would make any smart driver be careful) as I walked across the porch.

The man moved and the outside light came on, blinding me for a second.

I stopped to let my eyes adjust and heard, "What the fuck?"

I blinked, focused, and then I could do nothing but stare.

He did not look like what I thought a caretaker would look like.

He was tall, very tall, with very broad shoulders. His hair was dark, nearly black, wavy, and there was a lot of it sweeping back from his face like a stylist had just finished coifing it to perfection. He was wearing a plaid flannel shirt over a white thermal, the sleeves of the shirt rolled back to expose the thermal at his wrists and up his forearms. Faded jeans, thick socks on his feet, and tanned skin stretched over a face that had such flawless bone structure a blind person would be in throes of ecstasy if they got their fingers on him. Strong jaw and brow, defined cheekbones. Unbelievable.

Though, in my estimation, he was a couple days away from a good clean shave.

"Mr. Andrews?" I asked.

"No," he answered, and said no more.

"I—" I started, then didn't know what to say.

My head swung from side to side. Then I looked behind me at my car and the Cherokee, back around and up at the A-frame.

This *was* the picture from the website, exactly it. Wasn't it?

I looked back at him. "I'm sorry. I was expecting the caretaker."

"The caretaker?"

"Yes, a Mr. Andrews."

"You mean Slim?"

Slim?

"Um...," I answered.

"Slim isn't here."

"Are you here to give me the keys?" I asked.

"The keys to what?"

"The house."

He stared at me for several seconds and then muttered, "Shit," and right after uttering that profanity, he walked into the house, leaving the door open.

I didn't know what to do and I stood outside for a moment before deciding maybe the open door was an indication that I should follow him in.

I did so, closing the door with my foot, stamping my feet on the mat to get rid of the snow, and looking around.

Total open space, all shining wood. Gorgeous.

Usually, websites depicting holiday destinations made things look better than they really were. This was the opposite. No picture could do this place justice.

To the left, the living area, big, wide, long comfortable couch with throws over it. At the side of the couch, facing the windows, a huge armchair two people could sit in happily (if cozily) with an ottoman in front of it. Square, sturdy, rustic table between the chair and couch, another one, lower, a bigger square, in front of the couch. A lamp on the smaller table, its base made from a branch, now lighting the space. Another standing lamp in the corner of the room by the windows made from another, longer, thicker branch with buffaloes running across the shade, also lit. A fireplace, its gorgeous stone chimney disappearing into the slant of the A-frame; in its grate a cheerful fire blazed.

A recessed alcove to the back where there was a rolltop desk with an old-fashioned swivel chair in front of it, a rocking chair in the corner by another floor lamp, its base looked like a log and was also lighting the space.

A spiral staircase to a railed loft that jutted over the main living space and there were two doors under the loft, one I knew led to a three-quarter bath, the other one, likely storage.

The pictures of the loft on the website showed it held a queen-sized bed, had a fantastic master bath with a small sauna and a walk-in closet.

To the right I saw a kitchen, perhaps not top-of-the-line and state-of-the-art but it wasn't shabby by a long shot. Granite countertops in a long U, one along the side of the house, the other, a double top, a low, wide counter with a higher bar, both sliced into the open area, and the bar had two stools in front of it. A plethora of knotty pine cabinets that gleamed. Midrange appliances in stainless steel. Another recess at the back where the sink was, the fridge to the left. And a six-seater dining table at its end by the floor to A-frame windows, also in knotty pine, with a big hurricane-lamp-style glass candleholder at its center filled with sage-green sand in which was stuck a fat cream candle. Over it hung a candelabra also made from branches and also lit.

"You got paperwork?" the man asked, and I was so caught up in surveying the space and thinking how beautiful it was and how all my weeks of worries if I was doing the right thing and my seventeen hours of exhausting travel was worth getting to that fabulous house, I started. Then I looked at him.

He was in the kitchen and he'd nabbed a cordless phone. I walked in his direction, put the grocery bags on the bar, and dug in my purse to find my travel wallet. I pulled it out, snapped it open, and located the confirmation papers.

"Right here," I said, flicking them out and handing them to him.

He took them even though he was also dialing the phone with his thumb.

"Is there a prob—" I asked. His eyes sliced to me and I shut up.

His eyes were gray, a clear, light gray. I'd never seen anything like them. Especially not framed with thick, long, black lashes.

"Slim?" he said into the phone. "Yeah, got a woman here...a..." He looked down at the papers. "Miss Sheridan."

"Ms.," I corrected automatically, and his clear gray eyes came back to me.

It had also dawned on me, at this juncture, that he had a strangely attractive voice. It was deep, very deep, but it wasn't smooth. It was rough, almost gravelly.

"A *Ms.* Sheridan." He cut into my thoughts and emphasized the "Ms." in a way that I thought maybe wasn't very nice. "She's lookin' for keys."

I waited for this Slim person, who I suspected was Mr. Andrews, the absent caretaker, to explain to this amazing-looking man that I had a confirmed two-week reservation, pre-paid, *with* a rather substantial deposit in the rather unlikely event of damage. And also I waited for this Slim person to tell this amazing-looking man that there obviously was some mistake and perhaps he should vacate the premises so I could unload my car, put away the perishables, have a shower, talk to Niles, and, most importantly, *go to sleep.*

"Yeah, you fucked up," the amazing-looking man said into the phone. He concluded the conversation with, "I'll sort it out," beeped a button, and tossed the phone with a clatter onto the counter. After doing that, he said to me, "Slim fucked up."

"Um, yes, I'm beginning to see that."

"There's a hotel down the mountain 'bout fifteen miles away."

I think my mouth dropped open but my mind had blanked so I wasn't sure.

Then I said, "What?"

"Hotel in town, clean, decent views, good restaurant. Down the mountain where you came. You get to the main road, turn left, it's about ten miles."

He handed me my papers, walked to the front door, opened it, and stood holding it, his eyes on me.

I stood where I was and looked out the floor-to-A-point windows at the swirling snow; then I looked at the amazing but, I was tardily realizing, unfriendly man.

"I have a booking," I told him.

"What?"

"A booking," I repeated, then explained in American, "a reservation."

"Yeah, Slim fucked up."

I shook my head; the shakes were short and confused. "But I prepaid two weeks."

"Like I said, Slim fucked up."

"With deposit," I went on.

"You'll get a refund."

I blinked at him, then asked, "A refund?"

"Yeah," he said to me, "a refund, as in, you'll get your money back."

"But—" I began, but stopped speaking when he sighed loudly.

"Listen, Miss—"

"Ms.," I corrected again.

"Whatever," he said curtly. "There was a mistake. I'm here."

It hadn't happened in a while but I was thinking I was getting angry. Then again, I'd just traveled for seventeen-plus hours. I was in a different country in a different time zone. It was late, dark, snow was falling, and the roads were treacherous. I had hundreds of dollars' worth of groceries in my car, some of which would go bad if not refrigerated and hotels didn't have refrigerators, at least not big refrigerators. And I was tired and I had a head cold coming on. So I could be forgiven for getting angry.

"Well, so am I," I returned.

"Yeah, you are, but it's *my* house."

"What?"

"I own it."

I shook my head and it was those short, confused shakes again.

"But it's a rental."

"It is when I'm not here. It isn't when I'm home."

What was happening finally dawned on me fully.

"So, what you're saying is, my confirmed booking is really an *unconfirmed* booking and you're canceling at what is the absolute definition of the very last minute?"

"That's what I'm sayin'."

"I don't understand."

"I'm speakin' English. We do share a common language. I'm understandin' you."

I was confused again. "What?"

"You're English."

"I'm American."

His brows snapped together and it made him look a little scary, mainly because his face grew dark at the same time. "You don't sound American to me."

"Well, I am."

"Whatever," he muttered, then swept an arm toward the open door. "You'll get a refund first thing Monday morning."

"You can't do that."

"I just did."

"This is . . . I don't . . . you can't—"

"Listen, *Ms.* Sheridan, it's late. The longer you stand there talkin', the longer it'll take you to get to the hotel."

I looked out at the snow again, then back at him.

"It's snowing," I informed him of the obvious.

"This is why I'm tellin' you, you best get on the road."

I stared at him for a second that turned into about ten of them. Then I whispered, "I can't believe this."

I didn't have to wonder if I was getting angry. This was because I knew I was livid and I was too tired to think about what I said next.

I shoved the papers into my purse, snatched up my grocery bags, walked directly to him, stopped, and tilted my head back to glare at him.

"So, who's going to refund the money for the gas for my car?" I asked.

"Miss Sheridan—"

"*Ms.*," I hissed, leaning toward him and continuing. "And who's going to refund my plane ticket all the way from England where I *live* but my passport is *blue*?" I didn't let him respond before I went on. "And who's going to pay me back for my holiday in a beautiful A-frame in the Colorado mountains, which I've spent seventeen-*plus* hours traveling to reach? Traveling, I might add, to a destination I paid for *in full* but didn't get to enjoy *at all*?" He opened his mouth but I kept right on talking. "I didn't fly over an ocean and most of a continent to stay in a *clean* hotel with *nice views*. I did it to stay *here*."

"Listen—"

"No, you listen to me. I'm tired, my sinuses hurt, and it's snowing. I haven't driven in snow in years, not like that." I pointed into the darkness, extending my grocery-bag-laden arm. "And you're sending me on my way, well past nine o'clock at night, after reneging on a contract."

As I was talking, his face changed from looking annoyed to something I couldn't decipher. Suddenly, he grinned and it irritated me to see he had perfect, white, even teeth.

"Your sinuses hurt?" he asked.

"Yes," I snapped. "My sinuses hurt, *a lot*," I told him, then shook my head again; this time they were short, *angry* shakes. "Forget it. What do you care? I'm too tired for this."

And I was. Way too tired. I'd figure out what I was going to do tomorrow.

I stomped somewhat dramatically (and I was of the opinion I could be forgiven for that too) into the night, thinking this was my answer. This was the universe telling me I should play it safe. Marry Niles. Embrace security even if it was mostly boring, and deep down if I admitted it to myself, it made me feel lonelier than I've ever felt in my life.

Paralyzingly lonely.

Who cared?

If this was an adventure, it stunk.

I'd rather be sitting in front of a TV with Niles (kind of).

I opened the boot and put the bags back in. When I tried to close it, it wouldn't move.

This was because Unfriendly, Amazing-Looking Man was now outside, standing by my car and he had a firm hand on it.

"Let go," I demanded.

"Come back into the house. We'll work somethin' out, least for tonight."

Was he mad? Work something out? As in him *and* me staying in the A-frame together? I didn't even know his name, and furthermore, he was a jerk.

"Thank you," I said snottily. "No. Let go."

"Come into the house," he repeated.

"Let go," I repeated right back at him.

He leaned close to me. "Listen, Duchess, it's cold. It's snowing. We're both standin' outside like idiots arguing over what you wanted in the first place. Come into the damned house. You can sleep on the couch."

"I am *not* going to sleep on a couch." My head jerked and I asked, "Duchess?"

"My couch is comfortable and beggars can't be choosers."

I let that slide and repeated, "Duchess?"

He threw his other hand out, his gaze drifting the length of me as he said, "Fancy-ass clothes, fancy-ass purse, fancy-ass boots, fancy-ass accent." His eyes came to my face and he finished firmly. "Duchess."

"I'm American!" I shouted.

"Right," he replied.

"They don't have duchesses in America," I educated him.

"Well, that's the truth."

Why was I explaining about aristocracy? I returned to target.

"Let go!" I shouted again.

He completely ignored my shouting and looked into the boot.

Then he asked, what I thought was insanely, "Groceries?"

"Yes," I snapped. "I bought them in Denver."

He looked at me and grinned again, and again I thought it was insanely, before he muttered, "Rookie mistake."

"Would you let go so I can close the boot and be on my way?"

"Boot?"

"Trunk!"

"English."

I think at that point I might have growled but being as I was alarmed at seeing only red, I didn't really take note.

"Mr. . . ." I hesitated, then said, "Whoever-you-are—"

"Max."

"Mr. Max—"

"No, just Max."

I leaned toward him and snapped, "*Whatever*." Then demanded, "Let go of the car."

"Seriously?"

"Yes," I bit out. "Seriously. Let. Go. Of. The. *Car*."

He let go of the car and said, "Suit yourself."

"It would suit me if I could travel back in time and not click 'book now' on that stupid webpage," I muttered as I slammed the boot and stomped to the driver's side door. " 'Idyllic A-Frame in the Colorado Mountains,' not even *bloody* close. More like Your Worst Snowstorm Nightmare in the Colorado Mountains."

I was in the car and had slammed the door but I was pretty certain before I did it I heard him chuckling.

Even angry, I wasn't stupid and I carefully reversed out of his drive, probably looking like a granny driver and I didn't care. I wanted out of his sight, away from the glorious yet denied A-frame and in closer proximity to a bed that I could actually *sleep* in and I didn't want that bed to be in a hospital.

I turned out of his drive and drove a lot faster (but still not very fast) and I kept driving and I didn't once look into my mirrors to see the lost A-frame.

Adrenaline was still rushing through my system and I was still as angry as I think I'd ever been when I was what I figured was close to the main road but I couldn't be sure and I hit a patch of snow-shrouded ice, lost control of the rental, and slid into a ditch.

When my heart stopped tripping over itself and the lump in my throat stopped threatening to kill me, I looked at the snow in front of my car and mumbled, "Beautiful." I went on to mumble, "Brilliant."

Then I burst out crying.

* * *

I woke up or at least I *thought* I woke up.

I could see brightness, a lot of it, and a soft, beige pillowcase.

But my eyeballs felt like they were three times their normal size. My eyelids actually *felt* swollen. My head felt stuffed with cotton wool. My ears felt funny, like they were tunnels big enough to fit a train through. My throat hurt like hell. And lastly, my body felt leaden, like it would take every effort just to move an inch.

I made that effort and managed to get up on a forearm. Then I made more of an effort and pulled my hair out of my eyes.

What I saw was a bright, sunshiny day out of the top of an A-frame window through a railing. I could see snow and lots of it and pine trees and lots of those too. If I didn't feel so terrible, I would have realized how beautiful it was.

Cautiously, because my stuffed up head was also swimming, I looked around and saw the loft bedroom from the A-frame website.

"I'm dreaming," I muttered. My voice was raspy and speaking made my throat hurt.

I also needed to use the bathroom, which I could see the door leading to one in front of me.

I used more of my waning energy to swing my legs over the bed. I stood up and swayed, mainly because, I was realizing, I was sick as a dog. Then I swayed again as I looked down at myself.

I was in a man's T-shirt, huge, red, or it had been at one time in its history. Now it was a washed out red. On the left chest it had a cartoonlike graphic of what looked like a man with crazy hair madly playing a piano over which the words "My Brother's Bar" were displayed in an arch.

I opened up the collar to the shirt, peered through it, and stared at my naked body, save my still-in-place panties.

I let the collar go and whispered, "Oh my God."

Something had happened.

The last thing I remembered was bedding down in the backseat of the rental having covered myself with sweaters and hoping someone would happen onto me somewhat early in the morning.

I'd tried unsuccessfully to get the car out of the ditch and, exhausted and not feeling all that well, I'd given up. I'd decided against walking in an unknown area to try to find the main road or happen onto someone who might just be stupid enough to be driving in a blinding snowstorm. Instead, I was going to wait it out.

I also suspected that I'd never get to sleep. Not in a car, in a ditch, in a snowstorm after a showdown with an unfriendly but insanely attractive man. So I took some nighttime cough medicine, hoping to beat back the cold that was threatening, covered myself with sweaters, and bedded down in the backseat.

Apparently, I had no trouble getting to sleep.

Now I was here.

Back at the A-frame.

In nothing but panties and a man's T-shirt.

Maybe this *was* My Worst Snowstorm Nightmare in the Colorado Mountains. Weird things happened to women who traveled alone. Weird things that meant they were never seen again.

And this was all my fault. *I* wanted a time-out from my life. *I* wanted an adventure.

I thought maybe I should make a run for it. The problem was, I was sick as a dog and I had to go to the bathroom.

I decided bathroom first, create strategy to get out of my personal horror movie second.

When I'd used the facilities (the bathroom, drat it, was fabulous, just like in the photos) and washed my hands, I walked out to see Unfriendly, Amazing-Looking Man—otherwise known as Max—ascending the spiral staircase.

Like every stupid, senseless, idiotic heroine in a horror movie, I froze and I vowed if I got out of there alive I'd never make fun of another stupid, senseless, idiotic heroine in a horror movie again (which I did, every time I watched a horror movie).

He walked into the room and looked at me.

"You're awake," he noted.

"Yes," I replied cautiously.

He looked at the bed, then at me. "Called Triple A. They're gonna come up, pull out your car."

"Okay."

His head tipped to the side as he studied my face and asked, "Are you okay?"

"Yes," I lied.

"You don't look too good."

Immediately a different, stupid, senseless, idiotic feminine trait reared its ugly head and I took affront.

"Thanks," I snapped sarcastically.

His lips tipped up at the ends and he took a step toward me.

I took a step back.

He stopped, his brows twitching at my retreat, then said, "I mean, you don't look like you feel well."

"I'm perfectly fine," I lied.

"And you don't sound like you feel well."

"This is how I sound normally," I lied yet again.

"It isn't how you sounded last night."

"It's morning. I just woke up. This is my waking-up voice."

"Your waking-up voice sounds like you've got a sore throat and stuffed nose?"

I kept lying. "I have allergies."

He looked out the windows, then at me. "In snow?" I looked out the windows, too, and when he continued speaking, I looked back at him. "Nothin' alive in the ice out there that'll mess with your allergies, Duchess."

I decided to change the topic of conversation; however, I was becoming slightly concerned that I was getting light-headed.

"How did I get here?" I asked him.

His head tipped to the side again and he asked back, "What?"

I pointed to myself and said, "Me"—then pointed to the floor—"here. How did I get here?"

He looked at the floor I was pointing to, shook his head, and muttered, "Shit." He looked back at me and said, "You were out. Never saw anything like it. Figured you were fakin'."

"I'm sorry?"

He took another step toward me and I took another step back. He stopped again, looked at my feet, and for some reason grinned. Then he looked back at me.

"I waited a while, called the hotel to see if you'd checked in. They said no. I called a couple others. They said no too. So I went after you, thinkin' maybe you got yourself into trouble. You did. I found your car in a ditch, you asleep in the back. I brought you and your shit to the house. You were out like a light, dead weight." His torso twisted and he pointed to my suitcase, which was on a comfortable-looking armchair across the room; then he twisted back to me. "Put you to bed, slept on the couch."

I was definitely getting light-headed, not only because of being sick but also because of what he just said. Therefore, in order not to fall down and make a right prat of myself, I skirted him, walked to the bed, and sat down or, if I was honest, more like *slumped* down.

I looked up at him and asked, "You put me to bed?"

He'd turned to face me. His brows were drawn and he didn't look amused anymore.

"You're not okay," he stated.

"You put me to bed?" I repeated.

His eyes came to mine and he said, "Yeah."

I pulled at the T-shirt and asked, "Did you put this on me?"

The grin came back. It was different this time, vastly different, and my light-headedness increased significantly at the sight.

Then he said, "Yeah."

I surged to my feet and my vision went funny, my hand went to my forehead, and I plopped back down on the bed.

Suddenly he was crouched in front of me, murmuring, "Jesus, Duchess."

"You took my clothes off," I accused.

"Lie down," he ordered.

"You took my clothes off."

"Yeah, now lie down."

"You can't take my clothes off!" I shouted, but I heard my loud words banging around in my skull, my head started swimming, and I would have fallen backward if my hand didn't come out to rest on the bed to prop me up.

"I can, I did, it ain't nothin' I haven't seen before, now lie down."

I started to push up, announcing, "I'm leaving."

He straightened and put his hands on my shoulders, pressing me right back down. My bottom hit the bed and I looked up at him, suddenly so fatigued I could barely tilt my head back.

"You aren't leavin'," he declared.

"You shouldn't have changed my clothes."

"Duchess, not gonna say it again, lie down."

"I need to go."

I barely got out the word "go" when my calves were swept up and my body twisted in the bed. I couldn't hold up my torso anymore so it also fell to the bed. Then the covers came over me.

"You had medicine in your groceries. I'll get that and you need some food."

"I need to go."

"Food, medicine then we'll talk."

"Listen—"

"I'll be right back."

Then he was gone and I didn't have the energy to lift my head to find out where he went. I decided to go to my suitcase, get some clothes on and get out of there. Then I decided I'd do that after I closed my eyes just for a bit. They hurt, too much, and all that sun and snow, I had to give them a break. It was too bright.

Then, I guess, I passed out.

*　　*　　*

"Nina, you with me?" I heard a somewhat familiar, deep, gravelly voice calling from what seemed far away.

"How do you know my name?" I asked, not opening my eyes, and I would have been highly alarmed at the grating sound of my voice if I wasn't so very tired.

"You're with me," the somewhat familiar, deep, gravelly voice muttered.

"My throat hurts."

"Sounds like it."

"And my eyes hurt."

"I'll bet."

"And my *whole body* hurts."

"You've got a fever, Duchess."

"Figures," I murmured. "I'm on holiday. Fit as a fiddle through my boring bloody life, I go on holiday, I get a fever."

I heard a not in the slightest unattractive chuckle and then, "Honey, I need to get you up, get some ibuprofen in you, some liquids."

"No."

"Nina."

"How do you know my name?"

"Driver's license, credit cards, passport."

My eyes slightly opened and that was too much effort so I closed them again.

"You went through my purse."

"Woman sick in my bed, yeah. Figured I should know her name."

I tried to roll but that took too much effort, too, so I stopped trying and said, "Go away."

"Help me out here."

"Tired," I mumbled.

"Honey."

He called me "honey" twice. Niles never called me "honey" or "sweetheart" or "darling" or anything, not even Nina most of the time, which was my bloody name. In fact, Niles didn't speak to me much if I thought about it, which, at that moment, I didn't have the energy to do.

I was nearly asleep again before I felt my body gently pulled up, then what felt like my bottom sliding into a man's lap and what felt like a glass against my lips.

"Drink," that somewhat familiar, deep, gravelly voice ordered.

I drank.

The glass went away; then I heard, "Open your mouth, Duchess."

I did as I was told and felt something on my tongue.

The glass came back and then, "Swallow those down."

I swallowed and jerked my head away. The pills going through my sore throat hurt like crazy.

I ended up with what felt like my forehead pressed into someone's neck, soft fabric against my cheek.

"Ouch," I whispered.

"Sorry, darlin'."

I was moved again back between sheets, head on pillow, and before the covers fully settled on me, I was asleep.

*   *   *

I woke up when I felt something cool, too cool, hit my neck.

"No," I rasped.

"You're burnin' up, baby."

I wasn't burning up. I was cold. So cold I was trembling, full on human earthquake.

"So cold." The words scraped through my throat and I winced.

The cool left my neck and was pressed to my forehead.

"Nina, do you have travel insurance?"

I tried to focus but couldn't and asked, "What?"

"This doesn't break soon, I gotta get you to the hospital."

I stayed silent mainly because I was trying to concentrate on getting warm. I pulled the covers closer around me and snuggled into them.

"Nina, listen to me, do you have travel insurance?"

"Wallet," I told him. "Purse."

"Okay, honey, rest."

I nodded and pulled the covers closer but I couldn't get warm enough.

"I need another blanket."

"Honey."

"Please."

The cool cloth stayed at my forehead but I felt strong fingers curl around my neck; then they drifted down to my shoulder.

I heard the word "fuck" said softly and the covers were drawn away.

"No!" I cried. It was weak but it was a cry.

"Hang tight, baby."

The bed moved and I fell back as substantial weight came in behind me.

Then his body was the length of my back, fitting itself into the curve of mine. I nestled backward, deeper into his solid warmth as the tremors kept quaking my frame. His arm came around me, his hand found mine, and the fingers of both my hands curled around his—hard, tight, holding on.

"So cold, Max."

"Beat it back, Duchess."

I nodded against the pillow and said, "I'll try."

It took a while, the trembling keeping me awake, him holding me tight, his body pressed to mine.

What felt like hours later, when the tremors started to slide away, I called softly, "Max?"

"Right here," came a gravelly yet drowsy reply.

"Thanks," I whispered.

Then I slid into sleep, so exhausted it felt like I'd fought an epic battle.

*   *   *

The cool cloth was again against my brow, sweeping back across my hair.

"Max?"

"Fever's broke."

"Mmm," I mumbled, falling back to sleep.

The words, "Work with me, Nina," stopped my descent.

"Okay," I whispered, and I was moved to my back and my upper body was pulled up.

"Lift your arms."

I did as I was told and the T-shirt came off.

"You sweated it out, Duchess. You're in the home stretch."

"Okay."

"Keep your arms up."

"Okay."

I felt another T-shirt come down over my arms, over my head. I felt it yanked down at my belly, my sides. I fell forward and felt my forehead resting against something soft and hard. The material was soft and it covered what I figured was a hard shoulder.

"You can drop your arms."

"Okay."

I dropped my arms and slid them around what felt like a man's waist. Then I cuddled closer. It felt like arms came around my waist, too, and it also felt like a hand was trailing gently up and down my back.

"You're sweet when you're sick."

"I am?"

"Hellion when you're riled."

"Yes?"

"Yeah."

"Mmm."

Then he muttered, "Not sure which I like more."

I had no reply. Mainly because I'd fallen back to sleep.

CHAPTER TWO

Human Again

I woke up to crazy brightness and after a couple of seconds remembered where I was.

The A-frame.

And Max.

"Oh my God," I muttered to the pillow as I opened my eyes and rolled to my back, memories flooding my foggy brain.

I couldn't be certain I remembered every second but I remembered enough to be mortified. Mortified more than I'd ever been mortified in my whole, entire life.

I had to get out of there. Immediately.

I threw the covers back, tossed my legs over the side of the bed, and stood. I had to give myself a moment to adjust, so I did. I was light-headed and my nose was a bit stuffed up, but other than that I felt human again.

Human enough to escape.

I walked to the railing and looked downstairs, left then right. Max wasn't in the kitchen or living room.

I looked out the windows and saw the snow and pine trees, white and green jagged mountaintops breaking the blue sky, breathtaking landscape, a fabulous view as far as the eye could see.

I also saw that the drive had been cleared of snow, including a large, level area at the front of the house. The one-track lane that led to the road was also cleared, as was the road leading away. My rental car was sitting in front of the house shining in the sun, so bright it was eye watering. It looked like it'd never been touched by snow.

There was no Cherokee.

"Max?" I called, my voice sounded untried, weak. I cleared my throat and called louder, "Max?"

Nothing.

Thank God. He was gone.

Knowing I should get a move on, I just stood there, all I needed to do crashing in and pressing down on me. I didn't know what to do first.

I'd always had the terrible habit of looking at any problem, no matter how big, as a whole problem. Charlie was always telling me to break it down, make the big problem into smaller problems, take it one step at a time.

I looked at the bed and my suitcase.

Shower. Shower first, get dressed, get some food in me, a quick snack, energy. Water, I needed to rehydrate. And coffee. I needed caffeine. Then write a note of thanks to Max, pack up my car, drive down the mountain, and spend two weeks in Denver.

I'd never really been to Denver, just the airport and a grocery store, but it seemed like a lovely place. And people lived in Denver; there had to be things to do. Cinemas. Shopping. Museums. I could find stuff to do in Denver. Maybe I could find me in Denver. Maybe I could figure out my life in Denver.

Denver it was.

I went to my bag and pulled out things I needed, went to the bathroom, dumped them there, then back to the suitcase for clothes.

I caught sight of the bed and got sidetracked when I decided that I should probably change the sheets. No one wanted to sleep in a bed after a sick person had been there. Max might have been a jerk when I first met him but he'd been *not* a jerk when I'd been sick. He deserved clean sheets.

So I pulled off the big, fluffy, chocolate-brown-covered

down duvet and yanked the sheets off the bed, throwing them into a pile at the foot. The Internet advertisement of the A-frame said it had a washer and dryer. I'd put the sheets in the wash after my shower and tell Max in the note where to find his sheets so he wouldn't think I made off with them. Not that he'd think I'd steal his sheets but who knew. People did all sorts of weird stuff at a rental.

I went to the bathroom and halted in front of the mirror when I caught a look at myself.

"Oh my God," I whispered.

My face was pale, there were purple-blue shadows under my eyes, but it was my hair that caught my attention. My hair was a disaster.

I hadn't lucked out much in life but one thing I had lucked out with was my hair. I had a lot of it. It was thick and it looked good practically anytime day or night, even just waking up or when I hadn't washed it in a couple of days. I'd had a few unfortunate perms when I was younger but usually it looked great no matter what length or what cut or, being honest, what color. Currently it was highlighted a light blonde, the streaks of blonde liberal through my naturally somewhat mousy brown hair and I'd let it grow kind of long.

Now it was dank, partially matted, and frightening.

I pushed aside the frightening vision of me, brushed my teeth, washed my face, and jumped into the shower. This was taking a lot out of me. I'd just battled a serious fever and I hadn't had food in who knew how long. I should probably rest, definitely take a second out to eat a banana or something, but I had no idea where Max was. I was hoping he was at work. That would give me plenty of time to do what I had to do and escape.

I got out of the shower, lotioned my body, perfumed, pulled a comb through my hair, glorying in the feeling of being clean. I decided that showers worked wonders. They were mini-miracles. Especially Max's shower, which was separate from the bath, tiled in beautiful taupe and brown veined marble and big enough for two.

I pulled on my underwear and the pair of jeans I bought that Niles shook his head at when I showed them to him. Niles didn't understand the jeans or the other stuff I bought for my rustic, time-out adventure in Colorado, thinking my purchases would help me fit in with the natives. Niles wore suits to work and large whale corduroys and cashmere sweaters when he was relaxed and at home. I'd never seen him in jeans and definitely not faded, secondhand jeans.

I'd bought them specifically for my Colorado adventure in a secondhand clothing store on Park Street in Bristol that specialized in vintage American clothes. They were faded and there was a tear in the back pocket, the threads bleached white, and I thought they looked hip. They also fit like they were made for me and they made my somewhat generous behind look good. Therefore, I loved them.

I paired them with a wide tan belt and my lilac, long-sleeved T-shirt that had fitted sleeves so long they came over my wrists and had a boat neck that was so wide sometimes it fell off my shoulder.

I gathered all my stuff and walked out of the bathroom, smelled bacon cooking, and saw that the dirty sheets had been taken away.

I closed my eyes slowly.

I should probably not have taken time to strip the bed, though that would have been rude.

And maybe I should have left out lotioning and, probably, standing under the strong, hot spray of the shower for a full five minutes, just letting the water wash over me and bring me back to life.

Well, Max was home and I had no choice—I'd have to thank him in person. No, I'd have to face him, tall, amazing-looking, gravelly voiced Max Whatever-His-Last-Name-Was who had seen me mostly naked and took care of me while I was sick. *Then* I'd have to thank him in person.

Get it over with, Charlie would say to me. *Always good to do the shit stuff fast, get it out of the way.*

Charlie, as ever (if he'd been there but, unfortunately, he was not), was right.

I sighed, threw Max's T-shirt on the armchair, and dumped my toiletries in my bag. On bare feet I walked to the spiral staircase and descended.

When I hit the living room, I saw him standing at the stove, his back to me. He was wearing another thermal, no flannel this time. It was wine-colored and it fit him perfectly. Maybe a bit *too* perfectly. You could even see some of his muscles defined through the shirt and there appeared to be a lot of them. He was again wearing faded jeans. The waves of his thick hair at the back were just as perfect as they were from the front. Maybe even more perfect. Maybe even his hair was the definition of *perfection.*

I was five feet from the bar when he turned, fork in hand.

His gray eyes hit me. They did a sweep from head to toe and back again; he smiled and I stopped moving.

"She lives," he said in his strangely attractive, gravelly voice.

His eyes and his voice both felt physical, like a touch, a nice one. I felt blood rush to my cheeks as I lifted my hand to my hair and found it wet and slicked back. So I dropped my hand and my head, and, looking at my feet, I mumbled, "Sorry."

"For what?" he asked, and I looked at him again.

"For—"

"You inject yourself with a flu bug?"

"No."

"Shit happens," he muttered, and turned back to the stove.

Well, I had to admit, shit definitely happened. Though not much shit happened to me anymore. I did my best to avoid that for a good long while but it used to happen to me and I knew it still happened because I heard from my friends when shit happened to them.

"Anyway, I'll just—"

"Sit down," he ordered, dropping the fork on the counter and moving to the fridge.

"I'm sorry?"

He had the fridge open but he looked at me. "Sit down."

"I thought I'd—"

"You need juice," he declared, and pulled out what appeared to be the cranberry juice I bought in Denver.

"Really, I should just—"

He closed the fridge and pinned me with his eyes. "Duchess, sit your ass down."

Well. What did I say to that?

I didn't know but I started, "Max—"

"Ass on a stool or I'll put it on a stool."

Was he serious?

"Max, I need to—"

"Eat."

"I'm sorry?"

"You need to eat. You haven't had anything in two days."

I forgot about him being somewhat rude and definitely domineering and felt my head move forward with a jerk at the same time I felt my eyes grow wide.

"What?" I whispered.

"You been out of it for two days."

I looked out the window as if the landscape could tell me this was false (or true). Then my eyes went back to Max.

"Two days?"

"Yep."

"It's Tuesday?"

"Yep."

"Oh my God," I whispered.

"Sit down, Nina."

Too shocked by the knowledge that I'd lost two whole days of my time-out adventure, without another word I moved forward and sat down on a stool. Max poured me a glass of cranberry juice and set it on the counter in front of me before he moved away.

"Coffee," I muttered. "Please."

"Gotcha."

"Two days," I whispered to my cranberry juice before I took a sip.

"You remember any of it?" he asked, and my eyes moved quickly to him.

His back was to me and he was pouring a cup of coffee.

Now, what did I do?

Did I tell him yes, I remembered him taking care of me? Giving me medicine, keeping me hydrated, wiping my brow, getting into bed with me and holding me until the tremors went away, changing my T-shirt, stroking my back? Did I tell him I remembered him being so sweet?

Since I wasn't intending on thinking of any of that (ever), I decided to lie.

"Remember any of it?" I parroted.

He turned and walked the coffee to me. "Yeah, you were pretty out of it. Do you remember any of it?"

I nodded as he set the coffee cup in front of me and affirmed, "I was really out of it, so actually, no. I don't remember anything."

He watched me for several seconds; then he dipped his head to the coffee cup and asked, "Do you take cream?"

"Cream?"

He grinned. "Yeah, Duchess, cream. You got that in England?"

"We don't call it cream."

"What do you call it, then?"

"What it is. Milk."

"All right, you take milk?"

"Yes."

"Sugar?"

"One."

"One what?"

"One sugar."

He was still grinning but he shook his head and went to the fridge. He pulled out a gallon jug of milk and set it on the counter by me. Then he pulled out a huge, unopened bag of sugar and, if I wasn't wrong, I bought that bag in Denver too. He set that next to the milk, opened a drawer, and got me a spoon. Then he turned to his bacon.

I opened the bag of sugar while I said, "I don't think I could do bacon."

"Bacon's for me. You're getting oatmeal."

"Oh."

He cracked two eggs *into* the side of the skillet *with* the bacon *and* the bacon grease and I stared. Then he walked to a cupboard and pulled out a box of instant oatmeal.

I spooned sugar in my coffee, then stared at the gallon jug of milk. I looked at my mug. Then the milk. Then back.

How was I going to get a splash of the milk from that huge gallon jug into my mug without making a mess?

On this thought, I heard, "Honey, you gonna will it to pour itself in your cup with your eyes?"

I looked at him and asked, "Do you have a little pitcher?"

He threw his head back and burst out laughing. That was deep and gravelly too.

I stared again.

What was funny?

"What's funny?" I asked when he got control of his hilarity.

"Don't throw many tea parties, Duchess," he told me, still smiling like I was highly amusing.

I wasn't sure I liked him calling me "Duchess." Okay, so the way he was saying it *now* was kind of sweet in a weirdly familiar and even somewhat intimate way. The way he said it two days ago, I wasn't so sure. It was almost like he was making fun of me except now it felt like he thought I was in on the joke.

"Maybe you could stop calling me 'Duchess,'" I suggested.

"Maybe I couldn't," he returned, then came toward me, picked up the gallon jug, and splashed a huge dollop of milk in my mug, making coffee and milk plop up and out on the counter. He turned back and poured, without measuring, a bunch of milk into the instant oatmeal.

"My name is Nina," I told him.

"I know that."

"Maybe you can call me Nina."

"I'll call you that too."

"Rather than Duchess."

He'd put the milk in the fridge and walked back to me, grabbing the bag of sugar. His eyes came to me before he turned toward the oatmeal. "You want a little pitcher for your milk, you're definitely a duchess."

I decided to let it go. In about half an hour he wasn't going to be calling me anything because I was going to be in a rental car and on my way to Denver.

"Whatever," I muttered, and took a sip of coffee.

Then I watched as he spooned sugar into the oatmeal. One spoon. Two. Three. Four.

"Is that for me?" I asked on a rush when he dipped in for spoon five.

His torso twisted and his eyes came to me. "Yeah."

He was making me oatmeal and I didn't want to seem ungrateful, so I muttered, "Um, I think four sugars will do it."

Two would do it. Actually one would have done it, but I'd settle for four.

"Your wish...," he muttered right back, but he sounded amused.

I decided to let that go too.

He put the oatmeal in the microwave, started it up, and headed back to the skillet. He flipped his eggs expertly, then using the fork, pulled the bacon out of, and, without draining the grease off, put it on a plate I hadn't yet noticed. The plate already had two slices of toast slathered in butter and grape jelly.

Before I could stop myself, I announced in a wistful voice, "I miss grape jelly."

His head twisted toward me and he had an expression on his face that looked like he thought I was funny at the same time he was slightly confused. "You miss grape jelly?"

I took a sip of cranberry juice, surveyed the microwave, but didn't answer. Talking to him was taking a lot of concentration and energy, neither of which I had at that moment. It was weird. He was acting like I'd been there a year. Like we were chums. Like he didn't practically throw me out of his house two days ago. Like he *liked* me.

You didn't tease someone you didn't like. At least that was what my mother told me years ago when I'd come home, complaining that all the boys teased me. She said boys teased girls they liked, and one thing I learned in life, my mother was rarely, if ever, wrong.

Max decided to let it go, too, and dumped his eggs on the plate, turned off the burner, moved the skillet to a different one, and came to stand in front of me. He held his plate aloft and started eating.

"You need to rest today," he told me while eating.

"Yes," I agreed, and I would rest that day but I'd do that once I found a hotel in Denver.

He munched bacon before he bizarrely informed me, "In the wall outside the bathroom upstairs is the TV. You just slide open the doors. Same below it to get to the DVD player. Got some DVDs down there. Remotes are in the nightstand."

I stared at him as he forked up some egg. "Sorry?"

"You want to use the computer, the password is Shauna444."

"Um...," I mumbled, then repeated, "Sorry?"

The microwave beeped, he set down his plate, and turned to it, saying, "That's with a 'U.'"

I wasn't following. "A 'U'?"

He opened the microwave, got my bowl, walked back to me, opened a drawer, dropped a spoon in the bowl, and put it in front of me.

"Shauna. With a 'U.' S-h-a-u-n-a. Then 444. All together."

"But—"

"Computer's in the rolltop," he went on, picking up his plate and a rasher of bacon. His eyes went beyond me to the window before he took a bite.

"Max, I think—"

"You bought enough food to feed an army. You should be good for lunch."

Oh my God. Did he think I was *staying* there?

"Max—"

He looked back at me. "You should go bland. Make sure you're over it. Wouldn't be good to have anything rich in your stomach if you have a relapse."

"Maybe we should—"

I heard a car door slam. I stopped talking and twisted on my stool to look around. Outside, parked beside the Cherokee, was one of those sporty mini-SUVs and making it sportier, it was red. Bouncing up the steps was a young woman with a mass of thick, gleaming, wavy, dark brown hair. She was wearing a baby-pink poofy vest with a sky-blue thermal under it with what looked like tiny pink polka dots on it. She had on faded jeans and they were *tight*. She also had on fluffy boots with big pom-poms at the front that swung around as she bounced up the steps. She was pretty. Very pretty.

No, she was adorable. The epitome of a snow bunny.

And she was very, very young. Way younger than me. Way younger than what I suspected Max was.

I was thirty-six. He had to be my age, maybe older, maybe younger, but not by much either way.

She looked twelve. Though since she could drive, maybe she was sixteen.

She stopped on the porch and gave an overexaggerated, overcheerful wave in our direction, bouncing up on her toes. Even overdone, the wave looked adorable, too, like it came natural to her, which it probably did since she was likely a cheerleader.

Good Lord.

"Becca," Max muttered. I looked at him and he folded a piece of toast in half and said, "I'm gonna be gone awhile." He took a bite out of the toast and turned toward the sink.

"I—"

"Hey!" a bright, cheerful, *young* female voice called from the doorway.

I turned to look and Becca was inside, closing the door. Then she bounced toward the bar, her boot pom-poms swinging wildly.

"Hey, Becca," Max greeted.

"Hey, Max," Becca called. She looked at me and said, still bright, still cheerful, still *young*, "Hey there."

"Hello."

"You must be Nina," she announced, and I couldn't be sure but I think I gawped.

How did she know who I was?

Her eyes went around me. "She's pretty," she told who I suspected was Max since he was the only other person there. She looked back at me and her eyes fell to my chest before she declared, still bright and cheerful and also somewhat loud, "I dig that top! Where'd you get it? I gotta have one."

"I—"

"You can shop, Bec, but it'd be a miracle you find that top," Max told her, and she looked at him when he finished, "and be able to afford it."

I looked at Max and said, kind of snappish mainly because of the way he'd said what he'd said, "It wasn't that expensive."

"Since she's gotta get on a plane and fly to England to buy it, that makes it expensive," Max returned.

He had me there.

"*England,*" Becca breathed, but she did it brightly and cheerfully.

"Um…yes," I said to her.

"I forgot, Max told Mindy you were English."

Mindy? Who was Mindy? And why was Max telling her about me?

"I'm not English," I told Becca.

"I *love* your accent." She kept breathing.

"I don't really have an accent."

"It's so cool!" she cried, her eyes going to Max. "Isn't it cool?"

"It's cool," Max agreed, but he didn't sound like he thought it was cool. He sounded like he was trying not to laugh.

I was going to look at him to see if he was trying not to laugh and maybe ask what was so funny when Becca kept my attention.

"Oh my *God*. I'd *so* love to live in a different country," Becca declared. "You are *so* lucky."

Me? Lucky? England was beautiful but...

"Though, I'd wanna live somewhere where it doesn't rain," Becca decided.

"It does that," I told her. "Quite a bit."

"If I lived there, how long would it take me to get an accent?" she asked.

"Um...I'm not sure," I answered.

"I'd have to practice," she declared.

I thought of a bright, cheerful, bouncy American cheerleader going to England and practicing an accent. Then I tried not to wince.

"I'm gonna get my boots," Max said, and I saw he was rounding the counter.

"Max," I called, but he didn't stop.

"Be back in a sec," he said, not even turning.

"So are all the clothes in England as cool as that top?" Becca asked me.

"Um...not exactly," I replied, then asked, "Can you hang on a second?" I had one finger pointed up when I jumped off the stool and hurried after Max, who'd disappeared up the spiral staircase.

When I made it to the bedroom, he was sitting on the bed tugging on a boot.

"Max—"

He cut me off. "Extra sheets in the closet."

"Okay, but—"

He tugged on the second boot. "I don't know how long this'll take, so make yourself at home."

"I'm leaving," I said quickly.

His head arched back and he looked at me. "What?"

"I'm going to Denver."

"No, you aren't," he replied, and his answer, which was firm, unyielding, and also surprising, made me blink.

"I'm not?"

"Nope," he said as he stood, and he seemed very tall and very big. He was, of course, very tall and very big in the kitchen, too, but the kitchen was a brightly lit open space. The loft wasn't a brightly lit open space. It was more like a brightly lit, intimate cocoon. His very tall, very big body seemed to fill the loft, leaving very little room for me.

"But...I am."

He walked to me and I resisted the urge to retreat mainly because the spiral staircase was behind me and I'd already spent two days sick in his house. I didn't want to break my neck there.

He stopped a foot away from me and said, "You aren't."

I shook my head and asked, "Why?"

"You need to rest."

"I'll rest in Denver."

"Drivin' to Denver isn't resting."

"Okay, then I'll get a hotel in town and spend the night there, drive to Denver tomorrow."

"You aren't doin' that either."

"Why not?"

"Because you aren't."

I was beginning to get angry. I didn't often get angry, mainly because I'd made my life so that not much happened to me to get angry about. But I was definitely beginning to get angry right then.

"Why?" I asked.

"Nina, I gotta get this done. I don't have time for this."

He didn't have time for this? Time for what?

"Time for what?"

"Time to spar with you."

Now I wasn't angry. I was confused. "We're...sparring?"

"You're off. You were better the other night."

"Better at what?"

He didn't answer me. Instead he repeated, "I gotta go."

"Max—" I started, but he began to walk around me, so instinctively my hand shot out and my fingers curled around his bicep.

He stopped but my body had frozen and my eyes had dropped to his arm.

My fingers were there, holding what felt an awful lot like steel. Niles didn't have steely biceps. Niles had soft, fleshy biceps. One would think steely biceps wouldn't feel nice but they didn't only feel nice, they felt *nice*.

"Nina," Max called.

I jumped and yanked my hand away.

"I want to thank you for being so nice about me being... sick and, um... everything, but really, I have to go."

"Why?"

"Why?"

"Yeah, why?"

"Well, because."

"Because why?"

Was he crazy?

I didn't get it. Why did he want me to stay? Two days ago he didn't want me to stay. Why were we even having this conversation?

"You're home," I reminded him.

"Yeah?"

"And, well, we can't *share* the house."

"Why not?"

I didn't have an answer for that because it was such a bizarre question I figured there *was* no answer.

Then I did, so I said, "I don't know you."

To that he grinned and it was a grin that made me highly uncomfortable but in a weirdly good way.

"Duchess, I've seen you mostly naked."

At his words, I still felt uncomfortable, though no longer in a good way, weird or not. I also felt my eyes get big, I felt my cheeks get hot, and I felt my heart start pounding.

Then I felt my blood pressure rise.

"Yes, this is true. You've seen that against my will," I reminded him.

"It wasn't against your will."

I leaned forward and snapped, "I was unconscious!"

"There she is," he muttered, but he looked bizarrely pleased.

"Who?" I snapped again.

He ignored my question and informed me humiliatingly, "Last time I saw that body of yours, baby, you lifted your arms for me yourself."

I did do that. I remembered.

"I did not," I lied.

"You did."

"I was in the throes of a fever!" I said, my voice getting loud.

"You still did it."

I threw a hand out. "Okay, fine, you've seen me naked. That doesn't mean we know each other."

"Slept with you too." My mouth dropped open and he asked, "Do you remember that?"

"No," I whispered, but I did.

"You wouldn't let me go."

Oh my *God*. I remembered that too.

"I will repeat, I was in the throes of a fever."

"Don't care what you were in the throes of, you take care of a sick person, you sleep with someone, you get to know them."

"No, you don't."

"Yeah, you do."

"You *don't*!"

He rocked back on his heels and told me, "You got a borin' life so you got a wild hair up your ass. You're out here on some adventure, time-out, because you got a fiancé at home who doesn't give a shit about you."

My head jerked and I stared. I didn't remember telling him *that*. Any of it. Most especially about Niles.

"He gives a shit about me," I whispered.

"Then why hasn't your cell rang in two days?" he asked.

"I—"

"And why you been awake and functioning for at least half an hour and you haven't phoned him?" he went on.

Drat!

Max leaned into me and I watched with not a small amount of fascination as his face grew soft. His face was always amazing. Soft it was something else entirely and that something else was even better.

"You're half a world away, Duchess, you been sick as a dog, and your man doesn't contact you? Even not knowin' you're sick, a man gives a shit, he phones."

He, unfortunately, had me there.

Therefore, I just stood there staring at him not knowing what to say.

Max wasn't so uncertain.

His hand came out and grabbed mine, lifting it between us, his fingers in my palm, his thumb toying with my diamond engagement ring.

"I was your man you were halfway around the world from me, honey, I'd fuckin' phone you," he said quietly.

"Niles is reserved," I whispered.

"Niles is an ass," he returned, and my brows drew together. "You don't know him."

"I know men and I know he's not reserved. He's an ass."

I pulled my head together, my hand from his, and snapped, "Yes? And how do you know that?"

"Because I've seen you naked. I've seen you sweet. I've seen you unsure. And I've seen you riled, and seein' all that, I know, you were half a world away from me, I'd fuckin' phone."

"Perhaps that's not the kind of relationship Niles and I have," I suggested snottily, but his words hit me somewhere deep, somewhere I didn't know I had.

"You on a time-out?"

"What?"

"If you told me you needed a time-out, first, I wouldn't fuckin' let you have one. Second, I wouldn't give you reason to fuckin' *want* one. And last, you took off anyway, I'd fuckin' phone."

My head tilted to the side and I felt my body start warming up not, this time, with fever.

"You wouldn't *let* me have one?"

"Fuck no."

"Ergo, you would *not* be my *man*."

"Ergo?"

"It's Latin. It means 'therefore.'"

"Whatever," he muttered. "I gotta go."

"Hang on," I snapped. "You may *think* you know me but I was delirious. I didn't get to know *you*."

"You will."

"I won't."

"So you think you're leavin'?" he switched the subject.

"I *am* leaving," I declared, happy to be on this subject.

He stuck his hand in his front jeans pocket, pulled out the keys to the rental, and dangled them in front of me for a brief flash before his hand closed around them and he shoved them back into his pocket.

"Be hard gettin' down the mountain on foot, carryin' that huge-ass suitcase of yours, which weighs a goddamned ton, your overnight bag, your purse, and a shitload of groceries," he informed me.

"Give me those keys," I snapped.

"I'd tell you to go for them, honey, but don't have time to play."

At his words, my mouth dropped open again. He grinned, chucked me gently under the chin with the side of his fist (yes, I will repeat, he *chucked me under the chin*), and walked away.

I stood staring at the space he used to be in. When I heard the front door open, I ran to the railing.

"Max!" I shouted.

"Later, Duchess," he called, a hand up, two fingers flicking out. He didn't even look back.

Becca looked back, though, and up. She gave me a wince-I'm-sorry-face and a finger wave and I knew she'd heard everything. I'd totally forgotten she was there.

I watched Max throw his now-black-leather-jacketed arm around her shoulders and I wondered who Becca was and what she was to Max, who had just been upstairs, semi-fighting with me. And also, if I wasn't wrong, and I didn't think I was, flirting with me in a rough, macho, mountain man kind of way.

They talked for a few seconds at the side of her car before they separated. Becca got in her sporty, red mini-SUV. Max got in his black Cherokee. They both drove away.

I looked down at the bottom floor and saw my cranberry juice, my coffee, and my untouched oatmeal all sitting on the bar.

I looked out the window at the wilderness.

The Internet advertisement for the A-frame said it was fifteen miles away from the nearest town. Secluded, quiet, the perfect holiday destination for a calm, relaxing, peaceful getaway.

The Nightmare Holiday Destination if you had to walk fifteen miles to town carrying a suitcase, an overnight bag, a purse, and a shitload of groceries.

Tackle a problem prepared, Charlie advised in my head, and I nodded like he was there with me.

Then I walked downstairs, heated up my oatmeal, warmed up my coffee, and sat on the stool, preparing to tackle my problem.

CHAPTER THREE

Buffalo Burgers

AFTER I ATE, I did my dishes, Max's dishes, wiped down the counters, found the extra sheets in the closet, and made the bed. Then I found the utility room around the corner from the recess in the living room. The dirty sheets were on the floor. As the advertisement said, washer and dryer but also a bunch of man stuff that needed to be organized.

I let that stuff be. I put the sheets in the washer.

I packed my bags and decided that Max could have the groceries. He and Becca and the unknown Mindy could have a party. I didn't care. I was out of there.

Then I poured myself another cup of coffee and found the phone book. It was thin. I'd never seen a phone book so thin.

I realized why it was thin when I looked up taxi companies. There was only one. But one was enough.

I went to Max's phone, pulled it out of the receiver, and punched in the number.

"Thrifty's," a woman answered.

"Hello, my name is Ms. Sheridan and I need a taxi to town."

There was a pause and then, "Nina?"

My body jolted before I froze with the phone to my ear.

"Hello?" the voice called.

"Um . . . yes?"

"This Nina?"

"How do you know who I am?"

"Welp, Max called, said a lady with a fancy accent by the name of Nina would call, askin' for a taxi. You're a lady with a fancy accent and you're askin' for a taxi. Get some of those callin' with British accents, not a lot. So I'm takin' a wild guess. You Nina?"

I wondered if I could make it to Denver, then to England before anyone discovered Max's body. Then I wondered if anyone would bother with extradition if they figured out it was me who did the deed. That was a lot of paperwork for one big, tall, domineering, jerky mountain man. Then I wondered, considering Max was so tall and big, how I'd kill him.

I decided, poison.

Then I answered, "Yes, I'm Nina."

"Max said you been down with the flu. Girl, you need to rest," the woman advised me.

"I thought I'd check into a hotel room in town."

She hooted in my ear but said no actual words.

"What?" I asked.

"Girl, Holden Maxwell quarantined me to his house and he was in it, I wouldn't go lookin' for no hotel room."

I felt my brows draw together. "Who's Holden Maxwell?"

"Who's Holden Maxwell?" she repeated.

"Yes. Who's Holden Maxwell?"

"Girl, you're livin' with him."

His name was Holden? What kind of name was that? No wonder he called himself Max.

I decided not to ask about the origins of Max's name or explain the fact that I was *not* living with him and told her, "Well, he isn't actually here, so I'm quarantined alone."

"Oh, he'll be back."

I didn't doubt that.

"Since you probably know where he lives, will you please send a taxi?" I asked.

"Nope," she answered.

I was silent a beat, mostly shock, a little anger. Then I repeated, "Nope?"

"Nope."

"Why not?"

"'Cause Max says you need to rest."

Yes, definitely poison.

"I'll pay double."

"You still gotta rest."

I was seeing red again. I ignored it and offered, "I'll pay triple."

"Triple shmiple. You gotta rest."

"Listen—"

"Come into town with Max when you've recovered. I'll buy you a beer."

Did she just tell me she'd buy me a beer? How did we get from me ordering a taxi to her buying me a beer?

"What?" I asked.

"Name's Arlene. Come to The Dog. Show you the town only locals know."

"But—"

"Gotta go. Get some rest, you hear?"

Then she hung up.

I stood staring at the phone buzzing at me. I beeped it off and put it in the receiver.

The Internet advertisement didn't say word *one* about nutty townspeople. Not word *one*. If it did, I definitely would not have hit "book now."

I looked back through the phone book. No more taxi companies. There were three rental agencies but they rented ATVs and snowmobiles. I didn't think that would help.

It was either walk, when I felt like taking a nap, or I was stuck.

Which meant I was stuck.

Which meant I needed to take a nap so I could be energized and clearheaded when I plotted *Holden Maxwell's* murder.

Before that, I had one more thing to do.

I went to my purse, grabbed my cell, and saw the battery was low. I also saw I had a number of texts, all from friends, not one from Niles.

I climbed the spiral staircase, went to my overnight bag beside my suitcase, dug out the charger and the converter, and plugged them into the wall. I pulled the cord and phone with me and sat on the bed. Then I went to my contacts and hit Niles's number.

He answered on the third ring. "Hello?"

"Niles?"

"Nina?"

I tried to figure out how I felt about his voice coming at me over the phone and I couldn't figure it out. It wasn't relief or welcome familiarity. It was just... well, familiarity.

Then I tried to figure out how I felt about his voice coming over the phone not sounding relieved that I was calling from half a world away. Just sounding like Niles and as if I were at the store asking him what he wanted for dinner. I couldn't figure that out either.

"Hi, I'm here," I told him.

"That's good."

"I've been here for—"

"Listen," he cut me off, "I'm about to go into a meeting."

"What?"

"I've got a meeting."

I shook my head. "Niles, I just wanted to tell you, I've been sick."

"Yes, you said you thought you were getting a sinus infection."

"Well, it was worse than that."

"You sound fine."

I did. Miraculously, outside of being tired, I felt pretty good. My throat didn't hurt, and I wasn't coughing, though my nose was still kind of stuffy.

"I'm better now."

"That's good." He sounded distracted. "They're waiting for me."

"Okay," I said. "Do you want me to call later?"

"Later?" Now he sounded perplexed, as if he didn't understand the concept of later.

"Later, tonight, when you're home."

"I'm working late."

"Yes, but your late is my afternoon."

I heard his sigh. Then he said, "If you want."

If I want?

I felt anger again, surprisingly anger at Niles. I never got angry at Niles. He never did anything to get angry at, mostly because he never did anything.

"Niles, I'm half a world away."

"Pardon?"

"I'm half a world away!" I said louder.

"I don't understand."

And he didn't. Because he wasn't the type of man who cared if his fiancée needed a time-out and took it half a world away.

And I wondered what he'd think if I told him I was staying in the beautiful home with breathtaking views with an amazing-looking man who'd seen me naked (mostly), made me breakfast, teased me, flirted with me, and who I'd kind of slept with.

"Are you there?" he asked me.

"I'm here."

"I need to go."

"Of course."

"Call me later, if you like."

"Right."

"Are you okay?"

No, I was *not*.

I didn't tell him this. Instead I said, "Tired."

"Rest, that's what you're there to do."

No, it wasn't. I was there to take a time-out.

"Right," I said again.

"Talk to you later."

"Right."

"Good-bye."

"Bye."

Then he disconnected.

I stared at my phone, hit the button to turn it off, and set it on Max's nightstand. I flopped back onto the bed and bit my lip so I wouldn't cry.

Charlie had never met Niles and I wished he had. Charlie had always been sharp, good at reading people. Charlie would have given it to me gently but he would have given it to me straight.

Problem was, I didn't think I needed Charlie to give it to me straight.

I lifted my left hand to my face and with my right hand I touched my ring.

I'd been thrilled when Niles asked me to marry him because I'd been in love with him. He was steady. He was quiet. He was predictable. And he loved me in his Niles way.

He'd never cheat on me, which had happened to me, back in the day when shit happened to me. He'd never be mean to me, say mean stuff to me, not on purpose just to hurt me and not when he was drunk, which also had happened to me, back before I played it safe and shit happened to me. And he'd never lay a hand on me in anger, which, unfortunately, also happened to me.

So he wasn't affectionate. So he didn't hold my hand, hug me, cuddle me, hold me when we slept. So he didn't call me "honey" or "baby" or give me a nickname like "Duchess."

He was solid. He had a good job. He worked hard. He didn't play hard, just worked hard. He didn't have a lot of friends. He didn't like to go out much. What he liked to do was sit on the couch watching TV with me at his side. Or DVDs. He was content with that. In his Niles way, he loved that, just him and me, watching TV.

And I was content...*ish*. It wasn't exciting but it was nice...*ish*. It meant I'd never get hurt again. Truly, there was something to be said for steady, quiet, and predictable.

But was that enough for me for the rest of my life?

You know the answer to that, Neenee Bean, I heard Charlie say in my head, and I jumped, lurching up, and looked around, seeing no one.

I'd heard Charlie talking to me on occasion but it was remembering things he'd said or knowing what he *would* say. He'd never talked to me *talked* to me.

"Maybe this time-out wasn't a good thing," I whispered to the room. "Maybe it was a bad thing."

Charlie didn't answer. No one did.

And I decided, since I was hearing voices, that maybe a nap was a good thing.

*   *   *

"Nina."

My eyes opened and I saw Max's face close to mine. I also felt his fingers digging into my hip. I was on my side in his bed and he was sitting in the crook of my lap.

"Jesus, you sleep like the dead," he muttered, pulling back only his head, his hand stayed where it was.

I saw the TV was blue screen and the sun was fading. It was getting dark, which meant it was getting late.

I rolled my head slightly on the pillow to look up at him, still not quite awake and asked, "What?"

"I thought it was because you were sick but you sleep like the dead," Max informed me. Then he lifted his hand not at my hip and took a bite out of a chocolate chip cookie.

My eyes narrowed on the cookie. "Are those my cookies?"

He chewed, swallowed, and answered, "Yeah," then shoved the rest of the cookie into his mouth.

I got up on an elbow and said, "But those are mine."

"Honey, they're in my house, they're fair game."

"I see this sharing-the-house business isn't going to work," I told him, and he grinned.

"They're fuckin' good cookies, babe, but there're about three dozen of them. You gonna eat them all?"

"Yes," I bit out.

"Well, you'll have to eat them all but four," he told me.

"You had *four*?"

"Yeah," he replied, ignoring my tone and possibly the

lethal look on my face before he went on. "I'm hungry. Let's go to dinner."

"Dinner?"

His hand suddenly moved from my hip to my shoulder. His finger traced skin there and I felt that my shirt had fallen down. I yanked it up, sat up, and scooted up to the headboard.

His hand dropped to the bed at the other side of my thighs so he was leaning across me and he said, "Yeah, dinner. I'm takin' you to town for a burger."

"You're taking me to town for a burger?"

He tipped his head to the side and asked, "You gonna repeat everything I say?"

"No."

"Good," he said, pushed up off the bed, grabbed my hand before I could evade his clutch, and yanked me to my feet in a way I could neither ignore nor fight. "Get yourself sorted out. We'll leave as soon as you're ready."

He turned and started to walk away.

"I'm not going to town with you," I announced.

He turned back and asked, "Why not?"

"Because you called the taxi company and told them not to send a taxi."

"And?"

"And, as delighted as I was to be offered a beer by Arlene coupled with the opportunity to experience town like a local, I wanted a taxi."

He grinned again. "Arlene's friendly."

"I think Arlene's a little nutty."

"Friendly ain't nutty, darlin'. It's friendly."

"It would have been friendlier if she sent a taxi."

He tipped his head to the bed and noted, "You got a nap."

"Yes."

"And you got your color back."

I fought the urge to touch my cheeks, won my fight, and said, "So?"

"So, you got rest, except for bakin' cookies. It's what you needed."

"Max, what I need is to—"

He turned and started walking away, saying, "We'll talk over burgers."

"Max."

"Burgers," he said before he hit the staircase.

"Max!" I shouted.

He didn't answer.

God, he was *so* annoying.

He was hungry? He wanted burgers? He wanted to talk over burgers? I was hungry, too, actually famished. So we'd talk over burgers.

I went to my suitcase, pulled out my hair dryer and my makeup case, and snatched up the converter. He wanted to go to town to talk over burgers? He'd have to wait until I did my hair and makeup. I didn't go anywhere without doing my hair and makeup.

Unfortunately, that morning I didn't sleep. I tried but it wouldn't come. So I made cookies instead. Then it was time for lunch, so I made lunch. After that, I put the sheets in the dryer, cleaned up after the cookies and lunch, and tried to read but I was too tired so I went upstairs and slid open the doors to the TV and VCR.

Max had a selection of shoot-'em-ups, some Westerns, horror, a few espionage, lots of explosion movies. I picked an espionage, made the bed, watched the movie, went downstairs and folded the sheets, then went back upstairs to watch another espionage, which, obviously, I fell asleep while watching.

Now it was dinnertime.

I blew out my hair sleek, gunked it up with some stuff I liked that contained any fly-aways, and did my makeup. Not full-on Nina makeup since I was in the Colorado mountains, and if makeup-less, mountain-fresh Becca was anything to go by, the girls in the Colorado mountains didn't do full-on Nina makeup. I went light. I might have got some of my color back but not all of it and I needed a bit of help.

I walked out of the bathroom, put away my stuff in my suitcase, ever ready to escape. I spritzed with perfume, put in some gold hoop earrings, a bunch of gold tinkly bracelets, and wrapped a thin, lilac scarf edged with an inch of gold once around my neck, letting the long ends fall down the front. I pulled on some socks and my high-heeled tan boots. Then I stomped downstairs.

"Ready," I announced when I hit the bottom.

Max was standing in the kitchen looking like he was sorting through mail and he was eating another cookie.

"You're eating another cookie," I accused.

His head came up and his eyes did a full-body scan before he said, "Duchess, you were up there a year. I didn't have another cookie, I'd starve to death."

I'd made it to the bar and put my hands on it. "I wasn't up there a year."

"Felt like a year."

"It wasn't a year."

His eyes did a full-face scan before he said in a softer voice, "Though, it was worth it."

That voice and his words made me feel funny in a way I wasn't willing to explore.

Therefore I said, "Can we go?"

He grinned before he replied, "Yeah." Then he put the rest of the cookie in his mouth and dropped the mail.

"Do you know where my coat is?" I asked.

"Closet," he answered, going to the dining room table and nabbing his leather jacket off the back of one of the chairs.

I walked to one of the doors under the loft, guessing, and guessed right. There was a big storage room, some hooks on the wall, lots more man stuff. My tan, shawl-collared belt cinched at the waist, falling to the hip cashmere coat was on a hook. I grabbed it and shrugged it on, flipping my hair over the collar as Max stood at the open front door.

"You look like you're gonna meet the queen," he said, giving me an indication that even toned down I might be a bit more fancy than the normal Colorado mountain town look.

"You don't meet the queen in jeans," I explained, walking through the door and cinching my belt.

"You would know," he muttered.

I swallowed back a growl and headed to the Cherokee.

He flashed open the locks but didn't come around and open my door. This didn't surprise me. He didn't seem a door-opening type.

Neither was Niles. Then again, Niles didn't drive, didn't know how, never bothered to learn, and it didn't bother him that he couldn't. Firstly, I could drive and when we went somewhere together, I did. Secondly, he could take a taxi to a train and you could take trains most everywhere. Then, once you got there, you could take a taxi to where you were going. Any town, even small ones, had more than just Arlene at Thrifty's.

I pulled myself up into the cab, settled, and belted in.

"I'd like you to call Arlene and lift the boycott on a taxi for Nina," I told him once he started up, did a swift, somewhat hair-raising, three-point turn, and headed down the lane.

"You goin' somewhere?"

"I might wish to and without the keys to the rental that would be difficult."

"We'll see."

"We won't. You'll call her."

"Not big on women tellin' me what to do."

"Max—"

"Or anyone," he finished, and I turned to him, incredulous.

"You're not big on women, or anyone, telling you what to do but you've essentially stolen my car and told the only taxi service in town not to give me a ride. Which is, in essence, telling *me* what to do."

"In essence," he agreed pleasantly.

"I…I…," I stammered, "I don't even know what to say."

"Then don't say anything."

"I've decided to poison you," I announced acidly.

He burst out laughing and took a right at the end of the road. I looked out the windshield and crossed my arms on my chest.

"I wasn't being amusing."

"Impossible."

My neck twisted and I looked at him. "I wasn't!"

"Let me get this straight. I nurse you through a fever and you thank me by poisoning me?"

"You're holding me prisoner."

"Honey, you rented the house for two weeks. That's hardly holding you prisoner."

"I rented a house that was supposed to be *vacant*."

"Lucky for you, seein' as you got so sick, it wasn't."

He had a point there.

"And today it was, save you," he went on.

He had a point there too.

I decided to be quiet.

Quiet wasn't good because Max seemed comfortable with quiet and my mind wandered. It wandered to what he was doing all day. And then it wandered to what he was doing all day with Becca. And then it wandered to the fact he was with Becca at all. And then it wandered to wondering who Becca was. None of this was my business but I wanted to ask even though I knew I shouldn't care. I realized I did care and I worried about what that meant.

We hit town and it was busy, busier than I'd expect for a small town in the mountains on a Tuesday night.

It was also pretty.

When I'd driven through it, considering the snowstorm and my state of mind, I didn't pay much attention. I knew from the Internet advertisement that it was an old gold mining town that made it even after all these years, lately because of tourist trade due to its proximity to popular ski slopes, its shops, restaurants, and the fact that it was pretty. The buildings looked old by American standards, not, obviously, English. And the sidewalks were wooden boardwalks with wooden railings like you'd hitch a horse to. There were more than a few shops that looked interesting.

If I ever got my car keys back, I was definitely going to explore.

After I checked into the hotel, which, on our drive through town, I also noted its location.

"Can you walk in those boots?" Max asked into the quiet cab.

"Yes," I answered.

"I mean more than a few feet."

"Yes," I answered, this time curtly.

"Just askin', Duchess, seein' as we have to park a ways away."

"I'll be fine."

We parked in town, though I didn't know if it was "a ways away" from where we were going. However, when he parked, he parked with the passenger side by an enormous pile of snow that had obviously been created by removing it from the roads. And he parked so close I couldn't open my door.

I looked out the window at the mound of snow and back at Max.

"I don't think I can open my door."

He didn't answer at first. He just opened his door and got out.

Then he leaned in, reached an arm toward me, and said, "Crawl over."

"Crawl over?"

"Crawl over the seat."

"Are you serious?" I asked.

"Do I look like I'm jokin'?" he asked back, and the answer was no, he didn't look like he was joking.

I apparently had two choices. Sit in the Cherokee while he had a burger or crawl over the driver's seat.

There was really only one choice, so I expelled a heavy sigh, unbuckled my belt, hitched my purse up my shoulder, and started to crawl over.

I barely had a hand in the seat when his hands went under my armpits and he hauled me bodily across the cab. Automatically I reached out to clutch his shoulders and one of his hands went out of my pit and around my waist, the other one went around my upper back, and he pulled me to his body.

Sliding me down his body, he set me on my feet in front of him. Right in front of him. *Full frontal* in front of him.

When he didn't immediately let me go, I tipped my head back and told him, "I think I made it."

"You smell good," he said in return.

"I'm sorry?"

"You smell good," he repeated.

I pushed back against his arms but they didn't budge.

"Max—"

"You call him?"

I blinked at the same time I shook my head, confused. "Sorry?"

"Your man, you call him?"

Something strange shifted inside of me. I didn't know what it was but I knew I wasn't going to explore that either.

"Yes."

"You tell him you were sick?"

"Yes."

"What'd he have to say?"

My hands slid from his shoulders to his chest.

I put light pressure there but said softly, "Max, I'm not sure that's any of your business."

"Yeah," he said softly back. "That's what I figured he'd have to say."

"What?" I asked, back to confused, but he let my waist go, put a hand to my belly, and pushed me back several feet. He closed the door, beeped the locks, grabbed my hand, and started walking fast with wide, long strides. "Max . . ." I called, but stopped speaking.

We hit the boarded sidewalk and he answered, "Yeah?"

I decided to let it go, so I replied, "Nothing."

We walked fast, side by side, hand in hand. I let the hand-in-hand thing go too. He was often a jerk but he *had* nursed me back to health, and anyway, his hand was big, it was strong, it was warm, and the night was cold.

I saw ahead of us that there were people hanging outside

a door looking like they were waiting to be let in. When we passed the windows, I saw it was a restaurant, rough-looking but also welcoming. And packed.

Max opened the door the people were standing around, pushed me through using his hand in mine, and kept the contact as we went to the hostess station.

The hostess wore no makeup, a T-shirt that announced she was a fan of the Grateful Dead, and she had a mop of coppery curls pulled up in a mess on top of her head.

She also had on a pair of unusual, huge, silver hoop earrings, the silver hoop a wide, curled, web. They were stunning.

She looked up. Her face brightened immediately when she saw Max and she shouted, "Max!"

"Hey, Sarah," Max returned.

Her eyes came to me and did a body sweep and her face closed down. Just a little bit but it did it and I thought that was strange.

Max stopped us in front of her and didn't let go of my hand. "Got a table?"

"Yep," she said instantly, and I looked into the packed restaurant. Then I looked behind us. Then beside us. All the open space and outside was filled with people standing waiting for tables.

I also noticed they were kind of dressed like me, except different, slightly more casual. But they were obviously tourists on vacation wearing vacation clothes, not locals.

Locals, evidently, didn't have to wait for tables.

She grabbed some stuff from under the hostess station, turned, and walked into the restaurant. Max tugged my hand and we followed her. She took us to the far, back corner where there was an empty booth that a busboy was still wiping down. He scurried off with a smile and a, "Hey, Max," before he passed.

She slapped down white paper placemats, utensils wrapped in napkins, and a plastic bucket filled with crayons.

Then she turned to Max and asked, "Usual?"

"Yeah," he replied, using my hand to position me toward the side of the booth that had its back to the wall, facing the restaurant. "Two," he concluded.

"Gotcha."

"Wait," I called when she started to move away.

"Yeah?" she asked, eyes on me.

"I like your earrings," I told her. "They're stunning."

She looked surprised a second before she lifted the fingers of one hand to her ear and muttered, "Thanks."

"Did you get them recently? I mean, is there somewhere I could buy a pair?"

She studied me for a moment before saying, "Yeah, down the street. I got 'em a year ago but they carry 'em all the time."

"Thanks." I smiled at her.

"Sarah, this is Nina," Max told her, and she nodded to me.

"Hey, Nina."

"Hi."

"It's called Karma," she told me.

"What?"

"The silver place. They got other good stuff too. Karma."

"Karma. Thanks," I said again.

"No probs," she replied, then turned and walked away.

Before I knew what was happening, Max maneuvered me into the booth before I could take off my coat or purse. And again before I knew what was happening, he sat down in *my* side.

"Max," I said, but he wasn't listening. He was shrugging off his coat, his arm bumping into me twice as he did so. He threw it over the table to the opposite bench, turned to me, and said, "Coat."

I pressed back into the corner and pulled the purse off my arm. Max took it from me, threw it over the table, and it landed on his coat. I watched it sail. Then I watched it land.

"You just threw my purse," I informed him.

"Yeah," he replied, then demanded, "Coat."

I stared at him a second, deciding that fighting about

taking off my coat and the fact that I'd rather he not sit *by* me but *across* from me would keep me from dinner. Therefore, still pressed into the corner, I shrugged off my coat. He took it and threw that too.

Obviously a gentleman.

"Max—"

He twisted, leaned toward me, put one forearm on the table, the other arm on the back of the booth, and considering his sudden proximity, the sheer size of his frame, the effect of his clear, gray eyes on me and the fact I was pinned in a corner, I stopped talking.

"Tell me, Duchess, how does an American come to sound like you?"

I stared at him another second, then murmured, "It's a long story."

He looked over his shoulder at the restaurant, turned back to me, and noted, "This ain't fast food."

"That's too bad, considering I'm hungry."

"So, the American passport and the English accent?" he prompted, ignoring my comment.

"In England, they say I have an American accent," I informed him.

"They'd be wrong."

"Actually, they're right."

He shook his head. "You aren't answering my question."

I sighed. Then I said, "I've lived there for a while."

"How long?"

"Long enough, evidently, to pick up a hint of an accent."

"A hint?"

"Yes."

"More than a hint, babe."

I shrugged, looked at the table, and gave in. "If you say so."

Then I arranged the placemats and silverware, one for him, one for me. All the while I did this I tried not to think about how it felt, him calling me "babe." Unfortunately, I failed not to think of this and decided it felt nice.

When I was done arranging the table for our dinner, he asked, "How old are you?"

My eyes shot to his and I told him, "That's a rude question to ask a woman."

"It is?"

"Yes."

"Why?"

"It just is."

"You older than you look?"

"Probably." Or at least I hoped so.

"Should I guess?"

I felt my body get stiff and I declared, "Absolutely not."

He gave me a grin and got closer. "Give me a ballpark figure."

"Older than Becca, younger than your mother," I told him.

His hand not dangling from the table came up and touched my shoulder. I looked down to see my shirt had again slid off. I rearranged it so it covered my shoulder, his hand fell away, and I glared at him.

"That's quite a range," he commented, and I shrugged. Then he said, "You look thirty." Well, that was good. "You act ninety."

I stiffened, then leaned toward him. "I don't act ninety."

"Honey, it was possible, I'd think you were born two centuries ago."

"What's that mean?"

"It means you're uptight."

I leaned in closer and snapped, "I'm not uptight!"

He grinned again. "Totally uptight."

"I'm not uptight," I repeated.

"Don't know what to make of you," he said, his eyes moving down my torso to my lap and he finished with, "Contradiction."

"What does that mean?" I asked, but I really shouldn't have and I knew it.

His eyes came back to mine. "It means you look one way, you act another."

I leaned in closer. "And what does *that* mean?"

He leaned in closer, too, and we were nearly nose to nose. "It means a woman who owns those jeans, those boots, that shirt, deep down is not uptight."

"That's right. I'm *not* uptight," I snapped, and jumped when two bottles of beer hit the table.

I looked up to see a waitress standing there, tray under her arm, white T-shirt, jeans, ash-blonde hair in a ponytail, pretty mountain-fresh face, no makeup.

"Hey, Max," she said.

"Hey, Trudy," Max replied.

"Hey," she said to me then smiled.

"Hi," I replied, not smiling.

Her smile got bigger and without leaving menus she walked away.

I looked at the beer and Max thankfully moved away, grabbed both, put one in front of me and took a pull off his.

"Is that for me?" I asked, and his eyes came to me around his beer bottle before he dropped his hand.

"Yeah."

"I didn't order that."

"I did."

He did? When?

I decided not to ask and informed him, "I don't drink lager."

"What?"

I dipped my head to the beer. "I said, I don't drink lager."

"What do you drink?"

"Ale, bitter, stout."

"So, you're sayin' you don't drink *American* beer, you drink *English* beer."

"There are lagers that aren't American. Heineken. Stella. Beck's. In fact," I went on informatively, "I think lager was invented by the Germans. In *fact*, I think beer, on the whole, was invented by the Germans."

I didn't actually know this for a fact. I was just guessing.

"Jesus," he muttered, dropping his head.

"What?"

He looked back at me. "Duchess, you can argue about anything."

"No, I can't."

"So now you're arguin' about not arguing?"

I decided to be quiet.

Max twisted and shouted, "Trudy!"

Trudy turned from the table she was standing at, hands up, notepad in one, pencil in the other, table of tourists interrupted in mid-order, and she shouted back, "What?"

"You got any ale?" Max asked, and I shrunk into the booth.

"Ale?" Trudy asked back.

"Ale."

"I think so, sure."

"Get the Duchess here one, will you?" he called, dipping his head toward me.

Her eyes slid to me; she smiled and shouted, "Sure thing."

At the same time I leaned forward and hissed, "Max!"

He turned back to me and asked, "What?"

"Don't call me Duchess in front of Trudy."

He grinned and replied, "All right, you tell me how old you are, I won't call you Duchess in front of Trudy."

I looked at the ceiling and asked, "Why? Why me, Lord? What did I do?"

My body went stiff and my chin jerked down when I felt Max's fingers curl around the side of my neck and I saw that he'd gotten close. Not only did I see he'd gotten close, his face had grown soft and he looked amused and the combination was phenomenal. So phenomenal, I held my breath.

His eyes dropped to my mouth and my lungs started burning.

"Christ, you're cute," he muttered.

"Max!" I heard a man yell. Max's head turned and I let out my breath.

Max muttered under his, "Fuck."

I looked into the restaurant to see a tall man with a handsome, open, boyish face, light brown hair, and a lanky frame headed our way. He was smiling.

At his side walked a tall woman, thin and utterly beautiful in a very cool way. Flawless skin. Long, ebony hair, perfectly straight and gleaming, parted severely and pulled back just as severely in a ponytail at her nape. She also wore no makeup. She had on almost the same thing as Becca this morning except her poofy vest was less poofy and was a muted, sage green and her shirt wasn't a thermal. It was long sleeved, ribbed, and dusky blue. She and the man were holding bottles of beer, Coors Light to be precise.

Her eyes were on Max and she was not smiling.

Her eyes slid to me and for some bizarre reason her expression turned glacial.

"Max, didn't know you were back in town," the man remarked sociably as they made it to our table and stopped.

Max slid out of the booth and shook his hand. "Harry."

Harry looked at me and greeted, "Hey."

"Hello," I replied.

"Nina, this is Harry," Max said, then jerked his head to the woman and I noticed Max was also not smiling. "And this is Shauna."

Shauna? Shauna with a "U" of the password on Max's computer? No wonder her look was glacial.

Oh my *God*.

"Hello, Shauna," I said, trying to cover my surprise and discomfort.

Her eyes grazed over me and she said to the wall at my side, "Hello."

"Man, it's packed tonight," Harry noted, looking behind him. "They're clearing our table. You mind if we hang here with you while they do?"

Without allowing Max to answer, he shoved our coats and my purse to the side and slid into the booth opposite me. Shauna's entire face grew so tight I thought it'd split open but Harry just grabbed her hand and pulled her in, oblivious to her state of mind. Or maybe he didn't know his partner's name was the password on Max's computer and all that implied.

I looked up at Max and saw just his mouth had grown tight but his face had grown that scary dark I'd seen the first night I met him. Nevertheless, without a word he slid in beside me.

"So, Nina, you come back with Max?" Harry asked me.

"Back?" I asked him.

"Yeah," Harry said, grinning a somewhat goofy grin.

"Um...," I replied, answering his confusing question the only way I could. "No."

"Nina rented the house," Max told Harry, and Harry nodded.

"Yeah, fuckin' great house," Harry remarked, and took a drink of his beer.

"It is," I agreed, not knowing what to do in this situation and hoping the icicles Shauna was so obviously willing to shoot out her eyes and pierce my flesh wouldn't actually form.

"Pretty unbelievable, Max built it himself," Harry said.

I stopped trying not to look at Shauna without looking like I was trying not to look at Shauna and my eyes shot to Harry.

"I'm sorry?"

"The A-frame. Max built it himself from the ground up," Harry informed me, and my eyes moved to Max.

"You did?" I breathed, actually *breathed*. Then again, I was surprised. And impressed.

"Designed it too," Harry went on before Max, who'd turned his head to me, could reply.

"He did not," Shauna put in coldly, and I looked back at them.

"Well, Rudy helped." Harry grinned, seemingly impervious to her frosty demeanor. "He looked over the plans."

"Rudy's an *architect*," Shauna told me with great emphasis on her last word. "He *more* than helped."

I decided Shauna seemed kind of like a bitch.

"Still," I said. "Building it, that's—"

Shauna cut me off. "He didn't *totally* build it."

"Yeah, those windows would be hard to get in all by himself. But the rest of it—" Harry said.

Shauna looked at Harry. "He didn't do the wiring."

Harry looked at Max. "I thought you did."

Again before Max could reply, Shauna put in, "Not all of it."

Before anything more could be said, my eyes on Shauna, I swiftly and firmly declared, "Doesn't matter, laying a single stone to create that beautiful house would be impressive. The whole place is perfect."

Shauna's eyes locked with mine and we went into stare-down. The stare-down was interrupted by Max sliding his arm around my shoulders and pulling me into his side. Both Shauna and I broke contact. Me because I was shocked at his familiar hold. Shauna because she was clearly infuriated by it.

I tipped my head back to look at Max to see his head was tilted down to look at me.

"You think my house is beautiful?" he asked softly.

I was struck by something in his eyes, something intense and mesmerizing, and the restaurant faded away.

"Well...yes, because it is," I replied just as softly.

"Hey, you're English," Harry butted in, and I watched up close as Max's jaw hardened and his eyes sliced to Harry.

I looked at Harry, too, and unlike Max I was glad, for my sanity mostly, that Harry had butted into our little moment. It was a nice little moment and it made me feel warm all over. Something I knew I shouldn't feel.

"Not exactly," I said to Harry. "I just have a hint of an accent because I live there."

"Whoa!" Harry burst out, and such was his surprise at this news his body slammed back into the booth. "Really?"

"Yes."

Harry's eyes darted between Max and me and he asked, "You live in England, how did you two hook up?"

"Long story," Max's gravelly voice replied in a way that

said that particular long story was not going to be told now or ever to Harry but more than likely especially to Shauna.

Harry belatedly took the hint and asked me instead, "What do you do in England?"

"I'm a solicitor."

"A what?" Harry asked.

"It's what the English call an attorney," I explained, and I felt Max's hand tighten on my shoulder.

"Cool!" Harry exclaimed. "Like, 'Order in the court!' and 'I object!'"

"Not exactly. I'm not a barrister. I'm a solicitor. I don't often see court."

"Come again?" Harry asked, looking somewhat adorably confused.

It was then I decided that Harry was a bit of a goof, but I liked him.

"It's different there," I explained. "I'm not a litigator. I don't try cases in court very frequently and when I do they're usually minor ones, like small claims. Mostly, I write letters and such."

"Bummer," Harry muttered, looking crestfallen.

I grinned at him and said, "They're good letters and some of them are *really* long."

Max chuckled, Harry grinned, and Shauna was still trying to get her eyes to form icicle daggers.

Suddenly Shauna's gaze shifted to Max and she asked, "You talk to Dodd?"

For some reason this made Harry's good-natured demeanor slip a notch and he muttered, "Shauna."

But at the same time Max answered, "Nope."

"You should talk to him," Shauna advised.

"Yeah, you've told me that a fuckin' hundred times," Max said, his voice kind of scary. Not overtly so but the threat was definitely there.

Shauna ignored it, looked at me, and announced, apropos of nothing, "Max's dad gave him that land."

"Really?" I asked, puzzled at the turn of conversation.

"It's great land. Beautiful," Harry tried to lighten the mood again. "Thirty whole acres of God's country."

"Yeah," Shauna answered me, foiling Harry's attempt to lighten the mood. "He didn't buy it or anything."

Max's arm tightened around me, bringing me closer as I murmured the only response I could come up with: "Oh."

"No way, considering it's worth millions and he doesn't have that," Shauna went on.

I blinked at her in surprise, not only that Max owned millions of dollars' worth of land but the nasty way she shared that fact as Harry whispered, "Shauna."

"Can't afford the taxes on it. That's why he rents the house," Shauna went on, and I stared.

Max's entire body tightened, I sat up straighter in the curve of his arm, and Harry hissed, "Shauna!"

She shrugged, her gaze skittered over Max as if afraid of catching his eye, and she muttered, "Just sayin', she's with him, she likes that house, she should know."

"Maybe we—" I started to change the subject but Shauna plucked up her courage and looked at Max.

"Saw you with Becca today."

This was an accusation. I knew it because her gaze slid to me to catch my reaction.

And, frankly, I'd had enough. Shauna wasn't kind of a bitch. She *was* a bitch. I didn't think I'd ever met a bigger one.

"Yes, Becca's lovely," I announced, curling into Max's body but not taking my eyes from Shauna. "I met her this morning. She came by when Max was making me breakfast."

When I mentioned Max making me breakfast, the cold snap emanating from Shauna reduced the temperature of the entire restaurant by a whole ten degrees. It was a wonder I didn't shiver.

I ignored it and the frosty look on her face and looked up at Max. He was scowling at Shauna, so to get his attention, I placed my hand on his chest. I was interrupted from feeling the fact that his chest was as hard as his bicep and fortunately also interrupted from the instant impulse to explore that feeling further when his chin dipped down to look at me.

Yes, his face was dark *and* scary. He was angry, maybe even furious.

I ignored that, too, and said quietly, "I don't want to seem ungrateful but my oatmeal was kind of...too sweet."

He wasn't following, likely because he was too angry. "Too sweet?"

I pressed my hand against his chest, cuddled closer, and whispered, "Too sweet. Four sugars? Um..." I trailed off as his face cleared and he grinned.

"I'll make it with three tomorrow, Duchess," he whispered back.

"More like, one."

His brows went up. "One?" I nodded and his arm tightened again but he also pulled me up his body as he leaned down so my face was closer to his and still whispering, he said, "That's the way you like it, that's the way you'll get it."

I was so busy watching his mouth form the words and experiencing feeling my front pressed to his hard body at the same time I was wrapped tight in his arm, I almost missed Shauna making a weird noise in the back of her throat.

But I didn't miss it. Neither did Max.

My eyes went to his, I smiled at him, and he smiled back. His smile and his eyes in that proximity weren't phenomenal. They were sensational.

The loud thump of a bottle hitting the table made me jump and I turned.

"Ale," Trudy announced, a smile firm on her face, her eyes on me. She dipped her head to the new beer on the table then looked at Harry. "Table's ready, Harry." And without sparing Shauna a glance, she turned and walked away again without leaving menus.

"We'll leave you alone," Harry said, and I noticed he didn't look happy-go-lucky anymore. He looked pale and maybe a little frightened.

Because of that, I probably shouldn't have said what I said next. But for some reason I couldn't help myself.

No, I knew the reason. Because Shauna was far more of a bitch than Harry was a good guy and she deserved it. Not only for saying what she said and for obviously, and in an ugly way, pining for Max, but for being with Harry at all. I didn't know him but I knew he deserved better.

Therefore I snuggled my head into Max's shoulder, wrapped my arm around his belly, and invited, "Why don't you two eat with us? It'd be great, getting to know some people from town."

Harry grew paler, Max grunted in a way that made me think he was struggling with laughter, and Shauna's eyes narrowed.

"We're good with our table," Harry muttered. "You two look like you'd like some private time."

"You sure?" I asked graciously.

"Yeah," Harry answered.

"Well, maybe we can get together some other time," I offered, and looked at Shauna. "Does Max have your number? I'll call you."

Before Shauna could say anything, Max's voice rumbled from behind me but he sounded funny, like he was now choking back laughter. "I've got her number."

I lurched up a bit and doing my best imitation of Becca, I cheerfully cried, "Great!"

"See you around," Harry said as he and Shauna slid out of the booth.

Shauna didn't say anything.

Harry gave us a half-wave as he walked away. I waved back and Shauna didn't even glance in our direction.

They were five feet away when Max got my attention by curling me into his body front to front so close I was almost in his lap.

"Enjoyed the show, Duchess," he muttered, his other arm sliding around me and he still looked amused.

I pushed against his chest and muttered back, "Show's over, Max."

He ignored me and held firm. "Though, it was unnecessary."

I quit pushing against his chest and looked in his eyes. "I'm sorry, I know your computer password is her name but she's just...not very nice."

"She's a bitch," Max declared bluntly.

"Well..." I drew the word out and let it hang, allowing the way I said it to speak for itself.

"And her name is my computer password because she set up the computer *and* the password."

I tipped my head to the side. "So, she and you—?"

Max cut me off by informing me, "Yeah, I used to fuck her." My body jolted at his frankness but he kept talking, "But it's been over awhile."

"You should change your password."

"Not exactly a priority, so I haven't got round to it."

"I'll do it for you," I offered.

His arms gave me a squeeze and he grinned. "What'll you choose?"

Before I could stop my mouth from forming the words, I said, "Shebitchfromhell666."

He burst out laughing, giving me another squeeze while he did it.

When he controlled his laughter, he looked back at me. "That's kinda long, honey."

"Maybe so, but you won't forget it."

His face got closer when he murmured, "Don't figure I will."

I realized where I was and what I was about and I pressed against his chest again.

"Let go," I whispered.

"Like you here," he whispered back.

Something tingled someplace private. It felt altogether too good and I pulled in a breath. "I have to use the restroom," I kind of lied. I didn't have to use the facilities. I needed to blow my nose.

"Run away and remind yourself to be uptight?" he asked, again bluntly, and I felt my brows draw together.

"No. I need to blow my nose."

He looked at me a second, seeming at a loss, then said, "Do it here."

I wasn't going to blow my nose at the table *in front of him*.

"I forgot tissues," I lied outright this time.

He grinned again and declared, "You're so full of shit."

What? Did he have X-ray eyes and could see in my purse?

"I'm not full of shit," I returned, and his face dipped close again.

His arms got tight before he whispered, "You like where you are just as much as I like you here."

Before I could say a word, his hold loosened and he slid out of the booth, taking me with him and setting me on my feet.

"Hurry up. The food'll be here in a minute," he said when he let me go.

I looked at the table, then at him. "We haven't ordered yet."

"Yeah, we have."

"I haven't even seen a menu!" I said, my voice raised.

"You're gettin' a buffalo burger with jack cheese and onion rings, just like me."

I shook my head, those short, jerky shakes, and I wasn't certain I'd ever really done that before but I seemed to do it a lot around Max.

"But—"

"Go blow your nose, Duchess."

"But—"

"You a vegetarian?"

"No."

"Then trust me."

I leaned toward him and stated on a hiss, "You're impossible."

He leaned toward me, grinning, and returned, "And you're cuter than hell."

"Don't call me cute when I'm angry!" I exclaimed, now totally loud.

His eyes went over my shoulder before coming back to me and he asked, "You want the whole restaurant in on our conversation?"

I looked in the direction his eyes pointed and saw a lot of people, including Trudy, Sarah, Harry, *and* Shauna as well as others were watching.

Then I turned back to Max, gave him a glare that would have melted paint off the walls but didn't appear to affect him in the slightest, and I flounced (yes, *flounced* but I decided I could forgive myself for flouncing, as it was definitely a flouncing moment) in the direction where I hoped there would be restrooms.

Luckily, I was correct.

Once there, I blew my nose, washed my hands, and looked in the mirror, wishing I'd brought my purse so I could fix my lipstick.

Then I pulled in a breath through my nose, rested my hands against the sink, and whispered to my reflection, "What on earth am I doing?"

You're living your life, Neenee Bean, Charlie said in my head. He sounded pleased and I watched my eyes go wide in the mirror.

I looked behind me. Then I looked under the two stalls behind me. The room was empty, except for me.

"I'm going insane," I muttered. "Going insane in the snowy mountains like Jack Nicholson in *The Shining* except without the spooky hotel."

No one replied because no one was there.

I decided being alone wasn't good. I was hearing voices when I was alone. *Charlie's* voice and as much as I wanted to hear Charlie's voice, would have paid every penny I had, sold everything I owned, made a deal with the devil to hear Charlie's voice, I didn't want to hear it *in my head.*

I walked back into the restaurant, smiling at Sarah and

Trudy along the way, noticing Harry avoid my eyes and Shauna staring daggers at me, and then I looked at Max.

He was eating an onion ring while he slid out of the booth.

"I see you didn't wait for me," I noted, my eyes on his chewing mouth; then I slid into the booth.

"I ate a ring, Duchess, relax," he returned as he sat in the booth beside me.

"Whatever," I muttered, and looked at my food of which there was a lot. The burger itself could feed four people. All of it was in a red, oval, plastic basket protected by a sheet of thin, white wax paper.

It looked utterly delicious.

I reached for the ketchup.

"Got burgers in England?" Max asked.

"Yes," I answered, squirting ketchup in a pile by the onion rings and not sharing with him that English burgers were not much to write home about.

"Buffalo burgers?"

"At gourmet burger places, yes," I answered, dipping in a ring.

"Babe?" Max called, and I looked at him, onion ring halfway to my mouth. "Prepare to be dazzled," he finished on a grin, then turned to his food.

I turned to mine.

He wasn't wrong. The food was so good, I was definitely dazzled.

*   *   *

"Sleep," I muttered, wandering drowsily into the A-frame and sliding my coat down my arms as Max flipped on a light.

"Honey, I told you, you shouldn't have had the hot fudge sundae," Max said from behind me and I heard the door close.

He was right and he was wrong. The burger and onion rings more than filled me up but I saw the hot fudge sundae slide by on Trudy's tray going to someone else's table and I couldn't help myself. They didn't have hot fudge in England. Not like they had at home.

And anyway, I was on vacation.

Even so, the hot fudge sundae was definitely overkill.

But it wasn't the hot fudge sundae making me drowsy. It was the fact that we spent the last two hours sitting in a bar called Drake's a block down from the restaurant, listening to Max's friend Josh play guitar and sing while Max drank Budweiser and I drank Fat Tire.

Josh was good, really good, but even so I ended up slouched into Max's side, his arm around me, my head on his shoulder. I knew I shouldn't be slouching with my body resting against his and my head on his shoulder but I couldn't help it. It was comfortable, the beer tasted great but was mellowing me out, the music was nice, my belly was super-full, and I was tired.

I hooked my coat and purse in the closet, closed the door, and turned to Max.

"Who gets the bed tonight?" I asked, and he walked up to me and stopped, toe to toe, and I was too tired to back away.

His hand wrapped around the back of my head and he pulled me toward him and I was too tired to fight that too.

Then he kissed my forehead.

I blinked at his throat as his sweet kiss hit me like a freight train. It felt good. Better than any kiss I'd ever had and it wasn't even on my lips.

"You go on up," he muttered against my forehead, dropped his hand, then turned and walked away, shrugging off his coat.

I stared at his back and decided tomorrow I was definitely out of there. I might not even go to Denver. I might drive straight to Kansas City.

I was not, however, going to pass up sleeping in his bed, that was how tired I was.

Therefore, not giving him the chance to change his mind, I called, "Good night."

"'Night, Duchess," he called back, draping his coat on a dining room chair and not looking at me.

I turned and hurried as fast as my tired feet would take me up the stairs.

I rooted my stuff out of my suitcase, washed and moisturized my face in the bathroom, brushed my teeth, and changed into my nightgown. I left my stuff in the bathroom, deciding I'd pack it in the morning.

I opened the door, checked if the coast was clear, and hurried to the bed.

Even as tired as I was, the lights were on downstairs. Amazing-Looking Max was in the house. He'd bought me dinner, a hot fudge sundae, and at least four beers during what seemed a lot like a date even though we came home together. And it was a date I enjoyed even when we were clashing or, maybe, especially when we were clashing. So I didn't expect sleep to come quickly.

I was asleep within minutes. Out like a light.

That was why I didn't feel Max sliding into bed beside me fifteen minutes later.

CHAPTER FOUR

The Bluff

I WOKE UP, my eyes opening, and I registered immediately firstly, that it was the dead of night, dark with a hint of moonlight and secondly, that I was awake like I was ready to take on the day. This was likely because if I was at home I would already be up, taking on the day.

Then I registered that I didn't have my head on a pillow. Against my cheek I could feel sleek skin and hard muscle. It hit me that I had my head on Max's shoulder, my torso was part on him, part pressed to his side, my arm was resting across his belly and my knee was cocked, my thigh thrown over his. His arm was under me and up my back, his hand resting at my waist.

Oh my *God*.

I didn't speculate about what he was doing there. I just thought about getting away.

I rolled to my back and then to my side, wondering if I could get my car keys out of his jeans and my suitcase to the car without waking him up.

I slid partly across the bed but I felt movement then a strong arm hooked around my belly. A soft, surprised gasp escaped from my mouth when I was hauled back. I hit the wall of his warm, hard frame and Max leaned his chest into me, cocking a knee, taking mine with it so his heavy thigh was resting against mine.

"Max," I whispered.

No answer.

"Max," I whispered louder.

"Mmm?"

Then I felt his face in my hair and my body froze as his hand slid up my belly and his fingers curled around my breast.

I sucked in a breath and held myself still. He didn't move or say anything more.

"Max," I whispered, and his name was barely a murmur, as evidently my voice was frozen too.

Again, no answer except the heavy weight of him settled deeper in my back.

He was asleep but he hadn't let go of my breast.

I could, and should, lurch out of his arms and escape him and his house, maybe throwing a tantrum between the former and the latter.

He had no business detaining me, keeping my car keys, bossing me around, crawling into bed with me while I slept, even if he had nursed me back to health and made me oatmeal.

But I'd never been held like this, not in my whole life, and I couldn't ignore the fact that it felt good. So. Very. Good. To be held, in bed, in the arms of a tall, strong, handsome man.

Unbelievable.

And it was more than that. I tried not to think about it, to let it penetrate my brain but in Max's bed, in his arms, I not only (obviously) wasn't alone, I didn't feel lonely. I felt warm, safe, protected with his big body cocooning mine.

And it felt good.

In fact, since I walked into his A-frame, except for the time I spent in the backseat of the rental, I hadn't felt lonely. Not in the times I woke up during my illness when Max was there or even when he wasn't and knowing he was close. Not even yesterday when I *was* alone. It had been a long time since I felt that safe contentment of knowing my solitude would be fleeting, gone before the wretched loneliness settled back in.

And it was more than even that. His hand at my breast, his

leg cocked into mine, it felt sexy and it made *me* feel sexy. I hadn't felt that way in a while. A *long* while. Too long and I missed it.

Niles and I, when we first met, had a healthy relationship in every aspect. But once I said yes to marriage, for some reason that changed. The sex came less and less frequently until now it'd been months since we'd been intimate. More than a few months. In fact, way too many.

Niles and I didn't live together. He liked his modern three-bedroom flat in Bristol with its view of the river. He could walk to work from there and practically anywhere else he needed to go.

My place was huge, way too much space for me but I liked my rambling, four-bedroom semi-detached mainly because it had been Charlie's. But Niles couldn't walk to work from my place. He'd have to take a bus, which he would *never* do. And taxis every day would cost a mint. Unlike me, Niles *was* a barrister and he made really good money, not to mention his family came from it. Still, a taxi every day was a bit much.

Charlie had bought the house for a song and started to fix it up and when he was gone, I'd made it my mission to finish his work and I did. I couldn't let it go because it had been Charlie's and because I'd put so much into it, but Niles had no interest in moving there.

We were at a stalemate. Niles telling me to put it on the market and move in with him. Me resisting. And while I was resisting, I buried the feeling of resentment that if Niles paid attention, if he *listened*, he'd know how much that house meant to me and I wouldn't have to resist.

Furthermore, these days Niles and I rarely saw each other during the week. Maybe to have a drink, sometimes I'd go to his house and make dinner. But we spent most of our weekends together, usually me at his house again spending the night just sleeping.

But he didn't hold me when we slept. We didn't make love. He didn't curl his fingers around my breast in the unconscious but still possessive way Max was doing at that very moment.

And even though I tried not to think about any of that, told myself to move, to get out of there, to get away from Max, that it was insane to lie in this man's arms, I couldn't do it.

Instead I lay in the dark, the moonlight bright and coming through the A-frame window, held by Max and I decided to allow myself a moment of insanity.

He was asleep. He didn't know what he was doing, what I was allowing him to do. I was fully awake. There was no way I'd get back to sleep. I'd slide away from him later, after I let myself have this. This haven of safety. This feeling of being desired, and if I pretended (which I decided to do), even cherished. This feeling of being anything but alone and the opposite of lonely.

I let my body relax and I snuggled deeper into Max. In response, his fingers automatically tightened on my breast and he settled further into me. My torso went into the bed, his hand pinned under me, his chest pressed into my back.

I closed my eyes. That felt even better.

I slid my hand along his steely arm, allowing myself another forbidden treat. Then I pushed my hand under my body, my fingers wrapping around his strong wrist and holding on.

I lay there a long time, probably hours, dozing sometimes, sometimes alert. When I was alert, I took that time to memorize the feel of what I had in that moment, over and over. Liking it enough to allow myself a bit more, just a bit. I'd move away later.

Dawn was just beginning to light the A-frame when I fell into another doze that was more than a doze.

It was me falling fast asleep.

*   *   *

I woke, the sunlight bright against my eyelids and for a scant second I was confused.

Somewhere along the line I hadn't only fallen asleep, Max and I had both moved back to our original position of him on his back, me partly sprawled on him.

I felt myself being moved and I kept my eyes closed at the feeling of it. With an exquisite gentleness the likes I'd never experienced before, he slid out from under me. Then he moved me so my head was on the pillow. I felt the covers pulled up over my shoulder and I listened to Max moving away.

For a moment I just allowed the fact to wash over me that big, solid, bossy, ungentlemanly Max could move me that way, touch me that way. Not only that he could but that he would and he *did*.

Then I listened to the noises in the bathroom, taps turning on and off. He came out and a drawer opened, then closed. I felt his presence leave the loft.

Then reality intruded.

Drat it all! I was *such* an idiot.

I heard soft noises from downstairs, the kitchen sink going on, then off. I threw back the covers and ran to the bathroom.

I used the facilities, brushed my teeth, flossed, washed my face, my mind blank except for the fact I was an idiot. I should have taken my opportunity at escape. Max was apparently a heavy sleeper. I could have gotten away.

I gathered all my stuff in the bathroom and went out to the loft, going straight to my suitcase. I dumped the stuff in willy-nilly, frantic, sorting through my clothes to pull together an Escape Max Outfit.

I was so focused on this I didn't hear him hit the loft, and when his arm snaked around my waist, I jumped.

"Mornin', Duchess," he said into my hair when my back hit his front.

I went stiff and started, "Max—"

"Coffee," he interrupted me.

"Max—" I began again, pulling at his arm and he let me go.

I took a step to the side, turning to him, opening my mouth to tell him exactly what was on my mind (though I didn't know what that would be since nothing, at that moment, was on my mind) but he caught my hand. When I pulled back and took a step away, to my shock he twirled me, his arm lifting mine over my head like we were on a dance floor. He stopped me with my back to him and curled his arm around my belly, my back to his chest and he turned me toward the stairs.

"Coffee," he repeated, forcing me with his body to walk forward while I was still held in his arm.

He was stronger than me and way bigger, so instead of pulling away, I focused on a fight maybe I could win.

"You slept with me," I accused.

"Yep," he replied casually.

Yes, he replied *casually*. I'd known him essentially *a day*!

"You crawled in bed with me when I was asleep."

"Yep," he said again, and we hit the stairs. He let me go but put his hands firm to my waist and propelled me down.

"Max!" I snapped.

"Coffee," he said yet again.

His hand was now between my shoulder blades and he wasn't stopping. I was forced to descend the staircase with him behind me or be shoved down them.

Seriously, he was so annoying!

"I'd like to put on some clothes," I snapped.

"You've got on some clothes."

"I have on a *nightgown*."

"That's clothes."

"It's a *nightgown*," I said, hitting the foot of the stairs and whirling on him.

He grabbed my hand and headed toward the kitchen. I pulled back but he was stronger than me and he was apparently on a coffee mission.

He yanked me into the kitchen close to the coffeepot, which was filling, turned, and tugged at my arm so I was close. His hand dropped mine but his arm went around my waist, pulling my lower body into close proximity with his.

I looked up at him, opened my mouth, ready to let him have it, but he got there first.

"Oatmeal with one sugar or satisfy your hankerin' for some toast with grape jelly?"

I pulled in so much breath I felt my chest expand with it, filling me up, warm and sweet.

Men didn't remember things like you saying you missed grape jelly. Not if you just muttered it in passing. Charlie would remember that but he wasn't just any man. He was Charlie. There'd never been anyone like him.

Niles didn't remember things like that. In fact, the incident that drove me to deciding to take this Colorado adventure time-out was when I had trouble sleeping one night, dragged myself exhausted to his kitchen the next morning, and Niles, in an unusual mood, offered to pour me a cup of coffee. When I'd gratefully accepted, Niles asked me how I took it.

Since I'd known Niles for two years, had woken up in his house so often there was no way to count, been to breakfast with him, dinner, to his parents' house for lunch and dinner and he didn't know how I took my coffee, didn't pay even that amount of attention to me, it hit me I needed to think about our situation and I needed to do it fast.

"Duchess?" Max called, and I blinked at him, fighting back that warmth in my chest.

"Toast and jelly," I whispered.

"Gotcha," he said, letting me go but his hand came up, his fingers gliding along my jaw in a touch that was there, then gone physically. But the feeling of it remained. It tingled and it tingled in a nice way.

He turned to the counter and slid the toaster from the wall along the counter. Then he opened a cupboard and took down the bread.

"Thought I'd show you the bluff this morning," he said, and I stood there, watching him put slices of bread in the toaster, my mind blank.

Well, my mind was blank except for the fact that he was wearing flannel pajama bottoms, with a drawstring, a checked pattern in navy blue and charcoal gray on a lighter gray background. With these he was also wearing a gray T-shirt, which fit snug across his chest and tight around his bulging biceps.

I didn't think much of men's pajamas, ever. Only Max could make pajamas, even everyday pajama bottoms and a T-shirt like the ones he was wearing, look so darned good.

Then my mind moved to my nightgown, which was another purchase I'd made for the trip. Cotton, pale pink, spaghetti straps. The bodice fit close to my breasts. The back cut low, under my shoulder blades. The rest was empire waist, an A-line down to my upper thighs. The hem and the bodice were edged in a teeny-tiny line of cream lace.

My mind moved to wondering what Max thought of my nightgown and me in it.

I noticed he wasn't paying a lot of attention. He was getting out the butter and jelly. This was disappointing since it came to me that I *wanted* him to like me in my new, cute, little Colorado-adventure nightgown. I didn't normally wear nightgowns. I usually wore mostly what he was wearing except in girl style.

His eyes came to me and he called, "Hello? Nina?"

My body jolted and I asked, "What?"

He grinned and asked back, "Baby, you awake?"

"Um…"

"Sit down."

"But—"

"Sit down."

"All right," I muttered, thinking that was a good idea and walked out of the kitchen and to a stool. Then I sat down.

The toast came up. Max pulled out a plate, put the toast on it, buttered it (with far more butter than necessary), and put jelly on it (with a considerable amount of jelly, but I wasn't complaining).

Then he turned and slid the plate in front of me and went back to the coffeepot.

"Nina, the bluff?" he asked.

"Sorry?"

He poured coffee in a mug, spooned in a sugar, and went to

the fridge, pulling out the milk as he said, "I want you to come with me to the bluff."

"What bluff?" I asked, my eyes on what he was doing.

The toast close to my mouth, I took a bite.

Grape jelly. Ambrosia.

"Edge of my land, I want you to see it," he said, splashing milk into the mug, doing a swirl with a spoon and then turning and setting it in front of me.

I lost my concentration on the conversation and stared at the coffee Max set on the counter.

Once. He'd poured me coffee once. And he knew how I took it.

Niles had done it a hundred times and he never bothered to remember.

"Jesus, Nina," Max said, and it sounded like he was laughing through the words.

I shook my head and looked at him to see he was, indeed, laughing through the words.

"What's funny?" I asked.

"You. You're a zombie in the morning."

I felt my brows draw together and I said, "No, I'm not."

His response: "Babe," and then a grin.

He turned to the coffeepot, poured another mug, black, no sugar, sipped it, and slid some more bread in the toaster.

"Dress warm," he said, turning back to me and leaning his hips against the counter. "And bring your camera if you got one."

"My camera?"

"Views at the bluff, you'll want a photo."

I decided I needed caffeine, so I dropped my toast, grabbed my mug, took a sip, then another one because Max made good coffee.

Was I going to some bluff with him?

No, I was *not*.

Yet, I kind of wanted to. I'd never been to a bluff in the Colorado mountains. I wasn't sure I'd ever been to any bluff anywhere. Actually, I wasn't entirely certain what a bluff *was*.

And I was on an adventure, wasn't I? I was living my life, clearing the cobwebs, experiencing new things. I could move to the hotel in town or drive to Denver *after* Max showed me his bluff.

"All right," I said on another sip of my coffee, and then I took another bite of the delicious buttery, jellied toast.

Okay, so I was being an idiot. I could be an idiot for a few hours to see a bluff. Then after allowing myself to be an idiot, I could go back to being a smart, sane, rational person again. But being smart, sane, and rational was boring. I'd been doing that for a while and I could use a break. So I was going to give myself one.

"That was easy," Max commented, and I took another bite of toast and looked at him.

I chewed, swallowed, and asked, "What?"

He shook his head slowly and muttered, "Nothin', darlin'."

Then he took a sip from his coffee and his eyes went over my shoulder. His brows drew together and I watched his body get tight.

It was a fascinating, even thrilling but somewhat scary sight to see. He had a powerful body and seeing it come alert like that in an instant was remarkable.

"What the fuck?" he murmured, and I dragged my eyes away from his body, turned on my stool, toast in hand, and looked out the window.

Parking by the Cherokee was an army green SUV, police lights at the top, big star insignia on the door.

At the sight, I, too, felt my body get tight.

"Is that the police?" I asked, even though it obviously was.

"Yeah," Max said softly, but I could hear he was on the move.

A man got out of the SUV, jeans, heavy flannel shirt, padded vest, cowboy boots, badge, and gun on his belt. He was average height, salt in his pepper hair, a bit of a beer belly growing over his mammoth belt buckle but he still looked fit. He gazed up at the A-frame and headed up the stairs.

Max had the door open before he got there. I stayed frozen on my stool watching this play out.

"Mick," Max greeted the man.

"Max," the man greeted back, walking in through the open door.

"What's up?" Max asked.

Mick's eyes came to me and it was then, too slowly, I realized I was in a little, pale pink nightgown.

He looked back to Max, apparently unsurprised Max had a woman in a little, pale pink nightgown sitting at a stool by his kitchen and he announced, "Something's happened."

Max shut the door on the cold air, straightened, planted his feet, and crossed his arms on his chest before he asked, "What?"

Mick cleared his throat and his eyes came to me.

"That's Nina Sheridan," Max told him.

"Hey there, Miss Sheridan," Mick said to me.

I decided not to correct him about the "Miss" and instead invited, "Please, call me Nina."

"All right, Nina," Mick returned with an uncomfortable smile that made me, already ill-at-ease because of a morning visit from a police officer, more so.

"What's up?" Max asked again, and I wondered if I should run upstairs, put on a cardigan, my robe, maybe some jeans, a snowsuit (though, I didn't have one of those).

Mick walked farther into the house in my direction but turned back to Max.

"Gotta ask you a few questions," he said, and I decided not to go get dressed. The way he said that, I decided to stay right where I was.

"What questions?" Max asked, also walking in but he came directly to me, positioning himself behind my stool so close I could feel his warmth at my back.

Mick took this as an invitation to come in even farther and he did, stopping about three feet away.

"Gotta know where you were last night around two, three in the mornin'," Mick said.

I felt myself still and I stared at Mick, noting he was uncomfortable and not hiding it.

"What's this about?" Max asked, and I could tell by his voice he was not happy and also not hiding it.

"Just answer, Max," Mick said softly.

"In bed," Max said, his gravelly voice curt and Mick's eyes darted to me, then back to Max.

"Asleep?" he asked.

"Yeah," Max answered.

"Sorry, Nina." Mick's gaze came back to me, his eyes dropping to my nightgown for the barest of seconds before coming back to my face and he continued. "Could you corroborate that?"

"What's this about?" Max repeated.

But at the same time I said quickly, "Yes, I can."

"You sure?" Mick asked me.

"Of course I'm sure," I said firmly.

"Were you asleep too?" Mick pressed, and my back straightened.

"Mick"—Max was obviously losing patience—"what the fuck's this about?"

But again I spoke quickly. "No, I wasn't asleep." Mick opened his mouth to speak but I kept talking. "I'm here from England. I've got jetlag. I woke up around two in the morning, nine o'clock my time, and stayed awake until dawn. Max was with me the whole time."

Mick's face and body visibly relaxed, relief washing through him and he nodded.

"Now you wanna tell me what this is about?" Max's patience was gone; he sounded angry.

Mick's eyes moved to him. "Curtis Dodd was killed early this mornin'."

I heard Max pull in a breath, and even though I didn't know who Curtis Dodd was, I felt my eyes get wide.

"You're shittin' me," Max said quietly.

"Wish I was," Mick replied.

Then Max asked, "Murdered?"

"Yep," Mick answered.

"And you come to visit me?" Max didn't sound angry anymore. He just *was*. I heard it and felt it.

"Now, Max, just procedure. Everyone knows you don't get along with Dodd." Mick's tone was placating.

"Yeah, neither does most of the town," Max returned.

"Yeah, that's why I got deputies visiting a lotta folk. You're my third this mornin'," Mick explained.

Well, at least that was something.

"What happened?" I asked in order to turn the conversation and hopefully defuse the situation.

"Dodd was shot," Mick answered.

"Where?" Max asked.

"His house, guy broke in," Mick answered.

Max came closer, his body touching my back and I could feel something strange coming from him.

"Where was Bitsy?" Max went on, his voice cautious, or maybe concerned.

"Visitin' her sister. She don't like the spring break tourist season. Too many kids, teenagers gettin' sloshed." I felt something coming from Max; I didn't know what it was but it was also coming from Mick. He was uncomfortable again for some reason that was different than before and he hurried on, "You know she goes down to Arizona for a coupla months every March and April."

I felt Max relax before he asked, "Who found him, then?"

Mick shifted on his feet and I knew he would have adjusted his collar if he didn't think it would give him away.

"Dodd wasn't exactly alone," Mick muttered.

"Fuckin' hell," Max muttered back but his mutter was clipped and annoyed. "Shauna."

Surprise hit me and I looked at Mick, who was nodding, then over my shoulder at Max's hard, angry face.

"Shauna said she heard the break-in and went to investigate, then heard the shots. Lucky for her, seems the killer didn't know she was there, just did Dodd and took off. Hearin' the shots, she was scared shitless. Took her a while to get her shit together to leave the bedroom, find Dodd, then call it in. She was pretty shaken up. Still is."

"Bet she is," Max muttered like he did indeed bet she was and he didn't give a damn.

"What about Harry? I thought she was with Harry," I asked stupidly, looking over my shoulder at Max, and his eyes came to me. Then his hand came to my waist and he gave me a squeeze. He didn't have to answer and that was answer enough. Shauna was stepping out on goofy, sweet Harry. Therefore I whispered, "Poor Harry."

"Yeah, poor Harry," Max replied, his voice quiet.

I looked back at Mick and added, "And poor um...Curtis Dodd."

Mick examined me a second before his face split in a genuine, amused grin before his gaze shifted up to Max.

"Nina's new around here, I'm guessin'," he noted.

"Yeah," Max answered.

"I'm sorry?" I asked, and Mick looked at me.

"There's about two people in a four-county area that'd say, at learnin' the news that Curtis Dodd was murdered, 'Poor Curtis Dodd.' You and Shauna. You because you don't know him. Shauna because she was sleepin' with him."

"Oh," I mumbled, and wondered about Curtis Dodd.

"You want coffee?" Max asked, and Mick shook his head.

"Gonna be a busy day. Gotta get on my way."

"You have a travel mug in your truck?" I asked, and Mick looked at me.

"Yeah," he said.

"If you'll go get it, we'll give you a warm-up."

Mick's face changed. His eyes cut to Max, then back to me. He smiled and said softly, "Be kind of you."

"Well, not really. Max made the coffee, though I think he used coffee from my grocery stash. I'm finding Max isn't good with grocery boundaries."

A short, surprised laugh escaped Mick as his eyes shot to Max.

Max moved to my side and slung an arm around my shoulders, noting, "You'll find, Mick, that Nina's somethin' else."

My head tipped back and I looked at Max. "What does that mean?"

"Relax, Duchess." Max grinned at me. "It was a compliment."

"It didn't sound like one," I retorted.

He bent at the waist and his face got close. "Well, it was."

Mick cleared his throat and I decided to let it go. It was rude, arguing in front of other people, especially people you didn't know.

I looked at Mick and prompted, "Your travel mug, Officer?"

"Call me Mick."

I doubted I'd ever see him again, but on a smile I said courteously, "All right, Mick."

Mick went to get his mug. I went to the coffeepot. Max stood behind my stool and watched Mick.

"You okay?" I called.

"Shauna's a fuckin' bitch," Max replied.

This was true. Therefore I had no comment.

Max turned to me. "Bitsy, Dodd's wife, she's disabled."

I blinked then asked, "What?"

"Disabled, car wreck, ten years ago. Paralyzed from the waist down."

"Oh my," I whispered, and Mick came in, interrupting our conversation.

"Thanks for this. Been up since way before dawn. Figure coffee'll be my saving grace the next few days," he remarked, coming to me.

I poured him coffee, trying to ignore the fact that I *still* hadn't put on any clothes and was in a short cotton nightgown.

Mick didn't act like he noticed it and I guessed since he was a cop he pretty much saw it all. He told me he took two sugars and a "slug" of milk. I gave it to him, then gave him my farewell. Max walked him to the door, said his good-byes, stood in it as Mick jogged to his SUV, and only closed it when Mick started up the truck, gave a wave, and started to reverse.

Max joined me in the kitchen, reached around me, and grabbed his mug. Then he leaned a hip against the counter and, looking up at him, I did the same.

"Bitsy?" I prompted, curious. "And Shauna?"

"Bitsy's sweet. I've known her since we were kids. She's lived in town her whole life; everyone loves her. Shauna..." He didn't finish. I nodded that I understood and Max went on. "Dodd's loaded. Shauna likes that. Harry's pretty loaded, too, but not like Dodd."

"You're loaded too," I said to him, and he looked down at me.

"That I ain't, Duchess," he said honestly.

"According to Shauna, you're sitting on millions of dollars' worth of land."

I watched his face close down and he said, "Yeah, if I sell it."

"And Shauna wanted you to do that," I guessed.

"Yeah."

"To Dodd," I guessed again.

"Yeah."

I was right. Shauna was a bitch. She might be *more* than a bitch but I wasn't sure what that was.

"Tangled web," I whispered.

"It was then I scraped her off, got myself untangled."

I looked beyond him out the windows to the view.

There was nothing between him and that glorious view and I figured, for thirty acres all around, nothing beside him or behind him.

Like Harry said, God's country, unspoiled.

I looked back at Max. "What did Dodd want to do with your land?"

"He had a coupla schemes he was considering. Hotel and guest villas or a small, exclusive housing development."

I felt my lip curl. Max's eyes dropped to my mouth and he

did two things. He burst out laughing and wound an arm around my waist again, bringing our lower bodies close together but this time not in closer *proximity*, now actually *touching*.

"Max—" I whispered, my hands going to his arms.

He stopped laughing but smiled down at me. "That's what I thought, Duchess."

"What?" I asked, losing track of the conversation what with his biceps under my fingers and his hips fitted to mine.

"Your face, Dodd's plans, that's what I thought."

"Oh."

He let me go, turned to the coffeepot, and ordered, "Finish your toast, get ready, forget this shit. We're goin' to the bluff."

It took me a second before I could get my feet to move but I finally did, to my stool and I finished my toast. Then I went to the coffeepot, reaching around Max to give myself a warm-up as Max finished his own toast, his eyes pointed out the window, his mind on other things.

I took my coffee, walked upstairs, made the bed, grabbed my stuff from the suitcase, and locked myself in the bathroom, getting ready to be an idiot and go with Max to the bluff.

*　　*　　*

"I'm sorry?" I shouted over the noise from the snowmobile Max was sitting astride.

"Climb on!" he shouted back and I stared at the snowmobile.

"Can't we walk?" I asked loudly.

"No."

"Drive?"

"No."

I took a step back. "Maybe—"

"Duchess, get…the fuck…on."

My eyes went to his face and I snapped, "You're very impatient!"

"Life's short," he yelled over the noise. "Don't got a lot of it to sit and wait for you to climb the fuck on."

"I've never ridden on a snowmobile," I yelled back.

"Today's your day."

"I don't know if I *want* to ride on a snowmobile," I shared.

He muttered something I didn't catch, tinkered with the snowmobile, and the noise stopped. Then he climbed off.

Max shouted through the bathroom door to find him when I finally "fuckin' got ready." When I was finally ready, through the back door leading from the utility room, I found that Max's house butted up to a gradual incline covered in pine and aspen.

But around the side and up, there was a barn buried in the trees. In this barn were a variety of things, including an ATV attached to a snow plow, another ATV with no snow plow, what looked like a car under a tarp, and what looked like a motorcycle under another tarp. There was also a snowmobile, though by the time I met Max out there, the snowmobile was outside.

Max got close. I tipped my head back and he demanded, "Talk to me."

"It doesn't have seat belts," I told him, and he pressed his lips together. I didn't know why, maybe irritation, maybe quelling laughter.

"No," he said when he stopped pressing his lips together. "It doesn't have seat belts."

"Shouldn't we wear helmets or something?"

He got closer and I would have stepped back but his hand came to the side of my neck, his long fingers sliding up and into my hair behind my ear. His fingers were covered in a leather glove but it still felt good, good enough to root me to the spot.

He dipped his face closer to mine and whispered, "What're you worried about, baby?"

I took in a breath, let it out, and for some reason whispered back honestly, "It's just scary."

"I won't let you get hurt."

"But—"

"Nina, I promise. I won't let you get hurt."

I looked into his eyes and saw they were serious. He wasn't teasing, he wasn't impatient, he wasn't annoyed, and he didn't think I was a scaredy-cat. He was just...serious.

"Okay," I whispered.

"You gonna climb on?"

I nodded my head under his hand and he smiled.

Then he let me go. I pulled my cream-colored, cable-knit, close-fitting cap over my hair, making it bunch out at the sides. Then I pulled on my matching cream mittens. The sound came back when the snowmobile roared to life, and reminding myself I was out here for adventure and snowmobiling was definitely adventurous, or at least it was to me, I climbed on.

Max sat up straight, reached back, grabbed my wrists, and used them to yank me closer until my crotch was against his behind, my inner thighs running along his outer ones. He wrapped my arms around his waist, and before I could pull away we were moving. I had no thoughts of pulling away. The minute the snowmobile started going, I held on tighter.

At first I was terrified, my heart lodging firmly in my throat.

It filtered through my fear that Max had taken this route before; he knew what he was doing, where he was going, and I started to look around.

Then I felt the fear melt away as the trees slid by, the chill wind whipped at my cheeks, my body pressed to Max's solid one entered my consciousness, and I relaxed.

We hit a trail that ran the side of the mountain that had a river running the length of it and the views were unbelievable. So stunning, I didn't notice the sharp decline that was close to the side of the trail we were gliding across. Instead, I dropped my chin to Max's shoulder and drank in the view. All thoughts leaked out of my head. There was nothing but Max's back against my front, my arms around his waist, and that wondrous view.

Before I was ready for our ride to end, we hit the bluff by the river, the land seeming to fall away from the side, the vista it exposed heart-stopping, and Max halted the snowmobile, turning it off.

He sat back but I didn't take my arms from around his waist mainly because Max was right. The view from here was incredible and I was frozen in wonder. It was one of the most beautiful things I'd ever seen. But also the snow and the underlying quiet mixed with the landscape and the sound of the river rushing by it had to be the most beautiful thing I'd ever experienced.

"It's beautiful," I whispered, my chin still at his shoulder.

"Yeah," he agreed, his rough, soft voice bringing me out of my daze and I lifted my head and pulled away, coming off the back of the snowmobile.

I walked close to the edge and stopped, drinking in the view for long moments before I pulled my little digital camera out of my pocket. I started snapping photos, knowing the endeavor was useless. No photograph could capture this. This vista had to be experienced.

Max got close to my back and I couldn't avoid him without going over the edge and, furthermore, his arm came around me at my chest. He pulled me into his front, and before I could protest, he spoke.

"Dad used to bring us here all the time," he said quietly.

I stared at the landscape and something about his tone made me drop my camera.

"Us?" I asked, though I told myself I was no longer being an idiot. It was worse. I shouldn't ask. I shouldn't care. I shouldn't want to know.

But I did.

His arm tightened around my chest, bringing me closer. "Kami used to bitch constantly all the way. Said she wanted to be with Mom, which meant she wanted to be with her friends in town."

Before I could bite back the word, I asked, "Kami?"

"My sister."

"Your mom didn't come here with you?" I was looking at

the landscape, wondering who in their right mind wouldn't want to go there and mentally kicking myself for my questions, not wanting him to share and really not wanting to be the one who urged him to do so. He was fascinating enough just being him. I didn't need to hear his life stories.

"Mom and Dad were divorced."

"Oh," I said, and forced myself to leave it at that.

Max felt like talking, however. "Happened when I was about six, Kami four. Dad and Mom both lived in town but we still only saw Dad every other weekend, unless we ran into him or somethin' was happenin' at school."

"My parents were divorced too," I told him, and then clamped my mouth shut. I didn't need to know about him and he certainly didn't need to know about me.

"How old were you?" he asked.

"Young." I evaded a direct answer.

His arm got tighter, his fingers curling around my shoulder, not happy I avoided a direct answer.

"How old, Duchess?"

I sighed, then repeated, "Young." And before he could prompt further, I went on. "Very young. So young, I don't remember them ever being together."

"Rough, baby," he whispered, but I didn't tell him it wasn't. I didn't tell him it was sheer luck my father walked out of my life because not far down it, he came right back in.

I decided to change the subject and remarked, "It's lovely, your dad being able to give you this." I motioned to the panorama with my hand.

"Yeah, except it came to me because he died."

My body jolted and I turned in the curve of his arm so I was facing him.

"Sorry?"

"I inherited the land when he died."

His face was blank, which gave away the depth of emotion he was hiding.

"I'm sorry," I whispered.

"Long time ago, honey."

"I'm still sorry."

His arm around my shoulders gave me a squeeze and his other hand went to my waist.

I edged back a bit. He gave me some space but not much, so I was forced to stop when he stopped giving me leeway.

"But I meant," I went on, "what's lovely is that, when he was alive, he could give you this, bring you and your sister here."

He nodded and looked over my head to the view. "This was Dad's favorite place. He wanted to build a house on the land. All his life he wanted that. Couldn't do it but he talked about it all the time. But he'd never touch this place. Told me never to do it either."

There was something impressive and moving about Max building a house on the land where his father wanted to build, not to mention doing it with his own two hands.

"Your sister get land too?" I asked, and his eyes came down to me for a second before they went back to the view.

"Nope."

"He gave it all to you?"

"Yep."

"Wow."

His arm left my shoulder but only so his hand could slide into the hair under my cap as his other hand moved around my waist.

"She got everything else, his house in town, car—"

"The land is better," I announced, even though I had no idea what kind of house his father had or what kind of car. It could be a mansion and a Maserati; the land still would have been better.

Max grinned down at me and agreed, "Yeah." Then he continued, his eyes going over my shoulder, his expression moving far away. "She was pissed, though she never gave a shit about this place. She *did* know what it was worth."

I pressed my lips together to stop myself from asking questions.

Max didn't need me to ask questions and he looked back to me. "She'd sell it off. Dad knew that, even said it in his will, explainin' things. So he gave it to me."

"Did he make it a condition you never sell it?"

Max shook his head. "Just knew I'd never sell"—his eyes went back over my shoulder—"and I never will."

"I wouldn't either," I whispered, and bit the inside of my lip to remind myself to stop talking, mainly because Max looked back at me and his face had gotten soft, but his eyes had gone intense and his look struck me deep but in a good, warm, happy way.

"Been in my family since 1892," he told me.

My eyes grew wide and I asked, "Really?"

He grinned again and said, "Yeah, Duchess."

I opened my mouth to speak, put an end to this intimate tête-à-tête, which I was enjoying too much and I knew I shouldn't let myself, when we both heard, "Max!"

Max let me go with one arm but the hand at my neck slid around my shoulders as he moved to my side and looked up the trail.

"Hey, Cotton," Max said to a man who looked like he should be called Cotton.

Cotton looked like Santa Claus. Lots of white hair and a thick, full white beard that was a bit overlong, and one mustn't forget the big jolly belly, which Cotton definitely had. But he wasn't wearing a red suit. He was wearing a pair of jeans, a huge parka, and snow boots.

"Heya," Cotton said, eyes on me, ten feet away but I could see his nose and cheeks were red, just like Santa's.

"Hello."

"Cotton, this is—" Max started, but Cotton talked over him.

"Yeah, Nina, I know."

"What—?" I began, but Max gave me a squeeze.

"Trudy's Cotton's granddaughter," Max explained.

"Oh," I muttered.

"Small town," Cotton noted, stopping close. "We talk. Get used to it."

"Oh…" I said slowly, and finished, "'kay," uncertain I'd be around long enough to get used to it but I decided against sharing that with Cotton.

"Give me your camera. I'll take a picture of you both." Cotton dipped his head to my camera.

I got stiff. A picture of me and Max on Max's bluff? I didn't think so. And I didn't think so mainly because the very thought of having a photo of Max and me, together on his beautiful bluff, made me want it so badly I could taste it in my mouth and I knew that was wrong, wrong, *wrong*.

"Um…that's okay. I took some shots."

"Duchess—" Max said, but Cotton interrupted him.

"Give me your camera, girl."

"Really, that's okay," I said.

"Nina, this is Jimmy Cotton," Max told me under his breath.

My body froze and I stared. When I could again speak, I whispered, "No kidding?"

"Yeah, no kidding," Max said on a chuckle.

I stared at Santa Man.

Jimmy Cotton, the great American photographer. I'd seen three of his exhibitions, one at the Smithsonian, one at the Victoria and Albert, and one at The Met. He was a national treasure and his pictures were revered, including by me. I bought one of his calendars every year and had one of his Smithsonian posters framed and in my hallway at home.

He was also a recluse, never came to showings, never did interviews, famously eschewed the world that adored him. I didn't think I'd ever seen a picture of him, not even when he was young. I knew he lived in the Colorado Rockies, most of his photos were of the mountains. But I obviously had no idea he lived *here*.

"I'm…I'm…so pleased to meet you," I stuttered, feeling stupid and shy, both at the same time. "I saw your exhibitions at the Smithsonian and the one at the Victoria and Albert and—"

"V & A?" he asked, his eyes narrowing.

"Yes, it was spectacular. I was . . . it was amazing," I replied.

"Got a few of those they showed at the V & A up at my place. I'll go through my barn, wrap one up, bring it over to Max's."

My mouth fell open. I felt it but I couldn't do anything about it.

Max started chuckling and gave my arm a squeeze. "Give him your camera, honey."

Automatically, my hand holding the camera lifted up. Jimmy Cotton came forward, took *my* stupid little digital camera in *his* artisan's hand, and took several steps back. I was so stunned that Jimmy Cotton was holding my camera, I didn't fight against Max curling me so my front was tucked into his side, his arm tight around my shoulders, fingers shifting my hair around to bunch at my neck under his hand, forcing my cheek to his shoulder, his other hand going around my waist.

"Smile," Jimmy Cotton, *the* Jimmy Cotton, called from behind my camera and I smiled with all the happiness I felt that none other than Jimmy Cotton was taking my picture (not to mention, it felt good standing like that in Max's arms).

"That'll be a good one," Jimmy Cotton muttered, fiddling with my camera before he stepped forward and handed it back to me.

I took it thinking maybe I could die right there on the spot and do it happily, considering Jimmy Cotton just took my photo. Though that would mean I wouldn't have the chance to get his photo printed and hermetically sealed.

"You hear about Dodd?" Cotton asked Max, and Max kept the arm around my shoulders, hand curled around my neck but his other hand dropped away.

"Yeah."

"Thought the sun shone brighter when I woke up this mornin'," Cotton mumbled, and I let out a little surprised giggle.

"He was an ass," Cotton told me.

"I'm beginning to get that picture," I said back.

"Mick came up to the house this mornin'. Luckily Nina's got jetlag and she could tell him she was awake and in bed with me when the deed was done."

Cotton's face got hard and he asked, "What in the sam hill is Mickey doin', askin' *you* for an alibi?"

I was stuck on Max telling Jimmy Cotton (of all people) I was in bed with him but Max didn't seem to feel my displeasure, which I was pretty certain was so extreme it *should* be felt, and he spoke to Cotton.

"Not a secret we don't get along."

"Not a secret you ain't the type of man to do that kind of thing."

"Cotton—" Max started.

"Especially you," Cotton went on.

"Jimmy—"

"Especially with Dodd," Cotton continued, then looked at me. "Max had far more reason ten years ago to pull a trigger and take out that jackass, dang nab it." He looked back at Max. "And Mickey knows it."

"He's just doin' his job," Max said, but I was intrigued at what Cotton said. I'd heard the words "ten years ago" recently and just now and that seemed an interesting coincidence.

Unfortunately, Cotton was miffed and I couldn't get a word in to ask him to explain.

"Got a lot of nerve, showin' at your place."

"I wasn't his first visit."

"And won't be his last." Cotton looked at me. "Dodd wasn't much liked by *anyone*. Hell, Mickey could have come to visit *me*."

"You don't own a gun, Cotton. You're a pacifist, nonviolent, remember?" Max reminded him.

"Ever a man to test the mettle of pacifism and nonviolence, it was Curtis Dodd," Cotton shot back.

Max chuckled. I waited for more information to be shared but both men settled into silence.

It was either ask, when I told myself I didn't want to know, or keep silent. It took a lot of effort—I really wanted to know about ten years ago, Max, and Curtis Dodd—but I kept silent.

"Welp, you two young'uns don't need an old man spoilin' the mood. I'll just be gettin' on."

"You aren't spoiling the mood," I told him quickly, and he smiled at me.

"Any talk spoils *that*," he said, dipping his head to the vista behind me. "*That* you experience in silence, or better yet, with someone that means somethin' to you." For some reason, his eyes slid to Max when he said his last before he looked back to me and concluded, "Therefore, I best be gettin' on."

I didn't share that I barely knew Max, therefore he didn't mean anything to me (at least I was telling myself that) but Cotton was on the move and Max had bid him good-bye.

"It was an honor to meet you, Cotton," I called after him.

He stopped and turned back. Then he asked the bizarre question, "Yeah? Why?"

"Because..." I felt funny under his strangely intense scrutiny and finished lamely, "You're Jimmy Cotton."

"Just a man."

"A man with a way with a camera."

"Lotsa those," Cotton said dismissively, clearly not one who enjoyed praise from an inexpert like me but probably, I was guessing, not from anyone.

"I'm sorry," I said softly, but loud enough for him to hear. "I've been to my fair share of exhibitions, only yours made my heart hurt because my system couldn't process the beauty that met my eyes."

Max went still at my side and Cotton pulled in such a deep breath, his chest puffed out.

"So," I kept talking softly, "you're not just a man with a camera. Not to me. You're Jimmy Cotton. Your photographs gave me that. I loved it. I'm grateful and because of that, I'm honored to meet you."

He watched me for several moments, the cantankerous-old-man look he'd perfected slipping, his face getting soft. He tipped his chin up at me, gave a short wave, turned, and began climbing, rounding the bluff.

I watched him go and I suspected Max did too.

I watched longer because I felt Max's arm give me a squeeze to get my attention.

"Ready to go back?" he asked when I looked up at him.

"No," I blurted. His eyebrows came up in question and I blew out a sigh before suggesting, "Can we ride around on the snowmobile for a while?"

He grinned, then offered, "You want me to teach you how to drive?"

I shook my head fast and his grin turned to a smile.

"Baby steps," I said to him.

"You got it, Duchess," he replied, and walked me to the snowmobile.

We got on and Max drove me around for a good long while and, I had to admit, I enjoyed every single moment.

*   *   *

I rinsed the lunch plates in Max's kitchen sink and told myself it was high time that I got back to being a smart, sane, rational person again.

We'd driven around in the mountains on his snowmobile for a while, Max showing me more views, a few more of his favorite places, all of them beautiful, none of them quite as spectacular as the bluff. I took some photos, even one of Max I told myself I shouldn't take and hoped he didn't notice I was taking it. He was gazing over a valley, his handsome profile relaxed and, well...handsome. Too handsome not to capture on film with that valley spread out behind him. So I did and I did it quickly, prepared to pretend I was only taking a photo of the valley.

We rode back and I put together a late lunch while Max put away the snowmobile, then came in and built a fire in the grate in the living room.

We ate the shrimp, avocado, and mayo sandwiches on

white I made, me at my stool, Max standing at the counter in front of me, both of us silent. Max, seemingly comfortably so, me, not at all.

When he finished eating, I offered, "If you'll fire up the computer while I clean up the kitchen, I'll change your password."

"Sounds good," he muttered, sucking back a swig of cola and rounding the bar. I felt him get close to me as he went and was in the act of turning to him when I felt his hand curl around my neck, palm at my throat; then his lips were at my hair at the top of my head. His fingers gave my neck a squeeze, he let go, and without a word he walked away.

I sat there immobilized, uncertain what to make of Max's casual ability to be affectionate in pretty much every way, verbally, physically, with his face, his eyes. I knew how it made me *feel*, which was a dangerous feeling and I knew it would be dangerously easy to get used to it. I just didn't know what to make of it.

Yes, it was time to be smart, sane, and rational and get out of there before I let my mind wander to what I *wanted* to make of it.

I put the dishes in the dishwasher, wiped down the counters, and grabbed my diet cola.

By the time I hit the alcove, Max was sitting at the rolltop and the screen on the computer was lit.

"What do you want me to change it to?" I asked as he rose from the chair and held its back for me to sit in it. So I did and he stood at my side.

"I'm thinkin' shebitchfromhell666 might continue to be a reminder of Shauna," Max muttered drily.

I pressed my lips together in order not to laugh and slid my eyes up to look at him.

I unpressed my lips and asked, "So what do you want?"

"It doesn't matter."

"It has to be something you can remember."

"Nina, honestly, it doesn't matter. It could be one, two, three, four."

I shook my head in horror and advised, "It can't be one, two, three, four. That's *way* too easy to hack."

"Considerin' I check my e-mail about once every three months, dump most of it, check the weather every once in a while, and got nothin' else on there, ain't nothin' to hack."

I sighed and explained, "Yes, but you rent this place and other people could use it, look up porn, maybe even icky stuff."

He grinned. "Icky stuff?"

I ignored his grin and the way it communicated he thought I was adorable (and the way that made me feel) and continued. "Icky stuff, icky stuff that could get you into trouble. Don't you watch television?"

"Not much."

"Well, your everyday pedophile probably wouldn't hesitate renting a beautiful A-frame in the mountains and enjoying himself by accessing your one, two, three, four computer."

"Jesus, darlin'."

"Sick people are everywhere. Just watch *Criminal Minds*."

"If that's their subject matter, I'm thinkin' I'll avoid it."

"It's really good," I told him, warming to my topic because I liked that show and therefore I idiotically lost myself and did not keep my mouth *shut*. "They have this really smart, genius guy who's fascinating. And this really sharp, tough lady. And this hilarious computer mastermind who wears funky clothes and always has perfect lipstick. And they almost always get the bad guy."

He was grinning down at me again when he muttered, "Sounds like I'm missin' out."

"It's worth it just for Penelope Garcia's lipstick and the stuff she wears in her hair, trust me," I shared.

I stopped talking when I saw his eyes start glittering and his body start shaking and his face *definitely* said he thought I was adorable.

Instead, I looked at the computer and got down to business, clicking through the screens to take me to the window that changed the password and I asked, "What's your favorite number?"

"Lucky number's three."

I pulled in breath through my nostrils. That was my favorite number.

And it was Charlie's.

"Okay, then, something three…," I prompted.

"Make it up, Nina."

"Give me something to go on."

"Just make it up. I'll write it down and hide it somewhere."

I looked up at him. "Max—"

He cut me off and said, "Three duchess three."

I wasn't certain but I was pretty sure I felt the blood draining from my face.

I didn't shift my eyes from the screen when I asked, "Sorry?"

"Three duchess three. I won't forget that."

"But—"

"Type it in, babe."

"But, Max—"

"Type it in."

I sat there paralyzed and when I didn't move, Max leaned into me, picking out the letters on the keyboard with one finger, then again to confirm. His hand covered mine on the mouse and he clicked "OK."

His hand still on mine on the mouse, he twisted his head to look at me and he said, "That should do it."

"I have to go," I blurted, and watched his brows draw together.

"What?"

I slid my hand from under his, rolled the chair away as he straightened, and I stood, repeating, "I've got to go." I held out my hand, palm up, and requested, "Can I have my car keys?"

His brows were still knitted when he asked, "Where you goin'?"

"To town."

"To shop?"

"To check into the hotel."

He took a step toward me, murmuring, "Duchess."

I took a step back.

He stopped, his brows snapped together again, and his face grew dark. "What the fuck?"

"Thanks for, you know, today and last night and everything but . . . I have to go."

"Why?"

Why?

There were so many reasons we'd both be eighty if I took the time to enumerate them all.

"I just do."

"Give me a reason."

"Max—"

"One," he demanded firmly.

"Okay," I said to get it over with. "Maybe I've got it wrong, what's happening here, but if I don't perhaps I should remind you, I'm wearing another man's engagement ring."

"You don't gotta remind *me*, Duchess. You gotta remind *you*."

Oh drat.

I was getting angry; I could feel it.

"I'm sorry?" I said quietly.

"No woman had my ring on her finger when I got into bed with you last night."

"Yes, well"—I leaned toward him—"I'm glad you brought that up."

"Because you're pissed I did it?"

"Yes!"

"Then why'd you wake up at two and stay in bed with me until mornin'?"

I stared at him, at a loss for words, mainly because any explanation I could give him I was *never* going to give him. And I realized, belatedly, even if it was to give him something as important as a rock-solid alibi when the police popped by to question him as a potential murder suspect, perhaps I shouldn't have shared that tidbit.

Then I announced, "I'm leaving," and I started to walk around him but he took a quick step to his left and caught me by the waist, pulling me in front of him. "Take your hands off me!" I snapped, but his arms wrapped around me tight, bringing me up full frontal to his body.

"This is something we both wanna explore," he declared.

My eyes narrowed and I wedged my arms between us, my hands against his chest.

"This?"

"What we got, what's happenin' here, you and me."

"It is not!"

"No?"

"No."

He looked over my head and clipped out, "Christ, you're full of shit."

"I am not!"

He looked back at me, giving me a shake. "Oh yeah, Nina, you are."

"You don't even *know* me!"

"I know enough that I wanna know more."

"Well, you *can't* know more. I'm leaving."

"You're stayin'."

"You can't keep me here."

"I can."

"That's—"

"And you wanna stay."

I shook my head in disbelief and cried, "You're infuriating!"

"And you love every fuckin' second."

My mouth made a "poof" noise at such a display of arrogance and I pushed against his chest. His hand slid up my spine, bringing me closer, pinning my hands between us as I watched his neck bend.

I had a feeling I knew where this was going.

"Max," I warned, my body bracing.

"Quiet," he ordered softly. "Got a point to make, honey."

"Max!" I snapped.

"Let's see how good this could be," he muttered, his eyes on my mouth, and I knew, I just knew he was going to kiss me.

"Max, don't you—"

But his fingers had sifted into my hair against my scalp, cupping my head, holding me steady, and his mouth came down on mine, cutting off my words.

And considering my mouth was open, he didn't miss the opportunity to slide his tongue inside.

My body froze when his tongue touched mine.

Then my hands curled into his shirt and my body melted.

His tongue felt good, it tasted good, it was all just *good*. Not just good. It was better than good. I missed this. I loved kissing and, Lord, did I miss it.

My eyes drifted closed, my head tilted, and that was it, I was lost.

And then Max *really* kissed me and I became so lost, I never wanted to be found.

It wasn't good.

It was astounding. He was just as amazing a kisser as he looked amazing, maybe more, and that was saying something.

My toes curled in my boots, my hands glided up his chest to wrap my arms around his neck, my body pressed the length of his, and my stomach did a somersault before it plummeted in a delicious way. I felt a tingle between my legs that was more than delicious—it was *luscious*—and given all of that, I had no choice but to open myself up to him.

And I did.

When I did, Max took and he took and he took. And I gave and I didn't care if he drained me dry. In fact, I wanted him to.

His mouth broke from mine and his head came up. My fingers, which were in his hair, put on pressure, and he whispered, his gravelly voice actually hoarse, "Jesus, honey."

"More," I breathed, not even opening my eyes and his

mouth came back to mine. He gave me what I wanted and I loved every *bleeding* second.

Somewhere in the back of my head, I realized he was moving, taking me with him, shuffling us toward what I understood was the couch and I was happy to be going there, couldn't wait to get there, couldn't wait to explore Max *more* and let him explore *me*, when the phone rang.

On the second ring, Max's head came up and he stopped our movement.

"Don't." It sounded like a plea and it was coming from my mouth.

"I've gotta, Duchess." His voice was still rough and he sounded like he didn't want to but when his arm left my waist and his palm touched my cheek, I opened my eyes and saw in his face that I was right. He didn't want to but he had to. "Don't lose that look," he ordered, then bent forward, kissed my forehead, let me go, and with long strides walked to the phone on top of the rolltop.

I watched him go and listened to him answer with a, "Yeah?"

I shook my head, trying to clear it but I could still feel his arms around me, his lips on mine, his tongue in my mouth, his soft, thick hair under my hands, his hard body against mine, and I wanted it back. I couldn't shake off that feeling of want even though I tried. It was like it was born in me, natural, everything I was or everything I was meant to be and there was no way to get rid of it.

"Now?" Max asked, sounding incredulous and a bit annoyed but also sounding like he was trying to hide both. "Okay, yeah, calm down. I'll be there in fifteen minutes." I stared at him as his eyes sliced to me. His face wasn't soft with desire like it had been five seconds ago. It was tight and impatient. "Yeah, I said I'd take care of this, I'll take care of it." Another pause and he didn't unlock his eyes from mine before he said softly, "Don't worry, I'll be there. Fifteen."

He hit the OFF button, it beeped, and I felt my body twitch

at the sound. Sanity was returning but Max was right in front of me, impeding its progress.

"I gotta go."

I just nodded.

"I don't know when I'll be back."

I nodded again.

"Duchess, you with me?"

"Yes," I whispered.

"I'm takin' your car keys with me," he announced.

"Okay," I replied instantly.

His hands came to either side of my head and he tipped it back as he got closer. I saw his face was back to soft and he looked almost relieved.

"I made my point, didn't I?"

Oh, he made his point.

"Yes," I whispered again.

"We'll finish when I get home."

I didn't answer. I didn't know what he meant, finish talking or finish making our way to the couch so I could act like an even bigger idiot and behave like a screaming bitch besides.

"Nina?"

"It sounds like something important."

"It is or there's no fuckin' way I'd go." His hands at my head brought me closer and he finished, "I'll explain later."

"You better get going," I told him.

I felt one of his hands come down to my neck; then his thumb slid along my jaw.

"Be good," he whispered.

"I'll try," I whispered back. His eyes moved over my face. Then he bent his neck and touched his mouth to mine, giving me an exquisite, sweet, light kiss that was much like his forehead kiss except a whole lot better, and he let me go.

I watched him go to the closet. He disappeared behind the door and came out, shrugging on a canvas coat. His eyes came to me and he ordered, "Stay awake."

"Okay."

He lifted his chin and walked out the door.

I wandered to the computer even though I wanted to watch him leave. I didn't want him to see me watching.

I pulled the chair up to the rolltop. I sat down and clicked into the Internet browser in order to access my webmail.

I heard the Cherokee depart as I typed in the Web address, then my username and password. I heard silence when I clicked on "compose" and more silence as I typed in Niles's e-mail address.

Then I spent the next two hours writing to my fiancé, explaining, in detail, what a time-out meant. What it meant that he didn't know how I took my coffee. What it meant that he didn't understand how much it hurt when he asked me to sell Charlie's house. How lonely I was, even when I was with him. How it felt, him not making love to me, being affectionate, making me feel desired or desirable. How much it bothered me that, even though I'd talked to him about all of this, even wrote him other e-mails, it didn't ever seem to penetrate. And lastly, the part that took the most time, how it wasn't going to work out between us. Then I told him I'd call him in a few days and we would talk. I read it, edited it, read it again, added more, read it again, changed a few things, then I hit SEND.

It disappeared and I stared at the screen showing a list of my e-mails.

Well done, sweetheart, Charlie whispered in my ear.

He sounded sad but proud.

I started crying.

CHAPTER FIVE

Charlie

I OPENED MY EYES, blinked at the bright sunlight, and smelled bacon cooking.

I was alone in Max's bed. Max, evidently, was downstairs cooking breakfast.

I rolled to my back and stared at the point in the A-frame ceiling.

After sending my e-mail to Niles and crying my eyes out. Crying my eyes out so much I had to move to the chair by the couch and curl in it, holding a toss pillow to my chest in order to give myself a comfortable cocoon while letting go of a part of my life that was once important to me. In fact, I thought it was going to be my entire future but I'd figured out wasn't so important anymore. After doing that, I cleaned up my face. Then I threw another log on the fire. Then I stared at the log burning, trying to sort out my head. Then I failed at sorting out my head. Then when it got late, I made dinner for one and ate cookies for dessert. Then I read until it got later. When it got really late, I changed into my nightgown, put in a movie, slid into bed, and obviously fell asleep again while watching it.

Now, clearly, it was morning and Max was home.

And he said when he came home, we would finish.

And as I lay there staring at the ceiling, I decided I was going to have to figure out a way to tell him I wasn't ready for us to finish in whatever way that would come. I wasn't ready for what was happening in his A-frame on my Colorado adventure. I wasn't ready to explore what was going on between him and me.

I wanted to, honest to goodness. I wanted it so badly it felt like an ache.

But I was coming to terms with my life changing in one way. In fact, I had realized the day before as I stared at Max's fire, I knew before I even took this time-out that Niles and I were never going to work and I realized that I'd known that for a long time. I'd either fallen out of love with him or he'd bored the love out of me. But before I even left I had understood somewhere in my head that I simply needed distance to come to that conclusion and that distance would give me the courage to carry it through.

Therefore, I couldn't process, nor did I want to, the colossal shift back to Nina of Old. Nina who opened her heart, let loose, took adventures and even more risks. Nina who did that and got her heart trampled and her head messed with for her troubles.

I wasn't sure I wanted to play it safe and be smart, sane, and rational every second with every nuance of my life.

I *was* sure I'd learned my lessons way back when and I wasn't going back to *that*.

I couldn't live the life that I was living with Niles. I'd come to terms with that.

And I couldn't go back to who I used to be. Heartbreak lay down that road. Heck, it was paved with it.

And Holden Maxwell had "heartbreak" written all over him.

I pulled myself out of bed, went to the bathroom, did my routine, and then, deciding on propriety in the face of our impending conversation, I walked to my suitcase and dug around until I found my wool robe. It was like a big, long, buttonless cardigan sweater that went down to my calves. It was creamy green and had a hood. It cost a fortune and it was *lush*.

I shrugged it on, belted it up, and headed downstairs to face

Max. I hit the bottom, saw him in the kitchen, and stopped dead.

His back was to me and he was wearing pajama bottoms and nothing else. His shoulders, the muscles of his back, the wide expanse of smooth, tan skin was all exposed to the naked eye and I was blinded by the beauty of it. So much, it was a wonder I didn't throw out my hand and go reeling.

At that thought, he turned and gave me a view of his chest.

At this view, arguably better than his back, I sucked in a breath, then whispered to myself, "Oh my God."

"Hey, baby," he called, apparently (and luckily) not hearing me, and headed my way.

I stood immobile as he walked to me.

He stopped in front of me, his head tipped down, and his hand came to my jaw, tipping my head up.

"You sleep okay?" he asked softly, and I nodded. "Wake up at nine o'clock your time?" he went on, and I shook my head. "Sorry I was out so late." I shrugged and he grinned. "I see I got Nina Zombie."

"Um...," I muttered.

He shook his head once, still grinning, then dipped his face and touched his mouth to mine. My toes curled.

"Look after the bacon, will you?" he said when he lifted his head. "I'm gonna go put on some clothes."

"Okay," I whispered.

"Might be good you get some coffee in you before you get near sizzling bacon grease," he advised, still amused.

"Okay," I repeated on a whisper.

"God," he muttered, his thumb drifting across my cheek, his clear gray eyes watching it go. "You're cute."

I swallowed. He let me go and walked away.

I stood where he left me and realized that I was, officially, in trouble. If I couldn't function at the sight of his chest, how was I going to tell him we weren't going to explore what was happening?

Especially if he kept touching me and calling me "baby?"

I pulled myself together enough to take one step when the door under the loft opened. My body jerked in surprise and I gave out a small scream.

A girl walked out, a woman-girl like Becca. Wild, curly, almost frizzy strawberry-blond hair and a lot of it. Cute-as-a-button face. Cornflower-blue eyes. Long, thin, shapely legs that went on forever.

And last, but oh so definitely not least, she was wearing the shirt Max wore yesterday.

I felt like I'd been punched in the gut.

"Forgot to tell you," Max called from upstairs, probably because he heard my scream, "Mindy's here."

"Hi!" Mindy cried brightly, and skipped to me, actually *skipped*. "You're Nina, right?"

"Right," I said, immobile again, this time for a different reason.

"Cool!" she cried, grabbing my arm in one hand, my hand in the other, both with a friendliness that was unreal, and she jumped up and down twice.

"I, um...need to look after the bacon," I told her.

"Oh, sure," she said, looking suddenly confused at my behavior in the face of her outgoingness.

"Nina's a zombie in the morning, Mins," Max called, and I knew he could hear everything. "Maybe you should look after the bacon, darlin'."

Mins? *Darlin'*?

"Cool!" she cried again, as if looking after bacon was her heart's desire, her hands moving from me. "I can do that."

Then she turned and part skipped, part slid on the wood floors in her adorable baby blue socks with darker blue hearts all over them, part danced to the kitchen.

I followed with a lot less exuberance.

No, it wouldn't be hard to tell Max we weren't going to explore *anything*. He wanted me to be a member of his harem? No. Not me. I wasn't going to become a card-carrying member of that particular club with, apparently, Mindy, who he'd brought home when *I* was under his *bloody* roof, and maybe Becca not to mention the ex-member, bitchy, cheating, awful Shauna.

No way. No *bloody* way.

I went to the cupboard over the coffeepot as Mindy pushed the bacon around in the skillet and I took down a mug. Then I poured coffee. I spooned in some sugar. Then I went to the fridge and sloshed in some milk. All the while I did this, my mind tortured me.

Did he sleep with her on the couch when I was upstairs in his bed? He was a big guy but his couch was deep, long. Mindy was long, too, but she was also thin. It would be cozy but it would work.

Did they *do it*, Max knowing I slept like the dead?

Or maybe not caring if I heard?

And also not caring what I'd think that he had a predilection for young girls?

Not that he seemed to discriminate since he'd obviously wanted me, and Shauna seemed to be about my age. Maybe he slept with anyone. Maybe that was why Sarah, the hostess at the restaurant, gave me that weird, closed down look when I walked in. Maybe he liked buxom, copper-haired, Deadheads with fabulous earrings too.

I was sipping at my coffee and seething when Mindy turned to me. "So, you live in England?"

"Yes." My reply was short and curt and I didn't care. She might be okay with this arrangement, seeing as Max was gorgeous and had a fantastic house, but she was young; she'd learn.

"You like it?" she asked.

"Yes," I replied again, and saw Max rounding the counter in jeans, a navy T-shirt that fit him like the gray one he wore with his pajama bottoms. In other words, it fit him too well.

I had the urge to throw my coffee mug at him and then I squelched this mainly because he meant nothing to me. I barely knew him. This intensity of emotion was because I broke up with my fiancé via e-mail the day before. My emotion had nothing to do with *Max*.

He hit the range, his hand hit Mindy's waist, and my eyes narrowed on his touch.

"I got it now, babe," he said softly, and I felt that punch in my gut again when he called her "babe."

Mindy moved away on another skip. Then she rounded the counter and planted herself on *my* stool.

"Duchess," Max called, and my eyes cut to him. "Get Mindy some coffee, will you?"

He wanted *me* to get *Mindy* a coffee?

I was back to wanting to throw my coffee mug at him.

Max was oblivious. I knew this because he turned to Mindy and asked, "You take cream or sugar?"

"Lotsa milk, two sugars," Mindy ordered, and I moved to make her coffee mainly because this would give me something to do, something that had nothing to do with me inflicting bodily harm.

As I was filling her order, Mindy called out to me, "Hey, Nina, you ever wanna move home?"

"Home?" I asked, pouring coffee.

"America."

"No," I lied, because I did, all the time. I missed home constantly. The trouble was I was also home in England and I knew if I came back to the States I'd miss my other home so I couldn't win either way.

Which was, I realized at that dire moment, the story of my *bloody* life.

"Really?" she asked.

"Really," I answered when I poured in "lotsa milk."

"She misses grape jelly," Max muttered, and I ignored him and the memory he invoked and gave Mindy her mug of coffee.

"Hey, thanks!" she cried, like it was a surprise I made it for her when she'd watched me the whole time. Then she continued. "Why do you miss grape jelly?"

"They don't have it in England," I replied, and went to the fridge.

"What else don't they have?" Mindy asked with open curiosity.

"Quite a bit," I answered, not inviting further discourse.

I pulled out my yogurt and berries. Then I grabbed the bunch of bananas on the counter and I yanked one off. I pulled a knife out of the block by the range. I was going to eat my breakfast and if Max didn't give me my keys, I was going to throw such a fit that Mick, the nice police officer, would be called to the scene and *then* I'd damn well get my *bloody* keys.

"You all right?" Max asked quietly when I got close, and I could feel his eyes on me.

"Perfectly fine," I answered, not looking at him and I reached into a cupboard to pull out a bowl.

There was silence a second; then, ever game, Mindy called, "Why'd you move there? To England."

Not thinking clearly and it didn't matter anyway—I'd be out of there very, *very* soon—I answered, "I've sort of lived there on and off most of my life."

"But," Mindy said to my back as I started to slice bananas into the bowl, "Max said you were American."

"I was born here," I told the banana. "My mother is American. My father is English. They got divorced when I was a baby and my father moved back." I finished with the banana, threw the peel in the bin under the sink, and started to rinse the berries.

"So, you'd go back to see your father," Mindy guessed.

"No, my father forgot I existed until he got remarried and his second wife had a baby, my half brother." I turned off the tap and shook the berries in their plastic container, the water leaking out. "She wanted her son to know his sister."

"So, that's when you started going?" Mindy surmised.

"Yes, when I was around seven."

"Cool that you have a brother," Mindy announced happily from behind me, and my eyes closed automatically as I felt that punch in my gut again. This one was different but familiar. It had come at me a lot over the last three years but it never hurt any less.

"Yes, cool," I said, and opened my eyes, turned to my bowl, dumped some berries in, and set the rest in the container aside.

I looked at Max who was watching me closely, his face carefully blank but his eyes alert and asked, "Where's my granola?"

"Cupboard with the oatmeal," he answered, and I turned there.

"I've got a brother," Mindy shared. "We're close but he lives in Seattle now, which is a bummer sometimes and not a bummer others 'cause he can be kinda, *in my life*. YouknowhatImean?"

Yes, I knew what she meant. I knew if her brother knew that she was carrying on with a mountain man lothario who was old enough to be her *much* older brother, then her real, Seattle-dwelling brother would be *in her life*.

I didn't say this. Instead I said, "Of course."

"You close with your brother?" she asked.

I poured granola on my berries, then set the box down and answered, "I moved to England permanently because of him."

"Yeah?" Mindy prompted.

"Yes," I said, spooning out my yogurt and not measuring my words. Not even knowing why I was speaking at all. "He was in the army, sent to Afghanistan. When he was there, a bomb blew his legs off." I heard Mindy gasp and I felt something coming from Max but I was impervious, like I was in a different world. "My father, who is not a nice man, turned his back on his golden boy when he felt he was no longer..." I hesitated, then said, "*Golden*." I shook my head at the still-painful memory and put the top on the yogurt. "His fiancée broke things off with him and he was having trouble adjusting. So I moved to England to help."

There was silence as I mixed my fruit, granola, and yogurt and I turned to face the kitchen. When I did, I saw they were both staring at me. Well, Mindy was. It was more like Max was watching me, *closely*.

Mindy broke the silence, saying quietly, "Jeez, Nina, I'm sorry. He okay now?"

"No," I told her bluntly, looking right at her. "Charlie never adjusted. He committed suicide three years ago."

"Holy crap," Mindy breathed, and I watched the color drain out of her face.

"That pretty much sums it up," I told her.

"Mins, do me a favor. Go upstairs, get yourself one of my T-shirts to wear into town, yeah?" Max said, and Mindy's eyes moved to him.

She also saw him watching me, how he was watching me, her body jolted and she hopped off the stool.

"Yeah, right, um…a shirt…" She hesitated, her eyes going back and forth between Max and me.

"Just lose yourself for a while, okay?" Max ordered, not taking his eyes off me.

She didn't answer or maybe her answer was her skip-dancing away.

I looked at Max and took a bite of my breakfast.

"What was that about?" Max asked, not moving toward me.

"What?" I asked back, my mouth full, well beyond thinking it rude to speak with my mouth full.

"Closed up tight for two days, you share a tragedy and you do it like that?" Max asked, and it dawned on me that *he* looked angry. "What's that about?" he demanded to know.

"Mindy was asking," I explained after I swallowed.

"You didn't have to tell her like that," Max returned.

"Oh, sorry, Max," I said, my voice tinged with sarcasm. "Does she have a delicate disposition? Should I have shielded her from that?"

"Yeah, considerin' she was raped three weeks ago and her boyfriend's bein' a fuckin' dickhead, that would have been good."

I felt every cell in my body cease moving and I stared at him.

Then I whispered, "What?"

"Mindy was raped three weeks ago. She was in Denver with Becca. They were out clubbin' or whatever the fuck they do these days and got separated. Mindy was raped. She went through that, they haven't found the guy, she gets home, her boyfriend who she lives with starts actin' like an asshole. Then *more* of an asshole. Brody, her brother and my best friend who lives in Seattle, asked me to come home and look out for her, seein' as he can't."

Oh my *God*.

Mindy and her baby blue socks with darker blue hearts, skip-dancing, jumping up and down when she met me was *raped*.

"So, Nina," Max cut into my thoughts, "I'll ask again. What the fuck *was* that?"

"I thought…" I shook my head and looked away, closing my eyes, feeling like a bitch because I'd *been* a bitch. I looked back and whispered, "It doesn't matter."

"Well, yeah, it does, considerin' she's like my sister, too, and she and Brody talk and you didn't make a very good impression. This'll be all over town and to Seattle and people'll think I got another Shauna in my bed."

"I—"

He cut me off. "I don't care what people think but I do care what Mindy thinks and I care what Brody thinks."

"I—"

"Jesus," he muttered, looking away and I noticed he'd taken the bacon off the burner and it was sitting in its grease. He went on as if talking to himself. "Was I wrong about you?"

There it was. My opening.

"Yes," I told him, and he looked back at me. "I'm a scream-ing bitch." He stared at me and I went on, "It was jetlag, I think, making you think I was cute…or…whatever. Really, I'm like this. I act like this all the time." He didn't speak just kept staring at me, so unwisely I went on. "I'm over my jetlag. I'll probably be bitchy willy-nilly to just about everyone."

His head cocked to the side and his face got dark in that scary way before he repeated, "Willy-nilly?"

"Yes," I replied instantly, "to everyone."

"So, what you're sayin' is, you're actin' like a bitch to me and to Mindy in an effort to bullshit me into givin' you your car keys back so you can run away because you're scared as shit of what's happenin' with us?"

No, that wasn't what I was saying. At least, it didn't start that way.

I looked at him in an effort to assess my next move and he looked really mad, so I found it difficult to assess my next move.

Then I said carefully, "No."

He moved toward me. I retreated and hit the counter. He didn't stop until he was super close. He pulled the bowl out of my hand, set it to the side, and put a hand on the counter on either side of me and leaned in.

"Duchess, let me explain somethin'," he said in a low, quiet, *angry* voice. "Bitches, real ones, don't say the word 'willy-nilly.' "

"Oh," was all I could think to reply.

"You talk to him?" he asked, and I got confused because I was thinking he was changing the subject.

"Talk to him?"

"Yeah."

"Who?"

"*Him*," Max clipped, and I realized he *was* changing the subject and I tensed, didn't answer, and Max said in a low, warning voice, "Nina."

"Kind of," I whispered quickly.

"How kind of?"

"I sent an e-mail."

"You sent an e-mail," Max repeated, his face disbelieving of the fact I'd send a breakup e-mail to my fiancé, and even in my state, I had to admit it did sound bad.

"I'm"—I hesitated—"better at saying things when I write them down. I can edit. Make sure that it says what I need it to say and I don't"—I licked my lips—"that I can make it so it doesn't..." This was hard but for some reason I kept going. "I had to do it so it didn't...*hurt* too much."

Some of the anger slid from his features and he muttered, "Baby."

"Can you move away?" I asked quietly.

"No."

"Max, please."

He ignored me and asked, "That really happen?"

My head jerked and I asked back, "The e-mail?"

"Your brother."

My whole body jerked and I looked away.

"Nina, look at me." When I didn't, his hand wrapped around my jaw and he made me look at him or he made it so he could study me, which he did a long time before murmuring, "What else is behind that fuckin' shield?"

He really didn't want to know. If he did, he'd know why I jumped to conclusions about him with Mindy, with Becca, and he'd know just how messed up my head was. I wanted to be gone but I didn't want him to think I was messed up and just that was messed up.

I didn't answer and his hand at my jaw became fingers sliding into my hair.

"I'm sorry about your brother, honey."

I pressed my lips together, felt the tears hit my eyes, and then whispered, "Me too."

"You were close," he stated.

I nodded and when he opened his mouth to speak, I beat him to it. "Please, don't. Please don't, Max. You can't be nice to me, not about Charlie. You can't be nice. Anyone who's nice...when people are nice..." I stopped talking and tilted my chin down to hide my face.

His fingers were in my hair, cupped against my head, and he pulled me into him so my forehead was against his chest.

"All right, Duchess, I won't be nice."

My hands went to his stomach and I pushed at it as the tears clogged my throat and I choked, "You're being nice!"

"Honey—"

My fingers curled into his T-shirt and I demanded, "Stop it!"

His hand at my head twisted it so my cheek was against his chest, his other arm went around me, and he pulled me to his body, which was shaking. "Baby"—his voice had laughter in it—"I'm not doing anything."

I felt my breath hitch and at the sound, his arm got tight and his fingers flexed against my scalp.

"I miss him," I whispered, and I didn't know why. I didn't even think the words before they came out of my mouth.

"I can tell."

I pulled in a shaky breath, then another one, and the third went in smooth so I told him, "You can let me go now."

"Keep tellin' you when you're in my arms, I like you where you are."

"Max—"

His hand in my hair pulled my head back and when I was looking at him he declared, "Next up, we're talkin' 'bout your dad."

"I don't have a dad."

His brows slid together and he said, "You mentioned him earlier."

"No, I mentioned *my father*," I stated clearly. "I don't have a *dad*."

"All right, then we'll talk about your father."

"No, since I never talk about him."

"Nina."

"Max."

"Did I stay away long enough?" Mindy called. Max twisted, I got up on tiptoe to look over his shoulder, and Mindy halted at the counter. "Whoops. See I didn't."

"You did," I said quickly.

"I can come back."

I pushed against Max's stomach again. He released me and moved to my side as I said, "You're fine."

"Sure?" she asked.

"Definitely," I replied.

Her eyes hit the stove and she observed, "Bacon's all greasy, Max."

"I'll sort it out," Max told her.

She skip-danced around the counter, throwing him a cheerful smile, and I marveled this girl was raped three weeks ago. Marveled at the same time that the knowledge hit my stomach like a rotten pit.

"I'll do it," she offered, and I saw she was in one of Max's T-shirts and obviously her own jeans, for they fit perfectly.

"You need a shirt?" I asked, and she looked at me as she pulled a paper towel off a holder.

"Uh, last night, I kinda got beer on—" she started, but Max cut her off.

"Damon doused you with beer," he stated, and Mindy's eyes flitted to him.

"Damon?" I asked, grabbing my bowl.

"Her dickhead boyfriend," Max muttered, pulling down a plate and handing it to Mindy.

"He's just—" Mindy began, but Max interrupted her again.

"A dickhead," Max declared.

Her face fell and she arranged a paper towel on the plate.

I decided to wade in. "Why did he, um...I mean, how did he get beer on you?"

"He threw it at her," Max answered, and Mindy ducked her head and pulled bacon out of the skillet.

"He threw a beer at you?" I asked Mindy, not comprehending these words. At least not in recent Nina Land with Niles, who didn't even drink beer, just occasionally gin and tonics or wine with dinner and he wouldn't begin to imagine dousing anyone with any liquid.

Older Nina Land was the land where there were dickheads who might (though they didn't) douse women with beer. Though, maybe not women who'd recently been violated.

"He's not really...coping...uh—" Mindy stammered.

Max's hand went to the back of her neck and he said quietly, "She knows, Mins. I told her."

Mindy nodded but didn't lift her head from her bacon task and I squelched a new desire to throw my bowl at Max, for he may not be okay with me being a bitch to Mindy but he certainly wasn't handling this very well.

"He's not coping with what happened to you," I said to her, and she nodded and took the last piece of bacon out of the skillet when I went on. "Men are idiots mostly. Anyway," I changed the subject. "Upstairs, my suitcase is on the armchair in Max's loft. You can go through it, grab whatever top you want."

Her head twisted to me and her eyes slid along my robe.

Then she began, "I couldn't—"

"Why not? You can't wear that." I dipped my head to Max's T-shirt. "It's huge on you." And it was. She was swimming in it like I had but I'd worn his T-shirts to bed, which was acceptable.

A pretty girl who'd just been raped? No.

She needed to remember she could look pretty and it was okay.

"But your clothes are really nice. Becca said—"

I spooned up more fruit, yogurt, and granola and smiled at her before asking, "You have a flesh-eating virus or something?"

She grinned at me and replied, "No."

"Then go and pick something."

Her eyes moved to the ceiling, then to me, and she said, "Anything off-limits?"

"No."

"You sure?"

"Yes."

"You sure you're sure?"

I shook my head but smiled and promised, "I'm sure I'm sure."

"Cool!" she cried, dropping the bacon fork and skip-dancing out of the kitchen.

I spooned breakfast into my mouth. Max's eyes followed Mindy but since I was in the back recess, I couldn't see her. I knew when she was out of sight, though, because Max's eyes came to me.

Then *he* came to me.

Since I was already against the counter, I had nowhere to retreat.

He got super close again, took the bowl out of my hand, the spoon out of the other, dropped the spoon in the bowl, and set it on the counter.

I swallowed my food and demanded, "Would you quit taking that away? I'm trying to eat breakfast."

I said this as I looked at the bowl. I should have kept my eyes on him because when my head twisted back, his hand came to my neck and his mouth came down on mine.

I really tried not to respond this time. I knew how good it could be, so I thought I could steel myself against it.

I was wrong.

His tongue touched my lips, my mouth opened like it had a mind of its own, and then I was in his arms. Max deepened the kiss and my hands slid around his neck, my fingers going into his hair. I went up on my toes, pressed into his body, and he pushed me back into the counter.

It was as good as it was yesterday, just as good, which meant it might *always* be that good.

Which was bad.

His mouth broke from mine but he didn't move far away. His hand came back to my neck, curling around, his forehead rested on mine, and our heavy breathing mingled.

"Tried to wake you up last night when I got to bed. You were out like usual, didn't have the heart in the end," he whispered.

"Okay," I whispered back, not really thinking because my mind was on my nipples, which had gotten hard and were tingling and my stomach, which had somehow disappeared and between my legs, which was tingling even more.

"Mindy was on the couch," he went on.

"Oh."

"No Mindy tonight," he finished, and I found that my stomach *hadn't* disappeared because it spasmed in a way I really, *really* liked.

"Oh," I breathed this time, and I watched his eyes smile.

His thumb slid along my jaw. "You kiss like that, honey, lookin' forward to findin' out what else you can do."

I kissed like that? It was Max who was a good kisser.

I didn't tell him this. Instead, I shivered.

Then I muttered, "Um..."

He interrupted me with, "Men are idiots?"

"Mostly," I answered on a whisper, and I heard *and* felt him chuckle.

"Hey! I know!" Mindy shouted from somewhere not exactly close, but in Max's house nowhere was exactly far.

Max closed his eyes, rolled his forehead to the side, and his body unfortunately followed it.

I hastily grabbed my bowl.

"What?" I asked when Mindy hit the kitchen.

"You and me and Becca can go shopping in town this afternoon and later we'll take you to dinner."

"That's a great idea," I told her.

"We got plans," Max said from beside me, and I watched as Mindy's face fell.

I looked at Max and widened my eyes at him. He caught my hint, looked at Mindy, and sighed.

Then he said, "You bring her home, safe and sound, we can push 'em to later."

"Cool!" Mindy exclaimed.

"Doesn't anyone around here work?" I asked.

"I work at The Dog with Becca, so we work nights," Mindy said, walking to the cold bacon and picking up a slice. "I'm off tonight. Becca's gotta work but that isn't until later." Then she bit off some bacon and chewed.

I noticed that Max didn't answer my question.

"You're good to stay with Bec?" Max asked, and Mindy

nodded. "And we're movin' your shit there this mornin'?" Max went on. Mindy took another bite of bacon and nodded. "You're gonna stick with this break with Damon?"

"A week, Max," she said. "That was the deal we decided on last night."

"You stick with a week," Max returned, sounding exactly like an older brother, though I couldn't know; I didn't have an older brother, just a dead younger one. But I was guessing since, even younger, Charlie used to sound like that a lot.

She looked at me and rolled her eyes.

Yes, definitely an older brother.

"Mindy." Max's voice was a warning.

All right, maybe a somewhat scary older brother. Charlie had never been scary.

"I'll stick with the week," she answered.

"You make Damon stick with it too," Max pushed.

"Oh...*kay*," she replied impatiently, and I looked at Max to see he was grinning, which, when I looked back at Mindy, I noted she found annoying.

"I love that top on you," I butted in. "You should keep it."

Mindy's annoyed face disappeared and her eyes hit me. "I couldn't."

"You can."

"But—"

"I'll replace it in town this afternoon. It looked like there were some great shops."

"They're awesome!" Mindy cried. "I can't *wait* to show you."

"Me either," I replied, spooned up more of my breakfast, and when I was shoving it into my mouth, Max's arm hooked around my neck and he pulled me into his side.

"Make me some eggs and toast to go with that bacon, Mins," Max ordered. She rolled her eyes but headed to the toaster. I tested his arm around my neck and found it didn't budge. "Hand me my coffee, Duchess," he ordered me. I caught Mindy's eye and rolled mine back. She giggled and I reached forward, his arm still around my neck, grabbed his mug, and handed it to him.

So, in the end, I finished my breakfast pressed to Max's side, his arm around my neck, watching Mindy make eggs and toast while Max sipped cold coffee.

And I not only didn't tell him we weren't going to explore our situation, I also let him kiss me again, told him about Charlie, and made a date to spend the afternoon and have dinner with, essentially, his baby sister who'd been raped only weeks before.

Yes, I was officially in trouble.

*   *   *

I took a shower in Max's downstairs bathroom, hauling all my stuff down there to do it. There, I got ready while Max took a shower upstairs and Mindy sat on the toilet seat chatting animatedly to me like a girl who'd never experienced anything but extreme happiness while living in a land of golden rainfalls, fairies that granted wishes, and dancing leprechauns that showered treasure on you.

When I was done getting ready, which—if Max's impatient yet amused demeanor was anything to go by—took way too long, we all climbed into the Cherokee and went to Mindy's apartment, where we packed up a lot of her stuff. In fact, as far as I could tell since she and this Damon person didn't have much, outside of dishes and furniture, it seemed like most everything she owned.

On a trip to the Cherokee with a box, I caught Max, who was heading back in.

"Isn't this, um...," I asked quietly, in case Mindy could hear, "a lot of stuff for one week?"

Max put his finger to his lips, winked at me, then took the box from me and headed back to the Jeep.

When we were done packing up, we drove across town and Becca helped us carry it up the two flights of stairs to her third-story condo.

After we had Mindy safely ensconced in her new lodgings, Max took us out for lunch at a little rustic but lovely café by the river. We had a booth by the window and Max sat by me. Mindy and Becca did most of the talking, so much I didn't have time to think much less room to speak. Though I did manage to think it felt nice the way Max lounged beside me, his arm across the booth at my back, his bearing laid-back but possessive. And I also managed to remind myself I shouldn't be thinking that way, even though I couldn't stop myself from doing it.

The sun was shining and the cold snap had completely disappeared. It had to be twenty, maybe even thirty degrees warmer that day and the snow was melting so fast the gutters in the streets had turned to streams. The sun glistening off the water and the snow made the clear day so much brighter it was cheerful, like the town had its own brand of magic.

Experiencing it, I couldn't help but wonder if maybe Mindy had, indeed, lived an enchanted life prior, of course, to being raped.

When we walked out of the café, Mindy proclaimed, "All right, girl time! No boys allowed."

"Like I'd wanna go shoppin'," Max muttered, his arm sliding around my shoulders, pulling me into his side.

"Right, so . . . skedaddle," Becca ordered.

Max grinned and said, "She'll be right back."

Then he walked me to the Jeep, shoved me into it with a hand in my belly, followed me in, slid his fingers into my hair, an arm low at my waist, and he made out with me right there on the street, in town, in broad daylight.

Yes, *made out with me*. Tongues and all.

I did not fight this mainly because I was focused on fighting my body's reaction to his hands on me and his tongue in my mouth and, unfortunately, losing.

When his head lifted, I noted vaguely he didn't let me go.

"You gonna be all right with the terrible twosome?" he asked, and I found it unfair he seemed capable of breathing and standing erect. My knees had gone weak and my breath had gone funny.

"I think so."

"Don't let them get you into trouble."

"Okay."

His face came a few centimeters closer and he whispered, "Look out for her, yeah? She has"—he hesitated—"bad moments."

At this open evidence of his concern for Mindy, something I liked a lot, my hand moved of its own accord and slid from his hair to cup his jaw.

"I'll look out for her," I promised.

His beautiful eyes looked into mine for seconds that felt like minutes before he touched his mouth to mine in one of his sweet, swift kisses and he pulled me from the truck.

"I'll see you at home later," he said.

"Okay."

He chucked me under the chin and started to walk around the Cherokee.

I made a massive effort to pull myself together so I didn't watch him like a love-struck idiot and headed back to Mindy and Becca. He tooted his horn as he drove past us and I lifted my hand in a wave, hoping my wave didn't make me look like a love-struck idiot.

"I think he likes you," Becca said. She looked at Mindy, who was watching me and they both giggled.

"I need to spend money," I muttered.

"Yeah, me too," Mindy said, linking her arm with mine and we took off.

There weren't some great shops in town. There were some *really* great shops and considering I didn't have to pay for a wedding anymore and I'd been saving since Niles asked me over a year ago, I went crazy. I bought so much stuff both Becca and Mindy had to help me carry my bags. I also found Sarah's earrings, and feeling generous, I bought all three of us a pair even though they were more expensive than I was expecting, mainly because they were heavy with silver and beautifully crafted. Becca and Mindy tried to protest but I wouldn't let them. A girl who'd been raped and her friend who was looking out for her needed new, expensive, heavy, silver, beautifully crafted earrings. It should be a law.

We ran into practically everyone the girls knew it seemed, since we were constantly stopped in shops and on the boardwalk. There were a lot of introductions and gabbing. I was a curiosity since some had heard of me already and it was evident Max was a popular person and anyone associated with him was automatically an object of fascination, most especially an outsider with an English accent. Others, Becca and Mindy freely told, "Nina's with Max," which *then* made me an object of fascination.

After the curiosity about me wore off, most of the talk was about Curtis Dodd and who might have done the deed. Most of this was liberally interspersed with open comments about how no one was really going to miss him. Some of it was catty talk about Shauna, who, it was evident, was *not* a popular person. There were a lot of careful looks at Mindy, who seemed to have trouble dealing with these, as indicated by the pink that would tinge her cheeks. When that happened, either Becca or I would get close. Sometimes, if Mindy started shuffling her feet or chewing at her cuticles, I'd grab her hand. When I did this, she held on tight and I'd feel the sting of tears behind my eyes but I just held her right back.

We walked by a photography shop that printed digital photos and I asked the girls if we could go in because I was dying to see the photo Cotton took printed out rather than small on the screen at the back of the camera. When we entered, it appeared to be a shrine to Jimmy Cotton. The walls were wallpapered with his pictures. We hung out while the photos were printing, halfheartedly looking at photography stuff we had no interest in. When they were done, I paid for the photos and we stood a few feet from the counter looking through them.

I came upon Cotton's photo and stared, stunned at what the

man could do with a digital camera. The framing was magnificent. He managed to make the bluff, river, and mountains most of the photo, Max and me at the side.

But regardless of the beauty of the vista, it was Max and me that took my full attention.

Not surprisingly, Max was incredibly photogenic, smiling natural and casual into the camera.

Surprisingly, even with his supreme male beauty, I looked natural and casual, smiling at his side. My cream cap, blonde hair, and pale, wind-kissed skin were an attractive foil to his dark handsomeness. I liked the look of us together, maybe a bit too much.

And we didn't look like we'd just met and barely knew each other. We looked like we'd known each other forever, comfortable in our close hold.

We looked even like we belonged together.

I hadn't realized I'd put my hand to his stomach, my arm around his back, and I noticed that I fitted into his side like God created me specifically to slot right there. And his hand curled at my neck, gloved fingers barely visible through the strands of my hair, had the weird look like he was claiming me. I was, just simply, *his*.

"I freaking *love* that picture!" Mindy cried, standing close, staring at the photo, and Becca got close too.

"Wow, awesome shot," she breathed. "Max is hot and you've got the prettiest eyes I've ever seen."

I started, tore my eyes from the photo, and looked at Becca. "I'm sorry?"

Becca's gaze came to my face. "Prettiest eyes, Max said it too."

I blinked and felt my eyebrows go up just as I felt a pleasant warmth wash through me.

"I'm sorry?" I repeated.

"Max said you've got the prettiest eyes he's ever seen."

Oh my *God*.

"He said that?" I whispered, and Becca grinned.

"Yeah, the other day, when, um…" Her gaze slid to Mindy, who was listening, then came back to me. "He said it the other day when we were talkin' 'bout you. He said you were cute when you were pissed and you've got the prettiest eyes he's ever seen."

Oh. My. *God.*

I looked back to the photo and examined, for the first time in my life with any great attention, my eyes. You couldn't see it really in the photo but I knew they were deep set and hazel, more brown than green. I'd never thought much of them except wishing they were bigger, wider so I could use more flair with eye shadow and, even focusing on them, I didn't think much of them now.

"You do have really pretty eyes," Mindy said to me softly. "I noticed them right off the bat."

"I…they're…um….," I stammered.

"Really unusual, striking, eye-catching, no pun intended," Becca said on a grin.

"Can I have a copy of that photo?" Mindy asked, still speaking softly, and I looked closely at her.

She was gazing at the photo and her face was soft like her voice.

"Sure, darling," I said softly, and her eyes skittered to me.

"Thanks," she whispered.

I walked to the counter, handed my memory card to the clerk as well as the photo, and asked for another copy.

Then I turned to Mindy and told her, "Best part about it, outside the view, is that Jimmy Cotton took it."

"Jimmy Cotton does *not* take snapshots," the clerk said to me, his voice filled with unmistakable outrage.

I turned back to him, surprised at his entry into our conversation and the tone of it, and asked, "I'm sorry?"

"Jimmy Cotton"—he waved my photo at me—"does *not* take snapshots." He indicated the walls of his shop with a wave of his hand. "He's a *master.*"

"Yes, I agree, but he happened onto us at the bluff yesterday and he took our photo."

"With a digital camera?" the clerk shot back, now his tone was filled with derision as if digital cameras were the invention of the devil.

"Um..." I looked at the memory card and answered, "Yes."

"Jimmy doesn't *do* digital."

"Um..." I started, but I heard Mindy whisper from beside me. "The bluff?"

I turned to her and said, "Yes."

She snatched the photo out of the clerk's hand and looked closely at it.

"God, I was lookin' at you and Max. I didn't notice you were at the bluff."

"We were. Max took me there yesterday," I said, and her eyes moved quickly to me.

Then she breathed, "Wow."

"Sorry?"

"Wow," she said louder.

"Wow, what?"

"Wow, Max took you to the bluff." The strange wonder slid out of her face, it brightened and she smiled, blinding and huge. "He took you to the bluff."

"Yes," I said, drawing out the word because I was confused.

"What's the big deal?" Becca asked, getting close.

"The bluff is Max's favorite place in the world," Mindy answered.

"He seemed rather fond of it," I remarked, and Mindy giggled.

"Yeah, you could say he's 'rather fond of it,'" Mindy replied through her continuing giggles. "Brody told me he's *seriously* rather fond of it. It's his special place and he doesn't share it with *just anybody*. He didn't take Brody there for years. He didn't take me there until my sixteenth birthday and he's known me *since I was born*."

I had the strange sensation of not getting a good feeling about this information at the same time I *was* getting a good feeling about it.

"Really?" I asked.

"Yeah," Mindy said through a smile.

"Wow," Becca whispered.

Wow was right.

"I don't know what to do with that information," I told Mindy and Becca.

"I'll ask Brody what you should do with that information," Mindy offered helpfully, and I felt my lungs seize.

"No, don't do that."

"Oh yeah, *do that*," Becca encouraged. "I wanna know too."

"No, don't," I repeated.

"You gotta," Becca said. "This could be *huge*."

"Yeah." Mindy's eyes were bright with excitement and happiness. "Lovin' this. Brody'll love it too." Her bright, happy eyes came to me. "Maybe even enough to come home and check you out."

This was a nightmare.

"Um . . . that kind of scares me," I told her, and she laughed, linked her arm with mine, and put her forehead to my shoulder.

"My big bro is cool. You'll *adore* him. He's *awesome*," she said when she lifted her head.

I looked into her carefree eyes and I didn't have the heart to burst her bubble.

"Brilliant," I muttered, and she grinned.

"That'll be a quarter," the clerk said from behind us, waving the print.

"A quarter for a Jimmy Cotton print? Bargain!" Becca exclaimed, I thought mostly to annoy the clerk.

If this was her intention, she succeeded magnificently and the three of us walked out of the shop together under the weight of his irate scowl, Becca and Mindy gulping back giggles.

Me?

I found it funny, their giggles were infectious, and I definitely laughed.

That didn't mean I wasn't quaking in my boots.

*   *   *

We were sitting at a red-and-white-checked tableclothed table in the center of which was an enormous pepperoni and mushroom pizza that a family of five could assist us with consuming and everyone would be sated when Mindy started the conversation.

"Okay, it's none of my business, really, but it kind of is because I've known Max since I was born."

I looked at her around my beer knowing I wasn't going to like this.

I lowered my beer and asked, "What's none of your business?"

Her head tipped to my hand. "That diamond on your finger."

I was right. I didn't like this.

"Mindy—" I started.

"I know you've known him, like, real brief, but sometimes shit happens fast when you know it's right and you guys seem solid," she said softly. "Still, it isn't Max's."

Max and me seemed solid? Shit happens fast when you know it's right?

I ignored both of those and said softly back, "No, it isn't Max's."

"So, is it an heirloom or something?" she asked, and I pulled in a deep breath.

"No," I said on the exhale.

"So, whose is it?" she pressed.

I looked at Becca, who had a slice of pizza in her hand, her hand to her mouth, her teeth in the slice but her eyeballs were wandering around the room looking at anything but Mindy and me. If she didn't have the pizza in her mouth, I knew she would have been whistling.

Then I looked at Mindy and made a decision. "His name is Niles."

"Niles?" she asked, and I could tell she didn't much like his name.

Niles was a perfectly fine name, of course. However, it

didn't ring American Mountain Man like "Max" or "Brody" or "Damon."

"Niles," I repeated.

"Okay, so," Mindy went on, and I could see she was pulling up the courage to do so. I wished she wouldn't but I understood why she did, considering it was obvious she was close to Max and cared about him. "You're wearin' Niles's ring, why are you up at the A-frame with Max?"

"It's a long story."

"We got time."

"Mins," Becca whispered.

"No, it's okay," I said, but I didn't know why I said it since it wasn't.

Then suddenly it was.

And over beer and pizza, I found myself telling two twenty-four-year-old girls (I'd found out their ages) everything about my life, Niles, Charlie, my time-out adventure in the mountains, and my e-mail.

I did not, however, tell them about Max.

When I stopped speaking and grabbed another slice of pizza, Becca breathed, "Wow. You're goin' through *a lot*."

"Yes, that's about it. Wow," I whispered, then bit into my pizza.

"So, you aren't with this Niles anymore?" Mindy asked.

I chewed, swallowed, and licked my lips.

Then I whispered, "I don't think I've been with him for a while."

I suddenly felt tears hit my eyes.

"Oh, Nina," Mindy whispered back, her fingers wrapping around my wrist.

My neck twisted and I dropped my slice. Mindy's hand went away and I took a sip of beer.

I shared, "You know, the funny thing is, that part doesn't hurt. Losing him. Not at all." My voice dropped and my eyes went between them both as I asked, "Does that make me a bad person?"

"No," Becca said instantly.

"I don't think he's been with you for a while either," Mindy said. "By the sounds of it."

I nodded and told her, "I'm just sad because I care about him and I don't want him to hurt."

"Not sure he'll hurt," Becca muttered, and I looked at her.

"Sorry?"

Becca pressed her lips together, glanced at Mindy, then said to me, "He seems pretty clueless. Don't want to sound like a bitch or anything, but, way it sounds, not sure he'll even notice you're gone."

I had to admit, this idea had merit considering I'd sent that e-mail yesterday, Niles checked his e-mail frequently, and I hadn't heard from him at all. I did tell him I'd call in a few days but I'd also broken up with him. Like Max had said, a man cares, he phones.

And even though I said I'd call in a few days, if Niles cared I broke up with him, he'd phone, my offer to call in a few days be damned.

Ergo, it seemed Becca was right.

Nevertheless, I started, "He's just—"

"Clueless," Mindy said firmly.

"But—"

"Listen, Nina," Becca cut in, "you're gorgeous. You're classy. You're sweet. You dress *awesome*." She glanced again at Mindy, then went on with a sageness that was beyond her years. "See it all the time, a good woman settles for somethin' that feels good, in your case, it felt safe, but it ain't right. This Niles guy might be a nice guy, but he ain't right. It's good you realized it before it was too late."

She's right, Charlie said into my head, and my back went straight.

"I saw you look at me," Mindy said to Becca, and she looked somewhat peeved, so I couldn't focus on the fact that Charlie was in my head again. Or on what they'd both just said to me. Or on the fact that it made sense and I felt relief, deep down, to have two twenty-four-year-old girls I didn't know all that well assuring me I was doing the right thing. Instead, I needed to focus on Mindy and Becca.

"I did," Becca said honestly to Mindy.

"Damon's just havin' a rough time," Mindy told her.

"Yeah, you've said that, like, a million times," Becca said back.

"Well, that's 'cause he is," Mindy retorted.

"Girls," I waded in.

They ignored me. "For Nina, this Niles guy, he's boring and clueless and"—she looked at me—"Nina and Niles? That doesn't sound too good. Now, Nina and Max"—she grinned—"that goes great together."

"Becca," I said, but she looked back to Mindy.

"So she said yes because she felt safe. Now she realizes safe ain't all that. For you, Damon is hot and he's . . . well, that's about all he's got. Bein' hot. Mostly he's a jerk."

"He isn't a jerk," Mindy returned.

Becca looked at me. "He's a jerk."

I didn't know if it was the right thing to do but I decided to add, "Max doesn't seem to care much for him."

"Max never likes my boyfriends, neither does Brody," Mindy said to me.

"Maybe because they're all jerks?" Becca suggested.

"They aren't all jerks," Mindy replied.

Becca looked back at me. "All hot. All jerks."

"Looks aren't everything," I advised Mindy.

"Easy for you to say," Mindy muttered. "You've got Max. He's the hottest of the hot."

She had that right.

"You'll find um . . . hot and nice," I encouraged, though I wasn't certain I should. It was my experience that those two didn't go very well together. Niles was nothing to sneeze at. In fact, he was quite good-looking if not powerfully built and amazingly attractive. He was also nice. He was just . . .

Clueless.

"Easy for you to say again," Mindy said to me. "You've got Max. He's hot *and* nice."

I suspected she had that right, too, though the jury was still out on that one.

"Mindy—" I started, and she cut me off but before she did I noticed her color had gone high, the light had gone out of her eyes, and her shoulders had slumped.

I guessed this was all indicative of a "bad moment" coming on.

"Can we not talk about this?" Mindy asked, and I knew from the dead tone of her voice that I was right.

"Girl—" Becca began, but Mindy cut her off too.

"I asked, can we not talk about this?"

I looked at Becca, who was looking at me. I tipped my head at Mindy and Becca shrugged.

"All right, darling, we'll not talk about this," I said to Mindy.

"I need a drink," Mindy said back. "Let's go to The Dog."

"We're drinking here," I reminded her.

"The Dog's more fun," Mindy told me.

I was supposed to be back at the Mindy-less A-frame after dinner to meet Max. Max and his hands and his mouth and his tongue and his muscled back and amazing chest and queen-sized bed.

"I could go to The Dog," I decided.

"Brill!" Becca exclaimed. "My shift starts in half an hour. We'll get you at one of my tables and we'll carry on girlie time even when I'm workin'."

"I need to call Max," I told them, digging in my bag, looking for my phone. "Do either of you have his number?"

"Sure," Mindy said, but I was still digging.

Then I realized I'd left my phone on Max's nightstand. And Niles might have called while Max was at home.

Drat!

I dropped my purse to hang on the chair and turned to the table. "Actually, I forgot my phone."

Mindy's thumb was moving on her phone. She beeped it and handed it to me. "Use mine, should be ringing."

I took it, glanced at them both, and muttered, "Excuse me," before I got up and walked from the table the short distance to the lobby.

"Yeah?" Max answered.

"Max?"

"Duchess?"

"Yes."

"Everything okay?"

"Um...we're going to The Dog."

There was a moment of silence. Loaded silence.

Then, "What?"

"We had a somewhat...difficult conversation at dinner. Mindy needs a drink."

"Mindy's drivin' and she's supposed to be drivin' you up here. She doesn't need a drink."

"Trust me, Max. I think she needs a drink."

He was quiet a second. Then his voice was soft when he asked, "That bad?"

"Not really," I answered honestly. "Just that, if we don't do evasive maneuvering, it might get there."

"I need to come down?"

All right, maybe he *was* nice.

"I'll call you if I think you should."

"All right, Duchess," he replied. "And speakin' of callin'. Your phone's here." I held my breath and he went on, "You got a coupla calls. The display says they're from your mom."

"Oh."

Mom. She knew I was here. I was supposed to call her and talk through the Niles situation. With all that went on, I forgot.

"You want me to answer if she calls again, give her Mindy's number?" Max offered.

"No, that's okay. I'll call her tomorrow."

"Whatever you want, honey."

Yes, evidence was clearly suggesting Max was nice.

"I better go."

"Yeah, you go, the new plan is you have fun. Mindy has fun. I'll come down to pick you both up 'round eleven. That enough time for evasive maneuvering?"

The evidence was becoming overwhelming.

"You don't need to do that. I'll stay sober and drive Mindy home."

"How'll you get here?"

"Well, I could stay with Mindy and Becca and maybe one of them will bring me back tomorrow morning."

His voice was different, firm to the point of being solid when he stated, "Babe, that's not gonna happen."

"Max—"

"See you at eleven."

"Max—"

"Be good."

"Max!"

Wasted effort to say his name, he hung up.

I slid Mindy's phone closed and walked back to the table.

"Max has a new plan," I announced when they both looked at me. I sat down and I looked at Mindy. "He wants us to have fun. He's designated driver, picking us up at eleven."

"Killer!" Becca cried.

"Cool!" Mindy cried at the same time.

I smiled at them genuinely this time because really, if I got down to it, spending time with them, shopping at great shops, eating delicious buffalo burgers, snowmobiling, gazing at beautiful vistas, meeting Cotton and having him take my photo with Max, getting my head sorted about Niles, which was a relief even if it was a sad one, my Colorado adventure might have started out terrible and was trundling along the road of deeply confusing but still, it wasn't turning out half bad.

*   *   *

"Rat-arsed!" Arlene yelled through a guffaw. "That's just screwy."

"Well, then, what does shitfaced really mean?" I returned.

She considered this, head tipped to the side, then grinned somewhat crookedly and proclaimed, "You got me there."

"Ha!" I cried, and she and I both laughed.

I was right when we left the pizza place. My Colorado adventure wasn't turning out half bad and it was getting better.

The Dog was *fun*. It was well off the main drag out in the middle of nowhere. You had to know it was there to find it, which meant it was almost entirely populated by locals.

And it was *populated*. Even for a Thursday it was busy, nearly jam-packed. The music was loud and the beer was cold. It was *great*.

Arlene, my taxi nemesis, had hit Mindy and my table around forty-five minutes after we arrived. She introduced herself and without invitation sat herself down at a stool at our small, high, round table. She was older than me I guessed by about fifteen years or so. She was short, very round but had the daintiest feet and hands I'd ever seen. She had close-cropped hair that looked permed and it was colored a peculiar shade of peach that I thought was supposed to be strawberry blonde but missed the mark by quite a bit.

And she was hilarious.

"What other words do they have?" Mindy asked, leaning into me.

I was educating them on British English versus American English. I'd been doing this awhile and they thought it was *fascinating*.

"Um . . . ," I mumbled, sucking back more beer, of which I'd lost count how many I'd had. I swallowed, dropped my hand with bottle to the table, and stated, "Rubbish."

"Trash, you said that one already," Arlene told me.

"Bunged up!" I cried.

"What?" Mindy giggled.

"Means you have a stuffy nose."

"Love it! Bunged up!" Arlene said on a near shout.

"They also say 'head full of cold' when you've got a cold,"

I shared, and then carried on. "Pants are underwear, trousers are pants. Vests are called waistcoats, tank tops are called vests, and robes are called dressing gowns!"

"We speak the same language at all?" Arlene asked, and I smiled at her.

"Not much," I answered. "But it works anyway. Though never, but never, tell someone you were rear-ended. *Ever,*" I advised. "They don't say that but what they *think* when *you* say it is very *rude* because they aren't thinking of *cars at all*."

We all laughed uproariously as if this was the height of comedy.

"I like you," Arlene declared, grinning broadly. "Never thought I'd say this in my lifetime but I may even like you better than I liked Anna and she was a hoot."

"Anna?" I asked, wiping a tear of laughter from under my eye.

"Max's wife," Arlene replied.

I stopped laughing, her words hitting me like I was a cartoon character standing at the bottom of the cliff and the anvil fell on my head.

I didn't get the chance to crawl out from under because, shockingly, Mindy was suddenly yanked violently from the table.

"Hey!" Arlene exclaimed, hopping off her stool and I turned.

A tall, good-looking, dark-haired boy-man with scarily bulging biceps that did not look attractively powerful, just scary, had his fingers wrapped tight around Mindy's upper arm.

"Big, bad Max moved you out today, did he?" he sneered in Mindy's face, giving her a shake.

I hopped off my stool, too, as Arlene rounded on Mindy and the man.

"Damon, leave her be," Arlene ordered.

"Fuck off, Arlene," he clipped, and her upper body drew back in visible affront.

"You eat with that mouth, Damon Matthews?" she demanded to know.

"This ain't your business."

"Well"—I got up close to them and declared quietly—"it's mine."

He swung to me and gave me a head-to-toe. "Yeah? Who're you?"

"I'm Nina Sheridan," I announced like I was saying, "I'm Supergirl."

Damon was not impressed. "So?"

"She's Max's woman," Arlene proclaimed, and this wasn't taken favorably by Damon.

"Fuck," he muttered low, his eyes narrow and not leaving me. "That asshole gets all the sweet pieces."

"What's going on?" Becca arrived before anyone could say word one to his rude comment and Damon swung to her.

"You fuck off, too, bitch."

"Did you call me a bitch?" Becca shrieked, instantly beside herself with fury and I got closer in an effort to defuse the situation.

"Listen, Damon—" I started, but he jostled Mindy and began to move away.

"We gotta have words," he told Mindy, ignoring me.

"Damon, I told you, we're on a break for a week," Mindy said softly, planting her feet, twisting her arm in his hold. He stopped and glared at her.

"Funny, *you* get nailed in Denver and *we're* suddenly on a break."

Mindy went solid. Becca went solid. Arlene went solid.

I, on the other hand, saw red for the third time in my life and moved.

"Take your hand off her," I insisted, having got right in his face.

"Fuck off," he bit out, right in mine.

"Take your hand *off* her!" I yelled.

He leaned into me and clipped, "Fuck...*off.*"

I got more in his face. "Take it off. *Now!*"

He took it off and shoved my shoulder, shouting back, "Bitch! Fuck! *Off!*"

I went back on a foot and, so furious at what he said to Mindy, not thinking that, boy-man or not, he was bigger than me and his biceps were scary, I lifted both hands and pushed with all my might against his chest.

He went back two long paces and I shouted, "That's it, asshole, move along!"

Without delay, he took two steps forward, his arm went across, down, and then swung out and around, backhanding me viciously, his knuckles connecting with dazzling accuracy at my cheekbone.

I jerked to the side and bent double, my hand going to my face, my hair flying and settling around me, my eyes blinking away stars.

I was still blinking away stars when I heard Mindy cry, "Max!" and then Max's gravelly, frighteningly *furious* voice order, "See to Nina."

Then I straightened as I felt Arlene's hands on me and I watched Max do with one hand what I had to do with two. He planted his palm in Damon's chest and Damon went flying. Max stalked after him and did it again and Damon went flying again.

"This ain't your business, Maxwell," Damon snapped, trying to evade Max's hand, but, as if it were a magnet and Damon was steel, Max's hand hit his chest again and Damon was propelled back, right toward the door.

"You okay?" Arlene asked me, and all I could think to say was, "Max."

"Come on!" Becca shouted, grabbing my hand, and Mindy, Becca, Arlene, and I rushed to the door Max hustled Damon out of.

We were followed by a slew of people.

I didn't notice because the minute we hit the parking lot and shuffled between two cars to get to the open area I saw Max's fist connect with Damon's face and Damon went down to all fours.

"Enough?" Max asked calmly, and Damon's head twisted up to look at him.

Then he rose to his feet, lifted his fists, and said what I was guessing were two of the very few words in his vocabulary, "Fuck you!"

He lunged forward swinging. Max ducked away but righted with a powerful uppercut to Damon's ribs and Damon went back several paces.

Max followed him and landed two more blows, left then right, both to the ribs again then another one to the face and Damon went back down to his hands and knees.

"Enough?" Max repeated, towering over him.

Damon was coughing and he lifted one hand to his ribs as he pushed to his feet.

"Damon, boy, stay the fuck down," a man urged.

"Come on, Maxwell," Damon taunted stupidly, wriggling his fingers at Max.

"Be smart," Max replied.

"Fuck that," Damon said, and lunged again. Lifting a fist too slowly, Max easily deflected it and landed quick blows to Damon's belly, both of them causing Damon to expel painful-sounding "oofs." Then Max caught him under the chin and Damon flew back and fell down to his behind.

"Stay down!" another man shouted.

"Enough?" Max asked, standing over him.

Damon kicked at Max's feet but Max casually stepped away.

"Dick!" Damon spat, saliva flying from his mouth, blood dripping from his lip.

"I asked if you've had enough?" Max said to him.

"Enough of that twat Mindy?" Damon sneered, and Max's body, loose for the fight, got tight.

"You're the dick!" Becca yelled, and I looked to my left to see Arlene and another lady had hold of her and she was straining to get at Damon. I looked to my right to see Mindy, pale and visibly heartbroken, staring at Damon and Max.

I moved to Mindy and put my arms around her. She instantly leaned into my body, wrapped her arms around me, and put her head to my shoulder.

"You've had enough," Max decided on a mutter, turning away, dismissing him. His eyes came to Mindy and me, and even though I knew he wasn't mad at me, the look on his face still made me shiver. "Jeep," he clipped.

I nodded. "I'll run and get our purses."

"I'll get them for you," another lady said, and took off.

Damon pushed to his feet behind Max.

"Max, he's up," a man informed him, and Max, now two feet away from Mindy and me, turned around.

"Come back tomorrow, asshole, get *all* her shit. Don't want her back," Damon said to Max, swiping at his lip with the back of his hand.

Mindy made a funny, sad noise and my arms got tighter.

"Her name's only one on the lease, Damon, figure you should get *your* shit out. I'll be there, you give me the keys," Max called back.

"I ain't fuckin' movin'," Damon returned.

"Then you get home from work tomorrow, your shit'll be in the snow," Max told him.

"Touch my shit, we got problems," Damon threatened.

"We don't already got problems?" Max asked the obvious.

Damon glared at him and made another threat: "This ain't over."

"Damon, be cool, stand down," someone advised, but Max apparently had had enough.

He walked back to Damon and Damon tried not to appear to cower and mostly succeeded since he didn't retreat but he still looked a bit scared.

"You mistreated what amounts to my sister and back-handed my woman. How is it in that scenario that you're put out?" Max asked quietly but loud enough for everyone to hear.

"Mindy and me ain't none of your business," Damon shot back.

"There isn't a Mindy and you," Max returned.

"Your woman put her hands on me," Damon accused accurately, but he was beginning to sound like he was whining.

"She's wearin' heels, boy, but she's five foot seven. You got five inches and at least a hundred pounds on her," Max replied, and I figured he was being a might bit generous with the weight but I wasn't going to correct him, mostly because he wasn't done talking. "And, lastly, she's a *woman*. You don't ever strike a woman in anger." Damon continued glaring and Max continued speaking. "I'm feelin' generous since you're bleedin', so I'll point out you should learn a lesson from this. A man hurts your woman, you take yours from that man. You *never* take it from your woman." Damon just kept glaring at him, so Max asked, "You got me?"

To which Damon muttered, "Just fuck off."

Max's back was to me so I couldn't see his face but he didn't speak and I suspected he was examining Damon to see if he was really that dumb. Deciding that Damon was indeed really that dumb, Max shook his head, turned, and walked away.

"Here's your bags." The lady who ran to get them handed both to me.

"Thanks, um...?" I said, looking at her face.

"Jenna."

"Thanks, Jenna," I whispered. She nodded to me and I led Mindy to the Jeep.

The lights flashed as we walked to it and I knew Max was behind us. I helped her into the back, tossed our purses to the seat beside her, moved to the passenger side door, and saw Max there.

"You okay?" I asked, looking at him but he didn't answer.

His fingers and thumb caught my chin and he tipped my head up to look at me in the outside lights. His face, I noted, was no less scary and it got scarier when the entirety of it went hard and tight when he looked at my cheekbone.

"Max, I'm okay," I whispered, but I wasn't. Now that the commotion was over, my cheek stung like crazy.

"Need to get ice on that soon's we can," he muttered.

"Mindy should stay at your place. That man is...I don't trust him." I was still whispering.

"Yeah." He was still muttering. "She'll stay with us. Get in. I'll talk to Becca. I want her stayin' somewhere else tonight too. I'll be back."

"Okay."

He let my chin go and the backs of his fingers drifted along my jaw before he moved away and jogged to Becca.

I got in and turned to Mindy. "You're staying at Max's, okay, darling?"

"Yeah," she said, looking out the window.

"Mindy, look at me, sweetheart."

She didn't look at me. "He hit you."

"I'm okay."

"He hit you. I saw it. Becca saw it. *Max* saw it. *Everyone saw it.*"

"Sweetheart, I'm okay."

She started crying silently, I knew because her body was moving with her sobs and I crawled through the two front seats and got close beside her, pulling her into my arms.

Max got in and looked around his seat to us; his face, even in the shadows, I could see was still angry. Mindy didn't lift her head or stop crying.

"I'm going to ride back here with Mindy. Is that okay?"

His eyes went to Mindy in my arms, her face in my neck, and he nodded.

"Buckle up, Duchess," he said quietly.

I nodded, buckled Mindy first, used the middle seat buckle for myself, and held her shaking-with-tears frame all the way back to Max's house.

CHAPTER SIX

Somethin' Else

I WAS SLIGHTLY jostled but I was comfortable, warm and mostly asleep, so I didn't let it bother me. I could also hear a tone that was familiar but I didn't let that bother me either.

Then I heard a deep, gravelly voice quietly say, "Yeah?" but I didn't let that bother me either.

I also listened when the voice went on, still quietly, "Yeah, she's here but she's sleepin'." Pause. "Yeah, you want me to have her call you?" Pause while the sleep slid from me. It hit my consciousness that it was Max's deep, gravelly voice, it was his bed, and his body that were making me comfortable and warm and that the familiar tone was my mother's ringtone.

Then my eyes flew open and I shot up on an elbow, my thigh still thrown over Max's, my hand sliding up to his ribs when I pulled up.

Max's clear gray eyes locked on me.

"She's awake," he spoke into my phone.

I started panting.

"Hang on," he said to who I assumed was my mother, and held the phone to me. "You wanna talk to your mom?"

I took my hand from his ribs and snatched my phone away. Then I sucked in a breath and put it to my ear. "Mom?"

There was silence on the line.

"Mom, you there?"

More nothing and then, "Neenee Bean, are you in bed with a man with an *amazing* voice?"

I closed my eyes tight and twisted, getting up on my bottom, my knees coming to my chest.

"Mom," I said, opening my eyes.

"Holy cow, sweetie, holy … holy cow."

"Mom, um…" I twisted and looked at the clock, seeing it was seven thirty-two and also seeing Max lying on his back. The covers were down to his waist. He had one hand behind his head, the muscles in his bicep well defined and naturally flexed. His chest was exposed to the naked eye, nearly searing my retinas with its magnificence. And his eyes in his soft face were on me. I took this all in, the searing sensation in my retinas burning a direct path southward, and I twisted back saying, "It's early. Can I call you later?"

"I take it you made a decision about Niles without me," she noted the obvious.

"Yes."

"And, considering the situation as it seems, it was the right one."

I closed my eyes again, then opened them and said, "Mom, really, can we talk later?"

"He know about Niles?" she asked, indicating that she didn't feel like talking later, which was kind of her way.

"Who?"

"What's-His-Name who answered the phone."

"Yes, he knows."

"You work fast, sweetie," she remarked, then asked, "What's his name?"

I played dumb since Max wasn't moving in order to give me privacy. "Who?"

Mom didn't like me playing dumb. Then again, she never had, so she nearly screeched, *"The man who answered the phone!"*

I started to throw back the covers and find my own privacy since Mom was in the mood to talk. But Max was of a different mind and his arm hooked around my waist before I could even get the covers back. Then I felt him at my back and his other arm went around my waist.

My neck twisted so I could give him a glare over my shoulder.

His response: he dropped his head and kissed my shoulder.

I pulled in a breath.

"Nina!" Mom called.

"I'm here," I replied, turning back around.

"What's his name?"

"Max," I answered, and felt Max's arms get tight and his face went into my neck.

I put my hand over the phone and turned my neck. His head came up and I snapped, "Will you *stop*? I'm talking to my *mom*!"

He grinned and dropped his chin to my shoulder. I growled and turned away.

"...there?" Mom called in my ear.

"I'm here."

"What's going on? Are you okay?"

"Nothing. I'm fine."

"Have you broken it to Niles?"

I tested Max's arm strength, unsurprisingly got nowhere, considering their steely nature, settled in again, and said, "I sent him an e-mail."

Max's arms convulsed as Mom had the same exact reaction as Max.

"You sent him an *e-mail*?" she asked incredulously.

"I know, Mom, but you know I'm better with words when I write them out."

She didn't answer at first, then asked, "When?"

"Mom, can we talk about this later?"

"My daughter is in the wilderness with a strange man with an *amazing* voice having just changed the entire course of her life and you want to talk about it *later*?"

I sighed because it might be irritating but this was Mom's

way too. Then I answered her earlier question. "A couple of days ago."

"What'd he say?"

"Who?"

"Niles!" she cried.

"I don't know. Nothing. Unless he e-mailed back."

"E-mailing," she mumbled. "Insane."

"Mom—"

"He hasn't called?"

"No."

"That boy," she mumbled again.

"I . . . it's just the way he is."

There was a pause before she said, "You know I liked him, Neenee, you know I did. But I think you made the right decision."

"Mom—"

"I mean, you e-mailed or not, he should call you. It's not like you said, 'This isn't working out' after a couple of dates. First, you fly halfway around the world for a 'time-out,' whatever that is, which he allowed you to do, and in my humble opinion, that's *insane*. Then you broke off an engagement!"

This sounded familiar too.

"Mom, I know."

"He was any man at all, he'd be at your doorstep."

"Okay, but, Mom—"

"Though, don't think that would be good under the present circumstances."

"Can I talk, Mom?"

Apparently I couldn't for she kept going. "It's just that"— her voice got soft—"I think, sweetie, this is good. It shows you the way. It shows you that you've decided on the right path. And I know you were so worried and I'm glad you've found the right path."

I breathed in deep, let it out, and said, "Thanks, Mom."

"Now, tell me about this new one," she urged, and I envisioned her snuggling her behind into her chair and lifting up her coffee cup, getting ready for a good old gossip.

"I can't."

"Why?"

"Because he's right here."

That got another squeeze from Max's arms.

"Tell him to go."

"He's not the kind of man you tell what to do," I shared, and heard Max chuckle.

"Then *you* go somewhere else."

I sighed again and admitted, "I can't."

"Why not?"

"Because he won't let me."

Another chuckle from Max.

Another pause from Mom, then, softly, "He won't *let* you?"

"He's also not the kind of man who, he wants you around, he lets you go."

"Oh my," Mom breathed.

"Can I call you later?"

"He going to *let* you?" she asked, but she sounded like she was laughing.

"Mom, please."

"Okay, but call at a good time. I want *all* the dirt."

"All right."

"Love you, sweetie."

"Love you too."

"Neenee?" she called as I was about to take the phone from my ear.

"Yes?"

"You okay about the Niles thing?"

"Yes, Momma," I said softly.

"You happy about this Max thing?"

"I don't know yet."

Another pause, then, "We'll talk later."

"Thanks."

"Bye, sweetie."

"Bye, Mom."

I took the phone from my ear, hit the button at the top to

shut down the display, took in a deep breath, then twisted around to Max and let him have it.

"I cannot *believe* you!" I hissed.

"Honey," he muttered, but he sounded amused.

Amused!

"Don't 'honey' me," I snapped, and then tossed my phone around him toward the nightstand. It bounced off and fell to the floor. I didn't care because I was focused on giving him my full attention. "What was that all about?"

"I wanted to hear what you had to say."

"Does it matter that *I* wanted to have a private conversation with my mother?"

"You can have a private conversation with her later, after I go down and sort out Mindy's apartment."

"But I wanted to have it *now*," I told him angrily.

"Yeah, but later it won't be interesting. Now, it was interesting."

"Why did you answer the phone at all?" I clipped.

"She's called three times, Duchess. I didn't want her to get worried."

He had a point there and it was a thoughtful point but I wasn't going to give it to him.

"You're impossible!"

He grinned. "I think you've told me that before."

"Maybe because it's *bloody* true."

"Jesus, you're cute."

"Don't call me cute!"

Suddenly I was on my back, head on the pillow, Max's heavy body pressing mine into the bed all down my side and part of my front.

I blinked up at him in surprise. His hand touched my face and his thumb came to my cheekbone as his eyes went there.

"It hurt?" he asked, clearly finished with our other conversation and deciding to move on.

"No," I lied. It throbbed a bit, felt kind of tight, but it wasn't too bad.

I put my hands to his chest and gave a light shove.

His thumb swept along my cheekbone and he ignored the shove entirely.

His eyes came to mine and he informed me, "It's bruisin', baby, bit swollen but it doesn't look that bad."

"Thank you for that information," I replied snottily. "Now get off."

His hand moved away, his head bent, and then his face disappeared in my neck.

"Stop bein' pissed," he muttered his order in my ear.

"Get off."

"Nope," he said, and his head came up but it did it so his face was close. "You and me are both in my bed. No one's asleep. No one's delirious. I think we should take advantage of that."

My eyes got wide as my body reacted strongly to his suggestion and it was a positive reaction.

"Mindy's downstairs," I whispered, and he grinned, his face getting even closer.

"Not gonna fuck you, honey, just fool around," he whispered back.

"Max—"

"Shut up and kiss me, Duchess."

"Max!"

"All right, I'll kiss you."

Then he did and it was so good I forgot I was furious and my hands started sliding up the smooth skin and hard muscle of his chest when his head suddenly came up and his neck twisted.

"Fuck, what now?" he muttered. I tried to get a handle on the sudden disastrous change of circumstances but before I could do that he looked at me. "Someone's comin' up the lane."

"Who?" I asked stupidly, for Max couldn't see the lane from his position on me and as far as I knew Max was not clairvoyant.

"I don't know," he answered, being nice and doing it without pointing out that my question was stupid.

He did a push-up and knifed off the bed; then he yanked the covers from me, grabbed my hand, and pulled me to my feet.

"Put on your robe, Duchess," he said softly. It was an order but it was a gentle one. "That nightie's sweet but I think me and Mick are the only ones should get to see it. And Mick's was a one-time opportunity, yeah?"

He didn't wait for me to answer mainly because he really wasn't asking a question.

I stood unmoving as he walked to the dresser and grabbed a T-shirt, then turned and moved to the stairs, pulling it over his head. He wound around in his descent on the spiral staircase, yanking the shirt down to his waist and I lost sight of him.

For some reason, I liked it that he wanted me to put on a robe. For some reason, I liked it so much my toes were still curled like his gentle order was one of his kisses. And I liked it that he voiced it as a suggestion even though we both knew it was an order. An order not because he was being domineering but because it meant something to him that I didn't put myself on display. It was up to me in the end to do what I wanted but he'd made his wishes clear and I knew how he'd feel if I defied them. Still, he wasn't a jerk about it. He'd simply made his wishes clear in what I was guessing was a Colorado Mountain Man kind of way.

Or maybe it was just Max's way.

Not to mention the fact that he thought my nightie was sweet.

"What's up?" I heard Max ask.

I jerked out of my stupor and ran to the bathroom. I did my routine and left the bathroom, hearing voices but not making out the words. I grabbed my robe, shrugged it on, and belted it as I walked down the stairs.

Mindy was up on a hand, peering over the back of the couch at Mick, another man, and Max standing in the kitchen. She looked sleepy and adorable.

I glanced in the kitchen, caught Max's eye, then went directly to Mindy.

"Morning, sweetheart," I said to her.

"What're Mick and Jeff doin' here?" she asked, her voice sleepy.

"Why don't you go upstairs and lie back down?"

"Is everything okay?" she asked back, her eyes still on the police.

"I don't know. They just got here. You want to go upstairs?"

She shook her head but mumbled, "They should leave him alone. They gotta know what a visit from the cops would do to him." She looked at me and said, "He's a strong guy and it was a long time ago but you never forget that shit, ever."

I had no idea what she was talking about but I also had the feeling I really didn't want to know. But before I could make up my mind whether or not to ask, she threw back the covers and I grabbed her clothes from the armchair.

"I'll go upstairs to change," she said, pulling Max's T-shirt that she wore to bed down her thighs while still seated and I knew she didn't want them to see her.

I handed her the clothes and straightened, turning to the kitchen.

"Sorry, gentlemen?" I called, and when six eyes hit me, I said, "A lady needs some privacy. Can I have your backs?"

They all looked at the back of Mindy's head. She turned and gave them a wave over her shoulder. Mick and Jeff waved back but Max was smiling at me.

Then Mick and Jeff turned their backs to the living room and Mindy got up and darted to the stairs, whispering, "Thanks, Nina."

I watched her go and then walked to the kitchen, calling, "All clear."

They turned back to me and when I hit the kitchen, Max claimed me. There was no other way to put it. I was claimed. He did this by pulling me tight into his side with an arm around my shoulders.

"Nina, you remember Mick? This is Jeff," Max introduced, and I nodded to Mick and Jeff.

"Hi, gents," I greeted.

"Nina," Mick said.

"Nice to meet'cha." Jeff smiled.

Mick's eyes went to my cheek. Then they went to Max.

"Matthews?" he asked.

"Backhanded her at The Dog," Max answered.

"Fuckin' dick," Jeff muttered, and looked at me. "Uh... sorry."

"That's okay, as, last night, he proved your estimation of him to be true," I said to Jeff, and for some reason my remark received three man chuckles that made the spring coiling in my stomach relax. If their visit was bad for Max, I doubted they'd be chuckling.

"Heard there was a disturbance at The Dog last night," Mick commented.

"Damon make a complaint?" Max asked, and I tensed.

"Nope. Word I hear, enough folks witnessed the hit to his manhood, I'm thinkin' he's not gonna be big on spreadin' that word," Mick replied, and I relaxed.

"You fuck him up?" Jeff asked Max with an edge of enthusiasm. Then he again turned to me and muttered, "Uh...sorry again."

I smiled my "I'm okay with the f-word" to Jeff but even as I did I was feeling uncertain if Max should brag about parking-lot fisticuffs at The Dog to policemen and I opened my mouth to speak but Max got there before me.

"Got a few in. Best part, Nina shoved him and he went back at least five feet," Max replied.

There were more man chuckles at the idea of me shoving Damon and I wasn't certain how to take this but decided to let it go and change the subject.

"Does anyone want coffee?" I asked, and Max squeezed my shoulder.

"Love a cup," Mick replied, and Jeff nodded.

I started to move away and as I did so Max muttered, "Thanks, baby."

I liked those two words and how he said them so much, without thinking, I glanced over my shoulder and gave him a small smile, then went to the coffeepot.

"Mindy okay?" Jeff asked when I grabbed the pot and moved to the sink.

"Hangin' in there," Max answered.

"She shot of Matthews now?" Jeff continued with more than a hint of curiosity and I turned off the tap and moved to the coffeemaker, looking him over.

He was taller than Damon, lighter hair, leaner of build but fit and perhaps not as overtly good-looking he was also not unattractive in the slightest. In fact, since he was more obviously comfortable with who he was and how he looked instead of being in your face about it as Damon was, he was *more* attractive.

Hmm.

"I'm thinkin' ... yeah," Max said, but when I looked at him he was also studying Jeff closely.

"Good news," Jeff mumbled, and I lifted the top to the coffeemaker and poured the water in.

"So, Bitsy's home?" Max was obviously bringing the conversation full circle.

"Yeah," Mick answered.

"And you're here..." Max prompted, and Mick lifted a hand to the back of his neck.

"Wouldn't ask—" he started.

"You need me," Max cut him off, his words mysterious.

Mick dropped his arm and I turned my attention to the cupboards, finding the gourmet coffee I bought in Denver in the second one I opened.

"Yeah, Max. I know—" Mick said.

"She doin' okay?" Max interrupted again.

"Murdered, cheatin' husband and life ahead of her in a wheelchair, all alone?" Mick asked, then answered, "No."

"I'll go see her today," Max said, and he didn't sound like

he enjoyed saying those words because, I suspected, he knew he wasn't going to enjoy his visit, which was even more mysterious since, from what he said before about Bitsy, I thought he liked her.

I measured coffee into the filter and Mick mumbled, "Thanks, Max."

"You got any leads?" Max asked.

"Looks hired," Mick answered, and I was surprised he shared this information.

"Hired?" Max sounded surprised, too, but probably not that Mick was sharing.

"Hit was execution-style, no muss, no fuss, in and out. Dodd was dead before he hit the floor," Mick shared. "Didn't touch nothin'. Didn't take nothin'. Left nothin' behind."

"Got leads on who hired him?" Max went on.

"Leads? No. List of possible suspects a mile long? Yes," Mick replied.

I flipped on the coffee and pulled down mugs as Mindy hit the counter and slid onto a stool.

"Hey, Mick," she greeted. Her eyes skimmed over Jeff and then dipped to the counter. "Hey, Jeff."

"Mindy, darlin'," Mick greeted back.

"Hey, Mindy," Jeff said in a gentle voice. In fact, his whole face had grown gentle and my eyes went to Max.

Max was watching Jeff. Then his eyes came to mine. I bugged them out and jerked my head at Jeff and Mindy. Max shook his head and grinned.

"Coffee will be ready in a jiffy," I announced, leaning a hip against the counter.

"Kind of you, Nina," Jeff said, and I smiled brightly at him.

"Sure you boys could use some sustenance," I surmised. "Mindy makes some mean bacon and eggs. You want some?"

Mindy's head snapped up and my eyes slid to Max, who was looking at the floor but I could see he was pressing his lips together.

"Haven't had breakfast," Jeff replied too casually.

"Well, that's just awful," I noted, making this news sound dire, my eyes going to his hands. "No wife to fill your belly before a hard day of the God's honest work of tackling crime?"

Max's head came up and he made a strangled noise, which I hoped was him choking back laughter because he thought I was cute.

"Nope," Jeff answered through his grin.

"Good-looking guy like you? That's a miracle. Isn't that a miracle, Mindy?" I called, and looked at her. Her eyes were huge and her face was aflame.

"Uh...yeah," she muttered.

"Come here, sweetheart, let's make these local heroes some breakfast," I urged.

She reluctantly slid off her seat and headed into the kitchen. "You boys sit down. We'll have breakfast for you in no time," I said to Mick and Jeff as they shuffled out. Mindy shuffled in and Max came to me.

Max made a show of reaching into the cupboard for sugar, hiding me from Jeff, Mick, and Mindy but when his hand came down with the bag of sugar, his mouth went to my ear.

"Bullshit's so thick in here, Duchess, we might need gumboots," he whispered.

I tried to look innocent when I tipped my head back and asked, "Sorry?"

"Sorry my ass," he muttered on a grin, closed the cupboard, and moved around me to stand with his hips leaning against the sink and his arms crossed on his chest.

"So!" I called cheerfully to Mick and Jeff, who were both now at the stools. "With a town full of suspects and a hired killer, how do you go about nailing down the culprit?" Before Mick could speak, I turned and prompted, "Jeff?"

"Um...," Jeff mumbled, and Mick answered.

"Sorry, Nina, we don't usually discuss the specifics of an ongoing investigation."

"Oh, right," I murmured, foiled, as Mindy passed in front of me from getting the bacon and eggs from the fridge. Then

I suggested, "If it were me, I'd check bank records. A hired killer probably costs a lot of money."

"Good idea, Nina," Jeff said considerately since I was certain they'd already thought of that.

"Oh!" I cried, turning from pulling the bread out of the cupboard. "I know! See if anyone sold anything of value. You know, like their car."

Mick was smiling broadly. "You want a job?"

Before I could answer, Max put in, "I think they got a handle on it, honey."

I gave Max a look, put some bread in the toaster, and went to the fridge to get the milk, wondering what other topic of conversation I could put us on to make Jeff sound interesting.

"Why does everyone dislike this Curtis Dodd so much anyway?" I muttered as I closed the fridge and missed Jeff and Mick exchanging glances.

"Land developer," Mick said to my back as I started pouring out coffee.

"Yes?" I asked when he said no more.

"Folks like town the way it is, Nina," Jeff told me as I handed Max a cup, black, and I turned to take Mick's to him.

"What does that mean?" I asked Jeff, then smiled and inquired, "And how do you take your coffee?"

"Black, sugar, one spoon'll do," he replied.

"You see the housing developments on your way in, 'bout twenty miles out?" Mick asked as I went back to the coffee.

"Kind of, it was snowing. It doesn't snow much in England, so I was a bit anxious and concentrating," I explained as I made Jeff's and Mindy's coffee.

"Those're Dodd's. Even twenty miles out, they changed the landscape and the economy," Mick said. "Then he put in a coupla strip malls close to the developments, more change to the landscape and the economy."

"Houses are big, people in them loaded. They got money to spend. Sometimes that's good. Sometimes it isn't so good," Jeff put in.

I touched Mindy's back and set her coffee by the range where she was studiously frying bacon as if taking her attention from it would mean it would combust, igniting us all in a fiery inferno. I turned and walked Jeff's coffee to him.

"Money in the town would be good," I noted. "Wouldn't it?"

"Yeah, for shop owners, some more jobs. The rest live like they live. When there's not much to compare it to, they like that life just fine. When a bunch of fancy cars and folks with fancy clothes and fancy attitudes sweep through town, they find reason not to like their life so much," Jeff said.

I nodded and went back to the coffeepot.

Well that possibly explained Sarah the restaurant hostess's face closing down on me when she saw my "fancy clothes."

"People here like a small town, some good tourist trade, neighborly folk," Mick explained as I made my own coffee. "Town's bigger now, not everyone knows everyone else, not everyone's so neighborly anymore."

"And crime's up," Jeff added. "Petty stuff, nothin' big, but more people means more people misbehavin'. Last ten years, we've had to add three more officers to the payroll to keep up with it."

I turned and leaned against the counter with my coffee, taking a sip before saying, "I can see your point."

"Well, seein' it then knowin' that those developments you drove through, those are only coupla ones Dodd put in. He builds in four counties, changed them all. Within a twenty-mile perimeter 'round our town, he's put in twelve developments, four strip malls, and he was plannin' to put in even more."

"Don't strip malls have to be, um...on a strip?" I asked.

"Dodd's are in the middle of nowhere, though they're close to the road. Not exactly what you expect when you're drivin' through the beautiful state of Colorado," Mick answered.

"Again," I remarked, "I can see your point."

"And people here don't only like bein' in a small town, lots of them live here *because* they like it *and* they're pretty damn proud of the beautiful state of Colorado," Mick went on.

"If it's that unpopular, how'd he get zoning permission?" I asked.

"Can't say," Mick answered.

"Bribes?" I guessed.

Mick nodded but said, "Can't say."

"Really?" I whispered, my eyes big and they were on Mick.

Mick kept nodding and Jeff grinned at him as he repeated, "Really can't say."

I smiled at Mick. The toast popped up and I went to the fridge to get the butter.

"Anyone want jelly?" I asked the room at large.

"Not for me," Mick said.

"Nope," Jeff answered.

"Crazy," I muttered, and Max chuckled.

I took out a plate, grabbed the toast, put in more bread, and started buttering before I asked, "Mindy, darling, you working tonight?"

"Yeah," she answered, and I looked at Jeff.

"You know, Jeff," I called, and his eyes, which were resting on Mindy's bottom, jolted to me. I ignored catching him checking Mindy out and asked, "It's asking a lot, considering how much responsibility you carry in your day-to-day job—"

"Nina—" Max muttered low, but I kept going.

"Because I know your job is super important—"

"Nina—" Max muttered again, but I ignored him.

"But if you could look in on Mindy tonight at The Dog, it would be appreciated."

Mindy twirled around, fork in hand, and stared at me.

"No problem," Jeff said quickly.

"I'm...," Mindy whispered, and turned to Jeff, not meeting his eyes. "That's all right, Jeff. You don't have to do that. I'm fine."

"Don't have to, but I'm gonna," Jeff said, and Mindy's face flamed.

I smiled.

Then I was jerked back with a steely arm around my waist and my back hit a wall of solid Max.

"Stop it," Max whispered in my ear.

I twisted my neck to look at him and whispered back, "What?"

"Really, I'm good," Mindy said to Jeff, and I looked back into the kitchen.

"Yeah," Jeff replied firmly. "We'll see you stay good."

My smile came back.

The steely arm gave me a tight squeeze that pushed the breath out of my lungs.

I gave a quiet but happy wheeze when Mindy grinned shyly at Jeff, tucked her hair behind her ear, and turned back to her skillet.

Max's arm loosened but didn't go away and I heard him call, "What'd I say, Mick?"

Mick's eyes were moving between Max and me, Mindy and Jeff.

"Yeah, Max." Mick grinned in Max's and my direction. "You were right, Nina's somethin' else."

"I still don't know what that means," I complained.

"Trust me," Mick said, still grinning. "It's definitely a compliment."

"Well," I muttered, "then I guess that's all right."

Then the toast popped up.

*   *   *

I was making the bed upstairs and I could hear Mindy in the kitchen cleaning up after breakfast when Max came up after walking Mick and Jeff to their SUV.

I looked at him briefly but didn't pause as I smoothed the covers and bent my head to watch what I was doing as I rearranged a pillow that was slightly askew.

"Everything all...*oof*!"

I stopped speaking when I was hooked at the waist, pulled up, and twirled around. Suddenly I was falling back, Max coming with me. I hit the bed, his big body hit me, and the breath evacuated my lungs, but I didn't have time to process this predicament because his mouth came down on mine and he kissed me.

He did it *hard* and he did it *long*.

My body was liquid under his, my fingers in his hair, my other hand under his T-shirt at his back and I was breathing heavily when his head came up.

"What was that?" I asked on a mini-gasp.

"It was either kiss you breathless or tan your ass. First is quieter with Mindy in the house."

All the delights of post-Max-kiss *with* his hard body on mine *in* a bed *and* my hand experiencing for the first time the planes of his muscled back evaporated at his words. My brows went up and I asked, "Sorry?"

"Your intention was sweet, babe, and the way you went about it fuckin' hilarious. But my girl down there was raped three weeks ago and her man publicly proved himself an ass last night."

"Yes," I snapped quietly so Mindy wouldn't hear. "I was there."

"Yeah, so, fixin' her up with the first guy that strolls in maybe ain't such a good idea."

"The first guy who strolls in who has a badge, carries a gun, and looks at her like he wants to build a fortress around her so no one can ever hurt her again."

Max's head jerked and he asked, "What?"

"In other words, Max, he's sweet on her."

"Gotta be blind not to see that, Nina, and by the way, it's the whole damn reason Mick brought him up here in the first place, seein' as he coulda done his business alone or he coulda just called me and they both knew Mindy was here. But it still ain't a good idea."

"You're wrong," I snapped softly.

"No, I'm not."

I was so angry and Max was being so annoying, I didn't

pause to consider my next words. I just said them and in saying them, inadvertently I shared.

"Trust me, I know. You get messed up by a man, it's important to learn right away that there are good ones out there or you might find yourself so far down a *very* lonely road that you'll never be able to find your way back." His face changed. He hadn't been exactly angry, just wanting to make his point, but now his eyes were hyper-alert and intense, but I also had a point to make, I felt it was important, so I kept talking. "I'm not saying he's going to heal her wounds and watch her walk down the aisle to him in a month and they'll grow old together. I'm just saying he seems like a nice guy. There aren't many of those around and she needs all the reminders she can get that even a rare breed can be found."

"You get messed up by a man?" he asked, and I grew confused at his question, for I found this a change of subject and I was intent on the last one.

"What?"

"You get messed up by a man?" he repeated, and my mistake dawned.

"I'm a woman," I covered quickly. "That happens."

"How'd you get messed up?" He was Max. Therefore, he didn't let it go.

"Usual stuff, now get off me. I should go help Mindy."

"How'd you get messed up?"

"Max, get off."

"Nina, answer me."

I went silent, staring at him as I considered my approach to this current dilemma. Then I decided what the heck? I'd tried everything else. Why not just lay it on him?

Still, I tested the waters before diving in. "You're not going to get up unless I answer, are you?"

"Nope," he responded immediately.

I nodded and said, "All right, then, Max, you name it, it happened."

"What?"

I brought my hands up between us and counted them down. "My first boyfriend cheated on me with my arch nemesis, the homecoming queen no less, which was humiliating. My second boyfriend was just a jerk. Third and fourth, both cheated. The fourth with *my best friend*. The fifth stole from me, not much but not much is enough when it's stealing. The sixth got drunk a lot and got mean when he did it and he didn't care who he was mean around, and since a lot of the time he was around me, I got the bulk of it. The seventh beat me. The eighth asked me to marry him and two days after me telling him it's over, he hasn't called. I haven't been raped, thank God, but that's enough for a girl, don't you think?"

"The seventh beat you?" Max asked quietly.

"Twice."

"Beat you?"

My body tensed under his, which I realized belatedly was solid as a rock, as the tone of his words penetrated and, again, my mistake dawned.

I mentally made note that the sharing strategy might not be the right one either.

"Twice," I whispered in the face of what appeared to be his building fury.

"What happened?" he demanded, his voice getting loud.

"Max," I was still whispering.

"What…the fuck…happened?" Max was getting louder.

"Mom told Charlie. Charlie flew to the States and paid him a visit and I took a prolonged vacation in England while Mom moved my stuff out," I answered quietly.

"Fucking hell," Max murmured.

"Max—"

"Fucking hell!" Max shouted, and then I stared in terrified horror as his torso twisted away from me. He reared an arm back and slammed his fist into the bed at my side.

"Max," I breathed through frozen lungs. His hand instantly moved to cup my cheek and his face was hard but his voice was suddenly soft.

"Never hurt you, baby," he whispered, and tears hit my eyes.

"Don't—"

"Never."

"Is everything all right?" Mindy asked, and my head turned on the bed as Max looked up and we saw Mindy standing at the top of the stairs.

"Give us a minute, darlin'," Max said to her.

"Is everything all right?" Mindy repeated.

"We're fine, sweetheart," I said softly. "Down in a minute."

"Max?" she called, her eyes on him, her face pale.

"We'll be down in a minute."

She studied us a second, then whispered, "Okay," and turned and ran down the stairs.

"So that's the reason for the shield," Max said.

My head turned back and my eyes hit his. "Max—"

His gaze unfocused and he muttered, "Fucking hell."

"I made those choices. Max, I wasn't exactly blameless," I told him, and his eyes refocused so much my breath caught at their intensity.

"Don't you dare," he ordered.

"Sorry?"

"Don't you fuckin' dare take on that blame. Cheats, thieves, abusers, it's their problem. You take on that blame you got no choice but to build a shield."

"Max—"

"This guy now, the one you're shakin' off, he drink?"

"No."

"Say shit to you?"

"Max—"

"Does he?"

"No!"

"Lift his hand to you, without your brother around to have your back?"

"Of course not."

"Just doesn't fuckin' care."

I couldn't deny that.

"Max, please, get off."

"Lonely path," he said, and I didn't reply but he wasn't looking for one. He kept talking. "You hate it."

"I—"

"Searchin'."

"Max, please—"

His hand at my face slid into my hair and his face got close before he said, "I know this. Those assholes are assholes because they did what they did and because they did it to a good woman. Learned some things in my life, Duchess. One of the most important—you find a good woman, you take care of her."

"Please."

"This happens between us, Duchess, I'd take care of you."

"Don't."

"Die doin' it," he vowed.

My breath stuck in my throat as his words wrapped tight around my heart and I made a noise, half gasp, half moan.

"That's what I've learned," he finished.

"Please stop talking."

"You don't believe me?" he asked.

"Can we stop talking now?"

"You're so far down that path, you think you can't find your way back."

"Max—"

"Baby, wake up and look around. That path brought you straight to my fuckin' house."

I could take no more. I closed my eyes and turned my head away. If I couldn't escape him physically, I had to escape him mentally.

His thumb slid along my cheekbone under my bruise and his next words penetrated my mental evasion.

"Shoulda fucked him up worse."

I gulped back tears and pressed my cheek into the bed.

"I knew a man laid his hands on you, I would have."

I shook my head but kept it averted. Max fell quiet but his thumb slid back over my cheekbone and his fingers trailed through my hair and down my neck.

"See you've had enough," he whispered, and I nodded.

His weight left me but he wasn't gone but a second when I was on my feet in front of him.

I opened my eyes and tilted my head back to look at him as both his hands settled at my neck.

"I gotta go into town," he said. "It'll give you time."

I nodded again.

"I wanna know what's happenin' with Damon before Mindy gets near town. I need to leave her with you."

"We'll be all right," I assured him, and his forehead dropped to mine.

"Nina, I get Mindy sorted out, tonight I want you to talk to me."

"Max—"

"Think about it, honey."

I bit my lip and said, "Okay."

"All right." His thumb swept my jaw. Then his hands brought me closer and his lips went to my forehead. "Be back as soon as I can," he muttered there, kissed me sweet, then let me go and walked away without looking back.

The minute I lost sight of Max, I ran to the bathroom, closed the door, put my back to it, and lifted my hands in front of me. They were shaking.

I closed my eyes and tried to blank my mind.

I like him, Charlie said to me.

"Be quiet," I whispered.

Nina? Charlie called.

"I said, be quiet."

Sweetheart, see that light? he asked.

"Please," I begged.

Neenee Bean, it isn't a train, Charlie told me.

"Shut up."

You're almost there, he finished.

I closed my eyes, slid down the door, pulled my legs to my chest, and wrapped my arms around them, putting my cheek to my knee.

A knock came at the door and I jumped.

"Nina?" Mindy called.

"Be right out!" I called back.

"You okay?"

"Great, just going to take a shower."

There was a hesitation, then, "All right."

I waited for Mindy to come back, say something more, knock again, for Charlie to invade my mind.

When nothing happened, I took a shower.

*   *   *

Feeling the need to be prepared for what came next, I not only took a shower, but I did my hair and makeup too. Then I dressed in jeans and a thin, violet boatneck sweater that had a wide dip at the top of the back and a tie across my shoulders holding the sides together.

Dressed and ready to face my next ordeal, I wound my way down Max's stairs and saw Mindy sitting at his computer. All buoyant, skip-dancing Mindy was gone. What happened the night before had worn her innate cheerfulness clean away.

Last night she'd cried all the way to Max's house. She'd pulled herself together when we walked in but started crying again when Max got me some ice for my eye.

"Go upstairs, honey," Max had whispered while he held the ice to my eye. "Get ready for bed, lie down, keep the ice on as much as you can. I've got Mindy and I'll be up soon."

Considering the situation, I hadn't argued about him "having Mindy" or, more importantly, meeting me in bed. Firstly, since Mindy was sleeping on the couch, there was nowhere else for either Max or me to bed down. Secondly, I knew Mindy needed Max just then and me arguing about sleeping arrangements would delay her getting him. Therefore, I did as I was told, lying in bed and listening to their murmuring until I fell asleep.

Now I knew, even with all that crying last night, watching her despondently clicking on Max's computer, she was having a very prolonged "bad moment" and I had to do what I could to make it go away.

She tipped her head back to give me a small smile but that, too, looked dead. Then she turned back to the computer screen.

I walked up to her, but hesitated because it seemed we'd known each other an age with all that had gone on but we didn't know each other all that well. Finally, I went for it and gently pulled her hair over her shoulder.

"I have to check my e-mail, darling, then make a couple of calls. If you want to get a shower, I'll give you a facial after I'm done," I offered, drawing her long, curly, soft hair through my palm again and down her back.

She turned to look at me. "A facial?"

"Yes, I do an at-home facial every weekend. Brought all my stuff with me. It's fantastic. Your skin will never feel so good." I put my hand to her cheek and said, "Promise."

"Are you okay?" she whispered, her voice trembling with emotion or fear or both.

"I'm fine," I lied, because I . . . was . . . *not*.

"Max sounded—"

"He's fine."

She shook her head and my hand dropped away.

"He sounded *pissed*," she told me, and she was right, except it was a significant understatement. "Never heard him like that, seen his face like that. Even when he was fighting Damon last night, he was in control."

I pressed my lips together, uncertain how to proceed. Then I decided on honesty.

"You know what happened to you a few weeks ago?"

Her eyes got wide and her mouth got tight before she swallowed and nodded.

"One day, sweetheart, you're going to have to tell a good man what happened to you and, on your behalf, he's going to get like Max did earlier."

I watched her shiver, actually *watched* her *shiver*, before she whispered, "You've been raped too?"

I shook my head quickly and said, "Beaten."

"Oh, Nina." She was still whispering but now tears were in her eyes and I bent at the waist, got close, and put my hand back to her face.

"We girls, we're tough, darling. Soft on the outside but deep down, we're *tough*. Doesn't feel like it now but none of this is going to beat you."

She was trembling visibly, but she said, "Okay."

"I promise."

"Okay."

"Go get a shower, sweetheart, use my stuff." When she hesitated, I continued. "Showers work miracles." I ran my knuckles along her cheek and smiled before I finished, "And facials are even better."

She nodded and repeated, "Okay."

I pulled away and she got up and walked to the stairs as I sat down at the computer.

"Neens?" she called, giving me a new nickname that I instantly liked.

I looked to see she was halfway up the stairs, standing in a curve and looking down at me.

"Yes, my lovely?" I answered.

"You told Max about . . . what happened to you?"

"Sorry, it was bad timing. It just happened."

"I'm glad," she said. "I'm glad you trusted him with that and I'm glad that's why he was the way he was because he scared me but it doesn't scare me now that he was that way for you."

It was me who was now shivering.

I ignored this and said, "You need anything to wear, just dig in my suitcase."

"We left all your shopping bags in my car," she reminded me, then muttered, "Bummer," before she walked up the stairs.

I turned to the computer, and as the shower went on, I held my breath and checked my e-mail.

Nothing from Niles.

Drat.

I looked up the stairs. I could hear the noise of the shower but it was significantly muted and I suspected I heard it because I was listening. Max built a quality house.

I leaned forward and pulled my phone out of my back pocket. Then I called Niles. Then I held my breath while it rang.

Then I got voice mail.

"Niles?" I said into the phone after I heard the beep. "This is Nina. I called because I thought we could talk. We need to...finalize things." God, I was *such* an idiot. "I'll call back later."

I touched the screen to end the call. Then I called my mother.

"Oh my *God*!" she said instead of hello. "I thought you'd *never* phone."

"Hi, Mom."

"Get let out of Max Prison?" she asked, her tone amused as I shut down my e-mail and headed across the house to the coffee.

"I wasn't in Max Prison."

"He sounds interesting." Her tone now sounded nosy.

I changed the subject and informed her, "I just called Niles."

She was quiet a moment, then asked, "And?"

"Voice mail. I left a message."

"Did you check your e-mail?"

"Yes."

"And?"

"Nothing."

"That boy," she muttered.

"It's okay. We'll have dinner or something when I get home, talk it through, finish it up like two adults."

"Yes, it would be novel for you two to actually speak to each other in the same room while you break off an engagement. Not talk via e-mail and voice mail."

"Mom."

"Neenee, I'm just glad you've made your decision and you're moving on. And...speaking of moving on—"

While we were talking, I hit the coffeepot and poured myself a cup. I put the milk back and closed the fridge, cutting her off, "Mom—"

"Honey, spill."

I grabbed my mug, leaned a hip against the counter, took a sip, and stated, "I don't want to talk about Max."

"Why not?"

"Because I don't want to *think* about Max."

"Why?"

"Because I don't know *what* to think about him."

"Okay, you tell me *all* about Max and I'll tell you what to think about him."

"Mom."

"Nina."

"Mom," I said more firmly.

"Nina." She beat my firm by a mile. "Listen to me, let me explain something to you. You're my daughter. I love you. I learned a *long* time ago that I had to let you make your own decisions, your own mistakes, and then sit back and watch you learn from them. You're like me, honey—you don't learn from people telling you stuff. You learn from doing. But this is one place I want you to listen to me and learn. Don't make my same mistake. Don't close yourself off from something that might be good. Learn to take risks again, Neenee Bean."

I looked out Max's windows at the vista and took another sip of coffee.

My mother didn't open herself up to looking for another man after my father. When she'd found out about three weeks after she had me that he'd cheated on her and then he left her for the other woman and then left the other woman and left the country, my mother had been devastated.

And bitter.

He'd been the love of her life; she'd adored him and his betrayal had destroyed her.

It wasn't until six years ago that she met Steve. Steve, who for the first year she saw all the time but insisted he was her "friend." Then she gave in and for the next two years she called him her "companion." Now she called him her husband and she'd never been happier, not ever that I could remember.

"You don't even know him," I said softly into the phone, staring at the mountains.

"I know he has an amazing voice."

Max had an amazing everything pretty much, or at least as far as I could tell.

"Yes, well, he does have that."

"And I know he's got good enough manners to answer the dratted phone when your mother calls."

"Mom—"

Her voice got gentle when she finished. "And I know he talks real quiet when he thinks you're sleeping."

My stomach melted and my eyes drifted closed.

"Mom," I whispered.

"Honey, life has enough obstacles planned for you. Stop putting up your own and just live it."

I opened my eyes and blurted for no reason *whatsoever*, "He built his own house."

"What?"

"With his own hands."

"Really?"

"On land his father gave him, land his father always wanted to build on but he died before he could do it, so Max did."

"Wow," she whispered.

"I know," I whispered back.

"Are you there now?"

"Yes."

"Is it nice?"

"Oh yes."

"Where's he?"

"Taking care of some business in town."

"So the place you rented is just sitting there?"

"No, I rented his place. There was a mess-up with the reservation. I arrived and he was home but I had a really bad flu and Max took care of me while I was sick and...well...then I just—"

She interrupted me and asked, "You found this on the Internet?"

"Yes."

"Give me the website," she demanded.

"Sorry?"

"The website, Neenee Bean, I want to see photos."

I tried to decide if I wanted my mother to see photos of Max's A-frame.

Then I decided I wanted my mother to see photos of Max's A-frame.

I gave her the website but warned, "The photos aren't that good. The place is better."

"Oh hogwash, the photos are always better."

"Trust me, Mom"—I looked from the view through the house—"they don't do it justice." Then I cried, "Oh! And Jimmy Cotton lives in town, and when Max and I were out on his land, Cotton ran into us and *took our picture.*"

"You're kidding!" she screeched, excited since she took me to my first Cotton exhibition at The Met and she loved his work nearly as much as me.

"I'm not!"

"You have to send me the picture. Send it to Steve's e-mail."

Mom didn't do the Internet or e-mail or at least she told everyone in a superior way that she didn't do the Internet or e-mail. That said, she was on Steve's e-mail all the time if the many jokes and lessons on "sisterhood" and heartwarming stories she forwarded were any indication.

I tried to decide if I wanted my mother to see Cotton's photo of Max and me.

Then I decided I wanted my mother to see Cotton's photo of Max and me.

"I'll e-mail it in a while."

"Wonderful."

I heard the door upstairs open and I said, "Mindy's out of the shower, I have to go."

"Mindy?"

"Max's best friend's little sister. She's having some… um…difficulties and Max is helping her out. I promised her a facial. I've got to go."

"Okay, honey."

"Love you, Mom."

I heard the taps of fingers on a keyboard in the background over the phone and she said distractedly, "Love you too… erm, what's the town you're in called?"

"Gnaw Bone."

A pause, then, "*Gnaw Bone*?"

I laughed. "Why do you think I chose it? I had to stay in a place called *Gnaw Bone*."

"I love it!" she cried.

She'd love it more if she saw the shops.

"Neens?" Mindy called. "Do you want to do the facial upstairs or down there?"

"Upstairs!" I called back, then said to Mom, "Now I really have to go."

"Love you, sweetie."

"Love you, bye."

I touched the screen to end the call and yelled to Mindy, "We'll need a towel and washcloth!"

"Got it!" she yelled back.

"Do you want another cup of coffee?"

"Yeah, if you don't mind!"

"Okay!"

Then I put my phone on the counter, poured Mindy a cup of coffee, and prayed that facials could induce skip-dancing in recently raped, brokenhearted, twenty-four-year-old girls, and I figured I had my work cut out for me.

*   *   *

"What's your mom like?" Mindy asked. It was post-facial and she was sitting in the rocking chair that she pulled up next to the rolltop while I fiddled with the card reader I'd brought. I was sending my mother the Cotton picture of Max and me as well as the photo of Max I surreptitiously took.

"She's a nut," I answered.

"Like you?"

Surprised, I turned my head to look at her and stated, "I'm not a nut."

"You spent, like, a gazillion dollars on clothes and all sorts of shit yesterday and then ate more pizza than any girl I've ever met and then you laughed until you nearly fell off your bar stool about, I don't know, a *gazillion* times. Then you got right in Damon's face and no one, except someone as big as Max, gets right in Damon's face, not even Arlene and Arlene's ornery," she replied. Having stated her case, she summed up, "You're a nut."

"Well, I'm on vacation," I replied haughtily, haughty and vacation being my only two defenses. Seeing the attachment had loaded on Mom's e-mail, I hit SEND.

"You're not on vacation. You're a nut," Mindy said, and I could swear I heard a smile in her voice, so I looked at her and saw there was a smile on her face.

Maybe it was the facial that did it but I was thinking it was more me being a nut. I didn't care. Either way, I was relieved.

"Then I guess I'm a nut," I said, scanning my inbox to see if Niles had written. He hadn't, so I shut it down.

"Goodie!" Mindy cried while I was clicking the computer to turn it off. She jumped out of her chair and ran to the window. "Max is home for lunch. Brill!"

My heart skipped and my belly fluttered at the thought of Max being home for lunch.

"Shit!" Mindy hissed suddenly, and ran back toward me.

Then I watched in shock as she threw herself bodily onto the floor on my side of the couch. She curled up so she was as small as her tall body could be and she reached out a hand to me as if she was in a foxhole, I was standing outside it, and bullets were flying.

"Hurry, get down here. Maybe she won't see us!" She was still hissing.

My eyes went to the windows as I saw a fancy, shiny, black Lexus SUV slide next to my rental car.

"Who?"

"Kami!" Mindy whispered loudly. "Hurry!"

My eyes went to Mindy. "Kami? Max's sister?"

"Yes. She's *scary*. Hurry, before she sees you."

With sudden intense curiosity, I looked back to the window to see a woman getting out of the SUV. She closed the door, turned, and looked up at the house.

"But—"

"Neens, get down here!"

Too late.

Kami looked into the house, did a quick sweep, and stopped, her face pointed in my direction. I was pretty certain she saw me.

"She saw me."

"Damn!"

I stood. "Get up, lovely. She's Max's sister. How scary can she be?"

My point was not that Max wasn't scary. He was, *very* scary but he was scary in a lot of different ways for a lot of different reasons. Scary in a way women couldn't be. Though I didn't share this with Mindy.

I was watching Max's sister walk up the steps as her eyes stayed locked on me. She had Max's hair, but longer, the waves no less attractive. But she didn't have his height and she was carrying at least fifty (maybe more) extra pounds than her frame found comfortable. She also looked like she was in a bad mood.

"She looks like she's in a bad mood," I muttered, trying not to let my lips move.

"Great," Mindy muttered back.

I walked to the door as Kami walked through.

"Hi," I said.

"Hey, Kami," Mindy said from behind me, and Kami started when Mindy spoke. Her eyes narrowed on a spot behind me and I figured that Mindy had just righted herself.

"Mindy," Kami said severely. Her eyes, not clear gray but dark brown and not rimmed with fantastic lashes but makeup-less and nowhere near as spectacular as her brother's, then came to me. "You must be Nina."

I smiled and stopped in front of her. "Word travels fast, I'm learning."

"You *are* English, like they say," Kami noted, and she noted this like she would note, "You *are* a demon from hell, like they say."

I felt my neck start to get tight. "Well, sort of—"

She cut me off, looking around. "Is Max here?"

"No, he's in town," Mindy offered, coming to stand by me.

I tried to get things on the right track and lifted my hand. "You're Kami, Max's sister."

She stared at my hand, then at me. Finally, she sighed in a harassed way and took my hand. Hers remained limp as a dead fish and she replied, "Yeah." She dropped my hand and looked at Mindy. "When's Max gonna be back?"

"Dunno," Mindy answered.

"Well," she began, and walked to the dining room table, opening her enormous, well-made, designer leather purse, "tell him I stopped by and brought the papers for him." She yanked out some papers and slapped them down on the table.

"Papers?" Mindy asked as Kami turned back to us.

"Papers," Kami repeated. "Curt might be dead but that doesn't mean work stopped and Trev's still lookin' for a foreman and they still want Max. They're offerin' full benefits, have added a week on his vacation and another five thousand dollars. He'd be a fool not to take it and quit travelin' around like he's twenty-two and got no sense."

I wasn't sure I liked Max's sister and found myself

lamenting the fact I hadn't thrown myself on the floor beside the couch like Mindy.

"Kami, Max ain't gonna work for Dodd," Mindy said softly, and I looked at Mindy in surprise.

"Yeah? Well, then, it's good he's dead. Max doesn't have that excuse anymore," Kami shot back.

Now I was sure I didn't like Max's sister.

"Brody says he gets paid loads more on the jobs he takes out of town," Mindy told her.

"They sweetened the pot."

"I'm thinkin' they'll need to make it even sweeter for him to work for Dodd, even seein' as Dodd's dead. It's *still* workin' for Dodd," Mindy pointed out.

Kami directed her gaze to the floor, all the while shaking her head, walking toward the door and muttering, "Why am I having this conversation?"

"Would you"—I tried politeness again—"like to stay for a cup of coffee? We were just thinking about pulling together lunch."

Kami stopped at the door and looked at me. "Thanks but...no." She appeared to be fighting back a curl in her lip as her eyes traveled the length of me. "I'll pass on having coffee with another one of Max's women. We'll see how long *you* last. Then we'll think about coffee."

"Kami!" Mindy snapped, her back up, her courage slotting into place, her anger apparent.

"You should be warned, he's a player," Kami said to me, ignoring Mindy.

"He is not!" Mindy defended.

Kami's eyes went to her and she was definitely having trouble with her lip curling now. "Like you'd know."

"Know him better than you."

"Hardly," Kami said derisively.

To her tone, Mindy decided to deliver a twenty-four-year-old girl's lethal blow and it was good. "Know you better than you think, too, and I know you're just jealous because everyone likes him but everyone thinks you're a bitch and he's hot, you're not, and you couldn't get laid if you tried."

Kami leaned forward and snapped, "Mindy Smith, shut your mouth!"

"Make me!" Mindy snapped back.

"Ladies, please, this is—" I started.

"You can shut your mouth, too, Fancy Pants," Kami said to me.

My back straightened as well and I asked, "Did you just call me fancy pants?"

"Yeah, you got a problem with that?" Kami's voice was ugly and it was clear she was raring for a fight.

"No," I answered calmly, deciding cat fighting with Max's sister in his house wasn't on my agenda for the day. "Except it's weak." She opened her mouth to speak but I spoke first and I did it with glacial politeness. "Please, don't worry. We'll make certain that Max gets those papers. Enjoy the rest of your day."

Then I turned and walked toward the kitchen and heard Mindy following me.

"Don't say I didn't warn you," Kami called to my back.

"Careful on your drive down. Those roads are tricky," I called back, and opened a cupboard that hid my face from her but not one I needed anything out of. Mindy got close, I twisted my neck and I bugged my eyes at her. Mindy giggled.

When we heard the door close, I shut the cupboard and Mindy and I watched Kami stomp down the steps, get in her shiny SUV, execute a visibly annoyed three-point turn, and then drive, too fast, out of the lane.

I turned to Mindy and asked, "Did that just happen?"

Mindy turned to me and replied, "I told you."

I looked back out the windows and murmured, "How can she be related to Max?"

"Max's mom isn't much better. Then again she's mellowed with age."

This wasn't good news.

"You're good," she said. The huge smile spreading on her face was also brightening her pretty blue eyes.

"Sorry?" I asked.

"You went all Ice Queen on her, gave her no opening. It was awesome," Mindy complimented.

"Um…" I didn't know what to say but was strangely pleased with the praise. I finished with "Thanks."

"Anyway," Mindy said, clearly over it and onto better things. She turned to the fridge, opened it, and asked its shelves, "What's for lunch?"

"I thought I'd make toasted sandwiches with shaved chicken, Monterey Jack cheese, and avocado," I suggested, a suggestion that was met with silence.

I turned to see Mindy staring at me. Then she said, "Really?"

"Really," I answered. "Why?"

"'Cause that sounds freaking *great*."

I smiled and said, "It is." I reached past her into the fridge to get the cheese and chicken. "Fire up the stove, darling. Let's make lunch."

"Cool!" she cried, and skip-danced to the stove.

I looked from Mindy to the ceiling and silently said, *Thank you.*

Then I got out the cheese and chicken.

*   *   *

I was standing at the stove, stirring the chopped veggies in olive oil in the skillet when the lights of a vehicle flashed on the walls. I turned from the range and looked to the drive.

The Cherokee. Max was home.

I felt a pleasant shiver slide up my spine and looked to the waning light of a setting sun.

An hour ago, Becca had shown up with my shopping bags and the news that Max had given the green light for Mindy to go back down the mountain. We talked for a while, me ascertaining two things. One, Becca was still angry at Damon for "being such a dick" and two, she was "next in line" to get a facial.

They left and I checked my e-mail. No e-mail from Niles, so I sent him one asking if he was all right.

Then I sorted my shopping, clipping off the tags and putting things away before grabbing the creamer and sugar bowl I'd found in town. They were handmade, fantastic pottery by a local artisan, larger than normal creamers and sugar bowls, unusual squat shapes with equally unusual twisting handles and they were glazed cream at the top and inside, terra cotta at the bottom. Perfect. I bought them for Max's kitchen. A gift, a stupid one but my small way of saying "thanks for taking care of me when I was sick." He didn't need a creamer and sugar bowl, probably would never use them, but they sure would look good in his kitchen.

Therefore I took them to his kitchen, cleaned them, dried them, and filled them, leaving the small milk jug in the fridge and putting the sugar bowl by the coffeepot.

Then I sat at the dining room table and wrote a couple of postcards to friends that I'd also bought the day before.

After that, I'd started dinner.

What I did not do, but should have done, was sort out my messed-up head.

The casserole dish had the cubed salmon, king prawns, and quartered hardboiled eggs in the bottom. The mashed potatoes (flavored with a hint of English mustard), sitting in a bowl with a dishtowel over it, were ready to go on top of the casserole. The ingredients for the cheesy, mustardy, creamy sauce were by the range, ready to go in when the veggies finished cooking.

I heard the door open and I pulled in a silent breath. Then I looked over my shoulder.

"Hey, babe," Max called, shrugging off his canvas jacket and heading my way.

"Hi," I replied, and turned back to the veggies, stirring unnecessarily.

I heard the whispering sound of his jacket being hooked on

a chair. I felt him get close before I felt my hair swept off my shoulder and then his lips at my neck.

This time that shiver went from my neck back down my spine.

"Smells good," he murmured when his head came up.

"Fish pie."

"Mmm."

God, he could "mmm" *great* in that gravelly way of his.

"Sorry I been gone so long," he went on.

I picked up the cream and poured it into the veggies while asking, "Mindy's apartment sorted?"

"Couldn't find Damon. Did find out that the landlord has storage units at the complex. I got his shit out, put it in a unit, and the landlord changed the locks on Mindy's place."

I didn't like the idea of Mindy staying by herself, even with changed locks, so I turned to him and noted, "That doesn't sound exactly sorted."

"Yeah, but Mindy's stayin' at Becca's for a while, least until we know Damon's permanently out of the picture. After I stopped by Bitsy's, I went to the station, talked to Mick and Jeff, and they'll be keepin' an eye on things. Not to mention, Becca's talked with the totality of her neighbors and told them to keep an eye out for Damon and raise the alarm the minute he's spotted."

"That sounds more sorted," I muttered. He smiled and I turned back to the skillet, swirling the cream with the veg.

I felt his fingertips trailing across the skin of my exposed back, sweeping my hair along with it.

The shiver came back, this time with goose bumps. I turned back to him.

Before I could speak, his eyes went from my shoulders to mine and he whispered, "Like this sweater, honey."

Shyness hit me, sudden and nearly paralyzing. "Um...," I forced out, "thanks."

He grinned and moved away, asking, "You want a beer?"

I turned back to the food and told myself to get it together but I told Max, "I'm going to have wine."

"I'll get it."

I stirred the cream one more time, saw it begin to bubble, and turned off the stove, moving the skillet off the burner and adding in the rest of the ingredients for the sauce. Stirring it, I went to the casserole dish.

"You got three bottles of wine. Which one you want?" he asked, his head in the fridge.

"The Pinot Grigío."

"Gotcha," he said, and I heard the noise of a bottle sliding off a refrigerator shelf.

"How's Bitsy?" I asked, still stirring, waiting for all the cheese to melt.

"Pissed, scared, in shock," he answered. I heard him moving around. Then I heard kitchen noises and saw a wineglass hit the counter beside the dish and Max was at my side with a bottle and bottle opener.

"Is she going to be okay?"

"Will be. It'll take a while. She isn't cooperating, won't talk to the police."

I looked at him, surprised. "She won't?"

"Nope."

"Why?"

"She's pissed, scared, in shock," he repeated, and I guessed if my husband was murdered by a contract killer while I was on holiday in Arizona and he was in bed with the town ice queen, I might not feel cooperative either.

"Is that why they need you?"

He looked at me and pulled the cork out of the wine. "Yeah."

"I don't understand," I told him, because I didn't.

"We're close," he said, then said no more and I decided not to ask about Max being close to Bitsy, the wife of the dead man who sounded like his arch enemy.

It was strange, very strange, but I was presently dealing with another strange and not unpleasant feeling of moving around Max's kitchen with Max like we'd done it every night for the last ten years. I didn't have it in me to interrogate him about his relationship with the unknown Bitsy.

Instead I inquired, "Is she going to talk to the police now?"

"I'm takin' her in tomorrow."

I nodded and poured the sauce over the salmon and prawns before informing him, "Your sister came by."

"Yeah, I hear. Mindy called. Said you tag-teamed her but you dealt the death blow."

I went to the sink and dropped the skillet in it, saying, "I wouldn't describe it like that."

"How would you describe it?"

"Well, firstly, it wasn't that dramatic."

"Kami is all about drama, so I'm guessin' you're downplayin' the situation." Max finished pouring my wine, seemingly relaxed about the Kami situation, and set the bottle on the counter as I moved to stand in front of the casserole dish and pulled the towel off the potatoes. He slid the wine close to me and headed to the fridge, asking, "She act as big a bitch as Mindy said?"

I pulled in a breath and scooped potatoes on top of the sauced-up fish, uncertain how to answer.

I decided on, "She wasn't um…exactly pleasant."

Max sighed and I heard the top come off a beer. "She gets in moods."

He could say that again.

"She brought you papers," I told him.

"You look at them?" he asked, and my eyes shot to his face.

"Of course not."

He grinned and, coming close to me, leaned a hip on the counter. "Why not?"

My head shook once, it was quick and it was short. Then I repeated, "Why not?"

"Yeah, why not? I would. Anyway, you're a lawyer. Might be good to have you look 'em over," he stated before he took a drink of his beer.

"Are you thinking of taking the job?" I asked, again surprised.

"No fuckin' way," he answered instantly.

"Then why do you need a lawyer to look at them?"

"Just wanna know which way they're thinkin' of screwin' me."

"Kami said they sweetened the pot."

"Yeah, I'm sure they did. Don't mean there ain't fine print."

I went back to scooping potatoes. "It doesn't sound like these are nice people."

"They aren't."

"Then why would your sister want you to work for them?"

"I'm around more often, means she'll have help lookin' after Mom."

I finished putting the potatoes on top. Max noticed and took the bowl from me, turned and headed toward the sink.

"Is your mom all right?"

"Yeah," he said, rinsing the bowl and skillet. "Just alone and doesn't like it." He turned off the tap and headed back to me. "Today, took care of Mindy's shit, talked to Bitsy, hit the station, and went to visit Mom. That's why I'm late. She wanted to talk and then she wanted me to look at her kitchen sink. Spent part of the afternoon listenin' to her bitch, another part in the hardware store, another part on my back on the kitchen floor under her sink."

I looked down to the potatoes, smushing them around and coating the creamy fish, thinking of him taking care of Mindy, Bitsy, his mom and what that meant about him. Then I mumbled, "It's good you look after your mom."

"It's good but isn't fun."

I looked at him and said softly, "Sorry."

"It's okay," he said softly back. His hand came up and his finger touched my earring. I'd put my new ones in when I put away my shopping, impatient to see the way they looked. I'd liked the way they looked, so I left them in.

"You got 'em."

"Yeah."

He grinned and walked around me.

I grabbed the dish and put it in the preheated oven, closed

the door, tinkered with the timer, and set it. He came back when I went to the other counter, picked up my wine, and took a sip.

After I swallowed, Max took my glass, set it on the counter, and grabbed my right hand.

His head was bent to look at our hands but he was talking.

I was watching his hands working at mine.

"Went to Karma to get you those earrings you liked. They told me you'd already been by. Jenna was there, local jewelry artist who makes this stuff." I held my breath as I watched him slide something onto my ring finger; then he twirled it around and slid it off. "She said she had rings to match, doesn't make many of them, usually only does it special, so she doesn't sell them in the shop. She ran home to get one and brought it by Mom's." He slid the ring onto my middle finger and twirled it around; then his fingers curved around my palm, his thumb touching the ring as he muttered, "Fits there."

I looked down at a ring that was the same heavy, wide, stunning web design of my earrings with solid edges. It was gorgeous and it sat perfectly, from base nearly to knuckle, on my finger.

Then I continued to stare at it and all it indicated, including the fact that Holden Maxwell paid attention (which I was learning) and thus he gave thoughtful, generous gifts.

I felt tears sting the backs of my eyes and I tipped my head back to look at him.

"Max," I whispered.

His hand came to my cheek and slid into my hair before he asked, "You like it?"

I nodded, though I wouldn't say I *liked* it. I'd say I *more than* liked it.

He looked into my eyes. His face grew soft but his mouth grinned before he prompted, "Then you gonna kiss me or what?"

I really should have replied "or what."

But I didn't. I couldn't.

The ring was beautiful; it was special and his gesture was remarkable.

So instead of saying "or what," I did something not smart, not sane, not rational, and got up on my toes. Then I slid my fingers into his hair from the neck up. Then I grabbed on to his hard bicep with my other hand.

Max helped, leaning into me, bending his neck, gliding his fingers farther into my hair to cup my head and putting his other hand to my waist.

I kissed him, touching my tongue to his lips, which he opened for me, and I slid it inside, tasting beer, tasting Max, and thinking he was the most beautiful taste to ever touch my tongue.

He growled into my mouth, slanting his head, his arms coming around me, and he took control of the kiss.

His was better. So much better, I felt the need to slide my other hand into his hair and hold his head to me so he'd get the hint I didn't want him to stop.

Maybe never.

Maybe I *never* wanted him to stop.

We made out in the kitchen for a while. I had no idea how long and didn't care. I was simply loving the act of making out with Max in his kitchen partly because I loved kissing, but mostly because Max was a *really* good kisser.

Then he finally lifted his head an inch and, unfortunately, stopped.

"I'm guessin' you like it," he muttered, a grin playing at his mouth.

"Yes," I breathed, unable to grin and practically unable to remain standing. Luckily, he was still holding me.

"God, you're cute." He was still muttering.

I wasn't able to form a reply.

Then we both heard the loud knock of knuckles banging insistently on glass. This sound made me jump but Max didn't jump. Instead his mouth got tight.

Max twisted his neck and his torso, taking me with

him and we both saw Jimmy Cotton standing outside the door.

Jimmy Cotton opened the door, stuck his upper body into the house, and demanded, "Quit neckin' with Nina, Max, and get out here and help me." Then he disappeared, leaving the door open.

Max twisted back and looked down at me, and he didn't look happy.

His words proved my guess true. "Swear to God, this doesn't quit happenin', I'm gonna kill someone."

He sounded like he meant it.

"You can't kill Jimmy Cotton. He's an American treasure," I informed him.

"Right now," Max returned, letting me go, "he's a pain in my ass."

I watched Max stalk to the door, flip on the outside light, and exit, closing the door behind him. I didn't know whether to laugh, scream, or count my lucky stars.

I didn't do any of those. I got out a cookie sheet and the tube of crescent roll dough, popped it open, and started to unwind the dough.

I was forming the crescents when the door opened and Max walked in. His eyes hit me the instant he did. He had a funny look on his face and he was carrying what looked like a somewhat large frame wrapped in plain, brown paper.

I was forming crescents but I'd stopped breathing while I did it, my eyes on the wrapped package.

Without a word, Max set it on the floor, leaning it against the wall between the doors under the loft. He turned and walked right back out.

My eyes stayed riveted to the frame as my hands automatically rolled crescents.

Then Max and Cotton walked in together, Max backing in, Cotton moving forward, both of them carrying what looked like a huge frame wrapped in the same paper.

My heart stopped beating.

"Get over here, girl," Cotton ordered when they'd set it beside the smaller one. It was so big it engulfed the space.

Silently I grabbed a dishtowel, wiped my hands, and walked into the open space entry, my eyes still on the frames. I came to a stop right beside Max.

Cotton had moved forward. Taking out a penknife, he pulled it open and carefully slid it into the paper at the edge of the larger frame. Then he moved the knife through.

He did this all the while muttering, "Meant to do this when your dad was alive. Kicked myself when he passed. Holden didn't have a place on the land. He would have wanted this at his house, seein' as he had to live in town."

Then Cotton yanked the paper down and exposed a huge black and white panorama of the view from the bluff, and I caught my breath at the sight. It was all there, the river, the banks on either side, the mountains rising up them, all of it framing the river trailing away, leading to an opening that exposed a vista of valley, river, and faraway white peaks.

Without thinking, I reached out my hand and found Max's, my fingers sliding up and through the webbing of his, before I curled them, linking our hands.

Max's fingers curled back and his grip was tight.

When no one spoke for a while and I realized Cotton was staring at us, I struggled but found my voice. "It's…it's…" I looked at Cotton. "There are no words."

Cotton assessed the picture, mumbling, "Yeah, kinda like that one myself."

I couldn't stop the laugh that fluttered from my throat. "You *kinda* like it?"

Cotton grinned at me. "Yeah, it's pretty good." Then he looked at Max. "It'll look great here in the A-frame."

I felt Max's body grow tight and his hand flexed in mine.

"What?" he asked.

"Givin' it to you, boy," Cotton answered.

"I can't—" Max started, but Cotton waved his hand.

"You can, you will," Cotton interrupted. "I'm old. Wanna

know, when I die, my photos are in the places where they need to be. This one needs to be here."

Oh my *God*.

"Cotton—" Max started again, but Cotton had turned toward the other picture and he kept talking.

"This one's for Nina."

I started, this time my hand flexing in Max's and whispered, "I'm sorry?"

Cotton didn't answer. Instead he slid the knife in and along the frame, then ripped the paper down, bending to pull it away.

"V & A," he said, turning back to me, but I was staring at the picture.

I remembered it. It was a close-up photo of the rock on the side of a mountain, again in black and white, which was all Cotton did. The lines in the rock prolific and almost mesmerizing, sliding through in random undulations, one lone, yet utterly perfect wildflower growing out of the rock.

"Cotton," I whispered.

"I like that one too," Cotton declared, gazing at it critically.

"I can't take that," I said to him, and he looked at me.

"Why not?" he asked, sounding genuinely puzzled.

"I…it's…" *Why not?* Was he *mad*? "Because it's worth a fortune," I explained.

"I know," Cotton retorted. "Got about a dozen offers on it, all, like you said, a fortune. Didn't like the feel of any of 'em. Didn't want it hangin' wherever those folk would be."

"But—" I began, but Cotton cut me off.

"Like the feel of it hangin' wherever *you* might be."

At his words, which rocked me to my soul, I let Max go, my hands went to my cheeks, and before I could stop myself, I cried, "Oh, *bloody hell*! I'm going to cry!"

Then I did. I burst right into tears.

Within an instant, I was in Max's arms. I put mine around him and held on tight, shoving my face into his chest and crying like an idiot.

It was several moments later when I heard Cotton mutter,

"Women." Then sounding like he was on the move, he asked, "What's for dinner?"

I felt Max's body get tight against my wet cheek.

I tipped my head back to look at him, the tears subsiding when I saw his neck was turned and he was staring toward the kitchen, and regardless of the fact that Cotton just gave both of us priceless pieces of his art, Max's expression appeared murderous.

I followed his eyes and saw Cotton pulling himself up on a stool.

"Get me a beer, Max. It's been a long day," Cotton called, leaning forward to look at the rolls. Then he spun on the stool and exclaimed, "Right on! Crescent rolls!"

"Cotton—" Max started, but my arms gave him a squeeze. Max stopped speaking and looked down at me.

"He just gave us his photos," I told him. "We can give him dinner."

"Yeah, I haven't had a home-cooked meal since Alana died, or least not a good one." Cotton drew in an audible breath through his nostrils and he declared, "And whatever's cookin' smells good."

"Fish pie," I told him, and Cotton grinned.

"I like fish," he said.

It was low, it was soft, but I definitely heard Max growl.

I gave him another squeeze with my arms, let him go, and, slower, he let me go too. Then, wiping the tears from my face, I went back to the rolls.

Max got Cotton a beer and I had poured frozen peas into a bowl and was setting them in the microwave when lights flashed on the wall.

"This is a fuckin' joke," Max clipped from his place, hips against the sink, beer in hand, unhappy expression on his face as he stared toward the drive.

"Max is popular," Cotton noted.

"I'm noticing that," I replied, also looking out the windows.

I watched a figure come up the steps. I recognized

Arlene walking across the porch toward the door. Her eyes were on us and she didn't bother to knock; she just walked right in.

"Hey, y'all," she called, striding toward the kitchen like she lived there. "Hey, Cotton."

"Heya, Arlene. What's shakin'?" Cotton greeted.

"Don't shift some of this weight, everything," Arlene replied.

She stopped at the mouth of the U in the kitchen and looked at me.

"That don't look all that bad," she observed.

"Um...," I muttered, "hi, Arlene."

"What're you doin' here?" was Max's greeting.

"Damon whaled on her, had to check see she's all right," Arlene explained to Max, then turned to me. "Woulda thought it would be worse—thought he really walloped you one. Least it looked like that."

Something unpleasant was emanating from Max and I took a step closer to him. His response was to slide an arm around my waist and yank me back so the side of my back was to the side of his front.

"What's this about?" Cotton asked, and Arlene turned to him, walking to the bar and putting her forearms on it.

"Last night Damon Matthews backhanded Nina at The Dog," Arlene answered like she would say, "Last night, I made a TV dinner and watched the news."

"What?" Cotton exclaimed on a near shout, his eyes moving to me and then narrowing on my cheek. "Is *that* what that is?"

"Yeah," Arlene replied before I could speak. Then she turned to Max and ordered, "Get me a beer, will you, Max?" Without pause she turned back to Cotton and went on, "Damon came into The Dog, manhandled Mindy. Nina here didn't like that, got in his face. He gave her a shove, she shoved him right back, and he backhanded her."

Cotton was staring at me throughout Arlene's recitation and now *he* didn't look happy. "You shoved Damon Matthews?"

I shifted against Max's body and said, "He was being, um...rude."

"Girl, that kid *is* rude, came outta his mother's womb rude," Cotton told me. "But he's also solid as a rock and mean besides. What're you thinkin' gettin' in his face?"

Max entered the conversation at this juncture, saying in a dangerous voice, "He shouldn't have touched her."

"No, agreed, he shouldn't," Cotton returned instantly. "But he's Damon Matthews. Half the acts that boy perpetrates, he shouldn't do."

"Nina doesn't know him and didn't know that," Max replied.

"She could take one look at him and know not to get in his face," Cotton retorted.

"Bottom line, Cotton, he shouldn't have *fuckin' touched* her," Max stated, and the way he did, the room fell silent.

Arlene eventually broke the silence by sharing, "Max messed him up in the parking lot."

Cotton looked at Max and asked, "How bad?"

Cotton asked Max but it was Arlene who answered. "Figure it ain't a lesson he'll forget anytime soon. Whole town's talkin' about it. It's like Christmas and your birthday all rolled into one, what with Dodd dead and Max beatin' the crap outta Damon."

Cotton chuckled but I exclaimed, "Arlene!"

She looked at me and raised her eyebrows. "What? Not sayin' anything anyone ain't thinkin'." Then she moved to the other stool, slid onto it, and eyed the crescent roll dough on the cookie sheet. "Fantastic!" she cried. "Crescent rolls! Got enough for one more?"

"Jesus fuckin' Christ," Max muttered from behind me.

"Sure," I said to Arlene, and she grinned.

Cotton leaned toward Arlene and stage-whispered, "We're crampin' Max's style."

"Whatever," Arlene stage-whispered back, turned to Max, and called, "Max? Beer?" Then she turned back to Cotton and said, "What's up with the pictures?"

Cotton answered but it was Max who had my attention.

"I'm thinkin', Duchess," Max murmured in my ear, "that I'll give you the keys to your car but we're both gettin' in it, drivin' down the damn mountain, and checkin' into the hotel."

I bit my lip and turned to look at him. Then I smiled. He let me go. I got Arlene a beer, slid the crescent rolls into the oven, took the bowl of peas out of the microwave, and poured more in.

*   *   *

"I gotta carry you upstairs?" I heard Max ask, and I struggled with it but I opened my eyes.

"Sorry?" I whispered when I semi-focused on him.

"Never seen anything like it, honey. When you're out, you're *out*," Max said, taking my hand and pulling me out of the chair.

I blinked and looked around.

The last thing I knew, dinner was consumed, beers were consumed, three glasses of wine were consumed (all by me), to Max's displeasure. We moved to the living room with our uninvited guests and a plate full of cookies. Max made a fire while Arlene and Cotton ate my cookies and entertained me.

I didn't want to admit it but I thought Max put up with them and allowed them to stay because he knew that Arlene and Cotton were entertaining me. Arlene simply because she was entertaining. Cotton because he'd been a lot of places, done a lot of things, met a lot of people, and he was almost as good a storyteller as he was a photographer. I hadn't laughed that hard or that much since . . .

Well, since the night before, with Arlene and Mindy at The Dog.

But before that it had been years, before Charlie died or, more to the point, before he'd been so badly wounded.

Arlene and Cotton claimed the couch and I sat in the armchair. When Max was done with the fire, I was shocked when he sat in it with me, settling right down, forcing me to scrunch to the side.

I was right when I first saw the chair. It could fit two but it was cozy. Cozy, warm, snug, and safe and with three (work-ing on the fourth) glasses of wine in me, I curled up in it with Max. It was a little chair of heaven. He put his feet on the otto-man, crossed at the ankles. I bent my knees and put my feet in the chair, my thighs against his. His arm curled around my shoulders and, for comfort's sake (I told myself), my arm curled around his belly. I rested my head on his shoulder and I listened, laughed, and sipped wine while the fire burned in the grate and Max sat relaxed and close to me. Apparently, after that, I fell asleep.

Which, even standing, I mostly was at that moment.

I finished looking around, noting Arlene and Cotton were gone. The only light was coming from the loft and my eyes hit Max.

"Asleep," I mumbled.

"Yeah, baby," Max said on a grin, and tugged my hand, leading me up the stairs to the bedroom.

I did not argue with this. At that moment I needed Max's bed and I didn't care if he was in it.

In fact, if I was honest, that made the prospect even better.

I grabbed my nightgown from the suitcase, shuffled to the bathroom, changed, did my washing face, brushing teeth, moisturizing business, left my clothes in a pile on the floor, and shuffled out.

Max was in bed by the time I finished these onerous tasks.

His side of the bed was the side closest to the bathroom.

I'd barely enough energy to wash my face, brush my teeth, and moisturize. I certainly didn't have the energy to walk around the bed.

So I didn't.

I walked right to Max's side and he watched me do it. When I got close, he threw the covers back.

A wall of hard, muscled chest, cut abs, and pajama bottoms were all I saw.

The chair wasn't heaven, the bed was.

I crawled over him and flopped to my side.

He tossed the covers over us, switched off the bedside lamp, and turned into me.

Like it was the most natural thing in the world, his arms came around me, his knee went between my legs, my thigh moved to hook over his hip, and my arm slid around his waist as I got closer to his warm, solid body.

"You have a good night, darlin'?" he asked quietly into the hair at the top of my head.

Seeing as I was really mostly asleep, I didn't guard my words. I just said straight out, "Best night I've had since Charlie got hurt."

His arms got tighter. I nestled closer.

"What was he like?" Max asked, still talking quietly.

"Charlie?" I asked back, still talking in my sleep.

"Yeah."

"Best brother ever," I whispered, and snuggled closer.

"I'm gettin' that," Max muttered, but I heard a smile in his voice.

"You remind me of him," I said sleepily, not noticing Max's body tense. "He said it like it was. Didn't mince words but that didn't mean he wasn't kind. He was smart. He took care of his mom, me, his fiancée. He was thoughtful. Something meant something to him, he took care of it. Someone meant something to him, he let them know it. Never had a doubt about that, knowing how much Charlie loved me." I sighed, and concluded, "He was a good man."

"It's good you had that," Max whispered.

"Yeah."

"Means maybe you'll recognize it eventually."

"Mmm," I murmured, not processing words because I was just barely awake.

"Duchess?"

"Yes, darling?"

I didn't notice his body getting tense again; then his hand slid up my back and into my hair and he said, "Go to sleep, baby."

I did as I was told.

CHAPTER SEVEN

The Love of His Life

"Nina, honey, wake up."

My body was being shaken gently at the hip and Max's voice was coming at me.

I struggled up through the fog of sleep, turned my head on the pillow, and blinked at him. He was wearing nothing but his pajama bottoms, and for some reason, he was sitting on the side of the bed and had a carefully blank expression on his face.

"What?" I asked, still sleepy but also vaguely alarmed at his blank look. I didn't think I'd ever seen Max look blank.

"Baby," he said quietly before he continued with three words that made my drowsiness instantly disappear and my head figuratively explode. "Your father's here."

I shot up to an elbow and repeated, a lot louder this time, *"What?"*

I didn't give him the chance to answer. I threw back the covers and twisted my lower body around Max, got to my feet, and stomped (and obviously I could forgive myself for stomping this time) toward the stairs.

"Nina," Max called, but I didn't stop. I just tramped irately down the winding stairs.

Niles had phoned my father. He didn't talk to *me*. He talked to *my father*.

Which was the *very definition* of Niles not listening to me.

I told him my father had no place in my life but my father kept his place in it and he did this by keeping in touch with Niles. Niles had a great relationship with his family and therefore he never understood why I refused to talk to my father mainly because he never *listened* during *any* of the *vast* amounts of times I explained it to him.

And my father was here. *Here.* He'd dropped everything and flown halfway around the world to stick his nose into something that was none of his business. And I knew why he did it. Therefore, not only the fact that he was here but *why* he was here was absolutely, one hundred percent *infuriating.*

I hit the bottom of the stairs and rounded the corner, seeing my father standing tall and erect, wearing an expensive suit, shiny shoes, and a camel-hair overcoat. His fair hair was neatly trimmed with only a hint of gray, his cheeks were smooth, and his face was the face of a man ten years younger than him. And even though I knew he'd recently made the journey I'd made not long ago, he looked fresh as a daisy.

When I approached him, he didn't look at me. He was deep in the study of Cotton's pictures.

"Dad," I snapped.

"Are these Cottons?" he asked, still not looking at me.

"Dad!" I snapped louder.

"That one was at the V & A. I remember the frame. Unusual frame, perfect for that picture."

"Dad!" I shouted, and his head turned to me. His eyes did a sweep of my body in my nightie before they moved over my shoulder.

I looked over my shoulder, too, to see Max there, now wearing jeans and still pulling down a T-shirt but his feet were bare.

Again my father didn't greet me, didn't address me at all.

Instead he said to Max, "May I have a word with my daughter in private?"

Max didn't answer or I didn't give him the chance to mainly because I stomped to the door.

"No, you may *not*," I announced, opening the door and standing in the cool air that rushed in, looking at my father. "But you *can* leave."

"Nina," Dad said.

"Go," I said back.

Dad walked toward me and stopped. "We need to talk."

"We have nothing to talk about."

"Niles telephoned."

"Yes, I guessed that."

"Therefore, we need to talk."

"No, we do *not*," I reiterated.

Dad gave up on me and looked back to Max. "Really, would you mind?"

Max's eyes were on me but when my father addressed him, he looked at Dad, planted his feet, crossed his arms on his chest, and said, "Yeah, I'd mind."

If I wasn't so incensed, I would have rushed across the floor and kissed Max hard. Unfortunately, I was incensed.

"Dad, go," I demanded.

"Nina, listen to me," Dad said instead of leaving. "You're throwing your life away."

I shook my head and said, "No, no, I'm not. I *was* but evidence is suggesting that I'm not anymore."

Dad looked to Max, then glanced quickly around the living room and back to me, his eyes settling on my bruised cheekbone. His brows came up before he asked with only partially veiled derision, "Honestly?"

"Go," I repeated.

"This isn't you," my father told me.

"You don't know me," I told him the truth.

"Niles is a good man, works hard. He's from a good family."

"He's got money. That's what you're saying."

"I'm saying he's a good man and I'm reminding you about the fact that you haven't chosen many of those in your past. In fact, none at all."

My hand itched to slap him, which was surprising seeing as, outside of shoving Damon, I'd never acted out my anger physically on another human being. But I managed to hold myself in check.

"Go."

"You're repeating a pattern, Nina. As your father—"

But at his words and their implication, I was again seeing red and I shrieked, "How...bloody...*dare* you!"

Dad leaned slightly toward me and returned, "I'm being honest for your own good."

"You're talking about Max, a man you don't even *bloody* know."

"Yes, but I know *you*."

"No, you don't!" I shouted.

"Think about this, Nina. Your life, what you'd be throwing away."

"Go," I snapped.

"This is"—his hand, palm up, gestured around—"unseemly. May I remind you, you're engaged."

"I'm not. I broke up with Niles."

"You were engaged to him less than a week ago and you're standing in your nightwear, a bruise on your cheek with a strange man in attendance."

It was my turn to lean into him and I did, sneering and liberally lacing my words with grave emphasis. "Firstly, Max isn't a 'strange man in attendance,' considering this is *his house*. Secondly, are you *serious*? *You* are lecturing *me* about what's *seemly*?"

"Nina—"

"Sorry, but wasn't it *you* who was fucking around on *Mom* when she was pregnant with me?"

"Nina, for God's sake, that's hardly the point here."

"Yes? So, it's okay for you to sleep with another woman when your *wife* is *pregnant*, then *leave* her and *your child* all alone weeks after I was born?"

"You grew up with your mother, hearing her side of things."

I slammed the door and crossed my arms on my chest, putting out a foot and inviting, "Well, I expect *this* will be interesting. Do share, *Dad*. How is it okay that you cheat on Mom when she's pregnant, leave us both when I'm a newborn, and we never hear one word from you for seven years? Tell me, how is that okay?"

"Nina—"

"And," I cut in, "enlighten me about how that's okay and me breaking up with Niles and living my life—which is none of your *bloody* business I might add, something you can't declare ignorance of since I told you *to your face* at Charlie's funeral I never wanted to lay eyes on you again *in my life*, tell me—how this is *not* okay?"

"I'm glad you brought up Charlie," Dad said.

"Yes, pray tell, Dad, why are you glad I brought up Charlie?"

"Think, Nina." He did that sweeping gesture with his hand, taking in specifically Max, and then his eyes locked on me, his voice filled with obvious derision now. "Think about what Charlie would say about *this*."

I didn't think. My mind was blank, my fury so immense, I took two long strides to him and slapped him with all my might across his smoothly shaven cheek.

His head whipped to the side but suddenly I found my wrists imprisoned, pulled down and crossed in front of me. My back was pressed to Max and Max was pulling us both away.

"Out," Max growled.

"You dare," I whispered to my father over Max's growl.

"Get out," Max repeated.

"Nina—" my father began, his hand to his cheek, his face filled with shock.

"If Claire wasn't such a good woman, I'd wonder if Charlie was switched at birth and Charlie would have wondered too," I declared.

I watched my father's eyes narrow. "He was my son."

"You forgot that when his legs were blown off!" I shouted.

"Get out," Max ordered. "Now, before I put you out."

Dad ignored Max and glared at me. "Charlie would—"

But I interrupted him. "You have no *idea* what Charlie would or wouldn't. Charlie was good to the core. You have no *idea* what it means to be that way. Don't you *dare* tell me what Charlie would do."

Dad opened his mouth to speak but Max got there before him. "I'm not gonna say it again."

At this threat, Dad looked over my shoulder and back at me, declaring, "I'm staying at the hotel in town, Nina. This isn't done. We need to talk, calmly, if you can manage that."

Max let me go but pulled me back and stepped around me, moving toward Dad. Dad's glance shot toward him briefly before he walked swiftly to the door.

He opened it, stopped in it, and looked at me. "I'll be at the hotel."

"Enjoy your stay," I snapped nastily.

Dad's gaze rested on me a moment, and then he walked out the door.

I didn't watch him go. I stomped to the kitchen. When I made it there, I snatched up my phone from the counter and hit the button to turn it on.

"Nina," Max said from close by, and I felt his hand sliding along the small of my back.

I didn't look up, just lifted a hand, one finger pointed skyward and with the other hand went to my contacts, found Niles, and hit the button to connect.

"Honey, don't you think you should calm down first?" Max suggested, and I could feel the reassuring heat of his body but I was focused on the fireplace across the room, staring at it like I could ignite a fire in its grate with my eyes.

I didn't answer Max. I didn't want to calm down. I wanted this to be done and to do it I wanted what I had to say to be said.

I heard the phone ring once, then twice, and on the third ring Niles answered.

"Hello."

"Dad was just here."

"Nina?"

Nina? Was he mad?

"Yes, Nina!" I shouted into the phone. "What other American would call, informing you with barely controlled, therefore unmistakable fury that her father just paid her a visit?"

"Listen, I can hear you're perturbed but—"

"Yes, I'm *perturbed*, Niles. I'm very *perturbed* and if you tell me you have to go into a meeting, I swear—"

"Not a meeting but I have a client waiting—"

"Whatever!" I yelled. "A client is not more important than you listening to me. And, Niles, I want you, for once in your life, to listen to me. We're over. Do you understand? *Over!*"

His astonishing reply: "We'll talk when you get home."

I saw lights flashing in front of my eyes but I still managed to snap, "Oh no, we won't. We're never talking again. Anything I left in your house you can give to a charity shop."

"Seriously, I want to talk about this. It's just that now's not a good time."

"I know now's not a good time," I told him. "Reason number two why we're over. I'm not bloody important enough for you to *take* the time to listen to me. Reason number one, just in case you're curious, is that even when you do, you don't actually listen."

"I listen."

"Yes? If you listened, then why did my father fly to Colorado to have this morning's infinitely loving father-daughter chat?"

"He's just concerned that you're not making the right—"

"He's not concerned about that, Niles. He's concerned about my access to your trust fund and the cachet he'll lose when he can't link his family's name to yours."

"That isn't fair."

"It's not only fair, it's bloody *true*."

"You've always been too hard on him."

My vision covered in shiny, sparkling, white lights. I took

the phone from my ear, looked at the ceiling, and screeched, "Oh my *God*! Why am I even *having* this conversation?"

Max's fingers dug into my hip and he murmured, "Honey."

Again I didn't answer Max. I just put the phone back to my ear and said, "We're over."

"Who was that?" Niles asked, but I didn't answer him either. I brought my phone down, touched the screen to end the call, and threw the phone onto the counter with a clatter.

"Nina, please, baby, look at me," Max entreated, putting pressure on my waist but I yanked from his hold, put my fingers to my engagement ring, tugged it off, and then hurled it with all my might across the room.

I heard the tinkling sound of its bumpy landing but I simply picked up the phone again.

Max's hand came to my wrist, circling it with strong fingers and stopping my phone's progress, so I finally looked at him. He looked a contradictory mixture of concerned and amused.

"Duchess, I'm guessin' he got the message."

"You'd guess *wrong*," I informed him. "Niles doesn't pay much attention and when he does, he hears what he wants to hear. And anyway, I'm not calling him. I'm calling my mother."

Max gave me a look, squeezed my wrist, and then released it, muttering, "I'll make coffee."

"I'll take mine with a shot of tequila," I snapped, and watched him press his lips together and move away.

Then I touched and slid my finger on the screen on my phone until I found Mom and then pressed to connect.

She answered on the second ring. "You're an early bird today."

"Dad was just here."

There was complete silence.

Then a screeched, *"What?"*

"Yes. He. Was. Just. Here. Spreading his goodwill and love all around Max's entryway. It's a wonder there aren't cherubs flying around sprinkling rose petals and rainbows erupting through the windows, an aftermath of his delightful visit."

I heard the sink go off and then Max's chuckle.

I turned to glare at him. He grinned at me and opened the top of the coffeemaker to pour the water in.

"What was he doing there?" Mom asked.

"Niles called him."

"Why on earth would he do that?" Mom sounded justifiably flabbergasted.

"I don't know. Because he's Niles?" I sounded justifiably irate.

"That's just…that's…I don't even know what that is," Mom stammered.

"It gets better."

"Oh no." Now she sounded anxious.

"Dad said he's staying in town. He said, 'this isn't done.'"

"Oh no." Now she sounded panicked.

"Oh yes."

"What are you going to do?" Now she sounded hysterical.

"Well, the hotel is a pretty building, so I'd rather not set explosives." Max chuckled again and I glared at him again while he flipped the lid down on the coffeemaker and touched the switch.

"So, with that not being an option, what are you going to do?" Mom asked.

"Ignore him."

"He's hard to ignore."

"Yes, well, by a cruel twist of fate, I *am* his daughter. Two can play at stubborn."

Mom was quiet a moment before she said softly, "Sweetie, I'm worried."

"Why?"

"Because I got that picture."

"What?"

"The e-mail you sent," she said. "You look happy and he's…Max…he's…well, he's *gorgeous*." No doubt about it, she was right about that. "And, sweetheart, he looks happy too."

My anger took a hit and warmth started to slide through me.

"Mom—"

"I haven't seen you look like that"—she paused—"heck, I don't think I've *ever* seen you look like that."

"Mom—"

"I don't want your dad messing that up for you."

"But—"

"And he will. If he can, he'll do it."

"It'll be okay."

"You're sure? Because I'm not so sure."

"Mom, I really think I made my point this morning."

"How? Because when that man gets something in his head..."

I was watching Max, who'd taken down some mugs and just spied the new sugar bowl. He was grinning at it as he slid it toward him on the counter.

I was seeing this and I wasn't seeing it. This was because something had locked inside me, something unpleasant and ugly.

"I struck him," I whispered, and Max's head came up and turned toward me when he heard my tone.

"Sorry?" Mom asked in my ear, but my eyes connected with Max's.

"I hit him," I said more to Max than to Mom.

"You *hit* Lawrence?" Mom asked, but I was staring at Max, who took two strides across the room to me as I dropped the hand with my phone from my ear.

"I hit him, Max," I whispered as his hands came to my hips, then slid around and he pulled my body into his.

"Honey," he whispered back.

"I'm not like this," I said. "I don't... I've never—"

"It was an extreme situation," Max broke in gently.

"That doesn't excuse—"

One of his arms stayed around me but the other hand came to the side of my neck. "Duchess, hate to say this, but your dad's a dick."

"But—"

"I was havin' trouble not layin' a hand on him."

"But—"

"He was in my house actin' like that, never met me, didn't show you an ounce of respect."

"But that doesn't mean—"

"Then he brought your brother into it."

"I know, still—"

His arm gave me a squeeze as did his hand. He bent his head toward me and said, "You didn't hurt him, baby, and, honest to God, he got what he deserved."

"You don't think I'm—" I started, but I got another squeeze in two places.

"No, I don't think you're anything but what you are and most of that's good."

I felt the pressure release in my insides, the warmth seeping through, but my eyes still narrowed when I asked, "*Most* of it?"

"Duchess, remind me never to get you that riled. You're a handful when you're angry but you're hell on wheels when you're seriously pissed."

I was beginning to get slightly "pissed" when I heard faraway laughter coming from my phone. Then my eyes got wide and I jerked the phone to my ear.

"Mom, God, I'm so sorry. I forgot—"

She was still laughing when she cut me off by asking, "He calls you Duchess?"

Max was watching me talk and suddenly I was self-conscious. "He calls me that because he thinks I have an accent."

"Sweetie, that's because you *do*."

"I don't have an accent!" I snapped at Mom. Max threw his head back and laughed and he did it *loud*.

I glared at him.

He just kissed my forehead through his waning laughter, let me go, and went to the fridge.

"Oh my," Mom breathed in my ear, "he's got an amazing laugh."

She was right about that too.

"Mom—"

"I like him."

I felt my eyes get wide again and I reminded her loudly, "You've never even met him!"

Max, his hand curled around the filled creamer, turned to me, lifting the creamer, shaking his head and looking like he wanted to laugh again. At the creamer, my conversation or something else that struck him funny, I didn't know and at that moment didn't care.

"I still like him," Mom said in my ear.

"Mom—"

"I like the way he talks to you."

I liked that too.

Still, I said, "Mom—"

"And it sounds like he was there when Lawrence was being Lawrence."

"He was."

"The whole time?"

I thought about it and realized he was, the whole time. Except for the first few moments, when Max had quickly dressed, he was with me the instant he could get to me. He had my back the whole time, part of it literally.

"The whole time," I said more quietly.

"And he called Lawrence the d-word," Mom told me, and I couldn't help it, I giggled and so did Mom.

"Yes, he did," I said.

"You've *got* to like a man who thinks Lawrence is the d-word."

She was right about that too.

"Mom—"

"What's he doing now?"

I watched as Max poured coffee.

"Making me coffee."

"Steve does that for me too," she said contentedly. "Brings me a cup in bed nearly every morning."

I looked at the floor and said, "That's sweet, Mom, and I'm so glad you have that now. Anyway, enough of this. How's Steve? Is he doing okay?"

"He's Steve. Never has a bad day, God love him."

"And you do too," I said softly.

"Yes, sweetie, lucky I woke up and saw what life had on offer for me."

"Mom—"

"Hope, today, you woke up too."

"Mom—"

"Have coffee with your mountain man hunk," she urged. "I'll let you go."

I sighed and looked up when I saw Max's bare feet on the floor close to mine. When I looked up, he was putting a mug of coffee on the counter by me, his eyes came to mine, and he took a sip from his.

I looked at my coffee and it appeared to be just how I liked it.

I sighed again.

Then I said, "Thanks for listening, Mom."

"Everything's going to be okay," she assured me more firmly than I would have expected, considering she'd sounded hysterical not minutes before at the prospect of my father being in town.

"I know," I assured her back.

"Tell him I love his house. It's beautiful."

I looked away and murmured, "I'll tell him."

"Love you, sweetie."

"Love you, too, Mom, bye."

"Bye."

Then I touched the screen to end the call.

"You'll tell me what?" Max's deep, gravelly voice called, and my eyes went to him.

I put down the phone, picked up my coffee, and took a sip, then said, still feeling self-conscious, "She likes your house."

"What?"

"She thinks it's beautiful."

"How does she know what my house looks like?"

"I gave her the website."

He grinned. Then he lifted his hand and tucked hair behind my ear.

This gesture was so sweet, it made more warmth flood through me at the same time it caused me to shiver and the clashing sensations caused me to go temporarily insane enough to blurt, "She likes you."

His hand dropped and his brows drew together. "What?"

"Nothing," I muttered, then started to move way, saying, "You want break—?"

But I was drawn back with an arm hooked around my waist.

When my head tipped back to look at him, Max asked, "She likes me?"

I decided the safest explanation was, "She likes that you call me Duchess."

"That's a weird thing to like."

"Mom's a bit nutty."

"Not surprising," he mumbled. He went on when my eyes started to narrow. "She turn into a hellion when she's pissed too?"

I thought about this and answered truthfully, "Yes, probably worse."

"Steve her man?" Max asked, and I nodded. "Poor Steve," he muttered, and I grinned.

His face changed. It was that soft I liked so much but there was something more, something much more and I felt the change somewhere deep, private, and I held my breath for what was coming next.

He drew me even closer so our lower bodies were touching and he asked, "You okay?" I nodded but his arm gave me a squeeze. "Nina, I'm serious here. That was an intense fuckin' scene. You okay?"

From nowhere I understood what else was in his face and

when I understood it I realized why I didn't recognize it. The only male who'd ever looked at me like that was Charlie and he was my brother, so he was supposed to look at me like that in times like these.

It communicated a fierce sort of protection covered over with a tender mixture of worry and affection.

I couldn't bear the hope it made me feel, so I couldn't witness it anymore. I dropped my head and fell forward so my forehead was resting on his chest and I curled my fingers on his bicep.

"I pretty much hate my dad," I whispered to his chest as his hand slid from my waist, up my back, to wrap around the back of my neck.

"Reason why, darlin'. I'm now gettin' why you don't talk about him."

I nodded, my head moving on his chest, and admitted, "I hate that you saw me that way too."

He gripped my neck and used it to pull me back.

When I looked at him, he asked, "Why?"

"It's unattractive," I answered, my voice soft and there was a tremor in it I couldn't control, which denoted a fear I didn't want to admit but I still couldn't hide. "And it isn't nice."

His hand at my neck gave me a squeeze. He put his coffee mug down and circled me with his other arm.

Then he ordered, "Put your arms around me, baby."

I decided sharing time was over, so I suggested, "Max, we should make breakfast."

He gave me a steely look that said clearly he wasn't going to repeat his order, so on a sigh I put my mug down, too, pushed my hands under his arms, and wrapped them around him.

"There was nothing unattractive about what I saw."

"But I lost my temper," I explained.

"You stuck up for yourself and then you stuck up for the memory of your brother. You didn't take any shit, not even a little of it." His face dipped close and he whispered, "That's not unattractive, baby. That's beautiful."

My eyes filled with tears, my body melted into Max's, and the only thing I could think to say was, "Shut up, Max, you're going to make me cry."

He grinned a small grin, his head slightly slanted as he touched my lips in a light kiss; then, regrettably, he pulled away.

"I had other plans for this mornin', Duchess, and much as it kills me to delay them a-fuckin'-gain, I want to take my time. We'll have to save those for after we get Bitsy to the station and then take her home."

He might not have used a lot of words but all of them meant very frightening things since I had a pretty good idea what he meant by his "plans." I couldn't quite figure out what was *most* frightening, so I picked what was safest.

"We?" I asked.

"We what?"

"*We're* going to get Bitsy?"

His head gave a small jerk as if my question was surprising and he answered, "Yeah. Why?"

"I thought I'd stay home, read, maybe plot how I'll drug and kidnap my father, drive him to the next state, and dump him outside a police station with a note pinned to him saying that he killed JFK and was there to confess."

"As worthwhile a way that is to spend your time, you're comin' with me to Bitsy's."

"Maybe Bitsy doesn't want me to come," I suggested half-heartedly, for Bitsy lived in town and pretty much everyone in town had shown a rather healthy curiosity about me.

"Oh, Bitsy wants you to come. It was her idea," Max informed me unsurprisingly.

That was what I was afraid of.

I sighed, then asked, "How much of a chance do I have of getting out of this?"

"Zip," was his short, also unsurprising answer.

"Great," I muttered, looking at his throat.

His arms gave me a squeeze and he called, "Duchess."

I tipped my head back to look at him.

"She'll love you," he whispered.

While I was processing his words, he kissed me. I forgot about Dad, Niles, Bitsy, and his words.

I forgot about everything except the fact that his mouth was on mine, his tongue was in my mouth—which he could do amazing things with—I was in his arms, and he was in mine.

When he seemed happy to keep making out in the kitchen, I was more than happy to let him do it and I took advantage of the fact that my arms were around him. I pulled up his shirt and slid both hands in.

Then I explored. And I liked what I felt, too much. So much, I moaned a little in his mouth and pressed closer.

If I could think, it might have dawned on me that Max just meant to make out in the kitchen. When I pressed in closer, the kiss grew deeper, wilder, and his hand fisted in my nightie at the waist, bringing it up, while his other hand slid over my bottom.

I hadn't had that in a while. Too long. And more importantly, it had never felt like that. In fact, it felt so good I moaned again, lost the ability to stand, gave him my weight, and dug my nails into his back.

He growled into my mouth. I pressed my hips into his. His hand at my bottom slid up and then back down, this time *in* my panties.

That felt infinitely better.

"Max," I breathed against his lips, liking his hand there a lot.

"Fuck, Duchess," he growled against mine, then repeated, "Fuck."

His hand was moving over my behind and my head dropped forward. My lips against his neck, I touched my tongue there.

His lips went to my ear and his voice was even rougher when he asked, "You wet?"

I wasn't thinking, *couldn't* think. So, confused, I asked, "Sorry?"

"You wet for me?" His gruff words sounded in my ear and

they made me shiver from top to toe in his arms, and if I hadn't been wet before (which I was), his words would have done it.

"Yes," I whispered my honest answer against his neck.

"Fuck," he muttered into my ear.

"Max," I breathed again. I had no idea why but it sounded like a plea.

Unfortunately he was immune to my plea. I knew this because his hand came out of my undies, both his arms went tight around me, he buried his face in my neck, and he held me close for a good long while.

Eventually he said quietly into my neck, "After we get this done in town, we're comin' home and, swear to God, anyone gets close to this house, I'm fuckin' shootin' 'em."

I pulled my head back. His came up but he didn't drop his arms. Neither did I.

"Do you own a gun?" I asked.

"Yeah," he answered. "You have a problem with guns?"

I thought about this for a moment and realized I'd never really thought about guns, so I replied, "I don't know. I've never really thought about guns."

"I'll take you out shootin'," Max decided instantly.

I had a problem with that. "I don't think—"

"Later."

"Max—" I started to protest.

"Tomorrow."

"Max—"

His arms gave me a squeeze and his face grew attractively lascivious. "Maybe the next day."

"Max!" I snapped, losing patience.

He grinned and changed the subject. "You bought a little pitcher, baby."

I decided to let him change the subject, as this one was safer and less likely to make me angry. I'd been angry enough that day for at least a week. Maybe a year.

"It's a gift," I informed him, "for taking care of me when I was sick."

"You bought me a little pitcher as a gift?"

"Yes," I said. "And a sugar bowl."

He shook his head like I was adorable before he stated, "My gift was better."

"Sorry?"

"The ring."

I immediately pulled my hand from behind his back, placed it on his chest, and stared at the ring he'd given me, which I hadn't taken off.

Then I looked at him and said, "Yes, agreed, this ring is a whole lot better than a little pitcher even with a matching sugar bowl."

He threw his head back and laughed, one of his arms sliding high up my back as he crushed my arm between us and gave me a tight hug.

"Are you saying you don't like my gift?" I asked after he stopped laughing.

"I'll like the one you're givin' me this afternoon a fuckuva lot better," he replied, and I shivered again in his arms before his face got close and I saw he was fighting a grin. "Go take a shower, honey. I'll make breakfast."

"I can make breakfast."

He shook his head. "You take an age to get ready. You're gettin' a head start."

He wasn't wrong. I wasn't one of those women who was ready to face the day after a shower and an application of deodorant.

Though I didn't take "an age."

Even so, instead of arguing, I looked over his shoulder and mumbled, "Whatever."

His arms tightened before he let me go, grabbed his mug, and turned toward the fridge.

"What do you want, oatmeal, toast, granola?" he asked.

"Toast."

He opened the fridge and turned to me. "Jelly?"

"What do you think?"

He smiled, tipped his head toward the ceiling, and said, "Shower, it'll be done when you get down."

"Thanks, Max."

His head was in the fridge when, as if the two words he said didn't hold colossal meaning, he muttered, "Anything, baby."

Anything, baby.

Simple as that.

Anything, baby.

Before I could let those words settle in my soul, I grabbed my mug and nearly ran to the stairs.

I was quickly making the bed when Charlie spoke to me.

What'd I say, Neenee Bean?

It sometimes used to annoy me, but I had to admit, Charlie was rarely wrong.

"I think, just maybe," I whispered under my breath, but even I could hear the hope in my tone, "just maybe you're right, Charlie."

Charlie didn't respond as I finished smoothing the duvet and fluffing the pillows. Then I took a shower.

*   *   *

We were driving through the streets of town and I was looking out the side window, thinking maybe I could go for another buffalo burger sometime relatively soon when Max asked a question.

"Niles loaded?"

I turned to look at him. "I'm sorry?"

"Niles. Is he loaded?"

Something clawed at my insides, coming close to tearing away precious tissue.

"He makes good money," I said offhandedly, looking out the side window again. "His parents, however, *are* loaded."

"Your dad looked loaded."

I pulled in a breath through my nostrils and said, "Dad's loaded, too, but Niles's parents are on a whole other level of loaded."

There was silence a second before Max said softly, "Thinkin' today, Duchess, you might've gotten written out of your dad's will."

That claw curled up and slid away and the tension in my body relaxed as I murmured, "No big loss."

He glanced at me and stated, "You make good money too."

That claw came back with a vengeance.

"I'm not loaded."

"Nina, don't know much about 'em but your fuckin' purse looks like it cost more than my couch."

"It didn't," I replied sharply and hurriedly.

"You know how much my couch cost?"

"Unless you got a major bargain, it didn't cost less than my purse," I retorted.

He glanced at me again and said, "All right, relax."

"I'm relaxed," I lied.

"You're wound up tight," he observed accurately.

"I am not," I lied again.

"You got a problem makin' more money than me?"

"I don't know that I do."

"Honey, you're a lawyer."

"So?"

He didn't answer my one-word question. Instead he asked one of his own. "Can you practice in the States?"

I looked out the side window again and informed him, "I passed the bar and practiced here before moving there, worked for a small firm and I'm still licensed in America. I had to take a conversion course when I moved to England."

"Then you're set," he muttered under his breath, but I heard him.

I looked back and asked, "Set for what?"

He again didn't respond to my question but turned my attention back to one of his. "You didn't answer my question."

I was getting confused. "What question?"

"You got a problem makin' more money than me?"

"If that is, indeed, the case, why would I?" I asked.

"It's important to know."

"Why?"

He glanced at me again and repeated disbelievingly, "Why?"

"Max, seeing as you're a man and you brought this up, then my question would be, do you have a problem with it?"

"Nope," he replied immediately.

"Then why are we talking about this?"

We'd driven out of town and he made a turn into a residential area as he said, "You get used to that kind of life."

"What kind of life?"

"The life you get bein' with someone who's loaded."

I couldn't help it, I laughed.

"Duchess, not sure I get what's funny," Max said over my laughter.

I shook my head and looked out the windshield. "It isn't exactly champagne and caviar on his yacht. He doesn't own a yacht and I've never tasted caviar. Niles mostly watches TV."

Max made another turn out of the residential area, up an incline, and asked, "TV?"

"TV," I repeated.

"Think things'll be more excitin' in the mountains, babe."

He could say that again. Though I wondered why he said it at all.

After we went up a ways, he pulled into a lane that led to a huge, nearly ostentatious, weirdly almost overbearing house that looked down on the town as I said, "Now, can I ask, why we're talking about this?"

He stopped in front of the house, turned off the ignition, and undid his seat belt. I undid mine and Max twisted to me, draping one forearm over the steering wheel.

"Why?"

"Yes," I said. "Why?"

He looked slightly thrown, slightly annoyed. "Are you kiddin'?"

I felt my brows draw together in puzzlement and I replied, "No, I'm not."

"Duchess, what do you think is happenin' here?" he asked, his hand flipping out at the steering wheel with his question. Now he sounded slightly annoyed, slightly incredulous.

The claw was long gone. My insides were seized with something else. It didn't feel bad, entirely, but it was still downright terrifying.

"Max."

He took his forearm from the steering wheel, reached out, hooked the back of my neck, and leaned toward me as he pulled me toward him.

When we were close, he started talking. "You got a lot to think about but today you proved you can handle it so I'm layin' it out. When I say I want to explore this, what happens this afternoon is half as good as the promise of you, I mean that seriously. And I sure as hell am not gonna fuck around with this over an ocean and I'm also not leavin' my land. So that means you come here. You need to visit there, we'll do it as often as we can but you'll be here, with me, on my land. Yeah?"

"Sorry?" I whispered. Now *I* was thrown. So thrown I was having trouble breathing because I was mentally trying to catch up and he shook his head impatiently.

"I'm not doin' that long-distance shit," he explained.

"Long-distance shit?" I repeated, still whispering.

"Nina, we're as good together when we've actually *been together* as we are now, when we haven't, I'm not havin' you sleep in a bed half a world away from me."

"We're good together?" Yes, I was still whispering.

"You had better?"

"No," I said before I thought better of it.

His face got soft and he murmured strangely, "Yeah."

I blinked, then stammered, "Are you saying you want me to…to…to *move in*?"

He smiled and replied, "It works out, Duchess, I don't wanna live in the A-frame while you take a house in town."

"So, essentially you're telling me to move to Colorado?"

"Nothin' 'essentially' about it."

"But I live in Charlie's house," I whispered, and held my breath.

He didn't do what I thought he'd do or was conditioned to a man doing.

Instead, his face got even softer, his smile died, and he muttered, "Fuck."

"Max—"

"You don't want to let it go," he surmised astutely.

"It's all I have left of him."

Max's eyes held mine for a long time.

Then he sighed heavily, gave my neck a squeeze, and declared, "We'll work somethin' out."

This surprised me so much I didn't process what he was saying.

"I'm sorry?"

"We'll work somethin' out."

"What will we work out?"

"I don't know, somethin'."

"Max—"

He brought me even closer and he said in a voice that was strangely fierce and vibrating, "Listen to me, Duchess, you got somethin' good, you got somethin' solid, you find a way to work shit out. Your brother's place means somethin' to you, then we'll work somethin' out."

"Oh my God," I breathed, which was what, I suspected, if the moment was verbalized, any woman would breathe when she figured out she was falling in love with a Colorado Mountain Man she barely knew but that knowledge hit her with the certainty of a freight train.

"What?" Max asked.

"Nothing," I said quickly to cover.

He examined my face for a moment and he did this with an intensity that made me feel more than a little exposed before he said softly, "Crack."

"Sorry?"

He smiled, looking satisfied, and finished, "In your shield."

Yes, I was right. Exposed but more than a little.

Before I could say a word, he brought me to him, touched his mouth to mine, and then, when he pulled away, he muttered, "We'll talk tonight."

Then he let me go, turned and got out of the Cherokee.

I followed but I did it a lot slower, mostly because my legs were shaking.

I rounded the hood and looked up at the extravagant house. A woman in a wheelchair was waiting for us just outside the front door. She was watching me as I got close to Max. He took my hand and led us up the steps.

I was a little surprised by her. She had shining, heavy hair that wasn't light brown but wasn't dark either and had what appeared to be natural and appealing auburn highlights. She was dressed fashionably in a lovely, soft yellow sweater, jeans, and boots, all, I noticed with a practiced eye, of superb quality. She didn't look like she lived in that chair. Instead she looked like she'd just sat down in it to take a load off. As we got close, I saw she had a hint of a healthy, becoming tan and she was smiling at Max and me. Her smile was small but it was also genuine and friendly.

"Nina," she said. "'Spect you know I've heard a lot about you," she finished and lifted her hand toward me when Max and I made it to within a few feet of her chair.

"Yes, I figured that." I smiled back. "And you're Bitsy," I greeted, taking her hand.

She gave me a firm squeeze and then dropped mine.

"Yep, that's me, Bitsy, new widow," she replied, and I realized under her healthy tan and smiling face, she looked tired. Her words weren't sour, just real with a hint of forlorn she didn't try to hide, both making them heartbreaking.

"I'm so sorry," I said quietly.

"You, me, and Shauna Fontaine are the only ones in town who are," she responded with brutal honesty but still no bitterness, more like a sad understanding. Then she put her hands to the wheels of her chair, looked at Max, and continued, "Hey, Max, would you mind comin' inside a sec before we take off?"

Without waiting for us to answer, she deftly turned her chair and wheeled herself into the house.

Max glanced at me and with a tug at my hand we followed. He let me go when we got into the massive foyer and he closed the door.

"Don't mean to be rude, Nina," Bitsy announced after she turned her chair toward us again, her voice a bit hesitant. "But could you wait in the living room a minute while I talk with Max? Just need—"

I cut her off, letting her know she didn't need to explain anything to me; she could have whatever she needed. "That's fine. I'll wait."

"Thanks." She smiled again, a hint of relief in her expression, before she wheeled to my right and Max and I followed. She talked as she went. "You want a cup of coffee or a soda or somethin'?"

"No, thanks. I'm okay."

She swept out a hand to the room and invited, "Make yourself at home. We won't be long, promise." Then her eyes went to Max before she pushed herself toward the door.

"Be back," Max murmured, chucked me under the chin, and then he went after Bitsy.

I watched them go, then, in an effort not to think about what happened in the Cherokee (my habit of late, not thinking when I knew it would be far healthier, not to mention the whole bloody reason I took this adventure in the first place, to sort myself out), I walked to the floor-to-cathedral-ceiling windows and looked at the view.

It was different than Max's view considering it was on the opposite side of town and also on an opposite-facing mountain. It was also somehow a little less spectacular, seeing as it wasn't as far up the mountain, which limited the vista.

There was something else about it that struck me as strange. So strange it made me slightly uncomfortable. In an effort to understand this bizarre feeling, I settled in and took in the view.

I could see the whole town, its Main Street short—since I'd traversed it, I knew it was only five blocks long—roads leading off it, more businesses on them a few doors in but houses after that.

To the left, just out of town, there was a plain covered in two baseball fields, their outfields butting against each other. I could see small stands on either side of the dugouts. Next to this were two football fields running alongside each other separated by more bleachers. Small, white concession stands at either side of the complex. Probably where Little League was held in summer and Pop Warner football in the fall.

To the right, again partially out of town, was the high school, not large but not small. Another football field, far more bleachers available for onlookers, lined lanes of a running track around its perimeter. A baseball field on the opposite side of the school. Both of these had lots of lights, bigger concession stands, and looked more impressive.

It was clear the town liked its sport and supported its kids.

I thought about it and I knew, because I saw it on the little plastic displays on the tables, that The Dog had live music on Friday and Saturday nights. Drake's, the bar Max took me to in town the night of Shauna, Harry, and buffalo burgers, had acoustic music every Tuesday. I'd seen posters informing townsfolk of what was playing at the cinema that Becca told me was one town over. There were fliers on bulletin boards on the sides of buildings in town telling people that *Oklahoma!* was being performed at a dinner theater, which had to be close. Since I'd driven by it, I knew there was a mall about thirty miles out, which also had a multiscreen cinema. On the website where I found Max's house, it advertised that the town held two festivals, one a small music and arts festival in early summer, the other a larger Halloween/harvest festival in the fall. There were also a number of other festivals littered throughout the region.

Restaurants, shops, cinemas, dinner theater, sport, festivals, Denver only a two-hour drive away, small and large ski resorts very close, hiking and biking trails crisscrossing the mountains, it certainly wasn't like there was nothing to do in Gnaw Bone. In fact, it seemed a tranquil, pretty hub in the middle of it all.

I was thinking how I'd like to experience what a Halloween/harvest festival was like, not to mention a music and arts festival, when it hit me what was wrong about the view.

I realized that not only could I see all of town, if I was anywhere in town, I could also see this huge, grand house on its rise.

I hadn't exactly taken a tour of the entire town but from what I'd seen, the houses were smallish, some of them older, established, having been around for quite a while. Others much newer but not that new, looking like they'd been built the last few decades, not the last few years. They could all be described as comfortable but none of them could be described as luxurious. There were a couple of small apartment and condominium complexes like Mindy's and Becca's that seemed much newer, but mostly the town was settled and its income bracket was clearly identifiable.

This house and where it was positioned screamed "Look at me!" in a weird way. It demanded attention, I was guessing in order to rub people's noses in its obvious expense, constantly lord over the entire populace. You couldn't forget it was here because you couldn't escape it.

It wasn't an old house and I figured Curtis Dodd built it where it was for the reasons I deduced.

I felt a chill glide over my skin at what I suspected was not a popular decision on Dodd's part, not to mention what it said about him, and I turned away from the window and took in the enormous room. Even the furniture, decoration, and fittings were obvious in their lavishness. One could buy ten of my purses and five of Max's couches for one of Bitsy's.

I walked to a long set of interconnecting bookshelves that ran the length of the outside wall of the room, wishing to take my mind off my thoughts by perusing the many photos displayed in frames there.

From what I saw in the photos, the house and all its contents were not Bitsy's idea. Bitsy, it appeared as I studied the photos, decorated like me. There were tons of pictures of happy, smiling people who clearly cared about each other and who Bitsy clearly cared about. In some of them she was healthy, standing, smiling, laughing, and surrounded by loved ones. Others, I was heartened to see, she was in her chair, doing the same.

I decided then that I admired her. Charlie never got to that point. Charlie would smile after he lost his legs but it was never the same. Bitsy seemed to have come to terms with her life in her chair and continued to enjoy living it. Furthermore, it was apparent she didn't mind reminders of the life she had before she was put in it.

I stopped when I saw a photo of Bitsy with a man taken a long time ago, for they both looked young and they were both standing.

It had to be her husband, the now very dead Curtis Dodd.

I was surprised at the sight of him. Somehow I expected him to be short, maybe balding, looking squirrely, his eyes mean. But he looked kind of like Max, except not nearly as handsome or tall. But he was a Mountain Man, slightly rough, his hair fair to almost gold, his face tanned. He was smiling at the camera in a weird way, though, almost self-conscious, as if he wasn't comfortable being photographed and wanted to put his best foot forward. Bitsy, on the other hand, was smiling with abandon, clearly happy, both her arms around his neck and her cheek pressed to his. She didn't care what anyone thought and the only thing anyone could think was she was in love with the man in her arms.

I glanced through the other pictures, trying to find him in the faces, but that was the only photo of the two of them together and the only photo of him at all.

I moved to the last shelf, looking for signs of Curtis, my eyes grazing the limited books and knickknacks displayed between the photos when I stopped dead.

Three photos had their own shelf, a lower one, Bitsy's height, and they were arranged like it was a place of honor. Unlike the others, these pictures weren't shoved in, a jumble to exhibit as many as possible to surround Bitsy with constant reminders that she was loved and of the ones she loved. These were just those three, three different sizes in frames that clearly showed the photos were important.

I leaned down and it took everything I had not to reach out and grab one, bringing it in for closer inspection. But I couldn't touch them, couldn't let my fingers give the signal to my brain that they were real.

Max. Max and Anna.

In all that had happened, I'd forgotten what Arlene had said the other night at The Dog. It totally escaped me.

Max had had a wife. Her name was Anna and she was beautiful. Unbelievably beautiful. She matched him in her utter perfection.

Blonde to his dark, her hair long and wild, her complexion without flaw, her eyes gorgeous and dancing.

There was a photo, smaller, a snapshot of Max, Anna, Curtis, and Bitsy, all in a row, all with their arms around each other's waists, all smiling into the camera. Even Curtis looked relaxed and at ease. Good friends, out of doors doing something together, a picnic, a barbeque, enjoying good times.

There was another photo, much larger, more official, sitting in the center. Max and Anna's wedding day. He wore a tux. She had on a simple white dress that she made stunning, daisies mingled in her long, wild hair that she made look sophisticated. They were depicted full-length, standing outside, the river behind them. They were front to front, arms around each other, Max's head tipped down, Anna's head tipped back, broad smiles on both of their faces that you could see even in profile. Happy. Exceptionally so. They both looked young, maybe early twenties, their life spread out before them filled with love and wonder.

But it was the last that caught my heart, that claw coming

back to slash at my insides. It was a close-up, Max's arm around Anna's shoulders, her head against one of his, both of them looking in the camera, both of them clearly laughing, both of them deliriously happy and obviously in love.

Max's bluff was behind them.

Something blocked my throat as my eyes seemed to swell against their sockets and, suddenly frantic, I walked the length of the bookshelves examining the other photos again.

No sign of Anna. No sign of Max.

Back to the shelf of honor, I looked at the smallest photo. Bitsy, younger, standing, smiling, one arm around Curtis, who was to the outside, her other arm around Anna.

Then back through the shelves, Bitsy in her chair, no Anna, no Max.

"Oh my God," I breathed as it hit me.

Mindy telling me Max wouldn't forget what a visit from the police felt like. Max's fierce vow about dying in an effort to take care of someone you loved. Curtis, Bitsy, Anna, and Max, all standing linked and happy, friends once, good ones. Now Max was one of the earliest suspects questioned in Curtis's murder.

Something had happened, something that put Bitsy in her chair and took Anna away altogether. And that something, I was sure, had to do with Curtis Dodd.

My recent conversation with Max in the Jeep came back at me, striking me, scorching, like a bolt of lightning.

"You had better?" Max had asked.

"No," I'd answered.

Then he'd murmured, *"Yeah."*

His "yeah" didn't mean he felt the same. He hadn't agreed that *he* hadn't had better. He just knew I hadn't.

Because he *had*. He'd been *married* to her. Funny, beautiful, forever young Anna with her blonde hair and her knack for making daisies, of all things, look sophisticated.

And he hadn't said a word. Not one word.

All his pushing for me to share, *he* hadn't shared. He'd mentioned his father, his sister, his mother, his land, but not the fact that he'd quite obviously been married to the love of his life and she'd died.

Which was a bloody big piece of history to keep to yourself.

I heard the murmur of voices approaching and I quickly moved back across the room in order to appear as if I'd been studying the view. I turned my back to the entrance of the room and looked out the window, my eyes not seeing, my heart tripping over itself, that thing still lodged in my throat.

It would, of course, be me who would find an amazingly handsome Mountain Man with great hair, an attractive voice, an ability to show affection in a way that made you feel cherished, a protective streak that made you feel safe, and, lastly, a dead wife who was the love of his life.

Meaning that was something I would never be. The love of Holden Maxwell's life would never be me.

However, if we *explored* this, as Max wished to do, it was becoming more and more evident by the second that he could be that for me.

"Sorry, Nina," Bitsy called, and I swallowed against the lump, forced a smile on my face, and turned to her as she finished, "That took longer than I expected."

"That's all right," I said, trying to sound cheerful but my voice seemed higher pitched and false. I kept talking to hide it. "You have a beautiful view."

Bitsy wheeled herself close and looked out the window.

"Yeah," she said as if she wasn't entirely convinced. She looked at me and smiled her small, somewhat sad but still authentic smile. "Max's is better."

I nodded, for what she said was true.

"Let's get this done," Max announced.

I started at his gravelly voice and my eyes went to him.

He was looking down at Bitsy and he asked, "You want me to load up the motorized chair?"

"Nope, feel energetic today and not goin' very far. This one'll work," Bitsy answered, wheeling herself back into the hall. "I'll just get my coat and we'll be on our way."

I licked my lips and kept my eyes pointed at the floor as I headed to the front door.

"Duchess?" Max called when I was passing him.

I stopped, trying to clear my expression, and I looked at him.

"Yes?" I asked.

His head tipped to the side, his eyes scanning my face before he asked back, "You okay?"

"Fine," I lied, suddenly hating, no *detesting* the fact that, even knowing him only a week, he could read my mood so easily.

"Honey," he said softly, not believing me.

"I'm fine," I repeated, and he got close, hooking a finger in my side jeans belt loop, effectively, even affectionately, halting my progress when I moved to head to the door again.

"Nina," he said, and I looked up at him, wishing I didn't like his finger in my belt loop so darned much. "She's good," he told me in a hushed voice. "She's used to it. She adjusted a long time ago."

"What?" I asked.

"Her chair."

I blinked as I realized Max thought my mood had shifted because Bitsy was reminding me of Charlie.

This was thoughtful, as Max could be—I knew since he'd exhibited this ability on more than one occasion—and I suddenly decided I detested that too.

"That's good," I muttered, pulling from his hold on my belt loop and heading to the door where a be-jacketed Bitsy was pulling it open.

"God, it'll be good not to have to go somewhere in that stupid van," Bitsy commented, and looked at me, taking the sting out of her complaint by explaining, "I like the Cherokee."

"Then you get to sit in front," I told her, using this as my excuse not to be close to Max, not even in his car. I needed distance. I needed to think. I needed to process the knowledge I'd learned in Bitsy's house and what it meant to me.

"Oh, that's okay—" Bitsy began.

"I insist."

"Really—"

I cut her off again, saying, "Better views from up there."

She gave me another smile and a, "Thanks," then rolled herself out, down a ramp, and to the front passenger side of Max's Jeep.

Max opened the door and lifted Bitsy in without effort, like he'd done it more than once before. I grabbed the chair and wheeled it to the rear of the truck, thinking he was so obviously strong and detesting that suddenly too. Bitsy was thin, though not skinny, and looked fit regardless of the wheelchair. But standing, as I saw in the photo, she was Anna's height, and Anna, I guessed, was my height, which meant Bitsy was not exactly light as a feather.

I pulled the seat up at the middle, folding the chair as I'd done to Charlie's time and time again, thinking Anna was blonde and she was my height. She was also, according to Arlene, funny. She didn't look like me, I wasn't hideous, but I certainly didn't have her beauty or her obvious effervescence, but we resembled each other.

Maybe Max, at long last, thought he'd found a replacement. Not the real thing, never to have the real thing again, but close enough.

"I got it, Duchess," Max told me as I pulled up the back of the Cherokee to load the chair.

"Right," I muttered, and walked around him to sit behind Bitsy, not sparing him a glance. I got in and buckled up.

"It's nice that you came, Nina," Bitsy said into the car. "I know you're on vacation and this is probably the last thing you wanted to do."

I couldn't argue with that.

Max got in and I noticed he did this twisted so his clear, gray, too-intelligent eyes were on me. I looked out my window.

"Please don't worry. I'm fine," I told Bitsy, but spoke to the window.

"It's just that," Bitsy said as Max switched on the ignition and started to back out, "Max and I've been friends for a good long while and I'd heard about you, so I was curious. And, without making a big production out of it, I couldn't come to you."

"Really, it's okay," I assured her again. "It isn't every day a girl goes to a police station. I came out for an adventure and here it is. I'm having it."

She laughed quietly at my lame joke but she did it without a lot of humor. "Yeah, great adventure, huh?"

I didn't reply. Instead I hesitated, then leaned forward, reached through the seat, and curled my fingers around her shoulder. I felt it tense under my hand but I gave it a squeeze and then pulled away and sat back.

We rode in silence to the station, not exactly comfortable since everyone was in their own thoughts and none of our thoughts were good. However, fortunately, it wasn't a long ride.

I stayed silent and hung back as Max took care of Bitsy and she wheeled herself into the station.

"I'll go find Mick," Max said when we were all inside. He was moving forward, as usual taking charge, and Bitsy looked relieved to wheel herself to a bank of chairs.

I followed and she backed in beside one, giving me my cue to sit by her.

"This is stupid, this whole thing," she muttered when I sat down.

Her head was tilted down but she was looking under her lashes at the reception desk.

"What is?" I asked quietly.

"I shoulda let Mick come up to the house, talk to me there." Bitsy looked at me. I noticed her face had changed, the mask was falling, grief was moving to the surface, and she whispered, "I just couldn't."

"It's okay," I assured her.

"It's already a crime scene, my house." She was still

whispering. "I can't go to the utility room. It's roped off with yellow tape."

These words made my heart hurt for her and my stomach pitch in revulsion at the knowledge she shared with me. So without hesitation this time, I covered her hand with mine. She turned hers so our hands were palm to palm and her fingers curled and, when they did, so did mine.

"You do this as you have to do it," I said to her.

"I don't want any more of this in my house."

"Then that's how you're doing it."

She looked to the reception desk and back at me. "I'm sorry, Nina. Max has enough to do. Mindy, you, all the stuff he has to see to when he's in town. He doesn't need me adding to all that stuff."

I gave her hand a squeeze and said, "I don't think he minds."

She looked over my shoulder and replied, "He never minds."

No, she was right. Apparently Super Max was pretty content with taking care of half the town, such was his wonderfulness.

That, too, I suddenly detested.

Her hand gave mine a squeeze as her attention came back to me. "I promise, Nina, because Curtis is gone this won't get to be a habit. I've got people who look out for me, a lot of friends, family close, people who take me grocery shopping, a girl who comes in to clean the house, you know, stuff like that."

"It's okay," I promised, wondering why she felt she had to reassure me about these things. Then again she lived in town and pretty much everyone in town, including Max, thought that he and I were going somewhere and we were doing it together.

"You should know something else too," Bitsy said, calling my attention to her and she kept talking. "Harry came by yesterday. He's torn up." She shook her head but continued. "We won't talk about that but anyway, he said he met you and so did Shauna."

"Yes," I confirmed. She gazed at my face and I knew she read my opinion about Shauna because our eyes locked and we shared a silent moment of keen understanding about Shauna Fontaine.

Then her hand squeezed mine and she carried on. "He told me what Shauna said to you and, you should know, it isn't true."

"Sorry?"

"Max," she went on. "He takes the jobs out of town because he makes really good money doing them. He's never gone long, three months, sometimes six or eight, but not often and he never takes the big ones that last forever. He likes to be home and, sometimes, even when he's on a job, he'll come home for weekends and stuff." I nodded. She kept tight hold of my hand and continued speaking. "He doesn't rent that house for the money, like Shauna said. He's got money. Not only does he make good money but he's also got some besides, from, um . . . you know"—she hesitated—"a little nest egg."

I didn't know and I didn't get to ask, not that I would have, and she continued.

"It's just that he's smart. If he's going to be gone all that time, why not rent the house? He makes a bucketful when he rents it. He can get top dollar and he demands it. I would too. I mean, who wouldn't? His house is great."

I didn't want to be in another conversation about Max's finances, especially considering the reasons why I was in another conversation about Max's finances, so I said, "Of course," hoping that she'd be reassured and we could stop talking about it.

She nodded and went on. "The other thing . . ." She paused and her hand squeezed mine, not comfortingly, spasmodically, a reflexive action communicating something else entirely. Then this action was explained when she said in a low voice, the words coming fast and I knew it took a lot for her to utter them, "Beware of Shauna. I know why she was with Curtis and I know why she was with Harry. I'm guessin', from what Harry told me, that you figured it out, so you gotta know, she was with Max for another reason. She wanted him for a long time before she got him and she made no bones about it and when I say that, I mean a *long* time." She paused to let that penetrate, before she finished. "She still wants him, maybe even more now that she's lost him."

Considering the fact that I'd recently decided to go home to England as soon as humanly possible and never come back to Colorado again in my life, it was unnecessary for Bitsy to give me this warning. Although I didn't tell her that since her doing so was also kind.

"Thanks, Bitsy," I said, and then told her the truth, knowing, even so, she'd not understand my true meaning. "I'm not worried about Shauna."

She smiled at me. It was again small. Her face had not fought back the grief, but she wasn't letting it consume her, something else I admired her for, and she gave my hand a final squeeze before letting it go.

"Sucks," she started, looking back at the reception desk, and I saw her eyes lock on something and I looked to see Max and Mick were heading our way. "Finally, he's found someone he's into and it's during all this crap." I felt her eyes come back to me, so I looked back to her and she was again smiling. "But we'll get to know each other."

"I'd like that," I said quietly, even though I knew we wouldn't.

"Me too," she replied with feeling, not sharing my knowledge and making me feel guilty because she appeared to be looking forward to it.

"Bitsy," Mick greeted as he stopped in front of us and I stayed seated. I did this out of habit. It was something I did for Charlie, keeping myself at his level, not making him look up all the time, reminding him of what he'd lost.

"Hey, Mick," Bitsy greeted back.

"How's things, Nina?" Mick asked me.

"Interesting," I replied, and Mick smiled.

"Max, would you stay with me when they talk to me?" Bitsy asked, and then said to me, "Or, sorry, Nina, I should ask you. Do you mind?"

I shook my head and smiled at her. "I'll just go get a coffee or something."

"Thanks," she said softly. She nodded at Mick, started wheeling away, and Mick followed her.

Max stayed with me and I stood.

"Bitsy wants you," I reminded him.

"Somethin's up," he said straight out, watching me closely.

"You better go," I encouraged him, evading his subject. "Do you want me to bring you a coffee when I come back?"

He got close, tilting his head down to look at me but he didn't touch me.

"What's up?" he asked.

"I'll get Bitsy a coffee too. Do you know what she likes?"

His finger went into my side belt loop again.

Then he said in a low tone, "Not gonna ask twice, Duchess."

God. Seriously. He was *so* annoying.

"I'm fine."

"You're lyin'."

My eyes narrowed. I yanked my hips away but his finger held fast and instead of tearing my loop, I settled and repeated, "I said, I'm fine."

"Bullshit."

I leaned in and hissed my lie, "All right, Max, I'm going out for coffee and my dad's in town. I don't want to run into him and have another scene, this time in public."

His finger in my loop drew me closer as his face relaxed.

"Just stay at the station," he suggested. "I'll ask Mick to get someone to bring you coffee."

"Police coffee?" I asked, sounding horrified.

"Yeah, Duchess," he returned, grinning. "You think your system could stomach that?"

"No," I lied again.

His grin got bigger and he muttered, "Christ, you're cute."

I sucked in a breath, feeling those three words pummel me like blows to the gut.

Then I reminded him, "Max, they're waiting for you."

"Stay here. You want coffee, we'll get coffee with Bitsy after. She'd like that."

"Max, as I said, *twice*, I'll be fine."

He shook his head and his finger in my loop brought me even closer, inappropriately closer for a public place. A closer that was almost, but not quite, as close as making-out-in-the-kitchen close.

"Now you explained it," he said, "*I* don't like the idea of you runnin' into your dad in town without me havin' your back. So I want you to stay here. Yeah?"

I decided it was probably better to give in because Max wouldn't let it go and I needed distance immediately. What I did *not* need were more indications of all the reasons he could easily be the love of *any* woman's life.

I decided this but I also decided not to give in gracefully.

So I did it on the release of a heavy, annoyed breath. "Oh, all right."

His grin came back and his finger left my loop, but his hand lifted and curled around my neck, giving me a squeeze. Then he turned around and walked away.

Not five minutes later, a lady who introduced herself as Jane brought me coffee and when I took a sip, it was just how I took it.

Yes. Max was *so* annoying.

*   *   *

We were on our way back up to the A-frame.

It was after Bitsy's police interview. Max had taken us to lunch, again at that little café by the river, but this time it was warm enough for us to sit outside close to the rushing, snowmelt swelled river. And, after lunch, we took Bitsy home where she insisted we stay for a thank-you mug of her home-made lattes, which she created in a fabulous kitchen that also had a load of extra counters that had been built so she could reach them and, incidentally, her lattes were delicious.

Bitsy had been quiet and reflective through lunch and twice I caught her eyes filling with tears while she studied the river, though she never allowed the tears to fall. Max and I kept quiet with her. Me because I didn't know what to say and I was deep in my own thoughts. Max because, I suspected, he was leaving her be. When she went home, she seemed to perk up but I guessed this was because she wanted to entice us not to leave and I didn't blame her. Being alone with my thoughts in my current predicament was less than fun. Being alone with hers would be torture.

Now I was studying the beautiful landscape passing me by, wondering, if the cosmos had shined down on me and given me Max free and clear, if I'd have ever gotten used to the beauty of it. Thinking at the same time that Max thought that we'd be spending the afternoon further exploring our relationship.

I was also trying to form a plan on how I was going to avoid letting him do that and wondering, if he touched me and, God forbid, kissed me, even if I did form a plan, if I could manage to be successful in my endeavors.

"Duchess?" he called at the same time I felt his hand wrap warm and strong around mine.

"Yes?" I answered, looking from the side window to the front but not at him.

"What's on your mind, honey?" His voice was soft and he'd pulled my hand to rest the back of it against his hard thigh.

I hadn't felt his thigh until just then, but of course it, too, was hard, inviting touch. I decided this was most irritating even though my brain registered the feel was totally amazing.

I also decided not to fight at that juncture and leave my hand in his while I somewhat lied, though I thought of it more as not telling the full truth. "Bitsy."

His fingers gave me a squeeze as he said, "She'll be okay."

"She loved him."

"Yeah."

I bit my lip and pointed out the obvious because he more than anyone knew. "That means she won't be okay."

This was as good a time as any, in fact, better than most, for Max to share about his dead wife.

He didn't.

He just repeated, "Yeah."

Jerk!

"I'll talk with her later, after the funeral, maybe in a few weeks," he went on. "Get her to sell that house. Too many memories, too big for her, hell, it was too big for them when Curt was alive."

"Mmm-hmm," I mumbled.

He gave my hand a squeeze before he let it go to downshift in order to make a turn. He left it resting on his thigh and I moved it away, linking it with my other one in my lap, hoping he wouldn't reinitiate the contact as he said, "We'll look out for her. She'll make it through."

"Mmm-hmm," I repeated, hoping he meant "we" as in Wonder Max and the Townsfolk of Gnaw Bone, not him and me, something that would never be.

This was another decision I'd come to and I'd come to it in the silence over lunch, thus me knowing that being alone with my thoughts was not fun.

I couldn't live a life like the one I led with Niles.

I also couldn't live a life knowing the length of it, even if it was good, that I was second best.

No, there wouldn't even be a length to it because eventually, like everything else I'd risked, it would end in disaster. I'd had enough disaster with jerks, thieves, cheaters, and beaters. I didn't need the heartbreaking disaster that was all Max.

I needed to be the love of someone's life, like Mom was for Steve. They'd both waited a long time, Mom after a short marriage that ended in heartbreak, Steve after a long, loveless marriage that ended with his wife dying of a heart attack two years before he met Mom. I hoped I didn't have to wait as long as Mom but I also knew down deep in my soul I needed to wait for that special person who felt that way for me, just me and only me so I could feel safe giving that feeling back to him.

Max was silent through my thoughts; then, before he made the next turn, he asked, "You still thinkin' about your dad?"

"No," I replied truthfully this time. My father was the last thing on my mind, which was the only fortunate thing that came from the vicious twists and turns of my day.

"That Niles guy?" Max pressed.

"No," I replied, again truthfully.

Max was silent again while he made the next turn and he noted, "Somethin' else is eatin' you, babe." But before I could comment, he pulled in a sharp breath.

I looked at him, then followed his eyes. Then I pulled in a sharp breath too.

Firstly, there was a Subaru parked in front of the A-frame. Mindy and a tall man, the sun shining on their hair, were both leaning their backs against the Subaru's hatchback. Secondly, there was my rental car at the edge of Max's front clearing, obviously, and quite liberally, having been vandalized.

"What the *fuck*?" Max clipped as he turned into the lane, drove down it, and parked behind the rental.

He didn't glance at me when he got out. I followed him, my eyes also glued to the rental.

It had been nearly covered in spray paint, including the windows. The brake lights had been busted out, their plastic shards in the gravel of Max's drive. The tires were flat, all four of them. The wing mirrors were hanging drunkenly by wires, the mirrors shattered.

"Appears you got an enemy," the tall man said, he and Mindy walking up to us.

I glanced at him. He had dark red-brown hair, somewhat familiar blue eyes, and tanned skin. He was nearly as handsome as Max, and now that I was becoming somewhat of an expert at identifying them, I noted he was also total Mountain Man wearing a thermal under a jean jacket, faded jeans, and boots. His eyes were attached to me.

"I—" I began.

"I'm so sorry, Neens," Mindy interrupted me, coming to his side. She was biting her lip, looking worried, and her eyes appeared red-rimmed as if she'd been crying.

It was the red-rimmed eyes that took my attention. Therefore I forgot about my unknown new acquaintance and asked, "Are you okay?"

She shook her head and announced, "Damon did this."

"Did what?" I asked stupidly, feeling my heart start beating faster and my palms start itching.

"Your car, honey," Max answered, and I looked to him.

"My car?" I repeated, my mind stuck on thoughts of Damon getting to Mindy in town, doing something to make her cry and wondering where Max kept his gun.

He tipped his head to the rental and his arm slid around my shoulders. "Damon, he did that to your car."

I glanced at my car and my gaze went back to Mindy.

"Did you see him do this?" I asked.

"No," she answered.

My voice was softer when I went on, "Have you seen him at all, darling?"

"No," she replied.

"Did he call you?"

"No."

"Then how do you know he did it?"

"That's just"—she flicked a hand to the rental, her breath hitched, and she pulled in a deep one to cover it before she went on—"what he'd do." Tears gathered in her eyes and she concluded, "I'm so sorry, Neens."

Then she covered her face with her hands and burst into tears.

I pulled out from under Max's arm and swiftly walked forward, gathering Mindy in my embrace.

"Sweetheart," I cooed to her, "I have full coverage on that rental. It's no big deal."

Well, it was since I *really* now couldn't escape Max unless

I somehow managed to make off with his Cherokee in the dead of night, but I couldn't tell Mindy that.

I'd worry about that later, though hopefully not too much later. I had to worry about Mindy now, as she was hiccoughing and still hadn't taken her hands from her face even though I was holding her.

"Yes, but it's such a *dick* thing to do," Mindy said from behind her hands.

"You're right about that. Still, if he didn't do it, really I would just be throwing that insurance coverage away. I should find him, thank him for making that financial outlay worthwhile."

Her body jerked, her hands went down, and her head came up.

"What?" she whispered, and I looked over my shoulder at the car, then back at her.

"And, Mindy, seriously, he made that insurance *really* worthwhile. I mean he was *thorough*. Don't you think, darling?" I teased.

A surprised giggle came up her throat. She gulped it back and I smiled at her as I pulled one side of her hair over her shoulder.

Then I put my hands to her face and used my thumbs to rub away the tears as I said softly, "All right, you'll probably shed more tears over that Neanderthal before you're well and truly over him, but please, don't do it on my behalf. Okay?"

"You aren't pissed?"

Oh, I was pissed. Damon Matthews had taken away all hopes of escape and he was, indeed, a very serious dick. Still, Mindy didn't need to know any of that.

"I'm of the opinion that the more evidence he presents that you can *so way* do better than him, the better it is."

"Already, I like her." The deep, rumbling voice of the red-headed man came from close.

I dropped my hands from Mindy's face and stepped away, looking up at him.

"Brody," he introduced himself, hand up, eyes (Mindy's

eyes, which was why they were familiar) smiling and open as well as openly curious.

But I wasn't breathing.

Brody. Mindy's brother. *Max's best friend!* Here to "check me out" no doubt.

Why did this continue to get worse? Why?

"Nina," I introduced myself back, unquestionably unnecessarily, and I took his hand.

His grip was firm, strong, and overlong. Overlong in the fact that he didn't actually let me go. His hand, like Max's, engulfed mine.

"You're pretty," he told me.

"Um...thanks?" I answered on a question, giving a small, polite pull, which was met with firm, impolite resistance.

"You're right," he said, eyes still on me but I got the sense he was talking to someone else and his next words proved me correct. "She's got fuckin' great eyes."

I didn't know if he was talking to Max or Mindy but I didn't ask nor could I care because I was back to not breathing and he still hadn't let go of my hand; therefore I had more pressing things on my mind.

"Um...," I muttered.

"You wanna let her go?" Max suggested, and there was humor in his tone, humor mixed with an indication that his words weren't entirely a suggestion.

"Not really," was Brody's insane and alarming answer, and he coupled this with his grip becoming stronger.

"Brody," Mindy said on a mini-giggle. "Quit jacking around."

Brody obviously was in the mood to "jack around" and he didn't let me go.

Instead he remarked, "I thought you English people were reserved."

"I'm not, um...exactly—"

He cut me off, noting, "But you're sweet."

"Um..."

"Can you cook?" he asked, still holding on to my hand.

"Cook?" I asked back.

"I heard English food sucks."

I tried another pull, met with more resistance, and answered, "I think that's what Americans think when they go to England and eat American food. English food is delicious. English doing American food isn't as successful."

"Yeah, Arlene said she had some kind of fish casserole thingie-ma-bobbie over here last night that Neens whipped up and Arlene said it was *unbelievable*," Mindy put in.

Brody looked toward Max. "Arlene's havin' dinner at your house?"

Max came up close to my side and answered, "She's taken a shine to Nina."

This for some reason made Brody throw his head back and burst out laughing.

"Brody," Max said over his laughter, not a lot of humor in his voice. In fact, none at all. "Would you fuckin' let her go?"

Brody let me go. Then again, anyone would let me go with the way Max asked for it to be done. I stepped back, my shoulder hit Max, and his arm immediately curled around my waist from behind.

"Relax, bro, just bein' friendly," Brody said over my shoulder.

"Too friendly," Max said back.

"We're that"—Brody's eyes came to me—"friendly."

"I've noticed," I replied.

Then Brody asked, "Arlene?"

"We got slightly snockered with Arlene at The Dog before Max kicked Damon's ass," Mindy shared.

"Ah"—Brody nodded, light dawning—"Arlene held the sacred ritual. Snockered with her at The Dog. She's usually ornery as hell but you're in now, Nina, never to be let out."

"You make that sound not so good," I noted.

"Arlene's good people, if she likes you, but when she likes you, she's opinionated, in-your-business good people."

"Oh dear," I muttered, and Brody burst out laughing again.

Max gave my waist a squeeze.

"Either of you think to call the cops about Nina's car?" Max asked.

"Yeah, about fifteen minutes ago. They're on the way up," Brody answered.

"Mick should set up an outpost next to the house. He's been here so fuckin' much this week," Max muttered.

"Why's Mickey been here?" Brody asked, and I felt Max's body get tight against mine.

"Mins?" Max called. Mindy nodded, so Max carried on with a one-word answer that was obviously meant to explain all. "Dodd."

It apparently did, for Brody nodded.

"He needs you for Bitsy," Brody guessed.

"That and he wanted my alibi," Max informed him.

Good-natured, teasing Brody disappeared and his heavy, auburn brows snapped together dangerously before he bit out, "What the fuck?"

Here we go again, I thought.

"Brody, it's fine. He's talked to a lot of people," Max assured him.

"Yeah, but *you*?" Brody was still unhappy.

"Can we go in?" Mindy butted in. "I need a soda or somethin'."

"Yeah," Max said, his arm coming from around my waist but I felt his finger hooking this time in a back belt loop of my jeans and putting pressure on to propel me forward.

"Doubt Mickey'll come up on a vandalized car, not when he's workin' a murder," Brody noted as he walked beside us up the steps. "Probably send Jeff or Pete. Still, gonna have words with him 'bout visitin' you for an alibi."

"Let it go," Max said softly but firmly, sliding his key into the lock at the front door. "He's just doin' his job."

Max opened the door and pushed me in front of him but I still saw the look Mindy and Brody exchanged.

"I'll get the drinks," I announced, ignoring their looks,

telling myself all this mystery was none of my business any-more, not that it ever was. "Mindy, you want a diet?"

"Yeah, Neens," she answered, skip-dancing to a stool.

I shrugged my purse off my shoulder and plopped it on the dining room table, calling, "Brody?"

"Beer."

"Max?" I asked when I'd hooked my jacket around a chair.

"Beer, honey."

I nodded and hit the kitchen. Mindy sat on the stool. Brody pulled himself up to sit on the opposite counter. Max assumed his usual position with hips against the kitchen sink. I got the drinks and then took my can of diet and went to sit beside Mindy on the other stool. When I settled in, I chanced a look at Max to see I was right about feeling his eyes on me. He was watching me and I got the impression he didn't like that I put space and a counter between us.

"Stayin' at Mins's place in town," Brody declared, and Max's eyes went to him. "Gonna look for Damon, have a word, finalize shit."

"How much time you get off?" Max asked.

"Gotta be back Wednesday," Brody answered.

"Brody and I decided we're all goin' to The Rooster for steaks tonight," Mindy announced, bouncing twice on her stool with happiness at this idea, and Max's eyes took her in before they cut back to me. This was both good and bad. Good because his eyes cut to me rather than him going to his gun. Bad because he didn't look happy.

"Made a reservation and Mindy got Bonnie to cover for her at The Dog tonight," Brody added.

Mindy turned to me and explained, "The Rooster's steaks are *awesome* and you get to *dress up*!"

"Um...," I muttered, feeling the heat of Max's stare and feeling the pressure of his unhappiness.

"I'm wearin' high heels and this absolutely fab...you...las top I found at the outlet store. It's designer but they mis-marked it and I got it for *a song*. You'll *love* it."

"That's great, darling, can't wait to see it," I said to Mindy, and then glanced at Max to see he, unlike Mindy, was not thrilled at the idea of The Rooster and he, unlike me, could indeed wait to see Mindy's designer top.

"What're you gonna wear?" Mindy asked.

"Oh," I muttered, looking away from Max, "I'll find something."

"If you didn't bring anything, you could come into town with me and go through my closet and Becca's!" she finished, obviously excited about a girlie closet trawl.

"Um...," I muttered again.

"I'm sure she's got somethin'," Max put in.

"But maybe she—" Mindy started.

"She's got somethin'," Max repeated.

"But a girl's gotta—"

"Mins, babe, she's got somethin'," Brody said firmly, and Mindy looked between the men and me.

"Okay," she whispered, and grinned at me, bugging out her eyes.

I grinned back, then turned and saw Max's eyes go between Mindy and me to look out the window.

"Pete," he said, pushing away from the sink, and I twisted on my stool to see an SUV with lights on top and a star on the door rolling down the lane.

"We'll let you deal with this. Reservation's at six-thirty," Brody said. "You wanna meet us in town or you wanna meet us at The Rooster?"

"Rooster," Max answered as Brody walked by his side to the front door, still holding his beer.

"Gotcha," Brody replied.

"Honey," Max called to me when he had his hand on the door handle, "best get your rental papers."

"Okay," I replied, sliding off the stool and heading to the stairs.

"See ya later, Neens," Mindy yelled as I wound my way up the stairs.

"Yes, darling, see you," I yelled back.

"Nice to meet'cha, Nina," Brody called.

"You too," I called back.

Then I hit the loft and went to my overnight bag.

One thing I could say for Damon and his antics, he'd provided the perfect tactic for avoiding Max's afternoon plans.

Still, he was a dick.

*   *   *

I was sitting on my side of the bed finishing up my call to the rental car agency when Max hit the loft after sending Brody, Mindy, and eventually Officer Pete on their way.

After I met Pete, I decided if I were to stick around, if Jeff didn't work out for Mindy I was going to try to fix her up with Pete. He wasn't as cute as Jeff but he was still nice.

Unfortunately, it was highly unlikely I'd find out what Mindy's future held, since it was highly unlikely she'd keep in touch after I left Max and Gnaw Bone behind.

I tried not to think of how overwhelmingly upsetting this was. Instead, I told myself I barely knew her. I didn't believe myself, not even in the slightest, but that didn't stop me from repeating it in my head with hopes it'd sink in.

"That'll be fine," I said into the phone as Max came to a stop, standing in front of me. "Great, see you then. Bye."

It wasn't great, I thought as I touched the button on the screen to end the call. Seeing as it was late Saturday, they weren't sending anyone up until Monday. Which meant I'd have to come up the mountain to meet them there. Unless Max would let them get to the car without me, seeing as I would, if it all worked out, be staying at the hotel probably holed up in my room in an effort to avoid my father and, undoubtedly, curled into a ball with seven boxes of Kleenex lamenting my hideous luck that Max could never be mine.

How, a week ago, I had a boring, predictable life where nothing happened and now everything was a complete and utter mess, I had no idea. I wasn't rethinking my decision about Niles but I was rethinking my Colorado adventure and any future adventures I might be stupid, insane, and irrational enough to consider taking.

Therefore, on Monday afternoon, after the rental car person left, somehow, some way, I was heading to Denver and then I was changing my ticket and going straight home.

I could take no more of this.

I put the phone on the nightstand and looked up at Max. "They're sending someone Monday."

"Right," he replied, standing weirdly close to me so I had to tip my head back really far to look at him. Then he asked, "How long's it take you to get ready for somethin' like The Rooster?"

It was a weird question to which I didn't have enough information to provide a response. Furthermore, we had other things to talk about.

Still, for some reason instead of bringing up the other things we needed to talk about, I twisted on the bed, looked at Max's bedside clock, and saw it was four-thirty. Then I looked back to him.

"When do we have to leave?"

"From here, in an hour."

"It takes an hour to get there?"

"Yeah, how long's it take you to get ready?"

"I don't know. How fancy is this place?"

"For Colorado, fancy."

Hmm.

"Guesstimate?" I told him. "Half an hour, forty-five minutes."

His eyes went over my head to the clock and he muttered, "Not long, but it's somethin'."

Then he leaned down, put his hands under my armpits, and suddenly lifted me. Max's knee was in the bed, I was hauled farther onto it, and then I was on my back, Max on me.

Drat. Just where I didn't want to be.

Though with his heavy weight pressing me into the bed, I couldn't help but think it felt like *exactly* where I wanted to be.

"Max—"

"Quiet, Duchess, we don't got time to talk."

"Max—" I said again as his lips hit mine.

"Quiet," he repeated, and then he kissed me.

I pressed against his shoulders and bucked my hips, doing both only hopefully since he was big, heavy, and, apparently, determined. My hopes were dashed; he stayed put and his tongue touched my lips. As much as I liked the feel, which was a lot, I turned my head to the side. Undeterred, his tongue touched my neck.

That felt nice.

"Max."

"What?"

"There's something I need to say."

"Yeah?"

I opened my mouth to say it but his tongue slid up my neck and traced the outside of my ear as his hand slid down my side and ducked under my sweater.

"Max," I breathed since his tongue at my ear felt nicer than touching my neck, but I breathed it somewhat loudly.

"What, baby?" he murmured in my ear in his gravelly voice.

My body shivered against my will, his hand slid up my belly, then curled, warm and strong, around my breast.

Oh my God.

That felt beyond nice.

"Max—" I breathed again, a lot quieter this time. I was losing concentration since most of it was focusing on his hand and tongue.

"You keep sayin' my name, Duchess. I'm right here." Max was still talking in my ear but then his teeth nipped my earlobe as his thumb slid over my nipple.

Oh...my...*God.*

Of their own accord, my hands moved. One glided down his back. One went into his hair.

"Nina?" he called as his thumb slid back.

"Mmm?" was all I could say as I felt my nipple go tight and I felt it in two very good places.

His head came up, his thumb did another swipe, and my hips bucked involuntarily under him, this time not to push him off.

"You gonna let me kiss you now?" he asked, sounding amused.

"Uh-huh," I answered, unable to form words because his thumb was now rolling circles around my nipple and that was indescribably nice.

"Good," he muttered, and kissed me.

And he kissed me for a long time. While he did it, his fingers yanked down my bra and his thumb went back to my nipple, joined by a finger, the rolling sharper, sweeter, infinitely so. It felt more than nice. It was bloody brilliant.

My fingers were in his hair, keeping his mouth to mine. I was kissing him back as my hand pulled his T-shirt from his jeans and explored, taking its time, memorizing with my fingertips the feel of him, silky but solid, just like Max, sweet and strong.

I got lost in his fantastic kiss, in the feel of his skin, his muscle, in the throb between my legs. I didn't notice his hand leave my breast until his hips shifted to my side and his fingers ran over the zipper of my jeans.

"Max?" I whispered against his lips as his hand cupped me between my legs, his fingers pressing in and my hips lifted into his hand as I breathed, "*God.*"

"I wanna touch you, honey," Max said against my neck, his deep voice gruff.

"Okay," I replied instantly, unsure what he meant, seeing as he was pretty much touching me all over already, but I was happy for him to do more of it however that came about.

Max didn't explain and he also didn't delay.

He unbuttoned the button on my jeans and slid down my zipper; then his hand slipped inside. He not only didn't delay, he didn't mess with my panties. He went right in, fingers against wet, sensitive flesh, and the minute he touched me every nerve in my body zapped to life.

"Christ, I like that," Max's voice grated against my skin as his fingers explored.

I couldn't be certain at that moment, since I wasn't thinking all that clearly, but I suspected I liked it a whole lot more.

His mouth came back to mine as his fingers stopped exploring and found the prize. The instant he put on pressure, I moaned into his mouth and my hips bucked against his hand, telling him he'd honed in perfectly and hit the target with delightful precision.

"You like that?" he asked against my mouth.

"Yes," I breathed against his as his finger put on more pressure and started circling. Then I breathed again, "*Yes.*"

It was building fast. He was good, his finger strong, firm, working miracles, and it had been a long time, too long, *ages*.

My hand left his back and slid around his hip to his front, glancing over his crotch, finding him hard and liking that so much I felt a rush of wetness between my legs in response.

He pulled his hips away with a jerk and his hand slid out of my jeans.

"No," I whispered, my eyes flying open when I lost the beauty of his touch.

His fingers circled my wrist and pulled it over my head where his other hand captured it. Then he held it there as his body settled back into me, imprisoning my other arm as it was around his back, my elbow cocked, my hand still in his hair.

"What—?" I started.

His hand slipped back inside my jeans and he muttered, "Not me, baby, you."

"But—" I began again, and stopped when he resumed his play between my legs and I couldn't talk anymore. I could just feel.

"Feels so fuckin' sweet, Duchess," he muttered, his head up. His eyes, always beautiful, were more so now as desire was darkening them.

"Max—" I panted, my hips jerking under his hand, my wrist pulling against his hold, my fingers fisting in his hair. It was building again, fast, too fast and it felt good, too good, sensational.

"When I fuck you, wanna take my time," he told me, his voice hoarse, his gaze never shifting from my face.

I closed my eyes and arched my neck as the glorious pressure intensified.

His finger stopped but then it slid inside.

"*Yes*," I whispered, my eyes still closed.

"Christ, honey," Max growled.

"More," I begged, and he gave it to me, sliding his finger in and out in the space allowed, but it felt good, tight, close, intimate, his thumb hitting me at my sweet spot again, circling as he finger fucked me.

His mouth came to mine as I got close.

"I can't wait to get in there," he muttered, and my mouth opened under his, the moan gliding out as his tongue glided in and I came, hard. Harder than ever before. And longer. So much longer, it felt, for tense, wondrous moments, like it would never end and I didn't want it to.

And it was far more beautiful than anything I'd ever had.

Glorious.

Earth-shattering.

I came down slowly, my body feeling like golden, warm liquid. Sublime. Max kept his hand between my legs, his fingers slipping through my wetness, exploring, gentle, becoming intimately familiar in a way I liked. Tender, sweet, just like Max. His tongue was tracing my lower lip and his hand still held mine by the wrist over my head.

When I opened my eyes, I saw his were open, too, and he was watching me.

"How you feelin'?" he murmured against my mouth.

I felt *great*. And I felt scared out of my mind. And, for some reason, I blurted the latter.

"Scared."

His fingers stopped moving and his hand cupped me as his brows drew together. His head went away an inch and his face filled with puzzled humor.

"What?"

Now what had I done?

"Max," I whispered, "I—"

"Yeah," he interrupted as understanding came to him. It wasn't the correct understanding, not completely, but it was part of it. "You come harder than that when I fuck you, honey, you'll split straight out of your skin."

"Max—"

He kissed me softly and said, "Christ, Duchess, that was fuckin' beautiful."

"Max—"

"I nearly came just watchin' you."

My stomach dipped pleasantly.

"Max," I breathed, but he released my hand, pulled his other out of my jeans carefully, tugged me to my side and into his arms, and his face went into my neck.

"Drenched by the time I touched you, soaked right before you came. Gonna love eatin' you," he said against my neck, and my stomach dipped again, in a plummet this time.

"Max—"

His head came up and he grinned at me so big he looked like he was about to laugh as his arms got even tighter. "Baby, you keep callin' me and I'm right fuckin' here."

He looked at me, waiting for me to speak and I found I didn't know what to say.

Then I found myself saying, "I'm sorry."

His head jerked and his fight with his amusement became far more visible.

Even his voice vibrated with it when he asked, "What?"

"I...um, you didn't...I didn't..." I closed my eyes tight, then opened them and said, "That went really fast."

"Good thing, considerin' we don't have much time."

"But—" I started. He kissed me and I stopped.

"Like that you respond to me that way, Duchess."

"It's that, well, I respond to you—"

He smiled against my mouth. I felt it and I watched his eyes doing it and both were so marvelous, I stopped speaking.

"Oh yeah, you respond to me."

I decided maybe I should stop talking altogether. I didn't have my head or my body under my control and I didn't seem to be able to finish a sentence anyway.

So I dipped my chin, tucked my face into his throat, and slid my arms around his waist.

"How fast can you eat steak?" he asked the top of my head.

"I'm sorry?" I asked his throat.

"You need to make it record time, darlin'. I wanna get home in time to have my turn and I've noticed when you get tired you pretty much slip into a coma."

My head tilted back and I felt my brows come together as I protested, "I don't slip into a coma."

He didn't answer. He just raised his brows in return.

"Last night I drank nearly a bottle of wine by myself," I reminded him.

"Yeah, and the night before?"

"You were with Mindy."

"I walked up here to get Mins a T-shirt about five minutes after you came up and you were dead to the world."

"I was not."

"Babe, you were. I took the ice out of your hand and you didn't even flinch."

I'd wondered where that ice had gone.

I decided my best course of action was to stop talking about this, as it appeared my arguments weren't holding much weight.

I pulled my arms from his waist, put my hands on his chest, and gave a shove, saying, "I need to go get ready."

His head tilted back to look at the clock and his arms got tighter, locking mine between our bodies, rendering them useless.

"We got another twenty minutes," he muttered, and lifted his head. His face disappeared in my neck again as his hand slid over my behind and pulled my hips into his.

My fingers curled into his shirt as I steeled myself against a reaction and I tipped my head back and looked at the clock.

Then my hands flattened on his chest and I cried, "We don't have twenty minutes! I need to start getting ready now."

His tongue slid up my neck to my jaw and then along it before he responded, "You can hurry."

"Max! 'Makeup' and 'hurry' are two concepts that do *not* mix well together."

His head came up and he looked at me. "Then wash it all off. You look just as pretty in the morning as you do right now."

I felt my eyes grow wide in horror at the very thought and declared, "I am nowhere near ready to go Colorado mountain fresh makeup-free like all the natural beauties that seem to populate Gnaw Bone."

He grinned and repeated on a tease, "Colorado mountain fresh makeup-free?"

I decided not to rise to the bait and snapped, "Max, let me go."

I was pretty certain he was still teasing when he asked, "You sure you don't want to hang out in bed for a while and feel each other up?" However, even so, I paused to consider this idea, as it seemed interesting and more than a little appealing.

This was a mistake and I knew it when Max burst out laughing and kissed me quickly before knifing out of bed, taking me with him.

He set me on my feet and I concentrated on mentally solidifying my jellied legs as Max did up my jeans with swift, practiced hands, then curled his fingers around the back of my head, pulling me to him and kissing my forehead.

Then he turned and walked to the stairs, calling, "Want me to bring you a glass of wine?"

It was so very annoying when he was thoughtful.

"Yes," I called back.

"Duchess," he called again when I eventually turned to the bathroom. I stopped and looked to the stairs to see only his torso and head through the railings. "It might be fancy for Colorado but still, wear jeans."

Then he kept winding down the stairs and I was thankful that he told me. I'd hate to be too dressed up. That would be awful.

Still, it was also thoughtful, which again was annoying.

*   *   *

I looked at myself in Max's bathroom mirror, took in all that was me, and whispered, "What on earth are you doing, Nina Sheridan?"

My reflection did not reply, which was a bit frustrating since Charlie had also disappeared and I needed guidance.

I grabbed my empty wineglass from the tiled counter and walked into the bedroom. My eyes went to the clock and saw we were closing in on launch time, so I hurried to my luggage, set the glass on the nightstand, and dug through my bag to find my going-out clutch.

I'd functioned on autopilot getting ready mainly because if I allowed my mind to wander to what happened on the bed, I didn't know what I'd do. My options were to beg Max to call Brody and Mindy and tell them we'd go to The Rooster another night. Find Max and tell him he was good with his hands, his mouth, and other things as well and I was never leaving his house until the day I died. Or put my arms around him and my lips to his ear and admit I was falling in love with him.

As none of those were healthy ways forward, autopilot it was.

However, autopilot took me straight into a new debacle. For I'd washed my face and then applied Nina Going Out makeup, which was heavier, smoky, and likely seriously overdone for the Colorado mountains. I'd also curled my hair, not in curls, but to give it more waves and body. Then I'd slid in a headband made of three thin, gold leather braids that I'd used to pull back my hair softly from my face and I'd separated the braids along my crown to effect a kind of Grecian goddess look.

I'd slipped on my white mesh camisole, which was long, hugged my jeans at the hips (in fact, it hugged me everywhere), and had a low dip in the back. Under, it had a thin, stretchy, white camisole stitched in and on the outside it was covered entirely by little gold sequins.

Again likely overkill for the Colorado mountains but I didn't have anything that was fancy but not *that* fancy. Since I'd brought my strappy, stiletto-heeled gold sandals to go with the top on the off chance I needed something dressy, the only thing I could do to tone down this ensemble was buck the gold in my hair, on my body, and on my feet and I accessorized with nothing but my new silver earrings and Max's ring.

I found my envelope clutch, which was a soft fawn suede, understated and not gold, pulled out my fawn-colored pashmina that had a hint of sheen but wasn't overboard, spritzed with perfume, grabbed my wineglass, and headed downstairs.

"Max?" I called when I hit the bottom, and looked around to see he wasn't in the kitchen or living room.

Maybe he got tired of waiting and he'd gone without me, though I doubted this was the case and decided he was probably doing something Maxish. Chopping wood. Building a barn. Saving a child in distress or climbing a tree to rescue a cat. Stuff like that.

I dropped the clutch and pashmina by my purse on the dining table, walked to the sink, cleaned the glass, set it in the dish drainer, and walked back to my purse.

I'd put on my lip gloss and was filling my clutch with what I needed from my purse when I heard Max walk in from the back of the house.

I turned my head to see he was wearing his black leather jacket and he'd changed his jeans to a pair that was less faded but still faded. He had on a heavy black belt, black boots, and a midnight blue shirt that had wine and dark gray stripes in it.

His thick, dark hair was swept back from his face, and how he got it to do that so perfectly (since I'd looked and found no products in his bathroom) was a mystery.

He looked good enough to eat.

I felt my breasts swell as I watched his eyes hit me and for some reason, when they did, he suddenly stopped.

"Ready," I called with faux breeziness in an attempt to hide my response to his amazingness, and I looked back to the clutch.

I was flipping it closed when I heard his boots on the wood floors and then I felt him get close.

My head came up as his arms circled me from behind, high at my ribs, his hand flattening at the side of my left breast. Then I felt him bury his face in my neck.

I froze.

"All right, Duchess," he growled against my neck, "I won't bitch about waitin' for you to get ready if this is what I get."

The nipples on my swollen breasts got hard as his compliment struck deep.

"Max," I whispered.

"Fuckin' beautiful," he muttered, his nose brushing my ear. That, coupled with his sweet talk, sent a shiver along my skin.

My eyes caught on something sparkly and I focused on our reflection in the window. Max, his face still in my neck, his big body in his dark clothes surrounding me. Me, my light hair, my glittery top, snug and safe in his arms.

I liked what I saw so much, without thinking, my arms crossed and my hands covered his.

"We're going to be late," I said quietly, not able to tear my eyes from our reflection, not able to stop his words from making me warm, not able to call up all the reasons why he was so good, so wonderful, but he was no good for me. I could just call up all the reasons why he was so good and wonderful and got stuck on that.

His thumb moved to stroke the side of my breast and I melted back into him.

"Max, steak. I'm hungry," I lied. I could eat, definitely; there was rarely a time when I couldn't. But I would rather stay standing there in Max's arms maybe for the rest of my life.

His head came up but his arms gave me a squeeze and he kissed my temple before letting me go.

"Steak, yeah," he muttered with obvious lack of enthusiasm. He grabbed my hand, I grabbed my bag and scarf, and he pulled me to the closet.

"Am I too fancy?" I asked, settling my scarf around my neck with difficulty, as I also was holding my clutch in that hand as he opened the door, dropped my other hand, reached in, and grabbed my coat.

He closed the door and his eyes hit me. I stopped breathing under the heat of his stare. Then he gave me a one-word answer.

"No."

He shook out my coat and held it up and I realized he was holding it for me to slide my arms into. I turned my back and did so. He settled it on my shoulders; then his arms came around, his fingers curling around the edges of my coat, and he brought it closer around me. I'd had men help me with my coat but not like that. As with everything Max, he did it far, far better.

He let my coat go, grabbed my hand, and pulled me to the door.

We were standing outside while he locked it when he muttered, "Keep that top close."

"Sorry?" I asked his profile, and he turned to me. Moving fast, all of a sudden he reached a hand out to curl around the back of my head and he yanked me forward so I had to put up both hands to break my fall. I did and they hit the hard wall of his chest.

"That top," he said when he dipped his face close, and I realized his voice sounded funny. It was intense but it was also hoarse like when we were fooling around and I understood why when he again spoke. "Tonight, when I fuck you, I want you naked. Later, I want you ridin' my cock wearin' nothin' but that fuckin' top."

My knees buckled and my fingers curled, the nails of the hand not clutching my bag grazing his chest as they did so and I just stared at him, unable to function mainly because I was lost in his eyes at the same time I was focused on what my body was feeling and I liked both of these things so much there was no room for anything else.

"Babe, you don't move away, Mindy and Brody are gonna eat alone."

"Okay," I whispered, but didn't move.

We both stood there staring at each other, unmoving, in the cold night air on his porch.

His mouth twitched and he murmured his prompt, "Duchess."

I jumped and pulled away, mumbling, "Right."

He slung his arm around my shoulders and walked me to the passenger side of the Cherokee, beeping the locks as he went. He opened my door and waited for me to pull myself in before he closed my door again.

I was buckling up and Max was rounding the hood when I realized he'd helped me with my coat and he'd opened my door.

I was in trouble. Wonder Max was getting even more wonderful, something I didn't think was possible but there it was, all around me.

Drat.

Max got in, buckled up, started the truck, and backed out. We were out of the lane and on our way and I was trying to pull myself together, to remember all the reasons why Max equaled future disaster for me. I'd thought it through at lunch and I remembered I'd been pretty convinced. However, an amazing orgasm and Max's brand of flattery seemed to have built an invisible wall against my mind traveling down that path.

Max's hand found mine and his fingers laced through it, tugging it toward him and again resting the back of it against his hard thigh.

"Brody seems nice," I said into the silence, suddenly wanting it filled so I wasn't stuck in my head.

"He is," Max replied, and shared no further.

"How long have you two been friends?"

"Long's I can remember," Max answered. "He lived next to us while I was growin' up. His mom and dad got divorced; his dad moved away, remarried. His mom remarried, too, had Mindy and his mom and stepdad still live next to my mom."

"Oh."

He let my fingers go but, strangely, turned my hand and pressed the palm into his thigh, curling my fingers around its muscled contour. I pulled in a silent breath at this intimate gesture as he downshifted to take the turn, gained speed and then his hand came back to mine and his fingers laced through.

I understood it then. This was Max's way of telling me he didn't want me to pull my hand away when he had to let me go.

Yes, I was right. Max was becoming more wonderful and I was in trouble.

I swallowed and out of nowhere thoughts assailed me. His sister telling me he was a player. His unfathomable relationship with Shauna. His talented hand between my legs. His inability or perhaps unwillingness to share important facts about his life.

And this last leading me to remember the photograph of him and Anna on their wedding day.

All of this reminding me that Max had once been married and bringing to mind the fact that, for what I deduced was a good while, he had not.

However, it was my guess and Kami's insinuation that he had been busy.

None of which he'd shared with me but all of which he'd demanded I share with him.

"There were pictures in Bitsy's house," I blurted as he stopped at the intersection to the main road. His hand flattened mine on his thigh again and he looked to the left and right, waiting for his opportunity to turn.

"Yeah?" he asked distractedly, and I slid my hand way.

He stopped looking left and right, his head turned to me and his hand shot out and grabbed mine, bringing it back and pressing it against his thigh.

His voice was soft when he explained, "I like your touch, honey."

I left my hand where it was because I liked his explanation probably better than he liked my touch. I did this even though my protective instinct was waking up and it was likely I did it not only because I liked his explanation but also because I liked touching him.

His attention went back to the road, he found his opening, and turned right. After he'd gained our cruising speed, his fingers laced in mine again.

"There were pictures of you," I went back to my topic, and Max's hand squeezed mine.

"Not surprised," Max replied offhandedly. "Bitsy likes photos and I've known her a long time."

"How long?"

"Since school."

"She a friend that long?"

"Yeah."

"There was a picture of you and Curtis Dodd," I told him. "It looked like you were friends."

I thought he'd understand where I was leading with this and maybe share. But he didn't or at least he didn't share the important bits.

"Yeah, we were friends, long time ago. Brody, Curt, and me hung out together in high school. We all played ball."

"Ball?"

"Football."

"Oh."

He said no more and I waited, giving him his opening and he didn't take it.

"What happened?" I asked softly, thinking I knew and bracing for impact.

"Lotsa shit," Max answered. "After school, Curt and me were in business together, construction, small jobs. He wanted to take it in a different direction, the one he took, and he wanted me with him. He was determined and eventually got in my face. I didn't like it, not him gettin' in my face or what he planned to do and I knew the town wouldn't either. I tried to talk him out of it. He didn't listen."

He stopped speaking and I waited again for him to share further.

He didn't.

"But you stayed close to Bitsy," I remarked.

"Yeah," he replied, and he started to move his thumb, using it to stroke the back of my hand.

That felt nice in a way that interfered with my ability to put together the words to tell him I'd seen his wedding photo when Max changed the subject.

"Got an idea."

"An idea?"

"Yeah."

"What idea?"

"Next week, I'll introduce you to George."

"George?"

"Attorney in town, only one we got. Last time I talked to him, he was talkin' about expanding, findin' a partner. All the new folks around, work's pilin' up."

My heart started beating faster and I said softly, "Max—"

But Max kept talking, proving that while my mind was on future disaster, Max's mind was on other things entirely. "Best season to rent the house is winter. The A-frame is in demand, I jack up the rent, and still it's booked solid, back-to-back. Construction dies down in winter, too, jobs less easy to find. You and me can go to your brother's house after Thanksgivin', come back February, March. That enough for you?"

He was planning our future.

And it sounded like a good plan, a thoughtful plan, a generous plan. Max giving me what I needed, time in Charlie's house, time to spend in England, my other home. It was, if we could swing it financially, the perfect compromise.

Even so, I informed him quietly, "Max, we've known each other a week."

His hand squeezed mine and he asked, "And?"

I looked at him and repeated incredulously, "And?"

"Yeah," he replied, not taking his eyes from the road, "and?"

"We barely know each other," I explained unnecessarily.

"Met your dad, heard your history with all those dicks, and your mom likes me," he said, and this was, of course, all true. "Also seen you pissed, sick, sweet, you love my house, and it's fair to say we got chemistry."

"Yes, but—"

"No 'but,' just 'yes.'"

"Yes, but, that's *insane*."

He glanced at me and asked, sounding like he was getting annoyed, "Why the fuck's it insane?"

"Max, we've known each other *a week*," I repeated.

"You like the town?" he asked.

"Yes, it's pretty."

"You like Mindy, Arlene, Cotton, Becca, Bitsy?"

"Of course."

"They like you too."

That, I had to admit, felt nice since I liked them all a whole lot.

However, for sanity's sake, I kept fighting my corner and explained, "Max, you don't make decisions like this on the fly."

His hand tightened in mine and it was so tight it almost hurt.

"So...what? You're sayin' you sit, you wait, you let life slide by while you decide to make the decision you were gonna make in the first damned place and hope to God some shit doesn't happen, like you get in a car accident, lose your legs, or worse, your fuckin' life."

I felt my chest freeze at what I read in his words, so I could do nothing but breathe, "Max—"

He maybe didn't hear me, for he kept speaking. "Say you just lose your legs, then you got the rest of your life to think about all those months you wasted, not livin' it."

That I knew too well.

Still, I whispered, "Max—"

But he knew I knew it and his voice dipped softer. He was still irate but he was attempting to be gentle. "I figure, what you went through with your brother, Duchess, you get it."

"I just got out of a relationship," I explained, latching on to another defense, no matter how lame.

"You didn't just get out of that relationship, Nina, you been out of it for a while. You just recognized you were."

God, it was *so* annoying how bloody *smart* he was.

I yanked at my hand to no avail, so I let it relax but turned to look out the window and suggested sharply, "Let's not talk about this."

"Why? Because you know I'm right?"

I looked back to him and used my words as an accusation, a loud one, a loud one that bounced around the cab. "You're moving too fast!"

"Found somethin' I want. Don't tend to fuck around when that happens, Duchess. Ever."

Although his words made my belly feel kind of squishy in a good way, my mind reminded me he was annoying.

"Perhaps, Macho Mountain Man Max, you'll give me a second to breathe and get my head sorted before I decide to turn my life on a dime. Or would that be asking too much?" I queried sarcastically.

"You don't wanna breathe, babe. You wanna find time to repair your shield to hold me back. Since I'm guessin' I got in more than your pants today, the answer is, yeah, that's askin' too much."

I yanked at my hand, again to no avail, gave up, and snapped, "God, you're so *annoying*."

"You fight with Niles?" Max asked suddenly.

"No."

"Never?"

"No! And stop asking about Niles," I demanded.

He ignored my demand and kept questioning. "Didn't care enough to fight, didn't match you in fire, or was so lazy he just put up with your shit?"

My head shook back and forth, short, angry shakes.

Then I repeated, "My shit?"

"Yeah, babe, your shit."

I crossed my one free arm on my chest. It wasn't much but I suspected it made somewhat of a statement.

"I'm not talking about this."

"That's what I thought," Max said, not sounding annoyed anymore but amused. "All of 'em, didn't care, no fire, and lazy as hell."

I looked out the passenger side window, unable to retort since he was correct, on all counts.

"Poor Nina," Max muttered, lifting my hand in his and I felt his lips against my knuckles before he dropped it back to his thigh and he finished, still muttering, "You must have been bored outta your fuckin' brain."

I turned to look at him and announced, "Regardless of the fact that Brody has been your friend since childhood and you undoubtedly wish for me to make a good impression, I'm giving you fair warning that I am, as of now, officially no longer speaking to you."

This made him burst out laughing. I turned my head away and commenced fuming.

His hand gave mine another squeeze and he said, "Have at it, Duchess. Brody got you the minute you put your arms around Mindy this afternoon. You could probably set fire to the Cherokee in The Rooster's parking lot and Brody'd still like you."

"Don't give me any ideas," I muttered.

"Thought you weren't speakin' to me."

I clamped my mouth shut, tried once more to yank my hand from his, failed, gave up, and continued fuming while Max chuckled, thinking all this was hilarious.

So.

Annoying.

*   *   *

The Rooster was an enormous, beautiful building set high on the side of a mountain, a twisting, windy road leading to it. Its inside lights ablaze, and it had so many windows you could see *through* it.

I had, during the journey, managed to stay true to my vow and didn't speak to Max. For his part, he proved a new way he could be annoying, for this didn't appear to bother him in the slightest. In fact, after five minutes of silence, he let my hand go and turned on his MP3 player, filling the cab with seventies rock music. Good seventies rock music and I noted irately that Max even had good taste in music, something else I decided to find annoying.

I had, of course, taken this opportunity to pull my hand away.

To that, Max had, of course, grabbed my elbow, yanked my arm to him, trailed his hand down it until he caught mine, and pulled it right back.

I didn't fight this. Max was stronger than me and it would just be humiliating when I lost.

Now he had no choice but to let me go in order to park and once the ignition was switched off, I unbuckled my seat belt, opened the door, and jumped down. I then started marching toward the front door of the restaurant as fast as my high-heeled sandals would carry me.

My swift progress was hindered when Max's arm came around my shoulders and he hauled me into his side with such force I slammed against his hard body. My arm automatically wrapped around his waist and, for comfort's sake (I told myself), stayed there. I made no protest and Max said no words. Thus we walked the rest of the way together.

He opened the door for me and I saw the inside was not just windows but also gleaming, light wood, super high ceilings, some well-chosen Cotton prints, some antlers, a lot of comfortable-looking booths both big and small, and not a lot of tables but the chairs weren't restaurant chairs. They were cozy, high-backed armchairs, inviting you to stay awhile.

I decided I liked this place when I spied Mindy and Brody and started to smile, but Max stopped us, his arm curled me toward his front, and his mouth went to my ear.

"Somethin' you should know, Duchess."

I yanked my head back. Max lifted his and I glared at him silently.

He scanned my face, looked into my eyes, and grinned. "When I met you, my first thought was you were very pretty, great fuckin' eyes, but not my type. High-class, which means high maintenance. Then you got pissed and that was it. Even if you hadn't been in that ditch, now you'd still be in my bed. So if you think this attitude is a turnoff, baby, you're wrong."

I didn't know what to do with that, as it gave me nothing to go on, but I didn't have a chance to do anything because Max curled me back to his side and led us to Mindy and Brody.

When we stopped and Max's hands moved to take my coat, I announced boldly, "You should know, Max and I are fighting and I won't be speaking to him throughout dinner. I hope that won't ruin anyone's night."

Mindy's eyes got huge and Brody stared at me a second before he burst out laughing. Max, the jerk, could be heard chuckling behind me. Then he put a hand in the small of my back and pushed me into our booth.

I watched him hand our coats off to a white-shirt, black-pants, long-black-tie, long-white-apron-wearing waitress and then he sat beside me, not delaying in sliding his arm along the booth behind my back. I unwound the scarf from around my neck and tucked it next to me with my clutch when Brody spoke.

"Well," Brody started, still smiling, "this'll make an already rocky evening even more interesting."

"What?" Max asked, and Mindy, sitting on the inside of the booth across from me, leaned forward.

"Kami's here," she whispered.

I leaned forward, too, and whispered back, "Oh my God."

"It's worse," Brody declared. "Shauna's here too."

Mindy nodded to me and I repeated, far more appalled this time, "Oh my *God*."

"And . . . get this!" Mindy said. "Harry!"

"Shit," Max muttered, and it took all my control not to look around the room.

"Where?" I asked Mindy.

"We're the center," Mindy explained. "Kami's at one o'clock, Shauna's at five, and Harry's at nine."

"We're surrounded," I murmured, my voice horrified.

"Yep," Mindy agreed, and sat back.

Max's arm curled around my shoulders, his other hand coming to my jaw, and he turned my body and face to him.

Then he suggested bizarrely, "Feel like makin' out?"

"I'm sorry?" I replied snottily, forgetting from his strange suggestion that I wasn't talking to him.

"It'll piss Shauna off," Max answered. "Kami, too, I figure."

This idea had merit and therefore I considered it.

This was a mistake because Max knew I was considering it. He found this amusing therefore he burst out laughing, pulled me even closer and kissed me hard but not long, doing so even while he was mostly laughing.

His mouth broke from mine and he was spared the edge of my tongue as the waitress returned and asked, "Get you some drinks?"

"Vodka martini, up with an olive and lose the vermouth, please," I ordered. She nodded, bent her head, and scribbled and Max gave me a squeeze, gaining my attention.

"Duchess, you're in altitude."

"And?"

"And you had a glass of wine at home. You gotta be careful with booze when you're not used to altitude."

"I'll be fine."

"You weren't fine when you had a bottle of wine last night. You were out like a light."

"I was tired. It was late. Now it's six-thirty."

"It wasn't late. It was nine at night."

My brows drew together and I asked, "It was?"

"Yeah, honey, it was."

That was news. It seemed a whole lot later.

"Oh," I muttered.

"Take it easy, all I'm askin'," Max said on a squeeze of my shoulder.

"All right," I agreed, and Max turned to the waitress.

"Coors," he ordered. She nodded and wandered away.

"Lucky man, Max, seein' as Nina's silent treatment lasts about two seconds. Most women I know can hold on to it for days," Brody told Max, but his eyes were on me and I could tell he was teasing.

"Not quite, she was silent most of the drive here," Max shared.

"I could never do the silent treatment. I get too wound up," Mindy added.

"What are you two fightin' about anyway?" Brody asked nosily.

"Nothing," I replied immediately.

"Nina movin' here," Max said over my word.

"Max!" I snapped, turning quickly to look at him.

"You're moving here? Awesome!" Mindy screeched very, *very* loudly, and many of the other patrons turned to look.

In fact, when I swept my eyes self-consciously across the restaurant, I spotted Shauna, who, from the look in her eyes, which were glaring ice daggers at me, had heard every word.

As embarrassed as I was, since she was with another man, thus rubbing Harry's nose into her betrayal further, I forced an expression of surprised delight on my face, lifted my hand, and gave her a happy, "Hey, I know you!" wave.

She turned away.

"Christ, you're cute," Max muttered, and I looked at him, then caught Brody and Mindy both turning back from checking out Shauna, Mindy giggling, Brody grinning.

Our menus arrived at that point. Our drinks came not long after.

Kami came after we'd placed our food order and were enjoying a basket of fresh, warm, delicious bread.

She stood at the end of our table, her eyes were locked on Brody, and she said not a word of greeting to her brother, Mindy, or me.

"Brody, you're home," she announced as if Brody brought the black cloud of plague and death to Gnaw Bone upon his dastardly arrival.

"Yep," Brody answered the obvious, but shared no greeting either.

Her eyes came to me and she said, "Nina, congratulations, I see you've made it a week."

I opened my mouth but Max got there before me.

On a sigh, he ordered, "Kami, tone it down."

Kami's eyes went to her brother and she asked in a way that stated she thought I shredded them and doused them with gasoline and set them afire, "Did Nina give you the papers?"

"Yep."

"You talk to Trev?"

"Nope."

"Max," she hissed, and in doing so got his full attention. Or I could say his full, *scary* attention. So scary I couldn't help myself and partially shrank away from him.

"Not gonna tell you again, Kami, that ain't happenin'."

"So, it's up to me to take care of Mom all the time."

"She's not invalid."

"She's a pain in the ass."

"So don't give in to her shit."

"Easy for you to say, and *do*, not bein' here hardly ever."

"Maybe we can talk about this later when I'm not spendin' time with Brody, who I rarely see."

Kami didn't feel like being generous and therefore asked, "You rarely see Mom and me either. Brody more important than family?"

"Yeah, Kami, if Brody walked up to my table at a nice restaurant, said shit to my woman, and got in my face, he wouldn't be too important. Seein' as he don't treat me like dirt, then he is."

Kami's face got red. I took a hasty sip of my martini, thinking I'd need it and my eyes slid to Mindy, who looked pale. Her eyes were wide but she still appeared to be trying hard not to laugh.

Kami appeared to have found a new direction for her ugliness because her eyes came to me and I was glad I had taken that sip of martini.

Then she looked back to Max and asked, "You gonna jerk her around like you did Shauna?"

Mindy gasped. Brody sucked in an audible breath and straightened. Max just straightened.

"Kami, careful. Now you're pissin' me off," Max stated in a tone that underlined his words unmistakably.

"She know?" Kami asked, either not processing or ignoring Max's threat. "She know what you did to Shauna?"

"She knows we were together. She knows now we're not," Max returned. "You wanna carry on this conversation, we'll do it outside."

"You don't want her to know," Kami shot back, and Max slid out of the booth. But Kami's eyes came to me. "Led her on, took her ring shoppin', then scraped her off, givin' her no reason whatsoever. Just ended it." She lifted up her hand and gave a loud snap with her fingers.

"Where'd you hear that shit?" Brody asked, his tone scathing.

"Shauna told me," Kami answered.

"Shauna lied," Max stated, his hand on Kami's arm. "We're finishin' this elsewhere."

She pulled her arm out of his hold and took a step back,

accusing, "Shauna and I have been friends since forever and you treat her like that?"

Well that explained the attitude about Max and his supposed player status. Shauna had fed Kami lies and Kami, being what I knew of Kami, lapped it up.

My eyes went to Mindy and she bugged hers out at me in a "See!" look.

"Kami—" Max began, but she kept talking.

"That'd be like me messin' with Brody's head."

"Like that'd happen," Brody muttered, visibly shivering in revulsion at the thought, and it was my turn to fight back a laugh and I did so by taking another healthy sip of my martini.

Kami gave him a glare, then turned to Max and dealt her death blow. "Or like when you fucked things up with me and Curt."

My head snapped around at this interesting news and I stared at Kami.

"Uh-oh," Mindy muttered.

"Kami, for fuck's sake," Max bit out.

"Christ, Kami, that was twenty years ago," Brody put in.

"Not quite," Kami snapped.

"You wanna do this here, great," Max stated, and crossed his arms on his chest. "Curt fucked things up with you and him, not me. He always wanted Bitsy, Kami, even when he was with you. He got his chance, he took it. Truth hurts but there it is. Curt's dead, Bitsy's broken, and it's time for you to get the fuck over it."

"Bitsy's not broken. She may be stuck in that chair but she'll be rollin' in Curtis's money for the rest of her life."

This utterly nasty comment was when I felt it necessary to intervene. Why, I didn't know, it was insane. But I did it.

"You're a cow," I declared, and her eyes narrowed on me.

"What'd you call me?"

"A cow. We use that expression in England when we're talking about a bitter, whinging woman."

"What's 'whinging'?" Mindy asked on a whisper, and I didn't take my eyes off Kami as I answered.

"Moaning, complaining, nagging, *bitching*. That's *whinging*."

Kami leaned forward and hissed, "The nerve."

"No, nerve is described in England as 'cheek,' otherwise known as audacity or impudence, demonstrated by you walking up to our table and being a *cow*."

"Nina," Max muttered, but he didn't sound angry anymore. He sounded the opposite.

It was Max's sister and if he didn't want me to have a verbal altercation with her, that was his call. I'd said my piece anyway.

So I sat back, drained my glass, and declared, "I need another martini."

"You gave up Shauna so you could end up with the likes of *that*?" Kami asked, gesturing at me.

Kami's comment about Bitsy had been my final straw. Her insult to me was Max's.

"I gave up Shauna because she was fuckin' Curt at the same time she was fuckin' me, hedgin' her bets and tryin' to talk Curt into leavin' Bitsy so she could land him if she didn't manage to land me. And I gave her up because, once she thought she was in, she was mostly a bitch and thought she could lead me around by my dick. She couldn't, she didn't like that, so she got even bitchier. When I finally scraped her off, she latched on to Harry, who she *could* lead around by his dick at the same time spendin' his money and fuckin' around on him. Now, you got your explanation, you got your scene, go sit the fuck down, and I swear to Christ, Kami, you don't leave the drama behind next time I see you, I won't fuckin' see you. Yeah?"

My goodness. Max, I realized, was mostly patient in his Mountain Man way but when he was done being patient, he didn't take any shit either.

"High and mighty, always were," Kami shot back, still raring to go.

Max shook his head. He was done and I knew this because he slid in beside me and looked at Brody, remarking, "Remind me to thank you for this great fuckin' idea. Steaks at The Rooster. Fuckin' brilliant."

"Don't blame me," Brody muttered, grinning.

"Waitress!" I called, lifting up my martini glass when I caught her eye and then circling it around the table, indicating she should bring a fresh round for all.

"I love your top, Neens, I forgot to say," Mindy told me.

"Oh yes, darling, and yours is lovely. I forgot to say that too," I replied.

"And that thing in your hair," Mindy continued. "It's *fab*."

"Thanks." I smiled at her.

Kami emitted an annoyed, unladylike snort and stomped away.

When her lingering malevolent presence wafted away on her heels, Max's arm came around me and he suggested, "Maybe we should put Kami in a room with your dad, see who's the last one standing."

I looked at Max and proclaimed, "Dad would kick her ass."

Max grinned and stated, "Babe, Kami ain't no slouch."

"I can see, still, Dad hadn't given me the good stuff this morning. Probably jetlagged."

Max was still grinning when he muttered, "That ain't good news, Duchess."

"What's this about?" Mindy asked, and Max and I looked at her.

"Nina's dad's a dick," Max answered bluntly.

"What?" It was Brody's turn to ask.

I explained, "My ex-fiancé told my father I was here and my father is concerned about losing the social status he was counting on gaining through my marriage. Therefore my father flew out here to tell me I was making a big mistake. He did so this morning in his uniquely insulting way, managing also to utter slurs against Max, who he doesn't even know before Max had to chase him out of his house. However, he hasn't left town, which means he's at the hotel in Gnaw Bone likely planning to hatch a sinister scheme against Max, me, both of us, the town of Gnaw Bone and all its inhabitants, or maybe even the entire county."

Mindy and Brody both stared silently at me.

"Like I said," Max summed up, "Nina's dad's a dick."

"Wow, you've really had a bad day," Mindy said softly.

She didn't know the half of it.

"Thus me ordering another martini," I replied on a teasing smile.

Max's arm gave me a squeeze but when I looked at him he was looking at Brody. Then he spoke in a tone that could only be read one way and that was extreme approval.

"You should have seen her with her dad this morning, Brody. Christ, she chewed him up and spit him out. Thought I'd have to get out the mop and clean the floor."

Brody grinned but noted, "Bro, not sure that bodes well for you."

"I'm not a dick," Max replied. "I've noticed Nina saves the lethal stuff for bitches and dicks. Me, even pissed, she's tame."

My eyes narrowed on him and I asked, "Tame?"

Max's eyes came to me and he murmured, "Honey, with me, your claws are like a kitten's."

Mindy giggled. Brody chuckled. My eyes narrowed further and our appetizers arrived.

*   *   *

I'd finished martini number two and was enjoying the final sips of the glass of full-bodied, delightful red wine I had with my now-consumed, utterly delicious steak, its accompanying sautéed mushrooms and loaded baked potato after an individual, baked camembert, my appetizer, which was superb, when our next incident hit.

Shauna.

Brody spoke first and he did it the instant his eyes hit her standing at the end of the table.

"Seriously?" he asked disbelievingly.

She ignored him and everyone else. She only had eyes for Max.

"Max, can we talk a second?" she asked politely, her voice unlike it was the night of the buffalo burgers. It was lower, sultry, cajoling.

"Nope," Max replied curtly, and I noted happily he was immune to her sultry cajoling.

She leaned in and said softly, "Honey, *please*."

Even though Max asked me to be careful, I was, unfortunately, slightly inebriated. Therefore when she called Max "honey," I was not in any shape to fully consider my response as in, perhaps not have one at all.

Instead, my happiness about Max's immunity to Shauna melted clean away, my back went ramrod straight, I looked at Mindy, and I asked loudly, "Did she just call Max 'honey' in front of me?"

"Fuck," Max muttered, and his arm wound around my waist, pulling my lower body tight to his.

"I think she did," Mindy whispered, her face again pale and she was watching me closely, likely uncertain whether to jump across the table and hold me down or jump into the fray with me.

I looked at Shauna and told her, "You just called Max 'honey.'"

"I'm sorry, Nina, this'll only take a minute," Shauna said, having decided that she was not a cold, heartless, cheating she-bitch from hell, but tonight she was sugar sweet on the surface, however still unsuccessfully hiding the heartless, cheating she-bitch from hell she was to her core.

"No, it won't take a minute, Shauna, because in one second you're going to walk away."

"Nina, honey," Max murmured.

I threw out a hand, my eyes glued to Shauna, and declared grandly, "I got this."

Max's arm tightened and he said, "Shauna, Nina's unpredictable when riled. Do yourself a favor, take off."

"Max, seriously, this is important," Shauna replied.

"Let's go back to you calling Max 'honey,'" I suggested.

"Nina, again, sorry but I really need a word with Max," Shauna pushed.

"I might have been willing to allow that had you not called him 'honey' right…in…*front*…of…me. Now you'll get one over my cold, dead body," I retorted.

"Baby, calm down," Max said on another squeeze.

"It slipped, habit," Shauna said, the ice-queen frosting her features for a second before she could hide it, her words meant to remind me she'd enjoyed Max, even if just for a while. She fought it back and said, again low and fake sweet, "Sorry, really."

"Apology accepted," I declared magnanimously. "Now, please, we're nearing dessert, the best part of the meal. Don't ruin it."

She looked back at Max and said, "Max, you know I wouldn't bother you if it wasn't important."

"Spit it out, Shauna, and go," Brody ordered, sounding impatient.

She didn't pry her eyes from Max. "It's private. Max, *please*."

Max's mouth got tight as he tired of her game and stated, "We don't share anything private, Shauna."

"Max," she begged, and Max's patience slipped too.

"Honest to God, Shauna, Brody's in town and we're tryin' to have a nice meal. What the fuck?"

She realized she was getting nowhere, so she changed tactics and announced, "I'm pregnant."

The air at our table went static.

I was watching Max, my lungs burning due to the fact I was not breathing, wondering when he'd "scraped her off" and if there was a possibility this child was his as I watched him blink slowly.

Then he growled in his now lethally dangerous, deep, gravelly voice, "Come again?"

"Can we talk privately?" she repeated.

"No, Shauna, why are you tellin' me this shit?" Max asked.

"Because it's Curt's."

"Holy crap," Mindy whispered.

"Jesus Christ," Brody muttered.

"Oh my God," I breathed.

"What the fuck?" Max clipped.

She squatted at the table beside Max and looked up at him.

"Max, you have to talk to Bitsy," she entreated.

"Why in the *hell* would I do that?" Max asked.

"Because this is Curt's baby. Because Curt would have taken care of me, of the baby. He told me so. And because, now, Curt's gone," Shauna explained.

"You have got to be shittin' me," Max bit out and I could tell he was beyond angry. He was building up to enraged and it was my turn to put my arm around *his* waist.

"Can we talk about this privately?" she asked again.

"No, Shauna, fuck, I don't wanna talk about this at all. I don't even wanna *know* this shit."

She shuffled closer and put her hand on Max's knee and my eyes honed in on it as she begged, "Curt would take care of me, you know it. You *know* he would. I can't afford to raise a baby by myself."

"Are you mad?" I asked, and her eyes sliced to me.

"What?" she asked back.

"Mad? Insane? Crazy? Nutty? Bonkers? 'Round the twist? *Mad*?" I explained, my voice rising.

"Of course not," she snapped.

"Then first, get your hand off Max's knee," I snapped back and her hand shot away like Max's skin burned. "Second, trot away and find someone else who might be heartless enough to help you try to fleece Bitsy out of money. You have got to know Max would never do that."

"It's Curt's child and that's Curt's money and Max knew Curt and knows Bitsy and everyone knows Max is fair."

"And you were sleeping with *Curt* when he was married to *Bitsy*," I retorted. "Hard knocks but you live by the sword, Shauna, you must be prepared to die by it."

Her eyes narrowed and the frost started setting in. "What does that mean?"

"That means you played with fire, now you've been burned. Live with it. Now, honestly, just go away."

"This is none of your business," she snapped, standing. The mask slipping completely, now she was staring ice daggers at me.

"Sorry? *I'm* sleeping in Max's bed. They were *my* jeans Max's hand was down tonight. But it was *you* who called Max 'honey,' *you* who put your hand on him right in front of me, and *you* who walked up to our table, interrupting a lovely evening and laying this rubbish on us. So I'm making it my business. Go away."

"We're talkin' about an innocent baby here," Shauna returned.

"We're talking about you still digging for gold even though the vein has run dry *and* having the sheer gall to walk up to Max in a nice restaurant and try to drag him into it!" I shot back.

"What's happening here?" a man asked, and I looked over Max's shoulder with hopes of seeing a manager or someone of that ilk but Harry was standing there.

"Fuckin' A," Brody mumbled.

Max slid out of the booth. "Everything's fine, Harry. Shauna was just leavin'."

Harry ignored Max and stared at Shauna, asking, "Why're you botherin' Max and Nina?"

"Harry—" Shauna was back to her fake sugar-sweet pleading tone.

"Thinkin' you can fuck Nina over like you fucked over Bitsy and *me*?" Harry asked loudly, and I studied him somewhat drunkenly, thinking he was a lot less goofy when he was angry.

"Can we go somewhere private?" Shauna asked demurely.

"No, everyone in the restaurant already knows you're a fuckin' slut. Why would we need to be private about it?"

"Fuckin' A," Brody repeated on a mumble, and also stood. "Harry, man, seriously, let's you and me take a walk."

"Yeah," Harry answered. "We'll take a walk. When Shauna takes a hike."

"Harry," I called. "Why don't you pull up a chair, have a drink with us?"

Harry glanced down at me before his eyes cut back to Shauna. "I'd like that, Nina, and I'll be happy to oblige, soon as Shauna slithers away."

"Is there a problem, Shauna?" The man who was having dinner with Shauna was now there.

"Yikes-o-rama," Mindy whispered, and I gave her a wide-eyed look.

"It's fine, Robert," Shauna replied.

"You should calm down and sit down," Robert unwisely advised Harry, and he did it in a somewhat threatening way.

"Yeah? I should?" Harry asked, still loud. "She fuckin' you now? 'Cause you should know, a week ago she was fuckin' me, Curtis Dodd, and God knows who else."

"As I said, you should calm down," Robert repeated, stepping forward, and Brody brought up a hand to hold him back.

"Boys, this needs to go outside," Max ordered, getting closer to Harry.

"Fair warning, *Robert*," Harry declared. "She'll suck your dick great, but bein' a woman and able to multitask and all that shit, she'll have her hand in your wallet while she's doin' it."

I gasped. Mindy giggled. The manager approached way too late because Robert shook off Brody's hand and advanced, swinging, connecting with Harry's jaw and Harry went flying.

There were some shrieks as Harry landed on a table, taking it down to its side, glasses, plates, and salt and pepper shakers going flying. He righted himself, turned, and charged, bent double. He hit Robert in the belly with his shoulder and took him back six feet into another table. Glasses spilled, plates crashed, and the patrons jumped away as Robert landed, then pushed up. Harry couldn't find his feet, wrapped his arms around Robert, and they both went to the ground, wrestling around, grunting and cursing at each other.

I got up to my knees in the booth to watch them as did Mindy.

This didn't last long. Max and Brody waded in, Max taking Harry by the back collar and jeans, lifting him up to his feet and pushing him off. Brody did the same with Robert, pushing him in the opposite direction.

"Dumbass, motherfucker!" Harry yelled, steak juice, ketchup, and horseradish sauce and what looked like wine, butter, and sour cream on his shirt, Max's hand on his chest, pushing him toward the front door.

"Cool it, Harry," Max clipped, still pushing at his chest, Harry shuffling backward. "Outside."

I watched until the door closed behind Max. Harry turned jerkily toward the front steps, Max's hand came to his upper back, and they walked out of sight. Then I looked the other way and Robert and Brody had disappeared out a glass door that led to a back patio. Shauna, too, had vanished from sight.

"Wow," Mindy breathed, and I looked at her and she smiled bright. "Neens, babe, you're a *totally* fun date."

I grinned shakily at Mindy. Something caught the corner of my eye. I lunged to the side, grabbed our scuttling waitress by the wrist, and asked, "I know you've got cleanup but when you get a chance, can I have an amaretto on the rocks? A *big* one."

"Sure," she muttered distractedly.

"And you have one too," I told her. "Put it on our bill."

Her eyes focused on me and she said, "Hey, thanks."

I waved my hand, got off my knees, and sat on my behind. "No problem," I muttered, taking a deep breath and looking at Mindy. "You think we'll ever go out without the night ending in men fighting?"

"This one was more fun than the last," Mindy commented.

"Yes, this is true," I agreed.

"Still, it might get old," Mindy said on a smile.

"This is true too."

"I've never had amaretto. That isn't a big seller at The Dog. Should I try one?"

"You have to taste amaretto before you die," I informed her, my words dramatic but they were also true.

"Then that's a yes."

I smiled at her. She smiled back.

*   *   *

"My favorite part"—we were all standing beside the Cherokee, me swaying slightly and Brody was reminiscing about our night—"was when Nina told Shauna she was in your bed and your hand was down her jeans. That was fuckin' *awesome*."

"Say good night, Brody," Max ordered.

Brody grinned. "Just sayin'."

"I liked it when Nina came up with all those words for crazy," Mindy added, also feeling like waxing poetic about our fun-filled evening. "I didn't even know there *were* that many words."

"I forgot barking," I informed Mindy.

"I *so* have to live in England. You all talk *killer*," Mindy exclaimed.

"And barmy," I went on.

"Cool!" Mindy cried.

"And loopy, batty, and crackers," I carried on.

Max opened the passenger side door and his hands went to my hips. "Say good night, Nina."

"'Night!" I called when Max's hands turned my body toward the door and then lifted me up so I had no choice but to crawl in.

"'Night, Neens!" Mindy called back.

"Yeah, Neens, later. Max, bro, be safe," Brody said.

"Always," Max muttered, and slammed my door.

Max disappeared from the window but suddenly Mindy was there. I smiled at her through the window, then saw her flatten her hand on it. I lifted my hand and flattened it against hers. She gave me a funny little smile that I didn't quite understand before her hand disappeared and she walked away.

I hummed while I fastened my seat belt and Max got in beside me. My mind was on Mindy being so very sweet as well as the baked, marble cheesecake I most recently consumed, washing it down with amaretto.

"In a good mood?" Max asked, starting the truck.

"I love Mindy," I announced.

"Figure she loves you, too, Duchess. You're a match made in hell."

I didn't really listen to his words. I just kept talking. "That cheesecake was *yummy*."

"You blitzed?" Max asked, his hand on the back of my seat, his torso twisted to look out the rear window to pull out.

"I'm tipsy, not blitzed."

Max twisted back and pulled into the road. "What chance I got you won't pass out on the way home?"

I waved my hand in front of me and declared, "Oh, I'll be fine."

"Right," Max muttered.

"Can we listen to music?" I requested, and Max turned on the music.

Five minutes later I was dead to the world.

CHAPTER EIGHT

Concoctions

"OH...MY...GOD! I *love* your *house*!" I heard my mother cry.

I blinked away my weird dream into the morning sunlight shining into Max's loft and I saw his empty pillow. Why I was dreaming about my mother, I didn't—

"And *you're gorgeous*!" she exclaimed.

My heart stuttered and my eyes went wide.

"No," I whispered, threw the covers back and stopped dead when I saw my body. I was naked except for a pair of white lace panties.

My mind flew back to last night, waking up in Max's arms as he carried me from the car to the house. Me telling him I'd be okay to walk. Him putting me on my feet at the foot of the spiral staircase. Me stumbling up, taking off all my clothes but my underwear and my shoes, and falling facedown in bed.

And that was it.

Oh.

My.

God.

"*I love it here!*" my mother shrieked, the sound jerking my mind from my dismaying thoughts and my body into motion. "Steve, I want to move here."

I heard male mumblings but I'd located Max's shirt from last night on the floor and snatched it up. I shrugged it on, buttoning it at the same time I was running across the room and down the stairs.

I hit the bottom and saw Mom standing, looking out the window, her arms up and straight out at her sides as if she were calling to the mountain sun god to shine his blessing on her. Max was standing a few feet away from her, smiling, wearing nothing but his pajama bottoms. Steve was standing as close to her side as he could get with her arms spread wide, also smiling. Steve's smile was indulgent to Max's entertained.

"God's country!" Mom declared loudly.

"Mom, what on earth?" I asked, walking toward them, and Mom whirled.

"Neenee Bean!" she screeched, and rushed up to me, throwing her arms around me and giving me a fierce hug.

I forgot to be shocked by Mom's surprise visit when I felt her arms around me. Mine went around her and I hugged her tight.

"This feels good," I whispered into her hair.

"Oh yes, sweetie, the best," Mom whispered back.

I felt her hands gather up my hair and she pulled away, holding my hair at the back.

"I like your hair this long," she observed, her eyes doing a Mom Scan.

"Thanks, you look good," I observed, my eyes doing a Daughter Scan. I saw Mom looked fit and healthy, her skin tan, her hair perfectly dyed the blonde she declared she'd never let go and pulled softly back in an attractive, mature-lady's ponytail at her nape. Her turtleneck and slacks were trim, neat, and fashionable.

All pure Mom.

"Swimming three times a week, gardening, golf, and a good diet. And you have to moisturize, Neenee Bean, day and night. Don't forget."

"I don't."

"I know, sweetheart, your skin is *flawless*, always was. Though, Nina," she admonished, her eyes narrowing on my face, "you shouldn't go to bed with your makeup on. If I taught you nothing, I taught you *that*."

"You wanna let the big, bad stepdad get a hug in or are you gonna keep her all to yourself?" Steve's rumbly voice asked from close, and I stepped back and looked up at him.

Steve was big and tall, had gone only slightly soft, not losing his lean physique or his broad shoulders. His hair was all gray and he didn't care most likely because it was a thick, silvery gray and it suited him. Unlike Mom, who was dressed for lunch with the girls, Steve was wearing jeans, comfortable walking shoes, and a flannel shirt. He'd been a maintenance engineer and before he retired he'd supervised a complex of eight buildings.

He was also a lovely man.

"Hi, Steve," I said, and slid into his arms for one of his deep, tight, bear hugs.

"Good to see you, doll," he said to the top of my head.

"You too, Steve."

"Oh!" Mom cried, and Steve let me go so we could turn to her but he kept an arm around my shoulders. When we faced Mom, we saw she was addressing Max. "Once we get to know each other, I'll get to hug *you*."

It was then I remembered to be shocked by Mom's surprise visit. And at that moment, I added horrified.

"Mom!" I snapped, and she turned to me.

"I get to do it when he doesn't have a shirt on too. I'm calling it now," Mom declared.

"Speakin' of that," Max muttered, grinning broadly but heading to the stairs, "I'm gonna get dressed." He looked at me when he passed and said, "Babe, can you start coffee?"

"Um...yes," I replied.

His eyes dropped to my shirt and I caught them darkening before he turned his head away and went up the stairs.

"Nina, sweetie, this house, that view, that *man*. My *God*!" Mom cried.

"Nellie, darlin', this place is open plan. Max can hear you," Steve informed her.

"So? We're all family now. He'll have to get used to me," Mom decreed madly, and marched toward the kitchen. "I'll make coffee, rustle up breakfast. Neenee Bean, you go wash your face and *moisturize*."

I was still swaying from the force of Mom's "we're all family now" statement, so my protesting words were weak. "Mom, I'll get coffee and maybe we should meet in town for breakfast or something and you can tell me then what you're doing here."

"Oh, *tosh*!" Mom was in the kitchen, opening and closing cupboards. "That'll take too long. We'll have breakfast here," she declared. "I'll make pancakes. No! My famous scrambled eggs. Max strikes me as an egg man."

I decided speaking was giving my mother fodder to embarrass me further, so I grinned at Steve, ducked under his arm, and rushed to the stairs, saying, "I'll be back down in a second."

I hit the loft as Max came out of the bathroom wearing a dark blue henley thermal and jeans and I stopped dead.

"I'm so sorry," I whispered loudly.

Max got close and tilted his head down to me. "Yeah? Why?"

"My mother's...she's...well, my mother." I was still whispering.

"Heard the knock, honey, expected to see your dad at the door. Damn better sight seein' your mom smilin' and wavin' and jumpin' up and down."

I closed my eyes as the vision of Mom doing that, and she would do it, filled my head.

I felt Max's hands on my neck and he called, "Duchess."

I opened my eyes and repeated, "Sorry."

He used my neck to pull me closer. "Only thing you got to be sorry for is passin' out on me last night. Though, baby"— I watched up close as his eyes got warm—"you passin' out naked but leavin' on those fuckin' sexy shoes and now wearin' my shirt makes up for it."

"What?" I was lost in his eyes. I couldn't process words especially since his words were mostly scary.

"Not all of it, but it helps."

"What?" I repeated, still coping with the shocks of my morning and, of course, Max's warm eyes.

He got even closer and whispered, "Gonna fuck you in that shirt too."

I processed *that*.

"And those shoes," he went on as if deep in his thoughts. "Though, not at the same time."

My knees buckled and my hands shot up to grab Max's waist in order to stay standing. I found hooking my thumbs in his belt loops at the sides worked really well and I realized why he'd used that on me, though, obviously, his was different.

"You got any sisters?" Max asked for some reason, and I shook my head. "Brothers other than Charlie?" he went on, and I kept shaking my head. "Cousins?"

"Some of those," I whispered.

He grinned. "So is that who we can expect tomorrow?"

My cousins were as nutty as my mother and if she made calls to my aunts, who were also loons, this could be a possibility. Therefore, instead of answering, I fell forward and pressed my face into his henley.

"See I got mostly Nina Zombie," Max said, his lips at my hair. "Get yourself sorted out, darlin'. I'll go down and see that your mother doesn't move into the barn."

My head shot back and I whispered, "Oh God, Max, don't tell her you have a barn. Seriously, she'll consider it. She'll have contractors here tomorrow to talk about a conversion."

He was still grinning when he kissed me, pulled away, and stated, "My lips are sealed."

Then he let me go and walked to the stairs.

I ran to the bathroom and rushed through my morning ritual and didn't bother dressing because I didn't want to leave Max alone with my mother that long. And anyway, Max's shirt provided far more coverage than my nightie or even one of his T-shirts and it was Mom and Steve. Mom and Steve lived in Arizona now, so Steve had been seeing me in pajamas and bathing suits ever since he was promoted to "companion" status.

I ran down the stairs, rolling the sleeves up, and heard Mom banging away and talking at the same time.

"...then she got in a debate, with the *quizmaster*, on *television* and took him to task for his superior, sexist attitude."

Oh my *God*. Mom was sharing the Dreaded High School Brain Team Story.

"Mom," I cut in.

"Quiet, sweetie, I'm telling Max the Brain Team Story."

I hit the kitchen, seeing Max was at his usual place against the sink, Steve was at a stool, and Mom was at the counter surrounded by what looked like everything in Max's cupboards.

I had no time to ask about Mom's apparent surprise kitchen inventory. I had to stop the Brain Team Story.

"I know, Mom, and I wish you wouldn't."

She stopped and looked at me with raised brows. "I'll never know why you're embarrassed by that story."

"How many reasons do you want?" I asked.

"Three!" Mom shot back.

I lifted my hand and counted them down. "One, I did it on local television and everyone saw. Two, I was kicked off the Brain Team and suspended from school. And three, I was on the Brain Team *at all*."

"Men like smart girls," she retorted.

"Yes, that's what you told me when I didn't have a date to the senior prom."

She leaned forward and returned, "You didn't have a date to the senior prom because that silly Flannery boy broke up with you for that terrible Sipowicz girl." Mom turned to Max and added, "She had too much hair, always flouncing it around, and she was *loose*."

Mom spoke the truth. Perry Sipowicz had a lot of hair she was always flouncing around and she definitely was loose.

"Anyway"—Mom turned back to the counter and started moving stuff around randomly—"I was proud of my Neenee Bean for sticking up to that *awful* television person. He thought he was *God's gift* and everyone could see he was wearing a hairpiece. And he *was* being sexist. He wouldn't let Nina answer any of the questions and she was the only girl on either school's team. So I was *glad* she told him off." She turned back to Max and finished, "It was then I knew she'd make a brilliant attorney. She got into *every* school she applied to."

"Mom," I said, moving toward the coffeepot. "Enough."

"You did," Mom muttered, looked at Max and repeated, "She did."

I looked at Max and rolled my eyes. Max smiled.

I asked the room, "Who wants coffee?"

"Me!" Mom cried as if I wasn't standing right next to her, which I was.

I looked over my shoulder at Steve, pulling down mugs from the cupboard. "Steve?"

"A cup would hit the spot, Nina."

I looked at Max as I went to the fridge for milk. "Max?"

"Yeah, baby."

Mom leaned into me when I made it back to the counter by her side and she whispered loudly even though if she whispered softly Max could still hear her, as he was maybe two feet away. "I like that. The 'baby' thing. He's yummy."

"Stop calling Max yummy in front of Steve."

"Oh, Steve doesn't mind," Mom dismissed with a wave of her hand.

"Okay, then stop calling Max yummy in front of *Max*."

Mom leaned back to look behind me at Max and informed him, "Nina can be a bit uptight."

Max burst out laughing.

I cried, "Mother!"

Mom turned wide eyes to me. "You can!"

I looked to the ceiling and called, "God? Can I have a time machine? Please. I just want to go back thirty-five years, crawl out of my pram, get lost in the wilds, and be raised by stray dogs."

Mom leaned back and said to Max, "She can also be dramatic." She turned back to whatever she was doing at the counter and murmured, "Though, it's good. She's always had an *excellent* imagination."

I handed Max his mug and took Steve's coffee to him, saying, "Mom, Max likes me, okay? You don't have to convince him, seeing as I'm standing in his kitchen in his shirt."

"All right," Mom snapped, and looked back at Max. "She can get testy too."

I closed my eyes and dropped my head back. I stood there in supplication for half a second before an arm hooked at my waist and my back was up against Max's front.

"Grab your coffee, Duchess, and let your mom be," Max ordered in my ear.

I leaned forward and grabbed my coffee, muttering, "Whatever." Then I looked at Mom and found I couldn't let her be, so I asked, "What are you doing, anyway?"

"I'm in the mood to concoct something," Mom answered, and my entire body got tense.

"Mom—" I started, and Steve was with me, for he said in a low warning tone, "Nellie, not sure that's a good idea."

"My concoctions are the best," Mom declared in Steve's direction.

"Your concoctions are hit and miss. Mostly miss," I told her.

Mom whirled on me, aghast. "You *loved* my blueberry rhubarb soufflé."

"Mom, I *lied*. It tasted a lot like vomit."

Max's body started shaking against mine but I was forced to ignore it when Mom emitted an outraged gasp.

"It did *not* taste like vomit!"

"Please, just let me make toast."

Mom, if it could be believed, was even more aghast and she cried, "What will Max think, he gets toast?"

"It's his house, Mom, *you're* the guest," I reminded her.

"I'm the mom in *any* circumstance and children don't get toast. *Ever.*"

"She's got you there, Duchess," Max whispered.

I twisted and looked up at Max. "You're not a child, Max."

"As long as we're alive, you're always children, doll," Steve put in. I looked at him and my shoulders slumped.

But I didn't give in gracefully and therefore mumbled, "Ganged up on."

"Deal with it, sweetie," Mom muttered, then turned to the plethora of foodstuffs on the counter and went on, hands up, wiggling her fingers. "Now, I'm thinking...something *strawberry.*"

I decided to take a sip of coffee and let events unfold without my participation.

It was then I realized I was leaning against Max and he still had his arm around my waist. It wasn't weird or uncomfortable. In fact, it felt natural and entirely comfortable. It was also then I realized I liked this.

"Oh my *God*!" Mom suddenly shouted. I jumped and looked at her to see she was holding up the new creamer I bought Max. "This is *divine*, Max. You have *such* good taste."

"Nina bought that for me," Max informed her, and Mom's eyes got happy wide, her face beaming, and she looked at Steve.

"You hear that, Steve, darling? Nina bought Max a creamer." And Mom said this like she would say, "You hear that, Steve, darling? Nina just declared her undying love to Max and they're going to be surgically attached at the hip tomorrow."

"I heard it, love," Steve said, grinning at Mom's obvious happiness, for it was doubtful Steve was thrilled about the creamer.

"Lovely," Mom muttered, and put down the creamer and then started opening and closing cupboards, still muttering when she said, "Now, bowls."

"Max," Steve called. I looked to him and I suspected Max did, too, for Steve kept talking. "I hate to cut into the usual madcap Nellie-Nina reunion but we gotta talk about that jackass Lawrence."

There it was, the reason for their visit, just as I would have guessed if I'd had time to make a guess.

Mom was dumping stuff into a bowl but she leaned into me and stated, "Steve has a plan. Steve always has a plan." Then she winked at me and went back to dumping stuff in the bowl.

"What're you thinkin'?" Max asked.

"I'm thinkin' after breakfast we leave the women up here and go down the mountain and have a talk with Lawrence at his hotel."

My body got tense again.

"Works for me," Max said instantly.

"Um...I don't—" I started, but stopped when Max squeezed my waist.

"We'll be back, less than an hour," Max told me, and I twisted to look at him.

"Max—"

"Duchess," Max cut me off, "it's as good as done."

I hadn't had time to contemplate my predicament, my escape or to scrutinize the fact that I consistently seemed to allow myself to get thwarted and end each day in bed with Max. However, I was relatively certain that I didn't want Max to team up with Steve to send my father packing. I didn't know why. I just thought that was family business and Max wasn't family. And I didn't know why, but I thought if he *did* do this, he'd be that one step closer to *being* family. What I did know was that I *wanted* him to be family and I also knew I shouldn't.

"Max, can we talk about this?" I asked.

"We can, though you ain't gonna change my mind."

"Max—"

He used his hand at my waist to turn me to face him. Then his arm went back around my waist and pulled me close.

"Let me explain somethin', Nina. He's in town and he's

thinkin' about fuckin' with you. You said your piece yesterday, made your point clear, and he still thinks he can fuck with you. A man's any man at all, no one fucks with his woman, not even her father. He thinks he can, until I make it clear he can't, he'll always think he can. So better now than later he learns he can't. Yeah?"

"Max, I just don't think it should be you. Maybe I—" I stopped talking when I got another squeeze.

"Honey, he showed you zero respect yesterday and he upset you. You think I'm gonna let that happen again?"

"Max—"

"I'm not."

"Max—"

"He won't have a choice but to show me respect."

"Max—"

"Especially if I got your family at my back."

"Max!" I shouted.

"What?"

"All right, go see Dad."

There it was. I gave in again. I had no idea why I constantly did this, except perhaps the soft look and beautiful smile Max was giving me now.

To avoid it and its effect on my entire system, I turned within Max's arm and leaned against him again.

"Steve, when we get back, could use your help hangin' the Cotton," Max said to Steve, and I closed my eyes.

Steve was always busy, always doing something, always had a project. He'd *love* helping Max hang the Cotton.

"Sure thing, Max," Steve said amiably. I heard Mom sniff and looked at her but she had her head ducked.

Then she whispered, "Powder my nose."

Then she rushed away as Max called gently, "Door to the right, under the loft."

I sighed because I knew Mom was crying and I had a suspicion Mom had a lot more reasons to like Max now.

I looked at Steve and Steve was watching me. His eyes

dropped to Max's arm at my waist and came back to my face. His smile was slow and so was his wink.

I smiled back even though panic gripped me.

If I was honest, I knew why I didn't escape, even though I knew I was facing disaster.

Because I didn't want to escape.

Now, Mom and Steve might disown me if I tried.

I sighed and leaned farther into Max and his arm got tight.

I took a sip of coffee while the men stayed comfortably silent.

Then I asked, "Do you think we have time to sneak in some toast before she gets back?"

My timing was bad and Max's excellent construction foiled me, for Mom had opened the door and its noiseless hinges were my undoing.

"I heard that," Mom snapped, rounding the counter.

"No," Max answered my question, and Steve laughed.

I sighed again and took another sip of coffee.

"Not to be rude or anything, Max," Mom started when she hit the counter. "I adore the Cottons but I must say that piece of art you have out front is ... um ... how do I put it?" She paused, then finished in a tone that belied her word, "*Interesting.*"

My eyes went outside and I saw my vandalized rental car.

Then more than likely from stress, mild hysteria, and just Mom being Mom, I burst out laughing.

*   *   *

Max's phone rang after I walked out of Max's bathroom, dressed, made up, hair done and ready to face the day.

Max and Steve left to talk to Dad after "breakfast," which tasted mostly of strawberries, thank God, but the rest of it didn't bear thinking about. Mom said she'd clean the kitchen so I could get a shower. I left her to it and now was done and Max's phone was ringing.

I had no idea what to do, whether Max would want me to answer and take a message or if maybe it *was* Max, calling me to tell me he was in jail because my father was a big jerk and pushed him to lose control and Mom and I had to come down and post bail for him and Steve.

As I was making up my mind, the answering machine, which was at the rolltop but could be heard throughout the house, switched on. I heard Max's voice order, "Leave a message," there was a beep, and Bitsy's voice could be heard.

"Max? It's Bitsy. Listen, I was hoping you'd be home. You aren't answering your cell. I wanted to talk to Nina, could you ask her to..."

I ran to Max's nightstand and picked up the cordless, hitting the ON button and I heard the noise of the answering machine beeping off.

"Bitsy?" I said into the phone.

"Oh, Nina. Hi."

"Hi, sorry, I just got out of the shower."

"That's okay." She was silent for a moment; then she asked, "Is Max there?"

"No, do you want me to have him call you?"

"No, uh"—she paused—"really, I wanted to talk to you."

I wasn't sure how to react to this, so I gave myself a second and walked to the railing. I looked out and saw Mom sitting outside on the front steps, her legs stretched out in front of her crossed at the ankles, her hands back behind her, body resting on her hands, face tipped to the sun. It must be another warm day and the snow was fast disappearing.

Then I said, "Sure, Bitsy, what can I do for you?"

"It's just that, uh...Harry came by. He told me about last night."

"Oh."

"And, uh, so did Brody. He told me about last night too."

It must have been a busy morning for Bitsy.

"Oh. Yes, well, it was an interesting night," I said to her.

"You should know, Shauna lied to Kami. Max never took Shauna ring shopping."

"Oh. Okay."

"He, well, I don't know why he hooked up with her. She's

gorgeous, of course, and I don't think she ever showed him her, you know, true face until, you know, they got together."

"Bitsy," I broke in softly, hearing her hesitation, knowing it had to be hard to talk about the woman who'd been sleeping with her husband in her bed when her husband was murdered. "You don't have to talk about this."

"I know," she replied softly then suddenly asked, "Your brother lost his legs in the army?"

This hit me hard and I sucked in a breath. How she knew this, I didn't know. Could be Max. Could be Mindy. Could be Mindy telling Brody who told Bitsy.

It didn't matter. She knew. So I said, "Yes, Bitsy, Charlie lost his legs."

"Brody says Mindy says you looked after him."

So it was Mindy/Brody.

"Yes," I answered.

"So, I think…" She paused, then said on a rush, "You'd get me."

"I'm sorry?"

She was quiet a moment, then said softly, "No one gets me, Nina."

I walked backward to the bed, feeling my way with my feet, and when I hit it, I plopped down.

"Bitsy, I don't know," I said honestly.

"I know what happened to Charlie, Nina," Bitsy said gently. "So I know you'd get me."

I felt tears hit my eyes at what she was saying and I whispered, "Bitsy."

"I had my moments, Nina. It's terrible to admit but I understand Charlie."

I swallowed and whispered, "Okay."

"I'm sorry for you and for him."

"Thanks." I was still whispering.

"But my husband was fooling around on me," she whispered back. "And I don't blame him because, you know, the way I am. But I have to talk to *someone* about it. Someone who *gets* me."

I heard the tears in her voice when she stopped talking, so I said, "Oh, sweetheart."

"And you also get what it's like to have Shauna involved, seeing as she was after my man and she's after yours too."

"I'm not sure Max is my man."

"Oh, he is. Never seen him like that with anyone except Anna."

I sucked in a silent breath and my body locked.

She kept speaking. "The whole town's talkin' about it. We're all real glad. Thought Max'd never find anyone after Anna died. It's been ten years. That's a long time. Lord knows, I know that."

I couldn't think of her open talk about Anna. I had bigger things coming at me from her words.

It seemed now I was up against my own idiocy, my mother, Steve, and the whole town of Gnaw Bone. My only ally was my father and right then Max and Steve were running him out of town.

I wasn't in trouble. I was screwed.

"Bitsy—"

"Brody told me all you've done with Mindy, and I gotta say, I'm glad you're nice. Anna was my best friend and I loved her. She'd want Max to end up with someone nice."

Yes. Screwed.

"I don't know what to say. Um...thank you."

"Thank me for you bein' nice?" She had a smile in her voice.

"Yes, I guess, and thank you for trusting me to talk to."

She was quiet for long moments before she asked, "Do you think I'm crazy not to be mad at Curt?"

"I can't say you're crazy for anything you feel right now."

"These past ten years, even though...you know." She stopped and I didn't know but I didn't get the chance to ask before she went on. "I wasn't much of a wife."

I thought this was hideous if Curtis Dodd made Bitsy feel that way but I didn't tell her that.

"Things are hard, when this happens, on everyone," I told her.

"He loved me. People don't get that. We had a good marriage, considering. We were…uh…you know"—she hesitated—"*active* that way. It's just that it wasn't the same as, you know…Shauna could do." When I didn't respond, she repeated, "You know?"

"Of course," I said, thinking I kind of knew but mostly I didn't and I said a little prayer of thanks for that.

"And he's a man," she went on, defending her husband.

"Well, that explains a lot," I told her, and she gave a short laugh.

"Yeah."

"Bitsy, darling," I said. "You should feel free to feel how you want and don't think of what people think."

"No one liked him anyway. He died and his mistress phoned the police. It's hard not to think of what people think since everyone's thinkin' somethin'."

"Well, try. Anyone who truly cares about you will let you have your feelings, whatever they may be."

She was silent a moment, letting this sink in. Then she said, "Yeah."

"Do you want me to come and visit with you? My mom's here and she loves coffee. She'd really like one of your lattes. She's also a really good listener."

"Your mom's here?"

"Well, my dad came and he was being, well, my dad, which means he was being a jerk to me and to Max. I told my mom and Mom, being a mom and in particular, *my* mom, who's a little nutty, decided to bring her husband and have him help Max take care of Dad. So she's here, my stepdad Steve's here, and Max and Steve are in town probably threatening Dad and maybe earning themselves a lawsuit."

"Good thing you're a lawyer," she said, again sounding like she was smiling.

Well, there it was again, news traveled fast.

"Hey, speaking of that, would you help me draw up my

will?" she asked. "George is covered in work but he's read-ing Curtis's tomorrow and he said I should have one drawn up straightaway after Curt's is read. He wants to do it for me but says it may take a while because he has some big case pending, so he referred me to a guy next town over but I know him and he's a weasel. I'd rather you help me do it."

"Bitsy—"

"I'll pay you."

"It isn't that."

"What is it?"

"Um…" I tried to think of what it was but when I couldn't, I said, "Nothing. Sure, I'll be glad to help."

"It'll be easy. Just wanna make sure Shauna never gets her hands on any of it."

"Bitsy—"

Bitsy's voice got low and I realized Brody *really* shared when she said, "The kid's Curt's, I'll put some money aside for him to get when he comes of age. Till then she can blow."

And there it was. Bitsy was a good woman, through and through. She was also a woman scorned.

"Okay, darling, we'll tie it up tight," I assured her.

"I want a DNA test, though."

"Okay."

"Maybe three. Who knows who she'd fuck to get the test results back that she wants. We may need to go out of state."

It was my turn to talk through a smile. "Might be a good idea."

"Maybe you know someone in England. She's never been to England. Would better our chances, seein' she's been outta state."

I laughed and heard Bitsy laugh too.

I also heard the front door open and Mom call, "Neenee Bean, let's go hiking!"

"Be down in a sec!" I called back.

"That your mom?" Bitsy said in my ear.

"Yes."

"You can come over, bring her, too, anytime you want. Just give me a call, 'kay?"

"Okay."

There was a hesitation, then, "Thanks, Nina."

"Bitsy?"

"Yeah."

"You just give me a call, too, anytime. Here at Max's or I'll give you my cell, but it's an international number so—"

"Honey, I'm loaded. Haven't you heard?" I laughed again and she said, "I got a pen and paper right here. Sock it to me."

I gave her my number, she read it back, and then I offered, "Anytime, Bitsy, okay?"

"Thanks, Nina."

"No, Bitsy," I said softly, the tears hitting my eyes just as I fought them back. "You don't know how many times I tried to get Charlie to open up to me. So thank you again for trusting me."

"Oh, honey," she laughed, "my pleasure. I'll lay all my troubles on you, you like it so much."

I laughed back, which helped the tears subside and said, "Take care."

"Yeah, you too. Hope to see you soon."

"Bye."

"Later, honey."

"Who was that?" Mom asked, and I looked to see her standing at the top of the stairs.

"A friend of Max's," I told her, hitting the OFF button and vaguely hearing the answering machine beep again.

"Sounded like a friend of yours."

I sighed because there it was again, Max, his friends, and the whole town sucking me in.

"Well, I guess now she's a friend of mine too."

Mom grinned and walked into the room, threw herself on the bed, and bounced.

"This room is *divine*," she remarked, throwing out a hand. She looked at me. "Tell me all about your new friend."

"Well...I can't believe I'm going to say this but it involves murder."

Mom leaned forward and her eyes got wide. "No kidding? Do tell!"

I stood up and took the phone back to its charger. "Let's get coffee."

"Okay, bring mine up here. I feel like lounging," she said, and rolled to her back.

"I thought you wanted to hike?" I asked.

Mom gave me a look, lifted up a leg, and showed me a slender foot in a strappy sandal. "In these shoes?" she asked back. I smiled and she finished, "Temporary Colorado insanity."

"Your wish, Mom, my command," I replied, leaning into her, kissing her forehead. I then walked to the stairs to get my mom coffee.

I took it back up to her and we lounged on Max's bed and I told her about rape, parking lot fisticuffs, restaurant wrestling, ice queens, sweet and wise twenty-four-year-old girls, mountain men, and murder.

*   *   *

"Oh my *God*," Mom breathed, standing by my side on Max's porch, staring at Cotton walking up the steps. "Is that *Jimmy Cotton*?"

"How do you know what Jimmy Cotton looks like?" I asked her.

"Internet," she whispered, making her "I don't *do* e-mail and Internet" even more of a lie, her eyes still glued to Cotton and she appeared to be swaying.

"She swoons, Cotton, you're the male in this scenario. You've got to catch her," I told Cotton as he stopped in front of me.

"She wears fancy clothes, like you," Cotton observed, giving Mom a once-over and giving me further evidence that my shopping with the goal to blend in during my Colorado adventure had failed.

"She's my mother," I replied.

"I can see it," Cotton remarked.

"Oh my *God*," Mom breathed, staring at Cotton and looking like she was either going to faint, drop into a curtsy, or throw herself into his arms.

Cotton looked at me and asked, "She say that a lot?"

"Twice as much as me and I say it *a lot*, a lot." Or these days, I did in my head, but I didn't share that with Cotton. I just told him, "She introduced me to your work. She's a fan."

"No kidding," Cotton mumbled, and I smiled. "Came by to see where you two hung the pictures," Cotton told me, dipping his head toward the house.

"They're hanging them today. My husband is *helping*," Mom shared, sounding embarrassingly like a sycophant and Cotton's brows knit together.

"What's takin' so long?" Cotton asked me.

"We've been, um…kind of busy," I explained, and he grinned.

"Neckin'?" Cotton inquired cheekily.

I shook my head and hoped it didn't look like an "I wish" shake.

"Taking Bitsy to the police station and dealing with surprise visits from my dad yesterday and Mom today." I gestured to Mom. "Then my car got vandalized, we think by Damon." I pointed to the car and Cotton slowly turned to look at it, then back to me as I continued. "And Brody's in town, so we had dinner with him and Mindy last night. Dinner included our table being visited by an unhappy Kami and a not-so-nice Shauna and then Harry wrestled around on the floor of The Rooster with Shauna's date, turning over some tables and getting doused with ketchup and horseradish sauce." Cotton stared at me, speechless, so I finished, "In between that we slept and, yes, there was some necking."

"Nina gave me the lowdown a minute go," Mom told him. "It would seem that Gnaw Bone is the Rocky Mountain Peyton Place."

"Got that right," Cotton replied, and turned to look over his shoulder.

I looked, too, and saw the Cherokee heading up the road. I felt my heart skip and I didn't think this was because I was worried about the outcome of the confrontation with Dad. It was more likely because I was happy Max was home.

"Seein' as I'm here," Cotton said as he turned back to me, "I'll supervise the hangin' and bum a cup o' joe."

I smiled and replied, "You're in luck. We just made a fresh pot."

"I'm a lucky guy," Cotton said on a smile, and we all watched Max turn up the lane and park.

My eyes stayed on him as he got out of the Cherokee and one look at his face, my body tensed.

"Oh my," Mom mumbled.

She could say that again. Max looked *angry*.

Max hit the top of the steps at the same time an equally-unhappy-looking Steve made it to the foot.

Then Max's eyes came to me and without greeting Cotton he told me the outcome of the confrontation.

"Babe, your dad's a dick."

"Oh dear," Mom was still mumbling.

"What happened?" I asked.

"Your dad?" Max asked back. "Definitely jetlagged yesterday. You're right. He'd wipe the floor with Kami at the same time takin' on Shauna."

"That doesn't sound good," I noted.

"It wasn't," Steve, who had arrived at our group, put in.

"What happened?" Mom asked.

"Bottom line, he ain't leavin' mainly because Niles arrives tonight and they want Nina to 'appear'—Lawrence's word—at breakfast at the hotel tomorrow morning," Steve explained, and my eyes locked on Max as my heart skipped a beat, and this one wasn't happy.

"What?" I whispered.

Max got close and his hands came to either side of my neck. "You ain't goin'."

"But—"

"Fuck 'em, playin' these games with your head."

"Max."

"Nina, they can want whatever the fuck they want. That doesn't mean you have to do it."

I shook my head in short, dazed shakes and then it hit me.

So I said, "I'll go."

Max's brows drew together dangerously and he asked, "What?"

"I'll go."

His hands tightened on my neck and I felt his body tighten with them. "Why?"

"Because it's the right thing to do."

"Nina—"

"No, Max," I cut him off, hooking my thumbs in his belt loops at the sides of his jeans and I explained, "You don't break up with someone over e-mail or over the phone. You do it face-to-face. No matter what you may think, Niles isn't a jerk. He never hurt me, lied to me, cheated on me, *hit me*. He deserves me breaking up with him face-to-face."

"Your father's pretty convinced he and Niles can talk you into changing your mind," Max informed me.

"Well, they're wrong."

"Duchess—"

I interrupted him, this time by leaning into him and saying softly, "Max, they won't because you'll be there with me." His body jerked with surprise as his head tilted to the side. "And Mom," I went on. "And Steve. You'll all take care of me." I leaned in closer and promised, "It'll be okay."

His fingers at my neck tightened again and he whispered, "Baby."

"You've done a lot for me but can I ask you to do this too?"

Max's eyes held mine for a long moment before he replied softly, "Wouldn't want it any other way."

This was what he said. What he *meant* was he wouldn't

allow it to happen any other way. I knew that, and he knew it, too, but it was nice the way he said it.

And there it was again. Now *I* was inviting Max's deeper involvement in my life. What was wrong with me?

"What's all this?" Cotton asked, and Mom moved toward him, deciding she would stop fawning and start flirting (innocently, which was Mom's way and Steve thought it was annoyingly hilarious or hilariously annoying, I couldn't ever tell which) and hooked her arm through his.

"Coffee first. You need *at least* coffee before any conversation commences about Lawrence Sheridan," Mom told him.

They started walking to the front door, everyone moving in that direction, when Max's head turned toward the road. Then everyone's heads turned to the road. This was because three cars were speeding up it.

I stared at the racing convoy. Brody's Subaru, followed by Becca's sporty red mini-SUV, and trailing was a police SUV.

"What now?" Max muttered as he slung an arm around my shoulders and headed us both down the steps. For my part, without much choice, I wrapped my arm around his waist and hooked my thumb in his side belt loop.

Brody stopped his Subaru on a spray of gravel and was out of it practically before it came to a complete halt.

"You ain't answerin' your cell and your line's fuckin' engaged," he accused Max the instant he cleared the door.

"What—?" Max started, but Brody interrupted him.

"You seen Mindy?" he asked. His eyes were locked on Max but I felt something grip my insides, something vicious.

"No, why?" Max answered. His tone had an edge and I watched Becca pull in behind Brody's Subaru.

"She call?" Brody went on. He'd walked swiftly and come to a stop in front of Max and me. His face was a stony mask of worry.

"No, Brody. What's happening?" Max replied. His body had gone tight and alert at my side.

"You?" Brody turned to me. "See or hear from her?"

I shook my head. "No."

"Jesus, Brody, what the fuck's happening?" Max asked, his voice getting hard, not with anger, with what I saw in Brody's face.

Brody reached behind him and pulled a folded piece of paper out of the back pocket of his jeans as Becca made it to us and Jeff was jogging up.

"Mindy slipped that under the door to her apartment while I was out this mornin'," Brody told Max as he handed him the paper.

But I was staring at Becca's face and Becca was staring at the paper like it was going to grow claws and strike out at her and that grip on my insides not only tightened, it twisted.

I forced my eyes away from Becca, looked down at the paper in Max's hand, and read.

Brody,

I know what you're going to think but you don't know.
 I can't get clean.
 And I need to get clean.
 Every time I think I can go back to who I was before, I think I can forget, I think I can go forward, it fills my head and I remember how dirty I am.
 I need to get clean.
 And I know how.
 After last night, I know I can do it. I've been thinking about it and no time seemed to be the right time but I know I can do it now.
 You told me you were happy in your job, you love Seattle and Mom and Dad are moving to Arizona and they've wanted to do that for so long. And Max found Nina and she's sweet and they're happy together. So I can do it now. Everyone I love is happy. I know now it's all good.
 We had such a great night last night, the perfect ending, now I can go.

*Tell Becca not to be mad at me and tell her I listened
all those times we talked but she doesn't get it either.
She doesn't understand what it feels like to wash and
wash and wash and never feel clean.*

*So I'm going to the only place that can make me
clean, crystal clear, fresh and clean.*

*You don't be mad at me either, Brody. Please try to
understand.*

*Tell Mom and Dad, Max and Becca I love them,
okay?*

And I love you too.

xoxo Mins

"It's a suicide note," Becca whispered, but I knew that. I
knew it. I knew it reading it and I knew it because I'd stopped
breathing and I knew it because I'd read one before and I knew
it because that grip on my insides felt like a vice and I'd felt
that before too. "She talked about it to me. I asked her to go
see someone." Becca's voice dropped to nearly nothing. "She
promised she would."

"We got boys high and low lookin' for her," Jeff put in, and
his voice sounded tight.

I felt Mom, Steve, and Cotton had gotten close but they
stayed quiet, correctly reading the atmosphere.

I didn't look at anyone. I was simply staring at the note still
held up in Max's hand.

"Fuck!" Brody hissed. "She was okay last night, laughin',
eatin', drinkin'—"

"Crystal clear and fresh," I whispered, cutting Brody off.

"What?" Max asked, and I watched the note disappear as
his hand dropped away and his body turned to me as his arm
curled me to his front.

I looked up into Max's handsome face wearing a replica of
Brody's stony concern. "Crystal clear and fresh," I repeated.
"She said that to me when I was giving her a facial. She used
those words to describe someplace she really likes, someplace

on the river. She said the water was always clear there. You could always see right down to the bottom. Crystal clear and—"

"Holling's Bend," Max said, turning his head to look at Brody and then he suddenly let me go and he was running.

Not thinking, I ran with him—Brody did too—around the house and up the incline toward the barn.

Brody was yelling as he ran. "Jeff, take the road, scan the river as you go!"

They pulled ahead and I watched Max yank open the barn door on a mighty heave and disappear inside. I ran into the cold darkness to see him squatting in front of an open cupboard door. He twisted a knob on a safe and pulled it open, and I saw some keys hanging inside. He grabbed a set, turned and tossed them to Brody. Brody caught them and ran to an ATV. Max grabbed another set and ran to the other ATV.

He got on, and as he was slipping the key into the ignition, I climbed on behind him.

He twisted and clipped, "Nina."

"Go!" I yelled. "Go, go, *go!*"

He delayed no further, twisted back, started the ATV, turned sharply in the barn, and shot out behind Brody.

Max either was more experienced on the ATV or knew the terrain better, maybe both, but even with me holding tight to his waist, we passed Brody. The wind, chill on the ATV and me not wearing a jacket, whipped our bodies and hair and we were going fast, too fast, scary fast and I didn't care.

The wheels left earth as we flew over a rise and landed with a bone-jarring thud that made me glad I was holding on to Max for dear life. We barreled down it, heading toward the narrow, now muddy track running the side of the river that Max and I had taken on the snowmobile.

My heart in my throat hammering uncontrollably, I scanned the river as it flew by at our sides.

My eyes were on the river but my mind was on Mindy putting her hand to my window and giving me that funny little smile. That funny little smile I was too stupid, stupid, *stupidly* drunk to read. Max had asked me to take it easy on the drink. He'd told me she had bad moments. I'd even bloody *seen* them. But did I listen? Did I read the signs, signs I'd seen but didn't read before with Charlie?

No. No, I didn't.

We neared the bend and I saw her. Max did too.

"God fucking *dammit*," he clipped, and even with the wind, I heard the alarm and anger clear in his gravelly voice.

He hadn't stopped the ATV when I jumped off and started running straight to the steep incline that fell down to the river.

"Nina!" Max shouted, but I didn't pause and went over the side, running hell bent for my darling girl floating facedown, her body caught in some reeds and butting against some rocks, her long hair a darkened strawberry-blonde web drifting eerily all around her.

I lost my footing and fell to a knee, sliding down the incline on my lower side to the bottom. I felt the rocks and gravel scoring my thigh, hip, and calf but the pain didn't register. The minute my feet touched earth I ran again, straight to Mindy, straight into the water, and I heard Max shout my name again.

I ignored it and slid along the slippery stones under my feet, the snowmelt water rushing all around me, and the river floor fell away faster than I expected. The water was shocking in its bitter chill but I kept going. I was up to my breasts when I got to her.

Flipping her around, I slipped my arms under her armpits and started backward, pulling her along with me, which was difficult to do fighting against the mighty tug of the rushing river. I hit something and knew it was Max when I felt his arms hook under mine, anchoring me to him as I was anchoring Mindy to me.

We were waist high when Brody was there. He lifted her up in his arms and troughed through the water with long, determined strides. Max's arm went along my back, hand under my armpit, holding me close as he turned us and part walked, part dragged me back to the bank.

Brody had Mindy on her back and he was on his knees at her side, bent over her, ear to her mouth when Max hauled me out of the river and we made it to them.

Then his torso shot straight up, his eyes going to Max. "She ain't breathin'."

Without hesitation, I dropped to my knees and thanked all that was holy that I'd volunteered to go to that first-aid class, even though at the time I could have done without it because my caseload was heavy. Now, if this ended better than it looked like it would, I was personally going to hunt down my instructor and give him a huge, bleeding kiss.

Positioning my hands like I was taught, I put them to Mindy's chest and counted out loud with each compression.

Then I moved to her mouth, opened it, stuck my finger inside to make sure nothing was there, tilted her head back, pinched her nose, put my mouth to hers, and exhaled my breath into her body.

Back to the chest compressions, counting down.

Then I moved to Mindy's mouth, pinched her nose, and exhaled.

Back to the compressions.

Back to Mindy's mouth.

Then back.

Then back.

And again.

And again.

"Goddammit, Mindy," I shouted when she lay there lifeless, no longer counting out loud with my compressions but doing them all the same. "Don't let him beat you!"

Then I went to Mindy's mouth.

Back to the compressions.

And back.

And again.

"Nina," Max whispered. Dropping down beside me in a squat and I felt his hand at my back.

I looked up to see Brody standing. His hands were on the

top of his head. He was staring down at Mindy and me, his expression ravaged.

I ignored Max and Brody and bent to Mindy's mouth.

Then back to the compressions.

"Baby," Max was still whispering.

"When's Jeff getting here?" I snapped, then went to Mindy's mouth.

Then back to the compressions.

"Nina, honey," Max whispered. My eyes went to him, I felt my heart in my throat, the tears in my eyes, and I kept up the compressions.

Mindy choked.

My head jerked down and she was choke-coughing, the sound both heinous and beautiful, her hands lifting weakly before falling away and I moved her to her side as water flooded out her mouth.

"Get it out, darling," I cooed, bending close to her, pulling the wet hair from her face and neck. "Get it all out."

Liquid poured from her mouth and she kept choking, tipping her head forward, curling into herself after it was all gone.

"Mins." Brody was now squatting and he pulled her torso into his arms when she was simply spluttering. "Babe," he whispered, his hand cupping the back of her head, pressing it to his neck as his other arm held her close.

Jeff ran up to us. "Jesus, fuck, is she okay?"

Brody looked up at him. "Call an ambulance."

"No," Mindy whispered, her voice rough. "No."

"Babe, Mins, we gotta—" Brody started.

"They all know about me," Mindy said weakly into his neck. "They know everything. They all know. I don't want them to know this."

"The house," Max ordered, squatting and putting a hand under Mindy's knees, an arm at her back. He stood, pulling her out of Brody's arms and lifting her, striding away, still talking. "Jeff, you drive her to the house, Nina will ride with her."

"I'll ride with her," Brody declared as Max climbed the

steep incline with Mindy in his arms as if he did it every day for his workout. Brody and Jeff managed it too. I slipped and slid but not as badly as I did coming down.

"You take the ATV back with me. Nina's got her," Max ordered as he made it to the top and marched to the police vehicle.

"Max—"

Max stopped and turned to Brody. "Trust me, Nina's got her."

Then with Mindy in his arms, he used his hand to open the door and slid Mindy in the back. Without hesitation, the moment Max stepped away, I climbed up next to her and pulled her into my arms. She didn't put her arms around me but she cuddled closer.

I looked at Max and nodded. "We're good."

Max closed the door. Jeff slid in the front, turned the ignition, and reversed down the narrow track so fast all the hairs would have risen on my head if I wasn't concentrating on Mindy.

"You with me, sweetheart?" I asked her, but she didn't respond.

Jeff found a clearing he could execute a three-point turn in, then raced down the narrow one-lane track.

"Mindy, darling, you with me?" I repeated.

"Yeah," she whispered.

I snuggled her closer, moved my lips to her ear, and I promised on a whisper that was only for her, "You and me, we'll find a way to make you feel clean. You and me. Yes? We'll find a way." My arms tightened around her and I finished, "Just not that way."

She didn't answer and I smoothed the wet hair away from her face, down her back, my other arm holding her tight.

We made it to the front of Max's house at the same time the ATVs came into view, proving Jeff wasted no time getting us home. My door was pulled open and I jumped out. Jeff reached in and his arms went around Mindy but I didn't watch.

I turned and ran to Mom, who, with Cotton, Steve, and Becca, was running down the steps as Max and Brody both shut off their ATVs at the bottom.

"Thank God," Becca breathed, but my eyes were on my mother.

"Mom, run up to Max's bathroom and run a warm bath, okay?" I asked. She nodded and ran into the house. I looked to Cotton. "You know a doctor who'll come out here but won't talk in town?"

"Yeah, darlin'," Cotton replied, eyes glued to Jeff and Mindy.

"Call him," I ordered, and turned to Jeff. "Take her upstairs."

Jeff was already nearing the door. I followed Jeff into the house and up the stairs and Max and Brody followed me.

Jeff set Mindy on her feet in the bathroom where Mom was on her knees beside the tub, her hand under the faucet, her other hand controlling the taps.

"Can you stand, honey?" Jeff asked gently. Mindy turned her head away but her legs buckled and Jeff's arms went back around her.

"I got her," Brody said, pushing forward.

The bathroom was not small. It had good space, a bathtub, a separate shower, a sink built into a marble-tiled vanity, and a sauna.

Still, with Mom, me, Mindy, and three hulking mountain men, it was a close fit.

"Boys, out," Mom demanded before I could do it.

"She's my sister and I don't even know who *you* are," Brody shot back, and my eyes went to Max.

"Brody," Max said low, and came forward.

I went to Mindy.

"That's my mom, Brody, and we have this, okay?" I asked, nodding to Jeff that I had Mindy when my arms went around her and she transferred her weight to me.

I had to brace my legs but I took on Mindy as Mom got to her feet and moved in our direction.

Brody stayed planted.

I looked to Max and said, "Max, darling, get Brody to give us some time and send Becca up here, please?"

Max nodded and put a hand on Brody that Brody shrugged off.

"She's my sister!" he shouted, and Mindy flinched in my arms.

"Brody, man, pull your shit together and think about the last twenty minutes. Nina's fuckin' *got* this. Yeah?" Max was still talking low.

Brody glared at him. Then he glared at me. Then, when Jeff silently moved out, Brody followed him.

Max's eyes stayed on me until I nodded to him. He nodded back and then he followed Brody.

"Okay, Mindy, sweetie, I'm Nellie, Nina's mom, and I'm going to help you, all right?" Mom said to Mindy. "Now, let's get these wet clothes off, sweetheart. Can you help us?"

"It won't work. I can't get clean," Mindy told Mom, but she slowly lifted her arms, her wrists limp, hands dangling, and I held her upright as Mom pulled off her sweater.

"Your problem, sweetheart, is you're trying to get clean when you already *are*," Mom informed her, and bent at her feet.

Becca came in and I could tell she had been crying and was currently on the verge of returning to her tears.

Feebly, Mindy's eyes went to her friend.

"I'm sorry," Mindy said.

"I'm sorry, too, sorry I didn't take better care of you," Becca replied, keeping her emotions together, moving forward, dropping down to her knees to help Mom with Mindy's shoes. "Let's get you warmed up."

They got off her boots, socks, and jeans but when Mom moved to the tub and Becca moved to her undies, Mindy cried, *"No!"*

"We gotta get you warmed up," Becca told her.

"No! I don't take them off, just to change them. I shower in them," Mindy said, and at this horrifyingly sad news, my eyes went to Becca to see hers were on me.

"Then in you go with your undies on," Mom decreed, moving from the now-filled bath to Mindy.

We helped her in and I said to Mom, "My shampoo and conditioner are in the shower stall. Can you get them?"

"Sure thing, Neenee Bean," Mom replied before scurrying off.

"I'm not strong like you," Mindy mumbled, and I looked from Mom to her and dropped down to my knees by the tub.

"What, darling?" I asked.

She was shivering in the tub, her arms crossed on her chest, fingers curled around her shoulders, eyes glued to her toes.

"You're strong. I'm not."

"Mins," I whispered, and her neck twisted to look at me.

"You don't let anyone walk all over you. I'll never be that way."

If she hadn't already broken my heart, that would have done it.

"We'll talk later," I told her. "Let's get you warm."

Mom handed me my shampoo and conditioner. I set it on the side of the tub and moved down the tub to grab the hand spray in order to get to work on Mindy's hair.

"I'll get this, you go get out of those wet clothes," Mom said, bending toward me.

"I'm fine," I replied. "Mins, lean your head forward for me, will you?"

Mindy did what I asked but Mom got closer.

"Sweetie, you're soaked through and shivering. Go change your clothes. You can come back to Mindy in a second."

Mindy turned toward me and her eyes hit me but I smiled at her, realizing for the first time I was, indeed, shivering mostly because I was chilled straight through to the bone likely because I'd been in a snowmelt rushing river and also because of all that had recently transpired. I also realized that my clothes felt like they weighed a ton.

I ignored all of this.

"I'm fine," I replied on a small, trembling smile to Mindy. "Head forward, my lovely."

"Nina—" Mom started, and I turned and locked eyes with her.

"Mom. I'm. *Fine.*"

Mom stared at me a second, straightened, and I felt her presence move away. It took me a couple of tries to get the hand spray working because my own hands were trembling so much.

I distractedly heard Mom say, "Max," but I was able to get the hand spray working so my concentration went to getting the water warm.

"Cover Mindy," I heard Max's gravelly voice say from not too far but not too close.

"Gotcha," I heard Mom reply, and then she was for some reason holding up a towel lengthwise beside the tub, getting right in my space.

"Mom, you're in my way," I told her.

"Hand me the spray, Nina," Becca said, coming in behind me.

"But—" I started. Becca reached in and pulled the spray out of my hand, and then I was going up.

I looked to see I was in Max's arms. "Max! I'm washing Mindy's hair."

"You can do it after you change," Max replied, walking out of the bathroom and into the bedroom.

I saw Brody, back to the room. His clothes, likely Max's clothes, were dry and he was standing at the railing.

Max walked me directly to my suitcase.

"Max, seriously, I'm *fine.*"

"You're tremblin'."

"I'll be okay."

"Yeah, you will, after you get some dry, warm clothes on you."

"Max!" I snapped.

"Shut it, Duchess," he clipped, then put me on my feet.

I no sooner got steady when his hands were at my sweater

and it was over my head, its sodden weight lifted clean away
and I felt like I'd come out from under a boulder.

Even so, I breathed, "Max," and looked over my shoulder
at Brody, who still had his back to the room.

When I turned back, Max was digging through my suitcase.

"Bra off," he ordered quietly when he turned to me.

"What?" I breathed again.

He lifted up a clean bra. "Wet bra off, dry bra on."

"Brody's here," I hissed.

"Brody's not thinkin' about your body," Max returned.

This was definitely true.

I twisted my hands behind me and unhooked my bra. Max
handed me the new one before the wet one fell away and he'd
already turned back to my suitcase and was again rummaging
when I clumsily slipped it on.

When he was facing me again, he had my heaviest sweater
in his hands and he gave it to me. Then his hands went to my
jeans.

"Can you get your boots off?" he asked as the button came
undone and the zip went down.

I nodded and with some effort flipped my boots off with a
toe to each heel as he pulled the jeans down my legs. When he
did, I sucked in breath when surprising, stinging pain struck
my entire left side.

Max's hands stopped pulling down the jeans and they
went to my hips. He tilted them slightly, looked my leg up and
down, and whistled through his teeth.

"Scraped, honey, hip to ankle," he muttered, his fingers
probing gently at my flesh.

"I'm okay," I assured him.

"We need to get this cleaned up."

"In a minute."

His head tipped back and he looked at me. "Nina—"

"Please, Max," I whispered, my whisper heavy and
clogged, my tone saying I was holding on but my hold was
loose and slipping.

His eyes held mine for a long moment before he went back to my jeans and gently freed them from my ankles.

I stepped out of them and he tossed my jeans where he'd tossed my soggy sweater. He straightened and walked to the dresser as I tugged on the sweater. He pulled out a pair of his pajama bottoms. These were flannel, checked dark brown and red on a cream background.

"Looser, for your leg," he explained, and I nodded and pulled off my drenched socks and tossed them on the pile.

Max gave me the pajamas. I pulled them up and drew the drawstring tight. They were overlong and bunched at my ankles, covering my feet.

Still, Max went back to my suitcase. Then he was facing me again. He put a hand on my belly, pushed me back to the bed, where I fell to my behind, and got onto a knee in front of me.

He lifted a foot and put on one thick, wool sock. He dropped that foot and went after the other.

His eyes came to me.

"Am I done?" I whispered, staring at Max on a knee in front of me, both of his hands curled around my foot, and he had a look on his face as he gazed at me that I'd never forget in my whole life.

He let my foot go, leaned forward, lifted up, and, lips at my forehead, he murmured, "You're a lot of things, Duchess, dressed is just one of them."

Then he kissed me sweet, grabbed my hand, and pulled me off the bed.

I tipped my head back to look into his beautiful, clear gray eyes and suddenly I wasn't trembling anymore.

Then I ran back to Mindy.

*   *   *

We got Mindy cleaned, dried, and wrapped in my robe, putting a pair of Max's thick socks on her feet, as I only brought the one pair.

Mom shuffled off with Mindy, Max, Brody, and my wet clothes and Brody climbed into Max's bed with Mindy, holding her close as the doctor came up the stairs.

At this point, Max took my hand and led me to the bathroom, closing the door. Before I knew what he was about, the drawstring at my bottoms was pulled and the pajamas dropped to my ankles.

"Max!" I hissed on a whisper.

"Shower," he whispered back.

"Max," I hissed again.

His hands came to my waist and his face got in mine. "Two choices, Duchess. You get undressed and get in that shower, warm yourself up and clean those scrapes so I can put salve on 'em or we both get undressed, get in the shower, and *I* clean you up. You got one second, what's it gonna be?"

"I'll take a shower," I said immediately, because I knew by the look on his face that his threat was not idle.

"Right," he replied, and then he was gone.

I was putting my shampoo and conditioner back in the shower when the door opened, Max's torso slipped through, he tossed a pile of clothing on the counter by the sink, and the door closed again.

I took a hasty shower but even hasty, the warmth of the water seeped into my skin reminding me I was alive, I was healthy, and so was Mindy. It also reminded me of other things, other things I didn't want to be reminded of and that I could hold at bay if I was doing something, like saving someone's life or washing her hair.

I felt the tears threaten as I carefully cleaned my leg and I choked them back, my choking audible, reverberating around the marble-tiled shower. I had to keep it together. I couldn't let Mindy hear me. I could let it go later. Now I had to keep it together.

I got out, dried off, wrapped my hair in the towel, and had new, clean underwear on when Max was back in the room, closing the door behind him.

I covered my lacy bra-covered chest with my arms and hissed yet again, "Max!"

He completely ignored me, got close, then squatted down. I tried to take a step away but he caught me behind my knee and kept me close, his head tipping back.

"Stay still, Nina," he ordered.

"I'm okay. It's not that bad."

"Babe, the skin's broken in places."

"It'll be fine."

His fingers squeezed the back of my knee. "Honey, this'll take two seconds."

"Max—"

"Stay still, for me."

I closed my eyes and my body settled. Without thinking, my system knew it'd do anything, anything, for Holden Maxwell.

I opened them again when I felt Max's moist fingers gliding with care along the scrapes on my leg from hip to ankle. He had to go back to the tube of ointment several times and it took longer than two seconds but I didn't call him on this mainly because I was absorbed in watching his bent head, his fingers on my skin, both of these successfully shoving out the panicked, desperate thoughts and feelings that had me in their grip.

When he was done, he straightened and his eyes came to me. "All right, Duchess, take care when gettin' dressed."

Then he moved to the sink to wash the salve from his fingers and I grabbed the soft flannel pajama bottoms, not Max's this time, clean ones, mine. These were not checked in bold, masculine colors but were mint green with big pink, blue, yellow, and peach polka dots and had a wide, blue, satiny ribbon as a drawstring. They were also loose fitting, though not as loose as Max's, and I pulled them cautiously up my injured leg.

There was also the ribbed, long-sleeved, scoop-necked blue top that went with them. I pulled the towel from my hair and Max took it from my hands and wiped his own before he shoved it on the railing as I pulled the top on.

When he turned back, I grabbed my comb, yanked it through my hair, and whispered, "What'd the doctor say?"

"She's okay. All systems go. He doesn't figure she was in the water that long," Max whispered back. I nodded and kept yanking the comb through my hair when Max said, "Barb and Darren are out there. Cotton called 'em. They got here about five minutes ago." When I looked blank, he went on, "Her mom and dad."

"Oh."

I was still yanking the comb through my hair when Max reached out, his fingers wrapping around my wrist. He pulled my hand between us and pried the comb from me.

"I'm combing my hair," I informed him unnecessarily, and I watched his eyes slide from forehead to shoulders before they came back to me.

"You got it, Duchess."

"Oh," I repeated.

He tossed the comb in the sink and his hand at my wrist brought me closer. His other hand came to my hip and that brought me closer too.

"Baby," he said softly as he tipped his head so his face was all I could see and the emotion welled up in me, threatening to split open my skin.

I shook my head, short, quick, frantic shakes.

"No, Max, no. Not now, please," I whispered my entreaty.

He dropped my wrist but his hand curled around my neck and he gave me what I needed. "All right, honey, we'll talk later."

I nodded, grateful, then fell forward and pressed my forehead to his chest.

"I need a second before I go out there," I said quietly to his chest.

"You can have as many as you need."

I took in a shaky but deep breath before I muttered, "Stop being nice."

He didn't say anything, didn't move, just stood, one hand to my hip, one hand at my neck. My hands went to his waist and I held on.

After a while, I said, "All right."

He kissed the top of my head and repeated my words, "All right."

Then he grabbed my hand and walked me to the door, opened it, and led me out.

A redheaded woman, her long, strawberry-blonde hair streaked liberally and attractively with white, was sitting on the bed, her back to me, facing Mindy as well as hiding Mindy from me. An older mountain man stood by the side of the bed next to her, Becca next to him. None of them turned to me and the woman was whispering to Mindy.

Max silently walked me through the room and I started to pull my gaze away from the bed, knowing Mindy was okay, she was safe, she was with her family, but Brody's eyes came to me.

My step faltered at what I saw burning there and Max's hand tightened in mine. His arm curling, he brought me up close as he tucked our hands against the side of his chest. He kept me moving but my head turned as we walked, my eyes held by Brody's, tears pricking the backs of mine.

Brody nodded to me when Max and I hit the stairs. I nodded back and sucked in another unsteady breath when I watched one lone tear fall from his tough-guy, mountain-man eye.

He turned his head away and Max winded us down the stairs.

*   *   *

Mom and Steve had gone into town to go grocery shopping, which was needed even after my huge shop a week ago, considering Max had been hosting half the town for coffee, breakfast, and dinner for a week. Cotton had gone with them to show them the way, not that it would be hard to find but it was a nice thing to do.

The doctor had also left and Mindy, Brody, and their family were upstairs, murmuring to each other.

Max had taken a shower, then gone outside to return the ATVs to the barn, and I was cleaning to take my mind off everything. I'd dusted all Max's furniture in the living room and was sweeping his wood floors, my hand still around the dust rag should I find something to polish while sweeping when Max walked into the room.

I barely glanced at him and didn't stop sweeping when I did.

I heard his boots on the floor and had to stop when his arm hooked around my waist from behind.

"Max, I'm—" I started to protest, straightening.

"Stop cleaning, Duchess. When I'm home, I got a woman, Caroline, who comes up from town on Mondays, cleans the house," he said quietly into my ear, and I twisted my neck to look at him.

"No, you don't," I declared with authority, and his brows went up.

"Baby, I do."

"No, you don't. I was here last Monday and no woman named Caroline came and cleaned the house."

"You were delirious with fever last Monday and when you weren't you were out. She came, cleaned around you, and left," Max reminded me.

I'd forgotten that, not that I would remember Caroline but I forgot I was sick.

I was such an idiot.

"Oh," I said softly.

"You clean, she won't have anything to do. She's too proud to take the money anyway and she can't afford to miss a week. She's got two kids, an asshole husband who drinks too much, and not many clients. When I'm not in town, she cleans between renters too."

"Oh," I repeated softly.

He turned me to face him and took the broom from my hand and the dust rag from my other.

"You need somethin' to do, darlin', bake that cake mix you bought in Denver. Tonight we can use a fuckin' cake."

"That's a good idea," I whispered.

I could use cake, any cake, always could but I could especially use a yellow cake with that store-bought, thick, fudgy, chocolaty frosting. It was the lazy way of baking but they didn't have many cake mixes and not near the variety of store-bought frostings in England. I missed them.

He smiled. It was small, not Max's usual beautiful grin, but it was something.

Then he lifted his free hand and cupped my jaw before dipping his face close to mine.

"Anyway, duchesses don't clean," he whispered.

"I'm not a duchess," I reminded him.

"Yeah, you are."

"No, Max, I'm not."

"You're mine," he told me. I held my breath as I absorbed his words and they slid through me, soothing across edges that had come up jagged through the last hour, as he concluded, "And *my* duchess doesn't fuckin' clean."

His thumb slid along my cheek. Then his hand dropped as he turned away and went to the hall closet.

Before I could allow myself any reaction, which could consist of bursting into tears, loudly declaring he was the love of my life, or running upstairs, pulling Mindy in my arms and promising one day she'll find happiness, I hurried to the kitchen and baked a cake.

*   *   *

It was after Mom and I had made everyone sandwiches and heated Mindy some canned soup, serving it with fresh-baked bread Mom found in town and after the dryer expelled clean, fresh clothes.

Mindy was dressed in her dry clothes, Brody had the pile of his folded and in his arm, Mom, Steve, and Cotton were in the kitchen putting away the rest of what looked to be a year's worth of groceries, and Max and I were standing on the porch with Mindy and Brody.

Barb and Darren, who had been introduced to me, were in their idling car. Becca was already backing carefully out. Jeff was long gone.

I'd put on my woolly socks and Mindy was wearing Max's. Barb had taken her wet boots to her car.

"You're staying with your mom?" I asked Mindy, and she nodded. "That's good, sweetheart," I finished quietly. She nodded again and looked away from me.

This hurt but I also understood it or at least I told myself I did.

I looked to Brody when he spoke. "You'll come down tomorrow?"

It was my turn to nod and I did so to Brody. He nodded back.

"Neens?" Mindy whispered, and my eyes quickly went back to her.

"Yes, my lovely?" I prompted when she didn't say any more.

She pressed her lips together, her eyes still turned away.

"I never thought—" she started.

"Tomorrow," I said swiftly and firmly, now really understanding, and her eyes skittered to me, then away.

"But I—"

"Tomorrow, darling," I repeated, and her gaze came again to me but this time it stayed there.

"I didn't think you'd ever, not ever...not you...I wouldn't ever do that to you." She paused and then whispered, "I guess I just didn't think."

"Stop it, Mindy," I whispered back. "This isn't about me, sweetheart. This is about getting you back to where you need to be."

I watched the tears pool in her eyes and she was still whispering when she said, "Thank you, Neenee Bean."

I swallowed back a little sob. Max's arm slid around my shoulders and he curled my front into his side.

When I had control of my emotions, I said, "Tomorrow we'll talk. All right, my lovely?"

She nodded, now biting at her lips. Max gave me a squeeze. I looked at him and he gave Brody a nod.

Brody moved but Max suddenly said, "No, hang on."

Then his arm around me was gone and both of them were wrapped tight around Mindy. My hand went to my mouth and my eyes went to Brody.

"You're loved, Mins," Max's gravelly voice said, and I watched Mindy's fingers curl into his thermal at the back. "Maybe you don't get how much."

"Max." She choked back her own sob and I closed my eyes but felt Brody's arm replace Max's around my shoulders. I let my weight settle against his long body and he took it like Max did, without effort.

"You forget that again, you call me. I'll remind you," Max said to Mindy, then demanded, "Promise me that, babe."

"Okay," Mindy whispered.

"I want to hear you promise," he ordered, and I watched her fingers clutch his shirt.

She hesitated a heart-stopping second before she said, "I promise, Max."

He paused before he replied, "All right, honey."

He pulled away but caught her face in both of his hands, touched his lips to her forehead, turned, and took over for Brody holding me up.

Both my arms slid around his waist and both his arms slid around my back as Brody lifted his shoeless sister into his arms and carried her down the steps and across the gravel to the Subaru. Max and I held on to each other as we watched first Barb and Darren execute a three-point turn and drive down the lane followed by Brody and Mindy.

I waved just in case Mindy looked back or Brody looked in his rearview mirror. I couldn't know if they did but I kept waving even after they turned onto the road.

Max's arms gave me a squeeze and I sighed.

"Gettin' cold, darlin', gonna snow," he said, and I pressed my cheek to his chest and looked at the view, both my arms again around him. He was right. The clouds were covering the sun and there was a definite chill in the air.

"You okay?" I asked his chest, even though I knew the answer.

"No," he answered honestly.

"I'm so sorry, Max," I whispered.

"Me too," he whispered back.

We stood there a while silently holding on to each other. I was staring at Max's view and I knew he was, too, but he was doing it with his cheek against my hair.

It was then I wondered if things would have felt differently if Max had been around when Charlie died. If I'd have had this, maybe not the view, but his strong arms around me, his cheek to my hair. If I'd had him to hold on to.

I figured it wouldn't have hurt less, losing Charlie, but it *would* have hurt less, knowing after I did that I wasn't alone.

And I realized that losing Charlie was when the loneliness crept in and I had been in such grief, I hadn't been able to beat it back. So when I met Niles not long after and he'd been kind and in his way attentive, I'd fixed myself to him because with him I was no longer alone.

The problem was, I never stopped being lonely.

Max broke the silence when he asked softly, "This how you feel all the time?"

I tipped my head back to look at him. "I'm sorry?"

"Charlie."

I closed my eyes, then opened them and nodded the truth.

"Honey," he whispered, his face getting soft, his eyes getting warm, but there was something else there, an understanding that rent my heart.

"But you have a different ending, darling. She's going to be okay," I promised him.

"Yeah," he replied, giving me a squeeze.

"Nina'll freeze to death, you keep her on the porch much longer," Cotton called, and we both turned to see him leaning out the front door. "Anyways, we got pictures to hang, son. Get your hind end in here." Then he pulled back but left the door open.

The moment was broken, so I decided it was high time to lighten the mood.

Therefore as we walked, our arms around each other, to the open door, I said, "I think Cotton is trying to single-handedly increase your gas bill by two hundred percent."

"Did I say he was a pain in my ass?" Max asked loudly as we moved into the house, and Max closed the door.

"I give him my pictures, he calls me a pain in the ass," Cotton complained to my mother, who looked alarmingly like she was cooking. I hoped the mood to concoct was assuaged at breakfast because she'd also been to the grocery store, which meant her ingredients could easily have taken a creative, therefore alarming, turn.

"Children these days," Mom said back. "No gratitude."

"Max, Mom called you a child again," I told on my mother, even though Max heard it himself.

"Yeah, but she's making her Mexican casserole," Steve said. I sucked in an excited breath. Steve grinned at me, then looked to Max. "Nina likes her mother's Mexican casserole."

Max stopped me at the end of the counter and I looked up at him and explained, "You will too. You taste it, you'll think nothing but 'ambrosia of the gods.'"

Max smiled down at me and I was relieved to see this one was a little bit more like his normal, beautiful grin.

"Never thought those four words in my whole life, Duchess," he informed me. "In fact, I don't even know what one of them means."

"Food of the gods," I informed him.

"Then what you're sayin' is your mom's casserole is good."

"The *best*."

"And it was one of my *concoctions*," Mom put in snootily.

I got up on my toes and informed Max in a loud whisper, "A rare hit."

"I heard that!" Mom snapped.

Steve intervened by saying to Max, "We're gonna have to rig up some kinda hoist if you want that picture over your bed. It isn't gonna go up those spiral stairs."

"No problem. Had to do the same with the furniture," Max replied. "I'll go to the barn, get my tools."

"I'll go with you," Steve offered, and slid off his stool.

"I'll stay warm." Cotton declined participation and slid *onto* a stool.

"I'll frost the cake," I announced, and started to pull away from Max's arm but it tightened. I started to tip my head back to look up at him but stopped when his lips hit my temple.

Goodness but I loved it when he did things like that.

"Be back in a second, baby," he said softly, giving me a squeeze.

I loved it when he said things like that too. And when he gave me a squeeze.

He let me go. Steve joined him and I watched as they walked away.

"He's a keeper," Mom noted, her eyes on the space where we last saw Steve and Max.

She wasn't wrong but I was too emotionally depleted to deal with that fact right now or to process what I was going to do about it.

"Sweetie," Mom called. I looked at her and my hand came out to clutch the edge of the counter at what I saw in her face.

"Come here, Neenee Bean," she said softly.

"Mom."

"Before you frost that cake, I want a hug."

"Mom, you know—"

"Come here, Nina," she demanded firmly, and I did what I'd done since I was a child and I heard that tone from my mother. I obeyed and walked into her arms.

They came around me and the tears hit my throat, slid up my sinuses, and then leaked out my eyes. I couldn't control them and in the safety of my mother's arms I didn't try.

"Mom," I whispered, holding on tight.

"Lots of bad stuff coming up for you today and you can't hold it in, darling. You just can't." She held back just as tight and went on, "So you have to give it to your momma."

I stuffed my face into her neck and like I'd done countless times before, from falling off my bike to getting over terrible boyfriends, I gave it to her.

However, this time was different, for about halfway through me doing that, her arms went loose and her hands went to my shoulders. My head came up in surprise but I didn't see much partly because she was blurry but also because she turned me and I found myself in the safety of Max's arms.

Yes, the jury was now out. Verdict: Mom liked Max for certain.

Max's arms were different mainly because they moved. They lifted me, they carried me across the room, and they settled me into his lap when he sat in the armchair.

"You...you need to hang the pictures," I snuffled into his neck, hiding my face from view.

"Later."

"No, I'm okay," I lied, wiping my hand along my cheek and then letting out a hiccoughing sob.

"Later."

My head came up and I protested, "Max."

My head went right back into his neck when his hand cupped the back of it and forced it there.

"Duchess, I said *later*."

Max was obviously determined and I knew what that meant.

"Oh all right," I gave in tearfully but also grumpily.

Max made no response.

I slipped my arms around him and let his warm, solid body cradle mine.

Never said this, Nina, never thought I'd have the chance, Charlie whispered into my head, and the only response I could give was to hold Max tighter. *I'm so sorry, sweetheart.*

A new sob slid from my throat and Max held me closer.

*   *   *

After the pictures were up (yes, picture*s*, for Mom, Steve, and Cotton all demanded that mine be hung between the two doors under the loft, no one let me get a word in edgewise and Max sure as heck didn't intervene, not to mention, once up, they looked amazing). After Mexican casserole, which was even better than I remembered, and Max, who had two helpings, obviously thought so too. After three beers (for Max) and two (for me). And after coffee and yellow cake with fudgy, chocolaty frosting from a tub and a scoop of ice cream that Mom, Steve, and Cotton got from the store, Max and I stood at the front door saying good-bye to our guests.

"Where are you staying?" I asked Mom as I gave her a hug.

"Steve found a last-minute deal on a condo someone canceled. It's on the other side of town. We got it for a song. We're here all week!" Mom declared. My gaze slid to Max and I watched his eyes close slowly before he shook his head.

"That's great, Mom," I said, pulling away but holding on to her hands, and I actually did think it was great, mostly because I missed my mom and I didn't get to see her that often.

I hugged Steve next and then Cotton, who Mom and Steve were driving home. Snow flurries were falling as was night and Cotton had walked there because, I'd found out, he was Max's neighbor.

"I'll walk 'em to their car," Max told me. His eyes went to my stocking feet and he ordered, "You stay here."

I didn't argue. I'd had a tough day.

Instead I said, "Okay."

"'Night, Neenee Bean, see you in the morning." Mom waved, bouncing on her sandals, and then she turned to Max and declared, "I expect to be carried to the car by my daughter's mountain man hunk, seeing as I might break a heel in this snow."

"Mom!" I snapped. "None of it has actually stuck yet."

"Don't spoil my fun!" she snapped back, and then she screeched with delight when Max obliged her demands.

Steve grinned at me and shook his head. Cotton stared at Mom and Max and also shook his head, though for different reasons than Steve.

I watched through the windowed door for a while, then wandered to the armchair, plopped into it, and stared at the roaring fire, thinking Max was good at building fires.

Then again, he seemed good at everything.

I waved through the window when I heard the honking car drive by and watched Max walk through the door.

"Max, you shouldn't give in to her nuttiness. Trust me, it only makes her more nutty," I called.

"Your mom wants to be carried to her car, I can carry her to her car. Not a big deal," Max replied, bending and pulling off his boots.

"Whatever," I muttered, and turned back to the fire.

I felt him come to me rather than heard him and then I scrunched to the side as he sat in the chair beside me and propped his feet up on the ottoman.

I was about to open my mouth to say something, what I had no idea, when Max slid an arm around my shoulders and spoke.

"Two miracles occurred today. My woman saved the life of a girl I think of as a sister and it's eight o'clock, we're alone, and you're not sick, drunk, or asleep."

"Max," I whispered, and he turned from gazing at the fire to look at me.

"Never, Nina, never in my fuckin' life will I forget you racin' down that incline, jumpin' in the goddamned river, and breathin' life into Mindy."

I closed my eyes but opened them again when Max's hand came to my face and his mouth touched mine.

He pulled back an inch and murmured, "Thank you, baby."

"Max—" I started softly, and he cut me off.

"But you ever even *think* of jumpin' into a river again, I'll tan your ass."

My brows snapped together just as I felt my body jerk. "I'm sorry?"

Max's arm dropped across my lap, his hand at my hip, and he stated, "You scared the fuckin' shit outta me."

"Max—"

"Seriously, Nina, swear to God, I watched you go into that river—you didn't fuckin' hesitate—and my goddamned stomach dropped. I thought you'd both go."

"Max—"

"There'd be nothin' I could do. That river took you, it wanted you, it'd have you and I'd have lost you both."

"That didn't happen," I reminded him, trying to keep my patience.

"No, thank fuck, it didn't. Coulda, but it didn't."

"I had to get to her."

"I know you did."

"So I got to her."

"Yeah, you did. Nearly lost your life doin' it."

"That isn't true."

"A river's unpredictable, babe. You don't know that but I do. Especially in spring. You shoulda waited for me."

"Waiting wasn't an option."

"Not worth talkin' about now. It's done and thankfully everyone's all right."

"You brought it up."

"I brought it up in case you get a wild hair, which you seem to do a lot."

I pulled back as far as I could, which wasn't very far, and glared at him. "I'm not going to jump into rivers willy-nilly, Max. I didn't even *jump* in today. I just, kind of, *walked* in." His brows went up and I gave an inch. "Okay, *ran* in."

He shook his head and declared, "We're done talkin' about this."

I continued to glare. Then I started to push up from the chair but his arms tightened around me and he pulled me back down to him.

"Max, I'm going to go read or something."

"You're pissed I laid it out and you're gonna go nurse your snit."

Seriously, he was so annoying.

"Okay, so I'm going to go *nurse* my *snit*."

"No, you aren't. You're gonna sit here and we're gonna enjoy the fact that we're breathin', alive, and *alone*."

"Has anyone told you you're domineering?"

"Nope."

"Well, let me be the first. You're domineering."

He turned more fully to me and ran his forearm down the backs of both my legs, hooking them at the knee and pulling them over his legs on the ottoman. If I hadn't been in a *snit*, I might have noticed, firstly, that he did this gently so as not to hurt my scraped up leg and, secondly, that I was far more comfortable in this position.

But I was in a snit and he was talking, so I didn't notice.

"First, babe, seriously?"

"Seriously what?" I asked.

"If I got somethin' on my mind, you want me to keep it to myself?"

Well, it didn't sound very good when he said it like that.

"No, but—"

"Especially if it's important?"

"Of course not."

"Second, you get pissed at what I say, you want to go off in a huff rather than talkin' shit out?"

That didn't sound very good either.

"Well—"

"Yes or no."

"Maybe, yes," I snapped, and his face grew dark.

"You're shittin' me."

"If I go off in a huff, as you put it, I might have a chance to get my head together so we can talk it out, not argue about it."

"Babe, you're not kidding anyone. You want the chance to pull away, not get your head together."

Why was he so annoying?

I was angry enough to ask.

"Why are you so annoying?" I snapped again.

"Because I'm right, you're wrong, and you know it."

I shouldn't have asked.

I looked to the ceiling and told God, "God, next time I want an adventure, strike me with lightning. You have my permission."

"You know what sucks?" Max broke into my conversation with God, and I looked back at him.

"No, what sucks, Max?"

"It sucks you're so fuckin' cute even when I'm pissed at you."

My eyes rounded, my temper flared, even as my heartbeat spiked with a weird but palpable fear.

"You're pissed at me?"

"Duchess, you ran into a raging goddamned river and gave me attitude when I called you on it."

"Max, I ran in after *Mindy*, who was trying to commit *suicide* like my brother did *three years ago* and I *wasn't going to let that happen again*! Not to Mindy, not to Brody, and not *to you*!"

His face gentled but I wasn't done.

"And I don't get a wild hair *a lot*."

"Babe," he said low. His gentled face now looked like it was desperately trying not to crack a smile.

"What?" I snapped.

"You flew out to Colorado, drivin' into mountains you've never been to by yourself and harborin' a flu. You were alone, in a snowstorm, in the middle of nowhere in a house with a man you'd never met and you got into it with me. And, I'll just say, you might have a mouth on you, babe, but physically I can take you. Then you took on Shauna on what amounts to our first date. Then you took on Damon, who's a dick, could also take you, and, worse, *would*. Then you took on Kami and then Shauna *again*. You took one look at Jeff, decided he was a good guy, and threw Mindy at his feet. You didn't think for even a second before gettin' into it with your dad, just threw back the covers, blew from the loft, ran down the fuckin' stairs, and got right in his face. And this mornin' you acted out a hilarious but obviously practiced head-to-head with your mom." I was back to glaring silently at him since his facts made a pretty damning case, but he wasn't done. "And we won't get into you jumpin' on the back of an ATV a coupla days after you shied away from a fuckin' snowmobile, then jumpin' *off* it like you're a Hollywood stuntwoman."

"All right, Max, you made your point."

"Thank Christ," he muttered, then grinned.

"But you're still domineering."

"And you like it."

"I do *not*," I snapped.

"Baby, if I wasn't, you'd be at the hotel in town or, worse, in Denver and you wouldn't be right here."

"Which is where I don't want to be. I want to be upstairs, nursing my *snit*," I shot back.

"Too bad, darlin', because you aren't goin' anywhere."

"Fine, then I'll nurse my snit here," I shot back, crossing my arms and transferring my glare to the fire.

After a moment, Max sighed and his hand came to the back of my neck, and as he sat back in the chair, he forced my head to his shoulder. I let him do this but I still kept my eyes on the fire and my arms crossed on my chest.

We were silent awhile before Max spoke again.

"Becca told me about Mindy."

At his tone, I pulled in a breath, pushed down my irritation, and asked, "Sorry?"

"She told me that she was worried somethin' like today would happen."

I uncrossed my arms and lifted my head to see he was also gazing at the fire.

"Really?"

"Yeah," Max replied, not shifting his eyes from the fire. "That's why we moved her out of her place and into Becca's. Becca and I decided it on Tuesday. We needed to keep a closer eye on her, so we worked it and got it when Damon fell into our plans, bein' such a dick."

Something was wrong in his tone, in the blankness of his face, so I called, "Max."

"Shoulda kept her up here with us," Max whispered, and I knew what was wrong.

I slid my arm along his belly and curled it around his side, whispering, "Max."

"Shoulda told Brody."

"Max."

"Shoulda took her myself to talk to someone."

I gave him a squeeze and said more firmly, "Max, look at me."

Slowly, his eyes went from the fire to me and what I saw in them made me melt into him as my arm left his middle and my hand went to his neck.

"Darling, this stuff will torture you if you don't let it go."

"Nina—"

"I missed the signs, too, and I've seen them before."

"Nina."

"You couldn't have stopped today if this was where she was heading. You can't do that to yourself."

"Hard not to think I fucked up when all I got in my head is you jumpin' into that river and her floating in it."

Yes, I was *such* an idiot.

My fingers flexed at his neck and I pulled myself up to get closer to him.

"Max, you didn't fuck up."

"Coulda took you both."

"Max—"

"Woulda been on me if it did."

I pulled up closer and my hand slid into his hair.

"Stop it," I whispered. Max opened his mouth to speak and I moved to stop him, pulling up farther and pressing my mouth to his.

His hand slid up my spine, my head came up from my kiss, and I saw his eyes were still dark with bleak emotion.

I slid my nose alongside his and spoke again. "Max, stop it. Everyone's safe and I won't run into any more rivers, I promise."

"Baby—" he whispered, unamused.

"Sweetheart, don't go down that path. I've been down it and, trust me, it leads nowhere."

His eyes moved over my face and his fingers slid into my hair and he pressed my face into the side of his neck.

"Sorry, Duchess, you don't need this shit. The demons you been battlin' today," he muttered.

My arms slid around him and I kissed his neck. "You know, earlier today I wondered if it would have hurt less if I hadn't been alone when Charlie died."

His fingers slid through my hair and he asked, "Yeah?"

"I decided it wouldn't have."

"Probably not."

"But maybe if I hadn't been alone, I wouldn't have wandered down that path."

"Probably not," he repeated.

"So, since you're not alone, will you let me guide you away from that path?"

He was silent a moment. Then he asked an impossible question: "Where we goin', honey?"

"I don't know, just not there."

His body shook with silent humor. Not a lot of it but it still shook.

"That shield you got, babe, like titanium," he muttered, and I gave him a squeeze.

"I thought we were going to enjoy being alive, breathing and alone." I reminded him.

"Yeah."

"We're not really doing that."

"Nope."

"Let's move onto that phase of the evening," I suggested.

His fingers curled around my shoulder and gave me a squeeze.

"Good idea," he murmured.

"Do you want a beer?"

"No."

"I can make some hot chocolate," I offered.

"Thanks, but no."

"Do you want anything?"

"Anything?"

My stomach dipped and my body grew tense.

"Max—"

"There's somethin' I been wantin' awhile."

"Max—"

"Take my mind off things."

My head came up and I repeated, "Max."

His fingers slid into my hair again and his eyes focused on my mouth. "Be a good way to celebrate breathin', bein' alive, and bein' alone."

"I—"

"Kiss me, Duchess."

My hand went to his chest as his hand pressed my face closer to his.

"You're being domineering again," I informed him.

I felt his mouth grin under mine and watched his eyes do it.

"Yeah, baby, fair warnin', when we're naked, you better get used to that."

I gasped at his words. Then he kissed me.

It could have been the snow falling softly all around the A-frame, the fire burning in its grate, the soft lighting under the cupboards in the kitchen, and just the lamp by the couch being lit making the house more cozy and romantic than ever.

It could have been what happened that day to Mindy, Brody, Max, and me and relief that we were all here, still able to walk, talk, breathe, *kiss*.

It could have been Max's long fingers in my hair, his hard, warm body so close to mine, his mouth tasting vaguely of coffee and cake and strongly of Max.

It could have been that this was Max, and today he proved he was more Wonder Max than ever.

Or it could have been he was just a very good kisser.

But I melted into him and his kiss, tipping my head to the

side, lifting my hands to his neck and sliding my fingers into his thick hair, touching my tongue to his.

He growled in my mouth and at the feel of it, the sound of it, my body responded to just how much I liked that noise coming from Max and the fact that it was me who made him make it, and I pressed into him.

His hand went from my waist, up my shirt, and I felt the rough pads of his fingers against the skin of my back.

My body liked that too.

I pressed closer.

Max twisted his torso to me, pushing me back into the chair, his hand coming to my front, running over my ribs, my midriff, and up to cup my breast.

"Yes," I whispered against his lips when his warm hand closed over my soft flesh.

Then I kissed him, our tongues tangling, his thumb stroking my nipple. One of my hands went from his hair to tug up his shirt and it slid in, gliding along his hot skin and solid muscle.

His finger found his thumb and together they squeezed and rolled.

I felt this dance through my body, most specifically straight between my legs, and it felt so good, I liked it so much, I lost it.

I pushed him back and followed him, moving up over him to straddle his hips as my hands went to his shirt, lifting it up. Max helped, his hands going from me to the back of his neck, where he tugged the shirt over his head, down his arms and he tossed it away.

It was my time, my chance, his magnificent chest was right there in front of me and I wanted to explore.

So I bent, my lips going to his neck, my hands going to his body. Both explored. Fingers, lips, tongue, teeth. I slid down, bowed my back to get to him, taste his skin, drift the tips of my fingers across the ridges of his belly, run the edges of my teeth against his nipple, the sound of him sucking in breath forcing a surge of wetness to strike between my legs.

His fingers curled into my shirt and up it went, forcing my torso up, my arms. Then it, too, was tossed away and Max's hands came to my back, pressing in, forcing me to arch forward, pushing me up, and his lips fastened on my nipple over my bra.

"Max," I breathed as the sensation of his mouth closing on me rocked through my body, my hands sliding into his hair, and his tongue flicked out.

Even over my bra this felt better than his fingers, way better. He had a very strong tongue.

"More," I demanded on a whisper, my hips instinctively rolling against his hard crotch. His mouth went away but his hand pulled my bra down, his fingers curling around my breast and there it was, Max's mouth direct on me.

Divine.

I tipped my head down to watch and there was something so amazing about Max's dark head close to my skin. His tanned hand holding my breast to his talented mouth. I couldn't hold it back and I heard my moan as it escaped my lips.

His head tilted back, his face more beautiful suffused with want, especially his want of *me*, and he muttered, "Jesus, honey."

"More," I whispered again, and suddenly we were up, Max's hands at my bottom. My legs went around his hips, my arms went around his shoulders, and he was striding to the stairs.

I couldn't stop, didn't have near enough of him. Maybe I could never get enough. But I was going to try.

I bent my head and put my mouth to his neck, tasting it with my tongue, tugging his earlobe with my teeth.

Before I knew it, we were by the bed, Max bent at the hips, and the light went on.

"Drop your legs, Duchess," he ordered, and I did as I was told.

I no sooner got my feet on the floor than the drawstring was pulled on my pajama bottoms and they pooled at my ankles and then I was up again, only to be partially placed, partially tossed on the bed.

I watched Max follow me down but he didn't land on top of me. His hands slid up my inner thighs, spreading my legs, and then his mouth was on me, over my panties.

I heard the low, rough noise escape my throat as his mouth moved on me. Then he muttered, "Fuckin' soaked," before his fingers shoved the material of my panties aside and his mouth was *on me*.

I bucked against his mouth and moaned, "*Max*."

It was debatable whether his finger or his tongue was more gifted until his finger slid inside and his mouth covered my sweet spot and sucked deep. My whole body jolted at the sheer beauty of it and I knew a combination of the two was *the best*.

"Oh my God," I breathed, because it was coming and it was going to be beyond anything I'd ever experienced.

Then Max's finger slid away and his mouth moved up an inch and he kissed me over my panties.

My head shot up and I cried in protest, "Max!"

His hands went to my armpits and he hauled me up and twisted me in the bed until my head hit the pillows and he came down on top of me.

"You stopped!" I accused.

"We're comin' together this time, baby," he said against my mouth, and then kissed me, his tongue sliding inside. This time I tasted me on Max and it was so appealing, me mingled with Max, I forgot to be angry that he left me hanging and I kissed him back.

He rolled to my side, his finger hooking in my underwear, tugging it down, and I pedaled my feet to kick them off. They no sooner left my ankles than Max's arms came around me and he rolled to his back, taking me with him and I pulled up, straddling him, and my hands instantly went to his jeans. His hand went to the nightstand. I unbuttoned. He pulled open the drawer.

I slid down his thighs and bent low, touching my lips to

the flat, taut skin over the waistband at his fly as I kept unbuttoning. His hand came to my hair. I got the buttons undone and yanked the jeans partly down his hips and saw my first glimpse of the true meaning of Wonder Max.

He was beautiful all over.

My hand wrapped around him for half a happy second when I was pulled up, rolled over, and Max was on me.

"You keep stopping me in the middle of the good stuff," I snapped, my hands sliding down his back, one going in his jeans and over his bottom and it was soft (his skin) and tight (his muscle) and I immediately decided I *loved* it.

Max ripped open a condom with his teeth before he grinned, his mouth came to mine, and he promised, "You'll get the good stuff, Duchess."

His hand was working between us but his mouth was now covering mine and he was kissing me again and then his hips were between my legs and, just as I was really getting into the kiss, I felt the muscles of his bottom bunch under my hand and he thrust into me.

The feel of him, so big, so glorious, surging into me, filling me, connecting me to him, made me break our kiss as my neck arched reflexively and I committed that moment to memory, burned it into my brain, knowing I'd never forget it as long as I lived.

My other hand went into his jeans, both my legs bent at the knees to give him deeper purchase, and I pressed them against his sides as Max pulled out and rammed back in.

"That's beautiful," I whispered the God's honest truth.

"You're absolutely fuckin' right," Max muttered his agreement, pulling out so I could only feel the tip and then slamming back in.

My fingers flexed, my legs squeezed, and my mouth begged, "More, darling."

He gave me more. He gave me his mouth, his tongue, his right forearm in the bed beside me, his left hand fisted in my hair, and he thrust into me harder, faster.

It was back. It was coming. *I* was coming and he'd been right the day before—it was going to be so big, I was going to split straight out of my skin.

"Max—" I panted, my hips rocking with his drives.

"I can feel it, Jesus, Nina, you're ready," Max groaned. "Come for me, baby."

"Okay," I breathed, and did what I was told.

I closed my eyes and my head rolled back, my hips reared up, my hands went from his behind to become my arms wrapping him tight and I gasped as it tore through me, hard, long, and soul-destroyingly beautiful.

Max's face was in my neck and I felt his growled release against my skin half a second after I felt him drive in deep and stay planted there.

After, neither of us moved for a while. Max stayed buried deep, his face in my neck and my arms stayed wrapped around him, my thighs pressed to his sides.

Finally, Max rolled to his back, his arms coming around me as he settled me, straddling him and still connected, on top.

"Yeah," he murmured against my neck as his hand drifted along the skin of my back. "It's fair to say we got chemistry."

I closed my eyes tight and pressed my forehead into the pillow because the case for that was so strong there was no use arguing against it.

One of his arms curled tight around me as his other hand slid down and cupped my bottom.

"How's your leg, Duchess?" he asked softly.

"It's okay," I told the pillow.

"I didn't hurt you?"

God, he was so *wonderful*.

I shook my head.

His voice was even softer when he asked, "How's that shield?"

Before I could stop myself, I whispered, "Cracked."

"Finally," he muttered, both his arm and hand giving me a squeeze.

I sighed.

He rolled again, disconnecting us and laying me on my side. My knees came up as I curled into myself. Max's hand slid my hair from my neck and he kissed me there.

"Don't move, be right back," he ordered. Then he was gone.

I stared at his pillow, thinking I just had that, had him, and I wanted it again.

And again.

For eternity.

In the grips of a sudden, irrational panic, I whirled around and jumped off my side of the bed, thinking it would take too long to rummage through my suitcase and my pajama bottoms would take too long, so I ran to the dresser. I opened and closed the top drawer, then in the one down I found what I wanted. I yanked out one of Max's T-shirts and tugged it on. I was pulling up my panties, my mind blank, no thoughts in my head, none at all, no idea what I was even doing when Max came back in, his hair sexily disheveled from my hands, still in his jeans but they were only partially buttoned.

My mouth went dry. His brows snapped together.

"You moved," he informed me of the obvious.

"Yes."

"You dressed," he went on.

"Um…"

I stopped mumbling when Max started stalking.

I took one look at his big, tall, powerful body in stalk mode and I retreated. In about a step, I hit the dresser with my bad leg.

"Ouch," I said, but I barely got out that one syllable when I was up in the air and then I was down on the bed and Max was on top of me.

I looked into his clear, gray, *determined* eyes.

"Max—"

"I got in," he declared, and he could say that again.

"Max—"

"I'm in, Duchess. You think for a second I'm gonna let you push me out?"

"Um…"

"I'm not."

"Max—"

His hands started roaming and he stated, "No fuckin' way."

I forgot what we were talking about because his hands were up the shirt.

Then I asked, "What are you doing?"

"That was fast."

"Sorry?"

"Too fast."

"Um…"

I stopped muttering when his mouth came to my neck. "This time, gonna fuck you slow."

"Oh my God," I breathed out loud.

His head came up and he was smiling.

Then he said, "Yeah."

Then he kissed me. After that, he fucked me slow.

And it was even better.

*   *   *

We were in Max's sauna, which he had turned on after round one and taken me to after round two.

It was just big enough for two. Max had a towel around his hips and he was sitting on the little wooden bench. I had a towel wrapped around my body and I was on my back on the bench, my knees bent nearly to my chest with my feet against the wooden wall, my head on Max's firm, towel-covered thigh. He was using his fingers to sift through my hair, arranging it across his lap.

Heaven.

I had my eyes closed and my mind was wandering to nowhere, nothing. It wasn't filled with junk and garbage like it normally was. It was just drifting along peacefully. And my body was sated and relaxed so deeply, I didn't think relaxation *could* be that deep.

"What's in your head, Duchess?"

"You have a strong tongue," I blurted the first thing that entered my blank mind. Then my eyes popped open and I saw him looking down at me, his brows raised and his mouth twitching.

"What?" he asked.

"Nothing," I whispered, and turned my head to the side so my cheek was to his thigh and I hoped the hot sauna camouflaged the heat in my face.

His finger touched the hinge of my jaw and went down, along my neck to my collarbone.

"Nina—" he called, and I started talking, scared to death of what he might say. I had to stop him saying anything at all.

"I'm not sure sweating with a man in a sauna is a good thing to do."

"Why?"

"Sweat is unattractive," I told the wall.

"It wasn't when you broke one in my bed ten minutes ago."

He would mention that.

"Well—"

"Baby, look at me," he demanded gently as his fingers curled around my neck.

I closed my eyes and turned my head on his thigh to look up at him. His face was as gentle as his voice and I tensed.

"You're right, we've only known each other a week," he said, his thumb stroking my jaw, and my tense body went taut, all sated relaxation, garbage-free mind gone.

I knew it. I just knew it.

Wonder Max wasn't Wonder Max at all.

He had me naked(ish) in his sauna after having sex with me twice and he was done with me.

I just *knew* it.

"Yes, only a week," I agreed, pulling my face from his hand, lifting up and twisting so I was seated on the bench.

That was as far as I got before I was dragged across his lap. My eyes met his and I opened my mouth to speak but he got there before me.

"I wasn't done," he told me.

"What?" I asked briskly. His brows drew together over narrowed eyes and he examined my face.

"You pissed?"

"No," I lied.

"Yeah, you are."

"No, I'm not."

His eyes roamed my face and his arms tightened around me. "Jesus, Nina, how in God's name can you be pissed?"

"I'm not," I lied again.

"Babe, you are."

"Let me go. It's hot in here, hotter when we're touching."

"Nina—"

I pushed against his chest. "Max, let me go."

His tight arms gave me a shake and he clipped, "Nina."

I calmed and tried to look at him without glaring at him.

"Jesus," he muttered.

"You had something to say?" I prompted.

"Yeah," he bit off. "I was gonna say that I know we've only known each other a week and I know you're scared outta your fuckin' skull because I got you after all those assholes chewed you up but what happened today and what happened tonight even you can't ignore."

I managed to stare at him without glaring at him mainly because my mouth had dropped open and my mind had gone blank.

Then I whispered, "What?"

"We're connected now."

It was breathy this time when I repeated, "What?"

"*Very* connected."

"Max—"

"You think you can walk outta Mindy's life, Brody's life, *my* life after what happened today, what happened between us tonight—"

I broke in, saying, "I thought you were going to send me away."

His head jerked and it was his turn to ask, "What?"

"I thought you were done with me."

Max stared at me a second and I watched in budding, yet weirdly rapt terror as a dark, ominous shadow drifted over his face.

"I'm not those fuckin' guys," he growled so low I barely heard him.

My stomach pitched and I whispered, "Max—"

"Don't *ever* fuckin' mistake me for one of those fuckin' guys."

"I—"

"I don't know all they did. I just know what it did to you, and, Nina, I'm not one of those fuckin' guys."

"Okay," I said softly.

"And I cannot *fuckin'* believe, after I took care of you when you were sick, after this week, after today, after *tonight*, you'd fuckin' think that of me."

Even in the face of his obvious anger, I felt steel sheath my spine and I told him, "You don't understand."

"Explain it to me."

"It always starts good."

"Yeah?"

"Then it goes bad."

"And?"

"Sometimes very bad."

"You think I'm gonna cheat on you, lie to you, beat you?"

"I don't know."

That shadow darkened and his eyes again narrowed just as his arms grew tight.

"You don't know?" he asked.

"I didn't know with them either."

"Jesus, Nina, I give you *any* indication I'd fuckin' do that to you, to anyone?"

Actually, he hadn't.

Of course, there was the small matter of his dead wife that he still hadn't shared with me. Along with a lot of his life.

Whereas I'd shared a good deal of mine. Or it had walked in his front door, spilled out in phone conversations he was privy to, or come out when I was in a snit.

To explain this concept, I told him, "I don't even know how old you are."

"Yeah, that's because you haven't fuckin' asked. I don't know how old you are either but I've actually fuckin' asked."

Unfortunately, I had to admit, he had me there.

"What's your point?" he asked when I fell silent.

"Sorry?"

"What's my age got to do with it?"

"I'm just pointing out we barely know each other and, further, you're not exactly forthcoming."

"Not hidin' anything, Duchess, unlike you, who's secretive as hell and when you aren't, you're guarded."

I felt my own eyes narrow and I snapped, "I am not," even though I knew I kind of was.

"Yeah, how old are you?"

"Thirty-six," I replied immediately, and his face suddenly cleared.

"What?" he asked.

"I'm thirty-six years old."

"Jesus," he muttered, that shadow drifting back.

"What?"

"You're not thirty-six."

I stared at him for a second, speechless, in shock not only at his words but also at the firm, knowing way he said them.

"I am," I told him.

"You think that'll turn me off, you tellin' me you're thirty-six?"

What did he mean by *that*?

"I am thirty-six!" I snapped somewhat loudly.

He scowled at me, his eyes moving over my face. Then he asked, "Seriously?"

"Yes!" I snapped again, and then pushed at his chest to get away.

His arms got tighter. "Nina."

I stopped pushing and glared at him. "Obviously, since my age is such a turnoff, right about now I should be leaving."

His arms got even tighter but his head tipped back, his eyes rolled up, and he looked at the ceiling of the sauna.

"Grant me patience," he muttered his prayer to the ceiling, and I started pushing again so he looked back at me. "Stop pushin', Duchess."

"Let me go."

"Nope."

"Let me go!" I shouted. Max gave me another shake but I kept pushing.

"You don't look thirty-six," he told me.

"Let me go."

"Thirty, at a push."

"Max. Let. Me. Go!"

"I was surprised, surprised enough not to believe you."

"Let me *go*!"

"You wanna know how old I am?"

I gave up pushing since I wasn't getting anywhere and it appeared Max was determined to have this conversation. If I'd learned nothing in the last week, I learned that when Max was determined to do something, he did it.

Instead of pushing, I glared at him again and said, "Not particularly."

He ignored me and stated, "Thirty-seven."

He was older than me. That was good. Not that it mattered if he was younger, really. Actually, not that it mattered *at all* since I didn't care.

"Birthday's May eighth," he continued, breaking into my thoughts.

"Fascinating," I drawled sarcastically, even though it was because he wasn't a year older than me, he was a year and a half and his birthday was only a month away.

Max went on, "Dad died when I was twenty-nine, took me six years to build this house."

That was fascinating too. Six years was a long time. He must have been determined to do that as well.

Even so, I kept my mouth shut.

"He died of cancer, had it since I was sixteen, fought it back for thirteen years before it got him."

That was also fascinating but in a sad yet inspiring way.

Still, I demanded, "Stop talking," but he ignored that too.

"Don't know why Kami's such a bitch. Pretty much has been since I could remember. Mom, she fucked up, getting shot of Dad since she always loved him. They fought, fuck, you wouldn't believe it. Even when they were divorced. But she always loved him. Told me that after his funeral. His death broke her. She was so goddamned stubborn, so fuckin' proud, she let her life just slip away. Lived in the same town as the man she loved her entire life but was only with him for eight years. Now she's bitter for it."

Unwilling to let Max's sharing breach my defenses, I latched on to something he said and called him on it. "Are you insinuating I'm proud and stubborn?"

"Don't think you're proud, babe, but you're stubborn as hell."

"I am not."

"You sure as fuck are."

"No, I'm not."

"If you're not, then why, an hour ago, did you let me in—practically begged me to come in—and locked me tight when I got there and now you're doin' everything you can to shove me right back out?"

This time I ignored him and suggested, "Let's talk about your mother."

I saw his jaw flex in irritation at my change of subject before he asked, "What do you wanna know?"

"How about you explaining why you've had breakfast *and* dinner with *my* mother and she lives in *Arizona* and your mother lives fifteen miles away and I haven't met her?"

"This might have escaped you, Duchess, but we've been kinda busy."

I found it tremendously annoying when he was right.

Max went on. "There's also the fact that your mom showed up on the doorstep and then stayed."

Yes, totally annoying when he was right.

Max continued. "Not to mention, you already met Kami twice and I figured that was enough of my family for a while. I'm tryin' to find ways to make you want to stay, not give you reasons to run away."

This, too, was a good point.

"Perhaps we should stop talking and go back to relaxing," I suggested the impossible. I was never going to relax for the rest of my *life*.

"Explain somethin' to me, babe, why is it you always wanna stop talking when I'm winnin' the fuckin' argument?"

I decided to be honest. "Because you're more annoying when you're right than you are just normally."

Max stared at me a minute, visibly astonished by my honesty. Then he threw his head back and laughed while gathering me close to his amazing, sweat-slicked chest.

"Jesus, you're cute," he murmured when he quit laughing, and my face was stuffed into his throat.

"For the last time, Max, stop telling me I'm cute when I'm angry at you," I demanded, and he laughed yet again.

I shoved at his chest.

Max let me push back but unexpectedly I found myself suspended, then maneuvered until I was straddling Max's lap and my towel was whipped off.

I covered my breasts with my arms and snapped, "Max!"

One of Max's hands was at my hip, anchoring me to his lap; the other one was gliding up into my hair.

"Been wantin' to try this since you told me that first night your sinuses hurt," he muttered, his hand in my hair pulling my face to his.

"What?" I asked on a whisper, all of a sudden enthralled with watching his mouth get closer.

"Try and see how creative I can get, helpin' you work out that attitude of yours."

Even in the sauna, a shiver slid along my skin.

"Max—" I started, but didn't say more.

His head slanted and his hand tilted mine the other way. Then he kissed me.

Then he got creative, helping me work out my attitude, an endeavor at which he was staggeringly successful, for after we were done, the only attitude I had the energy to adopt was calm and serene.

*   *   *

Max and I made love in the sauna before he took me to the shower to rinse off. After our shower, he toweled me off and took me to bed.

He didn't like it when I put on my undies under the towel and tugged his T-shirt on over it before I pulled it free but when I explained I had never been comfortable sleeping nude, he didn't say another word.

As I lay on my side in bed, he soothed ointment onto my scrapes again while I tried with only small success to stay awake.

After he was done, he threw the ointment on the nightstand, turned out the light, tossed the covers over us, and pulled me into his arms.

As sleep started its invasion, I snuggled closer and whispered, "I'm sorry your dad was sick for so much of your life."

"Sleepy Nina," he murmured strangely. His hand had gone up the T-shirt and his fingers were drifting along my back. If I wasn't so sleepy, I would have keenly registered how incredibly nice his hand felt, drifting restfully along my back. Instead, I vaguely registered how incredibly nice his hand felt, drifting restfully along my back.

"What?" I asked.

"Sleepy Nina is Sweet Nina," he said quietly. "I see I got Sleepy Nina."

"No," I told him. "I'm Three Orgasms One in a Sauna Nina. That Nina is always sweet."

His hand stopped drifting, his arm wrapped around me, and he gave me a squeeze.

"I'll be sure to remember that," he muttered, and his mutter sounded like it came through a smile.

Sleep kept encroaching and I didn't have the strength, or will, to fight it.

But for some reason, my mouth kept talking. "Max?"

"Yeah, honey?"

"You scare me."

I felt his fingers tighten against my skin before he said, "I know I do."

"Every day it gets better, which makes it worse."

He gave me another squeeze as I pressed closer and wrapped my arm around his belly.

"Quit fightin' it, it'll just get better," Max advised.

I felt my weight settle into him as slumber slid over me.

But even so my mouth kept moving. "What if it doesn't?"

"Life doesn't give you promises, baby. I can't either but we'll do the best we can."

"Mmm..." Finally, my mouth started to go to sleep too.

But my mind didn't, not for a few seconds, while his words penetrated.

I didn't know for sure but I didn't think I wanted promises, not if they were empty. Honesty felt a whole lot better.

"Sleep, Duchess," Max urged.

"'Kay."

I got another squeeze and my mind processed this, too, mainly how much I liked it.

"'Night, baby," Max whispered, rolling toward me and wrapping his other arm around me, holding me close, holding me tight.

"'Night, Max," I whispered back.

Then I fell asleep in Max's T-shirt, in Max's bed, in Max's house, and in Max's arms and I did it before it fully penetrated my brain how I felt.

Not scared at all.

CHAPTER NINE

Settling

My EYES DRIFTED open and I saw the wall of Max's chest.

I was held tight to his side, my cheek on his shoulder and my arm draped across his belly. It was either dawn or clouds were covering the sun, for it was morning and there was light but it wasn't the sunny Colorado mornings I had swiftly become accustomed to.

It struck me that I felt rested, not like I'd spent the craziest week of my life, but like I'd just had a week on a beach with nothing to do but sit in the sun, read a book, and, if the spirit moved me, go play in the water.

And I knew it wasn't the three orgasms (one in the sauna) that I'd had last night.

It was something else, or a bunch of something elses.

And I knew all of them, every last one, and I decided to take that quiet me-awake/Max-asleep morning time, finally, to sift through them in my head.

Those something elses included Max calling me Duchess, not as if he'd christened me that name eight days ago, but like he'd called me that since birth.

And they included Max holding me while I was gripped in a fever, trembling with the chills.

It was Max making me oatmeal and telling me he'd never give me a reason to take a time-out and if I took it anyway, he'd phone.

It was buffalo burgers and the fact that he ordered them for me, not because he was domineering (or not entirely) but because he knew they were delicious and he wanted to give that to me. Coupled with that, it was the fact that he made sure I had an ale when he found out I didn't drink lager.

It was Max sharing his beautiful bluff and having his picture taken with me, a picture where he did, indeed, look happy. And so did I.

It was Max teaching Damon a lesson after Damon hit me.

It was him taking care of Mindy, talking to Bitsy for the police, on his back under his mom's sink because she needed it fixed.

It was Max hearing me tell Sarah I liked her earrings and going to buy them for me and after finding out I'd already bought them, bringing home the ring.

It was his voice when he spoke of Charlie, as if he respected him and he'd never even met him.

It was because he had my back with my dad, found my mom amusing, and got along with Steve.

It was because we fought all the time and he was right, I enjoyed it. It was challenging; he made me think, kept me on my toes. He wasn't boring, staid, and predictable. He didn't let me walk all over him. He was honest and if something was on his mind, he shared it even if it would anger me or he was calling me out on one of my many neuroses.

It was also because Max seemed not only to have patience with my many neuroses but most of the time he thought they were cute.

It was because he knew how I took my coffee, he held my hand, he kissed my forehead, and he draped his arm along the back of the booth when we were sitting together.

It was Max telling Mindy she was loved, she just didn't get how much.

It was because he was a good kisser and better in bed.

It was because he held me when we slept, like right then, his arm under my body, wrapped around me, holding me to his side as if, even in sleep, he had no intention of ever letting me go.

Even with all that, I knew I would never be the love of Max's life. I knew someplace deep he'd already had that and in that deep place it also hurt knowing I'd never be that for him. If it worked out with us, I wouldn't ever be the love of anyone's life. But that wasn't what bothered me. It was that I wouldn't be that person for Max. Especially Max.

But I also knew it had taken him ten years to find someone he'd like to explore sharing his life with again. And he'd made it clear that someone was me.

So I would never be what Mom was to Steve.

But being Max's second chance at something good was better than anything else I'd ever experienced. Nothing else even came close.

If I gave it a chance, it would be settling, definitely.

But I decided, pressed to Max's side, in his bed, in his A-frame in the Colorado mountains, after living the craziest week of my life and going through what we went through yesterday and still waking feeling rested and safe, I could settle for that.

Sweetheart, you're selling yourself short, Charlie warned in my head.

Go away, I replied, and shifted up, my decision made, which might be stupid, insane, and irrational, but I no longer had it in me to care. I put my mouth to Max's amazing chest and I trailed it down to his nipple. Once there, I flicked it with my tongue.

Max's fingers slid in my hair and I heard a drowsy-husky-gravelly, "Honey."

I'd forgotten about that, so I added it to my list. It was also the fact that Max called me "honey," "baby," "darlin'," and "babe."

Not to mention his gravelly voice.

I didn't lift my head when I heard him speak, just moved over him, straddling his body and adding my hands to my discovery.

I took my time and Max let me. Over to his other nipple where I played, then down, where I ran the tip of my tongue along the ridges of his belly. All the while my fingers moved along the contours of his chest, his sides, and down to his hips.

I moved down, too, my body and my mouth. He opened his legs for me and I positioned myself between them. Curling small, I wrapped my hand around his hard shaft and swirled the silky tip with my tongue.

"Fuck, baby," Max groaned, his fingers sliding back into my hair and fisting.

Encouraged, I swirled and swirled and swirled, then opened my mouth over him and sucked him inside, as much as I could take and I liked every inch I could get.

Max's fist twisted in my hair and he growled, "*Fuck*."

I was guessing he liked it too.

Taking him deep, I decided I liked more than the taste of him, the feel of him in my mouth. I liked knowing how much he liked it, so I slid him out and sucked him back in again and again and again.

Max's other hand went into my hair and suddenly, when I slid him out, his hips surged up, filling my mouth so full, I nearly took all of him. Then he pulled out and surged back in again and again and again.

It was Max taking over, as usual, Max being domineering and it was *delicious*.

So delicious, I felt the tightness and wet of excitement gathering between my legs and I moaned against his shaft.

When I did, he pulled out of my mouth. His hands left my hair, they went under my arms, and I was yanked up and over him. I didn't get the chance to process this quick change of circumstances, he knifed to sitting and before I knew it, my T-shirt was gone. He rolled me to my back on the bed and my underwear was gone. Then he somehow maneuvered me so I was straddling his face but was facing his hips.

"Wrap your mouth back around me, Duchess," he growled from between my legs before I had time to come to terms with my position, which under normal circumstances this early in a sexual relationship might be a little daunting. But I felt the vibration of his words between my legs and I liked it a lot. Enough to forget to feel daunted.

I leaned down and did what I was told. The instant I did, Max's hands went to my bottom, he pulled me down to his mouth, my knees slid out to the sides, and he returned the favor and the very idea of daunted was history.

It was spectacular, so spectacular it took every bit of concentration to keep giving him what I knew he liked when he was giving me what I absolutely adored. He groaned against my sweet spot; I moaned against his cock. It was taking and it was giving and it was sublime.

I was close to climax, I knew it, I wanted it, and I worked him faster because of it.

He lifted me up and half rolled, half tossed me to the side. Then he opened the nightstand drawer and grabbed a condom. Once he turned back to me, he wrapped a hand around my ankle and I gasped with surprise and excitement as he dragged me, spread-eagled, between his knees in the bed.

I sat up as he pulled the condom out of its wrapper and tossed the packet aside.

"Hurry," I whispered, my hands moving on his body as he began to roll it on.

"You'll get my cock, baby, lie back." Max's voice was hoarse and his eyes were not on his task. They were on me.

I waited and dropped my head to watch his hand at work. He really was beautiful *everywhere*.

It had only been a second but I decided he was taking too long.

"Max, hurry."

"Lie back, Duchess," Max growled. "I wanna see you naked, spread on my bed."

My gaze went from what his hand was doing to his face. I caught his beautiful but hungry gray eyes and I sucked in breath.

Normally I was uncertain how I felt about my body and didn't give it much thought. Though I was certain I didn't like flaunting it naked.

At that hungry look in Max's eyes, I forgot I didn't like flaunting.

So I whispered, "Okay," and lay back.

He leaned into me, one hand in the bed, one hand wrapped around his shaft. Then he slid the tip though the wetness between my legs, all the while his eyes roamed my face and down my body.

"Come closer," I urged.

"In a second."

He kept sliding his cock against me, rolling it over my sweet spot and all around, making me tremble and shift with impatience, my hands going anywhere on his body I could reach.

"Come inside," I begged, bending my knees and putting my feet in the bed to get closer to him while capturing his hips and giving them a tug.

"In a second, baby."

"Now, Max."

"I like that," he gritted. His head was bent, watching what he was doing. Then it lifted and his gaze locked on mine. "Beautiful."

He was right, so very right. I still wanted him inside.

The tip of his shaft rolled over my ultrasensitized sweet spot again. The feel of it shot straight through me. It felt great but it wasn't near enough and I lost patience.

"Max!"

I watched as he grinned slow and slid inside slower. My neck arched back.

Max's body covered mine and his hips moved in a slow, sweet rhythm while he wrapped my good leg around his back and I wrapped my bad leg around his thigh.

His mouth came to mine but he didn't kiss me. Instead he murmured, "So sweet, Nina, Christ, you feel so fuckin' sweet."

One of my hands trailed his back, my fingernails grazing him as the fingers of my other hand slid into his hair.

"I need you to go faster, darling," I whispered against his mouth, but he shook his head and pulled out, stilling with only the tip inside. "Max," I breathed, wanting him back.

"You like my cock," he stated somewhat arrogantly, and after he did his teeth nipped my lower lip, which felt wicked and sexy, so I decided to forgive him for being arrogant.

"Yes," I replied, "I like all of you but right now that's my favorite part and I want it back."

I was concentrating on what was happening between my legs, so I missed Max's body going tense.

Then he asked, "You like all of me?"

I was in such a state, I didn't think before I replied, "Yes."

He slid inside, and my eyes slowly closed. Then he slid back out so I only felt the tip and my eyes slowly opened.

"Max."

"What do you like best?"

My attention was elsewhere, so I had to ask, "What?"

"What do you like best? About me."

"Max."

"You want it, Nina, you gotta—"

"You know how I take my coffee," I said swiftly, and when his body didn't move, indeed, when he stared at me like I'd grown a second head, I desperately went on. "And you bought me buffalo burgers. You call me 'honey.' You kiss my forehead. You took me to your bluff and the ring is beautiful and thoughtful and may be the best gift anyone's ever given me. Now, *please*—"

He didn't let me finish. He drove inside and he kept doing it, not a slow, sweet rhythm this time, but fast, hard, rough with his mouth locked to mine and our tongues clashing.

My legs tightened and my fingernails stopped grazing and started digging as it built back up and then, without warning, overwhelmed me.

"You're there, baby," he muttered against my mouth, and

he was right. I was there. My lips parted in a silent moan and I heard him go on. "Christ, Nina, your pussy feels so fuckin' beautiful when you come."

"Max," I whispered as the climax he gave me continued to engulf me.

"Right here, honey." He kept driving deep, hard, and fast but his breath was ragged.

My arms and legs locked around him because he was right there, as close as he could get and I wanted him there forever.

I came down, holding him close, kissing him deep as he kept thrusting until he planted himself to the root, stayed there, and growled in my mouth.

Yes, I wanted this forever.

I kept Max locked in my limbs as he started drifting in and out of me. He kissed my mouth, my jaw, my neck, then rolled to his back, taking me with him and keeping us connected.

His hands glided along the skin of my back, over my bottom, aimless and soothing, and I lay on top of him, my face pressed into his neck. I gave him all my weight not because my recent decision weighed on me. No, that made me feel weirdly free. I gave it to him because I couldn't hold it and I knew he was strong enough to take it.

I liked that about him too.

"Duchess?" he called.

"Mmm...," I answered, and his fingers tensed into my skin; then they started gliding again.

"When you were sick, saw birth control pills in your bag."

"Yes?"

"You on the pill?"

"Yes."

His hands stopped gliding and his arms wrapped around me. "Next time, baby, don't want anything between us. Yeah?"

I had missed two pills while I was sick, so I doubled up for two days after. I had no idea if this strategy would work and I didn't care. Max didn't want anything between us, I didn't either.

"Yes."

His arms gave me a squeeze.

I raised my head and looked down at his content, amazingly handsome face, which, if this worked between us, could be mine.

This thought washed over me in a way that was so gorgeous, so warm, I automatically lifted up farther and put a hand to his face, using my fingertips to memorize the contours of one side, his cheekbone, his temple, his hairline, his lips. It didn't feel as good as it looked but it was close.

I was sliding the backs of my fingers along his stubbled jaw when he spoke.

"You okay?"

My eyes went to his and I saw his were searching.

"Mmm-hmm," I answered.

His mouth twitched and he muttered, "I got Morning but Naked Nina Zombie sittin' on my cock."

I shoved my face in his neck again.

"Mmm," was my response.

I felt his body move with silent laughter before he said, "I'm gonna shift you off me, darlin'. While I'm gone, you move from this bed, I'll—"

"I won't move," I murmured my assurance.

He was silent a moment before his arms gave me a squeeze and he called my name. "Nina?"

"Yes?"

"You sure you're okay?"

I nodded. "I'm good." I cuddled closer. "Very good."

I felt his body grow still under mine and his arms got tighter.

"How good are you?"

I snuggled even closer and answered, "Max, I'm very, *very* good."

He was silent again. Then his hand slid up my spine and sifted into my hair, cupping the back of my head and holding my face close.

"Thank fuckin' Christ," he muttered, keeping me close for a while before rolling me to my good side, pulling out at the same time. He got up on an elbow and leaned down, kissed my temple, and then he left the bed.

I was curled on my side, parallel to the pillows. I crawled back under the sheets and curled again with a pillow held to me.

I watched Max walk out of the bathroom naked and I decided I liked that too.

He pulled the covers up a bit, yanked the pillow out of my arms, tossed it to the head, then replaced it with his body.

This was much better.

He gathered me in his arms, sliding a thigh between my legs so I hooked one on his hip and pressed close, my hands at his chest.

"What happened?" he asked.

"What?" I asked back.

"You're different," he observed.

I was. And maybe he wouldn't like me different. Maybe, when the thrill went out of the chase because there was no chase, he'd lose interest.

All my contentment vanished and I felt my body get stiff.

"Shit, there she goes," he muttered.

I stuffed my face in his throat and lied in order to cover my sudden fear. "I just remembered what's on this morning's agenda."

He was quiet a moment; then his arms gave me a squeeze. "Fuck. Yeah. Jesus, I forgot all about that."

I tipped my head back to look at him and he dipped his chin down to catch my eyes.

"Maybe we can go on the lam, head to Mexico," I suggested.

He grinned at me but replied, "Nothin's chasin' me off my mountain, Duchess, not even your dick of a dad."

I sighed and pressed my face into his throat again. "It was just an idea."

Has fingers slid through my hair before he told me, "You say what you gotta say and then we'll get the fuck outta there."

I nodded. "Okay." I tipped my head back and noted, "Since what I have to say will take approximately five seconds, we should eat breakfast here. Do you know what time we're supposed to be there?"

He rolled, taking me with him and twisting his head to look at the clock. He rolled us back into place and said, "Eight o'clock."

I didn't catch a glimpse at the time, so I asked, "What time is it now?"

"Six-thirty."

I felt my eyes get wide and my body jerked. "Oh no! I have to start getting ready!"

I tried to pull out of his arms but this not only didn't work, he rolled again, this time *into* me so he was mostly *on* me.

Then he shoved his face in my neck and announced, "They don't get fancy Nina."

I felt his tongue where his gravel-voiced words just sounded and goose bumps came up on my skin.

"Max, *everyone* gets fancy Nina," I informed him, ignoring the goose bumps. "I *am* fancy Nina."

His hands started moving on my body and his lips slid up to my ear. "They can get wet-haired, makeup-free Nina."

I gasped, not in shock at his words, but in something else when his fingers curled around my breast.

"Max—"

His mouth came to mine. "Shut up, baby, and kiss me."

"Max—"

His thumb swiped my nipple and he repeated his demand, "Kiss me."

His thumb swiped back and I did what I was told.

*   *   *

"Nina, Jesus, babe, get a move on!" Max shouted from downstairs.

"Be right down!" I shouted back, and I looked at myself in the mirror above the bathroom basin.

Getting ready, I noticed that bruises had risen around the scrapes on my leg and it ached in a dull way. That was the bad news.

But the good news was, no one could see that with my jeans on and the bruise on my cheekbone was mostly faded and light makeup covered it completely. This was good because I didn't want Niles to see the bruise and jump to the same conclusions Dad had.

I grabbed my empty coffee mug, which had been filled and brought up to me by Max. This was after Max had made love to me (again), slower this time and with nothing between us, which, even for me, felt better. Then Max went downstairs, made coffee, came back, and we had a shower (together again). He'd gone back downstairs, brought up two full mugs, and shaved, wearing nothing but a pair of jeans while I stood at his side putting on my makeup. I found, although it was a single-basin sink, the counter was wide as was the mirror, so dual occupancy was quite comfortable. Not to mention nice.

Especially when I could see Max's chest in the mirror *and* right beside me.

Ready well before me, he'd left to do Max things, which I discovered, when I'd left the bathroom to go get my clothes, didn't include making the bed. But on the way back to the bathroom when I looked out the windows, I noted it did include shoveling the steps to the house. So I made the bed, got dressed, and did my hair.

Max could be dictatorial or, I should say, just plain *was* but I was ignoring his wet-hair, makeup-free edict. As ever, "fancy Nina" would be in attendance at the breakfast meeting that day. This was habit but it was also the fact that I was confronting my dad and I needed fancy Nina. Fancy Nina didn't take anything from anyone (anymore). I'd never tried out wet hair, makeup-free Nina. There was no telling what she'd do. She might be a wimp, who knew?

So I'd put on a designer sweater I'd bought at Harvey Nichols. Full price, it was a small fortune but it had a snag, so it had been marked down (and I had a friend who was a dab hand at knitting, so she fixed it and you couldn't even tell). It was a soft taupe with a hint of rose, loose-weave, and a bit see-through. It had long, wide sleeves, a deep V-neck that showed serious cleavage and a fair amount of chest, thus it necessitated a camisole. Therefore, I wore a fitted white one under it, which only seemed to pronounce the cleavage. I also wore my Colorado adventure jeans, my high-heeled tan boots, and the silver earrings and matching ring Max bought me. In fact, I'd never taken Max's ring off.

I walked into the bedroom and saw it was 8:02. It took fifteen minutes at least to get to town. We were going to be late.

Normally this would put me in a panic. I didn't like to be late, nor did I like it when others were late. Late was the worst, unforgivably rude. But since this was my dad and he was a jerk, I didn't much care. Though, to be fair, it wasn't nice to make Niles wait. To be unfair, I wondered if he'd even notice.

I scurried to my suitcase and gathered some clothes for the laundry. I didn't have enough lights, so I opened the walk-in closet and found a massive pile of Max's dirty clothes strewn all over the closet floor.

I stared at the mess, deciding he seriously needed a hamper.

I picked through them, not finding many lights, so I gave up on the lights, dumping them in a tidy-ish pile in the closet. I grabbed some darks—Max had loads of darks—and went back to my suitcase to get my own.

"Nina!" Max shouted.

"Coming!" I shouted back, and rushed to the stairs.

I went directly to the back room, shoved in the clothes, measured in soap, turned on the washer, and heard voices.

I walked out, still carrying my empty coffee mug and turned the corner to see Max in the kitchen, talking to a plump, petite woman with mouse-brown hair, which I decided in an instant would look fabulous with highlights.

I walked toward them, my heels sounding on the wood floors, and Max's eyes came to me before they dropped to my cleavage and stayed there. I ignored Max and looked into the warm, brown eyes of the woman to see she was smiling at me.

"Hi," I said.

"Hiya," she said back.

"Babe, this is Caroline. Caroline, you'll probably remember Nina," Max introduced.

"Hi, Caroline."

"So *cool* to meet you!" she exclaimed. "Last week, you were o-u-t, *out*. Never seen anyone that out and my kids get sick all the time. You even slept through me vacuuming, not just down here but the rug *under the bed*." I stared at her in horror when she informed me of this tidbit but she just kept talking. "Good to see you're feelin' better." I'd hit the mouth of the U of the kitchen, and I lifted my hand to pull my hair away from my face to hide my embarrassment that she'd vacuumed around a bed I'd been o-u-t out in and opened my mouth to say something, but her eyes zeroed in on my hand and she cried, "Oh my God! You have Jenna's ring!"

Before I could react, she rushed forward and grabbed my hand, pulling it down and yanking it to her.

"Um...," I muttered. Her head snapped up from her study of my ring and I saw she was wearing no makeup and she had the most beautiful peaches-and-cream skin I'd seen in my life.

"Jenna only makes these special and they cost a fortune!" Caroline cried out this information in an excited tizzy. "She says it's 'cause they're a pain in the ass to make, seein' as they're rings and all. They cost more than the earrings, which are a whack. I don't get it. It's less silver but what do I know? I'm no jewelry designer," Caroline told me.

"Um...," I mumbled again, not knowing what to say about the fact that Max bought me a ring that cost a fortune. I knew how much the earrings cost. If the ring was more, that was saying something.

But Caroline didn't give me the chance to say anything. She kept right on going.

"I've wanted those earrings for ages, had my eye on them for…ev…er. I keep startin' to save and then shit happens. Still, I hope someday to live the dream." The entire time she spoke, Caroline did it through a big smile. "The ring, shoo! No way!"

For some insane reason, I told her, "Max bought it for me."

At this news, her eyes bugged out and her mouth dropped open.

Then she twisted her torso to look at Max, still holding my hand and she practically shrieked, "*Killer*! I *love* this!"

My mind was racing to find a way to make this news a little less "killer" and thus stop it from being spread around town when her fingers curled tight around my hand. She turned back to me and shook it with excitement. At that my hopes were dashed and I knew this would be all over town in a matter of hours. Maybe minutes.

"Caro, you wanna let Nina go? We gotta get into town," Max said, and I knew from his voice he was grinning and also he didn't mind if news of his ring on my finger was around town within minutes.

"Oh, right," Caroline muttered. She dropped my hand and swept my empty mug out of my other one. "I'll take that. You two get."

"Nice to meet you," I said to her.

"Right back atcha, sister," she said to me, turning toward the sink, and I decided that I was definitely going to like Caroline. She had great skin and warm eyes, and any woman who calls other women "sister" was a woman you'd like.

Max caught my hand, I quickly grabbed my purse from the counter, and Max led me to the closet. Then he opened it, grabbed my coat, and helped me put it on. He took my hand again and without putting on a jacket, he led me to the door. He was, by the way, wearing a pair of jeans, boots, and a heavy, navy blue, flannel shirt over a white thermal.

"Later, Caro," he called as he opened the door.

"Later," she called back, and I heard the sink go on.

"Lock up when you leave, would you?" Max asked from the open door he'd pushed us through.

"Gotcha," she replied on a wave, and Max closed the door.

It was cold, definitely colder than it had been, and there was a new layer of snow over the other layer that hadn't quite gone away. It coated the landscape in white and made Max's vista brand-new again. There wasn't much snow, maybe an inch or more, but it was there and the effect was magnificent.

There were also clouds covering the sun and the steps had been cleared but the gravel drive was still blanketed with white.

"You gonna be safe in those heels?" Max asked, dropping my hand and sliding his arm around my shoulders as we started down the steps.

"I think so," I replied, but suddenly, on the last step, his arm disappeared from my shoulders and reappeared behind my knees, sweeping my legs out from under me.

I started to fall, a small cry escaping my lips, but he caught me in his arms, lifted me, and carried me to the Cherokee.

"Max!" I exclaimed, wondering what Caroline would think if she was watching and she was probably watching.

"I'm hungry," he stated, crunching through the snow to the Jeep. "You breakin' your neck will keep me from breakfast."

"I wouldn't have broken my neck," I snapped.

"Not takin' the chance."

"I've been walking on high heels since I was six and my mom bought me plastic, little girl dress-up shoes," I informed him.

"Still not takin' the chance."

I really had no option but to let him carry me, regardless of what Caroline would think (and tell everyone in town). I couldn't exactly wrestle him in my present position. He might drop me and I wouldn't win anyway.

Therefore I muttered, "Whatever," as he opened the door and set me in the seat.

He slammed the door, rounded the hood, and got in as I buckled my seat belt. He strapped himself in, started up, did a three-point turn, and drove down the lane.

"I'll take you, Nellie, and Steve to The Mark for breakfast after you do your thing," Max offered as he turned into the road.

"The Mark?" I asked.

"Where we had burgers," Max answered.

I liked the idea of revisiting The Mark where we'd had our first kind of date. And visiting it with Mom and Steve. Mom, like me, loved her food and Steve was a no-nonsense, stick-to-your-ribs-food kind of guy, so I knew he'd enjoy it. Something to look forward to after something definitely not worth looking forward to.

"They do breakfast?" I queried.

"Best biscuits and gravy you've ever tasted," he replied, and guided the Cherokee through another turn.

I scrunched my nose. "Um...I'm not a biscuits and gravy person," I told him.

He grabbed my hand and pulled it to his thigh. "They also make homemade granola. Never eaten it but everything at The Mark is good."

Homemade granola. I'd never had homemade granola. That *did* sound good.

We drove for a while in silence and when Max had to make another turn and downshift to do it, he placed my hand on his leg and this time, of my own accord, I turned it and curled my fingers around his solid thigh.

There was a fresh nuance to this action that I liked a great deal. I'd touched his hard thigh, naked in bed, in the sauna, and in the shower and I'd felt it between my legs. It felt better naked and in those places and touching it just then keenly and pleasantly brought up the reminder.

I let that nuance wash over me and closed my eyes at the happy feel of it. They popped open when an unwanted, unwelcome, highly intrusive, and intensely painful thought popped into my head.

That thought was to wonder if Max held Anna's hand while he drove and curved her fingers around his thigh when he had to let her go.

And that thought was so intrusive and so painful, it made me slide my hand away. I hid this from Max by using it to pull my hair from my face. Then I snapped down the visor, snapped up the cover for the mirror, and dug into my purse to find my lipstick.

We neared the main road and Max stopped to wait for a clearing to make a left.

"Nervous, Duchess?" he murmured softly as I uncapped my lip liner and focused on my lips.

I wasn't, not really. Instead I was thinking about Max and the dead love of his life and trying not to let those thoughts sear my soul.

"A little," I lied, and lined my lips with a slightly shaky hand.

"It gets ugly, honey, we're out of there," Max declared, finding his opening, taking the turn, and accelerating down the road.

"Okay," I replied, capping my liner, dropping it in my mini-makeup bag, and finding my lipstick.

I finished my lips, flipped the visor back up, and placed my hand on my purse, not on Max's thigh; although I wanted to do that, I just found I couldn't.

Max didn't notice. Instead, he pushed back into his seat and his hand dug in his jeans pocket. He pulled it out and without taking his eyes from the road, he held up my engagement ring, the ring between his finger and thumb.

"Found that after you had your thing the other day," he muttered as I stared at the ring. "Take it, babe, and do with it what you have to do."

I reached out and took it, still staring at it, remembering how I felt when Niles had given it to me. He hadn't gotten down on a knee. He hadn't slid it on my finger. He'd just placed the box on the table at the restaurant where we were eating, slid it next to my empty plate, and said, "I'd be delighted if you'd accept that."

And I'd been delighted to accept it, delighted at the thought of not being alone, of belonging to someone, and the ring was gorgeous. The diamond was over a carat and excellent quality, set in a thick, just-this-close-to-ostentatious band heavy with gold.

My mind moved from Niles, and like women so foolishly do when they meet someone they like, it flew forward months and months and I wondered, if things worked out with Max, how he'd propose.

Then suddenly I wondered how he'd proposed to Anna.

Then I shoved that thought aside and wondered what his ring would be like.

Then I wondered about the ring he gave to Anna.

Stop it, Nina, and talk to him, Charlie ordered in my head.

I swallowed, tucked the ring into my own pocket, looked out my side window, and didn't utter a word.

Max didn't take my hand again as we drove in silence into town and he parallel parked on the street three cars down from the hotel. I opened my door, jumped down, shut it, and rounded the bonnet, meeting Max on the sidewalk.

I had my head down but stopped when his hand took mine and he didn't move.

I turned, looked up at him, and saw his face was blank but there was something working behind his eyes. Something I didn't get but they were roving over my face.

Finally, Max spoke. "A warning, Duchess. I won't let your dad give you any shit."

The conflicting emotions I had in the Jeep settled at his declaration of support and I moved closer to him.

"Okay," I said.

His hand squeezed mine and then it tugged me closer and his other hand went to my hip.

"Another warning," he muttered, his eyes locked on mine.

"What?" I asked when he didn't say anything further.

He looked at me a second and I saw his jaw tense, his hand got tight in mine, and his fingers gripped my hip.

"Max?" I prompted. His apparent battle to gain control over something I didn't understand was beginning to worry me because it didn't seem at all like Max.

"The right thing to do would be to let you do what you need to do," Max stated.

I felt my brows draw together in confusion and I repeated, "What?"

"Not gonna do that, babe."

"What?" I asked again.

"You think to slide back, settle for something that made you run away because you think it's safe, because it's familiar, because you're scared of takin' a gamble on me, I'm warnin' you now, Duchess, I'm not gonna allow that."

Oh my God.

He was worried. In his Max way, he was worried I'd walk in, take one look at Niles, and go back to my old life. Or let Niles and my father talk me into it. That was why he was silent in the Jeep and that was why he didn't take my hand, because this was on his mind.

"Max—" I whispered, moving closer and putting my hand to his chest.

"You just need to know, I gotta fight to keep what we got so we can build on it, I will. Him, your dad, you, I don't give a fuck. In my life, I've learned when to let shit go and when to fight. This, babe, what we got, I'll fight for."

My hand slid up his chest and curled around his neck as I got closer. I felt tears prick the backs of my eyes and my stomach melted. I was back to thinking settling for Max would be perfectly all right. Definitely.

"Max—"

"Fair warnin'."

My fingers tensed on his neck and I squeezed his hand. "Okay," I whispered. "Fair warning."

He dipped his head and touched his mouth to mine and let

me go but his arm curled around my shoulders, mine curved around his waist, my thumb going into his belt loop, and we walked to the hotel. We no sooner opened the door when we heard it.

My mother screeching, "You *dare*!"

My head whipped to the side and up and I saw Max already looking down at me, his face both surprised and amused.

"Oh no," I whispered.

Over my words, I heard my mom scream, *"Let me at him!"*

Max's arm dropped but he grabbed my hand and walked quickly with long strides and I had to rush double time to keep up with him as he dragged me to the hotel restaurant. When we entered, we saw everyone in the restaurant had their heads turned to a corner table.

This was because, at the corner table, Steve was holding my mother back and her arms were outstretched toward my father, her fingers curled as if she was imagining strangling him.

Niles was standing, looking somewhat troubled and uncertain what to do, but Dad was sitting, staring up at my mother with an ugly smirk on his face.

Upon sight of this scene, I realized my mistake at being late.

Perhaps I should have come as wet-haired, makeup-free Nina.

"I see you haven't changed, Nell," I heard Dad remark acerbically.

Oh dear.

"I…you…I…*argh*!" Mom screeched.

Max and I hit the table and I opened my mouth to speak but Max got there before me.

"What's goin' on?"

Niles was now staring at Max. Not me, but Max, not looking somewhat troubled but looking like he'd been punched in the stomach, which, I had to admit, made me feel more than a little guilt. Dad still didn't move. Steve kept struggling to control Mom but she suddenly stopped fighting and turned to Max.

"You didn't say yesterday what *he* did!" she shrieked, her arm swinging out in an arc to point at Dad on the word "he."

"No point," Max calmly replied to Mom.

"No…no…no *point*?!" she yelled, staring at him with wide eyes.

"Mom, what on earth is happening?" I asked, but before Mom could answer, Dad spoke.

"Nina, good God. Aren't you even going to say a single word to your fiancé?"

I glared at my father. Then I looked to Niles and tried to rearrange my features into something a little less angry and a lot more sensitive.

"Hello, Niles," I greeted softly.

Niles's eyes had moved from Max to Max's hand clasping mine and he'd grown pale.

Then he looked at me and stated, "I don't understand."

I blinked at him, not understanding what he didn't understand.

"I'm sorry?" I asked.

"I don't…" His eyes went back to our hands and then came to my face. "What's happening?"

I felt Max tense beside me but I was still blinking at Niles.

"What's happening?" I repeated.

"This is…you're standing there holding hands with another man," Niles replied.

I pulled in a breath as the guilt hit me, harder this time. I gave a tug at my hand but Max held firm so I stopped tugging and said softly, "I know. I'm sorry, this must be shocking. It's—"

"How did you taking a holiday in the Rocky Mountains translate to you standing across from me, a week after you left, holding hands with another man?" Niles asked. His eyes had gone narrow and color had suffused his face.

"I wasn't on holiday in the mountains, Niles," I reminded him gently. "I was taking a time-out."

"Time-out from work," Niles said instantly.

"Time-out from you," I said back. "From *us*. I told you that, I don't know how many times."

Niles's head tilted to the side and he retorted, "I don't even understand what that *means*. I didn't then and I don't now."

"Then you should have asked me when I explained it to you, told me you didn't understand."

"I didn't think it was worth discussing and I certainly didn't think it would mean it would lead to *this*."

He didn't think it was worth discussing?

Now it was me who I suspected looked like I'd been punched in the stomach.

I let that go. It wasn't easy but I did it and instead asked, "Did you read my e-mail?"

"I scanned it. I didn't have time—"

Max got even tenser at my side but I was concentrating on the fact that I was getting tense too. Very tense. Ultratense.

"You scanned it?" I asked quietly, but I wasn't being quiet in an effort to be gentle. I was being quiet in an effort to control my temper.

"Nina, things are busy at work. You know that. That's why I couldn't come with you on your holiday," Niles replied, sounding like he was getting irritated, though only mildly so.

"Niles, I didn't *ask* you to come with me. The whole point of a time-out is to be *apart* so you can think about whether or not you want to be *together*. I explained that to you."

"That's ridiculous," Niles returned, and that dangerous film of red that boded bad things started to coat my vision.

"Fuckin' hell," Max muttered while I concentrated on trying to clear my vision so I didn't end up screeching like my mother.

"You can stay out of it." My father entered the conversation by speaking to Max.

"Sorry, Larry, I'm in it," Max shot back, and if things weren't going so very, very poorly, I might have laughed. Dad hated to be called Larry, *hated* it.

"And who are you?" Niles asked, scowling at Max.

"I'm Holden Maxwell," Max answered immediately, in other words before I could. "I own the house Nina rented. There was a mix-up. I had to be in town on personal business and Slim didn't tell Nina. She showed up at the house and I was there. Lucky I was. She was sick as a dog, lapsed into a fever so bad she was delirious for two days and I was worried I'd have to take her to the hospital. The fever broke and since then things have advanced between us. We've gotten to know each other, we both like what we know, and, bottom line, you didn't take care of what was yours. Now, as Nina has explained, you've lost it, I found it, and it's mine."

As usual, Max didn't mince words and Niles was now scowling at him but doing it with his mouth hanging open.

Max ignored Niles's scowl, and, his head swinging between me, Mom, and Steve, he asked, "We done here?"

I heard Steve chuckle.

However, Mom declared, "*I'm* not done."

"Yeah you are, sweetheart," Steve said, pulling her back a couple of feet.

"I'm not done either," Dad stated, and finally stood.

"You got nothin' to say. Far's I can see, this ain't your business," Max told him.

"She's my daughter," Dad declared.

"You fathered her but that doesn't make her your daughter," Max retorted, and Dad's face got red.

"As far as *I* can see, this isn't any of *your* business either," Dad returned.

"Then seems to me you aren't seein' very well," Max replied.

Dad didn't continue because Niles spoke.

"I lost *it* and you found *it* and now *it* is yours?" Niles asked Max, and Max looked to Niles.

"That's what I said," Max answered.

I decided to wade in. "Niles, please, listen to me—"

"This is unbelievable," Niles snapped at me, definitely mildly irritated. Maybe even more than that, though that surprised me. I'd never heard him snap, not in all the years I'd known him. "I heard his voice over the phone and I couldn't believe it, not even after Lawrence told me what was happening. I'm standing here looking at you now and I still can't believe it."

My patience waning, I explained, "I'm uncertain what you can't believe since things haven't been good between us for a while, a long while, Niles. And I told you I was taking two weeks to think about our relationship. Then I wrote you an e-mail, which, incidentally, took me two hours to write, explaining we weren't going to work and all the reasons why. Then I phoned you and told you we were over."

"Perhaps, if you were feeling this way, you could have spoken to me, face-to-face, not in an e-mail or over the phone," Niles suggested patronizingly. "And you wouldn't be acting like your mother, performing this drama, which forced me to leave work and fly halfway around the world."

That red film came back, this time with blinding white flashes, the anger so strong, pent up so long, I had to speak through my teeth in order not to scream.

"If you'll remember, Niles, I did. I spoke with you about Charlie's house and how I didn't want to leave it and you didn't listen. I spoke with you about how I was feeling about us, how I felt lonely even when I was with you and you didn't listen. I spoke to you about how my father wasn't a part of my life and here he stands." Like my mother, I swept my arm out to indicate my father but I didn't take my eyes from Niles as I continued. "I spoke with you about the fact we haven't been intimate, not in months and *months* and how that concerned me but you didn't seem to care."

At these words, I felt Max's hand convulse in mine but I ignored it and kept right on talking.

"I spoke to you about how all the times I've spoken to you about all these things—and there have been lots of times I've spoken to you about all these things, Niles—and how that bothered me deeply. And I spoke with you about how it upset me nothing ever seemed to get through, no matter what it meant to me, how important it was. And, finally, I explained exactly what a time-out meant, hoping maybe you wouldn't want me to go. That maybe, in the end, you'd do something to save us, to show me you cared. But off I went and you didn't even phone to see if I got here safely, which, in the end, I did but being as sick as I was, I actually *didn't*."

"And when you spoke to me about all these things, such as you holding on to Charlie's house, I explained that you needed to let them go and move on with your life and you agreed," Niles responded.

"I agreed?" I asked, my confusion mingling with anger.

"You're wearing my ring," Niles declared.

I stared at him a moment, thrown, not comprehending how my accepting his ring meant I agreed with him about anything. Then in order to get this done and get the heck out of there, I nodded and stuck my hand in my pocket.

"I'm glad you mentioned that," I said, pulling out the ring, leaning forward, and putting it on the table. "You can have it back."

"I can have it back?" Niles asked, incredulous, his eyes moving back and forth between me and the ring so fast I feared he'd give himself a seizure.

"Niles, for the last time, please hear me. We don't work. It's over."

Niles stared at me a second, his eyes getting cold in a way I'd never seen before. In a way that made my blood chill. In a way that Shauna *wished* she could go cold. He looked to Max and stated bizarrely, "I'll double his offer."

At this strange turn of the conversation, I was back to blinking but this time also shaking my head a little.

Max, however, didn't seem confused by Niles's words. Niles's words made Max go from annoyed to angry. I knew it because I felt it.

"Seriously?" Max asked disbelievingly.

"What offer?" I queried, but Niles and Max ignored me.

"Double, take it." Niles's eyes swept Max from head to toe and went back to his face. "Undoubtedly you can use it."

"What offer?" I repeated.

"Go to hell," Max bit out.

"Triple," Niles threw out instantly.

"I always liked you, not much, but I liked you," Mom hissed at Niles, also clearly not surprised at this turn in the exchange. "Now your true colors shining through, I don't like you. Not at *all*."

Niles didn't bother to look at Mom. He continued to stare at Max.

"You'd be a fool to walk away from that," Dad advised.

"What offer?" I asked, looking up at Max.

"Your father offered this . . . ," Niles started explaining, and my eyes went to him, "*man* two hundred and fifty thousand dollars to disappear out of your life. I'm making it three quarters of a million."

I gasped at this news and took a step back but Max's hand held mine fast. He took a step forward and he was stronger than me so I went with him.

He put the knuckles of his fist to the table, leaned toward Niles, and spoke quietly, cuttingly, in his rough, gravelly voice. "Fucked her last night, man, and this morning. Five times. *Five*. It was like she hadn't been touched in a decade. So fuckin' sweet. *Damn*," he taunted, his eyes locked on Niles. "You've had her. You gotta know, not enough money in the world's worth that."

Niles's torso jerked back and his face went pale again but it was my father who spoke.

"Honest to God, Nina, what on earth is the matter with you? You'd choose *this* over Niles?"

I stood there, shocked at what Max had said to Niles, shocked at what I was seeing from Niles, shocked that any of this was even happening, and I looked at my father, silent. Then I looked at Niles. Then I looked over my shoulder at Mom and Steve. Finally, I looked at Max.

What I had taken in consisted of both Dad and Niles wearing corduroys and nice sweaters. Both fair. Both slim. Both good-looking in a polished way. Both looking like money, breeding, class but not a lot of warmth. In fact, they both looked weirdly detached even though they were participating in this debacle.

I also saw Steve's attractive silver hair and I knew it had been dark before it'd changed its color. He was dressed much like Max without the thermal. No airs. No graces. All man. He had his arm around Mom's waist and her back was held close to his front. He was bigger and taller than Mom and looked like he could take on a bear and would if that bear threatened his Nellie.

And I'd seen Mom wearing lovely tweed trousers, a fitted black turtleneck, a tailored, trendy, black leather jacket over the sweater, and a neat, stylish black purse on her shoulder. Earrings, a pretty, unusual necklace glinting against her sweater, her hair pulled back softly in a ponytail, her makeup flawless. She stood in Steve's arm, dressed fancy, dressed somewhat like me, dressed like she liked to dress, standing there like she'd been built to stand held close to Steve.

And I felt Max's big, warm hand wrapped around mine, engulfing it, steady, strong, safe. He'd stood by my side through this fiasco and never let me go.

I stared at Niles and Dad across the table and I got it then. It penetrated.

Niles actually *didn't* care about me. Once he had me, he thought he had me and that was it. The world revolved around him, his wants, his preferences, his habits, and everything around him fit into that world. He didn't have to work at it, as partners always had to work at it. He didn't care enough to work at it. It was up to me to care, to fit, to revolve around him, his wants, his preferences, his habits. He didn't listen to me because what I said didn't matter. It didn't fit into his world and thus it didn't mean a single thing to him.

Even now, standing across from me, having lost me, he didn't try to win *me*. He was trying to buy off *Max*.

"You got nothin'?" Max prompted Niles, and my attention went from what was now screamingly obvious back to him.

"If you think you can goad me into getting physical, then think again," Niles snapped. His face had changed again to another look I'd never seen on him. Contemptuous, even scornful, and that hideous look shook me from my scalp straight to my boots.

"I just told you I fucked who you consider your woman, fucked her five times, and you got nothin'?" Max asked, disbelieving.

"This is hardly gentlemanly behavior." My father entered the discussion.

Max straightened and turned to Dad. "Not one fuckin' thing gentlemanly about protecting what's yours. Looks like you're gonna lose it, you do everything you can to stop that from happening." Max looked back to Niles. "And you didn't do that. She was a week away from me, she walked into a room I was in holdin' another man's hand, I'd lose my fuckin' mind. Not at her. Wonderin' where I lost my way and I'd talk to her about how to find my way back." I heard my mother make a noise from behind us but I was too busy staring at Max's profile, letting his words sink in and noting, as they were doing that, how good they felt. When Niles didn't respond, Max finished, "Christ, you stand there, starin' down your nose at me and you don't even get it's *you* who doesn't deserve *her*."

Moments passed and I continued to stare at Max's profile, his words rocking me in a good way but also wondering how rude it would be if I made out with him in front of Niles.

"Nina," Niles called, and I started, my eyes, with effort, leaving Max and going to him. "Perhaps we can speak alone," he suggested tardily.

"Too late, asshole," Max muttered, turning from the table and dragging me out of the restaurant.

This was because things had gotten ugly and therefore, as Max promised, we were out of there.

We exited the restaurant, Mom and Steve on our heels, and

I was still trying to come to terms with all that was said and all I'd discovered inside. Max, however, had already come to terms with it and the terms he'd come to was him being annoyed *at me*.

"Said it yesterday, babe, and you didn't listen," he muttered, dragging me down the wooden plank sidewalk with Mom and Steve following.

"Sorry?" I asked, walking swiftly to keep up.

"Said you ain't goin' to that showdown, them fuckin' with your head. Did you listen? Nope. Said you wanted to go. Jesus," Max explained tersely, and I tugged on his hand to stop him, which he did, right outside The Mark.

"Are you insinuating that was my fault?" I asked.

Max looked down at me and replied, "Babe, we were all there because you wanted us to be."

"Oh my *God*," I snapped, and tried to yank my hand from his but this effort failed so I gave up and went on. "Are you serious?"

"You were gonna marry him, Nina. Did that scene surprise you?" Max asked.

"Yes!" I shot back. "Yes, it did. I'd never seen Niles like that in my life."

Max's brows went up. "Honest to God?"

"Honest to God!" I cried. "I'd never marry *that*." I looked at Mom, who was staring at me with a mixture of anger, shock, and distress. "I can't even...I don't even..." I stopped, the entirety of what just happened hitting me. I tilted my head back and shouted, "I almost *married* that man!"

"Honey—" Max murmured, pulling at my hand, but I yanked it away, successfully this time, and took a step back.

"I almost married *my father*," I whispered, aghast, as I fully processed this monstrous realization.

"Duchess, baby—"

"He offered you money," I told Max.

"So did your father," Mom put in informatively.

"Nellie," Steve said low.

"I mean, who *acts* like that?" I screeched.

"It doesn't matter. It's over. You returned the ring. Done,"

Max stated, no longer annoyed, apparently now in control—another one of Nina's wild hairs modes. He knew me enough by now to know he didn't control me, I'd march back to that restaurant and wring Niles's neck and my father's, for that matter.

But Nina was not to be controlled.

"Two years. Two years I wasted on him. Oh. My. *God*." I threw my hands out. "What a fool! I'll never get that time back!"

Max looked over my shoulder, then at me, and said quietly, "Babe, calm down. Let's go in. Get food—"

I interrupted him, still ranting. "All that time I kept thinking and thinking, was I doing the right thing? Would I hurt him? How could I hurt him? He's a good man. Wondering, worried, my head filled with rubbish. I swear, I made myself sick with it. I did!" I shouted. "You were there! I actually made myself sick with it!"

Max caught my hips and pulled me closer to him. "Nina, it's done."

"I spent two hours writing an e-mail to him, Max, making certain it didn't hurt too much and he *didn't even read it*."

Max's hands gripped my hips harder and he said softly, "This isn't anything to be angry about."

My eyes grew wide and I yelled, "*You* didn't waste two years of your life on him!"

"And *you* realized it was a mistake. You did the right thing, the smart thing. You made the right decision and now you're free to move on with your life."

I glared at Max because he was right and I wanted to be loud and angry for at least a little while longer.

I mean, my God, I nearly married *my father*. And I hated my father!

"You know what's annoying?" I asked Max, and his hands slid around my hips to the small of my back, pulling me closer.

"What's annoying?" he asked back but I saw he was no longer in Control Nina Mode. Now he looked amused.

"When you're right and I want to be angry and you being right means I can't be angry anymore," I informed him.

"Baby," he muttered through his grin.

Yes, amused. My eyes narrowed on his grin and my stomach growled. I decided I could be annoyed at Max while I ate. Therefore I demanded, "Feed me."

"I'm guessin' about now if I told you that you're cute, you'd get pissed."

"Absolutely," I snapped.

"Then I won't tell you you're cute."

I put my hand on his chest, gave an ineffectual push, and demanded again, "Feed me, Max. I need homemade granola and you better hope they have yogurt or all hell's going to break loose."

His grin turned into a smile. He bent his neck, kissed my forehead, and, his lips still there, murmured, "Granola."

Then he dropped his arms but caught my hand and, glancing at a now-smiling Mom and Steve, he led us into The Mark.

*   *   *

It was clearly past normal breakfast time for mountain people because the restaurant was only a quarter full.

There was no Sarah. It was Trudy who led us back to the corner booth we'd had that first night and she did it while chatting to us, especially me, like she'd known me my whole life.

We sat, Max and I with our backs to the wall, and barely got ourselves sorted before Arlene marched up to our table, introduced herself to my mother and Steve, and then launched into a tirade about the proposed new plans for some strip mall. This tirade was directed mostly at me in a way that made it seem like Arlene and I had been in cahoots during a variety of shenanigans and therefore Arlene thought I'd agree wholeheartedly with her and together we'd start arranging meetings where we'd create signs and banners and organize townsfolk to picket the building site. Then she declared she needed to "get wrecked" and we were to meet her at The Dog at eight o'clock that night. Then without waiting for us to accept or decline this invitation, she marched away.

Trudy came back, took our orders (lucky for Max, they had yogurt but no berries), and walked away, but when she did, a woman approached. I remembered her from the night of Max teaching Damon a lesson. She was the one who ran in to get Mindy and my bags. She was also, I discovered, the designer who made my earrings and ring and although we'd spoken less than a dozen words to each other, she chatted animatedly to me and Mom, Max and Steve like we'd all been present when they'd taken the training wheels off her bike. Then a mountain man across the room called her name in much the same impatient tone as Max spoke to me before we left his house. She smiled at us, gave us a finger wave, and told me, specifically, she'd see me at The Dog as if we met there frequently for girls' night out, and then she left.

Everyone but Max watched her go.

Steve turned to me and said, "How long you been here again? I thought it was a week."

Max slid his arm along the back of the booth and burst out laughing.

I ignored Max's laughter and explained, "People here are friendly."

"I'll say," Mom muttered, and I heard Max's phone ring.

He leaned forward, pulled it out of his back pocket, and looked at the display.

I did too. It said "Bitsy calling."

"Sorry, gotta take this," Max murmured, and slid out of the booth, flipping it open.

I sat in the booth, watching him walk to the entry as he put the phone to his ear and deciding I liked the way he walked. He was tall, big, his body muscular but his gait wasn't lumbering. It was agile, fluid, almost graceful in a manly, macho way.

"Can I just say...," Mom started, and I looked at her to see she was also watching Max, "that I don't like him." She looked back to me, leaned in, her eyes alight, and she finished, "I *love* him."

"Mom—"

"No, I *adore* him," she amended.

"Mom—"

"No, I want to *adopt* him. But if I did, that might make it weird, seeing as you'd be brother and sister, in a way. So I'll just wait for him to become my son-*in-law*."

"Nellie," Steve said through a smile. "Enough."

"I'm moving to Colorado," I blurted my announcement, and both Steve and Mom stared at me.

"Come again?" Steve asked.

"I'm moving to Colorado."

Mom clapped loudly and cried, "*Yay!*" even louder.

I leaned forward and hissed, "Mom, be quiet! Max has asked, kind of, in his Max way, which means he told me I was moving here but I haven't agreed, yet. He doesn't know I've decided. I want to tell him, special if I can."

Mom leaned forward, too, and whispered, "Yay."

I smiled at her, shook my head at Steve, and sat back.

"This is wonderful." Mom was still whispering. "Marvelous, sweetie. Perfect timing. We haven't had a chance to tell you, with all the things going on, but Steve and I have bought an RV."

My heart skipped and I stared at her, knowing where this was going but I didn't get a chance to say anything before Mom carried on.

"We don't have it yet. We're getting it customized, so it'll take some time, but you see, now we can come up here for the summers!" she cried.

"Nellie—" Steve started.

"Mom—" I said.

"I just hope Steve can get it up that mountain, and if he can, we'll hook it up to the side of Max's house. It'll be perfect."

"Nellie—" Steve started again.

"Mom—" I repeated.

Mom waved her hand in front of her face and kept talking. "You'll be close again. I just *love* this. It's *perfect*."

"Mom—" I said yet again.

"Nellie," Steve said over me. "They'll just be starting out."

"Pishposh. Starting out. They act like they've been married for years and anyway, Max loves me," she declared. "And he's a man's man, like you. You can help him chop wood for the winter and, I don't know, other man stuff."

Steve stared at Mom for several seconds, then looked back to me. "Don't worry, doll. I saw a brochure at that hotel for an RV park. We'll haul the car up with us and hook up there."

"No, we won't," Mom told Steve.

"Yes, Nellie, we will," Steve told Mom.

"No, darling, we *won't*. I want to be close to my Neenee Bean," Mom shot back.

Jesus, I forgot how much I like your mom, Charlie said in my head, sounding amused, and I rolled my eyes.

"Mom—" I began, but Steve again spoke over me.

"We're not, love. We'll come up, we'll stay a few weeks, but we'll hook up at the park, give them privacy."

"There's enough privacy with us in the RV outside Max's house," Mom retorted, and looked at me. "Though, we'll probably use your bathroom and maybe your kitchen."

I sighed.

Steve spoke. "Nellie, it's not gonna happen."

"It is."

"No, it isn't," Steve said in a firm way that couldn't be denied, even by Mom.

Mom glared at Steve, knowing, by Steve's tone, there was no way she was going to get her way. Steve calmly accepted her glare. Trudy arrived with four coffees.

"Thank you," I said to Trudy, and tried not to smile at the realization that Mom had her Max. I'd been happy for her when she found Steve. Now, understanding, I was ecstatic.

Max came back and slid into the booth beside me while I poured milk in my coffee.

"Today's plans have changed, babe," he announced before taking a sip of his, and I looked at him.

"Plans?" I asked, not knowing we actually had plans.

"Yeah, gotta be at George's in an hour."

"George's?" I queried.

"Though, thinkin' this is good. You can meet him, feel him out."

"Meet him? Feel him out?" I parroted.

Max turned fully to me and put his arm on the back of the booth.

"Yeah, he's the attorney I was tellin' you about," Max reminded me, and I stared because the phone call hadn't been from George. It had been from Bitsy.

"Why do you have to go there?"

Max's easygoing nature vanished and his jaw got tight before he answered, "Curt's will is bein' read and, apparently, I'm mentioned."

I leaned into him and put my hand on his thigh before I breathed, "*Really*?"

"Yep," Max answered, not looking happy.

"What's this?" Steve asked.

I looked at Steve, then at Mom. "Curt is the man who was murdered."

Mom's eyes got wide. She leaned forward again and breathed, "*Really*?"

"Jesus, it's uncanny, like two peas in a pod," Max muttered, his eyes moving between Mom and me.

I decided to ignore that and told Max, "That's bad form, Max, informing you that you need to be at the reading an hour before the actual reading."

"Like I said," Max told me, "George is busy. Bitsy said he's covered. He set up the reading, told her when it was, and called her a while ago to get her help gathering everyone."

I didn't repeat it but this was bad form. Perhaps this George person *did* need help. That was good considering I needed a job.

"So, our plans?" I went back to the earlier topic.

"You and me go to the reading. Before that we find out when the insurance people are gonna come look at your car and then we go see Mindy."

I hadn't forgotten about Mindy but I also hadn't quite figured out my Save Mindy from Herself Strategy. I *had* forgotten about the car.

"Can we go to the reading?" Mom asked. "I've never been to the reading of the will of a murdered man." Her eyes searched the ceiling without her tilting her head up. She looked at us again and finished, "Or any man for that matter."

Max and I looked at Mom but it was Steve who spoke. "Nellie, you can't just sit in at one of those things like you're goin' to watch a play."

"Why not?" Mom asked Steve. "I'll be quiet."

"Like that'll happen," Steve muttered, and Mom gasped in affront.

Max chuckled.

"We'll go out," Steve said to Max. "Check out that RV park and we'll make dinner reservations for that Rooster place you were tellin' me about"—he paused and glanced at me—"for just Nellie and me, leave you two be for a while."

"RV park?" Max asked.

"I'll explain later," I told him quickly.

Mom spoke to me. "I want to know what happens at the reading the minute you know."

"Mom, it's not exactly your business," I informed her.

"Sweetie, everything that has something to do with you is my business," Mom informed me.

"Okay, agreed, but this has to do with *Max.*"

"And *Max* is with *you.* Therefore it has to do with *you,* so I want to know everything, *immediately.*"

"She's got you there," Max murmured, and she did, which was exasperating.

"Where's my granola?" I asked, craning my neck and searching for signs of Trudy.

"Max, sweetie," Mom called, but her head was bent as she dug in her purse. "Give me your phone number. Calling Nina is like calling England even when she's here. I'll call you."

"Don't do it, Max," I warned.

Max looked down at me, pressing his lips together, and when Mom pulled out her phone, he gave her his number.

And in case you haven't got it yet, I like him too, Charlie said in my head.

I sat back in the booth, defeated, and Max's arm curled around my shoulders, which made me feel not so defeated.

"Nina," Steve called. My eyes went to his and his were warm but the only thing he said, and he said it softly, was, "Doll," and that one word made me feel even better because I knew he'd make everything okay, even with Mom.

Softly back, I replied, "Love you, Steve."

Max's arm curled me close to his side but I only had eyes for Steve.

"Me too, darlin'," Steve replied.

Mom pulled in an audibly shaky breath and Trudy arrived with our breakfast.

* * *

"Thank *God* you're here!" Bitsy exclaimed on a whispered cry when Max and I walked into what a brass plaque outside the door announced was the office of GEORGE NIELSON, ATTORNEY-AT-LAW.

She'd positioned herself at the door, looking like she was waiting for us, and wheeled herself around before the door fully closed behind us.

She only had eyes for me and at one glance through the reception area I knew why.

Shauna Fontaine was sitting across the reception area smiling like the cat who got her cream.

"Oh no," I whispered.

"What the fuck?" Max asked, *not* on a whisper. His eyes were on Shauna and his face was hard.

"George says she's mentioned in the will," Bitsy told us, still whispering urgently, and she looked like she was struggling with tears or anger or both. "He didn't tell me until I got here. He didn't want me to be worried."

"Fuckin' Curt," Max muttered under his breath, and I tore my gaze off Shauna and looked down at Bitsy.

"Just breathe deep," I suggested, because I didn't know what else to say.

"I'd like to breathe *fire*," Bitsy said back. "What was Curtis thinking?"

"Curt didn't think much and when he did, it was about himself," Max told her bluntly, and I nudged him with my elbow, which I think had more of an effect on my elbow than on Max, for he didn't budge and his eyes remained in the unhappy scowl he was directing at Bitsy.

Bitsy pressed her lips together. I didn't know if this was to bite back a retort or to hold back tears. Then she looked to me.

"I'm just glad you're here. You can sit in, listen to the will. I'll make George let you look at it after. If he gives Shauna anything, or...everything"—she swallowed—"you can help me fight it."

"Bitsy—"

"Just listen in, okay? I already told George you'll be here. He says there's no reason to be worried but I want you in there, okay?"

I looked up at Max, who was looking down at me. He nodded, so I pulled in a deep breath and looked back to Bitsy.

"Okay," I told her.

"Thanks, Nina," Bitsy whispered. She took in a deep breath, too, turned her chair around, and wheeled into the room.

Max and I followed.

"Max," Shauna greeted him, her voice a contented purr; then she looked at me and her eyes grew cold. "Nina."

"She-bitch from hell," I replied. Bitsy's head shot around and she looked at me with wide eyes. Her fear had disappeared, delighted astonishment in its place, while Max grunted his amusement. I heard a few twitters from the others occupying the room but Shauna glared ice daggers at me.

A tall mountain-manesque person—"esque" because he

was wearing a suit but this barely concealed the mountain man within—with black hair cut super short even though there wasn't much of it to cover his scalp walked out of his office.

"Bitsy," he said, looking at her; then he looked at Max. "Max." His eyes scanned the room as he nodded to the others assembled, of which there weren't many: another mountain man, an older lady and gentleman, and me. However, they slid right past Shauna without acknowledging her and he announced, "Let's get this done so you can all get on with your day." He turned and walked back into the office.

We all followed.

"My next holiday is going to be to a nunnery in the depths of the highlands of Scotland. Maybe on an island," I muttered to Max, and he grabbed my hand and gave it a squeeze. I looked up at him to see he entered the room smiling.

Someone had pulled in a number of chairs and we all sat, Max and me on a couch in the back of the room. Bitsy was up close and she turned to look at us. I gave her a nod. She nodded back and looked at George.

George seated himself behind his big lawyer's desk, a desk nearly every lawyer except those who didn't happen to be partners in massive law firms seemed to have. Mountain man under his suit or not, George took his business seriously and he wanted those sitting across from him to take him seriously too.

I was wondering how much a desk like that cost when he began.

"Strangely enough, Curtis changed his will about a week before he passed," George announced, and I watched Bitsy stiffen and Shauna smile.

She'd told him she was pregnant around that time, I decided, and I got tense right along with Bitsy and Max, who shifted at my side to drape his arm along the back of the couch.

I dropped my hand to his knee and squeezed.

"We'll just get started," George said, and as he started, I listened closely.

Listening, there didn't seem to be anything Bitsy had

to worry about. Curtis had bequeathed her his business, his money, and the land he owned. He had made some generous bequests to his mother and father (the older lady and gentleman in the reception area) and a stretch of land he gave Trevor, a business colleague whose name I knew because Kami brought it up so often. There were a few personal items he also gave his mom and dad. The will wasn't very long but it was straightforward.

"To Holden Maxwell," George read, and I sat up straighter as Max's arm moved from the back of the couch to my shoulders. "I leave the acreage…" George went on but Max went completely still by my side and everyone gasped and turned to stare at Max as George read out the situation of the acreage he left Max, fifteen acres in all, apparently.

When he was done giving the estate description, George's eyes left the papers in his hand and they locked on Max as he said straight to Max instead of reading the words from the page, "Max, you win, buddy."

Bitsy emitted a little choked sob and Curtis's mother bit her lip, but I moved my gaze through them to stare at Max's profile, seeing his face still hard, his jaw tight, his gaze riveted to George.

George's eyes moved quickly back to the paper, and his lips twitched as he finished, "And finally, to Shauna Fontaine, I leave the knowledge that, when I started it with her, I got a vasectomy."

I felt my eyes grow so wide I feared they'd pop out of my head. I also tried and failed to stop a startled giggle from escaping my lips and my gaze flew to Shauna, who had gone pale but that didn't stop her from looking murderous.

I looked toward Bitsy when I noticed her turning in her chair and the minute she caught my eye, I saw she was struggling with hilarity.

"Welp, that's it," George stated. "Except he's left two personal letters. One to you, Bitsy." His eyes moved to us at the back of the room and he called, "And one to you, Max."

"Shit," Max muttered, and I looked up at him.

I'd failed to look to see if he thought Curtis's mention of Shauna was as funny as Bitsy and I did. But looking at him then, I noticed he didn't seem to think one thing was funny.

Max stood and I did it with him as the others also moved to their feet. Without looking at anyone or saying a word, Shauna left the room as the rest shuffled around murmuring to each other.

Trevor approached Max after he squeezed Bitsy's hand.

"Don't start," Max warned when Trevor opened his mouth to speak.

"Max, come on. You know, now especially, we could use you."

Max didn't respond and Trevor looked to me.

"You Nina?" he asked.

"Yes," I replied.

"I'm Trevor."

"Yes." I smiled at him. "I did hear your name read in the will."

He smiled back but my smile died when he spoke. "Rumor has it you caught the uncatchable." He jerked his head to Max. I was startled by his words and didn't have the chance to recover when he went on. "Talk to his stubborn ass. Get him to see sense."

"Um...," I began, my muscles growing tight.

"Trevor, shut it," Max growled.

"Curt's gone, Max, someone's gotta step into his shoes," Trevor told him.

"That'd be you," Max returned.

"Ain't me and we both know it," Trevor replied, leaning closer and saying low, "Now, you'd be doin' it for Bitsy." Max made no response. His face was stony and Trevor regarded him for several seconds before he finished, "'Spect, you think on that awhile. I'll see you at the office." He nodded to me, mumbled a, "Pleasure to meet you," and walked away.

I turned to Max and asked, "Darling, are you okay?"

Max looked down at me and said, "Gave me the acreage around my land."

"Sorry?"

"That fifteen acres? It's acres he bought up for what he was plannin' for my land. That's what he gave me."

I leaned into him and put my hand on his bicep as I whispered, "Oh my."

A muscle leaped in Max's jaw. He bent closer to me and whispered back, "Ain't what you think, babe. The inheritance tax on that land's gonna be crippling."

My hand flexed on his bicep as my heart squeezed and I breathed, "Max."

"I pay it, it'll cut deep and it'll be hard for me to keep all of it. Means I'll have to sell it. I'll make a whack on it but whoever I sell it to isn't gonna keep it clean. They'll build. Means I'll have condos or houses or somethin' restin' at the edge of my land. Land that's been unspoiled for . . . fuckin' . . . *ever.*"

"Darling," I whispered.

"And it's the land that butts the edge of the bluff."

My fingers spasmed on his bicep, my stomach dropped in an unpleasant way, and I stared at him.

I got closer and said, "Max, you can't sell it."

"He fucked me, babe. He said I won but that was his sick joke. He fucked me. Instead of givin' that land to Trev or Bitsy, who'd have to do somethin' with it themselves, which wouldn't be on me, he gave it to me knowin' I'd have to sell, knowin' he'd be makin' *me* ruin my mountain, destroy my bluff. When if I stayed with him years ago, I'd have my land, that land, and I'd be in a position to afford to keep both just like it is."

I felt my heart begin to race as that red started seeping over my eyes. I didn't even know him, but I hated Curtis Dodd.

"You can't sell," I declared.

"Got no choice, Duchess."

"I'll help you."

Max's already stony face turned to granite.

Then he growled, "Not gonna happen."

"Max—"

His eyes moved over my shoulder and he clipped, "Later."

"Max," Bitsy said, wheeling up to us with George at her side. She was beaming. "Curt finally did it. Healed the breach." She was apparently unaware of the catastrophe that had been perpetrated in this room. "It sucks that he did it after dyin', but at least he did it."

"Yeah," Max grunted, and Bitsy turned her smile to me.

"It's a long story but at least it ends well," she told me.

"Mmm-hmm," I mumbled, my hand traveling down Max's arm to grasp his and his fingers curled around mine in a death grip.

"You must be Nina," George said, and I nodded while trying not to wince. "Bitsy tells me you're her new attorney," he went on, and my eyes swung to Bitsy, who was still grinning ear to ear and then back to George as he kept talking. "And seein' as I don't exactly want to lose her as a client, thought we could talk while these two read their letters from Curtis."

"Nina's movin' to town, George," Max announced, and George's eyes, still on me, grew shrewd. "Yeah, I've seen her in action. You definitely wanna clear an office for her."

"You're moving here?" Bitsy asked, even more delighted at this news.

"Well—" I started.

"Yeah," Max stated.

"That's great!" Bitsy declared.

"Um …," I mumbled.

"Letters are on the desk. They're addressed on the envelopes. Don't know what's in 'em. It's weird, the timin', but Curt just gave 'em to me to give to you a coupla weeks ago," George told them, and moved to me, taking my elbow. Max dropped my hand as George finished. "We'll give you a minute."

He led me out as I looked over my shoulder at Max, who jerked his head at George; then he followed Bitsy, who was wheeling toward the desk. I lost sight of them when George closed the door. He led me a couple of feet away and stopped.

"You really movin' here?" he asked.

"Um...," I answered.

"Need help, seriously, divorces, adoptions, wills, a bunch of snot-nosed, rich kids doin' shit. Petty crime. Their parents always wantin' their kids to have their day in court rather than takin' their community service or payin' their fine like they should, teachin' the kids a lesson. I'm fuckin' buried."

I stared at him and said, "Well—"

"Don't want to lose Elizabeth Dodd as a client, either. If she keeps Curtis's business alive, she's a freakin' cash cow." My eyes narrowed and George said swiftly, "In a good way, of course."

"Yes, there are a number of good ways someone could use the term 'cash cow' when referring to a human being," I retorted.

"Still, you see what I'm sayin'," he told me.

"I do indeed," I replied.

"Send me your résumé, I'll have a look," he invited.

"Why don't you send me yours and I'll see if I want an office here or if I want to put up my own shingle," I returned.

His brows shot up and he asked, "Competition?"

"I know it'll be a new thing for you, as Max told me you're the only business in town but if I decide to go that way, I'm sure you'll get into the spirit of things."

His hands came up in a placating gesture. "I see no reason to shake things up, Nina. You got experience, we can work together."

"We *may* be able to work together if I never hear you refer to Bitsy or anyone else as a cash cow. They're clients with issues we need to help them sort. Not dollar signs. Or at least that's the way I work. Am I understood?"

He grinned. "So you're one of those?"

"One of what?"

"A liberal."

I rolled my eyes, but answered, "Yes."

"Make things interesting."

"I live to make things interesting."

"Yeah, I heard about The Rooster." My brows went up and he explained, "Brody stopped by yesterday morning. Heard you tore Shauna a new one."

"Well—"

"And Kami."

"Um…"

"Wish I'da been there, shit, just for the Kami thing— woulda paid money for that. She's somethin' else and I don't mean that in a good way. Hell, grew up with her and Max and everyone wondered how they could even be related. But would sell my kid to watch someone tear Shauna a new one. That woman, cold as ice, pure frost." He grinned bigger and stated, "Never in my life was I more thrilled to change a will. I typed the damn thing myself when Curt gave me the change."

I decided maybe I might like him.

"You wouldn't have to sell your children. I'm happy to do it for free anytime she pulls out her ice daggers and takes aim."

He tapped my arm and said frighteningly, "She's got her eye on Max, both Max and Curt for donkey's years. With Curt gone and him screwin' her so royally, I suspect you'll have a number of opportunities. I'll get Max to put me on speed dial."

Before I could respond to this horrifying news, the door to his office opened and we both turned to see Bitsy wheel out, her eyes red-rimmed, her face still wet and Max walked out behind her with an expression like thunder.

I felt a squeeze in the region of my heart, began to move toward them, but stopped when Max spoke.

"Another change of plans, babe," he said, his voice ominous. "We gotta go see Mick."

I stared at both of them, silent.

But George mumbled, "Uh-oh."

*   *   *

I stood on the porch of Max's A-frame watching the big tow truck with my rental in the flatbed maneuvering down the road.

Max, in his Cherokee, had seen it coming when he arrived. He went past the turn to the road and stopped, did a three-pointer, and was idling there, waiting for the flatbed to go the other way and give him full clearance to the road. When the truck turned and lugged away, Max turned in.

I had gone with Max and Bitsy to the police station, which was a block and a half away from George's office. Neither Max nor Bitsy had said anything while we walked and wheeled our way there. Bitsy was still struggling with tears. Max was still looking thunderous.

Max had walked right up to the reception desk and I stood by Bitsy, who took my hand.

"What's happening, Bitsy?" I asked, but she shook her head and choked back a sob, so I just gave her hand a squeeze and looked at Max.

He came back to us, his eyes on me, his face not having lost that stormy look of fury and he said, "You gotta get to the house, babe. The rental car people will be there in half an hour." I nodded and he went on. "I'll make a call."

The call he made was to Brody, who, after Bitsy and Max disappeared deep into the police station with Jeff, came to get me and he took me to Max's in his Subaru. He let us in using his key to Max's place and he'd stayed with me while the rental car guy took pictures of the car and talked to me. Then he'd stayed a little while longer while I made coffee and wandered to the utility room to discover that Caroline had taken care of the laundry. We drank coffee and I called Mom and asked Brody for Bitsy's number, which I used and left three messages because it took me so long to tell her what I had to say. This was essentially that I needed her to come to Mindy's mom's house and that she had to trust me, and I did all of that trying to be sensitive to whatever current calamity she was facing. Then after the tow had come, successfully backing into Max's lane and up to the car with a difficulty that was hair-raising just to watch and all seemed to be going okay, Brody had told me he wanted to get back to Mindy and he'd see me later.

He was not in a Brody mood, not that I really knew what a Brody mood was, but I knew the events of the day before were weighing on him. I knew this mainly because how could they not? I let them, not that I wanted to but because he was a mountain man and I figured he'd want to be left to his own thoughts.

He left and five minutes later when the tow truck was heading out, I saw Max heading up.

I watched him park, get out of the car, and crunch through the snow to the steps. The sun hadn't burned off the clouds. It was still chilly and I'd wrapped my pashmina around my neck and was in my coat, ready to go.

"Hi," I said when Max had gone up two steps.

"Babe," Max said back.

"You okay?" I asked when he made it to the porch.

"No," he replied when he made it to me.

It killed me. I could tell his thoughts, too, were heavy but there were other things going on. Too many of them and they were too important to delay.

"I'm sorry but can we talk in the Cherokee? We need to go back down, get to Mindy." He nodded but didn't touch me, which was strange and vaguely alarming. "You need to lock up. I've turned off the coffee. The house is good."

"Right," he said, moving toward the door, his keys jingling in his hand.

I licked my lips.

Something was wrong, very wrong. One couldn't say Max knew me through and through or I knew him the same way, not even close. But he was affectionate, touchy. He got close almost all the time. Most especially when something was on his mind or he thought something was on mine.

This distance was strange and I didn't like it.

To hide that, I walked down the steps to the Jeep, crunched through the snow in my high-heeled boots, and got in the truck. I turned to look through the driver's side window expecting to see Max approaching the SUV or at least walking toward it, but I saw nothing.

I looked up to the house and there was no Max at the door locking up. I twisted in my seat, looking all around.

No Max.

I looked back to the house to see him exiting. He locked the door and then jogged down the steps to the car. I buckled up as he slid in. I heard a jingle and I turned to see him holding up a set of keys.

"Keys," he muttered, shaking them between us.

"Sorry?" I asked.

"To the house, take 'em," he ordered, jingling them again.

Automatically my hand came up and my fingers closed around the keys. Without further ado, he let them go, started the ignition, and did a three-pointer.

I held the keys in my hand thinking this should be a bigger moment, Max giving me the keys to his house.

I waited a second for him to say something. He didn't.

"Max—"

He cut me off. "Nina, just...don't."

Don't? Don't what?

"Max—" I started again.

"Nina, seriously."

Seriously what?

I didn't ask. I swallowed, dumped the keys in my bag, and looked out the passenger window.

Max drove in silence. He didn't take my hand. He didn't turn on the radio. He just drove.

Something was very wrong and logically I knew it had to do with whatever was in those letters. Illogically, my garbage-fueled brain told me it had to do with me.

Logically, I thought, Curtis Dodd had something to do with Elizabeth Dodd being paralyzed and Anna Maxwell being dead. Now Curtis was dead and he'd not only screwed Max in his will, he'd also left him a letter that necessitated a trip to the police station. This would make anyone moody.

Illogically, I knew Max didn't have a problem sharing pretty much anything except stories about his beloved, dead wife. Therefore, his not sharing with me now, my garbage-fueled brain told me, had to do with me.

And my garbage-fueled mind reminded me that I'd fool-ishly offered to help Macho Mountain Man Max pay for his new land. He'd said he didn't mind that I made more money than him but my father and my fiancé had both tried to pay him to leave me alone, and, not two hours later, I was offering him money. Men were proud, especially, I figured, macho mountain men.

I was *such* an idiot.

We hit town and about two blocks in, Max turned right. He drove into a residential area and parked in the drive of a house that looked like it was built in the seventies and the Brady Bunch lived there. Max got out and I did too. He didn't wait for me to get to his side before he headed to the front door.

My stomach clutched painfully.

The door opened and Barb stood there.

"Max," she greeted. Her eyes came to me still making my way up the path and she said, "Nina."

"Barb, how's she doin'?" Max asked as Barb moved out of the door and Max moved in.

Barb held the storm door open for me as I made my final approach and she answered, "Hangin' in there." She closed the door behind me and turned to us, her gaze on me. "It's good you're here. She's talkin' a bit and the bit she says is mostly about you."

I nodded, unsure if this was good or bad, decided to go with good and whispered, "Where is she?"

"Upstairs," Barb answered, closing the front door on the storm door.

"I...planned something. I hope you don't mind," I told her, avoiding Max's eyes.

Barb studied me and her eyes filled with tears she didn't let fall and she whispered, "Glad someone has a plan. I have no stinkin' clue what to do."

I reached out and grasped her forearm, giving it a reassur-ing squeeze.

"How about I make some coffee while you bring her downstairs?" I suggested. Barb nodded. "Can Bitsy Dodd get into your house?"

I felt something come from Max and watched Barb's body jolt.

"Bitsy?" Barb asked.

I nodded again. "Yes."

"Sure, Brody's here. He or Max can get her in the house," she said. "They've done it before lotsa times."

"That's good," I told her, and turned to Max, who was studying me, his eyes intense but his expression blank. "Can you take care of Bitsy?"

"Yeah," he replied, and his eyes went to the door before going to Barb. "Someone's here."

Barb turned back to the door and I took off my coat. Moving into the house, I dropped it on the couch and I went in what I hoped was the direction of the kitchen. Luckily, my hopes came to fruition.

Max followed several moments later.

"It's your mom and Steve," he told me as I searched the cupboards for coffee.

"Good."

"Nina, you know what you're doin'?"

I found the coffee, took down the canister, and yanked out the pot from the coffeemaker.

"Not really," I replied.

Max got close as I filled the pot. "Don't know 'bout this shit but I'm guessin' now's a sensitive time."

I pressed my lips together and turned off the faucet.

Yesterday, according to Max, I had this. Yesterday, he trusted everything I did with Mindy. Yesterday, he let me take care of everything.

Today, or, I should say *now*, after whatever happened, he wasn't so sure.

"I figure what I have planned might not help but it won't hurt," I told the coffeemaker as I poured the water in.

"Nina, look at—" Max started, *not* calling me "babe," "honey," "darlin'," "baby," or "Duchess" but "Nina."

He didn't finish because my mom was there.

"Max, sweetie, there's a lady in a wheelchair outside who needs your assistance."

I was measuring coffee into the filter but I felt Max's hesitation like it was physical. Then I felt him leaving the same way.

Mom got close. "Did you learn what's going on?"

I had told her my plan for Mindy over the phone and I'd also filled her in a bit about the reading. I hadn't explained that Max couldn't afford to keep the land he was given, just that he was given it. I had told her about the letters, but as I didn't know what was in them, I couldn't give her that knowledge.

"No," I answered.

"He's not himself," Mom observed with what had to be her keen mother's sense since she'd been in his presence approximately twenty seconds and she'd known him less than two days.

Still, she could say that again.

"Hey," we both heard as I flipped the switch to the coffee and we both turned to see Mindy in the doorway.

She looked a little pale and definitely looked listless but other than that, she looked like Mindy.

"Hi there, my lovely," I said to her. I moved across the room, took her in my arms, and gave her a tight hug. I was pleased to note she hugged me back.

I pulled away slightly, gave her a smile, and told her, "It's already afternoon and I've not witnessed any brawls. Slow day."

Her head tilted to the side and her lips twitched before she said, "Well, I gotta be with you. I don't see any brawls either unless you're there."

My hands gave her upper arms a squeeze as my heart was processing her lip twitch hopefully. "Yes, I forgot about that."

"Max had a showdown with Nina's ex-fiancé in the hotel restaurant this morning, though, alas, no punches were thrown," Mom informed Mindy, pushing into my space, giving her a hug and kissing her cheek before pulling back.

Mindy looked from Mom to me and asked, "No joke? Your fiancé's here?"

"Unfortunately, yes," I answered.

"Ex," Mom put in firmly. "Ex-fiancé."

Mindy gave Mom another lip twitch before looking at me and asking, "Why's he here?"

"Because he's a jerk, like my dad, who's also a jerk."

"I thought you said he was—" Mindy started.

"I was wrong," I told her. "During the showdown, he exposed his true self and let's just say I won't be tearing up over pizza the next time we go out," I explained.

"Bitsy's here," Barb called from the doorway before Mindy could reply, and I looked at Mom, then at Mindy.

"Bitsy?" Mindy asked, now looking confused.

"Mindy, can you trust me for about fifteen minutes?" I inquired, and watched her body lock and panic fill her face and I thought for a second she would flee.

Then, seeming to struggle to push it back, she nodded and whispered, "I trust you all the time, Neens."

I pressed my lips together and swallowed the lump that formed in my throat as my eyes slid to my mom, who was smiling a gentle smile at me. This smile from Mom, as it always did my whole life, gave me strength. This was good. I needed it because I was scared to death my plan was going to go south.

Then I took Mindy's hand and gave it a squeeze. "Let's go into the living room."

I led her by the hand into the living room, Mom and Barb following. Bitsy was sitting in her chair by the couch and she looked run through the mill but when her eyes hit Mindy, her torso straightened and her gaze grew alert.

"What's up?" she asked me, but didn't look away from Mindy. "You said in your message you needed me here but you didn't say why. Is everything okay?"

"No," I replied honestly.

Bitsy's eyes grew wide and they instantly flew to Max, who was standing just inside the room by Steve, Brody, and some other person, a man I didn't know.

I thought Bitsy looking at Max was telling. I shoved that back, focused, and guided Mindy to the couch, where we sat, me at her left side.

"Bitsy, can you get close, please, right up here, in front of Mindy?" I called as Mom sat down on Mindy's right side.

Bitsy wheeled forward and got close to Mindy's front as Mindy looked between the lot of us.

I looked at Bitsy and stated softly, "I know you've had a tough day, a tough week, and I wish I had time to explain what was happening here so you wouldn't be blindsided by this. But I didn't and now I need you. This is going to be hard, but will you trust me?"

Her eyes were moving between Mindy, Mom, and me and then she looked at me and nodded.

"Can you take just a little bit more?" I prompted when Bitsy didn't answer.

"I . . . I think so," Bitsy answered.

"Neens, what's this—?" Mindy started, but I talked over her, keeping my gaze steady on Bitsy.

"Bitsy, yesterday Mindy tried to commit suicide," I announced.

Bitsy gasped and jolted back in her chair. Mindy tensed and then started to stand up but I grabbed her hand on one side and Mom grabbed the other side, holding her down.

I turned to Mindy and put a hand to her knee. "Yesterday, darling, yesterday you said you didn't want anyone to know. And I promise you, in anything else, *anything* else, I would respect your wishes." I lifted my hand from her thigh, cupped her cheek, and whispered, "Not this. This is too important."

"Neens, I can't do this," Mindy whispered back, tears filling her eyes, fear stark on her face, and my courage took a direct hit but I forged onward.

"Oh yes, you can, sweetheart. You can because you've got

strong women all around you and we're going to help you do this," I told her, and the tears slid down her cheeks. "You know I was beaten by my boyfriend. You know that Bitsy's legs were taken away and all that happened to her recently. What you don't know is that my dad cheated on my mom while she was pregnant with me and left her without looking back at either of us for seven years. She's now married to the love of her life and happy as a clam."

"Neens—" Mindy whispered on a ragged breath.

"What I'm saying is, life socks it to us and we survive."

"Neens—"

"We fight."

She shook her head and the tears continued to fall.

"And when we can't fight, we learn to turn to others who've learned life's lessons. Who've survived. Who'll gather close and help us make it through."

She kept shaking her head and tried to pull away but I dropped her hand and grabbed her face with both of mine.

My voice was fierce when I said, "Mins, we don't give up."

I heard crying, Mindy's and others, maybe Barb, but I kept my eyes glued to Mindy.

"We never give up."

"Neens—"

I interrupted again and said, "You're loved."

"I know," she whispered, her face blanching at the same time it flinched, what she did to those who cared about her the day before scored into her features.

"No one is angry at you," I assured her. "We all understand."

She shook her head. "No, you don't."

"Oh yes, darling, we do. And we hurt *for* you and that's a beautiful thing."

"It isn't."

"It *is*. To be that loved, Mindy, it's beautiful."

She closed her eyes tight and then opened them.

"You're strong." It was an accusation.

"I'm not. What I am is someone who has a great mom, I

had a wonderful brother, and I have a lot of good friends who helped me through. They taught me things along the way, filled me up with something that I could keep with me, and I didn't know what it was, not until now. I didn't know they were filling me with something I could give away when it was my time to give. Something that I'm giving now, to you."

She bit her lip and swallowed before whispering, "I can't stop thinking about it."

"Of course not, you were violated," I whispered back. "What happened to you was hideous."

"I'm weak."

I pulled her face close to mine as I leaned in and rested my forehead to hers. "Then promise to find help to get strong."

"I can't get clean."

"That's because you're polishing a diamond. How much more brilliant do you want it to shine, my lovely?"

Her body jerked so violently, her head came away from my hands.

"Mindy," Bitsy called. I dropped my hands and Mindy struggled but she looked at Bitsy, who lifted her arms toward the younger girl. "Come here, baby, I need you to listen to me now." Mindy shook her head. Bitsy leaned forward and urged, "Please, give me your hands."

"I can't," Mindy sobbed.

Bitsy leaned farther forward and took Mindy's hands. Lifting them up between them, she shook them hard.

"After this happened to me, I thought about suicide," Bitsy shared, and Mindy hiccoughed a loud sob and tried to pull away but Bitsy held on tight. "I did, so many times, God, so many."

"I can't do this," Mindy moaned.

"I wish someone like Nina knew," Bitsy talked over her. "I wish I had this kind of support around me. I had to fight back the urge on my own," Bitsy said. "I never told anyone, until I told Nina the other day. I don't know how I made it."

"You...you...," Mindy stuttered.

"I fought it back. Sometimes I didn't know why. What was the point? But I did it and I'm glad I did."

"Wh-why?" Mindy asked.

"Because I have nieces now and they're the loves of my life. Because, no matter what people think, I had more time with Curt and he was good to me; he made me laugh. Because I got to watch you grow up and grow beautiful." Mindy shook her head and tried to pull her hands away again but Bitsy held tight. "This kind of thing happens to you, one thing I learned is that you have to give away some of the pain. You can't carry it all with you."

"I…I've tried, with Becca. I don't know how to let it go," Mindy told Bitsy.

"It's easy, you just give it away," Bitsy explained.

"I—"

"Give me your pain, Mins," Bitsy ordered gently.

Mindy shook her head and pulled at her hands again.

"Give it," Bitsy urged, and the tears kept falling but Mindy just stared at Bitsy until Bitsy leaned in even closer and whispered, "Give it to me, honey."

Bitsy and Mindy looked into each other's eyes for long moments while I held my breath. Then suddenly Mindy fell to her knees in front of Bitsy's chair, shoved her cheek to Bitsy's belly, wrapped her arms around Bitsy's waist, and burst into loud body-rocking tears.

Bitsy stroked Mindy's hair with one hand, her back with the other and she curled around Mindy protectively while she did this.

I felt Mom's fingers take mine.

"That's it, beautiful, let it out," Bitsy cooed, and Mindy cried louder.

"Coffee now," Mom murmured, getting up and pulling me with her.

"Mom, we can't—"

Mom's hand tightened in mine and I looked at her. "Coffee."

I nodded. She let my hand go and rounded Bitsy's chair to me, her arm coming around my waist as she led me toward the kitchen. I saw Brody holding his weeping mom, Steve was moving toward us, the other person had disappeared, and Max was watching Bitsy and Mindy.

"They need some time," Mom stated to the gathering, and kept moving me toward the kitchen.

Steve followed closely, Barb and Brody after Steve and Steve had pulled me into one of his hugs when Max arrived.

Mom searched through the cupboards to find cups. I pressed my cheek into Steve's chest and avoided Max's eyes.

"Steve and I did some searching," Mom said softly to Barb and Brody. "There's a rape crisis center a couple of towns over. We contacted them. They said they do callouts and they're waiting for you to phone." When neither Barb nor Brody said anything, Mom went on. "Now's the time to call, to get her some help. I know it goes against the grain to push her after yesterday but it's the right thing to do."

"She didn't call when we asked her to call them before," Barb whispered.

Mom set the last cup on the counter, got close to Barb, and took her hand.

"Then *make* her," Mom whispered. "Or, better yet, do it for her."

Barb looked into Mom's eyes, anxiety, uncertainty, and fear in her own; then slowly she nodded.

Mom looked to Steve. "Darling, will you give me that number we wrote down?" Steve pulled it out of his pocket, gave it to Mom, and Mom asked Steve as she led Barb away, "Can you finish the coffees?"

Steve nodded, let me go, and moved to the coffeepot.

I stood swaying, hoping that my gamble would pay off and also hoping that Max would take over for Steve.

He didn't. Instead, to my surprise, Brody came close, grabbed my hand, and walked me to the kitchen table. He sat in a chair and I stood uncertain in front of him with my hand in his. Then he tugged my hand so hard my arm jerked in its socket and with a soft gasp I went down into his lap where both his arms came around me in an embrace so tight it forced the breath right out of me. His face went into my neck. My body stiffened in his arms and my eyes flew to Max, who was staring at us with a muscle jerking in his jaw.

Now what did I do?

I pulled in a breath, turned my head, and positioned my mouth at Brody's ear.

"Brody," I called.

He didn't answer.

Hesitantly, I put my hand to his hair. "Brody, darling, look at me."

He did, pulling his face out of my neck and tipping it back, looking at me as he spoke. "Owe you the world," he whispered.

I forgot my discomfiture, settled into him, and put my hand to his neck. "Brody—"

"She's my world, my baby sister," he said. "She'd not be here if not for you. Owe you the world."

I didn't know what to say to that because essentially it was true.

So I decided to change subjects. "Promise me we're going to have this moment and you're going to let it go."

"I'll never forget," Brody vowed.

I nodded and said, "Yes, I know, you'll never forget. I'll never forget. Max won't ever forget but after this, will you promise to let it go?"

His eyes held mine for several long moments before his lit and he asked, "If I don't, will you arrange an intervention for me?"

I felt my mouth move into a mini-smile. "Probably."

"I won't have to hug Max, will I?" he went on.

"Maybe, if you don't let it go," I threatened. "Cotton, Mick, Jeff, and Pete, too, since they're the only men I know in town. Oh wait, today I met George Nielson. I'll have to invite him along."

Brody gave me a small grin before it faded but the light in his eyes grew more intense and he whispered, "Then I'll let it go."

"Good," I whispered back.

"Coffee," Max grunted from close.

I looked up at him to see he was, indeed, close and he was holding a cup to me. I also realized that I was still in Brody's lap and I mostly realized this because Max was staring at my behind in a way that communicated a good degree of displeasure.

I scooted off Brody's lap, took the cup of coffee Max was offering with a murmured thanks, and made my way to the safe haven of Steve.

No one spoke, even when Mom and Barb came back. Max didn't get close. Instead, he seemed lost in his thoughts as he stared out the kitchen window to the backyard.

I tried not to look at him doing this but I couldn't keep my eyes from going to him as I sipped my coffee feeling, for the first time since I walked up the steps to his A-frame, lost and alone.

I felt this way until Steve got close, slid an arm along my waist, and put his lips to the side of my head.

"That couldn't have been easy, with Charlie and all," he murmured to me. "Proud of you, doll."

"Thanks," I murmured back, and Max must have heard, for his eyes came to us. That muscle jerked in his jaw again before he turned back to his intense perusal of the backyard.

*   *   *

At Bitsy's request, I stood in the sliding door of the van that brought her to Barb and Darren's house. The man I hadn't met who I saw in the house (his name, I found out, was Burt) was her driver.

"You okay?" I asked.

"Thanks, Nina," she answered, and my head jerked at her words.

"I thought you'd be mad at me, putting you on the spot in there, um—"

"Nope," Bitsy told me, smiling, but there was something sad about it. "You know, all these years in this chair, people still handle me like I'm made of glass. It sucks. Everyone's always taking care of me. That sucks too. Not once, not even once that I can remember for ten years, has anyone needed me, made me feel like I still had something to give." She reached out a hand to me and I took it before she finished, "In there, I had something to give. You knew my day was shit but you trusted me to do it. You trusted me to be strong enough. You knew Mindy's problems were bigger than mine and you treated me like a normal person instead of someone made of glass. So, thanks."

"Um . . . you're welcome?" I said on a question. She laughed softly and even her laughter did nothing to lessen the sadness in her features.

The laughter died away, her eyes went funny, and she whispered, "Wish you'd come here ages ago."

I studied her and asked quietly, "You okay?"

She pulled in a breath through her nose, seemed to shake off whatever had hold of her, and nodded. Her eyes slid over my shoulder before they swiftly shot back to me.

Then for some reason, she whispered urgently, "Take care of Max."

Her mood had shifted yet again, and surprised at her tone, her words, and the fervor behind them, I started to turn but heard Max's deep voice asking, "Ready?"

I nodded to him and looked back at Bitsy, leaning in, giving her a kiss on the cheek, and then moving away. Max moved in, slid the door closed, and pounded on the roof twice with his open palm.

When the counselor from the rape crisis center had arrived, Mom and Steve left (this was also in order that Mom could get ready for The Rooster). Shortly after that, Max and I said our good-byes to Mindy, Brody, and Barb and we went out with Bitsy and Burt to the van.

Now it was time to go back to the A-frame.

Max stood by me and watched Bitsy's van pull away and she and I waved at each other when it did. Max didn't move, just watched silently. Then without looking at me, he walked to the Cherokee. I followed.

He didn't open my door, just bleeped the locks and I climbed in and buckled up. Max had the SUV out of the drive before I got myself situated in my seat.

We were in town when I hazarded words.

"Everything okay?"

"We'll talk when we get home," was Max's alarming answer.

I wanted to push it. In fact, my palms were itching and words were on the tip of my tongue, I wanted so badly to push it. Something was wrong and I didn't know what it was. I didn't even know if I wanted to know what it was. I just knew I had to know. With effort, I kept silent all the way to the house.

Snow had started gently falling by the time we turned onto the road that led to his house.

Max parked and jumped down. I did too.

He hit the front door far faster than me, mainly because he wasn't wearing high-heeled boots, but this could also be attributed to the fact that his legs were a lot longer than mine.

I followed through the open door Max didn't close. I closed it and my eyes went to him as I shrugged off my coat. He was in the kitchen heading to the fridge. I hooked my coat on a dining room chair and heard the hiss of a cap coming off a beer. I turned to the kitchen and saw him with his head back, taking a drink.

I stopped at the edge of the counter and watched as he dropped his beer hand and leaned into his other hand on the counter.

I pulled up the courage to start. "Max—"

But Max spoke over me.

"I know the situation was extreme but is it too fuckin' much to ask you not to sit in another man's lap when I'm standin' in the room? Scratch that. Is it too fuckin' much to ask it even if I'm in another fuckin' *state*?"

I felt my mouth drop open and my stomach pitch.

"Sorry?" I whispered.

"For what?" Max asked.

Unnerved, I didn't know what to say. So I stammered, "I... but... but it was Brody."

"Don't give a fuck who it was."

"But—"

"Don't give a fuck why you did it either, Nina. Just don't do it again. Yeah?"

"He... Max, he pulled me onto his lap," I reminded him. "Under the circumstances, I could hardly pull away."

"No circumstances are the right circumstances for you to have your ass in another man's lap."

I shook my head, those short, quick shakes again.

"Are we... are we really talking about this?" I asked in disbelief.

"Positions reversed, Nina, you were in a room and I had a woman in my lap, would you like that?"

My stomach pitched again at the thought he planted in my head and at the fact he kept calling me Nina.

"No, of course not," I told him.

"Point made," he replied curtly.

"Unless it was Mindy or something," I added.

"I fed Mindy baby food. You've known Brody a coupla days. That's hardly the same fuckin' thing."

"In a way, it is."

"What it is, is, I've known you a week and you're fuckin' me. You've known Brody—"

I lost my incredulity at our conversation and my mild confusion and the fear that I felt whenever he was angry at me and that red film covered my eyes again.

"Don't you finish that!" I warned.

"Again, point made," Max shot back.

I leaned in and snapped, "You're impossible!"

"Yeah, you've mentioned that."

I glared at him and he held my glare. Neither of us

spoke, neither of us moved. I wanted to throw something at him but nothing was in reach and if I had to reach for something, I could swear at that moment my entire body would shatter.

Regrettably, I was unable to hold his clear, angry gray eyes, so I turned my head, looked into the house, and realized there was really nowhere to go to escape him. Except one place. So I went there.

I stomped across the room, my boots loud against the wood floors. Then I stomped up the stairs. Then I stomped to the armchair to see my bag was gone and I stopped, staring at the chair. Then I stomped to the closet, threw open the door, and turned on the light inside. I saw my limited amount of clothes hanging next to Max's, my sweaters tidily folded on the fitted shelves again next to Max's, and my shoes lined up on the tilted rods also next to Max's. My suitcase was folded up and tucked into a corner. All of my clothes had been laundered and, those that needed it, ironed and so had Max's.

Caroline was good at her job.

I turned out the light, slammed the door, and stomped to the bathroom. I opened the medicine cabinet and saw my toiletries tucked neatly away. Then I opened a drawer in the vanity and saw my makeup. So I stomped back to the door and saw my robe was on a hook at the back, and I felt like shouting with glee when I saw it. Then I slammed the door and locked it.

I drew a bath and started the long, complicated procedure of giving myself a facial.

What I wanted to do was leave Max's presence, his house, and the state in which he currently resided.

Something else I wanted to do was walk downstairs and scream in his face.

Since I didn't have a car and since I was so angry I couldn't trust my own mouth and since my mom and Steve worshipped the ground Max walked on and they'd planned a romantic dinner a deux at The Rooster. Thus I couldn't call them to come and get me. So I was stuck with the facial.

So I gave myself the longest facial in the history of me giving myself facials.

The water in the tub was cool but even after the facial, I had not cooled down when I climbed out and toweled off. I lotioned my body like I'd be graded for the endeavor and then I wrapped myself in my robe, grabbed my clothes and boots, and walked out.

The house was lit downstairs and up with both lights illuminated on both nightstands but I could see and hear no Max.

I dumped my clothes and boots in the closet and went in search of my underwear, which I found in one of the drawers (yes, by *Max's*). I snatched out a pair and put them on, pulled on my last pair of pajama bottoms and a shelf-bra camisole. The bottoms were cotton with tiny, retro daisies in sherbet colors against a raspberry sherbet background with the camisole being lime sherbet. I shrugged my robe back on and confiscated a pair of Max's socks, the best ones I could find, deciding I'd steal them just to tick him off. I yanked them on while hopping around foot to foot.

Then I went across the room, slid open the doors to the TV, selected the most gruesome horror movie I could find, even though I didn't normally watch horror movies since they were horror and thus scared the dickens out of me. Even the silly bad ones, which always made Charlie laugh his behind off when he used to force me to watch them with him. Then I curled up on the bed, shoving most of the pillows behind me, tucking one to my front, and I glued my eyes to the television set.

My stomach reminded me I hadn't had lunch and I silently told it to shut the hell up.

The movie had scarcely started before a young woman was being chased through the woods, the blood of her hacked up boyfriend covering her barely clad body when I felt Max's presence hit the loft.

Although a part of me I was *not* listening to was glad he was there (simply because the movie was scaring the dickens out of me), I didn't look at him. I kept my eyes fixed on the TV even as I felt the bed move when he sat on it and I heard one boot, then the other hit the floor. The bed moved again and I stayed completely still and focused on the TV.

Max slid in behind me, his arm went around my middle, and he pulled me into his hard body. With a forceful jerk I pulled myself forward and with an equally forceful jerk he hauled me right back.

I gave up and held myself completely still.

"Turn off the movie, Duchess."

Oh, so *now* I was Duchess. Now, after he proved, like most—no *all* men (except Charlie and Steve)—that he was a world-class jerk.

I didn't move or speak.

"Baby, turn it off."

Now I was baby. Nice.

He sighed, then pressed closer to my back.

"It's been a shit day."

I stayed silent and watched the young, barely clad damsel come to a bloody end in the woods.

"Curtis knew someone wanted him dead."

My body gave a small twitch at this news but I remained silent.

"He had death threats."

I watched the TV and somehow, shortly after the nubile young lady met her dastardly end, two other young, good-looking people were having somewhat raunchy sex in a cabin.

This, I knew from my experiences watching horror movies with Charlie, did not bode well. Sex was usually the last thing anyone did in a horror movie before their life was snuffed out with an ax, a hatchet, a glove made out of long, razor-sharp blades, or a common kitchen knife.

"Bitsy's life has been threatened too."

Thoughts of gloves made out of razor-sharp blades flew from my head, my body jerked, and my head swiveled around to look at him.

"Curt didn't tell anyone. He hired a PI," Max continued.

I broke my silence and asked, "Is she going to be okay?"

"Mick's set something up."

I thought of Bitsy alone in that big house, unable to move around except in a wheelchair.

"I should go stay with her," I declared to Max, and his brows knit.

"What?"

I yanked out of his arm, rolled off the bed, and threw down the pillow saying, "You'll have to take me."

"I'm not takin' you to Bitsy's."

"Then I'll call Arlene," I stated as I threw open the door to the closet and turned on the light.

"Nina, get in here."

I ignored him and walked to my chocolate-colored cords on a hanger, pulling them off.

"Nina," Max called, and when I continued to ignore him and examine my sweater selection on the shelves, I heard him mutter, "Jesus."

I selected a cream-colored cable-knit but I barely pulled it from its position on the shelf before it was yanked out of my hand by Max. Then he tossed it on the shelf (now not folded, which was a shame, Caroline was good at folding sweaters). Then, while I was still staring at the untidy sweater, my cords were yanked from my other hand and tossed onto the floor.

Belatedly I turned to look up at Max and exclaimed, "Hey!"

He grabbed my hand, flipped the switch to the closet light as he pulled me out, and then closed the door.

I twisted my hand in his and snapped over the dying screams of (undoubtedly) the young lovers on the television, "Let go."

"No, we're gonna talk."

"I think you said enough earlier."

"Babe, I was pissed and I'll admit I didn't handle that very well."

I felt my eyes narrow as I repeated, "You didn't handle that very well?"

Max ignored that and moved on. "You also didn't catch my meaning."

"Oh, no, you're wrong. I caught it all right."

"No, I don't think you did."

"Trust me, Max, I did."

"I'm not Niles."

That brought me up short and the only thing I could do was stare.

Then I hissed, "*What*?"

"I give a shit," Max stated.

"You give a shit about what?"

"Everything."

"Perhaps you'd like to give me more detail," I suggested, and tried to twist my hand out of his again, but he only used it to tug me closer and then his other hand lifted and his fingers curled in a way that could not be mistaken around the side of my neck. It wasn't painful, not in the slightest, but it was firm and it sent a message.

I stilled.

"All right, Duchess, you want detail, here it is. Brody's my best friend and I know he wouldn't fuck me over and I'm takin' a wild guess the amount of times you've been fucked over, you wouldn't either. It wasn't him. It wasn't that. It wasn't even you sittin' in his lap, though, I'll repeat, I didn't like that one fuckin' bit."

"That isn't detail, Max," I pointed out. "That's you repeating yourself."

"It was you callin' him 'darling.'"

I blinked and shook my head briskly, once.

"I'm sorry?"

"You sat in his lap with your hands on him and you called him 'darling.'"

My blood started heating and I cried loudly, "He was upset about his sister!"

"Yeah? Well, so am I."

"Yes, and if I remember, I call you darling too."

"Yeah, but you're sleepin' with *me*."

I pulled against his hand, sputtering, "I...you...I don't get—"

"That's mine," Max declared, and I stilled my struggling and stared at him.

Then I informed him, "You call other women 'babe' and 'darlin',' and—"

"You're my only Duchess."

He had me there.

"It doesn't mean anything," I told him, and his brows drew together dangerously.

"Duchess doesn't mean anything to you?"

"No, me saying 'darling.'"

"It means something to me."

"Well, I didn't know that," I defended.

"Yeah, so now I'm tellin' you."

"Well, maybe you should tell me *before* you get angry at me for doing something I didn't know you didn't want me to do. And maybe when you get angry, you'll find a way to let me know you are without being a total *jerk*."

"And maybe you'll cut me some slack when I got a friend with a murdered husband, a dead man writin' me notes, a sister who's been raped and we found facedown in a river, a new girlfriend whose dad's a dick and whose fiancé is an asshole and both of 'em are in town, and a future that means the end of my mountain as I know it."

"And maybe you'll cut *me* some slack when I've broken up with my fiancé *and* I just found out he's an asshole *and* he's in town *and* so is my dick of a dad. Not to mention, a girl I've come to care about tries to commit suicide like my brother did. *And*, on top of all that, I've decided to up stakes *again* and move to a different country *again* and gamble on a man I barely know but who is annoying, impossible, and can be a *jerk*. I've got to find a job and buy a big lawyer desk so people will take me seriously. And my mother and Steve are so excited about all of this, they're already planning to park their new RV beside your house and use your *bathroom and kitchen*!"

I ended this on a shout, so absorbed in my tirade I didn't see his expression change. When I noticed his eyes had gone warm and his face had gentled, I saw my mistake immediately but had no time to backtrack. Max dropped my hand but wound his arm around my waist and started shuffling me back toward the bed.

"Max—"

"I knew somethin' changed this morning."

"Max—"

"You're movin' here."

"Max—"

"You're buyin' a lawyer desk."

"Max—" I stopped talking this time because I fell back to the bed and Max fell on me.

Then his mouth went to my neck.

"Get off me!" I snapped.

"Nope," he said against my neck. Then his lips trailed up and his teeth nipped my ear.

I shivered.

Then I cried, "Off! We're not done arguing."

"We can pick it up after we celebrate," Max said in my ear, and I shivered again.

Then I pushed at his shoulders and bucked my body, neither to any avail.

"We're not going to celebrate. I'm changing my mind. I'm only coming back to look in on Mindy, have a beer with Arlene at The Dog, stop by Bitsy's, and have a latte and do a bit of shopping. Then I'm going right back to England."

Max's mouth came to mine and he said, "Cotton'll be pissed, you don't make him a fish pie."

"Then I'll carve some time out for Cotton, now get off."

He didn't get off. He slanted his head and kissed me. I tried to turn my head away but both his hands framed my face and kept me stationary. This didn't work so well for him, since I kept my mouth closed.

Max lifted his head and demanded, "Stop bein' pissed, Duchess, and open your mouth for me."

I glared at him. He grinned.

Then all of a sudden the grin died and his eyes moved over my face as his thumb stroked my cheekbone.

After he did this for a while, he muttered his confession. "I was a dick."

I pulled in a breath, shocked not only that he admitted it but that he understood he was being one.

"Shit comes up with Curt, history, for me, for Bitsy," Max went on, and my body tensed under his, for I knew some of the history and guessed the rest and wondered if now he was going to talk about it. "Normally, I can let it go. Today it was in my face and I didn't handle it very well."

I waited for him to say more and for a while he didn't. He just kept looking into my eyes. Then he did.

"It's been a long time since I've had someone I gave a shit enough about to share anything with and I'm out of practice."

This was something, a hint, and I waited for more. This time, I didn't get it.

Instead, his thumb drifted over my bottom lip while his eyes watched it; then he dipped his head and touched his mouth to mine before lifting his head again.

His hand cupping my jaw, he whispered, "I fucked up, baby."

I closed my eyes and turned my head away, disappointed—no, beyond disappointed.

But at least he could admit when he was wrong. That was something.

I opened my eyes, looked at him, and gave in. "Don't worry about it, Max. It's been"—I searched for a word and settled on, "Crazy."

He touched his lips to mine again before he pulled slightly away.

"Promise me you won't sit in another man's lap." His voice was gentle but serious and I nodded.

"I think I got that."

"And don't call anyone 'darling.' That's mine."

I swallowed, liking that he'd claimed that, and nodded again.

His forehead came to mine and he whispered, "Love it when you call me that in your accent, honey."

My body relaxed under his and my hands went to his waist but I reminded him, "I don't have an accent."

I watched from close as he grinned.

"Now, Duchess, what exactly is a lawyer desk?"

I couldn't help it, I grinned back. "Can I tell you while I make us something for dinner?"

Max lifted his head. "Yeah, dinner would be good. Then we're gonna celebrate."

"No, then we're going to finish my movie."

"Babe, that movie's shit."

"I know but I was kind of into it."

He grinned again and his eyes dropped to my mouth. "I want a kiss first."

My body relaxed even more under his and I whispered, "Okay."

"I want your mouth open this time."

I felt a shiver on my skin (and elsewhere) as I repeated, "Okay."

"Give it to me, baby."

I lifted my head and put my mouth to his and repeated yet again, "Okay."

Then I opened my mouth and kissed him.

*   *   *

We were in the kitchen, the water was at the boil, and I had the cookie sheet out as well as all the fixings for dinner.

Max had asked me what I wanted to drink. I'd requested a glass of wine from the bottle of Chardonnay he opened last night and he'd poured it for me.

Now he was standing, hips against the sink, drinking beer and watching me. I opened the packet of hot dogs and he burst out laughing.

My eyes went to him. "What?"

His head dipped to the counter. "This duchess food?"

"What?" I repeated, and he walked up to me, putting his beer on the counter and picking up the tube of biscuits.

"Mac and cheese and pigs in a blanket with white fuckin' wine," he stated through his smile. "Is this duchess food?"

"No, it's Nina's Home in America Food. They don't have macaroni and cheese in a box and biscuits in a tube in England and when I'm home I eat the food I like that I don't get in England." He kept smiling at me as he pulled the wrapper off the tube and rapped it on the edge of the counter so it gave a soft "poof" as it exploded open. "Max!" I cried. "You stole the fun part!"

His hand snaked out, caught me behind my neck, yanked me to him so he could kiss the top of my head, and let me go, muttering, "Sorry, honey," and twisted the tube open.

I pulled out some hot dogs, thinking that my telling him I was moving to Colorado wasn't exactly a special moment between us. I was also thinking that I had the Max I knew back after the Max I didn't know and who kind of scared me was around for the afternoon and I didn't want to go back to the other Max. I was also thinking I really wanted to know what was in Curtis Dodd's letters and I was thinking it was Curtis Dodd's letters that brought out the other Max.

But I really wanted to know what was in those letters.

"What was in Curtis's letters?" I blurted, tensing.

Max took a hot dog from me and started to wrap a biscuit around it.

"Bitsy's letter, a bunch of shit about Shauna, more shit about how he loved Bitsy and only Bitsy even though he was nailin' Shauna, and the fact that he'd received death threats," Max answered, not sounding angry, not looking broody, just being Max.

"And yours?" I prompted, wrapping a biscuit around a hot dog.

"A bunch of shit about how I needed to take care of Bitsy and take care of the business for Bitsy and how Bitsy had death threats too. And, seein' as I was readin' his damned letter, how I needed to take care of that and what he was doin' about it with the PI and how I couldn't tell Bitsy her life was under threat." He put the biscuit-coated hot dog on the tray and reached for another one. "Oh, and more shit about how he loved only Bitsy when he was fuckin' Shauna."

I tried to keep the tone light. "That's a lot. Was your letter ten pages long?"

Max's eyes came to me. "Curt had a natural talent with bein' able to be a serious fuckin' pain in the ass in twenty words or less, so no."

I smiled at him, put my hot dog down on the tray, and started another one, asking, "So, he knew someone wanted to kill him."

"Apparently, yeah."

"Why didn't he go to the police?"

"Question for the ages, babe, why did Curt do most of the shit he did?"

I had no answer for that.

"Does Bitsy know she's under threat?" I went on.

"Mick and I talked. We thought she should know, so we told her."

"Oh dear," I muttered, thinking that probably wasn't very fun at all.

"Yeah, she didn't know whether to be freaked or pissed."

I looked from my hot dog to Max. "Which did she settle on?"

Max grinned at me and answered, "Pissed."

I stopped wrapping hot dogs with gooey biscuit dough and leaned into Max. "Is she really going to be safe?"

Max stopped putting blankets on the pigs and held my eyes. "Yeah, she'd be here or we'd be there if I didn't trust Mick. He's got a man watchin' her house. Burt, who drives her everywhere she needs to go when she isn't with family or friends, has been told. Her folks and sister have been told. I talked to him and her brother-in-law is spendin' the night tonight. They got a huge security system in that house, never use it, but Bitsy's promised to keep it active when she's in or out of the house."

I was beginning to realize why the moody Max was in attendance that afternoon as I turned back to the hot dogs. "That makes me feel a little better."

"I'll feel better when they catch this fuck," Max muttered.

"Me too," I agreed, and then I caught sight of his hot dogs and informed him, "Max, you don't put two biscuits on the hot dog, only one."

"One don't cover it, Duchess," Max informed me, and I looked at him.

"Yes, well, this is true, but I don't have two hundred pounds of pure muscle to fuel. I have a behind that likes biscuits and asks them to stay awhile in the form of *fat*. Ergo, only one biscuit."

He grinned at me and proclaimed, "You got a great ass, babe."

"I've got a fat ass, Max."

Without warning, both his hands were on my ass and the front of my body was plastered to the front of his. Surprised at my new position and the swiftness I was in it, I put my hands on his chest and tilted my head back.

He wasn't grinning anymore when he repeated, "You've got a great ass, Nina."

"Max—"

"You aren't fat."

"Max—"

"Your whole body is fuckin' beautiful."

My heart skipped a beat and my stomach melted, as did my body and it did this into him and I said again, "Max—"

"Not a big fan of my woman running herself down, not even doin' it as a joke. You got an unbelievably pretty face, fantastic fuckin' eyes, and a spectacular body."

"Max, I—"

His hands squeezed my bottom and he interrupted me. "And I hear you say different again, Duchess, I'm not gonna like it."

I studied him and realized he was perfectly serious, about *all* of it, and I had no idea whatsoever how to respond to that.

"Yeah?" he prompted when I seemed unable to form words because I was too busy being moved by all he'd said and the fact that he meant it.

Then for some stupid, insane, irrational reason, five stupid, insane, and irrational words came out of my mouth. "Why do you like me?"

His hands slid from my behind to the small of my back as his head tilted to the side and he asked, "What?"

"Why do you like me?" I threw out a hand and continued. "Why are you so sure about all of this?"

His grin came back and he stated, "It ain't because you know how I like my coffee."

My stomach melted to nonexistence at him imparting the knowledge that he remembered what I said that morning and my hands slid up to his neck.

"You take your coffee black, Max. That isn't hard to remember," I told him, and my hands gave his neck a squeeze. "And it also isn't answering my question."

"Think I just mentioned your pretty face, your beautiful eyes, and your spectacular body," he reminded me.

"That's it?"

His eyes roamed the area of my head before they came to mine and he added, "You got great hair."

"Max."

He held my gaze for a long moment. Then his brows drew together and he asked, "You're serious?"

I leaned back a bit in his arms and answered, "Of course."

He watched me another moment and muttered in disbelief, "Fuck."

"Fuck what?"

"You can't be serious," he told me.

"I am," I replied.

"Babe," he said.

And that was it. I waited for more but apparently that really was it.

"That's it? Babe?"

"Nina, for Christ's sake." Now he sounded impatient and I started to get scared.

I drew back farther but his arms got tighter.

"Max, I asked you a question," I prompted, the fear becoming full-fledged as the impatience hit his features.

"Think you were there when you got in my face about rentin' this house," he told me.

"Yes, but—"

"And stomped on your high-heeled boots in your cute little tantrum when you walked out that first night and took me on again outside in a fuckin' snowstorm."

My tantrum wasn't *cute*. It wasn't even a *tantrum*. I was *angry*.

I let that slide and started, "Of course, but—"

"And you're a zombie in the mornin' and it's fuckin' adorable."

The fear started sliding away and I started melting back into him.

"Max—"

"You were also there when you told me you loved my house. And when you told me beer was invented in Germany. And when you told Cotton how his pictures made you feel. And, if I remember, you were there when you looked at the bluff like you'd stepped into heaven. And when you went on about some television character's lipstick. And you were also there when you took on Damon for Mindy. And when you practically threw Mindy in Jeff's arms. And when you threw down with Kami and Shauna, both in one night. And you were definitely there when you saved Mindy's life yesterday and you were also fuckin' there when you did what you did for Mindy today."

I couldn't believe he remembered all that. Heck, until then, *I* hadn't remembered all that. Some of it but not all of it and some of it I was trying to forget because it hadn't been all that fun.

"Max—"

"The people in this town are friendly enough with outsiders, Duchess, but only as much as they gotta be. They're friendly with you because they like you and they like you because, like me, they see all that. That's a fuckuva lot to like and they know that's just scratchin' the surface."

I couldn't take anymore. I wanted to, but I couldn't.

"Stop talking now," I whispered because if he didn't I'd start crying.

"You asked."

"Okay, I did, but you need to stop talking now."

"Baby—"

I looked down at the cookie sheet. "And don't be nice anymore. I prefer you annoying."

His body started shaking with laughter and he called, "Nina, darlin', look at me."

I kept my face averted. "No, I need to put the pasta in the water."

"Honey—"

I pushed against his shoulders. "Let me go, Max."

I felt his face in my neck. "You're demonstrating another reason I like you right now when you act crazy and cute."

Only Holden Maxwell would think my neurotic crazy was cute.

I kept pushing his shoulders and demanded, "Stop it, Max."

His hand slid up my spine, his fingers sifted in my hair, and his lips went to my ear. "All that, and there's a lot of it, Duchess, I can hold in my arms. You wanna know why I'm so sure, that's why."

I choked back my tears and this made a girlie noise so I shoved my face in his chest.

He held my face there with his hand in my hair and he held

me close with his arm around my waist. I held back the tears and I did this by deep breathing loudly.

Once I succeeded, Max kissed the top of my head again and offered, "I'll put the macaroni on."

Then he let me go and I turned back to the biscuits and hot dogs instead of downing the entire glass of wine, which was what I wanted to do or, better, move back into Max's arms.

*   *   *

We'd sat at the stools to eat the macaroni and cheese and pigs in a blanket.

We took our slices of cake up to the loft and ate them in bed while watching the horror movie.

The dirty plates were on the nightstand, and I had my wineglass in my hand. The pillows were piled up and I was in the curve of Max's body as well as his arm.

I was thinking that horror movies were a bit less scary watching them curled into Max, though not *that* less scary.

We were coming onto the climax and I was thinking we were in the homestretch. The heroine had to survive, of course, or how could there be a sequel? She was the only one left of the original crew. Someone had to survive.

Though it wasn't looking good for her.

She ran into the deserted, broken-down cabin, which was a mistake, seeing as the psychopath used to live there before he hacked his whole family up with an ax and that was his favorite haunt.

She turned a corner into a room and there he was, him and his ax and he was ready to strike.

So he did.

At the same time, Max's phone rang.

I jumped half a foot up from the bed and emitted a little terrified scream, nearly sloshing my wine on the bed.

Max started laughing.

Then he hit pause on the remote and leaned into me, grabbing the phone from his nightstand and beeping it on.

Up on my elbow, I took a calming sip of wine and twisted my head to look at him as he said into the phone, "Yeah?" My eyes caught his and he said, "Yeah, sure, she's here." Then he offered the phone to me.

I felt my eyebrows go up.

"Me?" I asked.

"Arlene," he answered.

"What?" I asked.

He shook the phone at me. I sat up and took it.

"Hello?" I said into it when I put it to my ear.

"Where are you?" Arlene queried.

"Um... watching a movie with Max."

"Watching a movie with Max?" Arlene asked as if I said I was strapping in to take a joyride with Evel Knievel.

"Yes," I answered.

"You're supposed to be at The Dog with me getting wasted."

Oh dear. I'd forgotten about that.

"Oh, Arlene, I'm so sorry. I... the day kinda got away from me."

"Yeah, I heard. Two blond English guys are at the hotel bein' snooty and actin' like their shit don't stink. Two blond English guys, word on the street says you, your ma, and Max faced off with this mornin'. That makes Damon, Kami, Shauna, and two snooty, blond English guys. Girl, what is it with you?"

"Um...," I answered, for there was no answer to give. I didn't know what it was with me.

"You fight with two English guys, then throw a fit on the sidewalk outside The Mark in the mornin', come night, you get blotto at The Dog."

Wow, the people in Gnaw Bone didn't mess around with gossip.

"Is that a rule?" I asked.

"Yeah, it's a rule," Arlene answered.

"I thought it would be better to give myself a facial and relax in front of a movie," I told her.

"You thought wrong," she replied, then demanded, "Give the phone to Max."

"Sorry?"

"Phone...to...Max," she repeated.

"Okay," I agreed, happy to give the unhappy Arlene to Max. I held the phone to him and said, "She wants to talk to you."

His mouth was twitching and he took the phone from me and put it to his ear.

"Arlene," he said. He paused to listen before saying, "Right." He bleeped the phone off and put it back in its charger.

I stared at the phone. Then I stared at him. Then I noted, "That was quick."

"Yep," he replied.

"What did she say?"

"You and your mom are meetin' her for drinks tomorrow night."

"We are?"

"She says she's arrangin' a girls' night out."

"Um..."

"Jenna's there now too. Arlene says she'll be there again tomorrow night. She says Jenna says she wants to get to know you."

"Um..."

"I'll go with," Max offered, and I stared at him.

Then I said, "Command performance girls' night out with Arlene I'm guessing doesn't include you being there."

"I'll take Brody and Steve. We'll let you do what you gotta do and we'll have guys' night out."

"I don't think girls' night out works when it happens at the same place and the same time as guys' night out," I supplied helpfully.

"Babe," he replied, grinning but saying no more.

Still being helpful, I explained, "I know you think that word speaks volumes, but I have to tell you, it actually doesn't."

His grin got bigger; then it changed and my wineglass was

no longer in my hand—it was on the nightstand. I had one second to look at it sitting there before I was in Max's arms and on top of Max.

"Max...," I started. His hand slid into my hair and he rolled, taking me with him so he was on top. "Max! The movie!"

His mouth was at my neck as he informed me, "The police guy saves her at the last minute; then he gets hacked in the first five minutes of the sequel."

"You ruined it!" I cried as his hand pulled my robe over my shoulder and his lips trailed its progress.

"Trust me, you didn't miss much," he said against my shoulder.

"I would have liked to see it play out."

His mouth moved back up my shoulder and down my chest as he changed the subject. "Like lyin' with you on my bed, watchin' a movie."

I liked that, too, a lot.

Still, I said, "Yes, well, then we should have finished the movie."

I was paying so much attention to his mouth I didn't notice his hand had slid up my side, my ribs until his fingers curled around the edge of my camisole at my breast.

"Prefer what we're gonna do now," he murmured against my cleavage, and before I could retort, his fingers pulled down my camisole, exposing my breast. They curled around it, lifting it up, and Max's mouth closed around my nipple and sucked deep.

My back arched as heady sensations shot straight from my nipple to between my legs.

My fingers slid into his thick, fantastic hair, I forgot all about the movie, and I whispered, "*Yes*."

His mouth pulled my nipple deeper and his tongue swirled. I closed my eyes and just let my body experience the beauty of it.

He released my nipple, moved up, and his lips hit mine.

"Bet you're already wet," he whispered there; then his fingers tugged at the drawstring of my pajama bottoms and his hand slid in. I gasped at his touch and his eyes darkened with desire when they found he was right. "Fuckin' love that," he growled, and kissed me, his tongue in my mouth, his finger slid inside me, and I moaned, not just already wet, but also already ready for him.

His finger slid out and hit my sweet spot and rolled and my back arched to get closer to him but also to show him how very, *very* much I liked what he was doing.

"Crazy," Max muttered against my mouth.

"What?" I whispered. My hands had pulled his thermal free and were gliding along the skin of his back.

"That asshole had you, had this"—his finger slid in and out and started rolling against my sweet spot again—"didn't take care of you," Max went on. "Didn't touch you for months. Let you walk out of that restaurant without puttin' up a fight. Fuckin' crazy."

"Max," I breathed, and he kissed me again, his finger still moving.

When he stopped kissing me, he told me, "Want you ridin' my cock tonight, Nina. Wanna see all of you. Wanna watch you fuck me, watch you make yourself come."

"Okay," I whispered, though I didn't know how I managed to speak since my entire body spasmed at his words.

He kissed me again, deep, hard, beautiful, then stopped and ordered, "You're gonna suck me first, though. I want your mouth on me again."

"Okay," I repeated in a whisper.

"Your mouth," Max growled. "Christ, nearly as sweet as your pussy."

I shifted with agitation under him. He was going to make me climax just by talking to me.

"This too," he said, but said no more.

"Sorry?" I tried to concentrate but it was difficult.

"This." His body pressed into mine, his hard crotch rubbed

against my thigh, his finger slid inside and started moving in and out, and his tongue swept my bottom lip, a combination that was mind-scrambling. "This, too, is why I'm so fuckin' sure about us."

My hand left his back and went to his face. "Max—"

Max cut me off, not that I knew what I was going to say. "Take your clothes off, baby. Want you naked while you work me."

"Okay," I breathed.

Then I took my clothes off while Max did the same.

Then I curled between his legs and sucked his cock until he yanked me over him. Then I rode it, fucking him while his eyes never left me, mine never left him, and his hands moved all over me. I rode him until I made myself come and kept going until he did too.

CHAPTER TEN

Follow Me into the Light

MAX WOKE ME with one hand between my legs, the other at my breast, and his mouth at my neck.

My neck arched upon waking and I whispered, "Darling."

His hands went away, he turned me, and he kissed me. Then he did other stuff to me. Then he took me, him on top, my knees bent, thighs pressed to his sides.

When I was almost there, teetering close to the edge, he pulled out, flipped me to my stomach, hauled my hips up, and rammed into me, hard and rough, again and again and again.

Delicious.

"Touch yourself, baby," he growled his order from behind me, and my face in the pillow, my fingers clenching it at the sides of my head, I did as I was told.

For about thirty seconds. Then I came, long and luxurious, my moans muffled by the pillow.

After I did, my hand slid away but Max's arm curled around my rib cage and he lifted my torso as he kept thrusting into me, his finger moving between my legs, rolling on my sweet spot.

I pressed back into his body, my hand curling around his wrist, and I moaned, "Max, I can't...too much."

He didn't listen. His finger kept rolling, his cock kept thrusting, his hoarse, gravelly voice demanding, "Again, Duchess."

"I can't."

"I want it again."

"Max," I whispered.

His other hand cupped my breast, his finger and thumb rolling on my nipple, too, and his touch shot through me like a dart.

I was right. It was too much. I was going to come apart.

"Give it to me," he growled. "Hurry, baby, I'm close."

My body jolted as it hit me, longer, past luxurious to sumptuous. So beautiful, I cried out, my other hand moving to cover Max's on my breast, fingers curling tight.

"Christ," Max grunted, "so fuckin' sweet." Then he drove deep with velvet brutality, once, twice, three times, groaning as he came through his thrusts.

He stopped and bent at the waist, pushing my torso down on the bed. He let me go and I collapsed back into the pillows. Max stayed where he was, his fingers moving on my behind, the small of my back, as his shaft gently glided in and out of me.

I let him, loving every plunge, his light, intimate touch, thinking this didn't exactly feel like settling. This felt like having it all.

He slid out and dropped to my side; then he pulled the covers over our bodies and gathered me into his arms. I pressed my face to his throat as I wrapped an arm around him, flattening my other hand against his chest.

"You okay?" he asked.

"Mmm-mmm," I answered, giving a little nod.

His hand slid up my back and his voice sounded like he was smiling when he made a query to which he already knew the response. "Was it too much?"

"Mmm-hmm," I replied, giving a little shake of my head.

His body shook, too, with laughter. I cuddled closer.

Then he asked, "How'd you do it?"

I tilted my head back to look at him. "Do what?"

"Go without for months?"

My head pressed into the pillow as it tipped to the side. "Sorry?"

"You're a hot little piece, Duchess. Can't imagine a woman like you could stand being without for very long."

I shoved my face back into his throat and didn't answer.

"Nina?" he called.

"Did you just call me a hot little piece?" I asked his throat.

I knew he was smiling again when he replied, "Yeah." One of his hands drifted over my bottom as his other hand slid into my hair. "'Cause you are."

"Mmm," I mumbled instead of getting angry, deciding in my current state to take that as a Max-style compliment.

"I see Nina Zombie beats out Pissed Off Nina," he observed.

Again, I decided not to reply.

Max rolled me to my back by rolling into me and got up on an elbow, his other arm resting across my belly, the front of his body resting along the side of mine.

"So?" he prompted.

"So, what?"

"You didn't answer my question."

I looked at his collarbone and shrugged.

"Musta been hard," he noted.

My eyes went to his and even though I would rather have luxuriated in the postglow of a double orgasm and a morning without one of my relatives at the door, I got serious and looked in his eyes.

"You know if I had a choice of either going back to Brent, who was the one who beat me, or going back to the time before and after Charlie died, finding myself so alone, so lost, so *needy* that I allowed myself to get tied to Niles, I would pick Brent."

His hand left my belly to cup my jaw and his face was soft when he whispered, "Baby."

"I'm not kidding."

"I know, that's 'cause it's fresh. Coupla weeks, you'll feel differently."

I sighed and closed my eyes, saying, "I don't know."

I opened my eyes when I felt his mouth touch mine.

"I do," he said when he lifted his head.

"Yes?"

"You gettin' lost, gettin' tied to that asshole, led you to me." He grinned and his grin was arrogant. "So, yeah, coupla weeks, you'll feel differently."

My eyes narrowed on his grin before they went back to his. "You know, you're not only annoying and domineering, you're also arrogant."

His mouth came back to mine and I saw his eyes were still smiling when he informed me, "Yeah, and you love it."

"I forgot, you're also impossible."

His eyes started dancing a split second before he kissed me, not a touch of the lips, but deep and long and he was mostly on top of me when he was done with my mouth. My arms were also around him with one hand wrapped around the back of his neck and his kiss was so good, the weight of him felt so nice, I forgot to be peeved.

"This is nice," I whispered.

"Yeah," he whispered back, and dipped his head, running his nose along my jaw.

I didn't tell him but Max doing that made it even nicer.

"Max?" I called, and his head came up.

"Right here, baby."

"Why Shauna?"

The minute I said the words, I wished I could shove them back in my mouth. I didn't even know why I said them. They just came out. We'd been "sparring," as Max called it. We were good at that, it had become us, and after, he was being so sweet, I felt safe asking.

I knew as the darkness swept his face, I shouldn't have asked.

"Sorry, I shouldn't have asked," I muttered, fear rippling through my belly because I knew I'd done something wrong and I didn't want him to go back to that other Max of yesterday afternoon. I decided to change the subject and tried to slide out from under him, offering, "I'll go make coffee."

His weight didn't shift. In fact, he gave me more of it, holding me in place and my eyes went to his.

"Why shouldn't you ask?" he inquired.

"You obviously don't want to talk about it," I pointed out carefully.

"Maybe not, that doesn't mean you shouldn't ask."

"Well—"

"You're naked in my bed, babe. You're cookin' in my kitchen. You're movin' to town, buyin' a lawyer desk, all of that to take a gamble on me. Don't you think you got a right to know?"

I did think I had a right to know, about a lot of things, about *everything*.

I didn't tell him this. I just held on to my courage and his gaze.

Max got up on a forearm but didn't shift the rest of his weight as his eyes went to my temple and the fingers of his other hand went there, too, sifting into my hair. He slid them down, through the tendrils, and then he started twirling a lock around his finger. I felt his touch and it felt lovely but I also watched his features, emotions drifting over them openly, too fast to read but most of them were not good. Then his eyes left the lock of hair even though his finger kept twisting it and they came to me.

"Long time ago, fifth, sixth grade, we had a posse. Bitsy, Brody, Shauna, Kami, Harry, and me."

"Harry?" I asked, surprised.

"Yeah."

"Kami?"

"Yeah, kind of, mostly she tagged along, didn't have many of her own friends."

I didn't find this surprising, if what Max said about Kami being a bitch since forever was true.

"Not Curtis?" I queried.

"No."

And not Anna? I thought but didn't speak the question aloud.

"We were tight," he continued. "Did everything together for years, into high school. Stayed tight, school to school, even though Bitsy and Shauna were a year younger, Kami, two."

I nodded, prompting him to go on as my hand slid around to rest on his chest.

"Kami broke off, findin' her own friends but she always stayed close to Shauna. Brody and me made varsity our freshman year, Harry didn't. That's when Brody and me took on Curt, who was a year older but we lost close touch with Harry. He was around, we hung out, but we were no longer tight."

"Did Shauna stay close?"

"Yeah."

"So she was your friend?"

He grinned. "I was in high school. High school boys do stupid shit around beautiful girls, and even though she was a conceited pain in the ass most of the time, she's always been beautiful, even back then."

I tried not to let the knifepoint of his words sink into my flesh but I didn't succeed.

The night before he'd told me I was *pretty* not beautiful and, as all women knew, there was a big bloody difference.

"Duchess," he said softly, obviously reading my expression, "doesn't hold a candle."

I forced a smile and tried to take us back to our earlier subject. "Go on."

Max stayed on the current subject. "Babe, seriously."

"So"—I steadfastly ignored him—"you were all friends."

As usual, Max steadfastly stayed on target. "She's beautiful but she's cold. Great with her mouth when it's on your cock. When she's usin' it for anything else, to kiss, speak, or frown, which she uses it for most, not so good."

"Max—"

"And she doesn't let go when you fuck her, wants control, of you, of herself, of everything. The whole thing was an exercise in manipulation, her tryin' to wrap you around her finger, catch you in her honey trap. But what she never got was, she's wound up so tight, so intent on her scheme, she never let herself enjoy it and if she doesn't, you can't."

My eyes caught his and I told him honestly, "I'm not sure I need this information."

"Never," Max said, again ignoring me. "Never did I walk into a room and see her dressed to go out and forget how to breathe like I did when I saw you before we went to The Rooster." I felt my eyes grow wide at this admission and I, too, forgot how to breathe.

When I remembered, I whispered, "Max—"

His thumb came up and slid back and forth along my temple. "Technical points at givin' head, Shauna's a ten. Artistic merit, zip." His mouth came to mine and he muttered, "You, babe, you get into it and *fuck*." His nose slid along mine and I watched his eyes get dark with good memories as he went on. "Watchin' you suck my cock, could swear you like it better than me. Perfect fuckin' scores." He kissed me lightly and continued. "Fuckin' her, she doesn't even rank compared to you. Different league."

As much as I didn't want to admit it, this pleased me greatly.

"And she's never, not once, not since fifth grade, made me laugh," Max finished.

That pleased me even more.

"Okay, I'm better than Shauna," I mumbled, feeling slightly shy and also self-conscious (even though I still felt very pleased). "Moving on."

"Yeah, we'll move on when you promise never to get that look on your face again when I'm bein' honest about her."

"What look?" I asked, although even though I didn't see it, I figured I knew.

"That look like I caught you off guard and shoved a knife in your gut."

Oh dear. Could he really read me that well?

"Yeah, that's what you looked like," he said, like I'd spoken my unspoken question aloud and I felt my eyes get wide.

"That's uncanny," I blurted.

"Babe, don't play poker," he advised, and then smiled before he finished, "ever."

"Good advice," I whispered.

His face grew warm and he bent his head, kissed my nose, and whispered back, "Cute." Then he rolled, wrapping his arms around and taking me with him so I was mostly on top.

I lifted up with an arm on his chest and an elbow in the bed and asked, "Are you going to finish your story?"

"Yeah," he said on a sigh. "Though not much to it. We graduated and Shauna went to CSU. She disappeared for a few years after that, got married to some rich, old guy from Aspen. Divorced his ass and fleeced him for as much as she could, though not as much as she wanted. She might be beautiful and he might have been old but he wasn't dumb. She came back and has been livin' on that payoff, lookin' for her next one ever since."

"Sounds like his payoff is dwindling."

"Yeah, she's fucked. She's been workin' Curt hard. One good thing about that will and those letters is that he knew it. She thought she was fuckin' him but in the end, he took what he wanted and fucked her."

"Literally and figuratively," I noted.

"Yep."

"And you?"

His head tilted on my pillow and he stated bluntly, "She's gorgeous. She's good with her mouth. She wanted in my bed. She worked at it. I let her in my bed. She played a game with me, hid a lot of who she was and I bought it. Right off the bat it wasn't near as good as she made it seem like it was gonna be. Then it got worse. When gettin' off wasn't worth puttin' up with her, I ended it."

"You didn't know she was also sleeping with Curtis?"

"That was part of gettin' off not bein' worth puttin' up with her, when I found out she was playin' me and Curt at the same time."

"So you don't like to share?" I asked, and his arms, which were resting around me lightly, tightened.

"Depends."

"On what?"

"Shauna, I didn't give a fuck. Even when we were together, it was casual. It's casual, I don't care." His hand slid up my back, bringing my torso close to his and I watched his eyes grow intense when he said, "It ain't casual, Duchess, like us, no, I absolutely do not like to share."

I bit my lip, liking his answer; then I inquired, "So, if you didn't mind—?"

Max cut me off, explaining, "It was Curt."

"And you didn't like Curt."

"Nope, didn't like him, didn't like a woman sharin' his bed and mine, and didn't like why she was doin' it."

"How long were you with her?"

"I work outta town most of the time, so it lasted a year. Probably would have figured it out a lot sooner if I'd been around. Don't know exactly but the time I was in town and with her probably was around a coupla months."

"When did Harry enter the picture?"

"A while ago, some time after I scraped her off and she figured out she wasn't gettin' back in. A year ago, bit more."

"How did they hook up?" I asked, and Max's face changed, his eyes growing distant.

"That's the fuck of it," he murmured.

"Sorry?"

His eyes focused and he looked at me. "Harry's always had a thing for Bitsy, always. Never had a thing for Shauna. Surprised everyone when they got together."

This was news, interesting news.

"Bitsy?"

"Yeah. The day she married Curt, he got so loaded, he tore The Dog apart. Mick had to put him in a cell to keep an eye on him and dry him out."

"Wow," I breathed.

"Yeah," Max said. "After Curt, Bitsy and Harry drifted apart. After she lost her legs, they became friends again, got close. Still are."

My mother was right. This was the Rocky Mountain Peyton Place.

"So Kami was with Curt before he was with Bitsy and Harry has always had a crush on Bitsy—"

"No, honey, Kami was with Curt until Bitsy broke up with Harry. Brody and I stopped hangin' with him in high school but that didn't mean we weren't still friends. We were. And Bitsy dated him through high school and after. Until somethin' happened, she broke it off and Curt wasted no time. He ended things with Kami and went after Bitsy."

I blinked at him. "So, Harry and Bitsy were together?"

"Yeah, six, seven years, at least."

"Oh my God."

"Long time ago."

"Motive for murder?"

Max burst out laughing and rolled again so we were on our sides, but he came up with his elbow in the bed and his head in his hand and I moved to my back so I could look up at him.

"Harry wouldn't hurt a fly, doesn't have it in him. He's never even been huntin', doesn't own a gun, far's I know," Max told me. "His folks left him a trust fund but he still opened his own lumber store. Does all right for himself on top of that stash. And even if he would go after Curt, he'd never go after Bitsy, not even threaten it."

"Oh."

He grinned. "Though, few months, I wouldn't be surprised to see him standin' on her front step, carrying flowers."

I liked this idea, so I smiled.

Max's eyes drifted over my face and then his head dipped close.

"That answer your question?" he asked quietly. I nodded and Max moved on to a different subject. "So what are we gonna do today?"

I thought staying in bed watching movies (or doing other things) held merit but I didn't suggest that.

Instead, I said, "I vote no brawls."

He grinned before he suggested, "I thought I'd take you out shootin'."

"Shooting?"

"Teach you to use a gun."

I closed my eyes, my eyebrows went up, then slowly I opened them. "A gun?"

"Yeah, you're in a house with one, you should know how to use it."

"How about I just ignore its existence?"

"How about you wrap up warm and I take you out and teach you how to shoot?"

"Um…"

His face dipped even closer. "Baby, guns are dangerous in the hands of people who don't know how to use them and people who do who mean for them to be dangerous."

"But—"

"I'm out on a job, you're here by yourself, it'll make me feel better you know where the gun is, how to get to it, and how to use it."

"Out on a job?"

"Yeah?"

"What do you mean, out on a job?"

"I work contract, take three-month jobs, sometimes six. Sometimes I take jobs and work fourteen-hour days, six days a week, three months on, one month off. Builds. Mostly in state, sometimes out. Thought you knew that."

"Well, kind of, but—"

"So, I'm gone, you're here, I'll—"

I cut him off. "Fourteen-hour days?"

"Yeah."

"Is that even legal?"

"When they pay you a shitload to do it, yeah."

I pointed out what I thought was the obvious, "But that's insane."

"You get used to it."

I didn't like that he worked fourteen-hour days. That was a brutal schedule. I also didn't like the idea of him being gone for three months straight, sometimes six. That would be brutal *for me*.

However, the current subject was a golden opportunity and I thought if I was careful, I could use it to suggest helping out financially.

So being cautious, I waded in. "Um, Max, after a while, if I move in—"

Then I stopped talking when I realized I hadn't been cautious enough and I hadn't even gotten to the meat of the matter.

I knew this because his eyes narrowed dangerously and he cut me off. "After a while?"

"Well, yes, I thought once I moved here I'd get an apartment in town, maybe a condo—"

"Those go on year leases," he informed me.

"Well, okay."

"You ain't stayin' in town a year."

"I'm not?"

"Fuck no."

"Where am I staying?"

"Here."

My eyes got wide again and I stared at him.

Then I asked, "*Here*?"

"Yeah."

"But I can't move here."

"Why the hell not?"

I blinked at him, uncertain how to answer, for the answer should be obvious. And that answer was, I couldn't move in here because we'd known each other a week.

Max kept talking. "I'm outta town, babe, I get back, I want you in my bed not in a bed in a condo in town."

"Max—"

"And bein' apart for months, I'm not wastin' more time waitin' for you to drive up the mountain or wastin' gas drivin' down to you when you should be here in the first place."

"Max—"

"Or fuckin' you in your bed one night, mine the other."

"Max—"

"Draggin' clothes everywhere."

"Max!" I said loudly to get his attention.

"What?"

"What about your rentals?"

"You live here, Duchess, I pull it off the rental market."

I blinked again and started to ask, "But what about—?"

"That's the reason I can't keep the land Curt gave me—losin' the rental income makes it tough, standard of living changes."

I stopped breathing at this news.

Then I asked, "Could you keep it if you didn't lose the rental income?"

"Yeah, but you're movin' here, I'm losin' the rental income."

Suddenly my day brightened and to brighten Max's I shared, "So I can help."

It was evident Max's day didn't brighten. I knew this because his face darkened. "No, you can't."

I put my hand to his jaw, my heart getting lighter. "If I move in, I can't live here and not contribute."

"Yeah, babe, you can."

I blinked again, my heart going right back to heavy as I grew confused and I asked, "What?"

"Things aren't tight. They're good, more than comfortable, solid. And they can stay good, we can live a nice life, we contain the acreage. That rental income means I already paid off the build on this place, got no mortgage, just taxes, utilities, and I pay those."

"But—"

"Not up for discussion."

"But—"

"You use your money for your fancy clothes and you can plant flowers and buy shit for the kitchen."

I stared at him in shock. Did he say plant flowers and buy shit for the kitchen?

Helpfully, I reminded him, "Max, we celebrated a new millennium a few years back."

"So?"

"So, I'll be earning money, I can help."

"No," he stated shortly, firmly, and with a definite finality.

I stared at him again.

Then I asked, "That's it? No?"

"That's it. No."

"I thought you didn't have a problem with me earning more than you?"

"I don't."

I was no longer shocked. Now I was back to confused.

"I don't get it."

"I don't have a problem with you earning more than me. I *do* have a problem with you payin' my bills."

There it was. Macho Mountain Man Max. I knew there was a hitch.

"If I lived here, they would be *our* bills," I pointed out.

"*When* you live here, you'll be my woman. I take care of my woman. Therefore they're *my* bills."

Losing patience, I called, "Hello? Max? I'm calling you into the twenty-first century. Follow me into the light of a world with cell phones and sat navs and computers you can carry around in a briefcase instead of them taking up entire rooms. Oh, and where women have been financially contributing to the household for decades."

His face remained dark and his voice was low and lethal when he told me, "Not findin' you funny, babe."

My body tensed but I felt my eyes get big.

"Are you serious?" I asked.

"Deadly," he answered.

We stared at each other silently as it hit me like a succession of blows to the stomach. I was lying on my back but I still felt winded.

I had conflicting information about the state of play with Max's bank account, but none of it had come from Max until now.

I took what I knew and I put together the picture.

I knew how much it cost to rent his house for a week; it was a small fortune. And what I paid wasn't even the top tier of on-peak rent. In the winter months rent was nearly double what I had paid. If he was only home two months of the year, and rentals were steady as he said they were, especially in winter, he made a fortune.

And he didn't have a mortgage.

And he had two ATVs, a snowmobile, a motorcycle, a car that needed to be kept under a tarp, a Cherokee that wasn't brand-new but it was far from old, and a housecleaner.

He might not be loaded but he certainly wasn't doing too badly for himself.

What he was was unwilling to let the little woman contribute to the household finances. He was such a macho mountain man that he would let his macho mountain man pride stand in the way of keeping his mountain clean.

Yes, here was the hitch. This was when the good part of starting out with someone turned bad. I felt the fear prickle my skin but I was too busy controlling the fury that nearly blinded me.

"Proud and stubborn," I whispered. My stare had turned into a glare.

"What?" he asked. His stare had turned into a scowl.

Quickly I rolled off the bed and searched frantically through the clothes we'd tossed onto the floor the night before. Latching on to his thermal, I straightened and struggled to yank it on, getting caught in the voluminous folds.

"Proud and stubborn," I muttered from under the shirt, battling the sleeves.

"Nina, get back into bed."

I successfully yanked the shirt down and glared at him.

"Just like your mom!" I accused, my voice getting louder.

His already dark face turned that scary dark and his voice turned into a warning when he repeated, "Nina, get back into bed."

"No!" I snapped. "You can handle me in that bed, Max, and when you do, I'll admit, I love it. But when you aren't fucking me, you cannot *handle* me."

His brows snapped together and his voice was a low, angry rumble when he asked, "What the fuck?"

I rolled the long sleeve on one side up my wrist and as I did so I leaned forward and fairly shouted, "You! Macho Mountain Man Max! You cannot *handle* me! Tell me the way it's going to be! Not let me participate in the conversation! Not let me participate in our *lives*!" I finished rolling the sleeve and threw my arm out. "Do you think, if I lived here, that *I'd* want that bluff to be desecrated? Do you think *I'd* want a condo on it or a house or a hotel? Do you think *I'd* want more traffic on the road, the quiet and peace of this place ruined? Do you think *I'd* want the erosion of the mountain that people and building would cause?" I started rolling the other sleeve and finished on a shout, "No! *I* don't want that! But are *you* going to give me a choice? Are *you* going to let me help? No again!"

He threw the covers back and I whirled and bent, digging through the clothes to find my underwear. As I did this, I saw the leg of his jeans slide away and I knew he was out of bed. I found my undies, snatched them up, and twirled, taking a step back from him as I saw he was close and buttoning his jeans.

I bent over and tugged my panties on, shimmying them up, abrading my scraped leg as I did but ignoring the pain.

"I can plant flowers and buy stuff for the kitchen. You're *mad*!" I yelled as I pulled on my panties.

"It's my house, babe, my land, my responsibility. This land has been in my family for over a hundred fuckin' years."

I straightened and faced off with him, still shouting. "Yes, you told me that and, if this works out like you're so darned sure it will, then won't I be your family?"

His upper body jerked and I knew I'd scored my point but I kept right on going.

"You're absolutely fine money-wise but you'll take this hit to have me the way you want me. *Not* the way *I* want *us* and that's with *me* being *your* partner, not your little woman!" I yelled.

"Nina, that's bullshit," he clipped.

"It is?"

"We're done talkin' about this," he declared.

"Oh, so now that *I'm* right and *you're* wrong, we're done talking about this?"

"Nina—"

I shook my head and lifted up my hand, still shouting, "No, no way. Proud and stubborn. That's you. I come here, I slot into *your* life. We don't build one *together*."

He took a step toward me and I took two quick ones back as he clipped, "Goddammit, Nina."

"I'm glad I know this now, Max. This is good to know," I snapped, and then I heard a rap on the door and my head twisted in that direction. From my position in the loft I couldn't see who it was but I suspected it was my mother or, if the turn of my morning luck held true, it was my father and Niles, so I instantly marched in the direction of the stairs, announcing, "I'll get it."

"Leave it, Duchess," Max growled, catching my wrist, but I twisted it free, not looking at him.

"Go to hell, Max," I bit off, and marched to the stairs and down quickly, my mind in turmoil, my heart beating too fast, tears threatening, hope dying, and that was the worst. It always was the worst when hope died.

I made it to the bottom of the stairs and I knew Max was close behind. I took two steps to the door, belatedly focused on it, and stopped dead.

Standing outside the door, the sun blazing on a new blanket of white coating the front steps, were Kami, Shauna, and an older woman who looked like Kami. Her hair was a beautiful, silvery white streaked with Max and Kami's almost-black and pulled back in a ponytail. She, like Kami, held extra weight but not as much as Kami, and even at a glance, I could tell she wasn't uncomfortable with it on her frame. She was attractive and wearing the mountain woman uniform of jeans, poofy vest, long-sleeved shirt, and boots.

Max's mother.

Wonderful.

I also took in the fact that both Kami and Shauna were smirking, though Max's mother was studying me through the glass, her face unreadable.

They'd heard.

Double wonderful. Darn it all to hell.

Max stalked past me straight to the door, which he yanked open.

"Now is not a good time," he announced on an angry snarl, barring entry with his big body.

"Yeah, we heard," Kami told him gleefully.

Yes, gleefully. She was *such* a bitch.

Then she forced her way in, scooting in between Max and the door frame. "It's cold, Max, and we need coffee."

With Kami already inside and with no other choice but to throw her out physically, which, in my state of mind, was a viable option, Max stepped aside for his mother to enter and Shauna gave him a sweet, satisfied smile, swinging that same smile to me as she came in too.

Shauna. In Max's house.

Seeing her smile pinned on me while she stood inside Max's door, I felt the pressure build and I stayed utterly still so as not to let it explode.

"You're Nina," Max's mom said.

I started, then looked to her.

Then I forced myself to walk stiffly toward her (yes, meeting Max's mom wearing nothing but Max's thermal and a pair of panties after just having been heard having a fight).

I also tried to force my voice to be kind but I only managed neutral. "Yes, and you're Max's mom."

"Linda," she said on a nod, and lifted her hand.

I took it. Unlike her daughter, her fingers curled around mine in a warm grip before she let go.

"Lovely to meet you," I murmured.

She watched me and I saw something flash in her dark brown eyes, a twinkle; then she doused it so quickly I was uncertain it was ever there.

She looked at Max and suggested, "Why don't you two get dressed? I'll make coffee."

"Like I said, Mom, this isn't a good time," Max told her.

"Dressed, Max," Linda ordered, and walked toward the kitchen.

Still smirking, Shauna and Kami followed.

I decided to take this opportunity to escape, which I did without looking at Max. I ran up the stairs and I didn't care what it looked like.

I was in the closet, my cords in my hands, my mind skittering from awful thought (meeting Max's mom during a fight) to terrible thought (Shauna and Kami being there) to horrendous thought (Max and me being over) when Max came in.

My intention was to ignore him, an impossible task when he grabbed my cords, tossed them onto the floor, and curled his fingers into my hips.

I tilted my head back to look at him and tried to yank my hips from his hands but failed at this when his arms locked around me. One hand sifted up into my hair and cupped the back of my head.

"Take your hands off me, Max," I hissed quietly.

"Shut it, Duchess," Max whispered back, and then his mouth was on mine.

The kiss was hard, long and closemouthed, communicating something I didn't get. I pressed against his hold and his shoulders while he kissed me but didn't succeed in getting away or yanking my mouth from his.

He lifted his head and I stopped struggling in order to glare at him. His eyes moved over my face. Then his arm at my waist drifted down to become a hand on my behind; then it slid up, taking the thermal with it.

Before I could protest what his hand was doing, he whispered, "You were right, honey."

With my history with men, most specifically Niles, who never listened to me, I found I was unable to process his words.

"Sorry?"

His fingers slid out of my hair and his hand went down, also under the shirt, and both of his hands were now traveling soothingly along my back.

"You were right. I was wrong."

My mouth dropped open.

Did he just say that? Did Macho Mountain Man Max straight out admit he was wrong?

I felt the anger flood out of me as the hope pushed back in and my body relaxed in his arms.

"Sorry?" I whispered.

He bent his head and his lips touched my forehead, where he muttered, "We'll talk about it later."

He kissed me sweet, then suddenly the thermal was pulled up, my arms going up with it and it was over my head.

I stood in nothing but my undies, watching Max walk away, pulling the thermal I just had on over his head. Then he disappeared. And I continued to stand there, staring at where I last saw him.

He'd just admitted he was wrong. He'd pulled me into his arms, gave me a hard kiss as his Max-style apology, and admitted he was wrong. And he'd done it last night, too, admitted he was wrong, told me straight out he'd "fucked up."

I continued to stare at where I last saw him, letting this penetrate and thinking that the most macho mountain man thing he'd ever done was have the guts to look me in the eye and admit he was wrong.

That was when I stood there, staring at where I last saw him but I did it smiling.

Then the murmuring of voices invaded and my mind flew

to the fact that Max's mom was downstairs having heard us fighting and so, for some insane reason, were the dreaded Kami and Shauna.

I snatched one of Max's shirts off the hanger without even looking at it, shrugged it on, and grabbed my cords. Then I flew into the bedroom, pulled underwear from the drawer, and, seeing the checked flannel of Max's that I was wearing (it was checked in gold, brown, and navy, perfect to go with my cords) I grabbed a cream camisole and hit the bathroom.

After I'd done my routine, dressed (including Max's flannel, which was huge but also warm, old, and soft from a million washings), and pulled my hair up in a ponytail at the back of my crown. With no other choice but to go makeup-free, I rushed out of the bathroom and across the loft.

I slowed my progress on the stairs, deep breathing to calm myself and repeating in my head, *Don't have a go at either Kami or Shauna in front of Max's mom.*

I was in possession of my faculties and hopefully in control of my mouth when I hit the bottom and turned toward the kitchen.

Linda was in it, bustling around in what appeared to be Mom Mode. Both Kami and Shauna were on stools. They all looked at me when I approached. I couldn't see Max until I got closer, for he was standing in the recess, hips against the sink.

"Coffee's poured, Duchess," Max told me when I hit the mouth of the U of the kitchen, and I saw his head dip to a mug that was steaming on the counter beside him.

"Thanks," I muttered, walking to the coffee and picking it up, feeling all eyes on me, and that feeling, needless to say, was uncomfortable.

"I remember that shirt," Shauna announced, and my eyes went to her over the rim of my mug. I nearly choked on my sip when she went on, "It was a favorite of mine too."

Out of the corner of my eye, I saw Linda's head jerk and right in front of me I saw both Shauna and Kami smile delightedly.

"It's good with your coloring," I heard Linda say, luckily

before I could utter a word or any of the twenty-five of them in my head and I looked at her.

"Sorry?" I asked, noting vaguely she had a bowl out and flour, milk, eggs, maple syrup, and measuring cups.

"Your coloring. That shirt. Looks good on you," she told me, and my mind focused, moving from Shauna's catty comment to the look on Linda's face.

She was making a point, a quiet one, but it was a point nonetheless.

Moments before I had the irrational desire to shrug off Max's shirt, take it outside, and burn it. At the present moment I remembered it was Max's, it was old, warm, and soft, and it was mine to claim when I wanted, not Shauna's, never again Shauna's.

And that was the point Linda was making, not only to me, but also to Shauna.

"Thanks," I whispered, my meaning deeper than the whispered word.

"Hope you don't mind, I'm making pancakes. Is that okay with you?" Linda asked, and I blinked.

Why was she asking me?

"Um . . . yes?" I answered.

She nodded and turned back to the bowl.

"Mom makes great pancakes, babe," Max told me, his finger going into my back belt loop and tugging me closer. "You'll love 'em."

I looked up at him and said, "Okay."

He grinned at me then he winked. It was the wink that got me. Max had never winked at me. I didn't think he was the kind of man *to* wink. But, like all things Wonder Max, he did it great.

Using my belt loop, he positioned my still-coping-with-his-wink body close to his side by the sink.

"Max, I like that sugar bowl and creamer, saw it in town, almost picked them up for myself," Linda noted.

"Nina bought 'em," Max told her over his mug, and took a sip.

"Good taste," Linda mumbled, looking at me and saying firmly, "Domestication."

"Sorry?" I asked.

"Cupboards full. Creamer and sugar bowl. You're domesticating Max." That twinkle hit her eye again. I caught it again but she extinguished it before she finished, "This'll be entertaining."

Oh my God. She liked me!

I couldn't help it. I smiled to myself and relaxed into Max's side. When I did, his arm slid along my shoulders, his hand dangling casually over the left one.

"You wanna tell me why you're here and not at work?" Max asked, and I tipped my head back to look at him, following his gaze to see his eyes were on Kami.

"Day off, Curt's funeral," Kami replied.

"You gotta take a whole day off for Curt's funeral?" Max asked.

"I'm grieving," Kami returned.

"Jesus, Kami, I hope they don't find out you're full of shit like they did at your last job. Be hard to keep that Lexus when you don't have a paycheck," Max remarked.

"Don't worry about me, got my Lexus and that's it. Don't have a barn full of stupid boys' toys I wanna fill with even more boys' toys," Kami shot back, adding nastily, "Maybe you'll grow up in this century."

Jealous, I thought, but kept my mouth shut.

"Kami," Linda said quietly, mixing batter.

"What?" Kami snapped, but before Linda could say anything further, Max spoke again.

"Now you wanna tell me why you're here at all?"

I looked up at him to see his eyes, cold and angry, resting on Shauna.

I'd never seen Max cold. I'd seen him angry but not cold and that cold was glacial. I took a sip of my coffee and looked at Shauna to see how she was handling it and noted she had her shields up and seemed perfectly at ease.

"Spending the day with Kami. We're going to the funeral together," Shauna answered.

I felt my eyes grow big and I also felt Max's body turn to stone at my side. Further, again out of the corner of my eye, I saw Linda's head twist around to look at Shauna.

"For obvious reasons, Shauna's grieving too," Kami put in.

"You have got to be fuckin' shittin' me," Max growled.

"What?" Kami asked, but Max ignored her and his eyes sliced to Shauna.

"You ain't goin' to that funeral, Shauna."

"Why not?" Shauna inquired with what appeared to be genuine curiosity, and I felt my lips part in astonishment, uncertain I'd ever seen anyone so inappropriately cavalier.

"I don't know," Max clipped sarcastically. "Maybe because you were fuckin' a married man and his wife, mother, and father'll be there?"

"I lost Curt, too, just like Bitsy," Shauna retorted.

"Yeah, but he loved her and was married to her for fifteen years. You were just convenient pussy," Max shot back.

I gasped, so did Linda. Kami and Shauna both glared at Max.

"Max." Now Linda said Max's name quietly.

"No, Mom, she's not goin' to that funeral." Max's eyes went to his sister. "And you've spoken about a dozen civil words to Bitsy in the last decade, so you shouldn't either."

"I'm not six, Max. You can't tell me what to do," Kami returned.

"No, you're not. You act it a lot of the time, but you're not. What you are is old enough to know better," Max shot back.

"We're goin'," Kami declared.

"Fuckin' hell," Max muttered.

"I was under the impression"—Linda entered the conversation and I looked at her to see she was regarding Kami—"after all that talk I heard in town about what happened with you two at Max and Brody's table at The Rooster that we were here so you both could talk with Max and Nina about your behavior that night." Kami opened her mouth to speak but Linda went on. "*Not*," she cut her off sharply and with obvious practice, "so you two could bring attitude into Max's house."

"I'm sorry, Linda," Shauna said readily, and looked at me. "You know Max and I have history, Nina," she reminded me unnecessarily. "I guess we rub each other the wrong way. I just wanted to spend some time with Kami today since it's gonna be a rough day for me but I probably shouldn't have come."

I stared at her, shocked at how good she was in front of Max's mom. Even I almost believed her.

"In case you feel like visiting again, Shauna, you can take it as read you aren't welcome," Max told her.

"Just because you two have broken up doesn't mean you can be an asshole, Max," Kami defended her friend.

"'Fraid it does, Kami," Max returned.

I was now stunned. These shenanigans made my mother and me, even my *father* and me, seem tame. Though, my father, mother, Niles, and me were still the worst, if you didn't count me slapping my dad during the Dad-and-me fiasco, of course.

"You know, Nina," Linda said matter-of-factly as she poured batter into the melted butter in a skillet, "a mother gets to the point when her kids are kids that she looks forward to them being adults." Her eyes came to mine as she set down the bowl. "I haven't reached that part of motherhood yet."

I didn't want to say that Max wasn't exactly acting like a kid, more like a pissed off mountain man whose bitch of a sister brought his ex-girlfriend to his house. So instead, I just smiled.

"Or at least I haven't with Kami," Max's mom went on. The twinkle came back to her eyes, it stayed there longer and my smile got wider.

"Mom!" Kami snapped, and Linda turned to her, leaned forward, and morphed into another woman altogether.

"What'd I say about this crap?" she hissed. "You two always fightin' with *you* always startin' it. Works my last flippin' nerve. Max is here, what? Practically never. And instead of enjoyin' the time you got, you get in his face. I've had it up to here, Kami." She lifted a hand up to her neck and continued. "And I've had it up to here with talkin' to you like you're five when you're thirty-five, dammit."

"I see, as always, perfect fuckin' Max," Kami shot back.

"Yeah, darlin', perfect fuckin' Max," Linda shot back. "Max comes over, fixes my sink, and doesn't whine at me for five hours. That's pretty fuckin' perfect."

Kami flinched and her face shut down.

"Same old shit," Kami grumbled.

"The same old shit is, Max has a new girlfriend and you bring his *old* one to his house, lyin' to me about why and makin' us look bad in front of Nina. That's the same old shit, Kami, and I'm sick and tired of it." Then Linda looked at me and mumbled, "Sorry, Nina."

"Um...that's okay," I told her.

"It isn't," Linda replied.

"Oh, so now it's gonna be perfect fuckin' Nina," Kami bit out.

Linda turned back to her daughter but I moved in quickly with hopes of lightening the mood.

"I'm sorry, Linda, but I don't know how to fix a sink."

Linda looked at me, her eyes caught mine, and she replied, "That's okay, Nina. Talked to Barb. What you know how to fix is a whole lot more important than a sink."

I stared at her, now understanding why she liked me, and Max's arm curled tighter around my neck.

"What's this?" Kami asked.

"None of your business," Linda said, her eyes going to her daughter, then to Shauna as she said, "You two are adults, so you gotta do what you think you gotta do but I'll tell you, you show up at Curtis Dodd's funeral, it'll make me think less of you." Her gaze hardened on Shauna and she finished, "It'll make me think less of you both."

Shauna's eyes moved quickly away but Kami glared at her mother.

"Maybe we should leave," Kami suggested.

"Since you're my ride up here, that'd make it difficult for me to get down the mountain," Linda replied.

"I'll take you down, Mom," Max put in smoothly.

"Perfect fuckin' Max," Kami shot at him.

"What is it with you?" Max shot back. "Seriously, Kami, I wanna know. Why are you such a bitch all the time?"

"I don't know, Max, maybe it's 'cause you were Dad's favorite and you're Mom's favorite and I could handle that if my nose wasn't rubbed in it *all the time*," Kami returned.

Jealous and juvenile, I thought, staring at her in amazement at her words, for her behavior was the norm, as far as I knew it.

"Honest to God?" Max asked.

"I'm sure it's hard for you to believe, seein' as you have no clue how it feels," Kami returned.

"Christ, I feel like I'm fifteen again," Max muttered. "Since we had this conversation when I was fifteen and fourteen and fuckin' twenty-five."

"Whatever," Kami muttered back.

"The other thing, Nina," Linda said to me, flipping the pancakes, "is all kids think a parent has a favorite. They don't. It isn't possible. You love your children, maybe not the same but always the same amount."

"Right," Kami said to her mother's back.

"Though," Linda said to me, "you can tell them that and tell them that but they'll never believe you."

"I'm an only child," I informed Linda, or at least I was now.

"That's too bad," Linda replied, reaching into the cupboard for plates. "I got a sister and brother, love 'em both to bits. Wish my kids had that."

"If Max'll take you down the mountain, we'll skip on the pancakes." Kami again spoke to her mother's back, clearly not allowing a single word her mother said to penetrate her rabid desire to be the martyr.

"All right, Kami," Linda replied, not turning, and Kami and Shauna both slid from their stools.

Linda continued with her pancakes and Max stayed still at my side, his arm around my shoulders as Kami and Shauna walked to the door.

"We'll see ourselves out," Kami called spitefully.

"All right, darlin'," Linda called back, and handed me a plate of pancakes.

The door closed and I offered the pancakes to Max.

"You eat, baby. I'll wait for the next round," Max said softly.

"And I'll apologize for Kami," Linda said as she put butter into the skillet. "She isn't like this all the time, honestly. Curtis's death has been tough on her."

"Then maybe she shouldn't be friends with Curt's piece of ass," Max muttered as I slid out from under his arm and walked to the butter.

"Max," Linda said quietly.

"Can't imagine why you brought them both here, Mom, especially Shauna," Max said, and Linda looked at him.

"I did because a mother always wants to believe the best of her kids. I had a word with Kami about the crap I heard in town. She and Shauna came and asked if I'd smooth the way with you. I had no idea that would happen."

"They played it so they could act just like that, get under Nina's skin and rile her up. Nina's hell on wheels when she's riled and they wanted to make her look bad in front of you," Max told his mother.

I stared at him, wondering if this was true and figuring, unfortunately, it was.

"Kami wouldn't do that," Linda returned.

"I'll give you Kami but Shauna?" Max asked.

"Known her since she was ten, Max. She's like one of my kids too," Linda answered.

"And she's also been up her own ass since she was ten," Max replied. "Christ, goin' to Curt's funeral? Jesus."

Linda sighed. I poured maple syrup on my pancakes and stayed quiet.

Linda went on. "Anyway, yesterday, I looked out the window and what did I see? You and Nina over at Barb and Darren's. I also saw you didn't bring her by to see me. You're at Barb and Darren's, you don't come to see me?" She shook her head and poured in more pancake batter. "It's all over town, you spendin' time with Nina's folks and you haven't brought her to see me. So you'll have to flippin' forgive me, darlin'. I needed an excuse to meet my own son's new girlfriend, so I brought 'em up here."

"The truth comes out," Max muttered.

Linda turned to him. "Yeah, there it is, Max. I found out from Barb why you all were there. That I can understand but I still don't get why you didn't walk a house away and introduce me to Nina."

I forked into my pancakes, avoided looking at either of them, and shoved pancake into my mouth (which, incidentally, Max was correct, was delicious) and stayed quiet.

"We been busy," Max told his mother.

"Yeah, havin' lunch with Mindy and Becca, with Bitsy, dinner at The Rooster with Brody, and breakfast with her folks. I heard about it all. Jesus, Max, Nina's made fish casserole for flippin' Arlene."

Seriously, the gossip tree in Gnaw Bone was second to none.

"Because she showed up at the house and stayed. Jesus, Mom, you know Arlene," Max explained.

"What I know about Arlene is she's had Nina's fish casserole."

I decided to wade in. "I'm thinking of making my pasta bake tonight, Linda. Why don't you come for that?"

"See?" Linda flipped a hand out to me but didn't take her eyes from Max. "Even Nina's polite enough to ask your mother to dinner." She turned to me and queried, "Are your folks comin'?"

I wondered briefly what Mom plus Linda would equal for the night's experience and I was guessing they'd probably enjoy it but Max and I sure as heck wouldn't.

But with no choice, I answered, "Um . . . sure."

Linda turned to the skillet and flipped pancakes. "Then I'll be delighted to come."

I chanced a glance at Max to see he was staring at me and I knew without him saying a word that he'd calculated the same equation and came up with the same answer.

I tilted my head to the side and shrugged. Max shook his head.

I ate my pancakes.

*   *   *

As Max taught me, I looked down the sight of the gun but I didn't really have to do much since he was standing behind me, his body pressed close to mine, his arms around me, his hands mostly around mine, aiming the gun.

"Shoot, baby," he said into my ear. I pulled the trigger. There was a loud rapport, and our hands jumped back with the recoil, and the can, dead center in the triangle Max set up on a fallen log, flew back, causing all of them to collapse.

"Yay!" Mom shouted, taking her hands from her ears and clapping, the noise muted by gloves. She was sitting on a tree stump Max had cleared of snow and I'd thrown a woolen blanket over. "Neenee Bean," she called, moving her eyes from the cans to me, "you're getting really good at that."

"Great," I muttered. Max chuckled and Steve spoke.

"Company."

Max's arms went from around me and he and I both turned to the drive, seeing a police SUV parking behind Mom and Steve's car.

We were outside and it was after pancakes. After Max had taken Linda back to town while I had a shower. After me getting ready. After Mom and Steve had arrived. After Steve had shoveled the steps to the house. And after Max got back in time for Mom to make grilled cheese sandwiches for lunch.

And, I guessed, watching Mick hop down from the cab of the SUV, after my shooting lesson.

"What now?" Max muttered, taking the gun from my hand, sliding on the safety, and shoving it into the waistband of his jeans as he watched Mick saunter over to us.

"Hey, Max, Nina," Mick called when he was close.

"Hi, Mick," I called back. Mick's eyes went to Mom and Steve. "These are my parents, Nell and Steve Locke."

"How d'ya do?" Mick greeted, arriving at our group.

I got a good look at his face and tensed.

Mom and Steve didn't answer because Max got there before them.

"What's up?" Max asked, and from his tone I knew he'd gotten a good look at Mick's face too.

Mick looked at Max. "You think we can talk privately?"

"Shit," Max muttered.

"Steve and I'll go in, make coffee. How's that?" Mom inquired, and I looked at her. She'd wrapped both her hands around Steve's bicep and she, too, was reading Mick's expression.

"Thanks, Miz Locke," Mick replied. Mom nodded and both she and Steve gave Max and me a look before they started moving toward the A-frame.

"Nellie, please. No one calls me Mrs. Locke," Mom invited from over her shoulder, still walking away.

Mick nodded at Mom, waited several moments as she and Steve made their way to the house, and then he turned to Max and me.

"I'll just...um...go with them," I offered, starting to move away.

"Nina, reckon you should stay," Mick told me. My breath caught and my body locked.

"What's up?" Max repeated. Mick looked at him and I slid my thumb through the belt loop at the back of Max's jeans.

"You know that PI Dodd hired?" Mick asked Max.

"Yeah," Max answered.

"Welp, we found him dead," Mick informed Max.

"*What*?" I breathed, moving closer to Max.

"Found him dead," Mick repeated, his eyes coming to me for his answer, then going back to Max. "Been dead awhile. Some boys found him at one of Dodd's building sites."

"When?" Max queried.

"Coroner's guessin' the same night Curt was done," Mick replied.

"How'd he die?" Max asked.

"Messy," Mick answered. "Not clean, not professional. He'd been tied up, taken there, killed. Shot four times. Twice in the head, twice in the chest. Whoever did it wanted to make sure he was dead."

Max stared at Mick and I moved closer, so much closer Max was forced to slide an arm along my shoulders.

"Can I ask why you're up here tellin' me this?" Max queried.

Mick shuffled his feet, twisted his neck uncomfortably, and looked Max in the eye. "Did you know your sister Kami bought a .38 'bout a month ago?"

I felt Max go still at my side. Then he answered, "No."

"Paperwork filed then," Mick went on. "Got it at Zip's Gun Emporium in Denver."

"You're tellin' me this because . . . ?" Max prompted.

"'Cause the PI was killed with a .38."

"Jesus Christ, Mick!" Max exploded. Coming unstuck, he leaned into Mick. "You tellin' me you think Kami murdered this PI?"

Mick's hands came up but he kept the dire information flowing. "She borrowed on her house, Max. Twenty-five K."

"Fuck," Max clipped.

"You know about that?" Mick asked.

"No," Max bit out.

"Jeff 'n' Pete are bringin' her in now," Mick told Max.

"My sister didn't kill any PI, Mick," Max returned. "And she sure as fuck didn't hire someone to kill Curt."

"It ain't lookin' good for her, Max," Mick replied.

I butted in, asking, "Why are you telling Max this, Mick?"

"I ain't tellin' Max, Nina," Mick said to me. "I'm tellin' you."

I blinked. Then I asked, "Me?"

"Heard word you're an attorney," Mick explained. "We been combin' Kami's records. She don't got a lot. Bank statements show she's pretty much got zilch, livin' from paycheck to paycheck, beyond her means, flyin' high in her Lexus cartin' around those fancy-ass purses on credit. Figure she'll need some help 'round about now and George isn't only covered in work, he's pricey."

"You're coming here because you want her to lawyer up?" I asked in disbelief.

"I'm here because I watched Kami Maxwell grow up and doin' that I watched her grow bitter." His eyes went to Max. "Just like her ma, wantin' a man she had but let him get away."

"Don't mean she killed a man, Mick," Max returned.

"If she did this, whatever pushed her to it, she's still one of our own and, right now, she needs help," Mick told him.

"This is fucked up," Max clipped.

"She's got motive and she had twenty-five large that went in and out of her account in about three days. We talk to her and she don't have an alibi, we may find she had opportunity," Mick said to Max.

"Kami ain't small but she's also not got the strength to subdue a man, tie him up, take him to a building site, and drill four rounds into him," Max retorted.

"Toxicology shows he was roofied," Mick stated.

"That's not good," I muttered, and Max's eyes sliced to me.

"Roofied?" Max asked.

"Date rape drug," I answered.

"Christ," Max bit out, and looked back at Mick. "Kami doesn't have it in her to shoot a man four times, he's drugged or not."

"That's what I'm hopin', Max. You got to know that. But I also gotta do my job and this is what we got. She don't have an alibi and some good reason to buy a gun and take a loan against her house and blow it all in three days, what can I say? Any way you look at it, with her history with Curt and Bitsy, the evidence we got, it ain't lookin' good."

"Do you have a ballistics match on her gun?" I inquired.

"Got a warrant to search her house. Jeff and Pete are bringin' her in. Other boys are goin' through her house. We find the weapon, we'll run the tests," Mick answered.

"You said they're bringing her in?" I asked.

"Yeah," Mick said to me. "You comin' down the mountain?"

"Fuck yeah," Max answered.

I let Max's belt loop go and muttered, "I'll go get my purse."

* * *

"I should sue you for wrongful arrest!" Kami shouted from her seat at the table beside me,

I drew in a calming breath and Mick, across the table from us, looked at me.

"Kami," I said softly.

"This is crazy!" she yelled.

"They're just asking questions, Kami," I reminded her. "You aren't arrested."

She twisted in her seat and glared at me. "Then I'm free to go?"

"Um...," I mumbled, "technically, yes."

She started to stand, declaring, "Then I'm goin'."

I reached out and grabbed her hand. "As I explained to you before we came in here, you're free to go, but if you do, you'll appear uncooperative and you don't want that."

She glared at me and I noticed while she did it that her hand was trembling in mine so I squeezed it.

Then I continued. "Or if you try to leave, you may force Mick's hand and he'll have to arrest you on what he thinks he's got."

Her hand jerked spasmodically in mine.

"You have nothing to hide, Kami, so sit down and take a deep breath," I advised, giving her hand a small tug.

She held my eyes. Then she looked at Mick and sat down, and I released her hand.

My gaze went to Mick. "Mick, you can start."

He nodded and looked at Kami. "All right, Kami, we'll begin at the beginnin'. What were you doin' between the hours of one and four last Wednesday mornin'?"

"I wasn't killin' Curt," Kami snapped.

"What were you doin'?" Mick pressed.

"I'd never hurt Curt," Kami kept snapping.

"Answer his question, Kami," I urged quietly.

She sighed in a harassed way and responded.

"Between one and four in the morning, I was sleepin'. What else would I be doin'?"

"Were you alone?" Mick asked, and Kami's face twisted bitterly.

"Yeah, Mick, I was alone."

Mick nodded and went on. "Did you buy a gun in Denver 'bout a month ago?"

Even though I told her that Mick had that on her, Kami's body jerked before she answered belligerently, "Yeah, so?"

"Why?" Mick queried.

"I don't know. Shauna and I were in Denver havin' a girls' weekend. We drove by this shop, saw they had a shootin' range. Shauna got a wild hair and we went in. Dad taught Max and me how to shoot. We used to go up to the land and do it all the time. I forgot I was good at it and we had fun. After we took turns at the range, Shauna mentioned she noticed I was good at it, too, and she convinced me to buy a gun."

My eyes on Kami slid to Mick to see he was nodding. But I was wondering why on earth Shauna would, first, get a wild hair to go to a shooting range and, second, after she did that, convince her friend to buy a gun. I wasn't a mountain woman. Therefore I didn't know what they spent their fun time doing but that seemed strange.

I just hoped Mick was wondering the same thing.

"You recently borrowed on your house," Mick informed Kami.

She nodded and asked curtly, "So what?"

"Twenty-five thousand dollars," Mick continued.

"Yeah, I remember how much I borrowed, Mickey," Kami snapped.

"It went in and out of your account in a few days," Mick told her, and Kami's eyes narrowed.

"So, you're lookin' into my accounts too?"

"Kami, you're a suspect in a double homicide," Mick said quietly.

She sucked in breath, her narrowed eyes went wide, and she sat back in her chair. I bit my lip. Mick had asked me not to mention that to her and as a favor I hadn't.

"Double?" Kami breathed, clearly astonished at this news, something Mick couldn't miss, which I hoped made my favor to Mick pay off for Kami.

"Curtis Dodd and Marco Fitzgibbon," Mick stated.

"Who's Marco Fitzgibbon?" Kami asked.

"The PI Curt hired to find out who was threatening his and Bitsy's lives," Mick answered.

Kami went stock-still before she inquired softly, "Curt got death threats?" Mick nodded and Kami went on. "Bitsy too?"

"Yeah, Kami," Mick told her.

"Shit," Kami whispered.

"The money, Kami," Mick prompted.

She shook her head and looked at me. "Is this confidential?"

"I'm sorry?"

"This interview, will this be made public or anything?" she asked.

"Why?" Mick butted in.

"Because I promised I wouldn't say anything," Kami told him.

"About what?" Mick queried.

"About the money, I promised I wouldn't say anything," Kami replied.

I leaned toward her. She hadn't shared this part with me fully; we hadn't had the time. What she had said was that it was all innocent.

"Kami"—I caught her attention—"if you had a reason to borrow that money, then you need to tell Mick what it was. He's trying to remove you from the suspect list. You need to give him all the information he needs to help him do that."

Kami looked at me and for the first time I saw she was uncertain. "But I promised."

I leaned closer and touched her arm. "You're being questioned for a double homicide. I think whoever you promised will understand. If something else is going on here, we need to ask Mick to leave so we can confer."

Her eyes held mine for long moments. Then she looked at Mick. "It was for Shauna."

This surprised me. Shauna again.

My gaze also went to Mick.

"Shauna?" he asked.

"Yeah, she's…" Kami paused, pulling her hand through her hair. Her eyes slid to me, then to the side and back to Mick. "She's in trouble. Money trouble. They were gonna shut off her electric, her water, gas. They already shut off her cable. Her cards are maxed. And she doesn't have any insurance and she's pregnant."

"You gave the money to Shauna?" Mick inquired.

"Yeah," Kami replied.

Mick turned slightly in his chair so his profile was facing the mirror behind him and he dipped his head, communicating to whoever was watching they were meant to do something.

"I got the permit and I got the gun," Kami went on, missing Mick's movements. "It's never been fired. It's never even been loaded. It's in a shoebox in my closet." Then she leaned forward and repeated, "Mickey, you gotta know, no matter what went down, I'd never hurt Curt, never send death threats, and I'd never, not ever, hurt Bitsy." She bit her lip as her eyes got bright and she finished, repeating, "You gotta know. You know me and you gotta know."

"All right, Kami," Mick said gently. "Let us check this out, yeah?"

Kami sat back and turned her face away, nodding. Mick looked at me, rose, and walked out of the room.

I turned to Kami. "Are you okay?"

Her eyes came to me and I noticed that Vulnerable Kami was gone. Bitchy Kami was back.

"No, I'm not okay," she snapped. "I'm sittin' in a police station being questioned as a suspect in a double homicide!"

"Mick's just doing his job," I told her. "He'll check your story and you'll be fine."

"I know I'll be fine. I didn't do jack, not to Curt, not to Bitsy. Hell, I wouldn't do that shit to anyone. But people'll know I was questioned."

"It's my understanding a lot of people were questioned. Mick even asked Max for his alibi."

Bitchy Kami escalated to Uber Bitchy Kami and she hissed, "*What*?"

"The morning after the murder, Mick came to Max's house, asked for his alibi."

"That's not even funny."

"No, it wasn't," I agreed. "But since he had one, it doesn't matter."

She looked away, her face tight as she muttered, "That's just whacked, totally whacked, and Mick knows it."

I was surprised at her defense of her brother but I wasn't surprised at her reaction to his news. Everyone felt the same way. More evidence that Curt was in some way responsible for Anna Maxwell's death and, in being so, the fact that Macho Mountain Man Max didn't exact retribution meant he was unlikely to do it now.

Before I could reply, the door opened and Max and Linda walked in.

"I'll be givin' Mick Shaughnessy a piece of my mind for this, make *no* mistake," Linda declared upon entry.

"What happened?" Max asked me.

"Since Kami explained things to me before we let Mick interview her, obviously she explained things to Mick and answered all his queries. He just needs to check their validity and we can move on," I told him.

"Thanks, Nina, for helpin' out." Linda expressed the gratitude Kami unsurprisingly had not.

"Not a problem," I murmured, and offered, "Maybe Max and I can go get some coffees? Would you all like a coffee while we're waiting?"

"That'd be nice, thanks," Linda replied.

"Knock yourself out," Kami muttered.

Max opened his mouth, possibly to protest at leaving his sister or to give Kami a piece of his mind for her attitude, but I gave him a look, got up, shrugged on my coat, grabbed my purse, and moved to the door. Max read my look and followed.

I waited until we were out of the station and on the boarded sidewalk before I spoke.

"You should know something," I whispered, squeezing his hand as he'd taken mine when we left the station.

"I'm guessin' this is somethin' I should know that I won't like," Max remarked, and I stopped and looked up at him.

Deciding to get it out, I did. "It was Shauna who talked Kami into buying that gun and it was Shauna who needed the money Kami borrowed on the house."

He stared at me a minute, his jaw tense, his eyes hard. Then he looked away and muttered, "Fuck."

I tugged at his hand until he looked back at me, and I said, "Okay, now I'm getting into possible slander here but... what if Shauna knew that Curt had made changes to his will around the time she told him she was pregnant?"

"What?"

"She didn't know that Curt knew he didn't father her child. What she knew was that there was a possibility he didn't since she wasn't exactly faithful to him. Kami said that they've turned off her cable and she was close to having the utilities stopped at her house. She needed money, Max, badly, especially having no insurance and a baby on the way. If she knew that he changed the will, she could speculate he changed it in her favor. She was smug before the reading. She thought she'd come out on top. But also she knew if she had the baby and he demanded a DNA test, she would lose everything she worked for. Which would mean she'd need him dead to collect before the truth came out."

"She doesn't have any money, Duchess. How's she gonna pay a contract killer?"

"She had twenty-five thousand dollars of Kami's money, Max," I reminded him. "And anyway, men do stupid stuff for women who are good with their mouths. We have no idea who she's been associating with."

Max, being a man, nodded curtly to the veracity of this statement before he pointed out, "She was in the house when Curt was killed."

"She made the call *after* Curt was killed, saying she was in the house *when* he was killed *and* time had elapsed between the killing and the call—she even admitted that." Max just stared at me, so I went on. "There's a break-in, you hear something, even if you're with a man and he goes to check on it, wouldn't you call the police?"

"Not if you don't want anyone knowin' you're there," Max pointed out.

I nodded, for this was true but suggested, "She could have done what she needed to do with this PI guy, then gone back to Curt's knowing what was going to happen there, made the call, and said she was there when she wasn't. Or she could have set the whole thing up to happen when she was in the house, knowing what was happening with the PI. Either way, she was giving herself an alibi."

"So who killed the PI?" Max asked.

"Someone else she scammed?" I proposed. "Or someone in on it, a partner."

"So you're sayin' she set Kami up?"

"How close are they?"

"For Kami, close. For Shauna, who knows? She's never demonstrated she's felt a genuine emotion since I've known her."

"Then yes, I think it isn't coincidence that on a girls' weekend to Denver, Shauna talked Kami into buying a gun and then borrowed an extraordinary amount of money from her. To come current on utilities and credit cards, who needs twenty-five thousand dollars?"

"Shauna, like Kami, lives large."

"From what Harry intimated at The Rooster, she's also had help living large, fleecing Harry and maybe even Curtis and, who knows, maybe even that Robert guy she was with at the restaurant."

Max stared at me again, then muttered, "Jesus Christ."

"Max—"

Max cut me off. "What d'you think we should do with this shit?"

"I think you need to look out for your sister and let Mick find the trail of breadcrumbs."

"That trail is leadin' him to my sister."

I got closer to him and advised, "You have to trust the truth will come out. If not, you have to trust that I'll do what I can to help your sister."

"Babe—"

"Watch out for Kami, that's it. Just look out for her. I'll do the rest."

I knew this was asking a lot of an action man to stand by and do nothing. I could tell by the internal struggle I saw waging behind his eyes.

Finally, he said, "Let's get my sister a coffee."

I leaned up and kissed his jaw before I agreed, "All right."

*   *   *

Coffees consumed, Kami was texting Shauna for the fiftieth time on her phone.

Shauna who, by her own report, was going to have a rough

day due to her beloved Curtis being put in the earth and thus needed her friend at her side, had somehow disappeared in Kami's hour of need, if Kami's unsuccessful attempts to contact her through fifty texts (maybe a slight exaggeration) and five phone calls (not an exaggeration) over the last hour were any indication.

I knew she hit SEND when I heard the beep. She flipped her phone shut and Max started, "Kami—"

"Don't, Max, just...don't," Kami muttered, staring at the wall.

The door opened and Mick walked in, shutting it behind him, and we all looked to him.

"Found your gun, Kami, right where you said it would be. Never fired, not loaded," Mick stated.

"Is that surprising?" Linda snapped, her eyes fierce on Mick's face, her bearing proving true what she said that morning, that a mother loves her children. Maybe not the same way but the same amount. She was deep in Lioness Mode.

"No, Lins, it isn't surprising," Mick said to her, and looked back at Kami. "Though Shauna doesn't have a deposit of twenty-five thousand in her account."

We all straightened and Linda and Kami grew pale.

"What?" Kami asked.

Mick pressed his lips together and went on. "Your bank reports that you made a check to a Robert Winston for twenty-five thousand dollars. Your check was cashed the day you wrote it but not deposited in his account, nor was any money deposited in Shauna's that day or since, except for a monthly deposit we've tracked to Dodd's business account."

"Holy crap," Linda muttered.

"Wh-what?" Kami stammered, her hand flat on the table, her face bleached white.

I kept quiet as I processed the news that Curtis was giving Shauna money through his business account. Not good.

"You know Robert Winston?" Mick asked.

"He...he's a...a friend of Shauna's," Kami answered

instantly, if stiltedly. "He lives in Chantelle, moved there, I don't know, not long ago. He has a house in one of Curt's developments. I think he's been around three months, maybe four. Shauna knew him from Aspen. She didn't want anyone to know about the money, you know, even the tellers talk. So she asked me to make it out to him. He was going to give it to her."

"Unless she's sittin' on the cash or she blew it as cash, she never got it," Mick told her. "Least, not in a way that leaves a trail."

Kami shook her head, visibly stunned at this news. Then she asked, "What about her bills?"

"Ain't my place to tell you but I'm doin' it all the same," Mick said to Kami. "Shauna's fully current on all her bills, never been in arrears. Far's we can tell, for at least seven months, Harry's been payin' 'em."

"Holy *crap*," Linda snapped on a near shout.

"He's also been payin' her doctor bills," Mick went on.

She had Curt giving her money and Harry paying her bills. She was being kept by two men. Now she had none, except, perhaps, this Robert character.

I looked at Max and resisted the urge to run to him, tackle him to the ground, and sit on him. He looked ready to explode.

"It's worse," Mick announced, and the room, already tense, became suffocating.

"What?" Kami whispered.

"Not too long ago, Shauna sold her house. She closed about a month ago, paid rent to the new owners to stick around."

"I don't believe it," Kami was still whispering.

"She's closed her accounts," Mick finished. "Closed 'em yesterday. She's also put orders in to shut down gas, water, electricity, phone, and cable, startin' first of May."

Kami wasn't letting this information sink in. "But if she sold her house, she'd have hundreds of thousands of dollars. She owned it outright. Why would she ask me for money?"

"Maybe because she hired a contract killer?" Linda screeched, and I changed my mind and decided I should

probably tackle Linda first before she continued. *"With my daughter's money!"*

"That's…that's *crazy*, Mom!" Kami shot back, deep in the pit of denial. "She'd never hurt Curt. He told her he loved her. He wanted to marry her. He was gonna leave Bitsy for her."

"Yeah, she told you that like she told you I took her ring shoppin'," Max clipped.

"But—" Kami said.

"I never took her ring shoppin', Kami," Max went on.

"But—" Kami repeated.

"Never fuckin' entered my mind," Max carried on.

"She said—"

"She lied, Kams, Jesus!" Max exploded. "We weren't even exclusive. I made it clear she could go her own way when I was gone and I'd go my own. I had a woman on the job I was on and she knew it."

My eyes got wide and my body grew still. *That* was news. Linda's gaze slid to me and I tried to act casual but I found it extremely difficult.

Kami was shaking her head and Mick entered the conversation. "Sorry, Kami, but thought you should know."

Kami just tipped her head back to stare at him and my heart went out to her. She looked beaten down by the betrayal. She might act like a bitch a lot of the time, but bottom line, she was a good friend.

Mick went on. "You're free to go but I might need to ask you more questions, so I want you to stick close to town."

"Why?" Linda was back to snapping at Mick.

"Because we need to talk to this Robert Winston guy and we need to ask Shauna a few questions and we can't find her. And seein' as this has all come to light, we might have a few more things to get clear with Kami," Mick answered.

"What things?" I asked.

"Don't know yet, just don't want her leavin' town," Mick told me.

"You can see that Kami had nothing to do with this. Her statement checks out," I said to Mick.

"Yeah, but—"

"Did you find anything to place her at the construction site? Dirt on her shoes? Rocks?" I pushed.

"No, but—"

"Did you find roofies in her house?"

"No—"

"Do you have any known dealers who have admitted to supplying roofies to Kami?"

"Nina—"

"Do you?"

"No."

"You have her gun in your possession and it hasn't been loaded or fired. A warrant to search her house has pulled up nothing or she wouldn't be free to go. A canceled check that proves what Kami told you she'd done with that money true, whether it was to a known acquaintance of Shauna's or Shauna, that doesn't change the fact the money was meant for Shauna. You have no physical evidence that places Kami at the construction site and no other evidence whatsoever to link Kami to either murder. All you have, as far as I can see, is the fact that Kami Maxwell was asleep between one and four the morning of the murders, which, by the way, so was the vast majority of the residents of Gnaw Bone and the entire Central, Mountain and Pacific time zones."

"Except we got the fact that Shauna Fontaine is on our suspect list, Robert Winston is now a person of interest, and Kami gave him twenty-five thousand dollars."

"And a jury will be made up of her peers and everyone knows Kami and Shauna have been close since grade school and friends help friends in a tight spot. It gets down to it, I'll call Max, Brody, and Mindy to the stand to testify that they heard Shauna announce to Max she was pregnant and needed money, thus corroborating Kami's story if not Shauna's lie. They'll also all testify to the fact that Shauna was with a gentleman by the name of Robert. He was protective of her, as in *over*protective considering he engaged in physical combat with Harry at The Rooster in front of dozens of witnesses in defense of Shauna."

Mick tried to interrupt. "Nina—"

I cut him off. "Kami thought her friend was up to her eyeballs in debt, had no insurance, and a baby on the way. Shauna asked for the transaction to be private, for her own ends but telling Kami it was to save face. We've all been there before, needing to save face or helping a friend who needs it. Every jury member will have faced that same scenario in their lives. But friends do what they can, which is what Kami did and a jury will believe that, too, and you know it."

"Shit, Nina, you're tryin' the case in this room," Mick mumbled.

"You wanted her to lawyer up, Mick, she's lawyered up. You don't want her to leave town, okay, where's she going to go? But she isn't leaving this room thinking this nightmare isn't over for her. She's got a life to live. Curtis Dodd meant something to her, his death is already taking its toll, and she doesn't need this hanging over her head."

"I'm just askin' her not to leave town," Mick noted.

"Okay, she won't leave town," I assured him. "But I'll remind you, on top of all that, there's a good possibility that she's just found out her friend took advantage of her, so she's dealing with enough. You need to question her, you call me and I'll set it up. Yes?"

Mick turned beleaguered eyes to Max but he was barking up the wrong tree. I looked to Max and saw he was leaning with his shoulders against the wall, arms crossed on his chest, eyes on me, and a huge grin on his face.

"Remind me never to do any more favors even if it's for one of our own," Mick muttered to no one.

"Are we done here?" I asked, standing and grabbing my coat.

"You movin' to town?" Mick asked back, and my head tilted with confusion at the somewhat nosy change of subject.

Even so, I answered, "More than likely, yes."

"You gonna practice?" Mick went on.

"Of course," I replied.

"Great," Mick muttered, sounding aggrieved and I understood, so I smiled.

"Don't worry, Mick, if it isn't a member of Max's family or a friend, I'm a pussycat," I assured him.

"Why don't I believe you?" Mick queried.

"Don't, she's on a tear, she's a tiger," Max put in. He had pushed from the wall and had his hand on Linda's arm, helping her from her seat.

"Yeah," Mick mumbled.

I headed toward the door. "By the way, it'd be nice, if anyone asks, you tell them Kami was assisting with the investigation and you might want to mention how cooperative she was."

Mick looked at me, clearly shocked. "Now you're askin' a favor?"

"I did you one. I'm calling my marker. Anyway, it might be good, me moving to town and putting out a shingle, you start collecting them," I advised as I grabbed my purse, and Mick's eyes again went to Max.

And again he was barking up the wrong tree. Max had opened the door for his mother and sister and he burst into laughter when he caught Mick's eyes. Then he slung an arm around my shoulders and guided me out the door.

As we neared the outer door, not taking his arm from around me, Max leaned down to put his mouth to my ear.

"Just in case I didn't mention it, Duchess, not so sure about the truth comin' out. What I am sure of is that I can trust you to take care of my sister." I pulled my head back as I twisted my neck to look at him but I had no chance to speak because he stopped me and he finished with, "Thank you, baby."

Before I could respond, he kissed me deep, with some tongue action, but although deep, the kiss was not long.

"Max!" Kami snapped when his head came up. "I need a drink."

I looked in their direction to see Linda's eyes were on me. "I think pasta bake is out. Can I treat you and your folks to a buffalo burger at The Mark?"

I glanced at Max and back to Linda.

Then I said, "They'd love that."

*   *   *

I sat on a stool at a high, round table at The Dog with a drunken Mom, Linda, Kami, Arlene, and Jenna. Becca was our waitress.

At Arlene's edict, with Mom and Linda backing her up, Max had been quarantined across the room in what had been decreed (again, by Arlene) as the Guys' Night Out Section of The Dog. He was playing pool with Brody and Steve and he was not to approach under threat of Arlene's wrath.

Regardless of my roller-coaster day and my current enforced separation from Max, I, too, was slightly inebriated. I'd been adventurous at The Mark, demanding to see a menu and ordering the chicken fried steak, which was made with an actual *steak* and therefore was *amazing*. I followed that with a Mile-High Mud Pie, which was five layers of chocolate cake, separated by dreamy chocolate mousse and covered with chocolate ganache. Becca had reported that not only had Mindy seen the rape center's counselor yesterday, she'd also gone down there to visit her again that day, asking Bitsy to go with her (and Bitsy did; even with the funeral, she'd carved out time). And I was finding out that Kami was a lot more fun when she was fed a buffalo burger and was also drunk. Therefore, I was feeling quite happy.

"You. Cannot. Be. *Serious*!" Arlene shouted, and I looked at her. Having been thinking about my evening, I hadn't been paying attention and I didn't know what she was shouting about. Then again Arlene, Mom, *and* Linda had been shouting everything they said for about half an hour, mostly while Kami, Jenna, and I giggled, unable to get a word in edgewise, so it wasn't the first time I lost track.

"I. Am. *Not!*" Mom shouted back, and I felt something, something warm and sweet, and instinctively I looked to the pool tables and saw Max, Brody, and Steve all looking at us.

Seeing Max looking so handsome standing across the room from me, holding a pool cue, its handle to the ground, I had an overwhelming urge and I didn't try to fight it.

"Be back," I muttered to Linda, who was sitting beside me. I slipped off my stool and weaved my way through the bar to Max.

When I got to him, I wrapped both my arms around his middle, pressed my front to his side, and tipped my head back to look at him as his arm slid around my shoulders.

"Hi," I said softly.

He grinned down at me and remarked, "Babe, you're breaking the invisible boundary between girls' night out and guys' night out."

"I think Mom, Arlene, and Linda are beyond enforcing the rules."

I looked across the room to see Mom hanging by her fingers from the table, her torso and head thrown back, laughing. Arlene was slapping the table with the palm of her hand, laughing. Linda was leaned all the way over, her forehead to the table, laughing. And Kami and Jenna were staring at each other, also laughing.

I looked back at Max and pointed out the obvious. "I don't think they even know I'm gone."

Max glanced at the girls; then his eyes came to me. "Doesn't look like it."

"You play pool?" Brody asked, coming up on my side, and I looked at him without letting Max go.

"No," I answered.

"Wanna learn?" Brody inquired on a smile.

"I'm beyond retaining new skills," I told him, and Max's arm around my shoulders gave me a squeeze, so I looked back to him.

"You smashed?"

"No." And it wasn't a lie; therefore I explained while pressing closer, "Just having a good night."

"You're up, Brody," Steve called. Then his eyes came to me. "Since the seal's been broken, gonna check on Nellie, make certain she doesn't fall off her stool."

"I think that's a good idea," I advised, and heard Max chuckle as I saw Steve smile and move away.

"You wanna get us another round?" Brody suggested, eyeing the pool table to line up his next shot.

"Yeah," Max answered, and then moved.

I was forced to drop an arm to move with him and we walked with our arms around each other to the heaving bar. Max pushed in, taking me with him, then lifted his chin to the bartender. It was then I saw Harry sitting alone at the opposite end of the bar looking more than a little unhappy and staring into an amber beverage that appeared to have been poured neat.

"Harry drinks bourbon when he's nursin' a bad mood," Max muttered, likely reading my expression.

The bartender came to us and Max ordered four beers.

I studied Harry, then turned into Max's body and wrapped my other arm around him too. "I'll go and keep him company."

Max looked down at me. "I thought you were keepin' me company."

"You have company." I tipped my head to Brody at the pool table. "Harry doesn't."

Max bent his neck so his face was closer to mine before he told me, "Brody's been my best friend for a long time, honey, and it's good havin' him home. Still, prefer your company."

This made me feel nice, *very* nice, and again I pressed closer but pointed out, "I can't do locker room talk."

"Not that I ever do locker room talk but if I did, I wouldn't do it with your stepdad."

I nodded my indication that I thought this was wise. "Then it's probably not good that I'm around, seeing as you won't be able to complain about my foibles and neither can Steve about Mom's."

"Foibles?"

"Faults, bad habits."

"Tellin' you a man secret, babe, but men aren't like women. We get together, we don't bitch. We just drink and, if we talk at all, we talk about the game." I smiled at him and he went on. "We did bitch, though, again, not sure I'd share my thoughts on your faults with Steve."

My happy mood evaporated, my body got tense, and my eyes narrowed. "So you think I have them?"

He grinned. "Baby, you set yourself up for that one."

"Okay, what are they, then?"

He didn't hesitate. "Your ass looks too good in those cords."

I blinked, for this was not what I expected as a response.

My "attitude," yes. My habit of trying to stop a discussion when I was losing an argument, definitely. My inability to say no to dessert, probably.

My bottom in my cords, no.

So I asked, "Sorry?"

"You walked across the room and practically every guy you passed looked at your ass. Hell, you're standin' here pressed up to me and *still* every guy who passes is lookin' at your ass."

I glanced over my shoulder to see if this claim was true. Max's body started shaking with laughter. Then he pulled slightly away to get out his wallet.

"You're lying," I accused.

"Nope," he said, flipping his wallet open and taking his arm from my shoulders to pull out some bills, so I dropped my arms.

"Well, if that's true, it's not my fault."

"Gotta put some meat on you, Duchess. No one's lookin' at Kami's ass." Max lifted his chin to the bartender to keep the change, flipped his wallet closed, and shoved it in his pocket.

"She's sitting down."

"They were checkin' you out when you were sittin' down too."

"My behind?"

He looked at me and stated, "Nope, your hair, face, and sometimes tits."

I gasped, then breathed, "They were *not*."

He grinned. "Babe, they were."

"You're full of it."

He shook his head and his eyes went over my shoulder; then he grabbed two of the beer bottles from the bar and handed them to a passing Steve, who was making his way back to the pool table. Steve smiled at me but said no more before he moved off to join Brody.

Max handed me a beer and took the other one. His arm slid around my waist and he pulled me to his front.

"Why d'you find that hard to believe?"

I explained it to him. "They're just looking at me because they're curious because I'm with you."

"Maybe that's why some of the women are lookin' at you. The men are lookin' at you because you got a pretty face, great hair, and nice tits."

"Max!" I snapped.

"It's true."

"You just like me."

He shook his head and his arm got tighter. "Shockin', Nina Sheridan fishin' for compliments."

His comment annoyed me, for it was patently untrue; therefore I pulled back from his arm but it just got tighter so I gave up and snapped, "I'm not doing that."

He was grinning again before he remarked, "Christ, you go from sweet to pissed faster 'n lightnin'."

"Only because five minutes ago I was in the mood to be sweet; then you were annoying."

His brows went up. "Tellin' you you're hot is annoying?"

"Telling me all the guys are checking me out when they aren't is annoying."

"Babe."

"Max."

We seemed to be at a stalemate and he sighed.

Then he said, "I'll tell you somethin', whether you believe they're lookin' or not, you gotta know, I don't care if they look. They can only guess what that ass, tits, and hair promises but I *know*."

I rolled my eyes, even though my stomach pitched in a good way. Max started laughing and I hoped, since I knew now that he could read my face, that what my stomach did wasn't written there.

"I'm going to go talk to Harry now," I informed him when he'd controlled his amusement.

"Yeah, you can do that after you kiss me."

I decided to give in and avoid the inevitable argument, so I leaned up, placed a hand on his bicep, and touched my mouth to his. Then I pulled back several inches, but Max jerked me forward again so I was plastered to him.

"That's a kiss?" he asked.

"Um... yes," I answered, surprised to find myself plastered against him.

"Honey, not even close."

My eyes got wide as I understood his meaning. "I'm not making out with you in a bar."

"Why not?"

"Why?"

His face again dipped closer. "Because, first, I want you to. And second, whether you believe it or not, guys are checkin' you out and that'd be me stakin' my claim."

"Staking your claim?"

"It's a guy thing."

"It's a Macho Mountain Man thing."

"Same thing."

"You're impossible."

"You gonna kiss me or what?"

"If I don't, you're just going to kiss me anyway, aren't you?"

Again, he gave me a grin. "You finally got that?"

"Impossible," I muttered.

"Kiss me, Duchess."

With nothing for it, I did with (possibly) my mother watching, his mother watching, and my stepdad watching. Not to mention his sister, best friend, Arlene, and half of Gnaw Bone. However, when he released my mouth, I didn't have it in me to care.

"See you're back to sweet," he muttered, his eyes moving over my face.

"You're a good kisser," I muttered back.

His forehead touched mine before he said words that changed my world.

"You're better," he whispered. I melted deeper into him and he finished, "Best I ever had and I mean that with everything you do with your mouth, even when you're usin' it to tell me I'm annoying."

My arms, which had gone around him during our kiss, tightened in a spasm.

"Really?" I breathed.

"Absolutely." He was still whispering.

Suddenly I felt like crying and to hide it I tipped my chin down and tried to pull away.

Unfortunately, during our kiss, Max's arms had gone around me, too, so this effort was moot.

"Duchess?" he called, and when I continued to avoid his eyes, one of his arms kept me locked to him while his other hand came to my chin and forced me to meet his gaze. When his caught mine, he murmured, "What is it, baby?"

What it was was a lot, including the fact that maybe, just maybe, I was going to be special in some way to him too.

And that meant the world to me.

I didn't tell him that. Instead, I said, "That was just a nice thing to say."

"I like that," he replied as his hand left my chin and curled around my neck.

I blinked in confusion and asked, "You like what?"

"I like that you don't believe guys are checkin' you out, you won't accept that compliment, but you get soft when I tell you I like somethin' you do for me."

I bit my lip and tried to look away but Max's hand at my neck tensed so I kept my eyes on his and demanded, "Stop being nice."

He grinned yet again and his fingers gave me a squeeze. "Duchess, you best get used to that. I know you haven't had a lot of experience with it but you should know, I intend to be nice to you on a regular basis."

"Now you're being nicer," I informed him, and it came out as an accusation.

"Yeah, babe, like I said, you better get used to it."

I wasn't sure that was possible. However, I was sure that I wouldn't mind trying.

I decided to change the subject. "Can I talk to Harry now?"

He looked at Harry and replied, "Yeah."

"Max?" I called, and he looked back at me. I got up on my toes to get close and I whispered, "You're the best I've ever had too. Not just with your mouth, with everything. And when I say that, I mean *everything*."

Then before I could witness his full reaction—for what I saw with his face softening but his eyes getting dark and intense was enough—I pulled free from his arms and hurried to Harry.

Told you that you were selling yourself short, Charlie said in my head.

Oh, be quiet, I said back.

I walked along the bar toward Harry, not looking back at Max, and I felt my mouth smiling slightly but inside I was smiling a whole lot bigger.

I noticed that Harry was being given a wide berth. Both of the stools beside him were empty and no one was standing close.

I slid onto a stool next to him. His neck twisted so he could look at me and I realized why he was being avoided. His eyes were red-rimmed with drink and maybe sleepless nights, for his face was haggard and, up close, he looked even less happy.

"Hi, Harry," I said softly.

"Nina," he muttered, and looked back down at his drink.

"You doing okay?"

"Nope," he answered instantly, and put the glass to his lips and threw back the contents in one gulp.

When he dropped his hand, the bottom of the glass crashed against the bar and I jumped.

Suddenly, and loudly, he shouted, "Jake!"

The bartender's eyes came to Harry and Harry rapped his glass against the bar indicating he wanted another. Jake nodded and turned to the bottles of liquor behind him.

"Harry—" I started.

He cut me off, "Heard you're movin' to town."

"Um . . . yes," I affirmed.

"Figures," he muttered strangely, and Jake was there.

I watched him pour bourbon into Harry's glass, Harry's hand still wrapped around it, and I looked up at Jake to see his eyes come to me. I shook my head slightly. He nodded, indicating he understood.

"Dude, you want another one after this, you gotta give me your keys," Jake told Harry.

Without hesitation, Harry reached into his jeans pocket, yanked out his keys, and slapped them on the bar. Jake snatched them up and walked away. Harry took a sip of bourbon.

"Max and I'll take you home," I offered, and Harry's bloodshot eyes came to me.

"You know, I don't get it," he stated.

"Get what?" I asked.

He looked from my face to my lap and up again. "You live in fuckin' England. *England.*" He spat out his last word and I jumped again, the venom in his tone surprising me. "You come to town, drive straight fuckin' through, straight to Max's. Now you're sittin' with his ma and his sister at The Dog, laughin' and bein' loud. Then you're pressin' up tight to Max and makin' out with him. I mean, what is that?"

I didn't know where he was going with this or why he was even talking about it or, most of all, why he seemed so angry about it, so gently I said, "Harry, I don't understand."

"It's just him," Harry told me. "Been that way as long's I can remember." Harry's eyes went across the bar to Max and his unhappy face went tight. "Always."

I was getting uncomfortable with the conversation and not knowing what to say I watched him take another sip.

"Harry, maybe—" I began, but Harry looked back to me and what he said shut me up.

"Knew Anna," he informed me. "Knew her for forever. She was a sweet little thing. Wasn't pretty, though. Sweet as hell, always. Funny, Jesus, so fuckin' funny. But not pretty."

I stared at him. Having seen pictures of Anna, I couldn't believe he didn't think she was pretty. She was beautiful.

Harry continued. "Then she got pretty. Like the ugly duckling story, in high school she turns into a swan. She'd had a crush on Max for fuckin' years. *Years*. He didn't notice her, didn't know she fuckin' existed until she got pretty. Then he noticed her all right. Everyone did."

I didn't want to hear this, not from Harry.

"Harry, Max and I haven't—" I started, but he kept talking.

"He asked her out and that was it. She was his. The whole town thought them bein' together was so sweet, so fuckin' sweet. Everyone thought it was like Cinderella. Anna wantin' him for so long, watchin' him from afar, never had a boyfriend, no one but Max. Max bein' Max, every girl wantin' a piece of him. Anna's impossible dream bein' possible and them hookin' up, gettin' so tight, fallin' in love." He shook his head and downed another healthy sip before continuing. "Even when he went off to CU, got that scholarship to play ball but got her pregnant his sophomore year. He quit school and came home and married her. Everyone thought it was so *romantic*. He was such a good fuckin' guy, givin' up his dream of bein' an architect, doin' the right thing by Anna. Jesus."

As this information pummeled me, I was beginning to breathe heavily and my heart was skipping in my chest. I wanted to run away, slide off my stool and run back to the safety of Max's arms, to the time when I didn't know this. I realized, after all that time thinking I wanted to know, that actually I *didn't* want to know.

"Please, Harry, listen to me a second—" I begged, but he kept talking.

"And you know what? He was never pissed about it. Never thought about what coulda been. Never angry that she derailed his life, gettin' knocked up. He was fuckin' *happy* about that baby, thrilled to put a ring on her finger. Over the fuckin' *moon*. She was happy too. They were so fuckin' happy. Even when she lost the kid. And the next one. And the one after that."

I was no longer breathing heavily. I wasn't breathing at all.

"They quit tryin' but hey"—he threw his hand out—"that's okay. They had each other and for the Great Max and the Beautiful Swan Anna, that was enough. It was everything. Fuck," he muttered, and took another sip.

I forced air into my lungs but didn't get a word in before Harry spoke again.

"Then Curt kills her."

The breath I'd pulled in squeezed out as my chest froze but Harry kept right on going.

"Jesus, tore the whole town apart. Thought they'd hunt Curt down. Hell, thought Max'd do it. Max was un…fuckin'… *done*. Never seen a man like that. Never. Fuckin' shit, he was wild. All anyone could think about was Anna bein' dead and Max losin' her and, finally, Max mannin' up and not seekin' retribution. And wasn't Max so *great* that he didn't lose it and whale on Curt? Wasn't he so fuckin' *wonderful* that, when his world came crashin' down, in the end he kept his shit together? No one thought about Curt takin' Bitsy's legs, leavin' her in that chair and Curt walkin' away unscathed. All anyone could think about was the end of Max and Anna. The death of a damned fairy tale."

"Maybe I should—" I whispered, wanting to get away, desperate to get away but somehow glued to my stool.

Harry kept right on talking. "Then everyone talks. They

see him playin' the field. They know he ain't serious with no one. Never again. Anna was everything to him. How *sad*," Harry hissed. "How *tragic*." Harry shook his head and took another sip before he continued his diatribe. "Such a good man, losin' everythin' at the age of twenty-fuckin'-seven, heartbreakin'. Max is untouchable. His heart's so broken, they said, no one'll ever get in again. No one noticed he was fuckin' everything that moved, leavin' 'em high and dry, never lettin' 'em get a piece of him. Everyone knew he did it everywhere, takin' jobs outta town, had women here, had women at his jobs, had fuckin' women *everywhere*."

"I should—" I started to slide from the stool but Harry's eyes pinned me to the spot.

"Then you blow into town, *you*." His voice got low, his eyes did a sweep of me again, and he continued. "The way you look, the way you talk, the way you dress, pure fuckin' class. No one knows who you are. You come from fuckin' *England* and suddenly you're makin' out with him at The Dog, pressed to him like he was some kind of god or somethin'. You're hot. You could have anyone. Point your finger at anyone in this bar, you'd have him," he informed me. "So of course he'd nail you."

"It isn't like that," I whispered.

His brows shot up. "No? So he's let you in? All the ones before you and he's let *you* in? You're hot, Nina, shit, I'd do you in a second. Count my lucky stars someone like you gave me a shot, twist myself into knots to lay the world at your feet, so maybe he has. What do I know? You can probably give him a baby. Anna couldn't do that. But you should know, girl, and not anyone's gonna tell you this but me, everyone hopin' you're the one, you're the one that'll heal all his fuckin' wounds. You're hot. You're sweet. You're even funny. But you should know, what you ain't is Anna."

It was a wonder I didn't fall off my stool straight to the floor, his verbal blow was so vicious.

Instead, I swallowed and suggested, "Maybe I should leave you to it."

He lifted his drink but offered, "You get the urge to heal my wounds, gorgeous, just say the fuckin' word."

I sucked in a breath, deciding this was not Harry. This was drink and anger and Shauna being such a bitch and him taking care of her for so long, it was all that talking. Therefore, I thought I should make some effort to help.

I leaned forward, telling him, "She isn't worth this, Harry."

Harry looked away and took a sip before he asked, "Yeah?"

"I know Max is a friend. He's been your friend a long time. You're saying this because you're angry about Shauna, and, Harry"—I put my hand on his forearm—"she isn't worth this."

Harry's eyes went across the bar to Max, his mouth got hard, and he downed the last of his drink.

Then he looked at me. "Yeah, Nina, you're right. 'Course. I got sloppy seconds from Max with Shauna. Thirds, you count Curt. So you're right, she ain't worth it."

"You're a good guy, Harry," I said gently, and Harry's face twisted in a way that was so hostile, so frightening, it was difficult to witness and I felt my body go completely still.

"Yeah," he said again, "a good guy." He leaned into me and whispered, "So good, I'll repeat myself because I figure you're a good woman and you deserve it and you might be wrapped up in him now but one day you'll learn you coulda done better. He loved her, Nina. She was his world. When a woman is a man's world and he loses her, ain't nothin' gonna take the place of that and you gotta know that. This is somethin' he wants. Max'll do good by you but he'll know and the whole town'll know, you ain't that to him, what Anna was. You never will be. So I'm thinkin', bein' a good guy and all, *you* should know that too."

I sat there, stunned silent, my heart beating madly, my lungs hurting, the tears burning the backs of my eyes, all my worst imaginings come true in Harry's brutally honest drunken blather.

Harry held my eyes and his hand covered mine on his arm, his face gentling and he kept whispering, "Shit, Nina, I'm a dick."

I leaned away and slid my hand out from under his, saying quickly, "That's okay."

"I'm just pissed. Shauna made me look the fool."

"I understand."

He leaned into the space I vacated, looking like he'd teeter right off his stool. "Nina, seriously. Don't listen to my shit. Max is a good guy. I'm just bein' an asshole."

"Right," I whispered. "I...I need some fresh air. Um... do...do you want a ride home? I could ask Brody, my stepdad, Steve—"

He shook his head. "I'll ask Jake to call Thrifty's, get me a taxi."

I nodded. "I'm just going to step outside a minute."

"Nina—" he started, but I moved as fast as I could to escape.

I left my untouched beer on the bar and started toward the door, lifting my hand to pull my hair out of my face. Holding it at the back of my head in a bunch, I looked over to the pool tables. Max had his back to me and I watched him lean over, lining up a shot.

I looked to Mom's table and saw Arlene, Linda, and Jenna leaned into Mom, listening with rapt attention likely to Mom telling some crazy, but true, story.

But Kami's eyes were on me.

That was fine. In the dark of the bar she couldn't see what I was certain my face looked like and even if she could, she was Kami. She wouldn't care.

I headed out the door without my coat, the chill night air instantly biting into my skin and I welcomed it. Something to focus on, something that wasn't the jumble of thoughts piercing my brain.

I looked to my right, my left, then headed right to the end of the building, where an overhead light illuminating the parking lot was out. Darkness, aloneness, somewhere to get my thoughts together or, better yet, force them out of my head.

I leaned against the building, taking in deep breaths,

feeling the tears hovering at the edges of my eyes. One escaped and I felt it slide down my cheek.

How could one minute, hope could be so precious in my heart that I'd be something to Max, something special, the best he ever had. And then the next...nothing.

Void.

Empty.

She was his world, Harry said about Anna.

She was his world.

She was his world.

Sweetheart, Charlie said into my head, *he was drunk, acting like an ass. Talking shit.*

"Go away," I whispered into the darkness.

"Nope, not until you tell me where Mindy is."

My head came up and twisted around and I stared in shock and not a small amount of fear at Damon Matthews standing three feet in front of me.

Just what I didn't *bloody* need.

I straightened from the building and looked over my shoulder at the entrance. Damon filled my vision, having moved to cut off my escape route.

"I'm talkin' to you, English. Where's Mindy?"

My eyes went to his. "Mindy?"

"Yeah, *Mindy,*" he clipped, his face snide. "Remember her?"

"Damon, she's—"

"Not answerin' her fuckin' phone, that's what she's doin'."

"Mindy is dealing with some things now," I explained.

"Yeah, who isn't?" He took a step forward, I took a step back, and he stopped. "See, she ain't home. She ain't at Becca's. She ain't comin' to work. She ain't answerin' her phone." He took another step forward and I took a step back, my legs hitting the bumper of a parked car and I stopped but he closed in. "Brody's stayin' at our place. The locks've been changed. I can't get to my shit. Landlord says Maxwell moved my shit into a unit and I gotta pay the rent on it before I can get my own...

fuckin' ... shit." On the last three words, he leaned into me, so close I was pinned to the car and I reared back as far as I could, putting my hand to the bonnet to stop from toppling over.

"Got a problem, Damon?" I heard, and I leaned to the side to see Kami standing behind Damon.

Damon straightened and turned to Kami. "Shove off, Kams."

"Don't mean to be tellin' you your business, Damon, but Max sees you out here gettin' in Nina's face, he's not gonna be pleased," Kami told him.

"Fuck Max."

"Just tryin' to be nice," Kami said, and normally I would have laughed at the concept of Kami being nice but I was too scared out of my wits to even crack a smile.

"You know where Mindy is?" Damon returned to his earlier topic.

"I know you get anywhere near her, I'll cut your balls off and nail 'em to the doors of town hall," Kami replied casually, and my eyes got big at her words and the coolness with which she delivered them, especially since Damon could probably twist her into a pretzel.

"Kami," I whispered.

"Yeah?" Damon sneered over my saying her name, leaning threateningly toward Kami.

Kami leaned in, too, and sneered back, "Yeah."

They had a staring contest while I held my breath and then surprisingly Damon looked away, muttering, "Fuckin' bitch."

"Word of advice, Damon, keep outta Nina's space, yeah? Mindy and Nina, boy, both off-limits to you. You hear me?"

"Fuck off."

Kami looked at me and stated, "He heard me."

Damon gave me a look that would blister paint off the walls but I just held his eyes until he turned and marched away.

I stepped away from the car and looked at Kami. "Thanks."

Her eyes were narrowed as she looked at me, ignoring my gratitude, and asked, "What'd Harry say to you?"

My body jerked; then I recovered, my eyes sliding from hers. "Nothing," I murmured. Suddenly I had an idea. It was probably a hopeless idea, seeing as this was Kami, but I had to give it a shot. I looked back at her and asked, "Listen, are you sober? You think that you could drive me—"

Kami cut me off by declaring, "Max is takin' you home."

I tried again. "But, see, suddenly I'm feeling—"

She cut me off again. "Then we'll go get Max."

Still knowing it was hopeless, as this was Kami, but Kami or not, she was still a woman and women knew women or at least the ones I knew did, I tried to communicate with her without actually saying anything and I whispered, "Kami."

"There they are!" my mom shouted, and I looked around Kami to see the entire group, sans Arlene and Jenna, flooding out the door.

"Darn," I muttered, and Kami shifted around so she was facing the party bearing down on us, Max and Brody bringing up the rear.

"Steve says I have to go home!" Mom complained. "Says Max says that overimbibing in altitude could be *dangerous*."

I avoided looking at anyone but Mom and told her, "I hear that's true if you aren't used to it, Mom."

"Oh, pishposh," she declared, waving her hand in front of her face, this movement sending her off-balance so she fell to the side, and Kami, Steve, and I all lunged forward to put a hand on her. "I'm fine!" she yelled when she was steady again on her feet, and we all moved back.

"You're rat-arsed," I told her.

"Whatever," she mumbled, then turned to Linda and announced, apropos of nothing, "I *love* your son and I love *you* and I *love* your daughter." She looked at Kami. "You have *the* most *beautiful* hair I've ever *seen*."

"Thanks, Nellie," Kami muttered, shifting on her feet, embarrassed by the praise. I stared at her a second before I heard Steve speak.

"Let's get you home, love."

Mom leaned forward and muttered to Kami and me, "He's always spoiling my fun."

Kami looked at me and I shrugged, for this was likely true. Then again, sometimes Mom's brand of fun needed to get spoiled before someone got hurt.

Mom hugged a surprised and stiff Kami, then released her and she got a return hug from Linda and finally she gave me one. After Mom was done embracing the female congregation, Steve kissed my cheek and said his good-byes and they moved to their rental car.

"I got work tomorrow," Kami announced. She gave me a look I couldn't read. Then, thankfully, she said, "Later," and moved away without giving anyone hugs but she did give a halfhearted wave, which I thought was quite nice, seeing as it was from Kami.

I was just grateful she didn't share the Damon Incident or her astute insight into the fact that Harry upset me before she went.

"I'm her ride," Linda muttered, her eyes on me. They were twinkling, for what else could she do? Kami, I was learning, was Kami.

Linda kissed Max's cheek and then Brody's. She was carrying my coat and purse and she gave them to me before she gave me a hug and when she did, she said in my ear, "Like you, Nina. You're a good kid."

I clenched my teeth and swallowed the tears as her head came up. I smiled weakly at her and nodded.

"I'm off," Brody announced as Linda moved away, and I shrugged on my coat. "Seein' as that shit went down with Mins, work gave me to the weekend, so we'll get together again before I leave, yeah?" he asked me.

"Sure," I said, even though I was not sure.

He gave me a mountain man hug. In other words I was engulfed in his arms and the hug was so tight I could hardly breathe. Then he clapped Max on the shoulder and took off.

I continued to avoid Max's eyes and I did this by watching Brody until he was out of sight.

"So, what'll it be, Duchess? You want me to teach you how to play pool or do you wanna go home?"

I looked at his collarbone and told him, "Let's go to your house."

I felt rather than saw the change in his mood before he asked, "My house?"

My eyes shot to his and I saw he was studying me intently.

"Um...suddenly I'm exhausted," I explained.

Max didn't look like he bought my explanation. He kept examining my face for several moments before he looked over his shoulder at the parking lot, then back at me.

"What were you doin' out here with Kami?"

I shook my head and stated, "I wasn't with Kami. I just got a little tired and I thought the fresh air would wake me up a bit." I licked my lips before I kept lying, "It didn't."

"Kami was with you when we got out here," Max pointed out.

"Um...she followed me out. I don't know why. She was only here a minute or so before you all joined us." At least part of that was true.

"What'd you talk about?" he asked.

"Nothing. You all came out before we—"

He cut me off, asking shrewdly, "What'd you and Harry talk about?"

I decided I needed to practice my poker face and I needed to do it very, very soon.

"Not much, he was kind of drunk," I lied again. "It's okay," I assured him. "Jake took his keys. Harry said he was going to call a taxi."

"Then what's the matter?" Max asked.

"I told you," I replied. "I'm tired."

"One second you're sweet and smilin' and the next second your eyes are dead and you're sayin' you're tired."

"My eyes aren't dead." But I knew they probably were.

"What'd Harry say?" Max pushed.

I sighed, not wanting to spar, not even wanting to talk, not even wanting to stand.

In fact, I *did* want to crawl into a bed, pull the covers over ~~e~~, shut out the world and anyone who could get in and hurt ~~e~~, and I wanted to sleep. Sleep for decades and wake up a ~~s~~pinster, go to the nearest shelter, adopt two dozen cats, and ~~th~~en live my life cleaning up hair balls and watching *Wheel of ~~Fo~~rtune*. That seemed like a happy life to me.

I didn't tell Max this. Instead I asked, "Max, can we just go ~~to~~ the A-frame?"

His eyes narrowed and even in the dim light I watched his ~~fa~~ce grow dark. "The A-frame?"

"Yes."

He took a step closer. I stepped back.

He stopped and whispered, "What the fuck?"

Even though I retreated, which I did so I could remain ~~sm~~art, sane, and rational instead of letting him touch me or ~~ho~~ld me or kiss me and make me the opposite, I leaned a bit ~~fo~~rward, looked him in the eyes, and softly begged, "Please? ~~C~~an we go up the mountain?"

He didn't answer for a long time. So long, since I was hold~~in~~g my breath, it seemed forever.

Then he said quietly, "Yeah, Duchess, we can go up the ~~m~~ountain."

"Thank you," I whispered.

I was careful to keep distance between us as we walked ~~to~~ the Jeep and stayed clear and not in arm's reach when he ~~o~~pened my door for me. I climbed up and belted in. Max got ~~in~~, started the car, strapped in, and we were off.

I was silent and avoided him taking my hand by digging ~~th~~rough my purse, pretending to look for a mint, which I didn't ~~h~~ave. Then I sighed my feigned defeat at the wasted effort and ~~lo~~oked out my side window, clutching my bag like it was a life ~~fo~~rce.

Max took the hint and he not only didn't try to take my hand ~~b~~ut he also didn't speak. And when we got to his house and out ~~o~~f the car, he stopped at the back of the Cherokee to wait for ~~m~~e to round it but he again didn't take my hand as we walked

up the steps. He let us in. I went to the closet, hooked my purs
and coat inside, and headed up the stairs.

Grabbing my pajamas, I went directly to the bathroom
cleaned my face, moisturized, and then looked in the mirror.

"Tomorrow," I told my reflection in a barely there whispe
"this will be over. I just have to get through tonight."

That's a bad idea, Neenee Bean, Charlie's voice wa
urgent in my head. *You'll regret it. You'll regret it, sweethear
until the day you die.*

"If I stay, I'll regret it in six months, a year, ten year
whenever it sinks in and turns bad and goes sour, knowing I'
second best." I was still whispering.

Nina, listen to me—

"She was his world. Don't I deserve to be that to someon
Charlie?" I whispered, and before Charlie could say more,
turned to the door and opened it.

I didn't look at Max but out of the corner of my eye I sa
him heading toward the bathroom as I came out. I quickl
went to the bed, got in on my side, turned out my bedsid
lamp, which Max had turned on, leaving his illuminated.
curled up, my back to the bathroom, and I took two very dee
breaths.

I heard Max come out and I felt the bed move when he go
in it. And even though I had my eyes closed, I saw the ligh
go out.

He didn't delay. He moved into me, his arm windin
around my belly, and he pulled my back into his front.

I didn't struggle. Instead my closed eyes closed tighter as
felt the warmth of him, the strength of him.

One last night.

"What'd he say to you, baby?" he asked softly into the bac
of my hair.

"Max, I'm really tired."

"What'd he say?"

I remained silent. His arm got tighter as he pulled me eve
closer.

"You know about Shauna, babe. You gotta know there ere others before you," he whispered into my hair.

Yes, your wife! The Beautiful Swan, Anna! I shouted in my ead.

"I saw your face in the police station, honey, when I talked out havin' a woman on the job when I was with Shauna."

"Max—"

"I told you this mornin', it's casual—"

"Please, Max."

"Her name was Shelly."

"Please."

"When I got home to look after Mins, the invitation to her edding was in my mail."

I drew in a sharp breath. His arm gave me a squeeze.

"It was nice. We both had fun and then it was over. She as fine with that. She knew the score. It ended good and we emained friends. I know the guy she hooked up with after me. e's a good guy. They're gonna be happy and I'm happy for em."

"Can I go to sleep?"

"You're different."

I clenched my teeth, then I tried, "Max—"

"We're not about havin' fun. We're that and we're a fuck-va lot more than that."

This was torture.

"We'll talk in the morning," I promised, for we would. He ust probably didn't know what I was going to say.

"Baby," he whispered his advice, "don't sleep on what's arin' you up inside."

"Nothing's tearing me up inside," I lied yet again.

"Duchess—"

"Max, please, it's late, I've had too much to drink, a crazy ay, a crazy *week*, and I'm just tired. Can't you just hold me nd let me sleep?"

At my request that he hold me, I felt his body relax into ine but he asked, "We'll talk in the morning?"

"Yes."

"You'll actually talk to me in the morning?"

"I said I would."

"None of this shit about not askin' questions when yo
think I don't wanna answer. We'll actually *talk*."

I swallowed, wondering why he remembered *everything*
then promised, "Yes, Max, we'll talk."

Max fell silent. I forced my body to relax. After a while, h
called my name on a whisper.

"Nina."

"Yes."

His arm got tight and he pressed his body to mine.

"Baby, that path you were on...?" he asked, but said n
more.

"Yes?" I prompted.

"Until you showed in that snowstorm, I was on it too."

Oh my *God*. Torture.

"Sleep, Max," I urged him, but I could hear my voic
clogged with tears I could *not* let flow.

"Forgot about this," he muttered into my hair.

"Sorry?"

"Forgot," he repeated.

"Forgot?"

"Forgot about carin' about someone so much you would d
everything in your power to stop them havin' pain."

No. Not torture. *Pure bloody torture.*

"Max—"

"And how fuckin' shitty it feels when there's nothin' yo
can do to stop it."

"I'll be okay," I whispered yet another lie, for I wouldn't
Not ever. Not ever again or, at least, not until I found someon
who thought I was their world.

If that happened.

"Yeah?"

"Yes, Max. So will you."

He fell silent again. I waited. Then I waited longer.

Then I moved my arm to drape it on his, I laced my fingers through his, and I whispered, "'Night, Max."

He shoved his face in my hair, his fingers tightened in mine, and he muttered, "'Night, Duchess."

For a long time I didn't sleep and I knew neither did Max.

Then slowly the impossible happened and sleep claimed me.

CHAPTER ELEVEN

Not If You're the Only One Fightin'

I WOKE UP to the bright Colorado sunshine, complete memory of my heart-wrenching night before, and an empty bed. I got up on my hand, pulling my hair out of my face, and listened to the house.

Nothing.

I started to look down toward Max's pillow but caught sight of the note on his nightstand covering the clock.

I scooted across the bed and grabbed the note.

Duchess,

Had to go into town, be back as soon as I can. Coffee's made, just flip the switch.
   When I get home, we'll talk.

                                                            Max

I looked at the clock and saw it was nearly nine. I'd slept in and, while doing it, as normal, I'd slept deep. I didn't feel him leave me.

I got out of bed, went to the bathroom, did my morning business, and went downstairs to flip on the coffee. I went back upstairs and took a shower. Then I wrapped up in my robe and went downstairs to get a mug of coffee. I took it upstairs and went to the closet, grabbed my clothes, went to the dresser, grabbed my undies, and went back to the bathroom. I did my makeup and dressed, hooking my robe on the back of the door. Then I did my hair.

What I didn't do was think. I'd have to do that soon enough.

When I was done with my hair, I turned off the blow-dryer and my hand froze in its descent to set the dryer on the basin because I heard my recorded voice.

"Oh, sweetheart."

"And you also get what it's like to have Shauna involved, seeing as she was after my man and she's after yours too."

"I'm not sure Max is my man."

I set the dryer on the counter silently as the next words in Bitsy's and my recorded phone conversation from days before drifted up to me.

"Oh, he is. Never seen him like that with anyone except Anna. The whole town's talkin' about it. We're all real glad. Thought Max'd never find anyone after Anna died. It's been ten years. That's a long time. Lord knows, I know that."

"Bitsy—"

"Brody told me all you've done with Mindy, and I gotta say, I'm glad you're nice. Anna was my best friend and I loved her. She'd want Max to end up with someone nice."

"I don't know what to say. Um… thank you."

"Thank me for you bein' nice?"

"Yes, I guess, and thank you for trusting me to talk to."

I walked woodenly out of the bathroom and across the room as the voices kept drifting up, relentless, the entire conversation.

I went to the stairs and wound my way down, my head moving, my neck twisting as I went so I could watch Max standing still as a statue staring at the answering machine.

"Bitsy, darling, you should feel free to feel how you want and don't think of what people think."

"No one liked him anyway. He died and his mistress phoned the police. It's hard not to think of what people think since everyone's thinkin' somethin'."

"Well, try. Anyone who truly cares about you will let you have your feelings, whatever they may be."

I stopped moving when his head tilted back to look at me. I stood in the curve of the stairs halfway down, trapped by the fierce anger in his eyes, and the conversation kept playing but I didn't hear it. I stood immobile, his eyes on me, his face carved from stone.

Then I heard my mom's faraway, disembodied shout from the answering machine recording. *"Neenee Bean, let's go hiking!"*

"Be down in a sec!"

"You know about Anna?" Max asked over the recording.

My stomach clutched, fear crawling insidiously along my skin.

"Max—"

"You know about Anna?" he repeated, his voice deadly.

"I—"

"Come down here."

"Max—"

"Get down here, Nina."

The answering machine message played out as I wound down the rest of the stairs and walked to within four feet of him. He watched the whole time.

"No, Bitsy. You don't know how many times I tried to get Charlie to open up to me. So, thank you, again, for trusting me."

"Oh, honey, my pleasure. I'll lay all my troubles on you, you like it so much."

"Take care."

"Yeah, you too. Hope to see you soon."

"Bye."

"Later, honey."

The answering machine beeped the end of the message.

"Max—"

He interrupted me, "How long have you known?"

"Um…"

Suddenly, he leaned forward and roared, *"How long have you known?!"*

My heart lodged in my throat. I jumped and moved back two paces, scared silent.

"Fuckin' answer me," he growled.

This was it. This was it.

Oh God, I knew it. It *always* went bad.

He couldn't even bear me knowing she existed.

I couldn't do this. I couldn't participate in this ending. I just had to get *out*.

I turned and ran to the stairs but didn't get there. Max's hand wrapped firm around my wrist. I came to a jerking halt and then he yanked on my hand, twisting it around my back, effectively twirling me so my front slammed into his. Then he released my hand but his arms came around me like vises.

"Don't run away from me, Nina," he clipped.

"Let me go," I whispered.

"Answer the *fucking* question."

I shook my head but answered, "Arlene told me at The Dog that night when Damon hit me."

"Christ, you've known a week." He bit this off as if it infuriated him even further.

"Yes," I whispered. "Please, let me go."

"You've known a week," he repeated.

"Yes, Max. Now, please, let me go."

"You didn't say a word."

I blinked and tried to focus through my fear on his enraged face. "Sorry?"

"You didn't say a *fucking* word," he repeated, squeezing me with his arms on the word "fucking."

He wasn't making sense and I decided to attempt to calm him down so I could get my head sorted, plan the steps to leaving him, take them one at a time, and then get out of there, out of Colorado, go home and find some way to pick up the tattered threads of my life.

"I know this upsets you," I said softly.

"Yeah, you do?" he clipped back sarcastically.

"I'm sorry."

"About what?"

"That I know."

His brows knit over narrowed eyes. "You're sorry yo know about Anna?"

"I know you didn't want me to."

His body jerked and he barked in my face, "What th *fuck*?"

"I know you were very—"

His face was still in mine when he growled, "You don' know shit."

I clamped my mouth shut and swallowed. Calming hir wasn't working and his intense fury was scaring the hell ou of me. I could feel my heart beating in my neck, in my wrists and even against his chest.

I finally pulled up the courage to whisper, "Max, please le me go."

"Explain," he demanded instead of letting me go.

I shook my head, short, confused shakes. "Sorry?"

"Explain how you know I didn't want you to know abou Anna," he ordered.

"I—"

He cut me off. "When *I've* been wrackin' my brain sinc you curled up to me in order to get in Shauna's face becaus you thought she'd humiliated me and you wanted to ge mine back for me and I knew. I knew a woman who'd stand by me, especially one I barely knew who'd do that for m thinkin' what you mighta been thinkin' after Shauna ran he fuckin' mouth, I knew what that woman would mean to me. So once it came clear how your crazy, fucked-up head works, I've been wrackin' my brain how to tell you about my dead wife."

I blinked, then breathed, "What?"

"You get a hangnail, Nina, you'd use it to drive a wedg between us."

"I—"

"Don't deny it."

"But—"

"And all this time, you knew."

"Max—"

He suddenly let me go and stepped away, glaring at me and stopped speaking.

"So, you knew the shit that's been goin' on in my head this last week."

I shook my head again, those short, sharp, confused shakes. "No."

"You know how she died?"

"I...I know Curt killed her."

"So you knew the shit that's been goin' on in my head this last week."

"Max—"

"Curt killed her and the week he dies, the week that shit comes back up after years of it stayin' buried is the week I fall in love with another woman."

A jolt of electricity bolted through me and all I could do was stare.

Max didn't seem to notice. "When Mick came to my door that night to tell me about the accident, to tell me Bitsy had to be cut clear and would probably never walk again, to tell me Curt walked away without even a fuckin' *scratch*, to tell me Anna was dead at the scene, I knew never again, I'd never let it happen to me again. Then you drove up to my house in a goddamned snowstorm."

"Max—" I whispered, my breath coming fast, almost in pants, but he talked over me.

"Then Curt gets murdered while I'm fallin' for you and this week it's been like lettin' her go again but I could deal with that, long's I had you. Your body in my bed. You bein' so cute all the time. You sparrin' with me. All that remindin' me life could be good. And I had your shit to occupy my mind, sort you out, get you to take a gamble on me and you fuckin' *knew* and you let me deal with your shit and you didn't ask that first *fuckin'* question. You didn't think *once* what I might be goin' through."

He was right, so right, and I hated when he was right.

Especially this time.

I didn't think. I even figured it out but I never thought c
him. I was so wrapped up in my own drama, my neuroses,
hadn't given it a single thought. Not once, not even when Cur
wrote whatever he wrote in his letter to the man whose wif
he killed, obviously in a car wreck, and Max went so strange
Bitsy had even *told* me to take care of Max, but did I?

No. I just thought about me.

I took a step forward but this time Max moved back and
stopped, actually feeling the blood draining from my face.

"Max, darling—"

"Nope, Nina, no way. Don't give me that fuckin' 'darling
shit now." He shook his head. "You were so busy worryin
about yourself, you didn't think to worry about me. So that shi
with Shauna that first night at The Mark, you cuddlin' up t
me, havin' my back…*fuck*." He ended on a snarl, so overcom
with fury and mountain man betrayal he couldn't go on.

"Max, let me—"

He cut me off again. "You know where I been this morn
ing, babe?"

"I…" I shook my head. "No, I…where have you been?"

"Talkin' to Bitsy," he replied, his voice terse. "See, yesterday
durin' our conversation, I realized I was askin' you to give u
everything for me, slot into *my* life. And I thought, you movin
all the way out here only to have me be gone, seein' you on week
ends or not for months, you make your sacrifice and what? That'
what you get? So I told Bitsy I'd take the job. I'd take over Curt'
business. I'd stay in town. I'd do that shit *for you*."

I felt my chest moving rapidly, the tears welling in my eyes
I couldn't believe it. Max didn't want anything to do with tha
job. He hated Curt's business. He hated Curt. Curt had killed
his *wife*.

"Please, Max, let me explain."

He shook his head and started to the door. "Figure this'l
be good, babe, but too fuckin' late."

I followed him, calling, "Max."

He turned to me with his hand on the handle of the door and I stopped at the coldness I saw in his eyes. A coldness I'd only seen once before. Coldness he'd aimed at Shauna.

"Told you, somethin's good, it's worth fightin' for but not if you're the only one fightin'."

Then he opened the door, slamming it behind him and stalked out.

My feet were bare so I ran up the stairs, pulled on boots, and ran down, threw open the door, and jumped down the steps, but when I got to the drive, I saw his Cherokee disappear behind the green pine and white aspen of his mountain.

CHAPTER TWELVE

Norm and Gladys

IT WAS STARTING to get dark. I was frozen nearly stiff but I sa
watching and listening to the rushing river by my cabin.

After Max left that morning, his parting shot so final, I knew
I only had one choice and having only that choice, in my head
broke down the problems facing me and tackled them one by one

I called Thrifty's and luckily got someone other than
Arlene who answered the phone. This person had clearly not
been informed of the ban on taxis to Max's house; therefore
when I ordered a taxi, he told me they'd send one and it'd be
there in half an hour.

While I waited for the taxi, I made the bed and packed
Then I went downstairs, booted up Max's computer, and
changed the password.

Then I wrote a note to Max. I wrote it longhand on a sheet
of paper I took from his printer. I didn't edit it or proofread it
just wrote it and left it on the kitchen counter. There wasn't
much to it anyway.

All it said was:

Max,

You're right. You deserve better.
Thank you for all you did and for being you.

Nina

PS: Your computer password is Beautifulbluff.

Then I got in the taxi and paid a fortune for him to take me to the closest rental car agency, which was three towns over. I rented a car, asking the clerk where I could book a few nights somewhere quiet, somewhere secluded. He told me he knew just the place, made a call, and wrote out the directions. I followed them and checked into my own little cabin among a bunch of other little cabins in a little wood by the river.

Then I texted my mom to tell her I was all right, not to worry about me, that I'd explain later, ignoring the fact that I'd had twelve calls and not even looking to see who they were from. I turned the ringer on my phone to silent and put it in the nightstand.

Then I drove to the market I saw on my way to the cabins and bought myself enough food to last a few days, drove it back to my cabin, and unpacked it.

I made myself lunch, ate it, but didn't taste it.

Then I took the chair that was on the tiny back porch of the cabin and moved it down to the river and sat staring at the water rushing by, my mind weirdly blank, my body totally numb.

What could have been minutes or hours later, I heard, "Nice view."

I looked to see an elderly man with a cane making his way to me over the snow, intermittent exposed rocks, and dead tufts of grass.

I smothered the desire to get up and aid his journey. Biting my lip as I watched his cautious approach, wielding his cane, thinking (what I didn't know was correctly) from my experience with Charlie, he probably didn't want some strange woman helping him and reminding him of a weakness he wasn't likely to forget.

I looked back at the river rushing across its rocks, the snow-shrouded banks, the green pine trees dotting all around.

It was a nice view and I hadn't even noticed. I hadn't really even seen it.

I looked back at the man and tried to smile as I agreed, "It's lovely."

He made it to my side and stared at the view.

After a while, not looking at me, he asked, "You all right missy?"

"Sorry?" I asked back.

I started when he replied perceptively, "Been on this earth a while. Know heartache when I see it. You been sittin' in the sun even though it's bitter cold, starin' at that river for yonks. You all right?"

I pulled in a ragged breath and lied, "Yes, I'm fine."

He nodded and continued his study of the river. Again, he did this for a while.

Then, after another while, he informed me, "I'm Norm. I'm in cabin number three with my wife, Gladys. You want company, she's a good cook."

Before I could say anything, he turned and picked his way back over the snow, rocks, and dead grass. I went back to my silent contemplation of the river and I stayed that way until now.

I got up slowly, my body creaky with cold and inactivity. I dragged my chair back to my porch and went inside. Instead of going to the tiny kitchen to make dinner, I went to the window, pulled the curtain back, and looked out.

There were seven cabins along the river, four across from them, dotted up an incline in the wood. There were two cabins with cars in front. Mine, number seven, was at the far end on the riverside, and Norm and Gladys's, all the way down on the riverside, number three.

I grabbed my cabin key, walked out the front door, locked up behind me, and headed to cabin number three.

*   *   *

"I'll see you at breakfast," I said to Norm and Gladys as I stood on their tiny front porch, illuminated by their blindingly strong porch light.

"We'll see you at eight-thirty, Nina, dear." Gladys smiled at me. "Cabin number seven?" she asked.

I looked into the drive area of the cabin complex and saw

ot much as the porch light was the only thing lighting the
arge, dark space. Then I looked back at Gladys and Norm.

"Yes, number seven. The silver rental car in front, can't
miss it," I told her.

"'Night, Nina, thanks for the company." Norm smiled at
me, his eyes searching but gentle.

I hadn't shared and they hadn't pried. They'd just given
me pork chops, mashed potatoes, gravy, and green beans and
finished it with homemade apple pie and ice cream, all of
which probably tasted good if I could taste anything. They'd
also told me about their three kids, seven grandkids, and one
great-grandkid. All of whom where spread across the conti-
nental United States. All of whom they loved dearly. And all
of whom I could probably recognize on the street after they
were done talking about them. And this was even before they
showed me pictures.

"'Night, Norm, Gladys."

"'Night dear, sleep tight," Gladys replied.

I turned on a small wave and headed back, and as the
night enveloped me quickly in its bizarre, dense darkness, the
thoughts I'd kept at bay all day flooded my head. Thoughts
about how, this time, I'd been the one who made the good part
of a new relationship go bad. How, this time, I'd been the one
who had a good thing and didn't take care of it. How, this time,
I thought I was guarding against something bad when someone should have guarded Max against me.

With some effort (and not entirely successfully), I shoved
these thoughts aside as I carefully made my way through the
darkness. I found my cabin by what could only be considered a
small miracle and then another miracle occurred when I found
the lock in which to insert the key.

When I opened the door, I was making a mental note to
turn on the porch light next time if Norm and Gladys invited
me over again when I was suddenly shoved through it. I emit-
ed a small, surprised cry but had no time for any other reaction when I was jerked away from the door, slammed against

the wall, my head cracking painfully against it. Then I had a strong man's forearm tight against my throat.

"Ain't no Maxwell here to have your back, is there?" Damon snarled in my face. I couldn't see him, not really, but I knew it was him.

I made no retort because I couldn't. I was choking.

This went on for a while as I scratched at his arm and kicked out at his legs, the whole time desperately fighting for breath. But he was stronger than me and the only time I connected with his shin, he pushed his arm deeper into my throat and the pain was excruciating.

"Been waitin' awhile, English, to get mine back," he whispered, then stepped back and released me.

My hands went to my throat as I started to bend double, my lungs on fire. I was drawing in a deep breath but he wasn't done.

As I bent, his hand came up and he backhanded me on the cheekbone, exactly where he'd connected before. This time, still breathless and nowhere near recovered from his choking me, I fell to my hands and knees.

I barely landed when he kicked me in the ribs and my body jerked with the blow as the pain, such pain I'd never experienced, not even at the hands of Brent, knifed through my middle like a wide, hot blade.

Focused on the pain, I didn't have it in me to evade or even struggle when his hands went under my armpits to pull me up to my feet. As I was favoring my ribs, my arm wrapped protectively around them, still trying to catch my breath, I couldn't even lift a hand to defend myself as his fist connected with my nose and I felt the pain followed by an instant flooding of fluid in my nose. He righted me for a better target and then his fist came back for the second round. The pain blew out in an array from my eye and I went back down to my knees and one hand, the other one still cradling my ribs, blinking away stars and sucking in breath.

Damon leaned over me. "Teach you, English. Yeah?"

Then, as quick as he came on me, the door closed and he was gone.

I pulled in breath, the ache in my ribs stabbing as I did it, but even so, I drew in another, then another. Then I crawled to the door, locked it, and, using the handle, pulled myself to my feet.

I stumbled to the bathroom and turned on the light, seeing the blood running from my nose, down my mouth, off my chin onto my sweater. I grabbed a towel, pressed it to my nose, peered into the mirror, and saw the swelling around my eye and cheekbone had already started.

Tears slid up my ravaged throat but I swallowed them down and tasted blood.

Sweetheart, put ice on your eye now, sit still, get your head together, then go to Max, Charlie said into my head.

I did what he said, though not all of it. I got ice and I lay on the bed holding the pack on my eye and cheek with one hand, the towel to my nose with the other, and I knew if I fell asleep without taking the ice to the sink there was no one to take it gently out of my hand. Instead, tomorrow, I'd wake up with a puddle in the bed.

But I fell asleep all the same. This was because, while I was lying there, I cried horrendous, body-wracking sobs that really, *really* hurt my ribs.

And crying always exhausted me.

*   *   *

My body jolted awake when the pounding came at the door, and I blinked into the darkness as fear shafted through my system.

He was back.

God, what was I thinking? I should have left. Driven to Denver. Gone anywhere. Why did I stay where he knew I was?

My mind blanked of thought and I jerked agonizingly upright in bed as I heard the door open.

Oh my God.

I was now *really* in a horror movie with a crazed mountain man gone bad stalker after me, in a *cabin* in the *woods* all *alone*. Everyone knew you steered clear of cabins in woods! They even had some crazy psycho serial killer who *owned* cabins in woods and tortured couples in one on an episode of *Criminal Minds*.

What was I thinking?

I rolled across the bed, ignoring the burning in my ribs, and gained my feet with the bed between me and the door when I saw the shadowed form in the door frame.

"Get out!" I screeched as loud as I could, knowing Norm wouldn't hear me—he wore hearing aids and asked "pardon" a lot, but hoping Gladys would.

The overhead light went on and Max stood in the door frame. The instant I saw him, I stopped breathing.

What was he doing here?

His face at first was searching but when his eyes took me in, his expression turned instantly ravaged.

"What...the...*fuck*?" he whispered, his gravelly voice so low, it slithered across the room at me like a snake.

I realized then that I was holding the sodden, now-iceless towel in one hand, the bloody one in the other, and I could just imagine what my face looked like. Not to mention my sweater, for I'd gone to sleep in my clothes, not even taking off my boots.

I ignored these things, stared at Max, then asked the first thing that came to my mind.

"What are you doing here?"

"What the fuck?" Max repeated.

"Max, what are you doing here?"

One second he was across the room, a bed between us. The next he was standing right in front of me, toe to toe. His hands were cupping my jaw and his eyes were moving over my face or, more precisely, my nose, cheek, and eye.

Then his gaze locked on mine.

"Duchess, what happened to you?" he asked softly.

"Max—"

"Baby, answer me."

"I don't—"

His hands tightened, not painfully but I knew he was done verbalizing his commands. He just simply wanted me to obey.

"Damon," I whispered, and watched Max's eyes close slowly.

Then he opened them and asked, "What happened?"

I shook my head but answered, "I don't know. I was here for a while, sitting by the river; then I went to Norm and Gladys's for dinner—"

Max blinked and asked, "Norm and Gladys?"

"My neighbors."

"Your neighbors?"

"Yes, cabin number three. We had pork chops and apple pie, um . . . not together, of course, apple pie was dessert. We had mashed potatoes, gravy, and green beans with the pork chops and, um . . . ice cream with the pie."

Why was I babbling?

Max pressed his lips together and I wasn't sure but he looked like maybe he was considering laughing or, alternately, yelling before he stopped pressing them together and suggested, "Let's get to the Damon part."

"Okay." I nodded, happy to be back on target and not making a prat of myself. "Anyway, I was walking back to my cabin from dinner and I opened my door. Damon was there. He pushed me through and . . . well . . ." I threw out a hand, for the rest was obvious.

"When did this happen?"

"I'm not sure but I'm guessing a while ago."

"You haven't been to the doctor."

This was a statement, not a question, but I shrugged my answer before I stupidly said, "No need. If my ribs are broken, then they can't do much of—"

I stopped talking when Max's eyes narrowed.

"Your ribs?"

I saw my mistake instantly but I had the distinct feeling Max wasn't going to let it go and I had this feeling because his eyes were narrowed but also since he pretty much never let anything go.

Therefore, cautiously I explained, "He kind of"—I paused—"um…when I was on the floor he kind of…" I hesitated again, then whispered, "Kicked me."

Max just stood there, stock-still, his hands still at my jaw, his eyes looking in mine, but his were dark, unfocused, and they were angry. Angrier than I'd ever seen them and that morning I thought he couldn't get angrier but there it was.

Which brought my mind to that morning.

"Max," I ventured when he seemed to be unable to move. "What are you doing here?"

He blinked again, his eyes focused on me, and he answered, "Bringin' you home."

This time I blinked and said, "But—"

"Now I'm takin' you to the hospital."

"Max—"

I didn't finish because Max was pulling the towels out of my hands, tossing them on the dresser behind me, and speaking. "I'll call Mick on the way, get him to round up Damon."

"I think—"

I didn't finish that time because Max's hand wrapped around mine and he was dragging me across the room as he said, "After the hospital, we'll go home."

"I can't go home," I told his back as he kept walking us across the room and he stopped and turned to me.

"What?"

"I'm making breakfast for Norm and Gladys. They're going to be here at eight-thirty. Norm's worried about me. I think Gladys is too. If I disappear in the night, I mean, they're not young, as in, they've got a great-grandchild not young. It'll give them a fright."

Max looked at me silently for several moments, his eyes gentle and warm but even so they were very active. Then he

urned fully to me, moved into me, his hand dropping mine
out coming up to wrap around the back of my neck. I watched
n fascinated shock as his head dipped. Then I felt the sweet,
swift touch of his lips against mine.

He pulled away barely an inch before he said quietly,
'Duchess, you're the only person I know who could be in a
goddamned cabin in the middle of fuckin' nowhere all of eight
hours and be on a first-name basis, sharin' meals, and makin'
breakfast dates with your neighbors."

I was not hearing his words. I still felt his lips against mine
and it was occurring to me, belatedly, that he was acting like
what happened between us that morning hadn't happened at
all.

"Are you still mad at me?" I blurted on a whisper, and I felt
my eyes go wide in fear that the question came out rather than
me just asking it in my head where it should have stayed even
if that meant it would go unanswered.

I pulled away but his hand only tightened on my neck.

"We'll talk about that later."

That meant yes. And he'd already been mad enough at me
that morning to last a lifetime, rightfully so, but I couldn't go
through it again. Not then, not ever.

I shook my head and pulled at my neck but his hand only
got tighter.

"I..." I swallowed, then went on. "Max, you don't have to
take care of me anymore."

"Shut it, Duchess."

"No, Max, you don't—"

His head dipped again and his mouth on mine stopped
mine from forming words.

Not taking his lips from mine, when the kiss was over, he
repeated, "Honey, like I said, we'll talk about it later. Yeah?"

"Okay," I whispered, because, really, what else could I do?

He lifted his mouth but only to kiss my forehead and say
there, "Let's go."

It was good he took my hand because from the minute his

lips touched my forehead, I closed my eyes. Therefore, blind and still feeling his sweet kiss, thus not processing anything else, I needed him to guide me out the door.

*   *   *

When Max brought me back to the cabin after our visit to the small local hospital, he had no trouble finding the lock to open the door, for he'd cleverly flipped on the porch light before we left.

Once he used his hand in mine to guide me through the front door, he hit the light switch and a lamp came on by the couch in the small living room. He closed and locked the door, still keeping hold of my hand, then his mobile rang.

He pulled it out of his back pocket and looked at the display.

Then he squeezed my hand and murmured, "You get ready for bed, darlin'. I'll be there in a minute."

I stared at him. What did he mean, he'd be there in a minute?

He let my hand go, flipped open his phone, and put it to his ear before I could ask my question (which I probably wasn't going to do anyway) and said, "Yeah?"

Beyond exhausted from fear, adrenaline, heartbreak, and a bout of crying unlike any I'd ever experienced in my history of bouts of crying, and I'd had a long history of bouts of crying, I realized I didn't have it in me to argue or even discuss what was going on. In fact, I barely had energy even to stand there. So I wandered to the bedroom, flicked on the overhead lights, headed to my bag, zipped it open, and dug out my pajamas.

I'd kind of thought he was just bringing me back so that I could make breakfast for Norm and Gladys and then he would be leaving. After what happened that morning, even if he had told me he'd shown up in the middle of the night to take me "home," I didn't exactly understand what that meant. Though my guess was that he was on an errand for my mother, who had his number, and Max being Max, regardless of what happened between him and me, he would run that errand for my

nother because he liked her and that's just the kind of thing
e did.

He'd kissed me, of course, three times in two places, and I
eally had no understanding of that.

Further, on the way to the hospital, as he said he'd do,
e'd called the Gnaw Bone police station and told them what
Damon did, saying I'd be in the next day to press charges.
After he did that, he took my hand but didn't pull it to his
high. Instead, he rested his hand on my thigh and released
nine to shift, then came right back to it, every time. Other
han that he didn't say much. He was acting gentle to the point
f being tender but he was also obviously lost in thought.

And, I figured, after that morning, not to mention him find-
ng me having been beaten up by Damon, they couldn't be
leasant thoughts.

The good thing about visiting a small local hospital in the
ead of night was that there was no waiting. We found out
ery quickly that my ribs weren't broken just bruised, same
vith my nose. Even though the swelling was contained by the
ce, the bruising was already coming up, including at my side
vhere there was an angry, curved mark the shape of the toe of
boot. To my horror, and at Max's demand, they took photos
f my midriff and my face, and when we left, they promised
Max and me they would send the photos and medical reports
the Gnaw Bone Police Department.

Max had been silent on the way back to the cabin, as had I,
ut he still held my hand.

I listened to the murmur of his conversation in the other
oom as I stripped off my clothes and put on my pajamas.
hen I looked around the room, taking it in for the first time.

The owners lived in a house about a quarter mile up the
ane that led to the cabin complex. It was definitely a family-
un business. They didn't even have an office, just a locked key
abinet behind the front door and a guest register book on a
pindly-legged table under the cabinet.

Now I saw that they took pride in their cabins. The room

was clean. The wood-planked floor looked recently redone
And the warm, sage-green walls also had been recently
repainted. There were touches here and there that showed they
made more than a small effort. Thick, blue, mushroom, and
green braided rugs. Prints on the walls that were chosen with
personal taste, rather than just a generic attempt at décor. The
bed had a duvet, not a comforter, and the duvet was soft and
downy, its cover a tasteful design of the green of the walls and
the blue and mushroom of the rugs as well as some browns
and grays. There were four fluffy pillows on the queen-sized
bed, not two thin, unappealing ones. There was even a gag-
gle of toss pillows that kept up the color scheme. And there
were attractive reading lamps on either nightstand with muted
shades, but at the top, there was an apparatus for the lamp to
swing inward so it could throw light where you needed it.

I was surprised that the cabins weren't booked solid, considering all of this and the fact that each cabin had a goodly
amount of space around it with trees and shrubs providing
more privacy, more quiet. Then again, this all looked pretty
fresh, so maybe the owners were new or they'd just done reno-
vations and hadn't had time to get the word out.

"Yeah, see you tomorrow," Max said into his phone as he
walked into the bedroom, and I realized that I'd been standing there in my pajamas staring stupidly at the room, examining the interior decoration.

I pulled myself together and walked to the bed, turning on
the lamp at his side as I heard him flip the phone closed. He
turned out the overhead light as I used the last of my energy to
scurry around the bed, throw the covers back, and get in, listening to his phone hit the nightstand.

I settled on my good side, facing the room, and I saw he'd
moved. He was now standing by my suitcase, which was resting on a chair across the room. He'd thrown his leather jacket
over the top and was unbuttoning his flannel. I watched silently
as he shrugged it off and dropped it on his jacket and both his
hands came up to the back of his neck where he pulled the

long-sleeved T-shirt over his head. Then he turned back to the bed and his eyes hit me as he walked to it.

My breath caught, not just per usual at the sight of his chest, but because it struck me suddenly he was there, I was there, and all day I'd been attempting to come to terms with the dreadful reality that I was never going to see him again.

I rolled to my back and closed my eyes, feeling him sit on the bed. I heard both his boots drop and felt him get up again. Then I heard the buckle on his jeans crack against the floor along with the swish of the fabric.

Then the covers moved and the bed rocked as he got in. The covers moved again, sliding down to my waist. My eyes opened and my head turned to him as his big splayed hand slided gently up to my rib cage.

It rested where Damon's boot print was and Max rested on his side, close to me but not touching me except with his hand. His elbow was in the bed, his head was in his hand, his eyes were on me.

Then his hand slid down to come to rest on my belly and I realized I was holding my breath, so I let it out and when I did, Max spoke.

"All right, baby, let's start this with you tellin' me what Harry said to you last night."

I held my breath again.

I wanted to ask him to turn out the light. I also wanted to ask him if I could go to sleep and we could talk about this in the morning (or never). Mostly, I wanted to ask him, before I'd so stupidly messed up and acted unforgivably selfishly, if he'd really been falling in love with me.

What I didn't want to do was tell him what Harry said to me, not only because of what Harry said, but because it was mostly about Anna.

But I knew I couldn't hide behind my neurotic behavior, not then. Max deserved better.

So I let out my breath and said softly, "He told me about Anna."

Max showed no reaction to this. His face didn't darken. His eyes didn't narrow. He just asked, "What'd he say?"

I pulled in air through my nose, then let it out and answered, "He said you loved her."

"I did," Max agreed readily.

I bit my bottom lip but let it go before I continued. "He said she was your world."

"She was," Max agreed again, and I struggled against the urge to close my eyes against a different kind of internal pain and won, miraculously holding his gaze.

"He said, after her, you had a lot of women."

"That's true."

I swallowed as this was confirmed and finished on a whisper, "He told me that you loved her so much, when she died you were undone. And he told me no one was ever going to be that to you, not ever again, and you and everyone would know it and he thought I should know it too."

Max had a reaction to this, his mouth got tight, his eyes got dark, and his hand pressed slightly into my belly.

Then he sighed and his hand lightened before he asked, "You know something?"

I pulled in both my lips and shook my head, though I did know a lot of somethings. Just not the something he was about to share. However, I wasn't certain I wanted to know what he was about to share. I didn't tell him this and, therefore, he shared.

"When Anna died, it was her world that ended, not mine."

I closed my eyes but Max whispered, "Honey, look at me." So I opened them again.

"You don't have to talk about this," I told him quietly.

"Yeah, I do."

I swallowed again and my hand went to rest on his at my belly.

"It took a while for me to understand that," he told me. "About ten years. I figured it out just over a week ago during a snowstorm."

Oh. My. *God.*

"Max," I breathed, and his hand slid along my belly to my side. He carefully pulled me to his body and leaned in.

"Harry doesn't know dick," Max informed me, his voice soft but slightly harsh. "He lost Bitsy and I don't know why, I don't care, it's got nothin' to do with me. It's his problem. He didn't fight to keep her and everyone knows he didn't. He just gave up and let Curt win. His story is different than mine. He gave up and had to live with his decision, Bitsy in the same town makin' her life with another man. I lost Anna because Curt was bein' Curt. It was outta my hands. He and I had our fallin'-out but Anna and Bitsy were tight. They tied one on at The Dog, Curt was designated driver, went to get them, take them home. About three weeks ago was the anniversary of it all, spring break, kids in town, doin' stupid shit, gettin' drunk like they always do. They fucked with Curt, shoutin' things out their car windows at him and he had a short fuse. He lost his temper, thought he'd teach 'em a lesson, decided to fuck with 'em back. Did it and lost control of the car. The kids swerved into a ditch. They were okay, goin' fast, shaken up but only minor injuries. Curt's SUV rolled four times and only stopped when it slammed into a tree."

"Oh my God," I whispered, turning slightly toward him, my hand automatically moving to rest at his waist.

"Yeah," Max grunted. "Worse, there was a factory recall on the SUV Curt had. Somethin' wrong with the back passenger side seat belt. Curt didn't bother takin' it in to get it fixed. Anna's seat belt snapped and when the truck rolled, she flew all over the inside of the cab, broke her neck."

At that, I rolled totally into him and wrapped my arm around his waist, whispering, "Max."

"Not a mark on her," Max whispered back, but his eyes had drifted away. Even though they were still on me, I knew he couldn't see me. He was seeing something else, something acutely painful. I knew it because it was etched in his face and witnessing it, I wished I had the power to put my hand there and absorb the pain.

But I didn't have that power. No one did. So I just gave his waist a squeeze and Max went on.

"When I saw her at the funeral home, no joke, she looked like she was sleepin'."

I wanted him to stop talking but I didn't request that. I just pressed closer and tightened my arm around him.

Max was still back there, I could tell by the look on his face and the words he said next. "Wanted to kill him. Christ, I was blinded by the urge, couldn't think of anything else. Not only did he kill her, actin' like an asshole, but he did it because he was a lazy son of a bitch, not takin' his car in to be fixed and he was careless, didn't even warn her to sit behind him." Max's eyes focused on me but they were still far away when he said, "You know, I woulda taken her like Bitsy, in a chair, been happy with that for the rest of my life."

I knew that. I definitely knew.

My hand moved from his waist to wrap my fingers around his neck and I whispered, "I know."

"He had Bitsy, alive and breathin', broken but still around to laugh, to talk, to share his bed. Fuck, he never got how fuckin' lucky he was, comin' outta that crash. Not that he didn't get hurt, but that he didn't lose Bitsy."

I stroked his jaw and stayed silent.

"It was Curt's negligence that he didn't take it in when the factory informed him of the recall. George told me I had a case but I let it go. Money wouldn't help but money meant everything to Curt, so he didn't get that. He sent Trev to offer me a settlement, didn't want me suin' him, the asshole." Max shook his head. "Christ, he was such a dick."

Yes, he definitely was.

Max carried on, "Anna had life insurance, got the payoff, never touched it. Not when I was buildin' the house, never. Touchin' it, usin' it, felt like givin' in."

"Giving in?" I asked, confused.

Max focused on me again. "To her bein' dead, makin' it more final."

"Death is pretty final, darling," I said softly but carefully.

His face changed, a wave of that pain sliding through it. His head dropped so his forehead was resting against mine and he muttered, "Yeah."

Still cautious, I guessed, "He mentioned her in his letter."

Max lifted his head and nodded and I knew that was why the other Max came out that day, why Bitsy told me to take care of him, because, bottom line, Curt was being a jerk.

"What'd he say?" I asked, my thumb still stroking his jaw.

"Told me he was sorry. Told me he loved Anna and it ate at him, what he did to her. I'm sure that made him feel better, writin' that out, makin' him feel like a better man, admittin' to that. What he didn't get was what that shit would make me feel. How no apology could change the decisions he made leadin' up to what happened that night. Nothin' could change the fact that his wife and my wife were in his car when he acted like Curt, not thinkin' that two precious souls were with him and the first thing that should be on his fuckin' mind was gettin' them home safe. Not pissin' in his corner, provin' to a bunch of kids who's the bigger man."

As usual, Max was right.

"The fuck of it is, he was writin' that letter at the same time he was fuckin' around on Bitsy with Shauna. God knows why, no excuse for it. And writin' that letter knowin' that his life was in danger, as was hers, and he was dickin' around with a PI and not gettin' the cops involved. He was writin' that letter apologizin' for his stupid, fucked-up decisions ten years ago at the same time still fuckin' makin' 'em."

Again, Max was right.

And something else Max was and it was clear as day, absolutely obvious.

He was not over his dead wife.

This hurt, worse than a kick in the ribs, a punch in the face, but I didn't let that show. Not that Max, in his current state of mind, would notice. He was far away, still reliving a nightmare.

Instead of pulling away physically or emotionally, which was what I wanted to do, my hand left his neck to become my arm wrapped around his waist and I rolled deeper into him, pushing him to his back and getting close, resting my cheek on his shoulder, wrapping him tight with my arm.

Max's hand slid under my body and curled around my waist.

"I saw her picture at Bitsy's," I told him, feeling his body get tight against mine and I hurried on. "She was beautiful, Max. You looked happy."

His arm gave me a squeeze and his body relaxed.

"She was," he agreed. "We were."

"You should know, Harry told me everything," I whispered warily. "About your scholarship, the pregnancies—"

His gravelly voice was back to harsh when he cut me off to remark sarcastically, "Remind me to thank him." I bit my lip and he continued. "And remind me, next time I'm enjoyin' your company and you get the stellar idea to leave me and go distract some bitter, drunk asshole from his fucked-up issues that are his own issues, ones he created his damned self, and he doesn't man up to that but takes pot shots at you, remind me, babe, not to let you go."

This sounded a good deal like Max thought Harry's tirade was my fault and to ascertain if this was true, I lifted my head and looked at his face. His unhappy, clear, gray eyes locked on mine and I saw that it was, indeed, true.

"He was just blowing off steam," I told him.

"Yeah, he was blowin' off steam at your expense, my expense, Anna's expense and she's fuckin' dead. Blowin' off steam, which meant you were nighttime Nina Zombie, actin' like your world had crumbled and you wouldn't let me in to help. Blowin' off steam, which reinforced whatever fucked-up idea you had about Anna and me in your head, which meant you didn't fuckin' talk to me about it and we ended up havin' a spat, you gettin' another fuckin' wild hair and takin' off and then gettin' worked over by Damon. Yeah, babe, Harry was just blowin' off steam."

I heard everything he said but there was only one part of it
that hit me like a bullet.

He called that morning a *spat*.

I got up on an elbow in the bed and looked down at him,
whispering, "Spat?"

His arm came up, crossing his chest, and his fingers curled
round the back of my neck to contain me should I wish to
retreat any farther, and he said, "Duchess, wake up. This is us.
We're gonna fight. You gotta learn how to shake it off."

I blinked.

"Shake it off?" I whispered, and this time my whisper was
both incredulous and lethal.

"Yeah, shake it off," he confirmed, ignoring my toxic tone
completely. "Either that or learn how to talk to me. How to ask
a fuckin' question once in a while without lookin' scared as a
jackrabbit about whatever answer you might get."

I blinked. Max kept talking.

"I ain't a figment of your imagination, Duchess. I didn't
start my existence the night you drove up to my house. I had a
life, a wife. I got a family, friends, a history. I fucked around a
lot, lookin' for somethin' and not findin' it, just like you."

I tried to contain my anger and reminded him, "Yes, Max,
you had a wife who was your world."

"Yeah, she was, until her world stopped. Mine kept goin',
babe."

"Harry said when a man has a woman who is his world,
and he loses her, nothing will take the place of that."

I watched Max's irritation grow to anger. He twisted toward
me and got up on an elbow, too, all without releasing my neck.

"Don't lie in bed next to me and throw in my face the shit
Harry fed you last night," he warned.

"But you admitted it," I told him.

"I fuckin' did not."

"You told me she was your world."

His hand tightened on my neck. "Yeah, she was, Duchess.
Was."

"Harry's a man and men know men."

"Harry's no man, Nina. Haven't you figured that out?"

Okay, he had a point there.

"All right," I agreed, and foolishly went on. "That might b
true but not five minutes ago you relived that nightmare, Max
I watched you do it and you cannot lie there and tell me you'r
over Anna. You loved her and her loss broke you."

His eyes turned to stone, indicating his anger deepening
quite significantly, and he clipped, "Jesus, you're a piece o
work."

"What?"

He rolled into me so I fell to my back and he was partially
on me, though not on my tender side, but I wouldn't have
noticed even if he pressed his full weight into me because he'd
gone way past angry right back to what he was this morning
He was furious and I braced for impact.

"You're a piece of work, babe." His voice was biting as he
repeated himself, his face dipping close to mine. "Is this wha
you wanna hear?" he asked, and didn't wait for my answer,
just kept on going. "She was beautiful. She was funny, sweet,
mellow, laid back. So fuckin' mellow, Christ. Life was good
for Anna. She loved livin' it and didn't let much get under
her skin. We probably had two arguments the whole time we
were together. Life with Anna was contentment, absolute. She
didn't get in my face. She didn't get in moods. She didn't throw
attitude. She woke up happy and went to bed happy and she
did everything she could to give me that same harmony and I
loved every fuckin' minute of it."

My mouth went dry at his words and I tried to slide out
from under him but he didn't let me move an inch as he carried
on.

"Not you, no. You get in my face. Your mood changes like
lightnin'. You throw attitude better'n any woman I ever met
and I grew up with Mom and Kami, so, seriously, babe, that's
sayin' somethin'."

"Get off me," I whispered, his words worse than Damon's

ows, far, far worse. I was pushing against his chest but it was
ke I didn't even speak and my hands on him didn't exist.

"You're blonde and Anna was blonde. That's about all you
vo share. You're night, Duchess; she was day."

I felt the tears hit my eyes and I couldn't stop them from
iding out the sides.

"Get off."

"She wasn't a fighter, though. She wasn't ready to take on
e world. She let anyone walk all over her and they did and
ie didn't react, not even a little. She just let it happen and
oved on, buryin' it deep, not lettin' anyone see, hidin' it even
om me, not lettin' me help. She was sweet, which meant she
t people in to walk all over her, never learned, did it all the
ickin' time. And she was a good listener but she was shy.
he'd stand at my side and bite her lip and look at Harry and
iink someone should help him but it wouldn't be her. She
ouldn't have the courage to walk through a crowded bar and
t by his side and take his issues on her shoulders. What he
iid to you would have wrecked her even worse than it did
ou. So I had to protect her from that shit and I did. She gave
ie harmony. I kept her safe so she could give it. That was us
id it was a good balance."

I didn't know how much more I could take and my voice
ad gone from demanding to pleading when I repeated, "Max,
et *off*."

"You wanted the comparison, babe, you got it. Now you
now what Anna gave me and what I gave her."

"I didn't want the comparison!" I cried.

"Yeah, you did. You're all fired certain you can't compete,
)nvinced yourself of it."

"Well, obviously I can't because, obviously, harmony is *not*
hat you'll get from me."

"There's no replacing Anna."

I looked away, closed my eyes, and quit pressing against his
iest. I was going to block him out. That was the only defense
e was giving me, so I was going to take it.

His words still came at me, though, unfortunately. I couldn't block them just by closing my eyes.

"You lose anyone, there's no replacing them. There'll never be another Charlie; you know that. And there'll never be another Anna. What you need to get is that's precious. You get to keep that. You don't *want* to replace it. That doesn't mean you can't find something else just as good."

Right, I thought, but didn't say it out loud but with his Wonder Max powers he must have read that word on my face.

"Christ," he gritted out. "I don't want harmony from you, Nina. I just want you."

"Can you get off me, please?" I asked quietly.

"Look at me."

"Please, Max."

"Dammit, Nina, look at me."

I looked at him and his eyes roamed my face; then his hand came up and cupped it.

"I see what I had with Anna for the gift it was but now that's gone. With this act, are you sayin', in this life that's all I get?"

"No," I whispered honestly, and the words I said next were coming from somewhere I didn't know I had. Saying things I didn't know I needed to say but things instinctively I knew he needed to hear and understand in a belated effort on my part to protect him for his own good. "What I'm saying is, you're you and you deserve better."

He looked genuinely confused when he asked, "Better than what?"

"Better than me."

I felt his big body jolt and it jarred me, sending a shot of pain through my ribs but I ignored that, focusing on his face which looked utterly stunned.

"You shittin' me?" he asked softly.

Yes, stunned.

"No," I replied just as softly.

His thumb swept my cheekbone and his face gentled as he murmured, "Jesus, baby."

"Think about it, Max," I implored urgently. "I'm argumentative and my head is messed up. Do you know Charlie talks to me?" I asked, but didn't wait for an answer, even as I took in his head jerking at the question. "He does. It started just recently but he does, like he lives in there. I'm not remembering him, things he's said. He's actually *talking to me*. And lately I've been talking back. It's insane."

"Duchess—" Max started, but I kept right on speaking.

"And I do stupid stuff all the time or at least I did before Niles and then there was Niles, who was stupid from start to finish. But before him, it wasn't just all the bad choices with men. I was always doing crazy stuff, like Mom but not benign stuff, like concocting disgusting food. The Brain Team thing wasn't the first or the last time I was off on one. I was *always* off on one. Do you know I've been arrested?" His eyebrows went up and I nodded my head on the pillow. "Not brawling, it was drunk and disorderly except I wasn't really drunk, more like tipsy but I was disorderly because I was yelling really loudly and, in the end, I kind of threw a beer bottle at someone." Max pressed his lips together. I again didn't know what this meant but I defended myself. "He deserved it. He smacked a girl's behind right in front of my friend, who was his *girlfriend*, and he was doing that kind of stuff all the time and it hurt her. So, being tipsy, I'd had enough and I let fly, shouting at him and throwing the beer bottle. Anyway, I wasn't aiming at him, so it didn't hit him, just smashed on a wall and got some girl's purse wet. She was kind of angry about it because the purse was designer so she was the one who called the police."

"Babe—"

On a roll, I talked over him and continued laying out my case. "And I'm totally neurotic. I know why, seeing as my dad left me and then I chose all of those stupid guys, so I have issues with that, as you know. I just don't know how to stop it. You told me all the guys at the bar were looking at me and even Harry said he'd do me but does that register with me? No.

I can't let people be nice to me, say nice things to me. I just can't accept it as fact and that makes me just plain *weird*."

This time, his brows knit and his face grew hard when he repeated in a low, dangerous voice, "Harry said he'd do you?"

"Yes," I told him, too caught up in relaying my urgent message to catch his change in mood. "Harry was drunk and acting like an idiot but I don't know why *you* want me. It's mad."

"Nina—"

"I mean, I go on a vacation to try to figure out my life and here I am. My leg's scraped up. My ribs are bruised. I've been backhanded and punched. I've been to a hospital once and to a police station three times. And I've been into it with practically everyone in town, and if you take out the time I've been sick, I've only been here *a week*!"

"Duchess, let me—"

"What is it with me?" I asked over him, then again didn't wait for an answer, just kept blathering. "I need a time-out to deal with my time-out! That's how messed up I am. And you're a good guy. The best. You take care of people, everyone respects you, you're nice and you're handsome, and you're generous and smart, and you don't need all that is messed up me messing up *you*."

"Babe, will you shut up?"

At his tone, which managed to be both commanding and gentle, my head jerked on the pillow and belatedly I focused on him.

"What?" I asked.

"Shut up," he said softly.

"Okay," I replied instantly, because his face was also gentle, gentle to the point of being tender, though his eyes were dancing like he was laughing inside. The combination of the two was so amazing, it was beyond amazing, indescribably amazing, and I could do nothing but what he told me to do.

"You threw a beer at someone?" he asked, still speaking softly.

"Not *at him*, it was a warning shot. But he smacked a girl's ottom in front of his girlfriend," I repeated on a near whis-er. "And I neglected to add that the girl's bottom he smacked wasn't happy either, seeing as she was my friend's friend too."

"Babe," he whispered, his eyes still dancing and his mouth was now twitching.

I went back to my point. "Obviously from my behavior the ast week and a half, you'll have noted there's a good possibil-ty I might do something like that in the future."

His mouth stopped twitching mainly because it had started grinning.

"Yeah, Duchess, that's been noted."

I swallowed and tilted my head on the pillow as I summed up quietly, my words heavy and utterly true, "I'm not har-mony, Max."

His grin didn't die even hearing my leaden words. "No, honey, that you aren't."

"You deserve that," I whispered.

His hand shifted so his fingers could trail at the wetness my earlier tears left at my temple as he said, "That's sweet you think that, baby, but that doesn't change the fact that that's not what I want."

I blinked slowly and asked, "Sorry?"

"To get that means not to get you, so that's not what I want 'cause, like I said earlier, what I want is *you*."

"My dead brother talks in my head," I reminded him.

"And I used to see Anna walkin' down the sidewalk when I drove through town. That shit happens in one way or another to everyone who loses someone. It'll pass."

Well, even though it made me sad he used to see Anna, still, that was a relief. I thought I was going crazy.

Nevertheless, I persevered, "I'm messed up."

"You're cute."

"Trust me, Max, you may think it's cute now but it'll get not so cute."

"What's not so cute is Harry tellin' you to your face he'd do you, he was drunk or not, but that's between me and Harry."

"What?"

He ignored my question and stated, "But the rest is you babe, and *you* need to trust *me*, it's cute."

"You deserve better," I reminded him.

"You repeatin' that means you haven't been payin' attention," he informed me.

"I'm sorry?"

His hand moved back to cup my face, his thumb moving over my bottom lip, and he spoke while he was doing this. "Harry didn't lie. I fucked around. After Anna there were a lot of women. After all of them, and there were some good ones, babe, but not even one sparked anything in me, nothin', after all of them, what do you think it says that I choose you?"

Oh my *God*.

My entire system went still from the inside out because I had to admit, he had a very valid point.

"I lucked out, baby," Max went on. "When I was young, life handed me somethin' beautiful. Then it took it away. Ten years down the road, somethin' different, but no less beautiful showed up right at my front door. I knew it almost the minute I saw it and nothin' has happened since to shake that. You think, findin' that in you, I'm gonna let you change my password, write me some fucked up note, and walk away?"

"But you were right this morning. I should have known what you were going through this week and I shouldn't have been so selfish."

"No, babe, I was pissed this morning, and in case you haven't noticed, when I get pissed, I mouth off and say shit I shouldn't say. What you gotta learn to do is call me on it, give me the attitude you serve up to everyone else like you did the other night when I was outta line."

"Max—"

"Or, at least, learn to control your wild hairs and let me burn it out and *then* call me on it."

"Max—"

His face got close, so close I could feel his breath on my lips.

s he said, "It kills me to say this, babe, the guilt burns so bad, ut this week I couldn't help but think about what life would e like with you and the ways it would be better than what I ad with Anna. And knowin' you throw beer bottles and give ack as good as you get, I like it, Duchess, that passion. It's in verything you do and, swear to Christ, I don't think I've ever een anything that beautiful. Anna loved life but, honey, when ou forget to let those little fears you got cobble you, fuck, you *devour* it. It's unbelievably amazing, awesome to witness. That assion makes you look at Cotton's pictures like you're experi-ncing bliss. And it makes you fight Kami's corner when she's een nothin' but a bitch to you and fight it like you'll go down vith her and so will the whole of Western civilization. And, Duchess, other people think it's beautiful too. It draws them o you, makin' friends outta folks like Arlene and your cabin eighbors Norm and Phyllis—"

"Gladys," I corrected him.

He grinned, his thumb caught on my lower lip, and he mut-ered, "Whatever."

Then he stopped talking, apparently thinking his final oint had been made.

I stared at him and I did this for a long time. And I came to he conclusion that Max didn't need to say any more.

His final point *was* made.

And I realized, very late, that he didn't even have to talk to nake it. He'd made his point hours earlier by showing up to ake me "home."

Though I decided not to share this with him. What I did lecide was we had to talk about one more thing.

So I called, "Max?"

"Right here, honey."

Yes, he was, right there, with me, in a cabin, by a river, fifty niles away from his house.

I closed my eyes, then opened them and admitted, "You scare me."

"You told me that before."

"I have?"

"Yeah, baby."

"When?"

"That first night I fucked you."

Oh yes, right. I was half asleep, I forgot about that. Of course, Max hadn't since he obviously had the memory of an elephant, which I figured did not bode well for me.

He was still grinning, likely reading my thoughts on my face (which, I should add, also didn't bode well for me) and his thumb went back over my lip before I asked, "What if this goes bad?"

"Like I said then, I can't give you any promises but we'll do the best we can."

"Is that enough for you?"

He stared at me and then burst out laughing. Collapsing on top of me for a second before his arms went around me and he rolled carefully, taking me with him until he was on his back and I was partly on top of him, partly pressed to his side.

I lifted my head, looked in his eyes, and asked, "What's funny?"

Still smiling big, he remarked in a way that I knew he was blatantly lying, "It cuts deep, Duchess, knowin' you're settlin' for me." His hand went into my hair and cupped the back of my head as my eyes got wide. He pulled my face closer and muttered, "But you should know, the answer is, yeah, it's more than enough and, you settle for me, I'll settle for that."

Then he pulled my face even closer and he kissed me.

And then, apparently our conversation was over because he kissed me for a good long while, so long I totally forgot about our discussion. When he stopped kissing me, he turned out the light, settled in, and told me to go to sleep. And his kisses were so good, his body so warm, he felt so good at my side, I was so exhausted, I just cuddled into him and did what I was told.

But I did it with that feeling of hope drifting back into my heart and this time, it drifted in with the clear intention of staying awhile.

CHAPTER THIRTEEN

Breakfast

I WOKE WHEN Max's heat moved away from my back, the weight of his arm gliding from around me. He did this carefully, with that exquisite gentleness unreal in such a powerfully built man.

I didn't open my eyes. I felt like I'd had around fifteen minutes of sleep and like I needed fifteen days to catch up.

And anyway, when Max was being gentle like that, I thought it would be better to shut off the other senses and experience nothing but the feel of it.

I was sliding back into dreamland when I heard the distinct murmur of voices. The owners of the cabin complex might have taken pride in their facilities but the cabins themselves were a fair shade less well made than Max's A-frame. With the way I could hear the conversation, I knew the walls were paper-thin.

"Nina had a rough night," Max's gravelly voice explained.

"Oh dear," Gladys replied, and my eyes flew open.

"And you are?" Norm asked.

"Max, Nina's boyfriend," Max answered.

"Nina's boyfriend who left her alone all day yesterday to do nothing but stare at the river like her world had ended and then left her alone last night to have dinner with two old coots like us?" Norm asked, sounding somewhat surprisingly belligerent. And his tone, not to mention what he gave away about me spending the day pining for Max, made me throw

the covers back and jump out of bed, ignoring the shot of pain
that emanated through my ribs as I did so.

"Norm!" Gladys cried on a gasp.

"Yep," Max replied, sounding not affronted but amused.
"That'd be me."

On Max's remark, I had made it to the door and I threw it
open, rushing out into the living room.

"Is it eight-thirty already?" I asked on a smile I hoped
didn't look fatigued.

Max, wearing jeans and his long-sleeved T-shirt but in bare
feet, turned to look at me and when he did, his lips pressed
together and weirdly, his ear tilted to his shoulder at the same
time he was giving short shakes of his head.

Both Norm and Gladys were staring at me, for some reason
openly gobsmacked.

Then Norm moved, luckily not quickly for I could see his
intent and I was able to cry out, "Max!" in time for Max to
turn back to Norm and then duck clear of Norm's flying cane.

"Norm!" Gladys screeched.

I ran forward as Max retreated, his torso swaying back to
dodge the swipes of the cane Norm was wielding like a rapier
as he advanced on Max.

I got in front of Max and threw my arms out, shouting at
Norm, "What are you doing?"

"Missy, your *face*!" Norm shouted back, swirling his cane
in the air before he planted it on the floor, leaned into it, turned
to Gladys, and ordered, "Go get our cellular whozeewhatsit
and call the police!"

Oh dear, even feeling the pain in my body, I'd still forgotten about my face.

"Max didn't do this," I told Norm, and Norm turned narrowed eyes back to me.

"I wasn't born yesterday, missy."

"Damon did it," I explained quickly, and when Norm
didn't look any less disbelieving, I continued. "He's kind of
my mountain man stalker. See, when he was little, Max lived

ext to Brody, who was his best friend and still is. A long time go, Brody's mom and dad got divorced. Then she got remaried and had Mindy, so Mindy is like Max's little sister. Then, few weeks ago, something bad happened to Mindy and he's not doing too well with it. So, since Brody now lives in eattle, Max was looking out for her, then I was looking out or her, and, well, Damon is her ex-boyfriend but he was her oyfriend-boyfriend then. And he came to a bar and was mean o Mindy, so I pushed him then he backhanded me, which Max saw because he was coming to pick us up because he vas our designated driver. Max got kind of mad about Damon ushing me and taught him a lesson in the parking lot of the ar, which, unfortunately, seeing as it was the parking lot of a ar, most of the town saw the whole thing. Damon didn't like hat, so he spray-painted my car and did other stuff to it too. And then, yesterday, he tracked me down and overpowered me vhen I was coming into my cabin after dinner. Luckily Max howed up a little while later and took me to the hospital." I ook in a deep breath and finished, "Nothing to worry about, hough. Max is here now and I'm okay."

Norm and Gladys both stared at me but Max's arm hooked round my chest from behind and he pulled me back into his ody. His body, by the way, which was shaking slightly so I new, even though it wasn't audible, he was laughing.

I ignored this when Norm noted, "Either that's the best tory ever made up or what you say is true."

"I wish it was a story but, unfortunately, it's true," I confirmed.

"Though, Norm, good to know, I didn't show last night, ou and your cane would have Nina's back," Max added, and I lbowed him in the ribs. His body twitched but that was mostly it.

"So, you're her boyfriend, where were you yesterday when Nina was tied up in knots?" Norm asked cantankerously.

"Norm!" Gladys gasped again, then looked at me. "Nina, I'm so sorry."

Norm's eyes stayed glued on Max. "Got two daughters, our granddaughters, and one great-granddaughter, son. I've

had my fair share of experience with pretty boys like you, s
you best be answering my question."

Gladys sighed. I pressed my lips together in order not t
laugh at Norm calling Max a "pretty boy."

Max, however, spoke. "We had a fallin'-out. Nina's pron
to gettin' wild hairs and she took off. I found her a coupl
hours too late. So, yeah, Norm, that's on me."

I stopped pressing my lips together, suddenly completel
unamused, and I turned in his arm.

"What Damon did to me isn't on you," I declared.

"I wasn't talkin' about Damon, Duchess. I was talkin
about you bein' tied up in knots, but now that you mention i
he's Damon. He spray-painted your car. I knew he wasn't don
with you, and yesterday, from the minute you left home to th
minute I walked in this cabin, you were unprotected. So, yeah
that's on me too."

"It is not."

"Babe, it is."

"It isn't!"

Max's hassled eyes went over my head and I knew he wa
looking at Norm when he stated, "She's up five minutes an
we're fightin'. Our first date, she fought about how German
invented beer."

"I did not!" I cried.

Max's eyes came to me. "Babe, you did."

I turned again in his arm, looked at Gladys, and announced
"He has the memory of an elephant, which you would *think* i
good for, say, anniversaries and birthdays and such, but day t
day?" I shook my head and concluded, "It's very, *very* bad."

Max's arm at my chest gave me a squeeze and my nec
twisted so I could look at him when he spoke.

"You didn't think that when I gave you that ring, inciden
tally a ring you haven't taken off. You said it was thoughtfu
and the best gift anyone's ever given you."

My gaze swung back to Gladys and, harassed, I declared
"See? He remembers *everything*."

I realized then that both Gladys and Norm were smiling at about the time I realized that Max and I were acting like lunatics.

"I don't think she's tied up in knots anymore, Gladie," Norm observed.

"She is, dear, just not ones she wants to untie," Gladys remarked.

"I should make breakfast," I mumbled, mortified, and to my further mortification when I tried to break free of Max's hold, it just got tighter and then I felt his lips kiss my neck.

"Why don't we make it lunch?" Gladys suggested, her eyes sparkling. She'd caught the neck kiss but then again, it would be hard to miss.

"No, I can make breakfast," I told her quickly.

"Lunch," Norm said firmly, reaching a hand out to Gladys and making a move to the door.

"We can't do lunch. Nina has to go to the police station to press charges against Damon," Max shared.

"Brunch, then. We'll be back at ten," Norm put in.

"Works for me," Max stated.

"Max!" I hissed on another twist of my neck to look up at him.

"Ten," Gladys affirmed. "See you then, dear."

And the door closed behind them. Max let me go to walk to it; he locked it and then turned back to me.

When he did, I asked, "How bad is my face?"

"Worse than when he backhanded you, better than expected since he connected three times."

Max said this while stalking toward me. Yes, stalking. Therefore, I didn't hear his words because instinctively I was retreating.

"What are you doing?" I asked as he kept coming at me.

"Veer right, baby," he directed, and I looked over my right shoulder to see the door to the bedroom.

Then I looked back, noting my mistake immediately, for he'd gained significantly and was right on top of me. His hands came to my hips and he veered us right.

"Max," I whispered.

"I know you're banged up, honey, so this mornin' all you gotta do is lay back and I'll eat you for breakfast before we have brunch."

My stomach dipped and my hands fluttered to his chest.

"Max," I repeated, but it was breathy this time. "I'm really tired. I was thinking of getting in an hour of sleep before they come back."

We were well into the bedroom and I knew this because my legs hit the bed. I went down and Max came down on top of me on my healthy side. Then his hand slid into my hair at the side of my head and his mouth came to mine.

"You sleep while I go down on you, Duchess, it's gonna piss me off."

I felt a quiver between my legs that radiated outward and I felt my lips quiver too.

"I'll try to stay awake," I promised him.

His mouth left mine but not before I felt it smile. It slid down my jaw then to my neck.

At my ear, he ordered, "Shimmy out of your pants, baby."

"Okay," I whispered, and pulled the drawstring of my pajamas as his tongue touched my earlobe, then the back of my ear before it slid down and out to the strap of my camisole on my shoulder.

I shimmied out of my pajamas and undies and I barely tossed them aside before his hand was between my legs.

"Wet," he muttered into my neck. His head came up as his fingers slid around. I saw his eyes had grown hungry and the sight made me wetter. He felt it and his mouth came to mine before he growled, "*Fuck*. I missed this, baby."

It had only been two days. It felt like two hundred years.

"Me too."

His finger slid inside and a moan slid out of my throat.

"Kiss me, Duchess," he demanded, and I gave him what he wanted as he finger-fucked me, his thumb pressing at my sweet spot as his tongue invaded my mouth.

He broke the kiss and muttered against my lips, "You're ready." Max used his hands at my waist to yank me farther up the bed. "Now I want you to open your legs for me, honey."

I opened my legs for him and he slid down and rolled between them.

Then his mouth hit me and he had me for breakfast and, at least for me, it was unbelievably *delicious*.

*   *   *

"Duchess," I heard Max call, and I blinked, then blinked again and dazedly looked around to see we were parked in front of the Gnaw Bone police station.

I lifted a hand to pull my hair out of my face, then dropped it and turned to the door to see Max standing in it.

"Did I fall asleep?" I asked stupidly.

Max leaned his torso into the cab and undid my seat belt, muttering, "Out like a light."

"Mmm," I mumbled.

"This'll be all over town next. Jeff gets Nina Zombie swearing out her statement against Damon." Max was still muttering but also grinning as he straightened and then slid an arm along my back and helped me hop down from the Cherokee.

After Max had "breakfast," we had a shower and I got ready. Then we had brunch with Norm and Gladys and after, we exchanged contact information and fond farewells. Then Max and I packed up the groceries, loaded the Jeep, checked out of the cabin, and Max followed me as we went back to the rental car agency.

The rental car agency, Max explained as we were packing up, was the downfall of my heartbroken getaway, considering, when Max got home, found my note, and saw all my stuff gone, he wasn't too happy and decided he was going to do something about it pretty much at once. Then again, he didn't get home until well after lunch—it took him that long to cool down—so I had a head start.

Deciding I had to get a taxi, Max called Arlene. Then Arlene called Bill, who was the person at Thrifty's who sent the taxi, and told him to tell her who my taxi driver was. Then Arlene called Alan, my taxi driver. Alan told Arlene, who told Max that Alan took me to the rental car agency, so Max called the agency. Since by then the rental car agency employees had changed shifts, Max made more calls and he found out that George knew the man who owned the rental car agency. George called him, that guy called his employee at home, and his employee told him where I was staying, the crux of my downfall. He told George. George told Max, thus Max found me.

The joys of small-town living.

When Max arrived at the cabin, he'd been pounding at the door because, as he put it, "Babe, seriously, you sleep like the dead," and eventually thinking he wasn't going to wake me with his pounding, he had to open the door with a credit card.

Yes, a credit card.

Those cabins were very pretty and they'd done a good job renovating but they definitely needed new locks. And, perhaps, better outdoor lighting.

After we packed up the Jeep, we turned in my rental. Then I climbed into the Cherokee and evidently fell fast asleep.

I had not been in favor of the turning in the rental car business. I thought it might be good for me to have a car so Max didn't have to drive me around everywhere. Max thought, since he wasn't working, there was pretty much no reason he couldn't take me where I wanted to go and, incidentally, be with me while I was there. Therefore, Max talked me into returning the car. Or, I should say, Max ordered me to do it and after we argued for ten minutes, I was too tired to keep arguing so I gave in.

Luckily, he did. It wouldn't do for me to fall asleep at the wheel. Though, I was *not* going to share that with Max.

Max still had his arm around me and he shuffled me to the side. He slammed the door to the Jeep and shuffled me back, stepped in until my back was at the Cherokee, and Max was pressed up against my front.

I tipped my head back to look at him, still partly asleep.

"Lucky you turned in that car, babe, or it'd be another call to Triple A to pull it out of the ditch, you fell asleep at the wheel."

God, Max was *so* annoying.

"You know, I think you're onto something," I told him. "A good way to get rid of Nina Zombie is to be *annoying*. And, seeing as you're that way a lot, it's too bad you like Nina Zombie because in future her appearances will likely be very rare."

He grinned. "You only think I'm annoying when I'm right."

"Yes," I agreed. "Take, for instance, *now*."

He burst out laughing but as he did this his hand hooked around the back of my neck, he pulled me up to my toes, and his mouth came down on mine.

I'd never had someone kiss me while they laughed. It was an experience.

A good one.

I'd also never had anyone kiss me (or do other things to me for that matter) when I had a black eye and a bruised cheekbone, not that I had them very often, just both the times my ex Brent had hurt me. When I saw my face in the mirror that morning, I found Max was right. It wasn't as bad as it could have been but it was definitely worse than before. And not exactly attractive. Though that didn't faze Max, not in the slightest.

After I'd melted into him, my forearms under his coat resting parallel along his spine, my hands flat on his muscled back, his lips released mine but he didn't move away.

He dropped his forehead so it was resting on mine and I saw his eyes were serious when he said quietly, "When you were sick, saw your plane tickets, honey."

"Yes?"

"You leave Saturday."

I felt my body lock as I pulled in a soft breath to fight the sharp, twisting pain in my stomach.

He was right. So much had been going on I hadn't even

thought of that. Unless I was telling myself I had to leave, I hadn't thought of actually *leaving*. In fact, in a weird way it felt strange thinking I had to leave. Not only did it feel like I'd been in Gnaw Bone a lifetime, England felt a million miles away.

And leaving meant leaving everything, everyone, the A-frame, The Mark, The Dog, Mindy, Becca, Bitsy, Arlene, Cotton, and, most of all, Max.

My flight left in, essentially, two days. And even though it felt like I'd been in Gnaw Bone a lifetime, I knew those two days would feel like two seconds.

And after that, what? The idea of a move and all that involved pressed down on me, especially since I had to do it without Max and I had no idea when I'd see him again.

What if, in my absence, he figured out I wasn't so cute?

My arms tightened against his back and feeling the pressure of all this weighing down on me like an anvil, I whispered, "Max."

"Any chance your work'll give you another week?"

Another week? Could it be that easy?

My eyes drifted to the side and that twisting pain subsided.

Yes, it could be that easy.

Then my eyes drifted back, I smiled, and pressed deeper into him when I said, "Yes. I've got loads of holiday. I'll call my assistant, get her to shift some things around. Then I'll call David—he's a partner and my boss. He'll be okay with it. He likes me."

Max's head went up slightly but his brows drew together sharply.

"He likes you?"

"Yes."

"How much?"

I was still smiling when I said, "A lot, seeing as I'm a good employee. His gay partner also likes me. No, his partner, Nigel, actually *adores* me but not because I'm a good employee—because I make fantastic martinis or at least that's what Nigel says. They like me so much, they've asked me to be godmother to their new Russian orphan baby."

Max's brows had unknit and his body was pressing me deeper into the truck when he smiled back and asked, "Did you say yes?"

"Of course. She's adorable and godmother duties include buying her ridiculously frilly dresses throughout childhood and then repeatedly explaining that men are idiots through her teen years. Then she's honor bound to come visit me at the nursing home when I'm old and gray."

One of his arms came from around me so he could cup my jaw in his hand and he was still smiling but his eyes were soft when he said, "Only you."

"Sorry?"

"Only you," he repeated.

"Only me what?"

"Only you would have some senior citizen swipin' at me with his cane. You knew him a day, he knew I could break him in two, and still he thought I laid a hand on you and he came at me. And only you would have a Russian orphan goddaughter you buy frilly dresses."

"It's a godmother duty," I reminded him.

His hand at my jaw tightened and he whispered, "It's Nina."

The way he said those two words made tears flood my eyes and my throat feel thick.

Okay, so again, Max had proved my fears moot. He wasn't going to figure out I wasn't cute because the fact of the matter was, he thought I *was* cute. And apparently there was no shaking that.

"Max," I warned, my voice sounding as thick as my throat felt. "You're being nice."

"Yeah," he agreed, then tipped my face up, touched his lips to mine, and when he was done he pulled back a bit, dropped his hand to curl around my neck, and changed the subject. "How would you feel if I was on that plane with you?"

I liked the lip touch and the heavy warmth of his hand at my neck and the fact that he was nice so much I was focused on those things and I wasn't following.

"Sorry?"

"Could talk to Bitsy. Trev can keep things goin' for a while. I could go with you, see Charlie's house, stay in England a couple of weeks."

"Are you serious?" I breathed, my eyes wide.

He looked at my face a second, then burst out laughing.

When he was done laughing but he was still smiling, he instructed, "Don't bother answerin' the question, babe."

"Okay," I whispered, too overcome with happiness that this meant another week with him in his A-frame and two more with *him* in *Charlie's* house.

I could show him pictures of Charlie!

"For once, I don't know what you're thinking," he broke into my thoughts, his smile now a grin, "except it's good."

"I'm thinking, if you come to England, I can show you pictures of Charlie," I shared happily, and watched with no small amount of fascination as his face got soft but his eyes grew warm.

"I'd like that," he muttered.

"Nina!" Niles's voice snapped from my left.

My head twisted to the side and Max's hand moved from my neck as I stared in shock at Niles in tan, large whale corduroys, a navy pea coat with a navy turtleneck showing out of the collar, standing on the wooded sidewalk facing Max and me, his tan-leather-glove-covered hands on the wooden railing. He was wearing this getup even though the weather had again turned and it had to be at least sixty degrees Fahrenheit.

The minute I looked at him, his face paled and his eyes grew huge.

Then, his voice almost shrill, he asked, "What happened to your face?"

"What are you still doing here?" I asked back.

"What happened to your face?" he shouted. His eyes went

traight to Max and he demanded to know, "Did *you* do that to her?"

"I'm gettin' tired of that shit," Max murmured as his body got tight in my arms.

"No!" I answered Niles sharply, giving Max a squeeze. "I have a mountain man gone bad stalker."

"A what?" Niles asked.

"It doesn't matter," I told him, reluctantly dropping one arm from Max and turning to face Niles. When I did, Max turned, too, his arm going around my shoulders and my other arm dropped to his waist, my thumb hooking in his side belt loop as I went on. "I asked, what are you still doing here?"

"I called you four times yesterday," Niles told me, not answering my question.

"And?"

"You didn't take any of my calls."

"And?"

"I'd like to speak to you," Niles clipped.

"Niles, honestly, I think we've said all there is to say," I pointed out the obvious.

Niles's face went hard and he informed me, "And I think the least you could do is allow me a moment to speak to you"—his eyes went to Max—"privately."

Unfortunately at this point, seeing as Niles had interrupted a nice moment between Max and me, and he was being kind of a jerk, I was starting to see red.

"The least I could do?" I asked irately.

"Duchess," Max muttered at my side.

"The least you could do," Niles affirmed.

"You've had two years of me talking with you privately and you never listened," I reminded him.

"But—" Niles started.

I was moving forward, taking Max with me, heading to the two-step opening at the railing by the police station just down from Niles. I wasn't going to get into this with him, not now, not ever. It wasn't worth it. *He* wasn't worth it.

Therefore, as I headed that way, I told Niles, "I need to go press charges."

"Against who?" Niles asked.

I stopped, glared at him, and answered impatiently, "Who else? Against my mountain man gone bad stalker!"

"Nina! Max!" I heard someone shout, and looked to the left to see Linda bearing down on our party. She got a good look at me, came to a juddering halt, and kept shouting, "Oh my *God*! What on earth happened to you?"

"Damon," Max answered without hesitation, and my head snapped back to look at him.

"Max!" I hissed.

"Everyone's gonna know," Max told me.

"They will now," I mumbled.

"*Damon*!" Linda yelled very loudly, proving my mumbled point.

"I'm fine," I told Linda.

"Nina, that word I'd like to have privately...," Niles butted in.

"Babe, seriously, get rid of him." Max's voice was getting a little scary.

"Niles, go home," I said to Niles.

"You don't look fine," Linda said to me, ignoring Niles.

"I am," I promised her. "Really, it just feels a little bit tight."

"That Damon Matthews," Linda spat. "You know, take one letter out of his name and it spells '*damn*' as in '*damn*, that kid's a worthless sonovabitch.'"

"Nina! Max! Hey!" I heard and looked to the right to see Becca approaching. Then she caught sight of me and skidded to a halt two feet from Niles. "Whoa! What happened to your face?"

"Fuck me," Max muttered.

"Damon," I told her, talking over Max cursing.

"That *dick*!" Becca screeched.

"Nina! For God's sake!" Niles bellowed, and I looked at him.

"Niles! Go! *Away!*" I shouted at him.

Becca's torso reared back, her eyes got wide, and they were on Niles.

"Dude," she said low. "*You're* Niles?"

Niles just scowled at her, so she looked at me.

"Seriously, Neens, Max is *way* better," Becca informed me. "Not only is he hotter, he's taller, has great hair, that awesome rough voice, and he dresses nearly as hot as he just plain is."

Becca was not wrong about that. Any of it. Therefore I had no response.

"Who's Niles?" Linda asked Becca, finally examining Niles.

"I'm Nina's fiancé," Niles answered Linda, now scowling more irately at Becca.

"Ex!" I shouted.

"Jesus, enough!" Max cut in on a sharp, impatient bark, and looked at Niles. "Man, it's over. Deal with it but deal with it somewhere else." He looked at his mother. "Mom, we gotta go in so Nina can swear out a statement. I'll call you later." He looked at Becca. "Babe, Nina'll call you, yeah?"

"Cool," Becca said on a grin.

"Is it pasta bake tonight?" Linda asked.

"No," Max answered instantly.

"When am I gonna get pasta bake?" Linda pushed.

"I don't know, Mom," Max replied, and I could tell he was losing it.

"Saturday," I told her quickly. "That's my parents' last day here. We'll have a little party."

"Duchess," Max said to me, sounding exasperated. "When I'm in England, we gotta get your shit sorted so you can move here and people'll get used to having you around so maybe they'll back the fuck off so I can spend some fuckin' time with you."

"You're moving here?" Niles asked on a loud, horrified whisper.

"Yes, Niles," I answered him.

"But you said you'd never leave Charlie's house."

Now he was hearing what I said a million times over the last year.

"I'm not leaving Charlie's house. Max and I are going to…" I stopped speaking as it hit me. I looked at Max and whispered, "We can't do that anymore, can we?"

Max's arm at my shoulders gave me a squeeze. "We'll talk about it later."

I ignored him, remembering what he'd told me the morning before about taking the job in town and how wonderful it was that he'd make that sacrifice for me, taking over Curt's business, but how he couldn't do it, seeing as it was Curt's business and Curt was a jerk, so I announced, "And you can't take that job."

"Babe, we'll talk about it later."

"What job?" Linda asked.

"*Fuck*," Max clipped.

"Nothing, nothing," I said quickly to Linda. "We need to go in."

"What job?" Linda repeated.

"Mom, *later*," Max bit out.

Linda's hands came up. "All right, all right. Yeesh. Later." Then she looked around Niles to Becca and asked, "Do you wanna get a coffee? I'm meeting Barb and Mindy at the café."

"Awesome," Becca answered.

"Mindy?" I asked.

"Yeah," Linda said to me, then invited, "When you guys finish, you can join us."

I smiled at her and said, "That would be lovely."

"Someone kill me," Max muttered. I looked up at him to see he was looking up at the blue, cloudless sky.

"Darling," I called, putting my free hand to his stomach. "We need to go into the station and get this done so I can see Mins and get a coffee."

Max's head tilted down and his frustrated gray eyes locked on mine. "Babe, just gonna say, you're lucky you're so damned cute."

That was when I curled my body into his, got up on my toes, pressed close, and smiled at him before I said softly, "I now."

And I did know. At that moment, with Max looking irritated but still amazingly handsome and I was tucked firm in the curve of his arm, I knew.

I knew I was possibly the luckiest woman in the world.

And Max proved me correct when his eyes moved over my face, his expression cleared, his face warmed, and his mouth came down on mine.

* * *

We were sitting in the little room that Mick had questioned Kami in, Max at my side, his chair pushed slightly back but close to mine, his arm draped around the back of my chair, his legs stretched out in front of him, feet crossed at the ankles.

This seemed like a pose of masculine relaxation but it wasn't.

I knew this when he clipped, "What's takin' so fuckin' long?"

I looked up from returning the texts my friends had been sending.

Before texting, I'd found that yesterday Niles *had* called four times, Mom three, and I had five calls from three numbers I didn't know. After interrogating Max, I found that one call was from his home phone (so I programmed it in), three from his mobile (so I programmed that in too), and the last one was from Arlene (which I also programmed in). Mom had given Max my number. Max had given it to Arlene and her message was mostly about how next time we were at The Dog I couldn't leave without saying good-bye and partly about her asking when I was making another fish casserole without any mention at all about my heartbroken getaway, which, I suspected, she knew would be foiled.

"They *are* investigating a murder, darling," I attempted to soothe the wakening beast.

His irritated eyes sliced from their impatient examination
of the door to me and I decided just to let the beast wake and
take my chances.

Thankfully at that point the door opened and Jeff walked
in carrying papers and a pen.

"Fuck, sorry, I mean, um..." He looked at me and repeated,
"Sorry."

"Max curses all the time, Jeff. You don't have to apologize
for saying the f-word," I assured him, smiling.

He smiled back, headed to the chair opposite us, dumped
his papers, and sat down.

"Shit, Jeff, we been here twenty minutes," Max put in,
proving me right about the swearing.

"Yeah, I know, things are crazy." He looked at Max, then
looked at me. "Sorry to say, Nina, we can't find Damon."

This wasn't exactly good news.

Max straightened in his chair and glared at Jeff. "Jesus,
we're talkin' Matthews here. He ain't the brightest bulb."

Jeff nodded. "I know but he's proving elusive. We been
lookin' for him since the spray-paint incident, talkin' to folks
all over town. His boss says he hasn't been to work since you
and he had your thing and he wants him to come back real
bad, mostly so he can fire his ass."

That wasn't good news for Damon but I couldn't find it in
me to care since maybe it would mean he'd be forced to move
away from Gnaw Bone, his self-appointed stalker duties, and
Mindy.

Jeff kept talking. "And none of his friends admit to knowin'
where he is. His old landlord said he caught him last Friday
tryin' to put a bolt cutter to the lock on one of the storage units
he's got. The old guy aimed some buckshot at him, chased him
off, didn't know we were lookin' for him. Other than that, we
got nothin'. Matthews is in the wind."

"He doesn't even know how to *spell* 'wind'; he can't be in
it," Max bit out, and I pressed my lips together to stop from
laughing.

"We'll find him," Jeff promised. "But we're low on resources, seein' as we got every man we can spare here, at the county sheriff's, and even the frickin' highway patrol tryin' to ack down Shauna and that Robert Winston guy."

Both Max and I stiffened but it was me who spoke. Really?"

"Yeah," Jeff answered, distracted and sorting through the papers he'd put on the table. "She's vanished. *Gone*." He ooked up at me and said, "We got a warrant to search her ouse. Nothin' there, no furniture, no clothes, nada. Totally lean. Last person to see her was Kami, and Mick said we an't talk to Kami, 'less we talk to you, so, by the way, Mick ays I need to set that up while you're here."

"Of course," I told him.

"Anyway," he went on, all business, "right now I'll take our statement, get Jane to type it out, and then you can read , make sure we got everything down right, then you can sign . Cool?"

I smiled again and said, "Cool."

"Then you can call Kami and we'll set something up," he nished, and I got an idea.

"Sure," I replied, then invited, "Maybe, while Jane is typ-ng out my statement and we're calling Kami, you can come nd have a cup of coffee with us."

"Babe," Max said low, reading my intent.

"Thanks but we're hammered. It's all hands on deck," Jeff nswered.

"Yes, of course," I agreed, then pressed, "But everyone eeds a break and the coffee at the café is better than station offee. I know, I've sampled them both. Anyway, it'll be my reat."

"Babe," Max repeated, still low.

"Really appreciate that, Nina, but, like I say, we're ham-nered," Jeff said politely.

It was time to dangle my golden carrot, so I did. "We're neeting Linda and Barb and Mindy will be there."

Max sighed. Jeff stopped looking hurried and distracte
and focused fully on me.

Then he said firmly, "Tell her I said hi."

I blinked and Max got tense at my side.

"Okay, let's start at the beginning," Jeff instructed, lookin
down at the papers and picking up the pen.

"Tell her you said hi?" Max asked, his voice even more of
gravelly rumble than usual, and his tone made me look at hi
to see he was staring intently at Jeff.

I looked back at Jeff and his head was up, his eyes o
Max.

"Yeah, hi," Jeff answered.

"That's it?" Max asked, beginning for some reason t
sound angry.

"Max," I whispered, putting a hand to his thigh.

"That's it," Jeff affirmed.

I felt Max go even more tense. I felt this both physically a
well as his tenseness shimmering in the very air.

Definitely sounding angry now, Max asked, "Coupla day
ago, you couldn't keep your eyes off her ass. Now all you go
to say is hi?"

My hand gave his thigh a squeeze and I again whispered
"Max," but this time I did it more urgently.

"Yeah, Max, now all I got to say is hi," Jeff stated, and
looked to him because now *he* sounded angry and when m
eyes hit his face, I noted he looked it too.

"Gents—" I started, but Max spoke over me.

"So you're happy to check out her ass until you find ou
she's dealin' with some serious shit; then you're not intereste
anymore?" Max inquired, his eyes narrow.

"No," Jeff bit off.

"Sounds like it to me," Max told him.

"Yeah, then I guess you don't know that I been by Barb an
Darren's every day since that scene at the river," Jeff returned
"And Mindy's made it clear she don't wanna see me and I fig
ured that out since each time I went she said she don't wann

ee me but she didn't say it to me—she told her mom to say it o me and Mindy didn't fuckin' see me."

"So?" Max asked, and Jeff's brows drew together.

"So, she don't wanna see me, that's it. I can take a hint."

"You like her?" Max asked straight out.

"Max!" I hissed, but Jeff answered.

"Not your concern."

"You like Mindy, it's my concern," Max countered.

"Better answer, it doesn't matter," Jeff retorted.

"Do you like her?" Max repeated.

"Max, please—" I began, but Jeff didn't answer and Max eaned forward, taking his arm from my chair.

"Jeff, man, I'm askin' you a question."

"She's the prettiest girl in town," Jeff clipped, obviously ot wanting to share but doing it anyway, probably knowing Max enough to know he wouldn't let it go. A lesson I, too, had earned and I'd known him a lot less time than Jeff. "She's also he sweetest by a long shot. So, yeah, I guess you could say I ke her."

My stomach melted and I stared at Jeff, seeing his anger t Max was covering a much deeper emotion. He didn't like Mindy. He *liked* her. And I liked that.

"Come with us to get coffee," Max ordered, obviously liking it too.

"I'm tellin' you, Max, don't have time," Jeff replied.

"Then get it to go."

"Max—" Jeff started, but Max leaned farther in and cut im off.

"A few days ago Nina told me, when a woman gets fucked ver by a dickhead, or a bunch of dickheads, she needs to learn here are good guys out there. You're a good guy and you like er. She's got serious shit to deal with now. She needs all the elp she can get, *especially* from good guys who like her." A uscle jumped in Jeff's jaw but he stayed silent, so Max fin-shed, "Nothin' worth havin', it ain't worth fightin' for even the thing you gotta fight is the thing you want. She don't

wanna see you right now because she's embarrassed, think
you think less of her because of what you saw and, I'm gues
sin', the guys she's picked in the past. Maybe she thinks she'
not worthy. You want her, man, your job is to convince he
she's wrong."

I'd stopped breathing and was staring at Max's profile as h
spoke to Jeff.

Every word he said about Mindy slid through me like a
invisible blade shrouded in velvet, cutting me to the quick bu
doing it in a way that felt like he was surgically removing
malignant tumor that I'd been carrying around for years. A
tumor that had been eating away at my insides. A tumor tha
with his words, suddenly was gone.

You love him, Charlie said in my head.

Yes, I replied to Charlie, scared at this sudden knowledge
but along with that fear, far stronger, I also felt joy.

There was no response from Charlie.

Do you think I'm crazy? I asked my dead brother.

Sweetheart, Charlie answered, *not anymore.*

"I'll come with," Jeff said, and I forced my mind off my
brief conversation with Charlie and my eyes away from Max
to Jeff as he finished, "Get it to go."

Max didn't reply, just nodded and sat back in his chair
and I leaned sideways until my shoulder hit his chest. His arm
went over my head to curl around me, my head dropped to hi
shoulder, and I gave his thigh another squeeze of my hand.

Then Jeff brought the matter back to hand, and looking a
me and lifting his pen to the paper, he stated, "All right, let'
get this done."

*　　*　　*

Seeing as it was sunny and warm, the snow again melting
Max and I, with Jeff trailing, walked through the café out t
the back seating area and Linda saw us immediately.

She indicated us to Barb, Becca, and Mindy with a nod o
her head and all of them twisted in their chairs to look at us

rb's and Mindy's eyes got wide when they saw my face but
ither of them said a word when Max and I hit the table. I
spected this was because Linda and/or Becca had already
ld them about Damon and I hoped they'd done it sensitively
r Mindy's sake.

"Hey again," Becca said to us, and I smiled at her and
oked between Mindy and Barb.

"Hi, Mindy, Barb," I greeted.

"Hi, guys," Barb greeted back.

"Hey, Neens," Mindy started; then her eyes slid sideways,
e caught sight of Jeff, pink hit her cheeks, and she bit her lip
fore saying, "Max."

Then she dropped her chin to look at her lap, ignoring Jeff
mpletely. I looked at Barb, who was studying her daughter
d also biting her lip.

"Mindy." Jeff rounded her chair and looked down at her.

"Jeff," she said quietly to her lap.

Jeff looked at me and requested, "Could you order me a
-go Americano?"

"Sure," I replied.

Jeff looked back at Mindy. "Can I have a word?"

There was silence for several moments before Max stated
ftly, "Mins, babe, Jeff's talkin' to you."

Mindy glanced at Max and then her head swung to Jeff.
e looked down and told the table as she started to rise, "I
ink I gotta—"

Jeff cut her off by grabbing her hand and pulling her fully
her feet. Her head jerked to look at him and he said, "Five
inutes."

"But—" Mindy began, and didn't finish.

Jeff pulled her chair from behind her and walked toward
e river, his hand firm in Mindy's, dragging her behind him.

I watched as he took her to the stairs that led off the back
ating porch and they walked down a cleared footpath until
stopped them out of earshot and close to the river.

"What's that all about?" Barb asked, her eyes on the couple

by the river as Max pulled a chair from an empty table an
flipped it around behind me.

I sat in it, throwing a smile over my shoulder at Max, an
answered, "Jeff just needs to get a few things straight wit
Mindy."

Max sat beside me as Barb, her gaze still on Jeff an
Mindy, her expression uncertain, went on. "He's come aroun
every day but I don't...is that..." She looked at me. "Do yo
think that's a good idea?"

I looked from Barb to Mindy and Jeff and I watched them
Jeff was standing close and doing all the talking. Mindy ha
her head tipped back, holding her body stiff, and she looke
scared as a jackrabbit.

"Um...," I started to mumble my answer, then watche
Mindy's head shake. Jeff got closer. Mindy prepared to retrea
and Jeff's hand came up to the side of her neck, halting he
retreat and his face dipped close to hers. He was mostly in pr
file but I could see he was still doing the talking. Mindy stoo
frozen, staring up at him; then suddenly her eyes closed an
her head bent. This placed Jeff's lips close to her forehead, bu
instead of moving back, he leaned in and kept talking.

I knew what it felt like when a mountain man did that and
hoped Mindy felt it too.

Then I watched Mindy's hand come up to curl around hi
wrist at her neck. At first I thought it was to pull away but the
I saw it was to hold on and I knew she felt it, the same as me.

When she touched him, Jeff stopped talking, his hand
her neck slid into the back of her hair, and he tipped her hea
down farther in order to kiss the top of it. When he pulle
away and allowed Mindy to look at him again, she was no lor
ger stiff, her face no longer scared. It was unsure but it wa
also soft and she'd leaned into him, just a bit but enough to te
the tale.

My stomach melted again and I turned to Barb and fir
ished my answer.

"Yes."

Barb's eyes caught mine and her smile was tremulous but it as a smile all the same.

When I looked away, I caught Becca's eyes and her smile asn't tremulous. It was wide and shining.

"Kami?" I heard Max say, and looked at him to see he had s mobile to his ear and his eyes on the couple by the river. We just got back from the police station. Jeff says they need talk to you again." He looked from the river to me. He gave e a Wonder Max wink and a small grin and kept talking. Nina's with me and she'll be with you when you talk to Mick. isn't a big deal, nothin' to worry about, but they need you to rop in and talk about the last time you saw Shauna. Can you wing by for a break or do you have to do it after work?"

"Why do they have to talk to Kami?" Linda asked me.

"Right, yeah, I'll tell Jeff. Later," Max said into the phone, nd flipped it shut.

"Max is right. It isn't a big deal," I answered Linda. "They an't find Shauna and Kami's the last person to see her."

"Damn tootin' they can't find her!" I heard from behind ne, and turned to see Arlene bearing down on us. "Get this!" he announced when she had everyone's attention, her arm naking out to snag a chair from a table with two people sitting t it. She did this without asking them if it was okay, which nade them look at her with a mix of shock and irritation even hough they weren't using it. Then she announced grandly, 'Shauna Fontaine has disappeared and they got an APB out on her." Her eyes rounded in the middle of making a circle of the table to gauge our reactions. They caught on me and she yelled, "Holy *shit*! What happened to your face?"

"Damon," Max, Linda, Becca, *and* Barb answered in unison and without hesitation.

"What?" Arlene asked.

"Last night, Damon got retribution," Max told her, and Arlene's eyes narrowed.

"Where were you?" Arlene returned.

"Not with Nina." Max's answer wasn't evasive. It was a

firm indication of where he wasn't and that the reason why I
wasn't with me was none of Arlene's business.

"Right," Arlene muttered, then noted, "Must be why th
call went out on him on the police band late last night."

"Yeah, Arlene, that'd be why," Max confirmed, and h
eyes came to mine. I gave him a placating grin; he shoo
his head and didn't appear very placated but instead mild
irritated.

Suddenly Arlene's neck twisted and she shouted across th
porch, "Fran, get me a cappuccino, heavy on the sprinkles!"

"Gotcha!" Fran, a waitress standing at a table several fe
away, shouted back and Arlene's head swung back to us a
her eyes took in the table.

Then they took in me and Max. "What's your problem
You ain't drinkin'?"

"We just arrived," I told her.

"Whatcha want?" she asked.

I answered for myself and Jeff, Max placed his order wit
Arlene, and Arlene twisted her neck and shouted again.

"Fran, Nina needs a skinny latte. Max wants an Amer
cano, black. And Jeff needs a to-go Americano, cream and or
sugar. Got that?"

"Yeah, up in a minute," Fran shouted, and turned to th
table that had twice been interrupted in placing their ow
orders.

Arlene plopped into her chair as Mindy and Jeff came bac
to the table, still, I noted with a warm feeling in my middl
holding hands.

"Yo, Mins," Arlene greeted, her eyes moving to the cou
ple's hands but fortunately, her mouth remaining shut.

"Hey, Arlene," Mindy replied.

"Jeff, what's shakin'?" Arlene asked.

"Everything," Jeff answered, releasing Mindy so she coul
sit down and his torso twisted, he glanced at a table besid
ours, put his hand on the back of a chair, gave them a chin til
and at their nod he rounded the chair to our table.

We all pushed our chairs out a bit as our group got wider we could fit everyone in and Jeff sat, his chair very close to indy's.

"So, Shauna Fontaine is suspect numero uno," Arlene said Jeff, and Jeff's eyes cut to her.

"Pardon?" he asked, playing dumb.

"Boy, you got an APB out on her," Arlene informed him of mething he obviously already knew.

"Arlene, can't discuss the specifics of the case," Jeff told r, and Arlene gave him a look but turned back to the table, claring, "Well, I can."

Jeff's eyes went to Max and both men sighed simultane- sly as Arlene launched in.

"Shauna Fontaine is gone, gone, gone. Her house has been ld, her shit's been moved out, and no one has seen her since y before yesterday," Arlene told the table.

"Her shit's been moved out?" Linda asked, her eyes wide.

"Yep, cleaned out," Arlene replied. "Cops went through it sterday."

"That's not enough for an APB," I noted, my eyes moving Jeff.

"Yeah, though she cleaned all the shit outta her house, n't mean she left the house clean. That dead PI guy was ne on one a' Curtis's construction sites in the bedroom of new, unfinished build. They were drywallin'. Cops found ywall residue inside Shauna's house, leadin' a trail from her ckdoor to her bedroom."

"Oh my *God*," I breathed, and Arlene looked gleefully me.

"Shauna don't work *and* it's doubtful she drywalls as a bby, so why's she got drywall dust in her house?" Arlene ked without really expecting an answer, and I knew this cause there was no answer to give and because she kept eaking. "So, the woman's got evidence in her house, motive, d she and her boy toy disappear into thin air." Arlene inned and finished, "A...P...B."

"Boy toy?" Barb asked.

"Well, more like man toy," Arlene answered. "Name Robert Winston and Winston's gone too. Neighbors of his sa he hasn't been home in days; they haven't even seen his ca Cops got a man parked out in front of his house and have sinc yesterday. No show. He's self-employed, real estate, if you ca believe that shit. If I remember, Shauna's wrinkled, old goat an ex-husband was also in property. Girl's got a type."

I looked at Max and he was glaring at Arlene, so I agai put my hand on his thigh. His eyes came to mine and I gav his thigh a squeeze. His hard face got a bit softer but that's a my effort achieved before Arlene was talking again and Ma looked back at her.

"Cops went to Winston's office. They say he's on vacatic and has been for two weeks. His leave is extended and he not due back in a while. 'Cept, he was seen brawlin' with poo old Harry at The Rooster Saturday night, so everyone know he isn't exactly outta town." Then Arlene leaned forward an shared on a very loud whisper, "And get *this*. He's got a wif In Aspen. He's supposed to be openin' a branch of his bus ness over here, which he's kinda done but he's also definitel on"—Arlene lifted her hands and made quotation marks wit her fingers—" 'vacation.' " She dropped her hands and carrie on talking. "The wife says she's been in Aspen, closin' up the house, gettin' ready to move here. Cops in Aspen who ques tioned her said she was pretty pissed when she heard the nam Shauna Fontaine. Apparently Shauna's got a history with th Winston guy. One dates back years. The wife took his a back after the *last* round of history and now Shauna's back fo round two."

My gaze slid to Jeff to see he was staring at Arlene in di belief or, I should say, somewhat *angry* disbelief as Arlen kept sharing her story.

"This is where it gets *really* interesting. See, last tim when the wife took him back, she made him sign everythin over in her name. She owns it all. The houses, the businesse.

en the bank accounts are in her name. She's got control of
e whole enchilada."

"Oh my God," I whispered. Now I was staring at Arlene.

"How do you know all this shit?" Jeff asked.

"Everyone's talkin'," Arlene answered.

"Not cops and this is confidential information," Jeff
urned. "You aren't hearin' this stuff on the grapevine or on
ur police band, Arlene."

"I got my sources," Arlene replied.

"They local?" Jeff returned.

"Not sayin'," Arlene muttered.

"Arlene, are they local?" Jeff repeated.

"Nope," Arlene answered quickly, and Jeff stared at her.

Then he muttered, "Chantelle." His eyes went intense
d he asked, "Your niece works reception at Chantelle PD,
esn't she?"

"Uh...she might," Arlene replied.

Max grunted (whether this was an amused or knowing
unt, I had no idea). Jeff looked annoyed and the rest of us
anced at each other as Arlene carried on, her eyes on Jeff.

"Anyway, Jeff, seems to me, unless this Winston fella finds
mself a sugar mama, his wife gets pissed, which she is, she
kes it all."

It was then Mindy entered the conversation and suggested
Jeff, "Maybe a sugar mama who thought she was going to
herit some, or all, of a local big man's construction empire
cause she told him she was pregnant with his child?"

My gaze snapped to Max, who was watching Mindy. Then
s eyes turned to me.

"That's what I'm thinkin'," Arlene responded to Mindy,
d looked to Jeff. "That what the boys at the station are
inkin', Jeff?"

At this point Fran hit our table carrying a tray filled with
ffees and Jeff stood, fishing his wallet out of the back of his
ans.

"What the boys at the station are gonna be thinkin' in about

ten minutes, Arlene," Jeff said, flipping open his wallet a
pulling out some bills, "is that the shit you shared at this tab
better stay at this table or someone's niece is gonna be out
a job." Jeff threw the money on the table and took his coff
from Fran before he concluded, eyes back on Arlene, "Yeah'

I looked at Jeff's angry eyes and set face and realize
when he was being macho mountain man police officer, I
was even more attractive than normal. In fact, as Becca wou
put it, he was downright hot.

Then I looked at Mindy and saw her gazing up at him wi
an expression on her face that said she thought much the san
thing.

Arlene visibly ground her teeth at having her gossip cu
tailed and then she muttered, "Yeah."

"Right," Jeff stated. His eyes went to Mindy and his s
face changed entirely before he said softly, "See you tomorro
night."

"Okay," Mindy replied back, just as softly, the pink aga
tingeing her cheeks.

"Kami's comin' to the station from work," Max told Jet
stopping to look at his watch. "In about half an hour. Th
good?"

"Yeah," Jeff replied on a nod. "I'll tell Mick." Then Je
looked at the table at large and said, "Later," as he moved awa

I watched him go, then twisted back and leaned clea
across Max toward Mindy.

"Tomorrow night?" I asked, and watched Mindy's cheel
get even pinker.

"He asked me out," Mindy whispered, leaning into me, ar
my hand reached out and snatched hers.

"That's great!" I whispered back, but my whisper wa
excited and kind of loud.

Mindy looked at me a second and leaned in farther to as
"Do you really think so, Neens?"

I nodded effusively.

"Seriously?" she pushed.

I squeezed her hand. "Yes, sweetheart."

Mindy bit her lip, then released it and stated, "I don't ow."

"Why not?" I inquired, and she got closer, her eyes going the side to take in the table and mine did too.

Everyone, except Max, who was forced to be a silent part it due to the conversation happening pretty much in his lap, d Becca, who was watching us and grinning, was studiously oiding our exchange.

I looked back to Mindy when she asked, "I think... don't u think it's, uh... too soon?"

I leaned farther over Max and squeezed Mindy's hand ain before answering. "My lovely, you can decide to start ing your life in a month, or two, or six, or next year and at'd be perfectly all right. It's up to you." She nodded and ontinued. "But my question to you would be, why wait?" I atched her swallow and finished, "Life's short, Mins, but you ed time, you take it. Jeff will understand."

"Uh... I don't know if he will. He was kind of"—she used, searching for a word, then found it and shared, "*deter- ined* when he asked me."

I noted that the way she said this was far from an objection. y eyes slid to the side and up and I saw Max watching us, his s pressed together, and my eyes slid back to Mindy.

"I've noticed macho mountain men can be that way," I told r.

She leaned closer to me, her eyes doing a quick glance Max; then she whispered very low, "Even though I felt nny... you know, talkin' to him seein' as, you know, he was ere... but..." She hesitated and I could barely hear her when e finished, "It was kinda hot."

"I bet it was," I replied. She tipped her head to the side in estion and I went on, "Been there, sweetheart, done that."

Max started chuckling and Mindy and I both jerked back d looked at him.

"You want me to move?" he asked.

"Would you, darling?" I asked back.

Max hooked a hand around my neck, pulled my temp to his mouth, kissed it, and got up, which was obviously h answer.

I got up, too, grabbed my latte mug, and scooted Max chair back a bit before I sat in it. Mindy scooted hers ba too. Becca got up suddenly, walked around the table, and sat Jeff's vacated chair.

"What's goin' on?" she asked.

I looked from Becca to Mindy and both Becca and I lean into Mindy as I demanded, "All right, sweetheart, tell everything."

Mindy gave me a tentative look before she gave me a hes tant smile. She swung it to Becca and leaned in close, Bec leaned in close, and Mindy told us everything. And what s told us about Jeff was definitely hot. But it was also even mo definitely sweet.

After Mindy was done, Becca noted, "I'm thinkin' Je isn't a dick."

I was thinking Becca was right.

"Neens?" Mindy called, and I looked at her.

"My advice, my lovely?" She nodded and I said, "Be ho est, take care of you first, and if Jeff doesn't take care of yo along the way, then move on." Mindy nodded again but wasn't done. "Though, I figure he'll take care of you along th way."

"I figure that too," Becca put in.

Mindy bit her lip and noted, "The timing sucks."

My eyes slid to Max, who was taking a drink of his coffe and listening to Arlene jabber; then they slid back to Mind and I replied, "Trust me, sweetheart, timing isn't everything.

Mindy looked at Max, then at me and she grinned.

*   *   *

We were back at the A-frame, my stuff was in the hous the groceries unpacked, and I'd just slid into the oven m

rld-famous nachos (this wasn't strictly true; I hadn't won
competition or anything, but I called them that anyway
cause they were really good). They were smothered in kid-
y beans and hamburger meat spiced with taco seasoning
d a mixture of three cheeses (cheddar, Colby, and Monterey
ck, the latter two they didn't have in England). After the
sired cheese melting, I would load salsa, sour cream, and
esh jalapeños with tomatoes for Max, which he told me he
ved but I hated. We were now tidying up the prep dishes as
e cheese melted into the corn chips in the oven.

This was after, at the café, Max and I ordered club sand-
iches for a late lunch.

It was also after Kami came down to the station on a pro-
nged break from work to tell Mick that after she and Shauna
cided not to go to Curt's funeral, she'd driven Shauna to
ami's house. Shauna had come around to her place that
orning rather than Kami picking her up. When they went
ick, Shauna got out of Kami's car, said good-bye and that
e'd see her later like always, got into her car, and left.

Kami also explained that she hadn't been to Shauna's house
weeks. She'd done this somewhat stiltedly, which meant she
as now embarrassed that she didn't see it for the cover-up it
as. But, honestly, how would she know? No one would think
eir friend was a murderess.

Lastly, she explained she hadn't heard from Shauna even
ter she'd left several messages and a number of texts (by
en I figured about a thousand), but, in Kami's words, "If that
tch fucking calls me, you'll be the first to know."

Then we left the police station and on the wooded side-
alk Kami let rip a five-minute rant about Damon, what he
d to my face, and the incident outside The Dog two nights
eviously.

This, unfortunately, reminded Max that he'd found out
out this incident for the first time during me giving my state-
ent to Jeff and I knew he was less than happy then, but he
dn't say anything in front of Jeff. Also unfortunately, after

Kami burned out her ire, she left me with a Max who'd be reminded he hadn't been happy.

I watched her go, having seen the look in Max's eyes a thinking for the first time since I met Kami that I desired h continued presence.

Max's hand curled around the back of my neck, and it us my neck to curl me to his front. I tipped my head back to lo at him and braced.

"Forgot to tell you this, babe, with Jeff and all, and consi erin' this shit's a one-time deal, what I'm gonna say won't m ter since this isn't gonna happen to you again but"—his fa got closer—"anyone, a guy, a woman, a fuckin' *martian* tra you against a car and gets in your face and the first person y tell ain't me and you wait more than two seconds to tell me, not gonna make me happy."

I started to defend myself, saying, "Max—"

He cut me off. "No response required."

I really wanted to make a response and further I want to make a response about him telling me I couldn't make response. However, he was, as usual, annoyingly rig I should have told him. So I pressed my lips together and pressed them together tightly. Max watched me for sever long seconds before his eyes dropped to my mouth.

Then he asked, "You gonna explode?"

I unpressed my lips and answered, "Maybe."

It was at that moment Max burst out laughing and at t same time my mother called. I decided a good evasive mane ver was to answer my mobile, which I did only to have h shout on the phone at me for ten minutes about my disappea ing act. She ended her tirade telling me she and Steve were Drake's and would Max and I "grace us with your presenc (her words) for a drink.

Since we were within walking distance, Max and I m Mom and Steve at Drake's. I had to calm Mom and Ste down when they saw my face. And, shortly after, Mom and had a heated discussion about the fact that Max and I werer

ing to some fancy seafood restaurant a town over with her
d Steve that night.

"I don't have anything to wear," I'd finally snapped.

"Nina!" she'd snapped back in horrified maternal affront
Mom style). "I taught you how to pack better, surely. You
ways bring something nice. I don't care if you're staying in a
ack in the Adirondacks. You come prepared for a nice night
ut!"

"I already used my fancy outfit when Max and I went to
he Rooster," I informed her.

Mom had a ready answer, which, by the way, was also an
t-used answer to nearly all Mom's problems. "Then we'll go
opping."

"I'm tired, Mom. I got beat up last night," I reminded her.
I want a cozy night in."

She waved her hand around and stated, "Good seafood will
ke your mind off all that. You love seafood."

"Mom, we're in *Colorado*. You eat *steaks* here and buffalo
urgers and, I don't know, elk or something. You don't go to a
eafood restaurant."

"I do," Mom retorted.

I looked at Steve. Steve shrugged.

Mom caught my look at Steve and gave in but the way
he did made that Max Unhappy Shimmer fill the air. "Okay,
ou're tired, then I'll make you two dinner at Max's house."

I opened my mouth but luckily Steve, likely noting the
himmer, intervened.

"Nellie, let Nina and Max have a quiet night."

"I can do quiet," Mom replied.

Steve stared at her, brows raised, and even Mom knew she
ad no hope of making the case for being able to do quiet.

Then Mom looked at me and her face fell before she whis-
ered, "I never see you."

I sighed, leaned into her, and took her hand. "Yes, but soon
'll be a short plane ride and a two-hour car ride away, not a
ontinent and an ocean away."

Mom's face grew gentle, her eyes moved to Max, nake
gratitude filled them, and she looked back to me.

"Right, tonight you and Max get a cozy night. Tomorrow
get you." She looked back at Max and asked, "Deal?"

"Deal," Max replied in his gravelly voice.

I started to release her hand but she held on tight and gav
my hand a rough shake. "And, Nina, sweetie, you *ever* ru
away from Max again and get yourself beat up, you'll answe
to me. Is that understood?"

Apparently I hadn't calmed Mom down about my face, s
in order to do that, I used my other hand to cup her chee
leaned even closer, and promised on a whisper, "Understood.

She smiled at me and released my hand. I dropped m
other one, and we finished our drinks without any furthe
drama before Max took me up the mountain.

Which brought me to now, tidying up the prep dishes wit
Max, in his kitchen, a new drama, at least for me.

This was because, firstly, Max was helping me tidy up
Niles could, if pressed (repeatedly), fill a dishwasher bu
mostly he ignored the dishes until his cleaning lady did then
once a week. If I cooked for Niles, I did the cleanup becaus
Niles's efforts were halfhearted at best and, if I let him try,
annoyed me, so to avoid being annoyed, I just cleaned up.

Max was a natural.

Okay, so he didn't wipe down the counters. He was more
rinse and load man. But he also was capable of putting awa
food, which was a clear plus.

This drama was, secondly, because it dawned on me tha
this was my future, making dinner and tidying up with Max.

Why something this simple seemed overwhelming in
weirdly spectacular way I had no idea, but it did.

It was so spectacular, I was standing there, the sponge i
my hand after wiping down the counter and staring unseein
at Max, deep in my thoughts when he called, "Babe?"

My body jolted and I focused on him.

"What?"

"You all right?"

Yes, I was all right. I was so all right I had the desire to ng the sponge aside and throw myself at him bodily and ow him how all right I was.

I didn't do this. I just moved to him and around him to get the sink and rinsed the sponge, saying, "Yes, just tired."

Max moved in behind me, curling an arm around my mid- le and using his other hand to shift the hair off my shoulder. hen I felt his lips at my neck and his hand slid up to my ribs.

"You haven't been favorin' this, Duchess. That mean it els okay?"

His hand, I realized, was over the boot bruise. A location, also realized, he'd clearly memorized for he'd honed in on it ith pinpoint accuracy.

My stomach melted yet again and I nodded, admitting, "A vinge here and there, if I move too fast, but mostly yes, I'm kay."

"Good," he muttered against my skin, and moved away.

I sighed happily and squeezed out the sponge, putting it on e edge of the sink.

Max got out plates. I got out the nachos. I loaded up our lates and gunked the chips up with all the extras while Max ot us both a beer.

Then we took them into the living room where Max had tarted a fire. Even though it was snug, we squeezed into the hair together. I put my beer on the table and Max wedged his etween his thighs, his stocking feet resting on the ottoman, nkles crossed. I curled facing him with my feet in the seat of he chair, my calves pressed tight against his lounging hip, and ve ate with plates in hand close to our faces.

"Do you think Shauna and Robert killed Curtis and the 'I?" I asked after swallowing a big, delectable bite of loaded orn chip.

"No," Max answered, and I stared at him.

"You don't?"

He shook his head and shoved nachos in his mouth.

"Evidence is indicating it's her," I pointed out.

Max swallowed, then unwedged his beer and took a pull.

Wedging it back, his eyes came to me. "Believed it th
other day, what you said. Now, the drywall dust? That I don
believe. Someone's framin' her."

"Really?"

He lifted a chip heavy with meat, cheese, and fixings an
replied, "Really." Then he stuffed it in his mouth and afte
chewing but before swallowing, he noted, "Your nachos a
better than your fish pie."

"You think?"

"Absolutely." He swallowed and finished, "Fuckin' great."

I smiled, pleased beyond reason that he liked my nacho
It felt like he'd told me he thought I could rule the world whil
carrying on a successful career as a supermodel.

"Thanks," I muttered, suddenly feeling timid, though stil
pleased and I looked at my plate and scooped up a chip.

"Duchess," he called, and my eyes went from my chip t
him to see he was grinning at me. "Honey, you gotta know yo
can cook."

"Um...," I mumbled, and he shook his head.

Then he turned his attention back to his plate, murmured
"Cute," and scooped up his own chip.

I decided, since he was being nice and I still wasn't used t
that, to change the subject.

"So, why does the drywall put you off the idea of Shaun
doing the deed?" I asked, and put my chip in my mouth.

"Woman isn't stupid," Max muttered after swallowing an
while digging out another chip.

"You found out she was fooling around with Curt while sh
was with you," I reminded him.

"She wanted me to, thought it'd make me jealous," Ma
told me.

"Oh," I whispered, and picked up another chip.

"Shauna wouldn't be sloppy. That's sloppy. Clearin' out he

ouse and not cleanin' away evidence?" Max shook his head, rabbed his beer, and muttered, "Sloppy."

He took a drink.

I twisted to get my beer and twisted back.

"So who did it?" I asked.

"Who knows? Someone who hated Curt, someone who ated Shauna, and town's full of them."

This was true and one could almost feel sorry for the both of them.

But only almost.

I sipped beer, then queried, "And Kami?"

Max looked at me. "Kami, I figure, got fucked. For whatever reason, Shauna was ready to move on, maybe with this Robert guy, and seein' as he stands to lose everything, he hitches his star to hers. Shauna wouldn't care who she ripped off to keep livin' the good life without workin' for it, 'cept on her back."

"Even Kami?"

"She'd take advantage of Harry, who isn't my most favorite person right now, but he's always been a good guy, she'd take advantage of Kami."

"But Kami's her friend, has been for years."

"If you think about it, so have I and so have Bitsy and Harry. She fucked us all over without blinkin'."

"Did you ever give her money?" I blurted, and only his eyes sliced to me, his head still faced his plate, and I whispered, "Sorry, dumb question."

"I ain't stupid either, Duchess."

"I know that," I said quickly.

"I know you do." He scooped another chip, shoved it in his mouth, chewed, swallowed, and continued. "Though, when we went out, she never reached for her wallet."

I bit my lip and twisted to put back my beer.

When I righted myself and studiously turned my attention back to my plate, at the same time vowing the next time we went out to dinner that I'd at least reach for my wallet, Max spoke.

"Different, babe, totally."

My eyes went to him. "Sorry?"

What he said next told me he'd read my face again.

"I was just fuckin' her. You're my woman, totally different."

"I wasn't your woman when we had buffalo burgers... steaks at The Rooster for that matter."

"Yeah, you were, for both. Especially The Rooster, babe. We fought about you movin' out here on the way there."

Okay, I had to give him that one.

"But I'd practically just met you when we had buffalo burgers," I pointed out.

"Yeah? So?"

"I wasn't your woman."

"Babe, you were."

"How's that?"

"You just were."

I stared at him and he returned my stare. Then he calmly turned back to his plate and dug out another chip.

After he chewed and swallowed, I asked, "So, you'd let woman pay for dinner?"

"Nope," he stated firmly. "But don't mind she goes for her wallet. She won't use it but I don't mind it."

"So I should have gone for my wallet?" I pushed, and his eyes cut back to mine.

"Did you not get my earlier point?"

"Max—"

He turned slightly toward me and dropped his plate to hold it at his thigh.

"All right, we should talk about this anyway and you're obviously twistin' this in that head of yours, so we'll get this straight. This works out, babe, I'm not gonna give a shit if a woman goes for her wallet because there won't be another one I take out, 'cept you. And *you* never go for your wallet. How we work out the money shit, we work it out private, at home. We go out, I pay, always. That work for you or do we have to talk about it for half an hour?"

"That isn't the point. The point is—"

"The point is, you're worried you've been rude when I'm ayin', Duchess, it woulda pissed me off if *you* went for your allet. Shauna, I didn't give a fuck because she didn't matter. *ou* matter."

This was a really good answer. So good I wasn't breathing roperly, so I kind of wheezed, "Okay."

"You get my point?"

I was still wheezing when I said, "Yes."

Max watched me wheeze awhile. When I controlled it and urned my attention back to my nachos, he queried, "How is it ou can be irritating and adorable at the same fuckin' time?"

"Just me, I guess," I quietly told my nachos.

"Yeah," he muttered, and I looked at him to see he'd rought his plate up and was digging back in but he was doing t grinning.

"Max?" I called, and he looked at me, chip held suspended.

"Right here," he replied, and put the chip in his mouth.

"About that job—"

He didn't swallow before he said, "Yeah, about that." He inished chewing, swallowed, and turned to me again to state, 'It's happenin'."

"Max—"

"Quiet, Nina, and listen to me, yeah?"

I had his attention, his full, somber attention, and I nodded.

"George and Trevor have explained to Bitsy that Curt has ontracts he can't renege on or Bitsy's gonna be fucked. I'll see hem carried through. Then Bitsy wants the business down-ized. She wasn't a big fan of Curt's work either. I got some deas that'll keep some boys employed and we got contracts hat'll stretch out a good long while. The guys who want to nove on'll have time to make arrangements. I ain't gonna live Curt's dream. I'm gonna make it so Bitsy's taken care of and hen it becomes somethin' that I can do to keep a roof over ur heads, food in our stomachs, and I can sleep at night. That vork for you?"

I was staring at him, being reminded, acutely, that tha thing eating me up inside was very, *very* gone when I whispered, "Charlie."

His brows drew together and he asked, "What?"

I swallowed, drew in a soft breath, smiled, and turned my attention to my plate again, saying softly, "Charlie. You remind me of him." I grabbed a loaded chip and looked back at Max. "He was able to make big problems little ones too. He was really good at it." I shoved the chip in my mouth, chewed swallowed, and concluded, "Like you."

I was preparing another chip with some beef, beans, and cheese that had slopped onto the plate when I heard Max command, "Come here."

My head came up and I asked, "Sorry?"

Then I saw the expression on his face and I started wheezing again.

"Babe, come here."

"I am here," I breathed.

"Closer," he ordered.

I moved my plate to the side and leaned in closer. Max did the same thing, hooked a hand behind my neck and pulled me even closer. Then he kissed me hard, closemouthed and short.

When his mouth released mine, his hand didn't move.

"You know, you can be nice too," he told me quietly.

I didn't answer.

"I like it, babe."

"Good," I whispered. He grinned, let me go, and went back to his nachos.

"How tired are you?" he asked after swallowing another loaded chip.

"I woke up tired but it's okay. It's nothing fifteen days of sleep won't cure."

Max chuckled, then, still grinning, suggested, "Another movie night."

I really liked that idea, so I agreed. "Sounds good."

"I get to pick the movie this time."

"Okay," I said, twisting to get my beer.

"Babe?" he called as I twisted back.

"Yes?"

"Still scared?"

I saw his eyes were dancing and I knew he knew the answer
to his question.

"A little," I kind of fibbed. I was but also I wasn't.

Max scooped up his last chip, muttering, "Another week,
you'll be good."

"Arrogant," I muttered back, then took a sip of my beer.

When I dropped my hand, I looked at Max to see him
chewing but doing it while smiling.

*   *   *

"Jesus, Duchess, you movin' in there?" Max's impatient voice
sounded through the closed bathroom door and I stared at my
black-eyed reflection in the mirror, trying not to hyperventilate.

I'd had an idea after nachos and during dinner cleanup and
now, putting it into action, I was thinking it wasn't such a good
idea.

"Nina!" Max called.

"I'll be right out!" I called back, and took in a deep breath.

So I was getting less and less scared about a lot of things
Max and me.

Which meant, to have a healthy relationship (or, healthi*er*),
I needed to be able to do this kind of thing.

I let out the breath, squared my shoulders, went to the back
of the door, put on my robe, tied it tight at my waist, and pulled
open the door.

Max was lying on his back on the bed, shoulders to the
headboard, a new beer in one hand, his other hand behind his
head, the pillows bunched up behind his back, my beer on his
nightstand.

I stopped a foot outside the bathroom door. His eyes traveled the length of me and came back to my face.

I was in my robe with bare feet and legs. He was still fully dressed, Therefore, he asked, "You gonna watch a movie or you goin' to sleep?"

I moved to my right, stepped back, and leaned against the wall.

Okay, maybe I couldn't do this.

Max studied me and turned to his side, taking his hand from behind his head to hold his torso up on an elbow and he called, "Honey, come here."

My feet moved me automatically toward the bed but they did this slowly. Max watched the whole time and I stopped by the side of the bed, stood stock-still, and stared down at him. He leaned to put his beer on the nightstand, moved back, and looked up at me.

"Jesus, Duchess, what happened in the bathroom?"

I pulled in a deep breath and before all courage fled, yanked at the belt of my robe. I shrugged it off my shoulders so it pooled around my feet on the floor and stood in front of him wearing nothing but a pair of Brazilian cut, white lace panties and my gold-sequined camisole.

Max's eyes moved to my body.

Then his body moved and before I could blink I was flying through the air. I landed on my back in the bed and Max rolled over me.

Holding his torso away, he ran his hand down my side, the calluses on his fingers snagging at the sequins, his eyes glued to my body. Then his head came up, he looked at me, and his beautiful eyes were unmistakably hungry.

"Baby"—his voice was thick—"you got this on, you better not be tired."

My hand came up to curl around his neck under his ear, my fingers sliding into his amazing hair.

Then I whispered, "I think I got my second wind."

His hand was at the edge of the camisole and it dipped under, then slid up my skin, and Max's eyes held mine as I shivered at his touch.

I put pressure at his neck as my other arm pushed under his body to curl around his waist and I demanded softly, "Kiss me, Max."

Max, unlike me, didn't have to be told twice.

*   *   *

After, we watched the movie, me pulling on my nightie, undies, and robe, Max yanking on a pair of pajama bottoms.

I lay cradled against his body, my head pillowed by his hard bicep, his forearm curled across my chest and his other arm draped around my waist as I watched a lot of things blow up, a lot of gunfire, and a lot of car chases.

Then I lost my second wind (this could be due to the three orgasms I'd had, yes, *three*; Max really liked the camisole and took his time, expending a lot of effort proving that) and felt my body start to settle farther into Max and closer to sleep.

"Am I losin' you, baby?" Max whispered into my ear from behind, and I nodded, so he offered, "I'll turn off the movie."

"No, sweetheart, you finish it. I can sleep through it."

I turned to face him, my back to the TV, and cuddled closer, pressing my cheek to his chest, twining my legs with his and my arm around his waist.

Max's arm tightened around me, his other hand sifting through my hair.

This felt good and dreamland beckoned.

"Nina, honey?" Max called.

"Mmm?"

"You happy?"

I turned my face and kissed his pectoral; then I turned it back and pressed my cheek into his chest.

Something exploded on the TV but Max muttered, "I'll take that as a yes."

"Mmm," I agreed.

I felt Max move slightly and I felt his lips at the hair on top of my head. He kissed me there and moved back.

"'Night, darlin'."

I was close to the edge, sleep's silken web weaving around me; therefore I didn't guard my words or even think about them when I mumbled, "'Night, Max." I gave a small sigh and snuggled closer before whispering, "Love you."

Then I fell instantly into such a deep sleep, I didn't feel Max's powerful arms convulse around me.

CHAPTER FOURTEEN

Manning Up

"TELL ME," Max growled against my lips as his hands at my hips ground me down on his cock.

"Darling," I whispered, not knowing what he wanted me to tell him but willing to tell him whatever he wanted to hear because I was so very, very *close.*

"Tell me, baby," he ordered, still growling, letting me move up and using his hands to slam me back down.

It was morning. Max woke me with his hands, then his mouth and now I was riding him but he was sitting up, my hands were in his hair, my head tipped down, my lips on his, and nothing was in my head but the beauty of the sensations gathering between my legs.

"What, Max?" I breathed. "What do you want?"

"Tell me you love me."

My closed eyes flew open and my fingers clenched in his hair. His eyes were open, too, and they were heated, hungry, and intense.

"Max," I whispered.

"Tell me, baby, before you come."

"Max—" I moved faster, riding him harder. I was urged by the sensations at the same time he demanded it with his strong hands.

"You love me," he stated.

Oh God, it was happening, all of it, everything.

"Yes," I whispered.

"Say it," he ordered.

He held my eyes and I said it. "I love you, Max."

His arms swept around me, holding me tight, and I watche his eyes get more heated, hungrier and so intense it felt lik they were burning into mine.

"Come for me, baby," he demanded.

"Anything, darling," I breathed, and then it hit me, my hea flew back, and I gladly did as I was told.

*　　　*　　　*

I wandered out of the bathroom, my eyes on Max, his eyes o me. When I got close to his side of the bed, he whisked th covers back, exposing the fullness of all things Wonder Ma and my soul sighed. Then I put a knee to the bed and straddle him in preparation for moving over him but he caught my hip and stayed my movement, pulling me down to him.

I didn't mind. Therefore I settled in, forehead to his neck torso pressed to his, knees to his sides, and his fingers starte to move randomly on the skin of my back and behind.

I lay there surrounded by everything Max, his body, hi arms, his bed, his home, thinking that I'd told him I loved him I'd known him two weeks and I told him I loved him.

He'd demanded I say it, of course. And it was true, c course. And he should know, obviously. And I *wanted* him t know.

That still didn't mean I wasn't freaking out because h should know and I wanted him to know but I wasn't sure should have told him *now*.

"You know, I do too." I heard his gravelly voice rumbl quietly.

"What?" I asked his throat.

He didn't answer and when his silence lasted a long time I lifted my head and looked down at his face to see he looke sated and serious.

"What do I know?" I queried.

His fingers stopped their roaming, one arm locked around my waist, the other hand slid up my spine and into my hair.

His amazing gray eyes didn't leave mine when he answered gently, "I do too. I said it the other day and I meant it." His fingers tensed against my scalp. "I'm in love with you, Duchess."

I stared at him, feeling the tears welling in my eyes because the feelings surging through my system were too much for them not to leak out somehow.

"Really?" I whispered as one tear escaped and slid down the skin of my cheek as Max's eyes watched it mark its path.

Then his hand moved out of my hair to cup my jaw, his thumb sweeping my cheek to dry my tear. His warm, sweet gaze came back to mine.

"Really," he whispered back.

I felt another tear escape and I bent my head and touched my mouth to his. When our lips connected, Max's head canted, his fingers sifted back into my hair to tilt my head the other way, and he rolled so he was on top. Through this, his lips didn't touch mine. They fused with mine, kissing me hard, long, deep, wet, and lastly, but most importantly, beautiful.

His kiss was a promise and it was a gift, both the best I'd ever received.

When he lifted his head, he cupped my face with his hand and his thumb traced circles at my temple.

"Are we crazy?" I asked him.

"What?" he asked back, lips twitching.

"Are we crazy? Is this crazy? We barely know each other."

All amusement left his face when his eyes locked on mine and he said, "Love isn't sane, darlin'."

"I wouldn't know," I admitted softly. "You're my first."

I watched with no small amount of fascination as his eyes grew dark and again intense and heated, before he growled, "Thank fuck."

Then he was kissing me again, his mouth and tongue working wonders, his hands roaming. My legs circled his hips, my fingers moved on the skin and muscle of his back, and I liked all so much, I barely heard the phone ring.

But Max's head came up when we both heard Harry's voic fill the loft.

"Max, buddy, it's Harry. I heard what happened to Nin and...uh...I called to—"

I heard him say no more because Max unfortunatel stopped what he was doing, reached out a long arm, yanke the phone out of its charger, beeped it on, and put it to his ear

"Harry," he said into the phone. I watched him listen an then he went on. "No, you can't talk to Nina but you can liste to me. Nina and I hadn't had the chance to talk about Ann and what you said was fucked up and it upset her. It upset he enough that shit went down that led to her gettin' worked ove by Damon. He caught her alone, freaked her right the fuck ou and damn near broke her nose *and* her fuckin' ribs. That's o you, *buddy*. All that shit's on you."

"Max," I tried to cut in, but Max's gaze was directed the pillowcase beside my head and his focus was directed o whatever Harry was saying.

"I don't care if you were drunk," Max went on. "She tol me the shit you said and she also told me while you wer fuckin' with her head, you told her you'd do her and you gott know, I do *not* like that. That is *not* cool. You know she's in m house, you know she's in my bed, and you know better than say that kind of shit to my woman."

"Max," I tried again when he paused to listen, but he kep right on talking to Harry.

"Yeah, we got problems. Fair warning, you need to avoi me for a while and you get anywhere near Nina or I hear yo tried to speak with her, our problems will get bigger. Are w clear?"

I lifted a hand and curled it around his neck. His eyes cut mine, his were very angry, and I braved the look on his fac opened my mouth to say something, but before I could, h continued.

"I don't give a fuck about that. What I give a fuck about is you tellin' me we're clear. Now, are we clear?"

"Please, Max, I think—" I started, Max's mouth got tight, his eyes narrowed, and his look was so scary, I clamped my mouth shut.

"Advice, Harry, grow a fuckin' pair. You got somethin' to say to me, you say it *to me*. You got issues, you deal with them like a man. What you don't do is, when my woman or *any* woman slides her ass onto the stool next to you to show you some compassion and kindness, you do not use that opportunity to let go of your shit by breakin' someone else's heart. You got a problem with the way your life's gone down, deal with it without draggin' someone down with you. Should have told you this a long time ago, Harry, but you need to man up, for fuck's sake. You need to man...the fuck...*up*."

With that, he took the phone from his ear and bleeped it off. Then he tossed it aside on the bed, and his eyes came back to me.

"Max—" I began again.

"Don't, Duchess," he cut me off. "Seriously, don't. It's a guy thing. I know you got an opinion about everything but the bottom line is what he did was not cool. He upset you and that led to a string of events where you got hurt. I know it was our shit that led to you gettin' hurt but what he did didn't help the situation. It's my job to protect you. What he did interfered with my ability to do that and I need to make certain that shit doesn't happen again. I'm doin' that. It's a guy thing and you need to know right now, you do not stick your nose into a guy thing."

"Okay," I replied. Max stared at me a second and blinked. Then he asked, "What?"

My hands moved on his back and I repeated, "Okay."

"Okay?"

"Yes, okay."

He stared at me again. Then he asked, "Easy as that?"

My hands slid around his sides, up his chest to curl around his neck, and I asked back, "Is this important to you?"

"Yeah," Max answered.

"Then yes." I lifted my head and touched my mouth to his before dropping my head to the pillow again. "Easy as that."

That's when, bizarrely, he said one word firmly and that word was, "No."

My head tilted on the pillow. "No what?"

"No to your earlier question. We're definitely not crazy."

I smiled at my man's amazing, handsome face. *My* man. And God, I didn't care if it was crazy, but I loved my man.

The fingers of one of my hands ran along his jaw and I asked quietly, "Can I tell you something?"

The fingers of both of his hands ran along my body as he answered quietly, "You can tell me anything, baby."

I planted a foot in the bed and rolled him to his back. Rolling over him, I looked down at his face as my thumb explored the contours of his cheekbone.

Then I whispered, "There was a time in my life when I used to roll the dice. I did it a lot and I always lost. Every time I lost and when I lost, I lost everything. So I got scared of rolling the dice."

My hair was hanging down, curtaining our faces, and one of Max's hands moved to pull one side up and hold it at the back of my head. I watched his face get soft and I knew that he knew what was coming.

So I gave it to him.

"Thank you for showing me it was worth taking a gamble again, darling." I dropped my head until my lips were against his and finished, "It feels good finally to win and win *huge*."

I saw the flash in his eyes and heard the rumble of his growl before his hand at the back of my head brought mine down the fraction of an inch it needed to go before his mouth took mine in another kiss.

Then he rolled me to my back and showed me yet again why taking a gamble on Max, on us, on Colorado, and on life was absolutely worth it.

*   *   *

I don't know, Neenee Bean," Mom said at the grocery store checkout, her face thoughtful, her eyes watching the clerk scan my purchases. "This feels like a celebration and a celebration doesn't say 'red wine, beer, and pasta bake.' A celebration says champagne and salmon en croûte.' "

Mom and I were shopping for dinner that night. Max and Steve were giving us Nellie and Nina time. They were leaving the next day and Mom had announced upon their arrival to the A-frame that she wanted a testosterone-free zone for at least two hours.

Prior to Mom and Steve's arrival, Max and my love fest was interrupted by a variety of calls that were, as Max decreed, only slightly less annoying than Harry's. They included Mom and Steve saying they were heading up the mountain. Linda saying Kami was coming with her for pasta bake. Brody calling to remind us this was also his last day in town and therefore getting an invitation for him, Mindy, Barb, and Darren to come too. And finally, since Gnaw Bone was Gnaw Bone, Arlene heard about the party and called to alert us to the fact that she and Cotton would be there. She didn't ask for an invite and she hung up before I could politely demur.

So our party of five turned into a party of twelve.

This did not make Max happy. Mom's decree of a testosterone-free zone made Max less happy. And what made him even less happy was when Mom pointed out his dining room table seated six and it needed to seat twelve. Thus she ordered Max and Steve off on the errand of buying more dining room chairs, this being her attempt to establish her testosterone-free zone.

Mountain Man Max, not exactly the kind of man to be sent on an errand, did this only after his eyes cut to me and he asked, "This gonna happen often?"

"Is what going to happen often?" I asked back.

"Half the town sittin' at our dining room table?"

I scrunched my nose and tilted my head because, at the look on his face, I didn't want to say yes but the answer *was* yes. I liked to cook. I liked to entertain. I liked my friend around me. So it was definitely going to happen often.

Max read my face, sighed, hooked me at the back of my head to pull me in so he could kiss my forehead, and then he took off with Steve to buy chairs.

"Individual," Mom, at the checkout, finished.

"Individual what?" I asked, handing my credit card over to the clerk.

"Individual salmon en croûtes," Mom answered, and looked at her.

"Mom, I'm not making individual salmon en croûtes for twelve people. That would take all day."

"It's a celebration, Neenee Bean! It doesn't matter how long it takes just as long as it's special."

I signed the credit card slip and handed it back to the clerk. "Firstly, I just signed the credit card receipt. I'm not going back through the store to buy ten more bags of food. Secondly, Max gave you two hours and I know you like Max because he's a great guy and there's a lot to like. He also likes you. But take my advice—you shouldn't test him. He's a great guy but he's also a mountain man. Mountain men aren't fond of being tested. And lastly, I think mountain people will be happy with red wine, beer, and pasta bake as a celebration. I think mountain people don't care what they eat during a celebration. They just care who's there to eat it with them."

"Damn tootin'," the clerk muttered under her breath, and I turned my surprised gaze to her, then smiled at her welcome solidarity. Maybe I was finding my mountain woman within.

Mom glared at the clerk. "Have you had salmon en croûte?" she asked.

The clerk's eyes came to me. "I saw five bags of grated mozzarella. Is that for your pasta bake?"

"Yes," I answered, and her eyes went back to Mom.

"Anything with mozzarella wins, especially five bags of it," she declared.

I laughed, thanked her, tugged Mom through the checkout, ommandeered our cart, and headed to the car.

Mom fell in step beside me and she did this while pouting. grinned at the cart full of food because I decided Mom was ute when she pouted. I had to admit I may have decided this ecause I had an amazing-looking mountain man who was in ve with me so pretty much anything would be cute.

Still, I said softly, "Stop pouting, Mom. We have today and en you're off home. Don't waste it pouting."

She bleeped the locks on the car and pulled up the boot. Okay, but only if you promise me you won't argue with what tell you next."

I didn't have a good feeling about this. If there was any- ing that could put a dent in my euphoria, Mom's craziness uld.

I pulled the cart to a halt and rounded it, yanking out bags put in the boot. "That depends on what you say next."

"You can't argue, Nina, because it's important."

I stopped loading bags because the tone of my mother's ice made it sound important. I straightened and looked at er to see her face communicated what she was going to say as important too.

"What?" I whispered.

"You know what you told me on the way here about Max's heritage from that murdered man?"

"Yes," I replied.

"Well, I'm going to talk to Steve about us giving you some oney to help with the taxes so Max doesn't lose that land."

I felt my face go soft and I moved closer to my mom.

"You can't do that, Mom. It's sweet but Max would never t you," I informed her.

"He won't have a choice. I've been thinking about it and as ar as I'm concerned, the way he is with you, the way you are ith him, I see good things and so I'm thinking it would be me vesting in my grandchildren's future," she replied. I pulled a sharp breath at a thought I'd never had, having Max's

children, giving Max a family, and I felt my body grow tigh
even as my heart wound up to sing. "He wants that mountai
clean, you want that mountain clean, and I want to do my bit t
help you keep it clean for you, for Max, for your children, thei
children, and so on."

"Mom—"

"Don't argue, sweetie, and don't tell Max until I have
chance to talk to Steve."

"You don't have to talk to Steve. I'm selling Charlie's hous
and using that money for the taxes," I blurted before I eve
thought about it and then my body got tighter.

"You're *what*?" Mom breathed, her eyes scanning my face
her face a mask of shock. She knew how I felt about Charlie'
house.

Oh my God. What was I saying?

Do it, Neenee Bean, Charlie said in my head. *It's time. Le
the past go. Just let it go. I'll always be right here.*

Charlie—I started to say back.

Let it go, sweetheart. I want you to give this to Max,
your future. You don't need that house to have me with yo
I'll always be with you.

Oh, Charlie.

Always, Nina.

"Nina!" Mom called sharply, her hand squeezing my arn
I focused on her face and stopped talking to my dead brothe
in my head. "Are you really going to sell Charlie's house?"

"He'd want me to," I told her the truth. "I…" I looked a
the grocery bags in the boot then back to my mom. "I thin
I was holding on to him through that house because I didn
have anything else. Not when I was with Niles. I was holdin
on to that house because I was trying to hold on to somethin
Charlie. But Max told me that having the memory of Charli
is precious. And he's right. And I have Charlie with me all th
time. I don't need his house to keep him with me. And I thin
if Charlie were here and he could give it, he'd want to do wh;
he could, just like you, to keep Max's mountain clean for Ma;

or me, and for…" I smiled but I felt my lips tremble as tears
lled my eyes and I concluded, "Our kids."

Mom's eyes never left my face as she lifted her hand to cup
ny cheek.

"Love you, Nina," she whispered.

"Love you, too, Mom," I whispered back, my hand coming
p to curl around hers at my face.

"And I'm happy for you, sweetie," she kept whispering.

"Me too," I kept whispering back.

"I think you're right about this. It would be what Charlie
wanted. He'd want you to have everything you want and he'd
want you to be happy." Her fingers curled around mine and
brought our hands down where she tightened her grip and
shook them between us. "He'd like Max," she finished.

"Yes," I agreed.

Yes, Charlie said in my head, and I laughed at Charlie.

Then I said to Mom, "Let's get back to the house."

We filled the boot and Mom got in the passenger side as
I hoofed the cart to the bay. I was turning around, my mind
on pasta bake, family, friends, and getting back to Max, so I
wasn't looking where I was going and I ran smack into something solid.

I took a step back, lifting my chin, muttering, "Sorry," when
I saw Damon standing in front of me and my body locked.

"Pressed charges, English," he hissed. "Stupid. Seems you
never learn but I'm gonna teach you."

My body prepared to take flight as my mouth opened to
scream but he landed a roundhouse punch to my temple and
everything went black.

*   *   *

I came to in a truck bouncing along the main street in town. I
blinked away the unconsciousness and could see I hadn't been
out for long. We'd barely left the grocery store.

My head turned left slowly and I pushed away from the
door I was leaning on. Damon was behind the wheel.

I lifted my hand to my pounding temple and kept blinking against the fog in my eyes.

"Damon, pull over," I said quietly.

"Shut your fuckin' mouth, English," Damon clipped back.

"Please, pull over."

"Shut your *fuckin'* mouth!" he snarled.

"Don't do this," I urged. "This isn't smart."

"Fuck you," he bit out.

"You're already in trouble. Don't—" I started to explain but his beefy arm shot out, his knuckles impacting on my lips, pushing them into my teeth, and I instantly tasted blood. My hand at my temple dropped to my lips as his arm disappeared.

"Like I said, bitch, shut your fuckin' mouth."

I shut my mouth. I didn't want to rile my mountain man stalker any further. He was already riled enough.

My mind was whirling but through the haze still over me from his first punch all I could think of was that if I opened the door and threw myself out, I'd likely give myself broken bones. I didn't want broken bones because it would be difficult to cook pasta bake after Max rescued me if I had broken bones.

I was still thinking this when I heard Damon mutter, "What the fuck?" and then I saw another truck speeding alongside us.

We were out of town and on the open road. I leaned forward, looked past Damon, and saw the driver was Harry.

Harry.

Thank God! Harry! He must have seen us and come to rescue me.

Harry sped several car lengths beyond us and then watched in shock as Harry cut the wheel and then his truck turned sideways into our lane, cutting us off. Damon stood on the brakes and I flew forward, throwing up a hand. It slammed into the dash as my body, not in a seat belt, flew forward, too, and kept going. My head cracked against the windshield and was immediately thrown left as Damon cut the wheel to avoid colliding with Harry's truck and then I was thrown forward again when we rocked to a bone-jarring halt in a ditch.

I was blinking away stars as I pushed myself back in the seat. It was pure instinct that lifted my hand and guided it to the door handle. I pushed my door open and nearly fell to my knees as I shoved myself out of the cab. My body was making its escape before my mind caught up with it but I lost my footing as I climbed the ditch, scrambling up the last of it on my hands and knees. I pulled myself to my feet at the top and rounded the back of the truck where I saw Harry standing, his eyes on the driver's side of Damon's truck.

"You fuckin' asswipe! Are you fuckin' *nuts*?" Damon bellowed, and I looked to him to see he was out of the truck and charging up the ditch toward Harry.

Then my whole body jolted as I heard the sharp crack of a gunshot and I stood stock-still when I saw the blurred, hideous spurt of blood spray from Damon's chest before he fell down to both knees.

Stunned to immobility, I stared as Damon's body dropped face-first to the grass, gravel, and mud beside the road. Then I slowly turned my head and saw Harry moving toward me, a peculiar look on his face, a gun smoking in his right hand, and he was shifting it to his left.

"Harry," I whispered, my voice trembling, my tone a mixture of horror and shock. "He hurt me but you didn't have to—"

I stopped talking when the look on Harry's face penetrated and his right hand lifted.

He no longer had the gun in that hand. He now held a syringe.

Too late I took a step back but he caught me at the waist, yanked me to him, and I felt the needle plunge into my neck.

Then his face was all I saw.

"Just like Max told me to do, I'm mannin' up, Nina. This is me mannin' *the fuck* up."

My lids lowered against my will. I forced them open as I felt my body lifted in Harry's arms and we started moving toward his truck.

Then they lowered again and I was gone.

*   *   *

My eyes opened and I was confused because I was certain m
eyes were opened but all I could see was dark.

I started to move and it was then I realized both my arm
were over my head. I thought this was strange until I tried t
move them and it was then I realized they weren't only ove
my head, there was something cold biting into my wrists an
it hit me my arms were secured over my head to something.

I went still and my mind raced. Then I remembere
Damon. Then thinking Harry was there to save the day. The
watching Harry shoot Damon. Then Harry taking me.

Oh my God. Oh my *God*!

I sucked in breath and that was when I felt the gag. Ther
was something in my mouth and something tied around m
head to hold it in place. I fought back the panic that surge
through me and tried to take stock.

I was on something soft, a mattress. It was cold, not bitte
but not comfortable. My limbs were stiff from inactivity an
lying in the chill. My arms were not only secured to some
thing over my head but my ankles were also tied together. My
head hurt like hell and I was still fuzzy from whatever Harry
injected me with.

And I was in the dark. Lying gagged and tied up in a for
eign location in the dark. Just like the heroine in a horro
movie *but real*.

I kept fighting back the panic by turning my mind to trying
to figure out where I might be. I was either someplace dark
like a room with no windows, or I was someplace seclude
and it was dark outside, someplace the moon couldn't light.

Either way, I was in trouble.

Cautiously, I tested my wrists against whatever they were
secured to and it made a clinking noise so I stopped.

"Nina?" I heard a woman call, and stilled.

Bitsy. Oh no, that was Bitsy's voice.

The mattress under me moved and I felt a hand light on me. Nina, it's me. Bitsy."

I rolled to my back, turned my head in her direction, and tied to see through the dark.

"Oh honey," she whispered, her voice breaking. "Oh God, Nina. Oh God. God. God. *God.* What have I done?"

I tried to say something from under the gag. She heard , her hand left me and I felt the gag being pulled from my mouth. When it was free, I spit out the material and then swallowed against the dryness coating the inside of my mouth.

"Are you okay?" Bitsy asked.

No. No, I very much wasn't okay.

"Harry's turned," I whispered, my words slurred. "I think, Bitsy, I think I watched him murder Damon."

The mattress moved again. I heard her dragging her body closer to me and I knew she was lying on it with me but apparently she wasn't shackled to the bed. Then again, Bitsy didn't need to be tied down. Bitsy couldn't go anywhere.

Her hand curled on my neck and I felt her face close.

"It's my fault," she whispered.

"Bitsy—" I started to tell her she had to find a way to get me loose so I could get out of wherever we were, get away from this true, real-life horror movie and get us some help but she interrupted me.

"It is. It's all my fault."

"Don't, sweetheart. We have to—"

I stopped this time because I heard the noise of a door opening and then light flooded the room, blinding me. Bitsy's body jerked away from mine and we both twisted as best we could. I blinked against the light and saw Harry walking in, the lower half of a woman over his shoulder.

Oh God, what now?

Then I saw him dump the woman on the floor, her long, straight ebony hair flying as he did it and he did it unceremoniously, not like she was a human being but like she was a sack of sawdust. Her head cracked against the planks just as her

body thudded against them. I watched in horror as her bod
settled, her hair slightly obscuring her beautiful face.

Shauna.

By the looks of her, clothes dirty and in disarray, hai
greasy, she hadn't seen the inside of a shower for a while an
I knew instinctively this was because Shauna Fontaine didn
take off with her man toy. Shauna Fontaine, like me, had bee
kidnapped by a mountain man gone bad.

The mattress moved again and I tore my eyes from Shauna
unconscious, or worse, dead on the floor to see Bitsy pushin
up on her arms.

"Harry—"

"It's okay, Bits. It's all gonna be all right," Harry cut he
off. "I got it all figured out."

"No, you don't, Harry. You don't," Bitsy told him urgently
"Listen to me..."

She trailed off when Harry moved to her side of the be
and sat on it. He twisted his torso to her. His hand coming u
to cradle her face, he leaned in close.

"I did, honey, I listened to you. I listened," he whispered.

"You didn't. This is out of hand. This is wrong. Shauna
Nina? Why—"

"He took away your legs," Harry explained.

"Yes, he did. *Curt* did. But Nina's Max's and—" Bits
started.

"He took away your legs," Harry repeated. "He kille
Anna. *Your best friend.* He fucked Shauna *in your bed.*" Hi
thumb lovingly swept her cheek. "I listened, Bits. I listene
to every word you said from that day I saw you in the hospi
tal after he crippled you. I listened and I was with you all th
way. He had to pay. You said it. You said it again and agai
and again as he fucked you and fucked you and fucked you
You didn't want him to do that to our town. You didn't wan
that big house up on the hill. You didn't want to be queen o
Gnaw Bone to his king. But he didn't care what you wanted
He never cared what you wanted. He only cared about on

ing. Curt. Curt was all Curt cared about. Wakin' up next to
ou and tellin' you he loved you and then goin' off and bangin'
hauna, givin' her money, makin' you the fool as you wheeled
our way through life. I listened, honey. I listened to every
ord you said. You were right. He had to pay."

"*He* had to pay. *Curt* did!" Bitsy hissed, yanking her face
om his hand, which stayed suspended in air for a second
efore he tried to touch her again but she dragged herself back
o his hand dropped.

"Bitsy, baby—"

"No!" Bitsy snapped. "We had a plan. You take care of
'urt and we play it cool. The money was untraceable. We'd
een putting it aside for *years*, Harry, *years*. No one would
ver know. No one."

Shock made every centimeter of my body lock. There it
vas but I couldn't believe my ears as I lay there and stared at
ne hideous scene playing out in front of me.

Harry *and* Bitsy had had Curt killed.

Bitsy.

Bitsy!

"He hired an investigator," Harry returned.

"So?" Bitsy shot back. "I knew that, Harry, and I told you.
'he guy didn't know anything. The game was to play it cool,
ou know that. No matter what, *play it cool*. That investiga-
or didn't know anything. I know because I got in Curt's desk
nd read his reports. He didn't even know *we* were sending the
eath threats! He didn't know anything. He didn't know *shit*!
'hen you off and kill him the same night that guy you found
illed Curt. Why? Why would you do that? And this"—she
hrew out an arm—"Shauna? Nina? It was only supposed to be
'urt. Only Curt. Why would you drag Nina into this? What's
he matter with you?"

"Shauna was fuckin' Curt *and* Max *and* me," Harry
etorted.

"I know that, Harry. It was part of the fucking plan for you
o look like you'd moved on from me," Bitsy returned.

"Jesus, Bits, I just told you she was fuckin' *me*," Harry b
out.

"Yes, Harry, *I know that*. That was the plan," Bitsy b
back.

"God"—Harry leaned back—"you don't even care. Yo
don't even care she sucked me off, that I had to fuck that col
emotionless piece of ass to keep up this shit so no one woul
guess."

"I cared but that was the plan, Harry. We both had to sacr
fice so we could have what we wanted. So we could be wher
we wanted to be," Bitsy reminded him.

"But she was tryin' to take Curt's money. *Your* money," h
clipped. "She got pregnant to do it."

"She's not pregnant, you idiot!" Bitsy, finally losing i
snapped. "She's as pregnant as *me*. She said it because Cu
always wanted a kid and obviously I couldn't give him on
so she thought she could play that but she wasn't going to g
dick. Not from Curt. He may have thought with his dick ha
the time but the other half wasn't stupid, Harry, and you kno
it. And you had to let her play you so you'd be with her whe
Curt was done and then no one would think a thing of it whe
you dumped her after I was available and you came back t
me. That was the plan, Harry. We've been talking about it fo
years. That was the plan. Simple, smart, patient, and cool. Bu
no. No, you go off and murder Curt's investigator and try t
pin it on Shauna and…and…and I don't even *know* wha
Nina's doin' here!"

"Shauna wants Max," Harry stated.

"So?" Bitsy yelled.

"So"—Harry leaned forward—"outside, her other asshol
is lyin' in the snow, four bullets in his chest and her finge
pulled the trigger, the residue will be on her hand. She was o
when I did it. She won't remember a thing. And it's the sam
gun that killed that Fitzgibbon guy."

I shifted my head to look down at the prone Shauna befor
I looked back at Harry in time for him to finish.

"The same gun that'll kill Nina."

My lungs seized and I felt the blood drain out of my face.

"Nina?" Bitsy whispered.

"Yeah." Harry's crazed eyes flicked to me then back to itsy. "Nina."

"Why?" Bitsy asked, then repeated on a shout, *"For God's ake why?"*

Harry surged from the bed and I tensed as he bent at the vaist, his face having gone red, his arms straight down at his ides, hands in fists, and he roared, *"He can't have it all!"*

Bitsy's upper body leaned away from him before she reathed, "What?"

"Max!" Harry spat. "Max! Fuckin' *Max*. Holden fuckin' Maxwell with his varsity letter his freshman year and his cholarship and his mountain that everyone thinks it's *so reat* he kept clean when all that buildin' was goin' on all ver the county. Max didn't let anything touch *his* land. Oh o. Not Super Wonderful Holden Fuckin' Maxwell. Not him. Ie could have made it rich workin' alongside Curt but he idn't do that. Not Holden Maxwell, man of integrity. Man of trength. He had Anna and they were always holdin' hands, lways laughin', always tight, lookin' at each other like the rest f the world didn't exist. Then he lost her but he didn't lose verything, not Max. No. After he lost her everyone thought e was even *more* wonderful how he stayed cool with Curt and tayed tight with you. How he *manned up*." Spittle flew out of Iarry's mouth on the last two words. "How he built that house or his dad. How he kept goin' even though everyone knew osin' Anna rocked his world. He didn't fall. He didn't even alter. Not Max. Everyone thinkin' how *strong* he was. How uckin' *perfect*. Then the finest piece of ass in two countries valtzes into town and before you could blink, she's cuddlin' p to him at The Mark. She's in his bed. She's makin' out with im on the street and at The Dog and two weeks later she's novin' from fuckin' *England* just to keep him warm at night."

He bent at the waist to put his face in Bitsy's.

"No," he sneered. "He can't have everything and I'm gonna make it so he doesn't. I'm tired of havin' nothin' and waitin' fuckin' *years* to make your play against Curt and all the while I'm watchin' Max have everything he wants. Every woman opens her legs for him and everyone in town thinks he shits roses. The same time, everyone in town thinks poor Harry, gettin' played by Shauna. Poor Harry, losin' Bitsy and pinin' after her all these years. Poor fuckin' Harry. Well, Bits fuck...*that*. Max told me himself just this mornin' to man up and I've decided I'm takin' his advice."

"But, Harry, Max doesn't have everything," Bitsy whispered.

"Yes, he does, Bits. He even has you. Even *you* think he shits roses," Harry retorted.

"You can't—" Bitsy began.

"I can and I can now especially because she knows every thing and I'm not waitin' ten years finally to have the only thing I ever wanted, except half of it"—his eyes dropped to her legs before slicing back to hers as I heard Bitsy gasp—"only to have Max's latest bit of pussy take it away."

"Harry," Bitsy whispered. "This isn't what we planned."

"No, Bitsy, it isn't but *I'm* the man and *I'm* sick of bein' led around by my dick so *I'm* changin' the fuckin' plan."

"You can't do that," she told him, and he leaned back throwing his arms out.

"No?" he asked, then planted his fists on his hips. "Watch me."

"Harry!" she shouted when he started to move around the bed. "If you hurt Nina, you won't have me," she threatened.

Harry's body rocked to a halt and he turned on her.

"Yeah? You gonna run away?" he asked snidely, and I watched Bitsy close her eyes tight. Then my eyes went back to Harry when he kept speaking as he untied my ankles. "This is what people know. Shauna wanted Max. She *always* wanted Max. And she used that Robert guy like she used everyone else. When he became expendable, he was gone. When Nina got in the way, she was gone. Shauna'll wake up and she won't

now shit. And all they'll know is that she's here with the gun
that made three bodies dead and she has the residue on her
hand. She fucked herself with her play on Curt, makin' her a
suspect in his murder so they'll probably pin that on her too.
But don't worry about Shauna, Bits. She'll make a good bitch
in prison. She'll have her shit sorted exactly as she wants it
before she finishes buttoning up her orange jumpsuit."

Then he was finished with my ankles and started walking toward me again and I started moving on the bed, inef-
fectually shifting my body to get away from him, running into
Bitsy as he pulled a set of keys out of his jeans pocket.

"Don't do this, Harry," Bitsy whispered from behind me
as he leaned toward my hands, and I kept trying and failing to
move away.

"Please," I begged, using Bitsy's words, "don't do this."

"Shut up," he muttered.

"Please," I whispered. "Please. You may think Max had
everything his whole life but you don't know me. I didn't. I
didn't have everything my whole life. My dad left me when I
was a baby—"

"Shut up," he repeated, still working at my hands.

I didn't shut up. "My boyfriends cheated on me, stole from
me, beat me—"

"Shut up," Harry said again.

"The brother I loved, I adored him, Harry, loved him
beyond anything, he had his legs blown off and couldn't hack
so he committed suicide."

Harry turned to me and clipped, "Shut *up*!"

I ignored him and kept going. "Today, I was happy, Harry.
It was the first day in a long, long time I woke up happy."

My wrists were freed but before I could make a move I was
being dragged from the bed.

"Harry! Don't!" Bitsy screamed.

I struggled but Harry was big. He was a mountain man and
he dragged and shoved me toward the door even as I twisted
and pulled and tried to flee.

"Harry! Please! Don't do this!" Bitsy screeched fro[m] behind us.

Calm, Nina, calm and think, sweetheart, Charlie said i[n] my head as Harry kept control of my struggling frame an[d] shoved me through the door into a dark hall. *Keep talking, ta[lk] to him.*

Instantly, I took my brother's advice.

"I understand what it means. I understand how it hurts [to] have everyone think poor Harry because they always thoug[ht] poor Nina. But now I'm happy. And I'm sorry if this hurts yo[u] but Max is what makes me happy. Please don't take that awa[y.] Not from Max, *from me.*"

He caught my wrist and yanked it behind my back, pullin[g] it high until it hurt so much I cried out. He positioned himse[lf] at my back and marched me forward, his lips to my ear.

"Keep your mouth shut, Nina, or I'll gag you again."

I clamped my mouth shut and clenched my teeth togeth[er] to stop myself from crying out at the pain in my arm. Harr[y] yanked me to a halt, reached beyond me, and opened a do[or.] The cold swept in as he pushed me outside.

Okay, Nina, he's just pulled out his gun. You need to g[et] his gun, sweetheart. He's holding it in his hand. You need [to] get it, turn it on him, and shoot like Max taught you to do. Yo[u] with me, Neenee Bean? Charlie said.

I'm with you, I replied, though I didn't think I was.

It was night, dark, we were in the mountains surrounde[d] by pines so thick it shrouded the space and kept out th[e] moonlight.

You've only got one hand, Nina, so you're going to have t[o] be creative. You're going to have to turn, very fast, very, ver[y] fast, sweetheart, and use your head. Aim at his chin and reac[h] for the gun at the same time you have to lift up your kne[e] hard, honey, as hard as you can, and aim for his crotch. Yo[u] got that?

I got it, Charlie.

Harry marched me forward and I saw the dark outline of

ody in the snow and I knew it was Robert Winston, dead, in
he dark, his body in the snow just like I was going to be if I
idn't get away from Harry.

I had to get away from Harry.

*Wait for it, sweetheart. Wait for me to say the word. You
et a hole in him, you go. You run as fast as you can. I'll guide
ou.*

Okay.

"Harry! Don't do this!" I heard Bitsy shout from far away.

Harry kept marching me, his hand at my wrist twisting my
rm so high and tight, the pain shot from my shoulder all the
vay to my fingertips.

"You're hurting me, Harry," I said quietly.

"I told you, Nina, shut up," Harry returned.

"You're going to kill me. I'm asking you to stop hurting me
efore you take everything from me."

His hand at my wrist squeezed tight but then it loosened
nd he moved my hand a couple of inches down my back so
he pain weakened and, although it didn't go away, it was
omething.

Well done, now wait for it, Neenee Bean, Charlie whispered.

I pulled in a breath.

We're close, sweetheart, Charlie told me.

I let out my breath and pulled in another.

Now! Charlie shouted.

I whirled at the same time I threw my head back. When I
vas facing Harry, I slammed it forward, my forehead connect-
ng with Harry's chin and pain exploded in my forehead but I
gnored it, lifting my knee, fast and vicious, and connecting
vith his crotch. Harry let out a startled, pained grunt. He let
ny wrist go and I reached for the gun, twisting it out of his
land and taking two running steps back.

Shoot him, Nina! Charlie yelled.

I lifted the gun and aimed it at Harry, shouting out loud to
Charlie, "I can't!"

Do it! Charlie urged.

Harry, one hand at his crotch, his upper body bent almost double but his head back and eyes on me started stumbling toward me.

"Charlie," I whispered, my hand holding the gun and trembling, "I can't."

Then don't shoot...run!

"Bitsy," I breathed.

Now! Now, Nina! Run!

I turned and ran.

My high-heeled-booted feet crunched through the snow and I heard Harry crunching after me. Pine needles whipped my face, snow flying off their limbs stinging me with pin points of freeze as I kept going.

Left here, veer left. Max is coming, Charlie told me.

Relief swept through me.

Oh thank God.

Keep running. Faster, sweetheart.

I veered left and tried to run faster but slipped and slid when my high-heeled boots hit rocks, finding purchase when they hit snow-covered turf, sliding and wavering again when they hit stone. Every step I took I heard Harry's pained grunting and his feet pounding behind me.

I looked back, just like all the stupid heroines in the horror movies do.

Keep going, don't look, Charlie instructed me. *Just keep running.*

I looked forward just when the toe of my boot caught on something solid and then I was flying. Yes, like all the stupid heroines in horror movies do, I fell, landing with a body-rocking jolt on my hands and knees at the same time stupid, stupid, *stupidly* losing the gun.

"Dammit!" I screamed.

Keep shouting! Max will hear you! He's close! Charlie yelled.

But I didn't get to shout. Instead I let out an "oof" as I tried to push to my feet and was tackled from behind by Harry. We

olled through the snow down the mountain, a tangle of arms
nd legs.

Fight, scratch, kick, bite, scream, sweetheart, scream!
Charlie ordered.

I screamed, loud and shrill and I kept doing it as I fought,
punching, shifting, flailing, scratching, and kicking. We'd
come to rest on an outcrop of rock that felt hard, cold, and
abrasive even through my clothes as we wrestled on top of it
and I kept screaming as I kept fighting. I gave it all I had but
Harry got me to my back and straddled me. I continued to
pound on his chest, scratch at his neck, and kick out with my
legs, bucking my hips and shrieking in terror as both his big
mountain man hands cupped either side of my head, yanking
it up so my chin was in my throat, and I knew he was going to
pound it into the rock. My fingers wrapped around his wrists
and I pulled out hard but didn't succeed in moving his hands.

SCREAM! Charlie shouted.

I screamed.

Then Harry was gone because Max was there, tackling
him from the side. They both went flying. I sucked in breath,
relief so extreme it felt like it ripped through me, shredding my
insides. I scrambled back on all fours and ran into something,
then hands were in my armpits and I was being dragged back.

I screamed again but over my scream I heard Jeff shout,
"Maxwell!"

My body stilled and my eyes searched through the darkness to see Max and Harry at the edge of the outcrop. Harry
was on his knees. Max was on his feet, one of his fists holding Harry up at the collar, both of Harry's hands scratching at
Max's forearm as his legs scrambled desperately in an attempt
to get his feet underneath him and Max's other fist repeatedly
connected with Harry's face with sickening thud after sickening thud.

"Max!" Another shout, this one from Mick as he ran and
skidded through the snow toward Max but Max didn't stop.

"You okay?" Jeff asked.

I nodded my lie, my eyes never leaving Max as I watched Harry's legs quit scrambling and his hands weakening in their struggles against Max's forearm.

Jeff took off just as Mick made it to Max. Wrapping both arms around him, he yanked him back but Max wasn't to be stopped. Jeff made it to the trio and then I saw Cotton materialize out of nowhere. Then Brody was there and Steve, Darren, George, some guys I'd never seen before, and finally Pete and it took all of them to pull Harry one way and Max the other.

Once they disconnected, Max jerked his body away and shrugged off the hands on him, standing still as a statue. Only his chest moving, his breaths coming heavy, the cold tufts of them gusting fast and hard from his mouth, lighting in the moonlight and his head was tipped down, his eyes glued to Harry. Harry had collapsed to his front but up on an elbow with his head bent as if he couldn't hold it up.

I pushed up to my feet, completely oblivious to the snow that covered me, matted wet and cold in my hair, embedded in my clothes, and I stumbled to Max. I was two feet away before he turned to me. I felt his eyes hit me through the darkness and my knees gave way before I made it those last two feet.

But I didn't fall because Max caught me in his arms and hauled me deep into his large, tall, strong body, holding me close, holding me tight, holding me safe.

Told you he was close, Charlie said in my head, his voice teasing but relieved.

It was funny and I would have laughed if I wasn't busy bursting into tears.

"I got you, Duchess," Max's gravelly voice rumbled in my ear.

I lifted my arms to wrap him as tight as I could with the little energy I had left and I shoved my face in his neck. One of Max's arms stayed locked around me and his other hand slid up, palm warm on my neck, fingers in my wet, snow-tangled hair, and he held my face to his warmth as I sobbed.

"I got you, baby," he whispered. "You're safe. I got you."

I nodded into his neck and when I had it together enough, I whispered, "Bitsy's up there somewhere. Shauna too."

"All right, darlin'," Max muttered. I felt his lips leave my ear and he asked someone else quietly, "You hear that?"

"We're on it." I heard Mick say before I felt Max's breath warm again on my neck.

"Hold tight, Duchess," he urged, and I did the best I could do and held even tighter. "That's it," he whispered, his arm returning the favor.

Things were happening around us. People talking, moving. Steve's murmur from behind me, his hand touching my hair before it fell away.

But nothing penetrated the fortress Max had built around me with his arms, his body, his strength. All that was my world was being held in his arms.

When I got myself together, I whispered, "Max?"

"Right here, Nina," he whispered back immediately. "I'm always right here, honey."

I hiccoughed another sob and pressed deeper into him.

Then I asked, "Will you take me home?"

Again, Max answered immediately, "Absolutely."

Then he bent. Lifting me in his arms, he carried me through the snow and pine trees of a Colorado mountain straight to his Cherokee, where he set me gently in the passenger seat, buckled me in safely, folded into the driver's side, and then he took me home.

EPILOGUE

Final Visits

I walked into the A-frame carrying my bags and shouting, "Max!"

I received no reply.

I dumped the bags on the dining table, considered for a moment how angry Max was going to get when he saw that I'd bought myself a whole new outfit (including shoes and underwear). Decided that he'd be pretty angry (until he saw the underwear). Then I shouted again, "Max! I'm home! Where are you?"

I was shouting because now, if you couldn't see the person whose attention you wanted, you needed to shout in the A-frame. This was because Max had built off both sides.

One side, off the kitchen, was a one-story, huge family room that was stuffed full of furniture that invited you to lounge and do it a long time (and we did), a big flat-screen TV on the wall, and inset shelves all around filled with books, CDs, and DVDs. There was another enormous stone fireplace in there that helped to heat the space in the winters and made it even cozier, and it was already, no matter how big it was, pretty cozy considering the high lounge factor of the furniture.

The living room also included an enormous wedding portrait taken by none other than Jimmy Cotton. It was a portrait that, personally, I thought was far and away Cotton's masterpiece.

It was a black and white candid of me in my ivory gown, ax in his dark suit. Max had guided me away from the party a private moment and he had an arm light around my waist. ad a hand light on his neck. My head was tipped back, Max's ped down so our faces were close. We were talking. About at I didn't recall, but whatever it was, even though we were th in profile, you could see Max had a small smile playing out his mouth and I had a huge one on mine, like I was about idy to burst out laughing. We both looked happy, we looked tural standing close and touching, and, best of all, we looked viously, unashamedly, and completely in love.

I adored that picture. It was my favorite thing in the house d I never tired of looking at it even though Max teased me equently) when he caught me lost in study of that picture.

At the other side of the house, off the great room, Max had ilt on two stories with two bedrooms and a bath downstairs. ostairs was Max and my master suite with a big bathroom d a sitting room. I loved that master suite. It was beautiful. it I missed being with Max in our loft, which we now used a guest room when Mom and Steve or friends from igland came visiting.

Therefore, considering the fact that even with me shouting, ax might not hear me, I went in search of him.

As I moved through our house, I tried not to think of see- g Shauna at the mall with her husband. I hadn't seen her in es. It had to have been at least two years. And seeing her ought up thoughts that hadn't occupied my mind in a long ne. Thoughts I didn't want to have but thoughts, whenever ey started to crowd in, I couldn't keep at bay.

Word was, Shauna lived just outside Carnal now, a town out thirty miles away. Gossip in Gnaw Bone reported she tually loved this guy. Seeing him for the first time, I was sur- ised. He was shorter than her, older than her, and not nearly physically attractive as her. Gossip also said he wasn't .actly rolling in the dough but she was content in her average ouse with her husband's average salary.

Max said it was bullshit since she still didn't work an
likely she had her eyes peeled for her next target just lik
always.

My thoughts were that it might not be bullshit. Even a
ice queen would rethink her life's path when, because of he
actions, her man toy gets murdered, leaving his kids father
less; her previous life path sets her up to be framed for mu
tiple murders; and when it came out she tried to fleece he
lifelong best friend, everyone in town stops not liking her an
starts actively hating her and they aren't afraid to show it eve
if she'd survived a significant trauma.

As they would, thoughts of Shauna unfortunately led
thoughts of that night and what came of it.

Mom had seen Damon carrying me to his truck and she'
called Max immediately. Just as immediately, Max sprun
into action, calling Mick at the same time he and Steve starte
their search for me. Max and Steve had found Damon n
thirty minutes later since he was not hard to find, seeing a
his truck and body were off the main road just a couple mile
out of town.

With Damon down and me gone, my purse still in Damon'
truck and there being no word or sighting to prove me safe
confusion reigned, so Max talked Mick into setting up an all
out manhunt or, in this case, a womanhunt.

It was not lost on Max that as word flew through Gnav
Bone and every man and most of the women in town droppe
what they were doing to join the hunt, Harry was the only on
unavailable to participate. Things became clearer when Bit
sy's sister reported that Bitsy was missing and they couldn
get hold of her and they never couldn't get hold of her. Mic
ran a search on properties that Curt, Bitsy, and Harry owne
and found a hunting cabin Harry had, and upon learning thi
knowledge, Max and Steve headed to the cabin and Mick, Jef
Brody, and the rest followed.

By the time Max found me, Harry had had me for seve
hours. It wouldn't be until much later, indeed when we wer

my bed in Charlie's house in England, that he would confess that those seven hours "were the worst seven hours of my ckin' life, Duchess."

I hated Harry because he made Max experience that fear. nd I hated him even more because he made my mom and eve experience it too. The only good thing to come of it was at I didn't stay in Gnaw Bone an extra week and Max didn't ome to England for a couple of weeks' visit. Instead, I stayed Gnaw Bone an extra week and Max came to England and ayed with me for three months as I worked my notice, sold harlie's house, and prepared to leave my old life behind.

Since that day, outside of working, trips to the mall or grocery store, when Max was in town doing something for his mom and other normal life things, Max was never far away rom me. He was usually right there and if he wasn't, he could e right there in under thirty minutes.

This wasn't suffocating. When you'd been kidnapped and narrowly missed being shot to death, having a mountain man t your back was reassuring.

And having an amazing man love you so much that experiencing the threat of losing you meant he didn't like you far away was beyond reassuring. It was beautiful.

Harry had shot Damon in the heart. Therefore he was dead before his face hit the dirt. He wasn't missed much because he was a serious jerk but no one believed that was appropriate comeuppance, even if he was a serious jerk.

Harry had confessed to three counts of murder, conspiracy to commit murder, and four counts of kidnapping, for in the end, he'd kidnapped Bitsy too. Despite confessing to the crimes, he still received a life sentence, as I thought he definitely should. Max was of another mind, namely the death sentence but since the state of Colorado had only put one man to death since 1976, Max had to make do with Harry not breathing free and having plenty of time to reflect on his actions for the rest of his sad, wasted life.

Bitsy had confessed to conspiracy to commit murder.

The fallout had rocked the town of Gnaw Bone, for no on suspected either Harry or Bitsy. Both of them were well like and the entire town was stunned that not only did they pe petrate this heinous deed (or, in Harry's case, *deeds*, plural they'd planned it for years.

That said, whether it was right or wrong, no one blame Bitsy much. Curt had crippled her, killed her best friend, fla grantly cheated on her, gave money to his mistress, and force Bitsy, in a variety of ways, into a life she didn't want to lea both in a wheelchair and also living in that house that lorde over the whole town. But the bottom line was, she spent yea planning her husband's murder. Nevertheless, her confessio and the extenuating circumstances meant her sentence wa relatively light but she was still in jail and would be for a whil

Although I had been caught up in their mess, Max als didn't blame Bitsy (much). This was because Bitsy, who ha been hiding her bitterness against her husband, didn't hid her repentance for what she, no matter what anyone told he (including me when I visited her), blamed herself that she' led Harry to do. She took responsibility for all of it, most espe cially what happened to me. The events leading on from Cu tis Dodd's murder broke her. It wasn't jail that broke her. Sh had, in her mind, the end of four lives on her hands *and* wha happened to me.

In an effort to make amends, she sold Curt's business t Max for a song. He argued with her about the deal but sh refused to listen. She wanted to do her bit to keep Max in tow with me and to keep Max and me fed and happy and she some how convinced Mountain Man Max to take the deal. He di and as he'd said he'd do, he downsized the operation. Eve so, with Max's reputation as a man as well as for his qualit craftsmanship, he kept his crew busy, his family fed and mor than comfortable. At the same time, we—since I bought m lawyer's desk and installed it in George's offices when he and formed a partnership—kept our mountain clean.

I completed my search for Max when I retraced my step

ck to the kitchen and I mentally, and thankfully, shrugged
f my thoughts. Then I saw Max's note.

Duchess,

Charlie and me are out.

Max

I held the note and stared at it.

They were out. Out. *Now*. When we should all be getting
ady.

I saw movement to my side and looked down at the big,
affy gray cat who had her bottom in the air, her chest to the
or, and her paws straight out in front of her, stretching and
wning at the same time, as usual oblivious to her mother's
ritation.

The cat was my idea. Max wanted a dog. He only capitu-
ted because when I really pushed him about the cat it was
hen I told him he was going to get Charlie.

So I got my cat.

"My husband is annoying," I told the feline.

She quit stretching and blinked at me, communicating
omplete unconcern.

I smiled at her, dropped the note, moved to my cat, and
ave her bottom some scratches before I walked out of the
-frame. I rounded it, saw the open barn doors, and rolled my
ves. Then I climbed to the barn, unlocked the safe, grabbed
e keys, and hopped on an ATV. I turned it in the barn and
ok off to search for my husband and son on our mountain.

I knew Max and Charlie had several special spots, but
henever I needed to drag them back home (which was often),
usually found them at the first spot I checked.

I rounded the trail at the top of the hill that rose up from
e back of Max's bluff and I stopped the ATV when I looked
own and my eyes hit the scene in front of me.

Max was down there, in jeans and a T-shirt, his skin tanner

than normal because he worked outside a lot and it was summer. He was sitting in the dirt (as he would since he didn't do the laundry), knees up, Charlie in his lap tucked between his chest and thighs. Max's head was turned away from me and toward the view. I couldn't really see my son's dark-haired head but I could see he probably wasn't studying the view because he was, at that moment, banging on his father's knee with his little baby fists.

I sighed my annoyance but even though I was the only one who could hear it, I didn't mean it.

Leave them be, Charlie said in my head.

"We need to get ready," I whispered into the wind.

Look at them, Neenee Bean, Charlie urged, but he didn't have to; my eyes hadn't left Max and our son.

Then Charlie twisted in Max's lap so he was facing his father, his little baby legs pumping and his little baby fists banging now on his dad's shoulders. Max didn't try to control Charlie's fists. He just wrapped his son in his arms and bent his neck so his face was in Charlie's. Therefore Charlie took that as his cue to grab Max's ear and I heard the wind carry my husband's chuckle mingled with my son's baby laughter back to me.

I felt my lips smile.

Leave them be, Charlie repeated.

"Okay," I whispered.

Love you, Neenee Bean, Charlie said to me.

"Love you, too, Charlie," I replied.

Then I turned the ATV around and headed home.

*   *   *

"When we get home, babe, we'll be talkin' about you goin' out on the ATV," Max growled into my ear, and I turned my head to him just as Charlie launched himself out of my lap and at his father's chest.

With practiced ease, Max caught the ever-active Charlie and pulled him close.

"What?" I asked with feigned innocence.

"Went to lock up the barn and saw one of the ATVs wasn't here I left it. Since Charlie can't sit astride one yet, that aves you and, like I said, when we get home we'll be talkin' out you goin' out on an ATV."

My eyes left Max's to look over his shoulder and they skid-d through the church pews that were full to bursting. I could e the entire church since we were beside Barb and Brody in e front pew. As I did this, I was thinking that I should have ken note of where the ATV was when I took it and I should ve put it back where I found it.

"Duchess, look at me," Max called, and I knew he wouldn't t up until I did as I was told so I did as I was told. "No more TV," he finished.

"I got home and you guys were gone," I explained.

"I left a note," Max told me.

"Yes, but we needed to start getting ready," I told him.

"We're here, aren't we?" he asked.

"Yes," I replied.

"And we ain't late."

"No, but we were close and you may have the memory of 1 elephant but you lose track of time *especially* when you're ut on the mountain with Charlie."

"Babe...we're...*here*," Max repeated. "And we're not te, so I didn't lose track of time. You know I wouldn't miss is, so you shouldn't have worried and in your condition you ould not, under any circumstances, be on an ATV."

I waved my hand between us and stated, "I'm good on an TV and I should be—you taught me how to ride one—and rthermore, I don't have a *condition*. I'm only ten weeks and ven if I wasn't, I'm perfectly *fine*."

Max's hand shot out and wrapped around mine tight as e, taking Charlie with him, leaned in and returned, "You're regnant with my child. I get that you're still my Nina and you aink you can do as you please even with my baby inside you. ut what you need to get is that you're my Nina, you got my

baby inside you, and I want you and our baby to be perfect
fine for the next six and a half months and then some. I'
gonna make that so and part of me makin' that so is not letti
you put your ass on an ATV."

"He's right," my mother butted in on a whisper, leanin
toward us from the pew she was sitting in right behind us.

"Nellie," Steve, sitting beside her, growled warningly.

Max ignored this and decreed, "No ATV."

I stopped scowling at my mother, my gaze passing throug
Steve then Linda then Kami, all of whom were in the pe
with Mom and all of whom were looking at Max and me wi
amusement (except Kami, who rolled her eyes and mouthe
"Bossy" at me).

Then I looked at my husband and started, "Max—"

His hand in mine pulled both to his chest so they we
tucked between him and Charlie and Charlie took that oppo
tunity to latch on to my hair.

But I only had eyes for Max mainly because he was th
only thing I could see.

"Duchess, no . . . A-T-*V*."

I glared at him and he didn't even blink so I knew M
Overprotective was going to get his way. I also knew M
Overprotective was partly Mr. Overprotective because h
first wife heartbreakingly lost a number of children befor
they took their first breath in this world. And even thoug
Charlie was a breeze, Max had lost enough that my easy preg
nancy wasn't going to change his perspective. He was also M
Overprotective because his first wife had been killed in a ca
accident that was beyond his control. And lastly, he was M
Overprotective because his second (then-soon-to-be) wife ha
been kidnapped by a mountain man stalker and then drugge
and kidnapped by a mountain man gone bad and nearly shot t
death in the snow.

So I gave in.

"Oh, all right," I forced out, grabbing my son and pullin
him from Max's arms into mine.

Max's answer to this gesture was to slide his arm along the ⸤w, curl it around my shoulders, and pull me snug and tight ⸤to his side.

The side door to the sanctuary opened and Jeff, looking ⸤andsome in his tux, and Pete, his best man, walked out to line ⸤ at the front of the church.

I felt my insides melt.

Then I felt Max's lips at my ear. "That new dress is sweet, ⸤by," he whispered. My lips started curling up but they froze ⸤hen he finished, "But we'll also be talkin' about that when ⸤e get home."

I turned my head and Max lifted his. Our eyes locked, ⸤hereupon I informed him, "I'll remind you that *you* were ⸤e one who wanted me to move out here before you really ⸤ew me and *I* shop. It's what I do. It's what I've always done. ⸤work hard. I shop hard. And furthermore, I'm not coming to ⸤is event, of all events, in anything other than a fabulous new ⸤ress. So, you win on the ATV but no, we are *not* talking about ⸤is new dress when we get home."

Though, we might be having a discussion about the new ⸤ds I'd bought Charlie. I really didn't need the dress but ⸤harlie really, *really* didn't need any new clothes. I should ⸤ver veer into the baby store but my feet always took me ⸤ere. There was no way to fight it, so I had long since stopped ⸤ying.

The good news was, Max didn't know about Charlie's new ⸤othes yet. The bad news was, I didn't keep anything from ⸤m so eventually I'd have to tell him.

I decided as I stared into his beautiful gray eyes that I'd tell ⸤m tomorrow.

"All right, I get the win on the ATV, you get the win on the ⸤ress," Max allowed.

I grinned and leaned in, touching my mouth to his.

I didn't move my lips away when I whispered, "Thank you, ⸤arling."

Then I watched as his eyes did what his eyes always did for

three years every time I called him darling. They got heated and they got intense. Then his hand curled around the back of my head, he tipped it down and kissed my forehead before he let me go.

I pulled away. Charlie collapsed into my chest and snuggled close in a rare but always treasured moment of cuddly baby affection. I wrapped my arms around my son and I took that moment as I'd taken many moments to congratulate myself for rolling the dice, taking a gamble on life, and heading off for my time-out adventure in the Colorado mountains where my gamble paid off every second of every day and it did this in spades.

I looked back to the front of the church, then looked to Brody as his head turned toward me and I caught his amused blue eyes to which I rolled mine to which his amusement became audible.

Then the music struck up and we all straightened and twisted in our seats to watch Becca walk down the aisle.

Then we stood and I held my son tight to me as Max's arm around me, hand resting protective at my belly, held us both tight to his body and my family and I watched a beautiful, glowing, smiling, happy Mindy walk down the aisle.

*   *   *

Holden Maxwell walked out of his sleeping son's bedroom carrying the spent bottle. He hit the great room, where he saw his wife tucked in the big armchair, her damn cat curled in a ball in her lap.

After the wedding and after the after-wedding drinks with Steve and Nellie, his mother and Kami, Brody, Cotton, and Arlene, he'd driven his family home and Nina had changed out of her pretty dress into a pair of loose-fitting but clingy drawstring pants and a tight camisole.

She wasn't close to showing yet and, with Charlie hadn't started really showing until early in her fifth month. Even so at the end she'd been very heavy with Charlie and Charlie d made it into this world weighing nine pounds and three nces.

This had alarmed Max, this late development, Nina's dy's swift change and heavy burden, a fact he didn't share ith anyone but Brody and his mother.

He didn't know it but he had nothing to worry about. Nina dn't slow down throughout her entire pregnancy, the labor d lasted three hours, and the delivery went so smoothly e doctor said he'd never had one that easy in ten years of actice.

When he'd visited Bitsy at the detention center to tell her out his new son and how he'd come into the world, she'd told m that she reckoned life had given him enough heartache, at he should have it easy for a while.

Bitsy had no idea that life with Nina was far from easy.

But that didn't mean it wasn't beautiful.

She kept him on his toes, his Nina did. His wife ate life, voured it daily with a hunger and passion that had not ceased amaze him as their days together slid by.

It wasn't lost on Max that life had handed him great bounty a young age and then had taken it away only to give it back. e knew the bitter taste of loss and so he understood Bitsy not king the taste of it.

And therefore, he never failed to savor the sweet taste of aving Nina fill his life. He remembered the second that bit-rness was swept clean from his tongue, when his now wife ad informed him her sinuses hurt when she'd bravely and lariously squared off against him in a snowstorm minutes fter they met. He'd been so used to the sour taste, it came as shock when it disappeared as he fought against laughter at e same time the sweetness invaded, so strong and foreign it ade his jaws ache.

He took the bottle to the kitchen and then went to join his ife in their chair.

He'd started a fire because Nina liked fires in the evening o matter if it was summer or winter. But he knew it was a

wasted effort. Just as with Charlie, in the early months of h
pregnancy she slept a lot. He knew she was probably out th
minute she rested her head against the high arm of the chair.

Gently, he moved her, her damn cat darting away as he di
He slid in next to her and then pulled her into him. She helpe
In her sleep she curled deeply into his frame, her arm snakin
around his gut, her head burrowing into his neck.

Through this, as usual with his Nina, she didn't wake an
she wouldn't. He'd have to carry her to bed. She'd had an activ
day, starting it with heading to the mall first thing and endin
with dancing like a madwoman at Mindy and Jeff's receptio
then laughing until she choked with her family and friends a
The Mark.

Max stared into the fire and held his wife close and as h
was doing this, a sweet, hushed voice he hadn't heard in thi
teen years spoke in his brain.

I'm happy for you, honey, Anna said, and Max closed h
eyes.

Then he opened them and pulled Nina closer.

"I'm happy too," he whispered.

*I'm going now. If Nina asks where he's gone, tell her I'
taking Charlie with me.*

Max didn't answer.

I love you, Max, and I love the way she loves you.

She would love that, Anna would. That was pure Anna.

"Find peace, Swanee," Max replied.

Already did, 'bout three years ago, baby.

Max's jaw clenched to fight against his throat getting tigh
Then there was silence except for the crackling of th
fire in the grate of the huge stone hearth he laid with his ow
hands in the house on the mountain his father gave to him
his son asleep in the other room, his wife carrying his unbor
child asleep and tucked to his side.

And Holden Maxwell stayed right where he was, stil
quiet, content, and staring into the fire until it was time to g
up and carry Nina to bed.

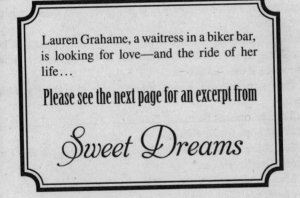

Lauren Grahame, a waitress in a biker bar, is looking for love—and the ride of her life...

Please see the next page for an excerpt from

Sweet Dreams

CHAPTER ONE

Bubba's

ᴀᴛ ɪɴ my parked car outside the bar.

It looked like a bar. It could be any bar anywhere, small
wn, big city, it didn't matter. It was just a bar. Bubba's bar,
parently, for it said ʙᴜʙʙᴀ'ꜱ in blue lettering on a black back-
ound in a huge sign at the top.

I looked out the window to my left. There were two Harley-
avidson motorcycles parked there.

I looked back at the bar, which it would seem might be a bit
a biker bar.

I looked out my window to the right. There was a beat-up,
d, blue Chevy pickup parked at the edge of the parking lot.

I looked back at the bar, which would seem was not high-
ass and not highbrow. They probably didn't even have mar-
ai glasses.

I looked at the window of the bar. In it there was a sign that
id ʜᴇʟᴘ ᴡᴀɴᴛᴇᴅ. In the little white space at the bottom of
e sign was written, ᴡᴀɪᴛʀᴇꜱꜱ.

I pulled breath in through my nose. Then I exhaled, got out
the car, and walked right to the door, through the door, and
to the bar.

I was right. Nothing special. Nothing high-class or high-
ow. It could be any bar anywhere.

There was a man sitting on a corner stool at the long bar
the back of the room. He had a ball cap on. There were two

other men playing pool at one of four pool tables. Two to the left, two to the right, the men were at one of the tables to the left. Evidently, bikers played pool. There was a woman behind the bar. She had a lot of platinum-blonde hair. She also had a lot of flesh at her cleavage. I could see this because it was bursting out the top of her Harley tank as well as straining the material.

Her eyes had come to the door the minute I walked in and didn't leave me as I walked to the bar.

"Hi—" I started.

"Chantelle's about twenty miles down the road. Straight on," the blonde interrupted me. "Just turn right out the parking lot and keep goin'."

"Sorry?" I asked, and felt the man with the ball cap turn to look at me.

"You lookin' for Chantelle?" the blonde asked.

"No, I'm—"

"Gnaw Bone?" she asked.

"Gnaw Bone?" I repeated.

"Gnaw Bone. Not too far away from Chantelle," she told me. "That what you lookin' for?"

I didn't know what to say. Then I asked, "You mean Gnaw Bone is the name of a town?"

She didn't answer. She looked at the man with the ball cap. I looked too. When I did, I saw firstly that his ball cap had definitely seen better days and those days were about four hundred years ago. Secondly, I saw that he was staring at my breasts.

I looked back at the blonde.

"I'm here about the waitress position."

For a second there was loaded silence. Then the man with the ball cap burst into a loud guffaw.

The blonde's eyes narrowed.

"Did Bubba put you up to this?" she asked.

"Bubba?" I asked back, at this point confused.

"Bubba," she bit out, then glanced around before looking at me. "This ain't funny. I got things to do."

I glanced around, too, and saw that she actually didn't have uch to do. The two guys were playing pool and didn't seem that thirsty. The ball cap guy had nearly a full draft in front him.

I looked again at the blonde.

"I'm not kidding," I told her.

"Bullshit," she replied irately, already at the end of her tience.

This was shocking. It wasn't like I'd never heard a curse rd before, or used them myself, just that I didn't tend to urt them out to strangers looking for jobs. Or strangers on e whole. And also I'd been there for about three minutes and dn't done anything to strain anyone's patience much less sh them to the end of it.

"No, seriously. I'd like to apply for the position," I plained.

She didn't answer for a while and took the time she was ent to study me. I decided to do the same.

She'd be pretty if she didn't tease her hair out so much and ear that much makeup and look clearly like she was in a bad ood and anyone could set her off. Though she really pulled f that tank top. I had serious cleavage, too, but it didn't come ith a petite, slim, but rounded body. It came with a big ass d a mini-Buddha belly and a hint of back fat. Not to mention mewhat flabby arms.

I decided to break the silence and announce, "I'm Lauren rahame."

I stuck out my hand. She stared at my hand and didn't get e chance to speak because the ball cap man spoke.

"Jim-Billy," he said, and I turned to him.

"Sorry?"

His hand was out to me, he was smiling, and this time look- g into my eyes. On the left side he'd lost the second tooth in d hadn't bothered to replace it. For some reason, instead of is making him look like a hillbilly with bad dental hygiene, made him look a little goofy and a little sweet.

"Jim-Billy," he repeated. "That's my name."

I took his hand and shook it. "Nice to meet you, Jim-Billy."

I repeated his name because I learned a long time ago at a training seminar to do that when you met someone. It solidifies their name in your mind so you wouldn't forget it. I was terrible with names and I found this worked and I figured a waitress in a small town needed to remember the names of the regulars at the bar. And Jim-Billy definitely looked like a regular.

It also worked that I chanted, *Jim-Billy, Jim-Billy, Jim Billy* in my head.

Then again, who'd forget the name "Jim-Billy"?

He gave me a squeeze, released my hand, and his gaze swung to the blonde.

"Tate'll like her. *Big-time*," he declared. "Bubba'll like her even better."

"Shut up, Jim-Billy," the blonde muttered.

"About the job...," I stated, bringing the matter back to hand, and the blonde looked at me.

Then she leaned into me. "Girl, take this as me doin' you a favor. Boys around here"—she threw out a hand—"they'd eat you alive. Go to Chantelle. Gnaw Bone. Woman like you has got no business in Carnal."

Carnal.

That was one of the reasons I picked that town. Its name was "Carnal." I thought that was funny and interesting but that was as interesting as I wanted to get.

I wanted to live in a Nowheresville town called Carnal. I wanted to work in an anywhere bar called Bubba's. There was nothing to either, except the names. Nothing memorable. Nothing special. Nothing.

"You don't understand," I told her. "I—"

She leaned back and stated, "Oh, girl, I understand." Her eyes moved from the top of my head to my midriff, which was all she could see with the bar in her way; then they came back to mine. "You're lookin' for a thrill. You're lookin' for adventure."

"I'm not. I'm—"

She threw her hands up. "You think I don't know it when ee it? Do I look like a woman who ain't been around? Do ook like a woman who feels like hirin' and trainin' and rnin' to put up with the new shit a new waitress is gonna d me? Then when she realizes that she wants her old life ck she ups and leaves and then I have to hire and train and rn to put up with new shit *again*?"

"I wouldn't give you...um..."

"Everyone shovels shit and I don't like the taste of it from kind. I already know I *really* don't like the taste of it from urs."

I again didn't know what to say because it was dawning on that she was discriminating against me.

"Not to be rude or anything," I said softly, "but you don't lly know me. You don't know what kind I am."

"Right," she replied, and there was derision heavy in her rd.

"You don't," I asserted.

"Girl—" she started, but I leaned forward and I did it for a ason.

I leaned forward because I needed her to hear me. I leaned rward because I'd been searching for Carnal a long time. I'd en searching for Bubba's a long time. I needed to be there d to be there I needed that job.

"Right," I repeated. "You think I'm some kind of lost oman like out of a book, traveling the globe on some idiot urney to find myself?" I asked, and before she could answer, continued. "Thinking I can go out there and find good food d experience interesting places while soul searching, wear- g fabulous clothes and being gorgeous and making everyone un into love me and, in the end, find a fantastic man who's lly good at sex and adores me beyond reason?" I shook my ad. "Well, I'm not. I know who I am and I know what I want d I know that isn't it because that doesn't exist. I also know hat I'm looking for and I know I found it right here."

"Listen—" she began.

"No, you listen to me," I interrupted her. "All my life, as long as I can remember, I thought something special wa going to happen to me. I just had this feeling, deep in m bones. I didn't know what it was but it was going to be beau ful, spectacular, *huge*." I leaned in farther. "All...my...life I shook my head again and put my hand on the bar. "It didn I waited and it didn't happen. I waited more and it didn't hap pen. I waited more and it *still* didn't happen. I tried to make happen and it *still* didn't happen. Now I know it isn't going t It's never going to happen because there isn't anything speci out there *to* happen."

I sucked in a breath. She opened her mouth but I ke talking.

"I had a husband. I had a home. I had a job. I had friend Then I found out my husband was sleeping with my best frien Not an affair—they'd been doing it *for five years*. When th cat was out of the bag, they decided to be together for re He divorced me and I couldn't afford the house on my ow so we sold it. Then, all of a sudden, after ten years of bei with someone, I was alone. They got the friends who alwa thought behind my back they were *perfect* together. They a knew. For five years. And no one told me."

"Fuckin' shit, woman," Jim-Billy muttered.

"Yeah," I said to Jim-Billy, and looked back at the blond "But, you know, after the shock of it wore off, I didn't care. swear. I didn't. Because all of a sudden I realized that I had shit marriage to a shit guy and I had a shit best friend and a sorts of other shit friends besides. And all that time I was li ing in a house I didn't want. It was too darned big and it wa too darned *everything*. A house should be a home, not a *hous* And that house was in a town I didn't like because every hous looked the same and every woman dressed the same and ever man played around the same and every car was shiny and ne and there was no personality *anywhere*. And in that town I ha a job I didn't much care about even though it paid me goo

oney." My voice dropped and I told her, "I realized I didn't
ve anything special. All of a sudden I realized that life didn't
ve anything special in store for me." I took in a breath and
ished, "And I'm okay with that. I don't want special any-
ore. I waited and I tried to make it happen and it didn't. So
it. Now I want to live someplace that is just a place. I want a
o where I can do a good job while I'm doing it and then I can
home to a place that's a home and just be home. I don't *want*
ything. I'm done wanting. I've been wanting and yearning
r forty-two years. The only thing I want is peace."

"You think you'll find peace in a Harley bar?" Jim-Billy
ked what was possibly a pertinent question, and I looked at
m.

"I think I can get to work on time, do a good job, feel good
out myself because I worked hard and did my best, and
home and not think about a Harley bar. I can think about
yself or what I have a taste to eat for dinner or what might
good on TV. Then I'll go to sleep not thinking about any-
ing and get up and get to work on time again." I turned to
e blonde. "That's what I think. I'm not looking for a thrill.
n not looking for adventure. I'm looking for nothing special
cause I can be content with that. That's what I'm looking
r. Can you give me that?"

The blonde said nothing, just looked me in the eyes. Her
ce was blank and no less hard and it stayed blank and hard
r a long time.

Then she said, "I'm Krystal. I'll get you an application."

*   *   *

stood at the window of my hotel room holding the curtains
ck with a hand and staring at the pool.

Carnal Hotel wasn't much to write home about. A long
ock of building, two stories, all the doors facing the front,
urteen on top, fourteen on bottom. I was on the bottom in
mber thirteen. The rooms were clean. Mine had a king-sized
d and a TV that had to have been purchased fifteen years

ago, which was suspended from the wall. The low four-draw
dresser and nightstands stuck out of the wall and had no leg
The closet had two extra pillows and an extra blanket. Th
bathtub and kitchen sink had rust stains, but even so, they we
clean too. The whole of it was below average but it would do.

That pool, though, that was something else. It wasn't b
but it was pristine clean. The lounge chairs around it were
top-of-the-line but they were okay, in great repair, and obv
ously taken care of.

I looked from the pool to reception. It wasn't so mu
reception as a tiny house. A tiny well-kept house with a l
tle upstairs. It also had big half barrels full of newly plant
flowers out front. It wasn't quite summer but it was the end
spring, so the flowers hadn't come close to filling out.

Carnal was in the Rocky Mountains. More precisely, it w
in a small valley surrounded by hills, which were surround
by mountains. It was closing on May, there was a nip in the a
and I wondered if those flowers were hopeful.

If they were, whoever planted them had the capacity for
lot of hope. There were more flowers in window boxes in th
front windows of the reception/house. There were also mo
flowers in half barrels intermittently placed by the poles o
the walk in front of the hotel rooms with more window box
on the railing of the balcony in front of the rooms upstai
And lastly there were more half barrels dotted around the po
area.

The parking lot was tidy and well kept and the hotel a
reception/house both had a good paint job.

All of this indicated that Carnal Hotel might be belo
average but the people who owned it cared about it.

I had checked in with a nice lady at the front desk who sa
anything I needed, change for the vending machines or lau
dry room, Wi-Fi access, menus for restaurants, and takeout
town, "just holler."

Then I'd unpacked my car. All of it. I unpacked it for th
first time in four and a half months. Then I cleaned it out. A

e junk food wrappers, discarded pop cans, fallen mints, st pieces of candy, bits of paper. The flotsam and jetsam of killer road trip. I lugged my suitcases (there were five) and xes (there were two) into the hotel room and took a plas- bag I'd found and filled full of trash to the big outdoor bin cked close to the side of the hotel not facing any streets.

Then I unpacked my clothes.

Over the past four and a half months, I'd been in tons of tel rooms but I'd never unpacked. I'd never stayed beyond ree days. I'd only stayed long enough to do laundry, take a eather, and decide where I'd head next in my search, zig- gging across so many states I'd lost count in my search for wheresville.

After I unpacked, I'd walked into town, which amounted to e walking by room number fourteen and turning the corner. rnal Hotel was on the edge of town right before the road ened up to nothing again. I'd found a deli, bought a pastrami rye, and ate it on the sidewalk, chasing it with a diet pop. en I'd walked the town up one side and down the other.

Bubba's was in the middle, five blocks from the hotel, and was definitely a biker bar because Carnal was a biker town. ere were two bike shops and one bike mechanic at the oppo- e end from Carnal Hotel and it had a sign that said WE TAKE RS TOO. There were also three motorcycle paraphernalia ops that, from what I could see looking in the windows, sold ot of leather bike accessories and more leather biker clothing.

There was also the deli, a diner, an Italian restaurant, a zza delivery place, and a coffee house, which was strangely lled "La-La Land Coffee." Again looking in the windows La-La Land, I saw it was not run by bikers but hippies who ere so hippie they wore tie-dyed shirts with peace signs on ont and had long hair. One of the two behind the counter had round, blue-tinted sunglasses even though he was inside d the other had a thin braided headband wrapped around her rehead. They looked in danger of dropping cross-legged on e floor and singing "Kumbaya."

This all was intermingled with a discount tobacco sto that sold all types of smoker delights for all types of thin you could smoke. There were two discount liquor stores, drugstore, and a tailor who seemed to specialize in stitchin biker patches into leather (or at least that was what the sign the window said). The town had two convenience stores, o opposite the hotel, one at the other end of town opposite t mechanic. It also had a busy grocery store about a quart the size of the mega-grocery stores that every other town the nation seemed to have, and it looked like it'd been the since 1967. And all this was rounded out by a bakery, a har ware store, a flower shop, a gas station, and a variety of oth Nowheresville places to fill a Nowheresville town.

There were people on the street and I knew they we friendly because most of them smiled at me.

After I checked out the Main Street (called Main Stre and it was also the only street with businesses, the rest w residential) of my new home, I went back to reception at t hotel. I bought a week's worth of Wi-Fi from the nice la who took that opportunity to share with me that her name w Betty. I shared my name, too, and decided to go ahead a pay a week in advance on my room when I got the Wi-Fi. Th decision overjoyed Betty and I knew that because she told m

"Sweetie! A week! I'm overjoyed!" she'd shouted.

She would be. Mine was the only car in the lot and she ha a flower and pool habit and those weren't exactly cheap.

Nevertheless, she was friendly and open and I decided liked Betty.

After telling her I was glad I'd brought her joy, I went ba to number thirteen and dragged out my laptop. Then I logg in. I ignored all my e-mail and sent a message to my paren and my baby sister that all was well, I was fine, and I'd che in with more information later. I saw that they'd sent e-ma to me but I didn't read them. I didn't read them because I kne they would freak me out because I knew my mom and d and sister Caroline were freaked out. They weren't big on n

ping stakes and roaming the country looking for nothing
ecial. They were bigger on me moving home, sorting myself
t, finding a decent man, and starting over (in that order).

I shut down my computer, sat on the big, soft bed, stared at
e wall, and thought about the next day when I was supposed
be at Bubba's at eleven to train to be a waitress and start my
w life.

Then I smiled.

Then I watched TV until it got dark and the pool beck-
ed me.

Now I was standing and looking outside to see the pool
oked clean and enticing and it was all lit up. In fact, the
rking lot was all lit up. Seeing it, I knew four things about
ception Betty. She was friendly, she liked flowers, she was
oud of her below-average hotel and small but clean pool, and
e wanted her guests to feel safe.

That's when I saw the car pull in. It was a convertible, an
d model something. It looked like a Chrysler, not great con-
ion but also not a junker.

It parked outside reception, the door opened, and a woman
lded out.

I stared at the woman.

She had thick, long dark hair and long legs, most of which
could see coming out the bottom of her very short, frayed-
mmed jean skirt. She had a tight tank top and more cleav-
e than Krystal (but as much as me). She wasn't petite or
m. She was long and *very* rounded but it was clear she didn't
re. A mini-Buddha belly and a hint of back fat didn't bother
r. Not in the slightest. In fact, she *worked it*.

She sashayed into reception and I saw a man was there. He
as Betty's upper-middle-age. He smiled at her like he knew
r and she waved and smiled back, giving the same impres-
on. I knew this was the truth when he handed her a key
ithout doing any of the usual checking-in business. She took
e key, put both her hands on the counter, lifted herself up,
oty pointed up in the air, feet in high-heeled stiletto sandals

on tiptoe. She kicked back one foot and leaned toward hi
giving him an across-the-counter air kiss. Then she strutt
back out to her convertible, got in, and drove through the pa
ing lot to park three spots down from my Lexus. She got o
didn't grab a suitcase, and walked toward a door where I l
sight of her.

I had a feeling I was going to have to buy some tank tops
fit in in Carnal.

I dropped the curtain and went to the dresser. Most of i
clothes were folded and sitting on top; there wasn't enou
room for them all in the drawers and closet. But at least the
been released from their suitcase captivity. In the drawers
put my underwear, socks, and pajamas. I'd also put my bathi
suit in there.

Seeing my clothes laid out, I thought it wasn't much bu
was more home than I'd had in a good long while and it ma
me feel weirdly settled.

It had been a warm day but it couldn't be over sixty-fi
degrees outside. Still, I loved pools, I loved to be in water, a
for some reason I really wanted a swim, so I figured it wou
be like any time you got in cold water. Once you were in, yo
get used to it. At least I hoped so. If not, so what? I'd just dr
my carcass out and come back to my room.

I changed into my swimsuit, put on a pair of track pants
sweatshirt, and some flip-flops. Before I could chicken out
grabbed a towel and my room key and headed to the pool.

I slipped off my shoes and sweats and decided to dive rig
in. Better to get it over with all at once. I moved to the side
the pool, braced for impact, and dove.

The pool was heated.

Heaven.

I swam five laps of the short pool and had to stop becau
I couldn't breathe. This, I told myself, had to do with the fa
that I was in the Rocky Mountains, at altitude, and it did *n*
have to do with the fact that I was seriously out of shape.

I forced out four more laps and had to stop again.

Then I forced out one more lap and put a hand to the edge
turn back for another lap when I heard the roar of bike pipes.

Stopped at the edge of the pool, holding on and peering
er the side, my eyes followed the black-and-chrome Harley
eaming in Reception Betty's parking lot lights as it glided
ong, pulled in, and parked next to the convertible. Then my
es watched the man shove the stand down with his booted
ot and swing his leg off the bike.

His back was to me so all I could see was that he was tall
d he had a *great* behind. He also had on faded jeans and a
ack long-sleeved, thermal T-shirt, and he had a head of thick
rk hair that also shone in the lights, just like his Harley.

One of the hotel room doors opened and the woman in the
an miniskirt ran out and threw herself at the tall man. Her
ms wrapped around his neck and I couldn't see it but I could
l her lips latched on to his.

He didn't even go back on a foot when her body impacted
s. He just curved his arms around her and leaned into her kiss.

That's something special.

The thought just popped into my head and I didn't know
hy. I didn't know what was happening. I didn't know these
o people. All I knew was that it *looked* special. So special,
I could do was stare.

They stopped kissing and she tipped her head back and
ughed with pure delight, the sound ringing through the air,
ling it with music.

I decided I hated her and I didn't know why. I didn't know
ho she was or what was happening. I just knew she had some-
ing special and I didn't and never would and that sucked. It
asn't a nice thought, which was unusual because I was nor-
ally a nice person. But it was the one I had.

She disengaged from him and came to his side, wrapping
er arm around his waist and propelling him forward.

He looked down at her and I saw his profile in Reception
etty's bright parking lot lights and when I did I held my
eath.

If he was that handsome in profile, so handsome he w
breathtaking, he'd be sensational full on.

That's when I decided I *really* hated her.

They got close to the door and he moved suddenly an
quickly. Swinging her up in front of him, she wrapped her le
around his hips, her arms around his shoulders and tipped h
head down to look at him. But he seemed to be peering in t'
room like he expected to see something or someone, som
thing or someone important, something or someone he w
looking forward to seeing. But before he found that somethi
or someone, she fisted a hand in his hair, tilting his back, h
mouth went down on his, and they entered the room necking

He closed the door with his booted foot.

Yes, sensational. If he could pick her up like that and car
her anywhere, he was beyond sensational.

"Like the pool?"

I jumped and pushed off the side with my foot, my hea
jerking around as I stared at the Reception Guy who check
in Lucky as Hell Girl, whom I hated. He was standing at t'
side of the pool and looking down at me. I'd been so engross
in Handsome Harley Guy and Lucky as Hell Girl I had
heard him coming.

"Sorry?" I asked.

"The pool," he answered. "Like it?"

"Um...," I mumbled, staring up at him. "Yes."

"It's heated," he informed me.

"Um...," I mumbled again. "I can tell."

"Betty 'n' me got it relined last year. One or t'other of
clean it every day. Best pool in the county."

I couldn't disagree. It was a fantastic pool, clean, heate
and everything.

Therefore I said, "It's really nice."

He rocked back on his heels and took in the pool with h
eyes before he looked back at me.

"Thanks. Ned," he said.

"Uh, no...my name is Lauren," I said back, and he laughe

"No, pretty lady, name's Ned." He jerked a thumb at himf. "I'm Ned."

"Oh," I replied, feeling like an idiot. "Hey, Ned."

"Hey back atcha, Lauren." He grinned. "Betty tells me u're stayin' awhile."

"Yeah," I told him, thinking he seemed friendly enough t not certain how much to share because, well, I didn't know m and every girl in a pool in the parking lot of a hotel on the lge of Nowheresville should be smart and not tell their story, rrent or past, to some random man who snuck up on them. fact, girls like that should get out of the pool, get into their om, and lock the danged door.

"That's great." Ned was still grinning. "We don't get a lot of ng-timers. Weekenders. Nighters. Yeah. Long-timers. No."

"Oh," I replied, my eyes going back to the long block of tel, specifically to my room, where I figured I should be at at present moment.

"That's Neeta," Ned said, and I looked back at him.

"Neeta?" I asked.

Ned nodded. "Neeta and Jackson." He shook his head. 3ad news."

My gaze slid back in the direction of the hotel. He'd misterpreted where I was looking. He thought I was looking at arley Guy and Lucky as Hell Girl's room.

I didn't inform him of his mistake. Instead, I asked softly, 3ad news?"

"Yeah," Ned answered. "She swings into town and shoo!" ly eyes went to him to see he'd put his hands up at his sides d had taken a step back. "We brace."

"Brace for what?" I asked.

He dropped his hands. "Brace for whatever Neeta's got up r sleeve."

"Is that"—I motioned toward the Harley and the convert-le with my head—"Neeta with that man?"

"Jackson, yeah. He's great, a good man, smart, solid, salt of e earth. Loses his mind around Neeta, though. Then again,

not many men wouldn't but I'm guessing you know all abo[u]
that."

My eyes had wandered back to the Harley as I treade[d]
water and Ned talked but I looked at Ned when I heard h[is]
comment.

"I do?"

His grin came back and it was bigger this time, brighte[r]
transforming his whole face, making me think he might ju[st]
be a friendly innkeeper in a biker town in the Rocky Mou[n]
tains, just like he seemed.

"Sure you do. Ain't shittin' me, pretty lady."

He was right. I wasn't shitting him mostly because I had n[o]
idea what he was talking about.

"Figure, though," he went on, and his eyes moved towar[d]
the Harley, "you'd be worth whatever trouble you might cause[.]"

"What?" I whispered, and he looked back at me.

"I'm a good judge of people," he informed me instead [of]
explaining himself.

"Yes?" I asked because I didn't know what else to say.

"Yeah," he replied quietly, moving closer to the edge of th[e]
pool and squatting. I kept treading water and staring at hi[m]
"See," he continued, still quiet, "any trouble you might caus[e]
I'm guessin' would be trouble you don't mean to cause."

"I've never caused any trouble," I told him.

This was true. I hadn't. I was a good girl. I'd always bee[n]
a good girl. I'd always made the right decisions and done th[e]
right things. I might have chosen the wrong husband and th[e]
wrong friends but they were the jerks in those scenarios, n[ot]
me. I was nice. I was thoughtful. I was considerate. I looke[d]
out for my neighbors. I got up when old ladies needed a se[at]
in a waiting room. I let people who had two or three items g[o]
in front of me at the checkout in grocery stores if I had a fu[ll]
cart of food. I kept secrets. I bit my lip when people I knew di[d]
stupid things I knew they would regret and then kept biting m[y]
lip when those stupid things bit them in the ass and they cam[e]
to me and whined about it.

I didn't wear miniskirts, not ones with frayed hems, not y miniskirts at all. If I did, I wouldn't wear them with high-eled sandals. Maybe flip-flops or flats but not high heels. I dn't air kiss front desk reception guys named Ned even if I ew them. I didn't drive a convertible. I didn't rush out a door d throw myself into the arms of a man.

And I'd never laughed so loud I filled the air with music.

"Betty's different than me." Ned broke into my thoughts d I focused on him.

"She is?" I asked, thinking I may have missed something.

"I'm a good judge of people; she's got the sight."

"The sight?" I repeated stupidly.

He grinned again while straightening; it was his big grin. e had all his teeth; the eyetooth was wonky but they were all an and white and the rest were straight. His hair was a little in, light brown. He wasn't tall, not short either. Lean and on e thin side. And, I was beginning to believe, a genuinely nice y, not the creepy night clerk at a hotel in Nowheresville.

"The sight." He nodded and looked toward the hotel before turned to me as I moved my arms through the water to take e back to the side so I could stop treading. I reached out and ld on to the edge as he kept going. "She told me she met you d she just knew."

"Knew what?"

"Somethin' big was gonna happen."

I blinked and it wasn't to get the water out of my eyes.

"Something big?"

"Yep."

"To me?"

"To you, through you, because of you, whatever. But what-er it is, it'll be big and it'll be good."

I didn't know what to do with this mostly because it was a tle crazy.

"She said that?"

He nodded and crossed his arms on his chest, rocking back his heels again.

"Yep. And she's never wrong. We been married twenty-five years and she gets these feelin's and, I'll repeat, she's never wrong. My Betty's always right. Always."

I didn't know what to say to that so I stayed silent.

"Anyhoots!" he exclaimed loudly. "Best leave you to your swim. You need anythin' at all, you know where to find me. hit the hay around midnight but you just gotta ring the buzzer outside the front door and it'll wake me up. Yeah?"

I nodded.

"Anythin' you need, pretty lady, I mean that," he said, and it sounded like he meant it.

"Okay," I replied.

"Glad to have you with us, Lauren."

"Thanks, Ned."

He lifted a hand in a wave and wandered back to the reception/house.

I looked at the Harley and listened to the quiet of Carnal.

Then I forced out ten more laps (with three more rest periods), got out of the pool, toweled off, grabbed my stuff, and ran to my room.

THE DISH

Where Authors Give You the Inside Scoop

♥ ♥ ♥ ♥ ♥ ♥ ♥ ♥ ♥ ♥ ♥ ♥ ♥ ♥ ♥

From the desk of Jennifer Haymore

Dear Reader,

When Lady Dunthorpe, the heroine of THE SCOUN-DREL'S SEDUCTION, came to my office, she filled the tiny room with her presence, making me look up from my computer the moment she walked in. The first thing I noticed was that she was gorgeous. Very petite, with lovely features perfectly arranged on her face. She could probably be a movie star.

"How can I help—?" I began, but she interrupted me.

"I *need* you," she declared. I could hear the smooth cadence of a French accent in her voice. "My husband has been murdered, and I've been kidnapped by a very bad blackguard…a…a *scoundrel*."

I straightened in my chair. "What? How…why?" I had about a million questions, but I couldn't seem to get them all out. "Please, my lady, sit down."

She slid into the chair opposite me.

"Now," I said, "please tell me what exactly is going on and how I can help you."

She leaned forward, her blue eyes luminous and large. "My husband—Lord Dunthorpe. He was killed. And his murderer…his murderer has captured me. I don't know what he's going to do…" She swallowed hard, looking terrified.

"Do you know who the murderer is?

She shook her head. "*Non*. But his friends call him 'Hawk.'"

Every muscle in my body went rigid. I knew only one man called Hawk. His real name was Samson Hawkins, he was the oldest brother of the House of Trent, and I'd just finished writing books about two of his brothers.

Yet maybe she wasn't talking about "my" Hawk. Sam was a hero, not a murderer. Still, I had to know.

"Is he tall and broad?" I asked her. "Very muscular?"

"*Oui*...yes."

"Handsome features?"

"Very."

"Dark eyes and dark hair that curls at his shoulders?"

"Yes."

"Does he have a certain...*intensity* about him?"

"Oh, yes, very much."

Yep, she was definitely talking about Sam Hawkins.

I sat back in my chair, stunned, mulling over all she had told me. Sam had killed her husband. He'd kidnapped her...and was holding her hostage...*Wow*.

"I need your help," she whispered urgently. "I need to be free..."

"Of course," I soothed.

Her desire to be free sparked an idea in my mind. Because if she truly knew Sam—knew the man inside that hard shell—perhaps she *wouldn't* want to be free of him. She was beautiful and vivacious—she'd lit up my little office when she'd walked inside. Sam had certainly already noticed this about her. Now...all I had to do was work a little magic—okay, I admitted to myself, a *lot* of magic, considering the fact that Sam had killed her husband—and I could bring these two together.

Sam hadn't lived a very easy life. He *so* deserved his very own happily ever after.

This would be a love match born in adversity. *Very* tricky. But if I could make it work—if I could give Lady Dunthorpe to Sam as his heroine—it would probably be the most fulfilling love story I'd ever written.

With determination to make it work, I turned my computer screen toward me and started typing away. "Tell me what happened," I told Lady Dunthorpe, "from the beginning..."

And that was how I began the story of THE SCOUNDREL'S SEDUCTION—and now that I've finished it, I'm so excited to share it with readers, because I definitely believe it's my most romantic story yet.

Please come visit me at my website, www.jennifer haymore.com, where you can share your thoughts about my books and read more about THE SCOUNDREL'S SEDUCTION and the House of Trent Series. I'd also love to see you on Twitter (@jenniferhaymore) or on Facebook (www.facebook.com/jenniferhaymore-author).

Sincerely,

Jennifer Haymore

♥ ♥ ♥ ♥ ♥ ♥ ♥ ♥ ♥ ♥ ♥ ♥ ♥ ♥

From the desk of Kristen Ashley

Dear Reader,

As a romance reader from a very young age, and a girl who never got to sleep easily so I told myself stories to get that way (all romances, of course), I had a bevy of "starts" to stories I never really finished.

Not until I finally started to tap away on my keyboard.

One of them that popped up often was of a woman alone, heading to a remote location, not feeling well, and meeting the man of her dreams who would nurse her back to health. Except, obviously (this *is* a romance), at first meeting him, she doesn't know he's the man of her dreams and decides instantly (for good reason) she doesn't like him all that much.

Therefore, I was delighted finally to get stuck in Nina and Max's story in THE GAMBLE. I'd so long wanted to start a story that way and I was thrilled I finally got to do it. I got such a kick out of seeing that first chapter unfold, their less-than-auspicious beginning, the crackling dialogue, Max's A-frame (inside and out) forming in my head.

But I had absolutely no clue about the epic journey I was about to take—murder, assault, kidnapping, suicide and rape, trust earned and tested—and amongst all this, a man and a woman falling in love.

The focus of the book is on Nina's story—oft-bitten, very shy, to the point where she's hardly living her life nymore, feels it, and knows she needs to do something about it even as she's terrified.

But whenever I read THE GAMBLE, it's Max's story that touches me. How he had so much from such a young age and lost it so tragically. How he took care of everyone around him in his mountain man way, but also was living half a life. And last, how Nina lit up his world and revived that protective, loving part of him he thought long dead.

The struggle with this, however, was Anna, the love Max lost. See, I knew her well and she was an amazing person who made Max happy. They were very much in love and neither Max (in my head) nor I wanted to give her short-shrift or make any less of the love they shared even as Max fell deeply in love with Nina.

I didn't know if this was working very well, for Nina was so very much *not* like Anna, but, at least to me, I found her quite lovable. This was good; you shouldn't try to find what you lost but simply find something that makes you happy. But still, it was important for me that the love Max shared with Anna wasn't entirely overshadowed by the love he had for Nina because Anna was in his life, she was important, and being so was part of what made him the man he turned out to be.

In a book that has a good deal of raw emotion, one line always jumps out at me and there's a reason for that. I was relieved when a friend of mine told me it was her favorite in this whole, very long book. So simple but also, by it being her favorite, it told me that I'd won that struggle.

It was Max saying to Nina, "*I see what I had with Anna*

for the gift it was but now that's gone. With this act, are you sayin', in this life that's all I get?"

In a book where grave tragedy had consistently struck many of the characters (as life often hands us our trials), I love the hope in this line. I love that Max finally comes to realize that the beauty he had and lost was not all he should expect. That he should reach out for more.

And he *does* reach out for more.

And in the end, he finds that it isn't all he would get. Being a good man and taking a gamble on a feisty woman who shows up in a snowstorm with attitude (and her sinuses hurting), he gets much, *much* more.

So I was absolutely delighted to take his journey.

Because he deserves it.

Kristen Ashley

♥ ♥ ♥ ♥ ♥ ♥ ♥ ♥ ♥ ♥ ♥ ♥ ♥ ♥ ♥ ♥

From the desk of Nina Rowan

Dear Reader,

What is the worst part of writing a historical romance? Once upon a time, I might have thought it was most difficult to unravel the plot and character motivations.

but the more I write, the more I realize the truth. It's the research! And I don't mean that in a moan-and-groan-it's-homework way. I mean that the more I research for the sake of a book, the more I get flat-out distracted by all the little golden nuggets I find.

When I start researching, I tend to trawl the London Times archives, which has a searchable database that is so beautiful and easy to use that it almost makes me cry. For A DREAM OF DESIRE, I started by looking up articles about prisons and juvenile delinquency, but got quickly distracted by other things like the classified advertisements. The Times was full of ads for polka and mazurka lessons, "paper hanging" sales, tea companies, and job openings for schoolmistresses and butlers. The "prisons" search term appeared in the classifieds in an advertisement for "prisons supply of coal, meat, bread, oatmeal, barley, candles, and stockings." The ad requested that suppliers submit an application to the keeper of the prisons to be considered for the position.

I also get distracted by other articles about criminal court proceedings (a goldmine of story ideas), new laws, intelligence from overseas, and details about royal court life, like the state ball of 1845 at Buckingham Palace, which was attended by over one thousand members of the nobility and gentry and where Her Majesty and the Hereditary Grand Duke of Mecklenburgh Strelitz danced the quadrille in the ballroom, which was festooned with crimson and gold draperies and lit by a huge, cut-glass lustre.

I find that fascinating. But distractions aside, it really is within the pages of the newspapers and magazines published in the nineteenth century that the most vivid details of a story can come to life. When I first started writing A DREAM OF DESIRE, I thought surely the term "juvenile delinquent" was a historical anachronism but it was used often in Victorian-era *Times* articles about "juvenile destitution and crime."

I've come to accept the fact that rather than being a dedicated, focused researcher, I'm more like a magpie whose attention is caught by shiny objects. But I've also learned to appreciate how much all those little tidbits of information come in handy when crafting a story—what might happen if the hero and heroine were in attendance at Her Majesty's state ball? What if the heroine was having a clumsy moment (or better yet, was distracted by the hero's rakish good looks) and tripped over the Grand Duke in the middle of the quadrille? What if she found herself face-to-face with a rather irate Queen Victoria?

Must go. I have some writing to do!

Nina Rowan

♥ ♥ ♥ ♥ ♥ ♥ ♥ ♥ ♥ ♥ ♥ ♥ ♥ ♥ ♥

From the desk of Jane Graves

Dear Reader,

I like wine. Any kind of wine. I've learned a lot about it over the years, but only because if you use any product enough, you'll end up pretty educated about it. (If I at

47 different kinds of Little Debbie snack cakes, I'd know a lot about them, too.) I can swirl, sniff, and sip with the best of them. But the fourth S: spit? Seriously? The theory is that one should merely taste the wine without getting tipsy, but come on. Who in his right mind tastes good wine and then spits it out?

My husband and I once went to a wine tasting/competition where we took our glasses around to the various vintners' booths and received tiny tasting pours, which we were to sip, savor, and judge. By the time we sampled the offerings of about two dozen vineyards, those tiny pours added up. At first we discussed acidity, mouth feel, and finish, then thoughtfully marked our scorecards. By the end of the event, we'd lost our scorecards and were wondering if there was a frat party nearby we could crash. Okay, so maybe that spitting thing has some merit.

In BABY, IT'S YOU, the hero, Marc Cordero, runs an estate vineyard in the Texas Hill Country that has been in his family for generations. As I researched winemaking for the book, I discovered it's both a science and an art, requiring intelligence, intuition, willpower, and above all, heart. The heroine, Kari Worthington, feels Marc's pride as he looks out over the grapevine-covered hills, and she's in awe of his determination to protect his family legacy. For a flighty, free-spirited, runaway bride who's never had a place to truly call home, Cordero Vineyards and the passionate man who runs it are the things of which her dreams are made.

So next time I go to a wine tasting, I'm going to think about the myriad challenges that winemakers faced in order to present that bottle for me to enjoy. But I'm still not gonna spit.

I hope you enjoy BABY, IT'S YOU!

Jane Graves

JaneGraves.com
Twitter @JaneGraves
Facebook.com/AuthorJaneGraves

♥ ♥ ♥ ♥ ♥ ♥ ♥ ♥ ♥ ♥ ♥ ♥ ♥ ♥

From the desk of Adrianne Lee

Dear Reader,

I have a secret to confess: I'm not creative with my hands.

My mother and sister inherited an artistic gene that I did not. My mother drew a Christmas scene on the mirror over the fireplace every year. Drawings I create look as though they were done by a toddler.

My sister can wrap a present that is too pretty to open. Gifts I wrap look as though I've hired a chimpanzee and given it ten rolls of Scotch tape, though that is probably insulting to chimpanzees.

I have zero skills at flower arranging. People think I'm joking when I say that, but it's actually true. If I set out to arrange a bouquet of my favorite blooms, by the time I'm done, I end up with two-inch stems. And if a food item needs to look as appealing as it tastes, I'm in trouble.

Therefore, when I set out to write the Big Sky Pie series, I had to imagine pastry chefs with the skills of sculptors, who create masterpieces, not with clay, but with pie dough. Molly McCoy is at loose ends after the sudden death of her husband. She has always dreamed of opening her own shop, a venue to sell her blue-ribbon pies, and she decides life is too short to not act now. But just as her dream is about to become a reality, Molly suffers a life-threatening health crisis. Worrying about the pie shop might be the end of her—if her son and his about-to-be-ex-wife don't step up and take over.

When my mother passed away unexpectedly, I was thrown off kilter so badly I lost forty pounds in six weeks. So I really understood how Quint McCoy could lose himself after his beloved dad died suddenly. Up to that point, Quint had always had a sense of who he was and what he wanted. He just didn't understand that work wasn't as important as family until after his grief caused him to push away everyone he loved.

Callee had grown up unable to trust that anyone would ever love her. Quint's rejection proved her right. She didn't fight for their marriage; she just went along with his request for a divorce. And that divorce is almost final when Molly collapses. She tricks Callee into agreeing to work with Quint to open her pie shop, but can this sizzling hot couple work together without their emotions setting flame to the Big Sky Pie kitchen?

I hope you'll enjoy DELECTABLE, the first book in my Big Sky Pie series. All of the stories are set in northwest Montana near Glacier Park, an area where I vacationed every summer for over thirty years. Each of

the books is about someone connected with the pie shop
in one way or another. So come meet the couples whose
relationships grow from half-baked into a love that will
melt your heart. Also, each book offers a different delectable pie recipe. What more could you want?

Adrianne Lee

FIC
ASHLEY

LIVINGSTON PUBLIC LIBRARY

3 1792 00491 0654

The gamble.

DATE			

004654   9104994